CHARMED
& Dangerous

CHARMED
& Dangerous

TEN TALES OF GAY PARANORMAL ROMANCE
AND URBAN FANTASY

EDITED BY JORDAN CASTILLO PRICE

jCPBOOKS.com

Charmed and Dangerous: Ten Tales of Gay Paranormal Romance and Urban Fantasy.

Compilation and introduction copyright © 2015 Jordan Castillo Price

"Dim Sum Asylum" copyright © 2015 Rhys Ford

"Swift and the Black Dog" copyright © 2015 Ginn Hale

"A Queer Trade" copyright © 2015 KJ Charles

"Magically Delicious" copyright © 2015 Nicole Kimberling

"Everyone's Afraid of Clowns" copyright © 2015 Jordan Castillo Price

"The Thirteenth Hex" copyright © 2015 Jordan L. Hawk

"The Soldati Prince" copyright © 2015 Charlie Cochet

"One Hex Too Many" copyright © 2015 Lou Harper

"Josh of the Damned vs. The Bathroom of Doom" copyright © 2015 Andrea Speed

"The Trouble With Hexes" copyright © 2015 Astrid Amara

Cover art by Jordan Castillo Price

ISBN: 978-1-935540-79-3

All rights reserved. No part of this book may be used or reproduced in any manner whatsoever without written permission except in the case of brief quotations embodied in critical articles and reviews.

First edition 2015

Contents

Introduction vii

Rhys Ford
Dim Sum Asylum 1

Ginn Hale
Swift and the Black Dog 49

KJ Charles
A Queer Trade 99

Nicole Kimberling
Magically Delicious 141

Jordan Castillo Price
Everyone's Afraid of Clowns 195

Jordan L. Hawk
The Thirteenth Hex 231

Charlie Cochet
The Soldati Prince 271

Lou Harper
One Hex Too Many 307

Andrea Speed
Josh of the Damned vs. The Bathroom of Doom 371

Astrid Amara
The Trouble With Hexes 393

About the Authors 469

Introduction

I was the weird kid who was always looking at monster magazines. Not necessarily because I loved the thrill of being scared—which I did—but because some of the so-called monsters gave me an entirely different kind of thrill. Maybe I wanted to romance them. Maybe I wanted to *be* them.

Sympathetic monsters can be found in plenty of stories, from Beauty and the Beast to King Kong. But the relatively young genres of urban fantasy and paranormal romance really gave the sympathetic monster a place to shine. I often joke about how nowadays the vampire nightclub owner is cheesily ubiquitous (and because there are no vampire nightclubs or their owners in this anthology, I can do that) but a century ago in most film and literature, vampires were icky, filthy corpses. With gross fingernails. Ew. But not anymore. Now characters are as likely to fall in love with demons as they are to slay them.

The theme of the sympathetic monster could be the story of us all finding our way in the world despite our flawed insides. Or maybe our insides are perfectly fine, and it's really the battle against hatred and fear at the core of the story, a battle that LGBTQ people know all too well. In these stories, our marginalized characters get a chance to be the hero.

-Jordan Castillo Price

Dim Sum Asylum
RHYS FORD

I HATED RUNNING first thing in the morning. Even in a fog-drenched San Francisco, it was too early to be pounding through the narrow sidewalks of Chinatown as merchants set up for a packed farmer's market. Towering over me, the *gōngyù* bridges cast long, hard shadows onto the pavement, the network of tangled arches burdened with the poors' makeshift villages, resting a disjointed mini-city above San Francisco's tall buildings. Someone in a *gōngyù* nearby was smoking ducks, the crisp, spicy smell of curing meat settling down to the street below.

Dodging a stall of dried fish, I rolled over the counter of the next booth, narrowly avoiding a line of bins filled with cuttlefish and rock cod on ice. The stream of Cantonese that followed me wasn't as hot and angry as the skein of Korean crested dragons flying in my wake. While the lizards were only the length of a dachshund, there were at least ten of them, with mouths filled with long pointy teeth and extremely angry. No matter how small something was, if it had teeth and it was angry, it was something to be reckoned with.

Luckily, I wasn't the one who'd pissed them off.

The man I was chasing was fat, wearing a badly fitting suit and smelled of bean burritos. I'd have given up chasing after him if it weren't for one thing—eight things—he'd stashed an entire clutch of the crested dragons' nest in his jacket's deep pockets.

For one of the few times in my life, I wished I'd inherited more of my mother's fae hollow-bone structure than my father's build. I could run faster if I weren't built so human. I wouldn't have said no to a pair of dragonfly wings either, even if they didn't work. I'd gotten some ancestor's long legs, and they came in handy to leap over a pile of decaying durian left on the sidewalk. My boot toe brushed one of the fruits, and I briefly wondered if I'd ever get the smell out of the leather as it exploded under the pressure of its rotted meat.

Above me, the crimson and green crested dragons dove past my head. They rode the air in undulating waves, their heads weaving side by side as they gave chase. Most draconian beings, big or small, flew using their wings. Asiatic lizards' flight was powered by the pearls in their foreheads so I didn't have to worry about being slapped in the head as they flew. I wasn't even sure if I registered in their tiny, pissed off little brains.

The odds of the dragons getting to him first were good but having them actually do something to him was slim. Crested dragons were scavengers down to the bone. I'd seen one run from a live rat one third its size but then savage a plucked turkey to ribbons after it had been left out for only moments while the cook heated up oil in the deep fryer.

The early morning chill made it difficult for them to gain speed and altitude. In the afternoon, the steady heat from the city's streets gave them thermals to ride, and if they'd been a more aggressive species, I'd be looking at Arnett's picked over carcass draped with full-bellied, contented frill-headed lizards. Still, they were motivated to get their eggs back and they buzzed around me, diving up and down above the heads of the morning foot traffic.

After the last wave of Asian immigrants a few years ago, the Chinatown district grew, extending down to Davis. The closed-in sprawl of the historic district migrated. Buildings were packed with entire generations of a single family and the area was difficult to maneuver in, walls moving as more or less space was needed by the inhabitants. I grew up in its sprawl. Arnett had not and now he was running blind.

"Arnett!" I yelled at his retreating back. Unsurprisingly, he didn't slow down.

The stream of people closed in behind him, moving uphill toward the business centers past Washington. One of the district's newer gates loomed over me, the large golden dragon on its crossbeam watching the skein carefully as it zipped by. It paid no attention to me. The draconian sentry sat purely for its own reasons, a bargain struck with the Triad Consortium long before the Golden Gate Bridge was built. Its tail swung and wrapped around the thick stone column supporting its perch. The rippling membrane at its end flowered, snapping out, nearly knocking me over. Despite or perhaps because of its criminal activity, the Triad knew what it was doing to keep its territories protected. The dragon was massive, a fierce reptilian watchdog mostly satisfied to remain on its post in exchange for a substantial amount of food every week.

So I couldn't count on its help with Arnett.

For a big man, Arnett could run—which was amazing, because for as long as I'd known him, he barely stirred himself to refill his coffee cup. He'd wait for a uniform, preferably one with round hips and pert breasts, and he'd beg her for a refill. It hardly ever worked, but he tried.

"Too damned early for this shit," I grumbled. "God, I hope they get him first."

Leaping to the side, I avoided running into a bicycle rack. The lizards moved faster, their legs tucked in tight against their serpentine bodies until they were brilliant streamers with bared white teeth. Closer to the pier, the air was cooler. Downhill, the streets opened up and the wind off the bay whipped quickly through the tall buildings. The chill was nearly arctic and the dragons hit the cold front, slowing their flight.

Arnett was heading down to the piers, probably hoping to get lost in the crowds of tourists. The dragons jogged to the right, and I skidded after them. They were following instinct, driven to protect their young, while I was chasing Myron because he'd pissed on our assignment. Once I caught up with him, I was going to kick his ass.

I spotted Arnett crossing over the BART tracks. His pockets swayed back and forth, heavy with eggs, and he kept his pace up, looking back every once in a while. He saw the skein before they honed in on him, and he bolted, crossing against the traffic. Horns blared and a truck's tires smoked as the driver slammed on his brakes. The burning rubber cloud filling the street dissipated as the dragons punched holes through it in their pursuit. I followed, a little bit warier of the traffic than Myron but no less determined than my serpentine rivals.

Morning commuters heading into the financial district were climbing out of the railcars, their minds on the day and not on the sweaty-faced man stumbling towards them. Lines of office workers and suits were forming around the scattered *bao* carts on the main causeway, vendors doing brisk business in *char siu* or lotus paste steamed in white bread balls.

Arnett stumbled through the commuters, jostling them from their orderly queues. Shoving began and it threatened to escalate when the dragons dove into the mix, their frilled manes puffed up around their triangular heads. Arnett nearly fell and fear closed my throat. The eggs weren't fragile, having to survive the jostle of their clutch mates and the skein, but the shells couldn't hold up to Myron's weight. Grabbing the handle of a turnip cake cart, he kept to his feet. I closed the distance between us, crossing the pavement with a few strides. Turning the cart, Arnett shoved it at me, knocking over customers. Hot oil splashed from the frying element, scalding the people nearby.

"Fuck you, MacCormick," he spat at me and tossed the vendor's kitchen utensils at my face. One of the smaller knives hit my cheek, digging the tip into my skin, and a splatter of blood hit my eye. Blinking, my eyes refused to clear and rubbing only seemed to blur things more.

One of the smaller dragons wove in, its talons bared and spread. Apparently no one told it that it was supposed to be fearful and docile so it attacked, its mane spread about its face. Arnett screamed and jerked away, his face scored with deep grooves. His foot hit the steaming oil, and he went down. The rest were on him and Arnett rolled onto his knees, a black steel service revolver in his hand. They scattered when he turned, frightened by the sudden movement.

He was up and off again before I could get a bead on him.

Front Street was closed to vehicle traffic in preparation for the Moon festival that weekend. Workers stood on spackling stilts, hanging banners and stringing fae lights along temporary canopies. Arnett twisted as he ran, shooting at me. His arm hit a support leg, pulling a man down onto the pavement. Something in the worker's body snapped when he hit the cobblestones, and my teeth ached in sympathy pains. A string of paper lanterns fell, rolling around underfoot as people scattered away from the concourse.

Wary, the lizards hovered above the heads of the fleeing crowd, their fierce draconian cries lost in the chaos and screams. Arnett took off, tucking his gun against his body and holding the flaps of his jacket down. Shaking my head, I ran after him with the dragons floating behind me.

"Sure, now you hide behind me, you damned scaly chickens." I panted, rounding the corner and almost falling into the heavy morning traffic near the Embarcadero. Arnett was only a few yards away but heading to the pier. A transport ferry from the other side of the bay was pulling up, announcing its arrival with a blare of its horn.

A pod of *uisge* bobbed up and down in the water, their merman handlers herding a smaller transport boat into its moorings. The ocean fae nudged their mounts around, smacking at the *uisges'* flanks with their tails to keep the creatures from approaching the pier. One of the larger water horses pulled up sharp, its attention drawn by the commotion on the pier. Its rider wrapped his hand in its seaweed entangled mane, forcing it to move into the rolling tide. The growing panic on the dock made each *uisge* nervous and they rankled, drawing their front legs out of the bay and slapping their algae-encrusted hooves against the water.

A dragon caught up with me, snagging a warm current from an exhaust vent in the sidewalk. From its aggressive crooning, I guessed it was the deranged mutant who'd attacked Arnett. Buoyed by the hot air, it shot forward, snatching a mouthful of Arnett's balding scalp.

Startled, Arnett let a shot off but the lizard refused to scatter. He grabbed at the lizard, reaching behind him with his free hand but the creature's sleek body was too slippery for him to get a stranglehold on and it slipped out between his fingers. Riding behind its prey's wake, the dragon plunged in again, snapping at anything it could grab before Arnett was out of reach. It hounded him, leaving bites and raw pock marks where its teeth hit.

"Get out of my way." He let off a shot into the air, and the crowd panicked, becoming a tidal wave of rushing bodies. The ferry's horn sounded again followed by the high shriek of its warning klaxon, sounding its imminent departure. Angling across the wooden planks, he ran straight for the boarding deck, the back of his suit dark with sweat and a thin streak of glistening scales chasing him.

I ran through the sea of frightened people, confusion reigning as they stumbled out of Arnett's path. Many were workers heading to their buildings but a few were tourists, up early for a tour of the fog-drenched bay. The skein kept pace with me, falling behind when they hit a cold pocket, but they were the least of my worries. If Arnett made the gate, he'd be on the ferry when it pulled out and there was no way I could make it on. I'd lose him, and with what he had in his pockets, he could make himself disappear for good..

From out of the corner of my eye, I saw a pair of fae women walking by Arnett, their nearly human faces sparkling with compound, pupilless irises, mascara-blackened eyelashes and gloss-painted lips. The one on the right was a set of curves in a red suit and pretty features while the other wore a velvet jacket cut to accommodate her slender wings. Red suit's waifish body and pert triangular face were typical of an Emerald Isle fae, but her bi-colored white and purple hair, cut into a messy bob, was rare. She was the type of woman most men would have stopped to talk to if there'd been time. As it was, I momentarily glanced into her widened eyes before Arnett blew a hole through her head.

Arnett's shot left a gaping black hole where her nose and mouth had been, and her chin crumbled as her skull collapsed. Her blood splattered my face, and I tasted her death on my tongue. Her slender butterfly patterned wings fluttered up, catching the wind coming up from the water. Their connective spines lost their rigidity as she died, and they framed her delicate body, blowing out as she fell forward.

A scream pierced the air. The woman walking with her broke down and keened, a haunting sound that ended in tears. Her sobs were heart-wrenching, and her hands trembled as they covered her mouth.

The round puff of a half-eaten *bao* tumbled from one of their hands, the bright *char siu* filling dull against the sharp red of the dead woman's blood.

People scrambled to get away from Arnett, but in the confusion the crowd thickened then thinned, making it nearly impossible for him to push through. I saw him turn, his eyes wild, and he reached for the screaming fae. Grabbing a handful of her long blue hair, he jerked the woman against him, placing the gun's muzzle on her temple.

"Back off, MacCormick. I'll kill this bitch, too."

Pulling out my gun, I came to a stop, panting hard. A cloud of fury and scales flew past me, then the skein retreated, hovering in the air.

"Let her go, Myron." I didn't have a lot of hope that he'd listen. Arnett never gave off the impression of being stable, and now as I stared him down, he appeared to have cracked open. "There's nowhere to go. Come on. Make this easier on yourself. You've already killed one person. Let her go."

"That insect? These aren't people! They're goddamned faerie," he spat. "Figured you'd take their side. Fucking splice! You're a disgrace to the badge. We fucking bled to protect this damned city, and things like you walk on it and take rank. Makes me fucking sick."

"Killing fae holds the same sentence as it does a human, Arnett," I said, trying for calm but my voice sounded unsteady, even to my ringing ears. Between the hum of the dragons and the shot going off near me, it was hard to hear myself think. "No matter what happens here, you'll be nailed for that. Don't make things worse."

"Shit, I should do SF Metro a favor and cap you. Damn cross-breed! I couldn't believe the Captain when he told me I had to work with a splice—"

"I'm not a splice, Myron," I said. "I'm natural born. It does happen. My parents didn't manipulate genetics to get me. I just happened. You know that."

"Bullshit. Your kind doesn't happen unless someone fucks with things. It's a damned conspiracy to pollute the human race. Is that what you're planning on doing, huh? Lay your fucking insect eggs in our bodies?" Arnett's lips were speckled with foam. "We should have gassed the lot of you a long time ago but now it's too late and you bastards are everywhere, like damned roaches."

The woman's dark eyes were wide, and she trembled in Arnett's grip. I didn't blame her for whimpering. With a gun pressed up against her temple and seeing her co-worker killed in front of her, she had every right to go into shock. What I needed from her was a shred of common sense and I hoped she understood me when I flexed my shoulders forward as I stared hard into her frightened face.

Hitching her breath, she groaned when Arnett pulled her further back. He held her tightly, wrenching her to the side. With her fae-fragile body, she was no match for his strength, but Nature had a way of equalizing things between predators. Biting her lip, the woman squared her body and lifted her shoulders, unfurling her thick-framed wings.

Most humans assumed a fae's wings were fragile, but the veins are rigid and as hard as steel. Her span unfolded swiftly, her wings slamming into Arnett's face and knocking him back when their radius struck him hard. Stumbling, he tried to maintain his balance and the skein hummed behind me, diving up and down in arcs, hungry to latch onto his exposed skin. Tucking her wings fully back, she hit him again and the pterostigma on her membranes flashed before she hit the ground and rolled away.

For luck, I thumbed the three black stars inked on the inside of my left wrist, sent a plea to Pele, then took aim, squeezing off a shot then another. The Glock jerked in my hand, pulling up slightly as each round went off.

Myron spun about, his mouth open wide in shock. The third bullet hit him square in the upper arm, burrowing into his torso. He spat, choking on a mouthful of blood, and the dragons fell on him, rage packaged in tight, serpentine bodies. The smallest one dug through Myron's jacket and shrieked loud enough to be heard over the ferry's departing bellow. I lost sight of it for a second then it surfaced, a faceted golden orb clutched tightly in its teeth. Another came up with an egg, spiraling upwards so another could forage through Myron's pockets. The others worked at his torn flesh, digging down to the bone and tearing out long strips of meat and muscle.

"Drop it!"

The rush of footsteps behind me wasn't enough of a warning and I staggered when the first uniform hit me, then went down under the next. My arms were pulled up behind me and a foot pinned my gun hand to my back. Handcuffs bit my wrists and my elbow was twisted sharply, pulling my shoulder blades together. Someone's fingers grabbed a handful of my hair and pulled it back. The sidewalk came up fast and painful when someone plowed me into the boards. I twisted around, spitting out the salty dirt carried over from the Bay's shore. The cut on my face reopened, and my blood dripped onto the pier. The wood was too damp to soak it in and it pooled, smearing on my chin as one of the cops dragged me across the plank then up to my knees.

"Hey!" I spat out the debris on my lip. "Check my belt. SF Metro. Detective MacCormick, Roku. Chinatown District."

A plainclothes cop fumbled around near my waist, the credentials on his lanyard hitting my face. He pulled my badge from its hook on my belt and stepped back, calling in the number for identification. I heard a squawk of a radio and then a string of Cantonese from the officer's dispatch. He approached me carefully, eyeing Arnett as the medical techs attempted to separate the dragons from their buffet.

"Let him up. He's C-Town's," he grumbled, holding my badge out to me as a uniform released my wrists. They hurt from being bound too tight, but I wasn't going to argue. If I'd arrived on the scene late as they had, I'd have taken down any shooter I saw too.

The wind grabbed my hair and whipped the white strands around my face, stinging my eyes. I'd left it long around my jaw to piss off the Captain but at times like these, I wondered if it wouldn't have been easier to cut it off. My long leather coat kept most of the chill out, but the knees of my jeans now had holes in them and the cold bit my legs. I thought longingly of the department vehicle I'd left parked on Kearny. It was too wide to drive hard through Chinatown after a fleeing thief but at least the interior had been out of the wind and warm.

The cop tilted his head up to look at me in the eye. "You okay? Who's the gunman?"

"My partner," I said, bending over to catch my breath. My lungs felt like I'd inhaled splinters and my ribs ached where I'd been slammed into the pier. "Detective Associate Myron Arnett. Raided a dragons' nest of eggs worth about eleven million yen. He's responsible for the civilian loss."

"Dirty? Damn," the officer said flatly, staring over my shoulder at Myron's twitching body. "What's this world coming to?"

"Yeah," I said shakily, taking my gun back from the uniform when he handed it over.

"Guess we should help the EMTs get those lizards off of him." He didn't look inclined to move. The force was spread too thin and catching one of our own with dirty hands didn't sit well among us.

"We could," I replied, watching the lizards getting their breakfast in. "Better yet, how about if you take her statement? I'll see about notifying the deceased's next of kin. The least I can do is let them know it was quick."

Unclipping his notebook, the cop said, "I'm sorry about your partner, Detective, but I'd have shot him too."

"Thanks." I nodded. "Hopefully the dragons will leave something behind. I'd like my Captain to have something other than my ass to chew on."

2

It's never a good thing when my day starts with me standing in Captain Gaines' office.

It'd been a week, and Internal Affairs still owned me. A lantern-jawed interrogator wrung me out for three days then left me with a toddler-sized pile of paperwork to complete by hand. They'd taken my badge and gun, leaving me with a cramped wrist and generally pissed off at the world. This went on until one afternoon I was told to head back upstairs to see my Captain.

It was almost too much to hope I'd be free.

I stood at the front of his desk with my eyes pinned to the wall directly behind him. I knew the wall intimately. It was close to the color of creamed peas and had a hairline crack running from the ceiling down to the large painting of a seascape hanging behind Gaines. It wasn't a good painting, but the sloppy G signature on the bottom right of the canvas kept me from making any critiques. It was the same signature as on my paychecks, and while I might lack common sense, no one could say I was stupid.

Even with me standing and Gaines lounging in his office chair, his head bobbed into my view, a tight military cut to his salt-and-pepper hair and the wink of gold from the rims of his glasses. Gaines' tailored uniform made him seem enormous, a thickly muscled strongman from an old-time carnival show with his full, heavily salted mustache a thick bush under his hook nose.

"Tell me something, MacCormick," he spat and I glanced down, inwardly wincing when I saw a vein jerking on his temple. "Explain to me how you shot your partner?"

"He indicated a desire to remove the dragon eggs from the nest we'd been tagged to barricade off from the general public, sir." I kept my voice even but the Irish in me rose, lilting my words. "While I was retrieving the barricade tape from our issued vehicle, Detective Associate Arnett approached the nest and extracted what appeared to be the entire clutch."

He didn't interrupt me so I continued, keeping my verbal report as matter-of-fact as I could. "He then fled the scene through the Chinatown warren, forcing me to follow on foot as the vehicle is too wide to be driven through that area. When he approached the pier, Arnett fired his weapon, killing a civilian and endangering not only the protected species but also other bystanders in the area, sir. I chose to respond accordingly."

"So you shot him?" Gaines' eyebrows lifted.

"Yes, sir." I shrugged. "I was aiming for his knee, Captain, but it was difficult to get a good aim with the dragons on him. Considering I was shooting him for taking the eggs, it didn't seem right to hit the lizards."

"You shot your partner in front of the morning ferry and let a pack of dragons ravage his still-breathing body?" he rumbled. "You don't find anything wrong with this?"

"As I told the officer on the scene, I intended only to slow him down," I said "I didn't think the dragons would eat him, sir."

"They tell me he'll recover in a few months. Just in time for a fall court session." The Captain's voice was a mix of resignation and disgust. "Sit down, Rokugi. I want to talk to you without having to strain my neck."

He'd used my full name and didn't say anything when I hooked my leg over the arm of his visitor's chair. Gaines was my godfather and my mother's partner until she'd climbed into the political pool. I'd grown up swimming in the backyard pool of the house he and his husband, Braeden, lived in and he was the one who found me in the middle of the Riots to tell me my boyfriend John and our two daughters were killed in the raging block fires. I called him Uncle Will until I'd joined his division, then he became *Captain,* but we still caught afternoon baseball games on hot summer days. The concerned look on his face was troubling.

"I have to ask this. I'm required to." He leaned back in his chair. "Was this a fae thing?"

"What?" The question confused me. "What are you talking about?"

"Would you have used less force if Arnett hadn't grabbed a fae or called you a splice?"

"He called me a splice. So what?" I snorted. "I'm half-fae. It's not the first time I've heard it. That's not why I shot him. I shot him because he was an asshole and killed an innocent bystander. IA called it a righteous shoot."

"You've met a lot of assholes in your life, Roku. You don't make a habit of shooting all of them. And I know what IA said. I have their report. I just want to know if you're okay and that this isn't something racial."

"He could have been a ninety year old grandmother with orphans hanging off of her teats and I'd have shot him. Arnett was armed and fleeing the scene of a crime." I exhaled, shaking my head. "He unloaded a few rounds into a woman. I had to go in front of her parents to tell them that their daughter was killed by a cop. It is not a fae versus human thing. It's a people thing."

"I believe you, kid, but God, you let the damned lizards *eat* him." He winced then rubbed his face, trying to scrub the weary out of his eyes. "IA's thinking you did it out of revenge."

"Revenge? I'd have done it if he'd shot a dog." I softened my voice. "He was one of ours, Uncle Will. She should have been safe. That girl shouldn't have died under blue fire."

"I know," the man agreed and nodded at me. "No one knew he was dirty. IA didn't even suspect him."

"He hid it pretty well. I only figured it out because I caught him red-handed. If I hadn't been early, we never would have known," I replied, sliding my leg down to sit into the chair. Gaines looked away but I knew him well. He was angry and ashamed of Arnett. One of his own let him down. "He sucked as a partner, and because of him, I'm still Internal Affair's bitch."

"Not anymore," Gaines said. He reached into his drawer and pulled out my badge and gun, placing them on the desk between us. "These are yours. As of tomorrow, you're back on duty."

"What's the catch? From what I was hearing, it was going to be another month." I didn't reach for my things. I knew that look in his eyes. There were going to be conditions of surrender, I could see it.

"You'll have to get a new partner." He placed a folder next to my gun. "I haven't figured out who's pissed me off the most yet. I've narrowed it down to two. You'll know in half an hour."

I left the folder where it lay but my fingers itched to grab it. "Can't I go solo for a bit? I just shot the old one."

"And be thankful he didn't die." Gaines handed me a grape lollipop. He'd handed me a lot of lollipops over the years, all of them grape or cherry. "If he did, Internal Affairs would be chewing on your badge for dessert."

"He could still die. Infection. Someone shoving a pillow over his face—"

"I need you to keep your nose clean. That's it," he replied, unwrapping a lollipop for himself. He stuck it into his mouth, sucking the candy into his cheek. "That folder? It's your IA release. They think you're a little crazy, kid, and I'm inclined to believe them. You haven't been the same since...."

He trailed off but I knew what he was saying. After I lost John and the girls, life seemed easier living on the edge. I took more chances than I should, pushed harder than I needed to. Of course if I'd pushed a bit harder, perhaps I wouldn't have worn that young girl's blood on my face. I wondered if the dead fae's parents would wear a black star on their wrist or if they'd pierce their wings with an onyx star. The fae wore their grief out in the open for all to see. I hated giving her parents the chance to decide how to mourn her. I knew how heavy a black star could get. The three I bore grew heavier each year.

"I'm good, Uncle Will." I crossed my heart with a finger. "Promise."

"Try to stay out of trouble for a few months. That's all I ask," he said. "Brae, on the other hand, wants you over for dinner next Saturday."

"Can't make it," I replied. "Girls' Day."

"That's why he wants you over."

"I'm not going to be good company after…"

"We're not looking for good company," the man replied. "We're looking for our godson. Be there, Roku. Seven o'clock and bring a bottle of good red. Brae's making lasagna. Don't be late or I'll stew your gizzard for a pie."

C-Town's detective area sat on an open loft above the uniforms' bull pen. I climbed a sweeping staircase, and I reclaimed my desk amid the quiet rumble of the night shift. It looked like I was alone except for the sparse light of computers flipping wallpapers of exotic beaches that none of us would probably ever see in our lifetimes. Someone kept cleaning the top of my desk, wiping it down and neatly stacking my cold cases. A bottle of tequila, complete with a worm on the bottom and wrapped in a blue bow, sat in the middle of my now organized mess.

"When you get a free weekend, we're so going to get hammered on this, V and B," I read with a grin. "Aw shucks, now I know you love me. You know I puke after about three shots of this shit. Thanks, Vasquez."

Detective Mike Vasquez was one of the good ones in Chinatown, as much of a legacy cop as I was. He and his partner, Thea Browning, shared the other half of the quad with me and Arnett. Myron hated both of them. Judging by the sparkling clean empty area that used to house Arnett's crap, Mike and Thea had no love for him either.

"Hey, my man! Rumor mill said you were back like five minutes ago." Yamada grabbed me from behind, lifting me up off the floor in a bear hug. Brian'd been a B-Class sumo wrestler before he became a cop but no one told him he didn't have to keep up the beefy physique he'd earned in the sumo stable. As my ribs cracked, I yelped out a squealing hello as he put me back down. "Good to have you back."

"Just in time for you to kill me," I gurgled, catching my breath as I slapped him on the shoulder. "Good to see you. What's up?"

"The Captain told me you were tagged to pick up some of my slack." Yamada wiped at his broad forehead, pretending to be overexerted. "Good to have you back. Even if you did let Arnett steal those eggs."

"Thanks, asshole." I made a face at him and sat on the edge of my desk. He lumbered off, his bristle head bobbing as he thundered through the maze of desks and chairs. Picking up the bottle again, I studied its label carefully, wincing at the worm bobbing about at the bottom. "So when are we planning—"

The chatter around me came to a dead silence when Gaines' slick leather loafers touched the bullpen's floor. He stood at the top of the stairs, a harbinger of good and evil with the power to lengthen our shifts with a single grunted command. As a Captain, he was one of the best. A cop never had to worry if Gaines had his back. That went without saying. Most badges would give their left nut, tit or wing to work under my godfather's command, which made Arnett's dirtiness an even greater betrayal. Smearing me and our partnership was one thing, but Arnett got his filth on the whole department and put a big black mark on Gaines' record.

My old buddy Myron would be lucky if he made it out of the local jail with the same number of teeth he had going in.

Gaines wasn't a surprise. The human behind him was, and from the looks of my godfather's squared up shoulders and steely-eyed glare, I was going to guess he'd brought me a new partner.

From his square jaw and beefy build down to his dirty blond fade haircut, everything about the guy screamed ex-hardcore military. He moved as if expecting a riot to break out on the upper loft, icy blue eyes scanning each of us, stopping only long enough to mark our presence before moving on to the next cop.

He found me first and then again, last. His gaze pierced through me, assessing and judging in a way that did not say cop. I wasn't sure what was found wanting, my shaggy mane or my odd ommatidia-faceted pupils, but something made his nostrils flare. I definitely spotted the moment he saw my pupils' copper-green sheen. His head jerked back a few millimeters and his chin jutted out.

If my new partner had a thing against fae or fae-bred, we were *assuredly* going to have a problem.

The guy wasn't young, not a starry eyed, fresh-out-of-Patrol newbie with milk still on his teeth. If anything, he might have been a year or two older than my own three decades, but it was sometimes hard for me to tell with humans. There were too many variables to their aging, from racial proclivities to diet, and for all of my own Japanese human half, I'd not spent any time with my father or his family.

The dark blue suit he wore was tailored to his bulk, fitted along his broad shoulders and cutting in slightly at the waist. Pity he hadn't worn his shoulder harness when he'd gotten the navy blazer altered, because his rig ruined the line of the coat, ruching up across his back where a strap hung up on the back seam. He wasn't short and definitely more evenly proportioned than me, but being human could do that to a guy.

Still, he was good-looking in a fit, thunder-god kind of way and my unruly dick was more than happy to make his acquaintance. If there was any part of me I regretted having human blood, it was my libido. Faes had it easy, a pheromone or two caught their attention and it narrowed the field down for them. Instead, I'd gone to a wider stream of lust and want. It was annoying. Especially when I found myself attracted to a man who looked like he'd rather be armed to the teeth and prowling war zones than be stuck in a car with me.

"Detectives," Gaines rumbled loudly. "I want to introduce you to Detective Associate Trent Leonard. He'll be joining our little family as of today. MacCormick, he's with you. I want the rest of you to make yourselves available to Leonard while he learns the ropes. He's just come out of Street so it'll be up to all of you to mentor him during his transition.

"Leonard, that's MacCormick," my godfather said, pointing at me. Detective Associate Trent Leonard practically snapped to attention and clipped his heels together when Gaines barked his name. "Keep tight on his ass, ask questions and you'll learn the job."

"Just don't be in front of him if he's got his gun out," someone teased from behind me. I'd have guessed Yamada but I was too engrossed in the whiff of musk kicking up out of Detective Leonard's skin. Something was queuing up his fight or flight responses and only a dead skink wouldn't know it was me.

I ate up the distance between us and tried not to let my metaphorical wings get ruffled when Leonard started, almost as if he were about to take a step back. Edging past Gaines, I stuck my hand out to my new partner and said, "Welcome to Dim Sum Asylum."

3

THE CHINATOWN RAIN was a pour of silky dark sheets as I drove through the lower reaches near the Bay. Damp rainy evenings are my favorite time in the city. The water spun out gossamer threads, misty batting thin enough to weave through the complicated loom of buildings set up on the city's hills. Neon signs bled into the fog, daubing reds and yellows across the air, a whore's lipstick smear after the end of a long night's work.

Passing under the Dragon squatting on the East gate on Grant and Bush, I saw its eyes gleam gold as it caught a whiff of something in the air. Its fin-like tail slapped at the green tiles on its long perch, rattling the chimes hanging from a broad support beam spanning the double-lane street. We had to stop for a minute as a car backed out of a spot, holding up traffic, and I made the mistake of looking around.

In the dark recesses below the prismatic reptile's squat, an old balding nun in muddied orange robes shook out fortune sticks onto an old TV dinner tray for a gaggle of Hawaiian-shirt wearing round men, either a tour group or rejects from a vintage Hilo Hattie advertisement.

A few feet away, her shaven fae apprentice fought to adjust her own robes around her tiger-moth wings, the upper end of her right span dotted liberally with tiny glistening obsidian stars. I counted an easy seven but it could have been more. After one or two, the count never really mattered, and her loss showed in the yellow weeping into her blue compound eyes. It was hard to catch a glimpse of her pain. I had my own, flickers of citrine at the edges of my irises when I thought of John and the girls, but the young fae's tragedy went beyond my imagining, and I was grateful when traffic began to move again so I could pull away from her anguish.

Despite the rain, I'd left the driver side window open a crack so I could feel the wind on my face and catch the scents of the streets we drove through. People were out in droves, both human and fae, tourists strolled up Grant, stopping sidewalk traffic as they peered at the street's storefronts. A red light brought me to a stop and I watched a stream of tourists and locals hurry from one corner to the next. The meat and dumpling place across from the Old Grant hotel sizzled with aromas, and my stomach growled, reminding me the last time I'd seen fit to toss something down my gullet, it'd been a scoop of cop cafeteria oatmeal before I faced the music in Gaines' office. That'd been hours ago, and the rows of suckling pig and tea-smoked duck hanging in the charcuterie's window made my mouth water something fierce.

The case we'd pulled—a missing shrine god—was a simple one on the surface, but when it was all said and done, anything in C-Town's inner coil was complicated. One thing always led to another in Chinatown. It was like pulling a loose thread usually meant things unraveling to a shit storm, and I never had an umbrella on me to take the brunt of the crap. My badge would take care of clearing away most of the shit I knew would hit us once we crawled into C-Town's underground but sometimes a flash of gold brought its own world of troubles and, glancing at the man sitting next to me, I realized I didn't quite trust Detective Leonard to have my back.

Still, my badge felt good. I'd never realized how much I'd miss its weight on my belt until IA took it off of me. The gun I could give or take but my badge, that was something different. It was as much a part of me as the three black stars on my wrist or the starburst on my shoulder blade, so it was damned good to have it on me again. Familiar. Comforting.

Unlike the bulky presence of Detective Leonard sitting in the passenger seat of our department-issued vehicle.

I didn't know what was more unnerving, the half-suspicious, odd looks I caught him giving me or the way he clutched at the door when I hit Chinatown's busy streets. Both were annoying, but short of shooting yet another partner, I didn't know what I could do to stop it.

I didn't have to wait long for something to change because Leonard cleared his throat and tossed in a bit of chaos he'd been cooking up while I drove.

"I read up on you. I mean, once I found out there was an opening in Arcane Crimes." He hadn't said much before then. A few grunts and a nice to meet you or two so I was surprised by his honey-smooth tones. With his bulk, I guess I'd been expecting something more guttural.

"There's a problem then. I don't know if I should be worried that you read up on me or that there's actually stuff *to* read up on." I could only imagine what Trent Leonard found in my files.

"Reports mostly. And well, rumors," he admitted. I eased into the next lane and rolled to a stop behind a delivery truck. There was a darkness to his tone as he muttered, "A hell of a lot of rumors."

"And you still wanted the job?" I whistled under my breath. "Brave man. Let's have them."

"Have what?"

"The rumors." I'll admit to a curiosity deep enough to rival any cat or dragon. "Beyond me shooting Arnett."

"He's not the only one you've shot." I hadn't needed *that* little reminder, and his jaw firmed up when I eyed him from across the car. "Mostly that you're a very human-looking splice and the department's—"

"I'm not a splice. Natural born. It happens." It was a common misperception. No matter how many times I corrected Arnett, he seemed to be stuck on that sorry refrain. "And even if I were, what difference would it make? Any splice made before the Demarcation Act is a legal citizen and any found to be created after that point is immune from prosecution. Life is life, Leonard."

It was an old soapbox. One I'd climbed up and down from time and time again. When CPS found Tara and Kristine in a back alley lab, they'd contacted John to help with placement. He hadn't planned on falling in love with them, and suddenly I found myself with two little girls who actually looked like they were mine. They'd only been mine a year before stupidity took them—and John—from me, but I was still willing to do battle for their right to live even as their ashes were scattered alongside John's in my fae clan's mourning pool.

My wrist itched and I scratched at the three stars inked black and deep under my skin.

"You asked for the rumors. That's one." He was right. It was stupid to shoot the messenger once I'd asked him to spill the beans. Gossip both fascinated and enraged me. I blame my fae blood. As a species, we found something oddly comforting about a murmuring under the shadows. "That and your mother bit and ate your father's head off."

"Wrong clan. My mother was Odonata. And the Mantoida haven't done that kind of thing in centuries." I sniffed in mock outrage. The truck in front of us began to move, and I eased in behind it. "And my father's fine. I think. Last time I checked he was alive and singing lullabies to otters. Why'd you want into Arcane?"

I had my own answer to that. Most of us in the Asylum did. Mostly it was from a fascination with the arcane as a whole. For me it was the exploration of the unknown and the hunt for people who violated the law. My shoulder blades itched for the chase, phantom wings frilling at the adrenaline in my blood. Even something simple as locating a shrine god got my blood up, and I could taste the possibilities in my mind.

"When I was a kid, I wanted to be a magician. Then I found out that kind of magic was all illusion and sleight of hand." He shrugged and his massive shoulders sucked up most of the space in the car until they settled back down. "So, I went chasing after the real thing."

I wasn't going to bring up the whole military presence rolling off of his skin or the hard eye scan he gave everyone we passed by. Detective Trent Leonard had secrets, dark ones from the clench of his jaw and the faint spiderweb scarring I could make out down the side of his neck. The damage had been patched up, nearly flawlessly, but I'd seen that kind of lightning strike bloom on someone before—a dead someone who'd tangled with the wrong qirin and had been served up as that week's stale yakitori by the time we'd found his body floating in the Bay.

Qirin were rare, and usually by the time one was spotted, the spotter was dead. But here was my new partner, with what appeared to be scars from a qirin. Looks like he'd found his magic and it'd bitten him back.

"Anything I should know about being your partner?" Leonard quizzed. "Other than you won't be biting my head off and eating it."

"That's an *only after sex* thing and once again, not my clan." My shoulder blades twitched again, keen on the hunt and this time, not for the case. My body sensed a thread of something erotic coming up off of my new partner. Either that or it'd just been too long since I'd last visited Madame Woo's Golden Dragon Club.

I actually couldn't remember the last time I'd been to Woo's. Hell, I wasn't even sure the bathhouse was still in business.

"Nothing much to tell you. I work, work some more then go home." My shrug probably wasn't as impressive as his but I could hold my own. "That's about it. You?"

"I needlepoint, but the rest of the routine is the same." I glanced at him, trying to see if he was serious, but Leonard's expression was stone cold hard. "What about your eyes? They're—"

I didn't get to tell him about my eyes or my opinion on his needlepointing. One second, we were following a delivery truck through slow traffic on Grant and the next we were staring up the short ceremonial robes of a squat two-foot tall Chinese man with an impressive Fu Manchu mustache landing on the windshield.

The glass gave under his—its—heavy stone feet, leaving two enormous starburst crinkles across the windshield. Part of me was amazed at the level of detail someone'd gone to, because the squatting golem's robes flapped as the wind caught up the hem, and we were gifted with the sight of its smooth, low hanging sac pressed into the glass.

It leered, waggling its tongue out at pedestrians. An old fae woman gasped when it grabbed the ends of its robes and pulled them up, unfurling the anaconda sex organ it'd been given. It shook its mighty cock at the people on the sidewalk, its raspberry red tongue circling lewdly around its fat lips. The lurid colors on its loose robes were vivid enough to burn the paint off of the car and its oddly carnation pink skin was mottled with faint dark crazing.

I felt the kick of its power, lust roiling under my skin and tightening my throat. Shrine god, my ass. The damned thing was fae-cursed, a fertility invoking totem someone'd inexplicably dumped too much mojo into, and now we were going to have to rein it in.

It was gone a second later, bounding off the car and scurrying down the sidewalk before I could catch my breath back. Beside me, Leonard was sucking in air, one hand on his gun and the other on the door handle.

"What the fuck was that?" he growled, struggling to get his seat belt off.

"Grab a containment bag!" I tucked the car up against the sidewalk curb and shoved an on-duty placard onto the dashboard. Loading zone be damned, I wasn't going to risk losing that thing. "*That* is our case. Lock the door behind you and let's go."

Tracking the cursed statue should have been easy. All we had to do was follow the trail of horrified looks and amused smirks along the way. The sidewalks were crowded and tracking a two-foot tall possessed statue was difficult in the best of times. These were certainly not the best of times. Either Chinatown was having a half-off egg tart day or someone'd dumped five busloads of tourists right at the corner of Clay and Grant, because Leonard and I suddenly found ourselves swamped in a sea of immovable people.

"Do you see it?" he shouted at me above the chatter around us. "I can't find—"

"There!" I pointed at a couple leaning against the wall next to a discount import shop. They were deep into one another's throats, hands groping whatever body parts they could reach. The fae's wings were plastered up against the bricks, a pair of badly painted lion dancers nearly hidden behind her fluttering spread. Her human companion was larger, dwarfing her slender body, but his shoulders were nearly buckling under her strong grip.

Normally, I'd have dismissed the couple as an inappropriate display of affection, but something told me the human cop and the fae delivery girl who'd dropped someone's noodle order all over the sidewalk hadn't planned on their torrid rendezvous.

The shrine god had definitely kicked up its juice. Gone were the smirks. Instead there were wing frills, furtive glances and even bolder touches scattered through the crowd. Heading up Sacramento in a full pound, I left Leonard behind, and I could only hope he'd catch up. The statue was moving quickly, driven by its curse, but I had no idea what it was chasing.

The people thinned out, and I found myself at Waverly, staring down the slender lane and peering off the lantern lit street in the hopes of spotting my tiny prey. Leonard caught up to me, slightly winded but not blowing out air. The hill was steep, I had to give him credit for taking it as fast as he did in his loafers. There were reasons I wore Converses and jeans to work. I never knew when I'd have to chase down something or someone through crowded or tight streets.

Waverly, unlike Sacramento, was a locals-only street. Only a few yards away from the main corners, it offered very little to the casual traveler. A church took up residence in an old brick building that once housed a triad's headquarters. The triad itself was still around, moved over to a more discreet location a few doors down, and marked as a benevolent society.

There was little benevolence to be found there behind the watermelon painted doors, but it looked like we were going to have to take that chance because one of the door's lower right hand panel had a suspicious two-foot tall hole in it.

My partner spotted the hole about a second after I did. Sighing heavily, he rubbed at his face then said, "Well, shit."

4

A BADGE COULD only get a cop so far through a door, and I didn't have a lot of hope the Wang Shi Benevolent Society would throw open their pink and green portal and let us in. An aged fae glowered at me from his doorway perch in the noodle shop across the way, but other than the rumble of traffic, the street was silent. No one came to the door when Leonard pounded on the frame, and he frowned at me, shaking his head as he pulled his weapon.

"We're going to have to go in," he grunted at me.

"Yeah, but not with guns out. How long have you lived in the city? Anyone tell you about places like this?" Leonard shook his head, and I suppressed a sigh. "Some of these societies—like this one—are kind of like a den of thieves. Not all of them just... some. This one's older. A lot of these guys are more into bouncing grandkids on their knees than breaking open heads, but they've still got a rep to maintain. We can't just bust in here. You've got a gun out and we're in civilian clothes, anyone in here is going to shoot first then ask questions. And that's if they don't rinse and repeat the shoot first part. Okay. I've almost got this open."

As odd as it might sound, the older triads fostered good relationships with the cops, especially as their criminal empires began to dissolve around them, and meetings became less about territory and more about whiskey, hanafuda and mahjong. It took me a while to work the door open, an exercise in milking the latch apart and praying they didn't have an extensive arcane alarm system.

"Write an apology note on the back of a department card. Say we're sorry for entering but we'll pay for the door." The flip lock was a hairsbreadth too far from my fingers, and I was straining to reach it through the now partially open door. "Put my name down. They won't know you."

I heard him scratching the message out, and I finally got a hold of the ball end of the lock. Sliding the hook free, I pushed the door open with my shoulder and shook the blood back down into my hand.

"Where do I put this?" He held up the card.

"Just tuck it into the trim on the door." Leonard gave me a skeptical look. "Trust me, no one's going to fuck with it. And the *lao* over there at the noodle shop is paid to watch the place. Chances are, the head guy here is going to know we're inside before we even find the damned statue. Keep your eyes open and whatever you do, don't shoot at the thing. Who the hell knows what'll happen then."

Trent was a big boy. His mass pressed up against the back of my senses, and while I had faith in Gaines' ability to pick me out a good partner—my brain hiccupped when I realized my godfather'd been the one who'd passed me Arnett. That had been a game of hot potato. No one'd wanted to work with Arnett, and I'd been the only other single in the department. Leonard was another thing entirely. Trained, focused and ready. Primed to work Arcane Crimes and hand selected from a stack of applicants.

But I didn't know him. Not really. And I wasn't willing to put him behind me and let him have a gun in his hand.

I also didn't want him to take point. Not on his first case out, and certainly not when we didn't know exactly what we were dealing with. I hadn't been kidding about the shoot first, and the society's cramped interior wasn't where I'd want a gunfight.

The building was a narrow rowhouse, an echo of a time when architecture ran to an East Coast aesthetic instead of adobe. As a result, the spaces were tight and dark, heavy with wood paneling and the stink of old men. A layer of antiseptic soap lingered in the air, thick enough to battle off decades of incense, cigarette smoke and a slight whiff of old blood.

Someone—maybe a lot of someones—had died in this place, and the smell of death clung to the building, sinking its nails into the wood. My fae blood ran thin but I could still feel the ripple of loss under my skin. The death wasn't recent, but it was violent and personal, leaving an echo residing in the walls. Death echoes were the reason most fae avoided cop work. They didn't happen all the time, and not every murder left the aftershock of its event, but when it did, the echo was like a hard blow to the nuts.

For me, it was more of a tickle. From a really ugly woman with sharp nails.

Something about the front room felt off. I couldn't put my finger on it, but it didn't seem right. The room was a long shotgun space, leading to a hallway dimly lit by the occasional sconce. Folding chairs and three card tables kept a small shrine company, a memorial space with a bowl of overripe tangerines and a handful of half-burned incense. The Formica topped tables were tired, their corners worn down to the pressboard, and the inset cushions on the chairs were faded and stained. At least two ashtrays sat on each table, a few overflowing with butts and soot, and on the table furthest from us, a beer bottle lay on its side, a yeasty liquid grave for a dead, floating cockroach nearly the length of my thumb.

"San Francisco PD! Entering the premises!" I called out, but other than my voice bouncing off of the buckling, drop-in tiles above us, there wasn't so much as a cricket chirping in the place. It *felt* empty—except for the crawling dead tickle—but I wasn't taking any chances. "Police! We are entering the building!"

"Nice place," Leonard muttered from behind me. "Can we find that damned thing now?"

"We don't even know where it is. Let's hope there isn't a back door." I couldn't see a staircase leading to the upper floors but that didn't mean there wasn't one. "Cover me. I'm going to upend one of the tables to block the hole it made. If you see it, bag it."

I liked the silence behind me even less than I liked the one filling the building. Turning, I caught my partner's sheepish grimace.

"Um..." Leonard scratched the back of his head. "Shit. Want me to go back and grab one?"

"No, I'll use my jacket." I eyed his suit. "Or yours. Let me guess—you didn't bring salt or black tea leaves either."

"I didn't know I was going to be in the field. First day and everything. Hell, I wasn't even expecting to get a partner yet. I thought it was just a meet-and-greet with Gaines then paperwork until IA cut you loose." He shrugged off his jacket as I maneuvered the table into place. "I fucked up."

It took a steady soul to admit he'd screwed up and an even bigger swallow of pride to sacrifice what looked like a custom tailored job because of it. I nodded to one of the chairs. "Leave that there. We'll use mine. It's old leather and can take more of a beating. And for all we know, the statue's going to spurt ectoplasm all over the place if we break its curse. Better something we can wipe off."

I dug the salt and tea packets out of my jacket pockets and handed half to Leonard. Locking the door behind us, I motioned for him to stay behind me, and from the ruffle on his forehead, bringing up the back wasn't in Leonard's behavioral profile.

"I've never de-cursed something before." He ground his words out. "But I read up on it."

I was trying not to resent Leonard's lack of arcane knowledge, his shiny loafers and even the massive gun he had tucked under his armpit in the shoulder holster fitted tight against his back and side. With his jacket off, Leonard was even more massive. I wasn't certain the seams of his dress shirt were strong enough to hold in his breadth and for some reason, I was fascinated by him unknotting his tie. His jacket's hem had been covering a taut, firm ass, his round cheeks filling out his pants nicely.

Leonard was human, built, a little bit seasoned and had a touch of stern authority on his strong, handsome face. He was like a marked off checklist of everything I liked in a guy. Except I wasn't getting the vibe I was anywhere near the type on *his* checklist.

When we got back to the station house, I was going to have a serious talk with my godfather about giving me a partner I wanted to lick chocolate off of.

"I'd feel better if we went in armed." His holster creaked a little as he walked, so maybe it was newer than I thought. My own rig was old, darkened by sweat and warped to fit my body, smelling a bit of gun oil and coffee.

"You are armed," I corrected. "I gave you salt and tea leaves. Watch our six."

Five feet in, a hallway jogged off to a tighter corridor, a dark thin space I had doubts my partner's shoulders could fit through. Since none of the main hallway doors were punched through or open, we were looking for our cursed prey somewhere down the building's side corridor. A door set into the end of the side hall was ajar so it was probably our best bet.

And there were other clues the damned thing fled through the cramped hall. The paneling bore signs of the statue's pinball-frenzied flight, long chalky scrapes and digs marking the thin wood veneer. Leonard's light flashed on something white near the second door, and I stopped before I stepped on the writhing object, angling my shoulder so I could see what it was.

"It's lost a hand." I had to step back quickly because the wriggling fingers hooked into the rough, industrial carpet to work its way toward my foot.

As tempting as it was to step on the damned thing, it looked to be porcelain, and all I'd end up doing would be grinding sex-spell cursed powder into the carpet. If shooting a society member was bad public relations, leaving a lust curse behind so its elderly patrons would be driven to hump themselves raw probably wasn't the best course of action.

It was a toss up between salt and tea leaves. I didn't know if the statue's owner was human or fae or even if they leaned Asian or Western in their beliefs. Since the statue was Chinese, I was going for the leaves.

Grabbing a pinchful, I muttered a standard remove curse at the wiggling hand as I sprinkled.

It continued to wiggle for a moment then went inert, stiffening back into what probably was its original position, a curled in meditation pose of fat fingers and paint. Picking it up off the carpet was a bit difficult, I had to work the thing loose and when I got it free, I passed it over to Leonard.

"What do you want me to do with that?" He recoiled slightly as I held it out.

"Put it in your pocket. I'm in jeans. You're wearing slacks. They've got more of a give and won't smash the thing." I shoved it into his hand. "Besides, you're the one who forgot the bag."

"I am never going to live that down, am I?" It was a grumble, but he tucked the hand into his pocket.

"Not as long as we're partners, no."

He looked skeptical but resigned. "Okay, so leaves, then?"

"Yeah, leaves." I checked my supply as I headed to the open door. "Hope we've got enough."

Leonard was right up against my back, a long hot presence in the hallway's murky air. His breath ghosted over my neck. The death tickle was gone, replaced by another, deeper kind of caress. My balls were growing tight, roiling about from Leonard's proximity. I wasn't liking the dark, and I sure as Pele's breath wasn't fond of what my partner was doing to me.

I didn't know what pissed me off more; wanting Leonard or him not reacting to me in the same way.

"Don't go borrowing trouble, Roku." I kept my muttering to myself and took another step. More crunching, and this time, the ground buckled under my foot. "You've got enough already."

The quiet should have warned me. I laid the blame on the death echoes, but I should have known better. The building was too quiet, too still, but my nerves were already on edge with Leonard's presence and my first day back on the job after a long stint of regret and second-guessing. We made it another foot into the thin hall when the walls fell back and an old, violence-scented fae exploded from a false panel near my elbow. The ceiling bristled with lights, drowning my vision out in a startling white wave and I blinked furiously to see beyond the flares spangling my eyesight.

It was an old trick, one I'd known since I was knee high to my grasshopper-winged neighbor. The door should have been a clue since the walls were up tight against its frame and bowed slightly at the ceiling. At one point someone—maybe even the ancient fae frilling in front of me—built out false walls and placed them on tracks to keep any intruders in a tight line, making them easier to attack.

That knowledge did me no good now, but my gun did, and I ached to draw it before the fae could take another step. Bringing a gun to a knife fight was only going to escalate things and something about the old fae assured me that I'd not win.

Barely coming up to my shoulders, the fae was ancient, his dove-gray, papery skin stretched tight over his skeletal frame and his once flame-red hair turned to a ginger and cloud skull cap above his thin, nearly white eyebrows. He led with his enormous hooked nose, and his still-vivid green-purple compound eyes twirled, catching every single movement we made. The hall was now wide enough for him to spread his wings, and they ruffled out behind him. Monarch dappled and tailed, their long trailing tattered ends waving when he moved. Dressed in simple cotton pants and a button up shirt, he would have fallen away from my attention if I'd passed him on the street—if it weren't for the sea of red faceted stone stars set into the uppermost black swatches of his wings.

They glistened, a death-wink gleaming from each one. Leonard had his gun out. In the ripe panic of walls, old fae and bright lights, my senses kicked up, and I could smell everything, from the oil Leonard used to clean his Glock to the faint sticky copper of blood under the ancient fae's long fingernails. I left my gun where it was, focused on the bloodied knife the fae held in his hand. I was too busy fighting the urge to shoot the fae in front of me, the hunting instinct in my bloodline ramping up until my head swam with hunger. There might have been a Glock in my holster but the crimson universe marbling the fae's wings reassured me my bullets would probably be wasted. He was a lifelong killer, wearing his victims in a brazen display of disregard for any law of the land.

"Shit, it's just an old man," Leonard muttered, putting away his gun. The fae caught Leonard's murmur and smiled, a peek of tool-sharpened teeth hiding a sharkish maw behind his thin lips.

I wasn't going to correct my partner. The old fae probably encouraged people to view him as harmless, and tipping him off that I knew better wasn't going to help us. I couldn't be sure our badges would do anything other than incite him to add cop-killing to his long career of sowing murder and mayhem.

Most humans didn't know the subtleties of fae cultures. Hells, most fae shed customary formalities in the past few decades as our species integrated, but standing in front of us was an Ancient, a sentinel of traditions and old ways. There were probably more than thirty death markers on his wings, but it was hard to get an accurate count as his wings shifted and danced. I was also more interested in keeping track of the chef's knife he gripped in his left hand.

"Did you bring that *wūgòu* into my house?" His chin lifted, challenging me to deny it.

"It escaped the one who made it. We're sent to contain it." I kept Leonard back with my elbow, angling my body to prevent him from approaching the old fae. "Did you not hear us earlier?"

"I didn't care about your police business. Not until that filth ran over my food like a sewer rat. Now I have to throw away a whole chicken because of its touch. Who is going to pay me for that, *wáwá*? Who is going to pay for my chicken?" The knife remained at his side but that wasn't any consolation.

"The department will pay for your loss, but right now, we have to contain the statue. Did you see where it went?" I spoke as respectfully as I could but his eyes were wild, spinning red along their edges. "It is lust cursed. We need to—"

"I know what it is." The scarlet spread, lighting up most of his compound eyes. There was longing in his expression, a simmering desire edging through the green of his lenses. "Flesh was never my weakness, *wáwá*, not in that way. But you know that, yes?"

I understood what he was saying. Sex drove most humans and fae. Death drove this one, and the urge to murder probably was overwhelming him. I couldn't tell when he'd killed last—it could have been decades ago or just a day—but if we didn't slip away soon, he'd kill again and wear two new stars on his wings.

"Which way did it go?" I asked, my hand drifting to my side. I'd be lucky to get a shot off before he fell on us, but it would slow him down enough to give Leonard time enough to escape. "And are you going to let us pass?"

"I want no trouble with the police. I haven't lived this long only to bring that wolf to my door." He jerked his head to the door at the end of the hall. "That leads up. To the *gōngyù*. You'll probably find it up there."

"Thank you," I muttered, giving him as wide a berth as I could given the space. He pressed himself back into the false panel he'd come through, and as I passed, the death tickles began again. His victim that night might have been a chicken, but recently—very recently—something with a greater intelligence suffered a long, agonizing death at the old fae's hands. "Leonard, go up first. I'll follow."

"You don't trust me with your pet monkey?" His words slithered out, a spit of Mandarin I was certain Leonard didn't understand. My partner gave me a curious look but I motioned him on, urging him toward the stairwell tucked behind the door.

"No, old man, I don't," I responded softly, leaving off the respectful honorific most Mandarin speakers would afford an elder. Keeping my back to the wall, I followed Leonard down the span. "Thanks for your time."

For an old man, he was quick, slithering across the carpet on his gnarled bare feet. It took him less than a blink of an eye to reach my side and I had my gun out without even realizing I'd drawn it. His knife clanged against the muzzle of my Glock, his face pressed in against my upraised arm with only an inch separating my flesh from his sharpened teeth. Leonard was back at the doorway, his gun up, but I nodded him off when the old fae took a step back.

"Do yourselves a favor, *chóng*, and listen to me." His breath left a wash of decay in my lungs, hot despite the distance between us. "You look for another way down once you find that thing. It would be better for all of us if my knife was only used on chickens today."

5

THE TWO-STORY BRICK square that housed the Wang Shi Benevolent Society hosted one of Chinatown's most famous features, a rooftop ghetto the locals called a *gōngyù*. Connected by bridges, the *gōngyù* spanned many of Chinatown's taller structures, often so thickly built they blocked the sun from getting to the street below.

Several wide bridges connected the rooftop to the *gōngyù* directly across from it. Like countless others, these stacked rooftop dwellings were cobbled together out of scrap material, becoming a foundation for others to build on. From the looks of things, the tight maze of alleys below were covered by interconnecting residences, a crazy quilt of colors, building materials and angles.

With night almost on the city and dark clouds rolling in, the tight walkways between the rows were nearly pitch black. Small dots of light penetrated the dimness, cast off from bare windows or cracked open doors. The place smelled of people, both human and fae, with a lingering overlay of bird shit, either from pigeons or rooftop chickens kept in hutches beside their owners' doors. Typical family sounds drifted out, someone's loud laughter cutting through a low rumbling argument.

The roof access from Wang Shi spat us out into the middle of a large span stretching over a few streets, jogging across the nested buildings with several arched bridges connecting to other rooftop islands. Finding the shrine god in this *gōngyù* was going to be a mess.

"There's only one access point onto this span." Leonard pointed to a wide cobbled together bridge a few buildings down. "Thing moves fast but is it smart enough to head over there? How intelligent is it?"

"Cursed relics aren't necessarily smart but they're kind of like chickens. They know what an axe looks like." I stepped around a toppled over tricycle, its purple handlebar tassels faded to a gray from the sun. "Go left. I'll take right. Let's hug the outside and see if we can spot it."

A few strides took me into the maze, and the rooftop village swallowed me up whole. Keeping my breathing shallow, I listened to the area around me. Normal sounds echoed between the tight buildings, drops of family life coming down like rain. A few feet down, a window was open and someone was singing, an old operatic tune about the Monkey King.

Within a few minutes of twisting and turning down tight corridors with not a sight of anyone else, I heard a footfall then a shuffling as someone behind me skidded to a stop. It was too light of a weight to be Leonard and in the warren of a *gōngyù*, I couldn't count on it being someone friendly. For all I knew, the old fae from Wang Shi gave in to his lust and wanted a pair of badges to hang from his earlobes. He'd survived triad wars, probably slipping out from between cop fingers for longer than anyone remembered. When I got back to the station, the Violent Crimes squad and I were going to have a serious talk.

Pretending to ignore the footsteps behind me, I continued on my way, pulled my Glock from its holster. A quick two-step jog around a corner hid me from view. The deep shadows camouflaged my gun, its long black shape hidden by pressing it against my leg, and I waited to see what would come out of the dim light.

It was definitely a fae, just not the bloodthirsty killer we'd left downstairs.

"Why you here?" An older Okinawan fae-woman shuffled into the light. Her eyes gleamed, fractured pearls and starlight beneath a furrowed brow. "You are police, yes? With that badge?"

Wearing neon green plastic house slippers and a pink flowered housecoat, the elderly woman was a fierce defender of her *gōngyù*, brandishing a thick bamboo pole. Her hair was nearly pure white, pulled up into a skewed bun. Her round gossamer butterfly wings sparkled opal, even in the dim light and she held them firm, not a quiver of nervousness in her proud set shoulders.

"Arcane Crimes. We're looking for a shrine god, cursed." I gave a quick description of the statue, leaving out the bit about its elephant testicles. "Have you seen—"

"Holy motherfucking Hells! What is—Kami! Where are you? There's a damned—" The broken granite tones of an old man punched through the street sounds coming up from the city. "Oh God, what the hell?"

In the tangle of the *gōngyù's* makeshift pathways, it was difficult to tell where the shouting was coming from but the woman apparently knew because she scurried away, her pole raised up over her shoulder as if a battle awaited her. Knowing the lascivious nature of the statue's curse, I was more worried for her heart surviving the rush of its presence than any damage it could do.

Luckily, I could outrun an old woman.

"Leonard, over here!" I bolted down the walk, heading towards the shanty she was aiming for.

Lights were going on around us, precious resources for anyone living off the grid in the *gōngyù*, but things greater than poverty lurked in the shadows. Built out of old wooden garage doors, the shack was topped with mismatched tin sheets for a roof and its cutout windows were sealed with agriculture tarp to keep the heat and bugs out. Someone with an optimistic bent decided the structure needed a coat of orchid paint and it'd been haphazardly slapped on, too thin to mask the former doors' beige and moss green planks. A stovepipe cut up through a corner of the roof, silver ducting tape sealing off the hole to protect it from rain. A thin thread of smoke wormed its way out of the cap, worrying me.

If the shrine god upended whatever the old couple was using to bank their fire, the flames would quickly eat through the *gōngyù* before the moon could rise above the cloud bank gripping the district.

More crashes followed and the old man's shouts grew strident. I was through the door with a push of my shoulder and prayed Gaines would sign off on more damages.

From the sounds of things inside the shack, there were going to be plenty of damages.

The old man was human, mad and armed with a mallet which he wielded at my head with a deadly accuracy. I saw stars and stumbled, nearly going down on one knee. His eyes were pale, nearly colorless and as wild as a cheated whore. A loose kimono covered most of his scrawny body but it did nothing to hide his distended pot belly or knobby knees. The snaps on his robe gave under the push of his stomach, popping open when he took another swing, and I was treated to the sight of his time-grayed BVDs, its front pouch sagging with worn elastic.

He hit me again, striking my jaw hard enough to rattle my teeth. A plastic vegetable crate caught my fall, a corner digging through my jeans. The mallet swung again and the old man screamed for his wife to flee while he kept me back. Another swing and I caught the wooden hammer with my shoulder, nearly dropping my Glock when my fingers went numb. As much as I didn't want to shoot the old man, it was tempting, especially when he raised the damned mallet again. Flashing my badge, I shoved him back with my aching shoulder, tumbling him through the open door.

"I got him!" My partner appeared in the frame just as the old man began to spit curses at me, and Leonard's massive arms closed around the old man's chest, pulling him back out of the shanty. The cursing continued, this time in a fae-accented Cantonese, either from the woman I'd met earlier or some other resident in the loony bin we'd stumbled upon. Leonard jerked the man clear, setting him down outside of my field of view, and I turned, leaving him to handle the rest of the insanity outside.

Because my prey was rattling around someplace in the cramped shack and I just had to find it.

There were no interior walls to the shack although there'd been an attempt to provide some privacy with screens around a makeshift camp toilet. The couple either were readying to go to bed or simply left their futon open because it stretched out along one wall, propped up on shipping pallets and away from the flattened cardboard boxes they used for flooring. The stovepipe was connected to a converted keg, insulated with thin firebrick and set into a propane tank rest. Their lives were stashed away into colorful crates marked for apples and cabbages, and judging by the bubbling set of beakers and tubes on a card table, they also appeared to be brewing some kind of hooch.

Books and knick-knacks made up most of the mess around me, spilling out from bookshelves lining the shanty's walls. A clothesline stretched across a space I gathered they used as a kitchen, a basket of daikon and carrots airing out below a flutter of drying panties and worn t-shirts held on by binder clips. The place wasn't as bad as some I'd seen, and despite the old man trying to play whack-a-troll with my head, they seemed like a nice couple.

It was a pity I was going to have to tear the place apart to look for a malevolent statue with too much magic shoved up its ass.

There was a movement near the futon, a rustle in the pillows that was big enough to catch my eye, and I prayed it wasn't a cat. I shoved my gun away then reached for the tea leaves. I didn't have time to shut down the fire in the keg. It would take my attention off of the statue, and I couldn't trust the people outside to keep the thing contained. From the sounds of things, Leonard had his hands full with the couple, and a murmuring rabble was forming just outside of the broken in door. We'd tapped for backup on our phones as soon as we hit the roof, but dispatch hadn't promised anything other best wishes and maybe a cup of hot coffee when we got back.

Arcane Crimes, while glamorous and exciting, didn't carry as much weight as homicides and burglaries. We were on our own and armed with plastic baggies of black tea leaves.

The cursed thing broke free of the futon, and I lunged at it, knocking over a pile of books on advanced mathematics. Pens from a fallen cup scattered over the cardboard and the shrine god scrambled to get a purchase on the floor, its three good limbs windmilling about. Loose cardboard slid out from under my foot and I tumbled forward, smashing my head against the palettes. My forehead stung, and a wet red dribble flowed down into my eyes.

"Fuck!" The last thing the already cursed statue needed was my blood. I was a hybrid, an unnatural fluke of conception no rampaging fertility icon needed to be bathed in. Grabbing a towel from the floor, I wiped off my temple and stood up.

There was a track of bloody prints on the cardboard and the glistening wet path was leading straight for the door.

"Leonard! It's headed your way!" I dropped the towel, exchanging it for a plastic tote bag lying nearby. It was big enough to hold the statue and a damned sight better than my jacket. The cold air was beginning to hit the city and it found every inch of my over-heated skin through the shanty's walls.

I watched the door, stepping around more books and papers to get to the front of the shack. Pulling my jacket on, I juggled the bag and peered around a long kitchen cabinet the couple somehow shoehorned into the space. Part of a door served as a countertop and it was relatively stable, barely rocking when I put my hand on it to steady myself.

The damned statue exploded out of its hiding place and rushed past me. I made a grab for it. Its hat broke off in my hand, a long chunk of black painted porcelain embellished with gold ribbons and red mesh. The ceramic was oddly fragile, crumbling on my palm. It rounded the corner of the cabinet and was out the door.

I was as hot on its trail as I could be, but a small rhubarb near the shack's door was difficult to negotiate, especially since it looked like my new partner let the old man keep his mallet. Their grumbling was loud, pitched up into a hot fury, but their anger quickly turned to a simmer once the statue wove through their legs.

The shrine god was leaking its magic, bleeding it off into any fae and human around it.

"Get back into your homes! There is a police investigation in—" Leonard let out an outraged yelp as a dreadlocked young woman grabbed his crotch. "Hey!"

"Leonard, quit fucking around and come on!" I yelled over my shoulder. "It's heading to the edge!"

Magic wasn't the only thing the statue was leaking. A wide trail of fine specks splotched the criss-crossed paths along the society's roof. Moving carefully, I kept my eye out for the statue, drawn to the side by a rustling pot of rosemary. A one-eared cat popped its head out of the greenery and hissed at me as I spotted the shrine god dragging its fracturing body up the length of the *gōngyù's* sole bridge.

Leaving the cat behind, I bolted toward the bridge.

Like all *gōngyù* construction, the arch leading to the next building was held together by a hope, a prayer and a lot of duct tape. In some cases, there was actual engineering, but oftentimes, the *gōngyù* residents struck up a mostly illegal deal with whomever owned the building and built a way across from another *gōngyù*. Some bridges were broad, wide enough to build stacks of one room hovels on either side, while others were barely wide enough for a single person to scurry across while holding their arms out for ance.

This particular *gōngyù* bridge was more hope and prayer than engineering.

It was old. It had that much going for it, but still it swayed slightly when I put a foot on it. Made up of old ladders and plywood, it rocked and bounced, tilting alarmingly, forcing me to come to a complete stop before I was tossed from the bridge onto the street below. Like the headless chicken it was, the statue continued to clump-stomp across.

Whoever cursed it was intelligent enough to cast a powerful, probably custom-made spell, but lacked the common sense to hobble the magic's inherent need to survive. Magic, a force like water and fire, often looked for any means to continue forward. The statue was no exception, and its owner infused it not only with a fertility spell but also a drive more ferocious than a forest fire. It was going to take any path offered to it to spread its arcane seed.

It reached the other side where the bridge's supports had been lashed to a fire escape trellis, creating an eight-inch jog from the bridge's landing to the next building's parapet. Most people living on a *gōngyù* liked uneven bridges. They were nearly impossible for the average rat to traverse, but easily navigated by an able-bodied human or fae.

The statue fell into the rat category, especially since it appeared it was missing both of its hands and part of one leg.

Unfortunately, the statue thought *any* kind of movement was forward.

And that included down.

"Oh come on!" I cried out when the statue inched closer to the edge of the bridge.

It bucked under me, and I flailed, trying to keep my balance. Not for the first time in my life I wished for my mother's blood to have given me a set of wings. Even if they were useless for flying, they did a kick-ass job at providing balance. As graceful as I was, gravity still wasn't my friend.

Around us, the city continued on. Ferries lit up the water, carrying people across the Bay and beyond to homes tucked into the hills.

The Golden Gate sparkled, a jeweled string of steel bands and beams. Chinatown was in full swing, its mysterious lure too great for many a tourist to resist and a comfortable den of depravity and security for those who liked to live in the shadows. I could see my own building off in the distance. A few blocks away, the mangy calico kitten I'd pulled out of a dog-bait pen five years ago was waiting for me to return.

Waiting was probably too strong of a word. Bob wasn't a waiting kind of cat. She was more of a piss on my bedding if a leaf landed too close to the litter box on the back balcony kind of cat, but she was there. In that building. Amid all of the chatter, neon and savory aromas, my life waited while I tried to wrangle someone's fuck up into a plastic bag I'd stolen from an old fae-woman living in a shitty four-walled *gōngyù* shack.

The statue didn't seem concerned. Realistically, it was impossible for it to change expressions since its face was molded into immutable porcelain and paint, but I could have sworn the fucker smirked at me as it bounced on the bridge's outer rail.

I didn't want it to go over. We were more than two stories up and there was no way in hell that thing would survive the fall. Instead, it would explode like a magic stink-bomb, and the wind would pick up its dust, carrying its diluted spell into anyone nearby. It would be an ugly night, fueled by sex and jealousy.

If I thought Internal Affairs owned my ass after I shot Arnett, it would tar and feather me if I brought a lust-fueled rampage to the city's streets.

"No. *No. Don't* go anywhere," I cajoled, inching my way towards the statue. If I could grab at least most of it, the spell could be contained. "Be a good…thing. Come here."

It was like talking to a deaf old cat.

"Roku! What are you doing?" Leonard shouted at me as he jogged up to the bridge. He grabbed my leg and I hissed, nearly losing my balance. The bridge churned and I held my breath, expecting to plunge to the cement walk below. "Come back here."

"The fucking thing is going to jump. It does that, and that damned spell gets into people's lungs. You think people are fucking animals now? Wait until their inhibitions are stripped away because some asshole wanted to get laid. It is going to be ugly, Leonard. I promise you that, and it's *not* something I want to explain to Gaines." I shook loose of his grip and took another tentative step. "*This* is why people aren't allowed to do magic without a license. You get shit like this and—"

The weight of the statue was too much for the span's railing and the bridge tipped, its laden side dipping far enough to pitch the cursed porcelain god over the edge. I might have screamed, frustration tends to do that to a man, and in that moment, two things happened.

One, it began to rain. A pounding furious thunderstorm I'd not been paying attention to when it crept up on the city and released its watery anger. The statue's powdery neutralized remains would stick to the sidewalk or drain down into the sewer.

The second thing was I fell.

As small as the statue was, it was heavy. Heavy enough to break the windshield on our sedan and definitely weighted enough to buckle a bridge's tenuous hold on its moorings. I wasn't prepared for the bridge's sway and I tumbled back, unable to keep my footing when the planking rocked back.

Physics really *did* suck.

The skin around my teeth tightened, terror making my spit slick in my mouth. I twisted around, throwing out prayers to grab at any bit of the building's brick façade. My hands skimmed the rough stone, scraping my fingertips and palms. There was nothing under my feet. Nothing but yards of empty space and the promise of a painful ending.

Something firm snapped around my wrist and my shoulder popped, strained to the point of breaking at the sudden jerk. I swung, slamming into the side of the building, and my ears rang from the impact. A rushing whistle screamed about my head and through the aching pain, I heard my partner yelling my name.

"Grab my arm, Roku!" His face came into focus amid the swirl of brick, mist and rain. "Hold on to me!"

His other hand dangled near my face but some sensible, conscious part of my frightened brain told me his forearm was a better purchase. There was an odd detached whisper from somewhere inside of me wondering why he'd called me by my first name, and not just once. That pondering slipped away when Leonard jerked me up, dragging me along the building's side. My feet kicked into motion a second later, and I dug my sneakers in for a better purchase, climbing up the façade as Leonard pulled me over.

I'd never felt anything as sweet as the tar paper and gravel beneath my feet right at that moment. At least not until Leonard grabbed me in a tight embrace.

He caught me up, wrapped his arms around me, then dragged a hand through my sweat damp hair as the storm raged over us. The rain was cold, shot through with ice crystals, and despite the storm's pounding, neither one of us made a move to find cover.

Trent Leonard felt good—too damned good—pressed against me. His thickly muscled body curved into mine and the sear of his breath whispered over my face, burning its touch into my skin. My heart was still going at a machine-gun-fire beat and my body roiled with the stink of a fearful sweat, but the tightness in my mouth was gone, replaced by a hunger for the man holding me.

Water sluiced over us and the heavy weight of his hard cock pressed into my hip as he rocked me and sighed. I affected him as much as he affected me—or watching someone almost die got Leonard's rocks off.

My shoulder hurt and my cock was probably hard enough to pound nails into the swaying bridge behind us, but I was alive. And being held by a partner I'd only had for one day who'd not only saved my life but brought my blood up to boil.

"Pele's teeth, you fucking scared me," he finally gasped. We were both shivering and my teeth chattered loud enough to nearly drown out the sirens drawing in on us. "Are you *trying* to get yourself killed?"

"You know, you'd think so, right?" I laughed, catching on to his curse when I reluctantly pulled away. "Hey, we swear to the same god. How cool is that?"

6

My bone marrow was weeping with fatigue. I'd been up for more than twenty-four hours and most of those hours were spent either running after some demented asshole's idea of a sure-fire way to pick up lovers, or finishing the paperwork to repair the damage Detective Leonard and I did to the couple's shack. Oddly enough, the benevolent society's rooftop access was locked, and SFPD's reconstruction unit had to find another way up.

This led to a new bridge and a long of discussion about paperwork duties between me, Gaines and my new partner.

That was the last time I saw Detective Associate Trent Leonard.

I unlocked the door to my corner loft, unsurprised to find Bob passed out on the sectional I'd shoved up against the long wall. She opened one eye, exhaled deeply then flipped over. I took that as a rousing huzzah that I'd come home to her.

"Hey, Bob." I waited for a meep or a purr, but nothing. She remained a mostly white, orange and black splotched fur bump in the middle of the red cushions.

Bob and I owned the loft, a large rectangular space set at the top of an old Chinatown building I suspected was once owned by a tong. Its ceilings were high, stripped down to the rafters and left open. The space was bisected by a few eight-foot tall cut-through shelving units I'd bribed a carpenter to assemble. It gave the illusion of separation but let me see through the whole space.

My bed sat against the solid short wall, the bathroom and closet built in behind it, giving me a sound buffer between my place and the woman who owned half a dozen fluffy white yappy dogs with names like Reginald and Princess Poo. Bob wasn't impressed by their existence, and promptly served one up for slaughter when it accidently bolted into the loft when I'd opened my door.

In a corner near the windows, Bob had an enormous cat post she never used in front of me, but I suspected there was lounging based on the white hair I found covering its stapled down carpet. A few old area rugs and I'd called it done.

I didn't need much—not anymore—and the loft was close to the Chinatown station so I could walk to work if I wanted to.

The sun was already dropping from the horizon, staining the sky with orchids and pinks. Chinatown stretched out beyond the loft's bank of windows, a confetti of lights and sounds spread out to the Four Point gates. The western dragon was awake, arching its wings in the failing light, the sun's dying rays turning its iridescent membranes to a fiery opal. It stretched and yawned, sparking the air with light motes from its gaping maw. A flock of somethings shot by, but with their dark forms cast into silhouettes against the glass, I couldn't figure out what they were.

A few cranks opened the window panels, letting the city bleed into my loft. Even five floors up, the clink of plates from nearby restaurants accented the indistinct murmurs of conversation and street noises slipping in. The fickle rain began again in earnest and seconds later, the clouds swallowed the city, a torrent nearly obscuring the gate and its dragon. There was an odd calm to the shushing sound of water pouring from the building's roof tiles. A gargoyle waterspout jutted out from under the eaves, its fins and tail wrapped around a thick pillar running up the side of the building.

The stone sentinel had kept me company through many a bottle of whiskey as I lay in my bed and watched the city slip into darkness.

I'd chosen the loft because of its view. It was also miles away from the home I'd shared with John and the girls. I'd needed distance from the suburbs, away from backyard BBQs and mowing lawns on my days off. I needed a space empty of school bus stops and hordes of power-walking moms with strollers. My life was different now, barren except for a cat named Bob and a quasi-uncle who was both my boss and my mentor.

But I still kept my family's photos on the mantle, their smiling faces as bright and hopeful as the day I'd last seen them.

A shower revived my skin but energized me too much to collapse into the enormous bed shoved up against the north wall. After pulling on a pair of black sweats and padding back into the living space, I debated checking my small kitchen for food, then settled on a cold bottle of beer. Popping off the cap, I saluted my disinterested cat and took a deep swig.

Since I didn't get many visitors other than the stray white fluffball from across the hall, I couldn't have been more surprised by the knock on the door than if Bob suddenly began to sing a Korean opera for me.

I was wrong. I was definitely more shocked to find Trent Leonard standing on my doorstep.

And I choked on my beer.

If he was hot in his dark suit and loafers, he was deadly in old blue jeans and a tight white shirt.

I liked that he was a little bit shorter than me. It balanced out the sheer bulk of musculature perfection he'd worked himself into. His T-shirt was from an old tearoom up the street, a place I often hit up in the dead of night for *xiaolongbao* and *char siu*. His shirt was worn nearly to transparency so his nipples were dark murmurs on his chest, their points pricked hard and firm. He'd left his shirt hem out but it cut in close to his body, fitting in against his ribs then tucking in toward his lean hips. His jeans at some point objected to holding back his thigh muscles because there were tiny rips through the pale denim, giving me peeks of tanned skin dusted with faint golden hair.

"Hey." Master of wit that I was, it was all I could say around the burn of beer in my throat.

"Can I come in?" Leonard rumbled at me. "We need to talk."

I stepped back and he brushed against me to get by. The back of his hand barely skimmed my thigh but it felt like my skin was on fire. I emptied my beer before closing the door behind him.

"Um... Tsingtao? It's what I've got—" I stopped talking, leaving the fridge ajar, its bulb a dim wash of yellowed light in my eyes.

Bob—my Bob—who couldn't be bothered to come see me when I came home and left hairballs the size of Chihuahuas on my pillows was cuddling up to my partner, rubbing her tiny triangular face against his fingers as he stood by the back of the couch.

"What's her name?" He scritched under her chin and Bob began to chirrup her pleasure.

"Bob," I replied, wondering what'd happened to my cat.

"But she's a girl."

"It's short for Kate." I studied Bob. Yep, it was definitely the cat I'd paid thousands of dollars for the vet to open her up after she'd eaten the buttons off the television remote and refused to pass any of them.

"What happened to her tail?" It was a stubby thing, cut to half the natural length of a tail, and it shivered erratically when Leonard stroked her back.

"Don't know. Seemed impolite to ask. I figured when she was ready to talk about it, she'd tell me." I grabbed another beer, twisting it open. I held it up for him to see but Leonard shook his head. Taking a quick sip, I swallowed carefully when he left off adoring Bob and turned his pale gaze towards me. "She's shy, you know. So, what's up with you?"

"I wanted to talk to you about... yesterday. At the rooftop... you. Shit, you scared the hell out of me and I..." He stepped away from Bob, crossing the floor over to me in a few strides.

It was hard to focus on Trent's face when he was inches away but I gave it my best shot. Sadly, my eyes seemed to find my new partner's lips and my crotch murmured its approval. Shifting back onto my heels, I said, "Yeah, well I kind of scared the shit out of me too. Thanks for pulling me back up."

"You don't get it, do you?" He cocked his head, the scruff of dark blond hair on his jaw nearly as long as the fade along the back of his skull. "I worked so fucking hard to get here... to be your partner. I spent every waking moment I had studying your case...studying you—"

"You're drifting into stalker territory there, Leonard." I needed to use his last name. Needed some sort of distance between us, but he wasn't going to let it go.

"Yeah, in the beginning, it was about transferring to Arcane Crimes but then... I saw you, going into IA after they'd taken your badge and..." He exhaled hard, blowing out his cheeks. "Gaines was bringing me in for my second interview and all I could think was... shit, I wanted you. I didn't even know who you were until later and by then—"

"You were on your way into the Asylum," I finished for him. "This... you...me...it's not going to go well. You know that right? We're partners. Our first case pretty much blew up in our faces and—"

"I'm always going to be a step behind you. I know that. You've got rank and well, you're all cop. You went in today like there wasn't any damned choice."

"There wasn't. That thing could have broken a lot of people down today. It's the job, Leonard—"

"Trent. For fuck's sake, call me Trent." He leaned in, putting his hands on either side of me. "I've got to get you out from under my skin, Roku. I don't know if that thing made things worse or what, but there's something about you I need. I want to get it out of my system and you can't tell me you weren't as jacked up on me as I was on you yesterday. I felt you get hard when I touched you. And it couldn't have all been that fucking statue."

There were times to be honest and times to lie. When my youngest daughter asked me if there was a Santa, I'd lied and said yes because little girls needed to know there was a mythical happy man who only wanted to bring her joy, especially after the shit life she'd started off with. I'd been honest with Gaines when I told him I didn't care if Arnett called me names. I'd have shot him more than once that day if only I hadn't been afraid of hitting the damned federally protected flying lizards.

Trent Leonard needed honesty from me and no matter what happened after tonight slipped away, we'd just have to deal with it because he was right. I was so damned hard it hurt.

"No, it was just the statue. Don't feel a damned thing."

"Tell me you're joking."

"Totally joking." I ran my fingers over his mouth, catching the swirls of my prints on the chap of his lips. "But I'm not... I'm not going to be good for you, Trent. You've got to know that. If you know anything about me, you should know *that*."

"I'll take what I can get, Roku. For now." Leonard—Trent—pushed up against me, angling his body into mine. I jerked my chin up, unsure of what he wanted at first but the thick press of his cock through his jeans gave me a good idea. Taking the bottle from me, he took a quick sip then placed it on the counter, trapping me against the cold quartz stone top. "God, you are so fucking damned beautiful. I—"

His hands were in my hair, a painful clench against my skull as he tugged my head back, exposing my throat. Trent's mouth was on mine before the soft moan escaping me had a chance to linger on my tongue. He held me there, pinned to the cabinet, the stone digging into my hip as he pushed my lips open with his tongue, taking what he wanted—needed—from my mouth.

If my skin was on fire before, it was now molten from the heat he'd pulled up from my core.

I dug in, shoving my hands up his shirt and across his chest. Finding the hard points of his nipples, I pinched and twisted, matching him tug for tug as he yanked my hair, angling my head so he could bite my neck. His teeth sank in and I gouged my nails into the tender buds I'd captured between my fingertips.

His eyes ran to storm when he lifted his face. The sun was long gone and we stood in the faint light coming up from the mist-veiled city. Shadows filled every crevice of his strong face, casting his fine bones into a pale granite. I could see the Nordic in his blood, a wildness tempered by fire and cut sharp from ice. His massive thighs kept me prisoner, holding me in place as he tugged off the SFPD t-shirt I'd tugged on after my shower.

"Pele and Morrígan, look at you." He skimmed my shoulders, his rough fingers tracking the markings he found there. "You've got *wings*. Under your *skin*. How far...? I need to see you. Have you. You have no idea how much I wanted to taste you last night, Roku. *No* fucking idea."

Common sense wiggled its way into my brain. I didn't want it there. No, what I really wanted was to have Trent Leonard spread me out onto my bed and fuck me senseless with the iron-hard cock I could feel through his jeans.

"Hold up." It felt futile pushing at Trent's chest, but being part fae had some advantages, strength being a definite benefit as I shoved him back a step. "I don't have anything here. I mean... fuck. I don't even think I've got anything in the kitchen we can use."

"Yeah, well I do." His grin was both boyish and sly.

"Thought I was a sure thing?" I tilted my head back to get a good look at him.

"No. Figured if you turned me down, I'd end up driving someplace to jack off my frustration." He gave me a quick suckle on my lower lip. "Now, why don't we go find that bed of yours."

7

I'D NEVER FOUND my markings all that fascinating. To me they were pale echoes of my mother's dragonfly green and gold wings, scattered hexagonal shapes loosely arranged into a spread of colors and darker spines as if they were folded down in rest. The colors ran over my shoulders, down my ribs and to the back of my knees, vibrant and bright against the pale of my skin. I'd been torn between putting my mother's star on my shoulder, or where it should be on my mottled skin wings.

I'd decided on my shoulder because I didn't want to put my mother's death marker on my ass.

Especially since my new partner intended on being there.

Trent's fingers were in me, deep and slick with oil. I panted, arching my back as he pushed in further, spreading me apart. I could barely grasp the head of his dick with my hand, stroking at him in time with his curling movements and I growled when he pulled himself free of my grip.

"Keep doing that and I'm going to come all over your bed," he growled into my back. My skin there was wet, laved and bitten where he'd explored me.

I'd taken my time with him, leaving nips of purpling skin where I'd tasted him. He'd moved too quickly and I'd drawn blood, my sharp canines nicking his skin, and I laughed, lapping it up with my tongue.

There were reasons the fae were known to consume their lovers. The need to hunt ran deep in some bloodlines—my bloodline—but my hunger ran to sex more than death throes. Still, it was better to shove down the instincts calling me to take mouthfuls of Trent's flesh down my throat and concentrate more on getting him inside of me.

Or I just really liked biting.

"Turn over. I want to see your eyes go green." He eased me onto my back, guiding my hips with his strong hands. We were both sticky and wet, sloppy with spit and lube. The bed sheets were clinging to me and he tugged away the linens wrapped around my calves. Trent waited until I settled then bent over me, our mouths barely a whisper away. "Swear to any God you want, Roku. This isn't because of that damned statue. I want you. Since the first time I saw you. Even before I knew we were going to be partners, I'd wanted you."

The thought of the cursed icon affecting him crossed my mind. More than once. We'd been prodded by and chanted over by the department's arcane expert who'd declared us both free of any supernatural influence. Still, the wondering clung to me, a barnacle of doubt I couldn't pry free.

"Trust me, Roku," Trent whispered against my lips. "I pulled you up the side of a building."

"I know," I said, running my fingers over the fine-lined scrapes on my chest and belly. "My shoulder still hurts from it."

"Hurts too much to do this?" His cock was at my taint, nudging along the velvet of my balls. I spread my legs, arching my back up until his head ghosted over my hole.

"Nah, I'm on my back." I bucked again, squeezing my ass checks over his head. "I'm going to let you do all the work."

He was in me before I could take another breath, filling me up until I could almost feel him in the back of my throat. It'd been a long time since I'd been with someone other than my own hands and *that* was few and far between. Hitching my legs up, Trent supported my thighs on his. He rocked, driving himself in, and I rose up to meet him, curling my spine and opening up for his cock.

I grabbed his arms, his biceps bunching and giving under my fingers. His powerful body rocked and quivered, strong enough to hold me steady but I'd broken his control, turning him to liquid with every clench of my body around him. Trent retaliated, grabbing my hips to steady himself…or steady me. I wasn't sure which. The bite of his fingers into my side was exhilarating, sending a hum along my nerves.

A shift of his position and his cock seemed to have grown another inch in girth. My hole was being stretched nearly to the point of pain then everything ghosted over to pleasure. I held on tight, riding Trent's thrusts into my core. We groaned and swore, panting to race to a finish neither one of us wanted.

I tried telling myself to slow down, to prolong our release because I wasn't sure when I'd have another chance to wrap myself around another man. Willing to take what Trent gave me seemed best, but I cupped his ass, squeezing it and wishing I'd have a crack at it later.

If there ever was a later.

All that mattered was the now. Our tongues lapped into a hot, searing kiss, his mouth savaging mine as he climbed his peak. My own cock was leaking heavily, smearing our bellies with pre-come. My own pleasure sang and dove. I felt it bleed over me, touching my eyes and mottling in a volcanic blush of gold and reds.

"God, your eyes," Trent whispered reverently, stroking my cheek as he drove up into my heat.

He kissed my shoulder, his face caught in the glow roiling under my skin. My fae blood delighted in the chase, rising up to embrace our pleasure until my submerged wings sparkled and veined. My thighs were bright but not as bright as my shoulders or sides. Those gleamed, dancing firefly lights under my pale skin. The glow caught on my freckles, sparks of darkness in the bright and Trent's body cast long shadows across the sheets where it frustrated the light.

I was close. Too close to do anything other than fall into the tightness coming to engulf me. It built up from my balls, working outward and into my belly. My cock jumped and I clasped my hand around it, working the loose skin of my shaft up. It was nearly too sensitive to touch, a delicious anguish I could almost taste. It left a metallic edge in my mouth, a razor of pleasure I'd sucked on too long, leaving my tongue shredded with the sharpness of it.

Then Trent came and the world blew back into the night.

I followed him over the edge, throwing myself into the sensations pouring out of my center. He milked me, stroking at the tendrils of nerves in my body until I shivered, too overwhelmed to protest and too weak to cry out. I gave myself one last jerk and my cock gushed hot, filling the thin space between us as Trent slumped down over me.

He must have pulled free from me. I wasn't aware of his body leaving mine until Trent returned with a couple of beers. He used his t-shirt to wipe our mess while the beers sat on a prayer table I'd gotten at a garage sale for fifty cents. I couldn't steady the jaggedness of my breathing, torn apart by the violence of my orgasm and fretful of his tenderness as he tossed his shirt to the floor.

My skin ached where my mottling sat inert, a litter of colors subdued by my release. Trent stroked at my belly then carefully rubbed at the long threadlike scabs along my chest.

"What are you thinking, Roku?" he whispered softly, lying on his side. Even soft, his cock was something to be wary of. I'd be afraid of rolling over onto its girth in the middle of the night, hurting him and probably scaring me into thinking I'd somehow caught Bob under me. "I swear, I can hear you thinking."

"What are you thinking?" I ventured. I sucked at post-coitus small talk. Every bone in my body was sinking down into my flesh, reminding me I'd not only been awake for nearly a day and a half but also just been fucked into the mattress. I wanted to sleep until I was hungry and then maybe eat until I was sleepy but most of all, I wasn't sure what to do with the low simmer of horniness Trent seemed to have awakened in me.

"I'm thinking I'm really going to enjoy being your partner," he confessed. "You want to know something?"

I was afraid to ask. Afraid to know. A few weeks ago, I'd shot my last partner and now, I'd just fucked my new one. Still, I nodded, watching his face soften its harsh planes with a wash of tenderness.

"I think...if you let yourself, you'll enjoy it too. We fit well together. Work well together. And I think, do *this* pretty good too."

"Maybe," I conceded. "Let me get a nap and we'll switch over. I'm going to have to take a full accounting of it all before I decide."

"You do that," Trent said, stretching out beside me. Chinatown continued its dance outside of my windows, the western gate dragon coughing out a challenge to the moon as it broke through the clouds. "Gaines was right, you know."

I dreaded to hear what my godfather had to say about my existence but I bit anyway. "Oh? Right about what?"

"He said you were a pain in the fucking ass," Trent smiled broadly, working our fingers together. "But he said you were worth every damned second of time I'd spend with you. You, Roku MacCormick, are going to be one hell of a ride."

Swift and the Black Dog

Ginn Hale

"We were just kids," Jack muttered.

Shafts of afternoon light speared through the blinds, illuminating the hard angles of his lean face. He exhaled a cloud of pale blue smoke and ignored the glare of the well-dressed diners seated at other tables. In a moment a maitre'd would appear and smoothly suggest that he remove himself from the building.

Then, inevitably, David would intervene, flashing his ministry badge and pronouncing Jack's full name a little too loudly, a little too officiously. A halting apology would be offered and followed by requests for autographs and photos. Behind it all Jack would hear the whispers.

That's Jack Swift?

God, did you see his hand?

He looks like some ragman from the Bone Ledges.

I've heard he's a queer.

Lifting his scarred hand, Jack drew the smoke down to ring his fingers. Let the surrounding diners see that the ragman in their midst was a wizard. They didn't need to know which one. Any wizard was too much trouble for most decent folk.

And indeed suddenly all eyes were averted. All except David's, but then David hadn't been paying attention to him in the first place.

He sat across from Jack in a tailored blue suit, clinking his gold ministry ring against the side of his fourth emerald gin. He liked the gin, David did. Liked that and girls. But he couldn't handle either well.

"It was fun though, wasn't it? Rachael says it was all a lot of laughs back then," David said.

"Sure. It's fun to kill a tyrant when you're just kids," Jack replied quietly.

It hadn't been, really. It had been agony—bloody, ugly agony. But not at the start. At first it was a challenge—him and his pals defying night-curfews and breaking open the lightning vaults. It had been heart-pounding, wild fun, like fucking in a falling plane. But then the Fireguard had caught wind of them and they'd learned what it was to bleed. They found out just how quickly they'd abandon one of their own to the dogs if it bought the rest ten more minutes to save their own sorry asses.

But those stories didn't sell theater tickets or glossy books. Certainly, didn't make for the pretty child-heroes people liked to think had liberated them. And David wasn't asking because he really wanted to know. He wanted to be reassured that Jack wasn't going to become an embarrassment, like Beadle had.

It never did for child-heroes to grow up into faggots, dykes and trannies.

"Rachael says it was fun, then it was fun. Hell, maybe we should crash the palace again for old times' sake." Jack couldn't help the menace in his tone, but David didn't seem to perceive it.

"Of course it was." David smiled and Jack knew the other man was thinking of the latest film version of the revolution where all the blood had been cherry syrup and the twenty-two year old trollop playing Rachael had waggled her tits and giggled like a stripper.

"Look, Swift, I know it's hard to put the glory days behind you." David clinked his ice obtrusively at a passing waitress. "But you're not a ruffian on the street anymore. You're a hero of the Republic, a grown man who has a responsibility to be a role model for our youth. You understand what I'm saying."

"You want me to get a hair cut?" Jack suggested.

David frowned at him but said nothing while the waitress took his glass. For a moment David's gaze followed her ass as she walked to the bar to refill his gin then he returned his water-blue gaze to Jack.

"I'm talking about the big picture here, Swift."

"I won't quit the smoke," Jack told him flatly. He had too much magic wrapped up in the rhythm of burning paper, striking matches and the slow exhale of poison.

"No. The Ministry of Health understands that they're part of your image. Part of the whole devil-may-care package of our Jack Swift…. Your Way, isn't that what you wizards call it? Your Ways?" David flashed a smile at the waitress' cleavage and took his drink from her manicured hand, with a little too much overlap of fingers. Jack noted her shudder at the contact. He felt some sympathy, having earlier shaken that frog-belly soft hand.

"Look, I'm just going to come out and say it, all right?" David turned his attention back to Jack after the waitress made her escape to another table.

"Really wish you would."

"You and Rachael."

"Me and Rachael what?" Jack asked, though he already knew. He knew and dreaded it. Hell, Rachael would dig up the ivory gun and fire the five names of death into Jack's heart if someone suggested it to her...he hoped.

"Rachael's a good looking woman and you're.... You're single." David took another dive into his gin as if it would cover the gaffe. Jack just laughed. A ring of smoke rose around his fingertip, feeling hot as a live wire. Tantalizing electric charges jumped inside the tiny gray cloud, flickering like distilled lightning. It only took a little electricity to stop a heart, a tiny lightning strike that would leave only a small burn scar on Jack's right hand. One of many.

But he was done with that. Now the smoke was just a habit, a prop, a toy he played with to keep his mind out of the real clouds and away from that far fiercer fire.

"It would be the match of the century," David said. "You know, comrades and lovers stuff."

Jack did know, but only because he'd seen it. Rachael and Amelia had been all that, certainly done it better than he ever could have with the men he'd knocked around with. No, Rachael and Amelia had been the real thing all the way up to death do us part, and then Rachael had eaten the ashes.

She and Amelia were one, forever and always.

"That's not going to happen." Jack kept it simple.

"Why not?" David asked in a whisper, which told Jack that he knew exactly why not.

"Have you run this by Rachael?" Jack demanded.

"She's the one who suggested it," David responded.

Tiny tongues of lightning flicked between Jack's fingers like nervous snakes tasting strange soil.

"That's not possible," Jack said. Not for the Rachael he knew, anyway.

"I spoke to her again this morning—"

"Where?" Jack demanded.

David smiled a nervous, darting smile, like he knew that it ought to be slapped off his face.

"She hasn't been well," David began but didn't go on.

Jack felt the blood draining from his face. Oh, those familiar words. The same ones offered to him for Beadle's absence and then six months later his body lay in a lovely golden casket.

"Take me to her."

2

Godscliff, the immense city-state, rose up either side of the winding jagged canyon in steppes and terraces. Eight hundred years of wizardry and engineering defied gravity and the relentless erosion of the wild river below. But nothing altered one law of nature: shit always flowed down.

Jack could see it all so clearly from his airplane seat.

Workhouses, apartment blocks and factories crowded the lower terraces, and beneath each terrace, cascades of sewage spewed from huge pipes. Shit, piss and flat tires rained down the mountain walls to fill the river below. Just over the filthy water, the Bone Ledges of the west bank jutted out, affording hook-and-pole scavengers a last chance to make use of the refuse, corpses and trash abandoned by the rest of the city. Fires smoldered all along the ledges, where scavengers incinerated bones to produce the ash needed to craft the fine porcelain that graced tables fourteen thousand feet above, in the Ministry Palaces.

Now, the stench and steam of the lower terraces lay so far below the airplane that the iron bridges spanning the Red Chasm River looked like spider webs, spun to entrap all the silver airplanes that darted and dived from the profusion of landing strips populating the higher terraces.

Up here, in mid-air, all that filth, rubber and refuse became distant, glittering minutiae. Here, an airhostess in a short skirt served Gold Label brandy and the security men standing at the cabin doors smelled like hundred dollar cologne.

These were not the heights Jack remembered. Certainly not the smoking, shrieking wrecks he'd brought down the last time he'd been this far up in the clouds.

He held his drink, but didn't trust it. In the leather reclining seat across from Jack, David snored into a satin pillow. The airhostess looked quietly pleased. Jack assured her that he needed nothing else and neither did David.

The plane's engine purred through walls of mist as it rose. Jack felt the ascent in his blood. Nearly ten thousand feet up and still rising. He rolled balls of smoke over his fingers as if he were toying with the supple cumulus clouds that slid across the plane's sleek wings. Through a pink-glazed portal Jack watched the land of a high ledge spread out below. Dwarfish gardeners looked up from the manicured terrace that had once been a cloud forest full of thorn trees and leopards. Now exotic gazelles and deer grazed within topiary mazes, awaiting their sporting executions.

And on the ledge above the Minister of the Interior's hunting garden stood the Perpetua Sanatorium. The plane alighted there on a private runway and the airhostess took Jack's untouched drink without comment.

The sanatorium walls were the color of onion skin and were guarded by clean young men in crisp uniforms. Each of them cradled a black machine gun like it was a lady's handbag. Jack guessed that they'd hefted and shot those guns plenty of times in the neat stalls of firing ranges. But meeting their eyes as he passed, he knew that not one of them had seen their bullets grind a man into meat.

They smelled like infants to Jack.

The fleet of pretty little nurses who staffed the reception desks and wandered the sanatorium halls reminded him of all those albino rabbits stage magicians pulled out of their top hats. They needlessly multiplied as he was escorted deeper and deeper into the heart of the sanatorium. And they watched Jack—their uniform dark eyes peeking from beneath identical blonde bangs—like they knew he could stuff them back into the satin darkness from which they'd come.

Gardenias and sweet alcohol perfumed the pearly gold halls, but beneath that lay a dry, vegetal aroma of feed and dung. David requested and was supplied with another drink. He gave a nurse a sloppy smile, and the four security men escorting them averted their eyes as David made a clumsy grab for the woman's breast.

"Quick little minx." David grinned when the nurse darted behind a desk. "That's the sort of thing a man ought to go after, Swift! You know what I mean? Pussy." He drew the last word as if he couldn't stand to let it get out of his mouth.

A grimace crossed the face of one of their armed escorts. Drunk as he was, David still caught it, but apparently didn't understand its cause. He turned on the guard and waved his soft white hands at Jack.

"Do you know who this man is?" David demanded. "Do you? This is Jack Swift. Yes, Jack fucking Swift! You can't smirk at Jack fucking Swift, not even if he's dressed like shit and he smells like a sewer! He's a national hero! You can't criticize a fucking national hero!"

Jack wanted very badly to make David kiss the cement at that moment. One of the guards seemed to see that in Jack's face. For just an instant their gazes met over David's head.

And there was something in the young man's expression, a little spark that made Jack suddenly think of Beadle—not the dead thing he'd been in his casket but alive and teasing him with that elusive, amused smile, daring him to do his worst.

For the first time in years, Jack felt his pulse skip like his heart was laughing. And feeling as stupid as the first time he'd laid eyes on Beadle, Jack let the old power surge and prick over his fingertips.

He tapped David's back, felt the electric crack and sear, and David went down. No one even moved to catch him as his unconscious body belly flopped onto the marble floor. His glass hit, spilling ice and liquor, and bounced from his grasp but didn't break. David would have a hell of a hangover when he came to.

The nurses stood at their desks, staring. An amber call light began to silently blink from the far wall.

"Never could hold his drink." Jack only spared David's prone body a glance, feeling both alarmed and pleased at his own sudden actions. He didn't want to look at the guard again and yet he found himself meeting the man's gaze and enjoying the quick smile that spread across his lips.

"Don't think he broke anything important." Jack turned to one of the dozen nurses now creeping in from the complex of corridors and doorways. "Take care of him, will you?"

The nurses watched him and then nodded as one.

They were rabbits and this was their warren, Jack realized. That disturbed him far more than David's fallen body. Creatures had been the Tyrant's Way. Attack dogs transformed into gape-mouthed human forms and stuffed into uniforms. Rats teeming the streets in the bodies of child-snitches. Sharp teeth and bright eyes hidden in human flesh, those had been his assassins, spies and soldiers.

And now wary animal gazes followed Jack again.

"I need to see Rachael Keys."

A nurse led him and the guards followed. Jack felt them staring at his scarred hand and walking at just a little more distance from him. The guards, at least, were human men. Jack could feel that, just as he knew the fine-boned blonde in front of him was a half-wild hare. But who had stitched her and her sisters into these new demure bodies and what had they done to his Rachael?

Jack knew which room held Rachael even before the door was opened to reveal a chamber of brilliant light, surgical steel and porcelain-white bedding. In the midst of so much illumination and reflection, Rachael was a darkness that drank in everything: light, heat and sound.

During the revolution they had called her the Shadow of Death and even Jack hadn't crossed her then. But now she looked like faded velvet, laid out flat and bleached to a dusky gray.

"Jack." She hardly mouthed his name and he went to her. Seeing her like this scared him almost enough to want to touch her, to hold her. Rachael opened her eyes and Jack saw the warning in her glance. He stopped at her bedside and shoved his hands into the tattered pockets of his overcoat.

"You look like shit," Jack said.

"You're one to talk," Rachael whispered. Then she drew in a deep breath and Jack could feel her dragging feebly at his life. He didn't fight her and only felt the briefest moment of weakness in his knees. Behind him, his escort of armed guards swayed. One went to the floor. Two others hit their knees and that last one—the one with the quick smile—staggered back to the door. He slammed it shut, as the final brilliant flickers of life were drawn from his collapsed comrades.

Rachael looked only a little better. Her dull eyes had turned from gray to obsidian.

"You need more?" Jack asked and he could see that it pissed her off. She never asked and he should have known better than to offer.

"Shut the fuck up, will you? I don't have time for it." She turned her head with great difficulty. "That fuck-up David actually found you for me?"

"I found him. Hadn't seen you in any of the newsreels for two months. Started to worry," Jack told her. "David said some crap about you wanting to make me your blushing bride."

A snort of laughter escaped Rachael and she shuddered like it hurt her.

"Better than an S.O.S., that," Rachael replied. "I knew he'd pass that on to you.... Stupid prick actually thought I'd gone straight. Like any wizard ever could. I knew you wouldn't make that mistake. You'd know it was all wrong."

Jack nodded.

She looked so different, so small and sick. Even when he'd seen her in the newsreels, made up like a doll and standing next to Peter under a Ministry of Security banner she hadn't looked this tamed, this defeated.

"You want me to get you out of here?" Jack asked.

He saw hope in her expression and he reached to lift her from her cocoon of white blankets but Rachael caught his hand. Her fingers felt cool as snakeskin.

"You can't just carry me out, Jack."

"What? You've gotten too fat to lift?"

"Pull back the damn blankets."

And all at once he was afraid to do as she said. Suddenly he could smell blood and sickness in the bedding. He gripped the downy comforter and the soft blankets and drew them back.

A gold spike jutted from Rachael's belly, its shaft impaling her naked body like a pin holding a butterfly to a display. Not even the Tyrant had broken wizards like that.

"Who?" Jack could hardly speak. His hands shook like the blankets they gripped were electrified.

"Don't be a cunt," Rachael warned him.

"Peter?" The gold spike. He should have known the moment he saw it but he didn't want to. Peter was one of their own. A sick shit and a fucker, but one of them.

"He's Minister of Security and he'll know you're here any minute," Rachael said. "I need you to keep a promise you made me."

"No." Jack dropped the blankets and stepped back from the bed.

It had been sixteen years, but Jack knew exactly what she meant. The first rewards for them had just been advertised. Huge red numbers had been printed below a grainy photo of Jack's wild laughing face.

"That was never a promise," Jack said. "Never."

"Words between wizards are binding, no matter how drunk you may have been. Now don't waste my time whining. I need you to harden up and make the fucker pay for what he's done—and not just to me." She paused, staring hard into Jack's eyes.

"He did this to Beadle?"

Jack could hear a security buzzer sounding in the hall outside and far more distantly the stomp of boots hitting the marble floor. Men with machine guns were marching to kill him. A sound so familiar that it felt like a memory, like he'd already done this over a hundred times before.

But Beadle's death felt fresh, a deep wound, open and aching. He'd known that it had been murder. But he'd blamed other Ministers, other devious bastards. He hadn't ever thought Peter could have been on the dealing end of it. He'd given Beadle up to Peter and then he'd slunk back down to his Bone Ledge beginnings because he couldn't bear the sight of them fondling and fucking in front of him.

Rachael reached out and dug her thin fingers into Jack's wrist.

"He wants to devour our Ways, mine and Amelia's. But I'm not giving up what's ours, not to that shit." Rachael fell silent a moment as an obvious shudder of pain rippled through her. Her dark eyes went glassy but her stare didn't waver. She pinned Jack with her anger and agony. "He'll be after you next. You have to swear to me that you'll dig up the ivory gun—"

"It's been in the ground ten years. It'll be rotted through—"

"Swear it to me, Jack," Rachael ground out.

He could feel her trying to claw at his arm. Once she could have turned his bones to dust, but now her grip was like a child's, clinging to him.

"I swear." Jack relented. Even if he'd find nothing but pebbles, it was the least he could do for her, when he hadn't been there to stop this from happening in the first place.

"You'll make him pay, you understand." A tear tracked from the corner of her eye and dribbled down the side of her face.

"Yeah, he'll pay." He couldn't stop himself from reaching out to her then and wiping the tear away.

"Don't turn soppy on me, Jack." Rachael scowled at him. "Not now."

"Never." Jack drew his hand back.

"Let's have this done with then. You said that if I ever took the Tyrant's coin you'd strike me dead, now I'm calling you on it. I kept some old-throne pennies for just this occasion." She opened her right hand and Jack saw the three copper coins stamped with the Tyrant's crown. "Now do it, Swift!"

"I won't."

But it didn't matter. She had taken his drunk teasing and made it binding.

The glory of light and fire came down from the turbulent heavens and surged into Jack as if it had missed him madly every minute of the last ten years. It gushed through his bone and muscle, awakening every nerve in his body. Oh, it felt good as an orgasm; all that light came bursting from him, bathing the room in thunder and fire, spilling across the floor, scorching the walls.

Then it was done and all that remained of Rachael was ash and three drops of molten copper.

A new, red burn-scar steamed across the back of Jack's hand and up to his elbow. Sirens wailed through the sanatorium like they were screaming in horror. By the time armed guards opened fire through the door, Jack was already out the shattered window. When they tracked him to the terrace edge he jumped.

In a recent color film, the antiseptic young actor portraying Jack had swooped gracefully in front of a backdrop of painted clouds like gravity had no hold on him. The same film cast him and Rachael as reformatory runaways and best friends. They'd got a good half of it all wrong, of course.

Jack couldn't fly for shit.

Flight compromised trajectory and destination. It implied directed motion full of intent and, like the path of any passing bird, it could be predicted. Anyone with a rifle and a sight could shoot a man in flight.

What Jack did was plummet while savage winds kicked and threw him through frigid banks of clouds. His course jerked and forked like the lightning crashing around him. His erratic battering was chaos, thunder and cloud cover. Not even a trained sniper could peg him once the wind took him. He tumbled erratically, rising, falling, twisting like a candy wrapper caught in the storm's fury.

At last he dropped through a rotted roof into an abandoned swimming pool full of rainwater, lotus flowers and inner tubes.

He floated on his back, dazed and aching like he'd gone ten rounds boxing a cyclone. It'd been years since he'd taken a jump that rough. His nose was bleeding, but not broken. He couldn't hear anything over the ringing of his own ears.

Above him, reflected light from the pool danced and broke across a high ceiling that once had been painted like an uninterrupted blue sky. Now gaping holes exposed the dark storm clouds that Jack had called down. Warm water lapped around Jack's body. The inner tube buoying his head felt like velvet and smelled like moss. A fine rain began to fall and Jack simply closed his eyes. He let it come, wetting his cracked lips, streaking his face. He thought he should be crying, but he couldn't. For now the rain was enough.

3

He only knew that he'd slept after he woke and then nearly drowned. He fought up to his feet and realized that he'd drifted into the shallow end of the pool. Algae green water lapped around his waist as he waded to a set of granite steps and slogged his way out of the pool.

Thick moss lined the murky water's edge. Past that, yellow dandelion flowers sprouted up between broken floor tiles, and hillocks of wild morning glory vines spilled over moldering beach chairs and twined up long-forgotten parasols.

He must have fallen to an old ledge on the far eastern slope. The Hanford Terrace, Jack guessed from the ornate abandon. Once a resort for favored subjects, the ledge had been evacuated at the end of the Tyrant's reign after Amelia had immolated half the Fireguard and herself, igniting the Tyrant's fuel reserves. Only a ragged overhang remained of the ledge above Hanford. For days after the initial explosion smoldering limbs and burning petrol had rained down on the hotels and spas.

No one returned to Hanford Terrace, even after David's colleagues in the Ministry of Health declared the ledge habitable. People were probably right to stay away. Even now bitter, faint traces of Amelia's killing magic still lingered in the air and drifted up from charred bones lying underfoot.

Jack shoved his way through a weed-tangled door and stumbled out onto the cracked remains of an open balcony. A red sunset colored the dissipating storm clouds and gold ministry planes swarmed in the heights. Lower down, walls of black security choppers hovered over the ledges, raking the streets with searchlights. Alert stations pumped out a recording of the High Minister Campbell's calm voice, thanking the population for their participation in this Ministry of Security drill. As far as Jack could see, the streets were empty, and only the lights of the lowest ledge bars still illuminated their decrepit landing pads.

Just like old times.

Only he was alone now and he'd lost his taste for the fight. He felt old and already beaten by the last decade.

Jack crouched down in the long shadows of rusted iron railings. Miles below, the river rolled by. One deep plunge and he could float out to sea along with the rest of the republic's garbage. Him and the sewage and a thousand unwanted flyers demanding rights for queers and dykes. They could all be washed away and forgotten.

Even beaten, Jack hated that idea. He leaned his face against the rough metal and tried to think, not remember, not regret, but think.

He wasn't a boy burning with arrogance anymore, but he couldn't let Peter get away with murdering Beadle or spiking Rachael, either. Fuck the Ministries and their bigotry, it was Peter who had done him one worse. Anger smoldered in Jack's chest and he let it grow, let it warm him deep in his bones.

It was time to dig up the ivory gun like he'd promised Rachael and fire the five names of death into Peter's chest. But first, Jack realized, he was going to need a shave and a change of clothes. And money, a good deal of money. The abandoned wealth of the Hanford Terrace seemed to open to him like Amelia's last smile.

4

FIVE MILES EAST and five thousand feet higher than Hanford Terrace, Mayer Ledge still rose nowhere near the frigid elevation of the Ministry Palaces but hints of winter swept down on sharp winds. The glory of the Tyrant's botanical gardens still stood in a circus of ornate greenhouses. Palms, ferns and huge canopy trees clouded the glass windowpanes with their humid exhalations.

Jack inhaled cinnamon and the musk of hot compost, and he remembered the taste of Beadle's breath in his mouth, the smell of his sweat on his skin. For a moment he wondered if that smiling guard at the sanatorium had survived Rachael's hunger. He wanted to believe that the man had. The fact that it mattered worried Jack a little. Now was no time to start caring about anyone, much less indulging in fantasies of a future where he got through all this alive.

Jack turned his thoughts from the guard's knowing glance and inviting smile. Above him a bird with a brilliant blue tail took flight from its perch, shrieking at a cluster of schoolgirls and their flashing box cameras.

Jack bowed his head, letting his black vintage hat take the brunt of photos. He walked past the girls in their yellow uniforms as if he was wandering, awestruck as any of the well-groomed tourists who'd ridden the funiculars up from their dull middle-ledge lawns to gawk at wilderness under glass.

And it was lovely—even constrained by cement beds and gardening wire. So many pungent blossoms, thrusting stamens and sensual, clinging vines spilled through the space that even the air felt lush and wanton in Jack's lungs. Flowers, at least, had the freedom to fuck how they pleased.

Jack imagined saying as much to the prim couple who stood scowling at their botanical map.

"There are supposed to be ghost orchids in this bed," the dowdy little woman complained.

"What do they look like?" The man peered between the simple map in his hand and the chaotic display of verdant foliage and dangling orange mangoes rising over him.

"I don't know. That's what I came here to find out..." The woman pulled off one of her gray gloves and stuffed it into her pocket. "Maybe that white flower over there..."

"They're behind you," Jack said. "The pale flowers floating over the lagoon."

"Oh." The woman blushed a little as she met Jack's gaze and he watched her for any sign of recognition. Despite the high rotation of security announcements flashing his grizzled image in the golden glow of the Perpetua Sanatorium, the woman didn't seem to recognize him. A shave, a haircut, a change of clothes, a pair of expensive shoes, he was no longer the filthy rag-man wanted by the Ministry of Security for questioning. Now he appeared to be someone a little better than these two, someone to stare at.

"You're staring," Jack told the woman.

She flushed and spun around to the lagoon display.

"There!" The woman exclaimed a little too loudly to the man accompanying her. "Oh there they are!" The man shot Jack a petulant glare and then joined the woman. Both of them carefully ignored Jack, which suited his purposes perfectly.

He slipped off the path and stepped into the dark tangle of ferns and foliage surrounding the mango trees. The soft carpet of soil and loam gave beneath his feet, silencing his quick strides into the shadowy heart of the old exhibit. He ducked and bowed as he moved beneath the cascading leaves of the mango trees, careful to keep skin contact to a minimum. Clever little chemicals lurked in the leaves and sap of the trees; they could leave welts as nasty as poison sumac.

Jack had known fuck-all about flowers and trees before he'd met Amelia but she'd been born to the high, decadent ledges, where all the debutantes kept perfumed greenhouses and wore silk gloves even while gardening. She'd known the name of every deadly fruit, root, leaf and seed by the time her aunt caught her kissing a maid and tossed her down to the Canigard Reformatory. There, she'd fallen in with him and Rachael.

Before they'd broken out of the place, Jack had shown Amelia where to bite to crack a man's trachea. Amelia had told him of all the poisons lurking in yew leaves, foxgloves and apple seeds. But it had been Rachael who'd shaped her Way and who'd awakened the fire and lightning brooding within his and Amelia's seething spirits.

Not that the magic could be easily shared or taught—that was the mistake straights always made about magic, thinking that it ought to be orderly, uniform and as easy to master as grammar. But magic arose from deep within the dark and churning realm of the subconscious mind. And every wizard had to find a personal Way to understand, accept, and embody the magic. Ways were like dreams, often holding meaning and power to only the dreamer.

But Rachael and Amelia had dreamed together: fire and shadow. For Jack, magic had been something far up in the clouds and he'd found his Way to it on the rising smoke of his illicit cigarettes. Week after week, he'd been caned black and blue for smoking but he hadn't been willing to stop.

Feeling sorry for him, Amelia had tried to teach him how she embodied her power—scattering flower seeds and then releasing the life within them in bursts of flames—but Jack hadn't possessed the temperament to snatch up another wizard's Way, not even when it was offered up to him so freely. He'd only managed to draw a few swirling flowers in the clouds. Those at least had made Rachael and Amelia laugh.

His memories of those months felt strange now, and fragile. He couldn't really picture Amelia's or Rachael's young faces anymore. Instead slurred, vague approximations lay over visages of corpses, their deaths distorting his recollections like dry rot creeping deep beneath woodwork.

Jack slunk past the trees and stepped over clusters of orchids until he reached the far wall and the nondescript door hidden behind a flowering coffee shrub. He tickled the cheap lock and it opened easily to him. Through the door, he stepped into a dank concrete maintenance corridor. Dozens of water pipes gurgled over the whine of banks of dehumidifiers. The air reeked of fertilizers and fungicides. Jack stalked along the narrow space silently taking in all the unlovely necessities that supported the illusion of vibrant nature at liberty.

As a boy he'd sneered at the thought of the common slobs who toiled in these corridors, but now he felt something near respect for the unseen and uncelebrated souls who held all this wonder together through constant mundane labor.

He'd never had it in him to be one of them, but that, he now realized, probably signified his own deficits more than theirs.

He found the disused exit easily enough and stepped out into the biting cold of a small, neglected courtyard. Stunted weeds grew in patches and heaps of decomposing compost formed a line of dark hills at the far end of the yard. Just ahead of Jack the broken granite base of a statue stood carpeted in lichen and frost. Not far from there a dark-haired man wrapped in a heavy black coat hunched on the single stone bench, arms crossed over his chest, hands jammed beneath his armpits. He looked up, nose red from the cold and eyes narrowed against the wind.

So he'd survived.

A warm rush of relief flooded Jack's chest. Then recognizing the stupidity of his happiness at the sight of the other man, Jack grew disconcerted.

The young guard sniffed and stood. The barrel of his machine gun scraped the corner of the stone bench as he rose.

"Jack Swift," the young guard called and he strode closer. His machine gun swung from its shoulder strap taking on the easy cadence of his steps. A few feet short of Jack, the young man stopped. "I thought you'd come here."

"Did you?" Jack didn't see any one else in the courtyard and the frost plating the heaps of compost appeared undisturbed. Still, royal assassins had survived the old days and those bitches could hide themselves in the crack of a man's ass. "And why's that?"

"To retrieve the ivory gun that Jon Beadle crafted for Amelia Currie." The guard flashed the gap of a broken tooth in an otherwise perfect smile.

Jack studied the guard's wind-chapped face. Still too young to wear the lines of kindness or cruelty that betrayed an innate character, he looked handsome in the bland manner of all the broad shouldered, dark-eyed boys Peter preferred for the honor guard.

A breeze lashed the guard's hair and Jack wondered if he knew how much it made him resemble Beadle and the way he'd grinned into every rising storm.

"You think the gun is here somewhere?" Jack asked, hoping that somehow it could have been a lucky guess.

"Not now," The guard replied. "But I dug it out of the mud right there."

He pointed to the base of the statue that had once commemorated the Tyrant's favorite bitch: the black mastiff that whelped so many of his most relentless soldiers until Peter had slipped into her kennel and gutted her. Strange to think now that it hadn't disturbed any of them, seeing Peter's bloody grin as he bragged over the ease of hacking apart a chained animal.

"Nine years ago, during the Damcrack Floods, a bunch of us Bone Ledge kids were evacuated up here to the heights," the guard went on, his gaze still resting on the lichen-crusted granite.

Jack nodded. He recalled the floods vaguely. He'd been drinking hard then and had ridden out the deluge in a drag bar, toasting Beadle's short life.

"The rain must have brought it up.... I was so excited and then I thought that it couldn't actually be the original ivory gun.... But it felt real to me. I hung on to it, for luck as much as anything else. Never could convince myself completely one way or the other that it was the real thing. But I hoped.... And now here you are."

Again Jack nodded. He and Rachael had buried the ivory gun deep and beneath murderous incantations. No way had a little rain brought it floating up through the earth and mud.

"So you took it?" Jack asked. He glanced as causally as he could at the surrounding walls, watching for the glint of a gun sight or the flicker of a killing curse. He found nothing. The courtyard seemed as abandoned as the cold evening when he and Rachael had come here to hide the gun and make what peace they could with the furious spirit of the Tyrant's bitch.

The guard shrugged, looking a little shy.

"I used to imagine that it meant something," The guard said after a moment. "That the ivory gun came to me."

"Sure. Maybe it did," Jack replied. Or maybe Peter finally found a proxy to get past that slavering ghostly mastiff and pull the ivory gun from between her skeletal jaws.

Jack moved carefully, reaching into the pocket of his coat to bring out a lighter and a cigarette. The guard watched him intently as he lit the cigarette and blew out a cloud of thin blue smoke.

"The smoke, that really is part of your Way, isn't it?" The guard's gaze followed the smoke as it curled and sank to ring Jack's scarred right hand. "It's not just from the films."

"It's part of my Way," Jack acknowledged. Lightning flickered between his fingers as he twisted the smoke into rings.

The guard watched Jack's hand with an expectant expression, as if he were waiting for Jack to preform a trick. Turn smoke into a dove, or a dozen gray roses.

Jack exhaled another coil of smoke. If he killed the guard now he might never find the ivory gun. That was if the guard wasn't lying about having taken it. Jack studied the young man. Dark hair, nice build, ears a little big, smile a little too easy.

"So how has the ivory piece held up?" Jack stepped past, striding to the remains of the monument. The dirt beneath him felt dumb. That smoldering fury beneath had at last slipped away into sleep. Neither the bitch nor the gun answered when Jack reached the granite and blew a long trail of blue smoke over the ragged stone.

"It looks the same as in the old photos." The guard watched Jack but not with the measured gaze of an assassin taking aim. "Though it sort of...." The guard frowned, seeming to weigh his words for the first time.

"It stinks pretty bad."

Jack laughed despite himself.

"Yeah, they never put that in the films, do they?" Nothing could lift the rotten stench from infant's bones and teeth that Beadle had crafted into the gun. The thing reeked of rot and shit. That had been half the reason Amelia always wore gloves, to keep the stink off her fingers.

"So, why are you here now?" Jack asked.

The guard's smile faded. His gaze slipped back to the craggy remnants of the statue. Granite flowers curled around the remains of a stone paw.

"I've always wanted to meet you…I guess a lot of people say that. But after what happened at the sanatorium, I thought you might need help. Maybe I could help you."

"Yeah? Well, that's uncommonly big-hearted of you. And after what I did, do you really think you want to help me?" Jack crushed out his cigarette against the monument and watched the guard. He looked young, earnest and a little excited. Like so many other young men Jack had put in the ground.

"You were set up. I heard the nurses reporting your arrival and calling in the strike forces when they thought I was dead on the ground. You were set up to take the blame for killing Rachael Keys." The guard spoke with certainty. And he wasn't wrong, though Jack doubted that he knew that it had been Rachael herself who'd used him for her own assassination.

"Maybe I deserved it," Jack suggested.

"No." The guard shoved a strand of hair back from his eyes. "Everyone in the Ministry of Security knows that she and Minister Tyber were at odds."

Strange to think of Peter and Rachael as *Security Minister Tyber* and *Security Secretary Keys*.

"They always flared up like kerosene and matches," Jack admitted.

"That's what everyone said. But after the shooting on Redding Terrace, it was pretty clear that Secretary Keys really did intended to bring the Minister up on charges for breach of public trust. Maybe even have him held responsible for the murders." The guard's expression grew troubled. He scowled down at the chapped red knuckles of his bare hands.

A group of striking miners gunned down behind the bar where they regularly met, was all Jack recalled of the Redding Massacre. He'd figured it for a Ministry assassination but hadn't had it in him to feel anything but disgusted and resigned at the time. Hell of a thing, when the Shadow of Death cared more about murder and corruption than he did.

"Rachael really made a stink about it?" Jack asked.

"She was furious." The guard's expression briefly lit with admiration then dimmed. "But then she suddenly disappeared and we were all told she's sick, but we knew.... We knew. Some of the men were happy about it. But most of us...were just cowards, afraid of ending up like the Secretary ourselves...."

Had he still been the fifteen-year-old delinquent who'd rushed into a revolution, Jack would have sneered at the idea of such caution, but he'd since witnessed the ruin that rolled in the wakes of brash men of action. Often as not, friends, lovers and family suffered and died because some ass needed to feel he was a hero. Often as not, that ass had been Jack.

"Yeah, well you're none of you wizards, so what were you going to do to a fucker like Gold-Spike Peter?" Jack replied. "And on top of that he has half the ministry guns behind him, doesn't he?"

"He does." The guard nodded but for some reason he seemed cheered. "But it wasn't the Gold-Spike who defeated the Tyrant. That was you, Jack Swift. And I just want to say that it would be an honor to help you in any way I can."

"I'm not the guy from the movies," Jack said. "I'm nothing like that."

"I know. I can see that. But you're...." The guard cocked his head to glance sidelong at Jack but then turned his gaze down to the frost glinting over the withered patches of weeds. "I always thought.... There were those rumors...."

The guard lapsed into silence and Jack took a moment to consider that jumble of words and awkward pauses. He understood right away what the young man hinted and stammered at. How much of it he believed, he wasn't certain. It seemed so very unlikely that Peter wouldn't have already laid far more then his eyes on the young man and screwed him well past playing bashful. So was this flustered fumbling an act for Jack's benefit? But what would be the point? Jack hadn't ever gone for coy types.

The guard dropped his gaze from Jack's face and ran a hand over his brow with the disheartened expression of a boy who'd lost his first job.

"I'm not normally like this," he muttered. "It's just you're...."

"Yeah I know who I am." Jack cut him off. "How about you tell me who you are."

The guard's head came up quick with a painfully hopeful expression.

"Finch. Owen Finch. Security, First Division." He didn't salute but

Jack could tell it had taken an effort not to. "I'm registered to the Bone Ledge, like you were. But I volunteered for security after the floods."

"Volunteered?" That didn't sound like any Bone Ledge boy Jack had ever known, but then he'd always run with a rotten crowd.

"I was seventeen and I needed secure work," Finch said, shrugging.

"You like it?" Jack asked.

"Does anybody like work?" Finch asked back. "Up until now, it's been an honest job. Beats scavenging off corpses on the Bone Ledge, doesn't it?"

"Suppose it does." Steady employment wasn't unknown to Jack but certainly didn't come easy. The same day in and day out felt unnatural and ominous after years of surviving on the run. What career he'd managed to make for himself—machine work mostly—hadn't come with gold epaulettes or a private airplane.

Not that he wouldn't have screwed it up if it had. He knew that much of his own character. He couldn't keep things nice, not even his own life.

Jack frowned at Finch's happy expression.

"So, what you said earlier, those rumors about me? That's something we have in common, is it?"

Finch flushed red all the way to his ears and at the same time Jack caught that look of hunger. He wasn't feigning just to flatter Jack into a back room where he could blow his brains out. Though that didn't mean this pink-cheeked guard wouldn't murder Jack after he'd gotten his rocks off.

Still, there was something touching about that blatant look of longing. The mix of desperation and tenderness made Jack too aware of how lonely he'd been these last years. And it made him resent the knowledge a little as well.

"Where's the ivory gun?" Jack demanded.

"At my flat," Finch replied. He answered so easily, just the way he smiled. As if there could be nothing to hide, no reason for him to fear that Jack might reach out and with a flick of his smoke-ringed fingers burn his heart to ash. After that Jack could just take his keys, find his registered address in his wallet and have the ivory gun in his ugly hands before sundown. He could do it in an instant.

He'd be no better than Peter after that but he wasn't certain that being better ever meant much to him. He wasn't some gullible boy who believed the moral fables that had been made out of his early bloody exploits. He'd been faster than the Tyrant but no less murderous, no less cruel. He could claim to have killed for a cause but then causes were easy to acquire if you were already intent upon murder.

He had one now.

"You shouldn't have just told me that, you know," Jack said.

"Why not?" Finch asked.

"Because now I've got no reason not to kill you, have I?"

Finch stared at him appearing nearly too surprised to be afraid. Then his expression turned disappointed. Likely he'd expected more of his childhood hero.

Well, hadn't they all?

Jack extended his smoke-ringed hand but Finch didn't balk. He stood his ground and met Jack's gaze like he meant to burn Jack's image into his eyes. And Jack couldn't do it. Once he would have scorched Finch's heart to gristle without a second thought—but somewhere in the slow passage of years since he'd been a boy, he'd grown soft and sympathetic toward people kinder than himself.

He brushed the shoulder of Finch's coat, then drew his hand back and stuffed it in a deep pocket.

"Well, let's go to your flat then, shall we?" Jack said at last.

Finch grinned, relief and happiness lending radiance to his nice features. Jack wanted to ignore that affectionate expression but he felt it like sunlight warming his skin despite the surrounding frost.

"It's not too far," Finch assured him.

Jack allowed himself to be led from the frigid courtyard down to the sheltered platforms where battered red funiculars whisked couples and families six thousand feet down worn tracks back to the narrow lanes of brick apartment blocks, crowded diners and rundown theatres of the Salthollow ledge.

5

FINCH DIDN'T TAKE him straight up to his flat. Instead he bustled Jack past a crowd of raucous off-duty maids into a small, busy diner. Afternoon light spilled long yellow shafts through the narrow windows and lit up the haze of steam and smoke hanging in the air. Sizzling oil, cheap beer, lively conversations and the snappy tenor of a radio newscaster washed over Jack like an atmosphere. Finch swiveled and turned between the packed tables and hurried waitresses. He tucked his machine gun close to his body but no one gave it or Finch undue interest. He was familiar with this place and to these people.

Jack hung back, half-listening to Finch's conversation with the raw-boned old woman at the battered register, while also contemplating the clusters of customers coming and going.

A working class crowd, for the most part. Though the profusion of missing fingers, feet, eyes and ears made Jack guess that veterans of the revolution numbered largely among the diner's clientele. At one table, a group of weathered women in their forties shared a platter of fried onions and rice, while discussing the merits of the various hooks and clamps that served as their hands.

Nearer Jack, two men sat nursing beers and sorting political leaflets. The younger of the two stared past Jack with one milky, spell-blinded eye while the elder massaged the stump of his right knee. The glossy black foot of his artificial leg jutted out from under the tablecloth at the odd angle of an optical illusion or a bad joke.

"Nobody's come sniffing around yet." The gray-haired woman at the register spoke softly to Finch but her gaze moved constantly over the room. Jack pitied the idiot who tried to dine-and-dash at this joint. Despite her age, the woman stood nearly as tall as Finch and looked tough enough to beat a mule to death with her bare fists.

She scratched the white gash of the scar running across her chin. Jack noticed another scar just rising above the flower-patterned choker the woman wore around her throat. Neither her delicate wedding ring nor the prayer bracelets adorning her wrists diminished the masculine strength of her muscular, crossed arms. Her fingernails gleamed like scarlet razor blades.

Years before, a woman very like this lady had treated his injuries and hidden him from the Tyrant's Fireguard. Despite her glower, Jack warmed to Finch's landlady.

She, on the other hand, glanced over Finch's shoulder to Jack with the expression of a woman who knew a bad apple when she saw one. Her white brows creased and then flattened to the same hard line that made up her thin mouth.

"Thanks for watching for me, Linda," Finch said.

"No problem." The old woman's expression softened for Finch. "Do you think you'll still be able to collect signatures for the Redding petition, next week?"

"Absolutely," Finch replied and Jack didn't miss the warmth of his smile. He obviously adored this tough, old gray-hair and Jack supposed that the old woman was fond of Finch, as well.

"I'll send some beer and supper up for you boys later, shall I?" The woman's assessing gaze settled again on Jack. This time he felt certain that she recognized him, but she said nothing and turned her attention back to Finch. "Make sure to light the shrine before you go up."

"We will," Finch said. Then he gestured for Jack to follow him back behind the woman and through a steel door and into a busy kitchen. Heat billowed over Jack like breath, pungent with spiced oil and onions.

Six burly cooks dressed in little more than aprons and slotted shoes sweated over old-fashioned soot-flame stoves and steamers. They swore and laughed while grease spattered and flames briefly erupted from their huge pans. A gangly youth clanged dishes and pots through the sudsy gray water of a wash sink. Two of the cooks called out greetings in passing to Finch but otherwise no one paid him or Jack any particular attention.

At the back of the kitchen an iron-rung ladder rose from a dark basement and reached up to the second floor. In the shadow of the steps, stood a small, stained table, which supported three gaudy brass incense burners. Taped to the wall just behind the burners was an aged propaganda poster. One of the simple ones printed just after the Revolution.

THEY FOUGHT
FOR OUR FREEDOM

The bold block letters at the center of the poster had faded to gray suggestions, and a patina of kitchen grease dulled the stark white paper to yellow. As they drew closer, Jack made out the halo of twelve red-framed photos that encircled the faint words.

Jack picked out Rachael's face at the very top of the circle easily, then scowled at Peter's imperious portrait. Blond and bright, he'd been as highborn as Amelia and even more bitter about his rejection; his own folks had tried to put him down with a pillow over his face. Jack wondered suddenly if murdering his own father to escape had somehow twisted Peter even more than any of them had realized.

He'd never been kind and his Way—those dramatic golden spikes and silver knives that he employed to drain the souls and lives from his enemies—placed the very worst of his character on display. He'd meant to terrify and he did. The Tyrant's people tried to dismiss Peter, comparing him to a mosquito. Only his delicate limbs and ferocious appetite were built into a limber body standing six feet tall, and he left his victims impaled and screaming.

But he hadn't been a remorseless monster, at least not back then.

Jack even remembered one night, after they'd pulled off a brutal series of assassinations, hearing Peter gagging and sobbing. Killing women had often made him sick but that night it had been worse than just puking. Peter had cried like he was dying. Beadle had been the one to go to him, creeping into the stinking cramped bathroom.

Beadle had soothed him by showing Peter how to keep himself separate from the anguish of the wizards whose Ways he devoured.

Jack vividly recalled crushing his ear against the flimsy door and listening while Beadle whispered gentle confessions to Peter. He had told Peter about his Way and how he'd learned to hide himself in mirrors while the men at the brothel did what they would with his little body. Then one day he'd realized that he didn't have to be the one locked away in a reflection; he could trap, punish, and even kill his tormentors in the mirrors. He'd even confessed that he'd stolen the Way of crafting bones from another wizard—the first man he'd captured in a whorehouse mirror. Beadle had teased Peter that he could catch him in the reflection of the toilet water, and that at last had won a laugh from Peter.

After all that Jack had been sure that Peter had been head over heels for Beadle. He'd been certain that he'd recognized complete adoration on Peter's face each time he glanced in Beadle's direction.

How wrong he'd been... about so much.

Jack passed a dismissive eye over his own young, wild grin. He'd been such a jackass back then. It embarrassed him that his image could claim any place in this shrine. He hadn't fought for anyone's freedom. He'd just been an angry shit, spoiling for a fight.

Then he took in the other small gray portraits: Cricket, Moon, Timmy, Amelia, Haddad, Pip, Fishy, Grant... They all looked so young to him now.

It seemed wrong that all he remembered about most of them was how grotesquely they'd died. Especially Moon. The Tyrant had released flashy footage of her torture, and slow execution as a newsreel. It'd played twice a day in every theater for months. Jack stared intently at the grainy image of fourteen-year-old Moon, smiling shyly from beneath the shadow of her thick black braids. He wanted to remember her like that, not naked and bleeding to death on the end of an executioner's lance.

Then he saw Beadle. The picture had cropped off half the mask he gripped in his long, dark hands, but Jack clearly remembered the graceful planes of polished white bone and Beadle staring out from behind them. Here in flat print, his face laid bare and frozen in one moment, Beadle didn't look quite as Jack remembered. He appeared thinner and more angry.

No doubt, Beadle had resented exposing his real face for the photographer. Likely he would rather have kept his mask down and posed as anyone else in the poster—or everyone else. In fact he would've had a laugh doing that. Turning himself broad boned and hirsute as Haddad and then melting into Amelia's delicate features, Beadle had always been his happiest when fooling everyone around him with his impersonations.

There'd even been days when he'd been a better Jack Swift than Jack had managed.

Beside him, Finch picked up a worn matchbook and lit several amber lumps of copal. Blue, perfumed smoke rose from the incense burners, curling and twisting in ghostly ribbons. Jack rubbed at his eyes, like the smoke could be blamed for making them go glassy and red.

"I'm sorry." Finch's quiet, low voice broke into Jack's melancholy reverie.

"What the hell for?" Jack snapped.

Finch didn't say anything, just looked him in the face. Then he handed the matchbook to Jack.

"Thanks," Jack managed, feeling like an ass for letting his sorrow turn him pointlessly surly.

Jack set fire to another three studs of copal. The fragrant smoke drifted over his fingers but he didn't hold it. Instead, he released the smoke to rise up into the lazy blades of a ceiling fan.

Then, following Finch up the rung ladder, Jack made his own ascent.

6

He supposed that it reflected something unseemly about him that he found the clean comfort of Finch's flat strange.

Dirty dishes, empty beer bottles and a trashcan overflowing with the remains of cheap dinners wouldn't have taken him aback. The tidy square sofa-bed, neat bookshelves, and four wooden chairs gathered around a simple dining table, however, surprised him.

Ugly memories had turned his expectations dank and sour, he realized. Probably because of that damn poster.

With Rachael and Beadle so present in his mind, he'd only been prepared for filthy floors, moldering walls and mattresses blanketed in wads of stiff, blood-soaked bandages. A funk of sweat, vomit, and spunk wouldn't have alarmed him any more than stockpiles of porn, bones, and guns.

But that was a past that Finch didn't inhabit. Instead this place smelled like fresh laundry. It felt warm and unguarded. Jack glanced over the framed photographs hanging on the far wall. A smiling couple posed with a slim boy hugged between them. A large family grouped around a holiday dinner table dressed in their modest best. In another two tin frames, a glossy black mastiff flopped across a grinning boy's lap. Something in the boy's smile made Jack feel certain that he was looking at Finch as a youth.

Jack wanted to move nearer and study those happy faces more closely, but resisted. That was a world that didn't belong to him.

"Make yourself comfortable," Finch said. "Linda will probably send up the beer in a few minutes."

While Finch disarmed and locked his machine gun away in its rack, Jack took in the straight line of paperback spines on the nearest bookshelf: history, philosophy and poetry. Odd reading for anyone born to the Bone Ledge. Odd for most of them to read, at all.

Then Jack noticed the neat stack of political flyers on the table. Finch lay his coat across the back of one of the four chairs and offered Jack another of his easy smiles.

"The toilet's through that door and if you pull back the drapes there's a fire balcony, if you want some fresh air."

Jack nodded and absently pulled a cigarette from the pack in his pocket.

"Let me get the ashtray," Finch offered and then turned into the small nook that served as his kitchen. A toaster stood beside the sink but there was no sign of either an icebox or a stove.

Jack picked up one of the flyers while Finch brought a tin ashtray from his cupboard.

"New Progressive Party?" Jack asked.

Finch grinned like Jack had mentioned his favorite singer and set the ashtray down on the table.

"Support has been slow growing but this year we'll likely win a majority in the Ministry of Justice and in the Ministry of Health." Finch swung down into one of his straight-backed chairs and stretched his legs out beneath the table. "That would be something, wouldn't it? Decriminalization of consensual crimes and financial programs for the low ledges."

Jack nodded though Finch's words didn't quite seem real to him. It had taken seven years of blood and murder to pull the Tyrant from his throne. After that, did anyone believe that the fat tics who had seized the ministries after his demise would relinquish their power when threatened by mere votes? What force did people imagine their political posters and ballots actually possessed? Who fought ministers and wizards with mere scraps of paper and actually expected to win anything?

"We took a significant percentage of positions across all the ministries in the last major vote."

Jack frowned. He couldn't remember if he'd bothered to weigh in the last time the polls had opened. Though he distinctly recalled getting booted out six years back, when he'd shown up too filthy and foul-mouthed for the liking of the prim volunteers running the place.

"It's going to happen," Finch said and he sounded absolutely certain. "You made it possible, Jack. We aren't ruled by a Tyrant anymore. Our leaders are answerable for their actions. Common people have a vote and we're going to use it to make things better for all of us." Taking in his handsome confidence, two very different thoughts occurred to Jack. First, he hoped that somehow Finch could be right, because it would be an amazing and beautiful thing if justice and equality could be more than empty words splashed across propaganda posters. Second, Finch was nothing like Beadle, despite a slight similarity to their eyes and jawline.

He wasn't anything like any of them had been back in the revolution. If anything Finch resembled one of those ideal, film incarnations, who truly believed that a better world was possible and worth the struggle. Idealists like that only survived in fiction. If Peter discovered that Finch had helped him—even this much—he'd gut Finch and let him die slow in a dank cell.

Jack dropped his cigarettes back into his coat pocket.

"I just came for the gun," Jack said firmly.

"Right. Of course." Finch sounded a little disappointed but immediately pointed to a tin box on one of his shelves. "It's there."

Jack set the flyer back down on Finch's table and went to the shelf. The tin box felt hot as he picked it up and when he opened it, that familiar choking stench rose up from the sleek, pearly body of the gun.

Finch made a sour face and bounded up from his seat to draw back his pale green drapes and throw open the door to the fire balcony.

Jack carried the tin box out, like he was removing the decomposing carcass of a rat. The late afternoon breezes swept away the worst of the stink, but couldn't clear it all. The odor rose in waves.

"I can't help but think that you might not have to shoot anyone with the thing to overwhelm them," Finch commented.

Jack laughed and then coughed on the foul air.

"Has it gotten worse? Or was it always so...strong?" Finch asked.

"Hard to say. It's been a while, but it does seem remarkably pungent, even for what I remember."

In fact, Jack had expected that with Beadle's death the gun would have diminished to a shade of what it had been. He'd seen it happen before, spell-bound bone thinned to a frail lattice, steel turned translucent and brittle as glass. The Tyrant's spells had all dissipated within two years of his death. Even the blazing horrors of the Fireguard dulled to char and dust eventually.

But the ivory gun appeared as solid and polished as the day Beadle had made it. The red scrimshaw spider still crouched just below the hammer looking bright as a drop of blood. The fine lines of its web decorated the grip like a veil of lace. Small skulls grinned over each of the chambers of the cylinder and a delicate script curled down the barrel proclaiming, *you're already dead, Fucker.*

The words echoed a quote from one of the pulp novels that Beadle had loved.

He was already dead on the inside. I just drove in the bullet hole to drain the corpse.

Jack had never bothered to read the book. He'd never liked stories about lovers murdering each other. But he wondered now if he shouldn't have.

Even from within the tin box, the gun felt heavy and warm. The sickly fumes coiled up around him like a shroud of revulsion and guilt. If the stench hadn't grown stronger it had certainly become more grasping and corrupt.

Maybe there was something about Beadle's Way—the fact that he'd stolen the bone-craft from another Wizard—that had imbued the ivory gun with greater permanence.

Another uneasy thought skittered through Jack's mind. He remembered Rachael's cold, assessing gaze moving over him. She'd sent him to retrieve the gun for a reason and she'd known it would still be strong and deadly.

A sick feeling churned up from the pit of his stomach. He wasn't sure if it was his suspicions or the reek of the gun getting to him. He closed the tin box and set it down on the iron rungs of the balcony floor.

"Something wrong?" Finch asked.

"Plenty," Jack replied. "I'm spoiled for choices."

Finch smiled at that and nodded. He leaned on the railing and looked out across the clutter of old brick buildings and fire escapes. Gold light from the sinking sun skimmed low across the ledge, casting shadows nearly as long and blue as the sky.

Then three black security choppers swept up from the ledge below and roared overhead. For a moment Jack's heart pounded with the heavy thuds of their whirling blades. Finch shifted, stepping smoothly between the choppers and Jack. One of the black machines dipped and Finch offered the men inside a relaxed wave. The gunner waved back and then the chopper whirred away. The other two followed.

"Friends of yours I, take it?" Jack asked.

"Friends of yours, as well," Finch replied. He looked Jack in the face with that same calm expression he'd given him at the shrine. "You aren't alone in this, you know. There are a lot of us who want to bring the Minister to justice. We just haven't had the means before—"

"Well, I'm a hell of a means, that's for damn sure." The words came out more bitter than Jack meant them to. He was thinking of Rachael, using him to kill herself. Using him even now that she was dead.

"No," Finch cut through Jack's anxious thoughts. "I meant a legal means."

"Legal..." Jack glanced at the tin where the ivory gun lay. What could possibly be legal about breaking into Peter's home and blowing his brains out?

"When Secretary Keys died we realized that Minister Tyber would take advantage of her weakened spells to break into her records and destroy the evidence she'd gathered against him." Finch spoke quietly but with a calm certainty. "One of the Secretary's loyalists realized that as well. She took everything she could carry and turned it over to our friends in the Ministry of Justice."

"To press charges, you mean?" Jack struggled to imagine that going well. Certainly wouldn't for the arresting officers. He couldn't see any wizard who'd fought in the revolution meekly accepting cuffs and shuffling into a holding cell. No, there would be blood, bullets and in the end a lot of smoldering bodies.

"That flyby overhead was the signal that they found what they need to lay charges," Finch said. The long gold light lent radiance to his broad smile. He struck Jack as so handsome, good-hearted and doomed that it made him a little sick.

Jack pulled a cigarette free from his pack and quickly lit it. He drew in a deep hot breath of smoke then exhaled and pulled the gray haze down to ring his fingers.

Finch watched him expectantly.

"So, you and your friends think that the minister is just going to roll over and let you lock him up, do you?" Jack asked.

"No. We know Minister Tyber won't surrender peaceably." Finch shook his head. "But there are ways to break a wizard's power, aren't there? A deputized wizard could come along on the arrest—"

"Fuck no!" Jack cut him off.

"Why not?" Finch didn't raise his voice. He just asked and his calm cooled Jack's outrage, though it certainly didn't change his mind.

"Because going against him right up front would be suicide. He'd see you coming miles away and be ready."

"But if you broke his power first—"

"It's not that easy." Jack dragged in another burning column of smoke. Bitterness filled his lungs and breath. "Not only would I need to catch him off-guard. I'd have to have something of his—something so personal that it gave me a means to tap directly into his Way. Even then I'd still have to ring him, to hold him where I wanted. That's hard magic and he'd be kicking the life out of me while I tried to build it."

"But you killed the Tyrant in his own palace." The admiration in Finch's voice and gaze was flattering. It disturbed Jack to notice how much he liked that. Jack clenched his hand around the hard edges of the tin box, feeling it bite.

"Yeah, I killed him. Took him by surprise in the dark and murdered him before he knew I was there." Agitated sparks flickered between Jack's fingers.

He hated the memory of that bloody fucking night. The charred remains of the two young boys who'd burned to death in the Tyrant's bed with him, flared through Jack's memory. He hadn't known they were there—hadn't known they were chained and couldn't escape the fury of lightning and fire that Jack unleashed into the dark chamber.

Jack scowled at the scars marring his hand.

"If I'd broken in there and tried fucking around encircling and breaking the Tyrant, it wouldn't have just been me who died. That fight would have torn down the entire palace on top of us. Even then I wouldn't have likely won."

Finch frowned deeply but didn't argue.

"It's the difference between shooting a helicopter down and trying to catch one with your bare hands," Jack said. He didn't want to feel guilty for refusing. Finch had to see reason in this, didn't he?

"I understand," Finch told him, but he didn't meet Jack's eyes. Instead he turned and gazed out to the far mountain peaks where the sinking sun glowed gold-red through the distant valleys. "I'm not going to ask you to do something that could get you killed.... You've already done more than anyone had a right to expect of you."

Finch turned back to him, his expression determined. The wind tossed a strand of his hair into his eyes and he shoved it back in annoyance.

"But I will ask that you let us try to do this legally before you resort to assassination. Because what's the point of murdering a man for unlawfully killing other people? As a society we have to find better ways of enforcing our laws. Common folk or wizards, there have to be fair trials. We can't just keep resorting to murder—"

A bell jangled from inside the flat.

Finch sighed heavily and then just shook his head as if even he wasn't quite sure why he bothered to talk about these things anymore.

"That will be Linda with the beer." Finch pulled a smile that looked too hard and proud. Somehow it seemed to suit him though. He strode past Jack back into the flat.

"You drink Brass Monkey, don't you?" Finch called.

Nine years back Jack hadn't done much of anything else, but he'd eased off since then.

"It's a favorite but I'm not picky." Jack followed him, with the tin box tucked under his arm and rings of smoke swirling around his fingers. He placed the tin on the bookshelf where he'd found it and then seated himself at the table.

In the kitchen, Finch pulled open a cupboard to expose the interior of a dumbwaiter. He withdrew two yellow bottles, labeled with the red-eyed monkey that had stared Jack down on so many drunken occasions. Finch placed the bottles on the table and followed that with a huge platter of pigeon rice and fried onions. Fragrant spices filled the kitchen and all at once Jack felt how little he'd eaten in the last week. He just hadn't had it in him to care.

Now he was ravenous.

Finch brought bowls and silverware to the table and then, to Jack's surprise, also set down two spotless beer glasses. White cloth napkins followed. Jack eyed the napkins and glasses.

How did anyone born to the Bone Ledge develop a habit of decanting beer into glasses, much less flashing cloth napkins?

"I feel like we're going to be saying our prayers over the feed in a minute," Jack commented.

Finch glanced to him and following his gaze to the napkin, laughed.

"I'm not putting on too fine of airs, am I?" Finch asked. He sat down across from Jack and poured Jack's beer and then his own.

"No," Jack replied. "I'm just not used to anyone so well mannered being born to the Bone Ledge."

Finch looked a little embarrassed. He served Jack two heaps of the steaming pigeon rice and then spooned some onto his own plate, but he didn't eat.

"I was born there but my father landed a job when I was two and our whole family moved up."

"Yeah?" Jack wetted his mouth with a slug of the mellow beer. Then he tucked into the rice. It tasted spicy and warming. "Up where?"

Finch picked up his fork and turned it over in his hand.

"Both my parents and my uncle were good with animals..." Finch stalled, taking a long drink of his own beer. "The family needed money and the palace kennels paid better than anywhere else."

"They took the Tyrant's coin?" Even as he spoke Jack realized he was an ass for asking. There'd been thousands of people who'd served the Tyrant. From maids, cooks and gardeners to entertainers and investment brokers. Even in the last days, the Tyrant had controlled entire economies. Not everyone taking his coin had supported his reign. They'd just needed money to survive and support their families.

Jack glanced to Finch. The other man bowed his head, working his fork through his rice. A shamed flush colored his cheeks like he'd been slapped in the face. Jack felt like a shit for doing that to him. He wished he possessed the finesse to seamlessly shift the subject but that wasn't in him. Instead he pushed on.

"You couldn't have been too old then. You remember much of the place?" Jack asked.

"Some." Finch stole a glance up at him and seemed to find reassurance.

"I heard that the stables and kennels were huge." Jack took another drink. "All I ever saw of it was after the palaces were sacked.... All burnt out. But I always did wonder."

"The kennels and hunting grounds were actually beautiful places. Big open fields for the horses. Giant runs for the dogs, and of course mews the size of townhouses where you could watch the hawks and owls flying." Finch took a tentative bite of his rice. "I used to trail after my mom and help her feed the dogs."

"Yeah?" Jack thought of the tyrant's bitch and the statue where he and Rachael had buried the ivory gun. Finch nodded. Some of the flush had faded from his face and he looked more at ease now. He sipped his beer and pointed to the pictures hanging on his wall.

"There was one big black mastiff that I loved. Bess. I think I spent more time with her and her puppies than I did with any of the other servants' kids. I used to wander all across the woods and wilds playing with her."

Jack stared at the photos, recognizing the joy and innocence of both the beast and the boy.

"I didn't really understand what the revolution was at first. I was nine when the fighting began." Finch took another drink and stared at the suds sliding down along the inside of his glass before he met Jack's eyes again. "By the end though, I knew what the Tyrant had been and done. My uncle hated him with a passion."

Jack nodded. By the end most people had hated the man. Though thinking back on it now, Jack wondered how much of that anger had stemmed from years of his seeming inability to secure the streets and ledges from the terror that Jack and his lot had relentlessly unleashed.

"Just before the palace fell, my uncle managed to smuggle me back down to a friend of his on the Bone Ledge. Linda, actually. Three months after that the Tyrant was dead and the purges started." Finch left off there and Jack understood why.

He'd been at the palace back then and seen it for himself. A seat of honor had even been provided for him at the start of the purges. It had been then that he'd lost what few illusions he'd held about the moral superiority of the men and women filling the seats of power after the Tyrant's death.

They'd staged a few sham trials for newsreels, then ordered so many summary executions that firing squads had worked for months like assembly lines specially designed to turn out corpses. Every evening a fleet of garbage trucks had hauled away the bodies of maids, accountants, butlers, tailors, singers and nearly every other hapless worker unlucky enough to be deemed loyal to the Tyrant's coin.

Finch would have been sixteen when he was orphaned and every childhood friend he'd known had been dumped into the mass graves that now made up the public gardens of the Palace Ledge. Wasn't any wonder he'd signed on for the three square meals and free bunk of a Ministry of Security recruit. Cradling a gun had probably been its own kind of comfort then too.

Though, these days it was hard to find anybody who didn't have a sad story if you dug deep enough. Still Finch didn't seem the type to work that angle or want pity.

"You've obviously done good for yourself," Jack commented. "This is a nice place. Better than my lodgings, I'll tell you that."

Finch indulged in a smile and looked relieved at the change of subject.

"I'm part owner of the café." Finch's pride in the fact sounded through his voice.

"Really? At your age?"

"I'm not that much younger than you," Finch replied, then he shrugged. "I didn't have anything to spend my pay on and I knew Linda and her husband, Adil, could run a place like this in their sleep. It was a little rocky the first two years but now they're doing great and I have room and all the board I could ask for."

"The food's certainly fine by me," Jack agreed.

Jack helped himself to some onions. They tasted good, in a way that he could never make his own cooking taste. Sweet and hot. Perfect with the cheap beer. Across from him, Finch relaxed in his chair. He ate, sipped his beer and cast Jack one of those flattering smiles that warmed Jack deep inside.

Briefly, Jack indulged in the peace and ease of the moment. How good would it be to have a whole life like this?

Then his gaze caught again on the pictures hanging on the wall. That happy boy and his huge mastiff stared back at Jack. He knew that animal. Jack turned his attention to Finch.

"Are you going to tell me how you really got your hands on the ivory gun?" Jack asked.

"I told you," Finch replied but he stole a telling glance to the photos. "I went poking around in the mud and just found it."

Jack scowled and considered Finch.

"But what got you poking around out there?"

"I..." Finch frowned, his gaze shifting into a distance that Jack couldn't see. "You're not going to believe me."

"Well, that's my problem then, isn't it?" Jack responded.

Finch picked up his beer glass but then put it back down.

"I was evacuated just like I said. I woke up in the middle of the night and Bess was there beside me."

"The Tyrant's mastiff?"

Finch nodded.

"She was standing over my sleeping mat. I knew she'd been killed and that I had to be dreaming but she seemed so real.... I got up and she led me out to the courtyard and lay down. I hardly noticed how hard it was raining, I felt so happy that she was with me again. But when I reached out to pet her, my hand sank through her into the mud. The gun was just there."

Finch picked up his beer again and this time drained it. "She's come to me a few other times since then. Led me to lost things or missing people. She kept one boy who we pulled from the river from freezing. Laid down on him... though none of the other guys with me seemed to see her."

"Well, fuck...." Jack stared at Finch.

"It's the truth. I know it sounds crazy—"

"Not crazy." Jack cut him off. "Sounds like you're a wizard."

"What? No." Finch protested. "It's Bess. She's the one—"

"She's your Way," Jack told him. "You work your magic through her form because deep inside you, she symbolizes something important and powerful to you."

It made sense now, how the gun had come to Finch and how Finch had known exactly where Jack would go. Neither luck nor chance was at play here, but the subtle magic of a young man who didn't recognize how powerfully he compelled the world around him to his will.

No, Jack thought, Finch didn't compel anything. He wasn't a tyrant or a revolutionary. He found what was lost and with a modesty that made him unaware of even his own power.

"Wouldn't I know, if that were the case?" Finch's tone sounded somewhere between argument and question.

"Wizard's Ways aren't like what they show in the films," Jack replied. "It's not like we sit down and decide. I didn't think to myself, I'm gonna work magic by smoking and being kicked through a six-story window. My Way just came out of that." Jack considered Finch's unconvinced expression. "You know Haddad, right?"

"Haddad, the Hawk." Finch brightened, clearly relieved not to be discussing himself anymore. "Of course, who doesn't?"

Jack nodded. Of course everyone knew Haddad—except almost no one had really known the gentle, deeply religious boy he'd truly been. Posters and propaganda had transformed him into a stoic, bearded man flanked by blood-soaked birds of prey. The images probably would have made Haddad's pacifist mother cry—if she'd lived to see them.

"Well, let me tell you something you probably don't know about him. Before they were torched by the Fireguard, Haddad's family raised temple pigeons. Haddad loved the things. When he first discovered he was a wizard it was after the fire, when he was homeless and starving. All of a sudden pigeons started flapping out of his coat to bring him bits of food and keep him warm. Like you, Haddad didn't believe that the birds were actually part of him—his Way of using magic. He thought they were the ghosts of his family. Wouldn't be convinced otherwise, by anyone." Jack sipped his beer, savoring the edge of bitterness, and then went on. "But later, when the fighting turned ugly, Haddad…changed and so did his birds."

At the time Jack had been delighted to see all those white, cooing little birds molt into blood-spattered monsters with beaks like knife-blades and steel scythes for talons. He'd been so delighted in their violence that it hadn't even occurred to him that the change in Haddad's Way reflected a much deeper break in the youth himself.

To this Day, Jack wasn't certain if it really had been an assassination at the end of the revolution or if Haddad had simply gone to the burnt out remnants of his parents' temple-house and slit his own throat.

"He didn't want them to be, but those birds were him," Jack said at last. "His Way."

"I can see how that might be true for Haddad," Finch conceded. "But I'm not—"

"Don't worry, I'm not going to out you to anyone," Jack said. "You can make what you will of what you've been given. Call it what you want.

Your Way or just sheer luck. You decide for yourself. That's what we all do."

Finch seemed to consider Jack's words as he studied the chapped knuckles of his hands.

"You really think that I could be—that I am—a wizard?" Finch lifted his head to meet Jack's gaze.

"As much of a wizard as I am," Jack replied. "But that doesn't have to mean anything more than you want it to. You're still the same man."

"Like you?" Finch smiled slightly.

Likely better than me, Jack thought but he nodded. Finch appeared to take comfort in the comparison. Jack did too, a little. Had things been different, maybe he could have been the sort of upstanding man that Finch imagined him to be—that Finch actually seemed to be.

Music from a neighboring theater drifted in and Jack realized that it would be dark soon. Already, sunset colors backlit the drape hanging over Finch's fire balcony.

The ivory gun waited in the tin box on a shelf, but there were still a few hours until Jack would have to go and keep his promise to Rachael.

A little time still to enjoy what last pleasure he could.

Jack stood. "Why don't you show me what else we have in common?"

He took Finch's hand and drew him to the neat sofa-bed.

7

JACK HAD ANTICIPATED something quick and off-handed, like any of the boozy blowjobs he'd enjoyed in bathrooms and alleys. A little fun to fill the time, maybe make him feel alive, but nothing serious or sweet.

Only he wasn't drunk enough for that unconcerned fumble for his fly. He felt far too clear-headed and too aware of Finch as more than a well-built lay. He had too much of an idea of Finch as a man—as a human being.

The few moments they bent together, unfolding the couch into a bed, seemed both foolish and friendly. The springs squeaked and squealed.

"Doesn't get unfolded often, I take it?" Jack commented. Finch flushed and Jack felt like an ass. But then Finch tossed one of the cushions at Jack's head and hit him square in the face.

"No. You are among the esteemed few to merit the trouble of bringing up the stairs." Finch replied in a facetious tone and yet Jack didn't think he was lying.

"I better be worth the trouble then, yeah?" Jack asked.

"Yeah, you better," Finch said, laughing.

Then he dropped to the edge of the bed to pull off his boots and socks. His bare feet struck Jack as strangely exposed and intimate. For the better part of a decade, Jack hadn't bothered with beds or full names, much less the odd little striptease of removing his clothes. He'd fucked standing up and with his boots on.

The music drifting from nearby theaters lent a dreamy tempo to the quiet of the room. Jack watched as Finch unbuttoned his crisp uniform shirt and hung it neatly over a chair back. He pulled his undershirt over his head, exposing the muscular expanse of his bare chest. A single fine white scar slit through his dark body hair. It looked neat and surgical, the result of an appendectomy maybe.

Nothing like the ugly coils of burns marring Jack's right arm or the jagged and puckered contortions carved into Jack's body by knife blades and bullets. The two of them might have only been seven years apart in age but in comparison to Finch Jack felt like a broken old man.

Finch glanced up at him and a wave of nervousness came over Jack.

"You're a looker, that's for damn sure," Jack said.

Finch didn't ask but Jack read the concern in his expression. Then Finch reached out and caught Jack's belt loops and pulled him closer.

He unbuckled jack's belt and opened the front of his pants with a quick certainty. Jack's erection jutted up at Finch's smiling mouth and Finch obliged, making Jack feel good and wanted.

Jack kept himself from clenching fistfuls of Finch's thick, dark hair like a man desperate not to be thrown. Instead, he stroked Finch's head, felt the softness of his hair and at the same time shuddered as ecstasy sparked up and deep down the length of his dick.

Afterwards, when he had come down Finch's throat, and should have been done with the other man and this place, Jack found himself dropping down onto the bed. He kissed Finch's mouth, tasting himself amidst the spice and heat of Finch. He pushed Finch back and returned the pleasure he'd been given. Finch gasped and groaned with pleasure, thrusting and clutching at Jack with a flattering abandon.

Then they lay together.

Jack drifted but didn't sleep. He allowed Finch to ease away his clothes to stroke and caress him. It had been so long since anyone had bothered to treat him like this. So long since he'd allowed it.

But then, he didn't suppose he'd live long enough after tonight to feel like he'd made a fool of himself over a few kisses and caresses. He could afford a brief romantic indulgence.

Jack wrapped his arm around Finch and hugged him to his side. He breathed in the scent of Finch and himself, which saturated the sheets and filled the air, and he felt oddly calm.

Bright colored theater lights flared and flashed outside, casting a diffused glow through Finch's drapes. A little spotlight fell across Finch's hip and another lit Jack's right shoulder. A cat yowled off key to the melody piping up from some dancehall.

They fucked and held each other.

Belatedly Finch remembered that he had to set his alarm. He and his friends planned to deliver the warrant of the Minister's arrest first thing in the morning, before word could get out. He didn't ask Jack to join them, but simply lay down with him and fell asleep in his arms.

Jack waited until he was certain Finch wouldn't wake. He eased himself out of the bed, dressed and found the ivory gun. Then he stepped out onto the fire balcony and was away on the rising wind.

8

THE WIND HOWLED and thunder drowned out the shouts of the alarmed security men. Teams of them fired into the crashing clouds. The muzzle flash of their machine guns sparked like cheap firecrackers as blinding bolts of white lightning tore through the steel gates surrounding Peter's stately home.

Jack watched from the rooftop as the grand theatrics of the storm drew more guards from the house. Shadows and wind lent the illusion of forms to clouds and each man on the ground seemed to see Jack up in the lightning. They emptied their guns and screamed into radios for more ammunition.

Jack exhaled a final breath of smoke, drawing the blue streams around his fingers. Then he crushed out his cigarette.

He eased himself down the slate tiles to the eaves and then dropped to an ornate balcony. Two stone gargoyles glowered at him, but the pin tumbler lock gave way easily enough. Jack let himself into a large, dim bedroom. The vague forms of naked figures loomed from picture frames on the walls. Jack padded past the immense empty bed and its disarray of twisted silk sheets. Full-length mirrors stirred with Jack's reflection and his own face scowled at him through the gloom as he passed dozens of gilt-framed looking glasses.

Jack slipped out into the hall where light flared from cut crystal fixtures overhead and glinted off of more silvery mirrors.

Two doors down a guard stood but his attention was obviously absorbed by eavesdropping on the orders shouted from behind the door he defended. A voice rose over the noise of the storm outside and Jack knew it at once. Peter snapped annoyed commands into the hiss and crackle of a radio. The guard sighed and rocked on his heels then he started to turn in Jack's direction.

Jack took him fast and could have killed him with a gesture. Should have.

But he looked so young, so scared.

Like a fucking idiot, Jack thought of Finch and paused.

Pale-faced and gaping, the guard fired off a single round. Jack felt the bullet kick into him like the blow of a sledgehammer.

There was where sympathy for an enemy led.

Wet heat seared down Jack's ribs but the pain of the bullet wound hadn't hit him yet. The guard's hand squeezed around the grip of his pistol but Jack didn't give him a second chance.

Brilliant volts exploded from Jack's hands, slamming the guard through the door and dropping him to the woven carpet in a steaming heap. Lights all down the hall burned out and the air crackled with bursts of wild electricity.

"Damn, Jack! You do know how to make an entrance." Peter's smooth voice rose from beyond the broken door. He sounded relaxed, almost amused.

Amber emergency lights flared and dimmed, flashing like strobe lights in a stage play. Jack bound past the crooked remnants of the door and sidestepped the guard's burnt body. In the sputtering light the heavy wooden bookshelves, classical sculptures and solid desk seemed to jig in and out of shadow, while gold flares burst up from dozens of mirrored surfaces. Peter's angular face leered at him from as many reflections.

Small green lights glowed from the mahogany case of the two-way radio that sat atop Peter's desk. Tinny, distant voices called through a hum of static. Sitting up straight in his leather wingback chair, Peter held the transmitter in his left hand and leveled a silver pistol at Jack with his right.

Peter's long shadow jumped and jerked with the eerie speed of a spider as he stood.

"Everything's fine, here," Peter informed the men on the other end of the radio signal. "Carry on."

The amber security lights dimmed, then surged back to life and Peter fired. The wooden shelf behind Jack splintered and he dived behind a marble plinth, which supported a life-size alabaster bust of Peter.

"Oh come on, Jack!" Peter called to him. "I'm standing right here. Aren't you going to bring down the sky?"

A second shot cracked over the thunder and gunfire outside. Stone splinters sliced across Jack's ear. With each fast breath he drew, Jack felt the wound in the left side of his chest spearing through his nerves. Blood already soaked the waistband of his pants; it felt warm as piss, but thicker.

"Did you cringe and hide like this when you killed the Tyrant?" Peter demanded. "I expected more from you."

"Seriously, Pete? You want me to burn you to ash right where you stand?" Jack asked. He peered into one of the mirrors as the lights again flashed to brilliance. Peter had moved closer, but that wasn't what concerned Jack.

"I'd expect you to try!"

No doubt he did. Jack standing up in a volley of light and power was just what he needed to capture Jack's form and Way in his mirrors.

If the condition of the ivory gun hadn't made Jack suspicious of the real situation, then all the mirrors would have. As it was, he took them in with the sick feeling of certainty. Rachael might have done him the favor of telling him the truth. But then she had probably feared that Jack wouldn't have had it in him to put things right, unless he had the evidence shoved in a battered tin in his coat pocket.

"Nice looking place you got here," Jack called as he tugged the reeking ivory gun out of his pocket. That wouldn't stay a surprise for long. "You know I'd feel bad scuffing the floors."

Peter snorted.

"Stop making me laugh, Jack." Another bullet tore through the corner of the plinth. "I'm trying to kill you."

"Yeah, about that." Jack stalled, waiting for the lights to again offer him a glimpse of the room. "What exactly did I do to piss you off?"

Just as he finished speaking the security lights flared and then steadied. Jack stole a glance around the plinth. He had the mirrors fixed in his mind. What he needed to find were the bone masks. On the shelf behind Peter's desk, two stood as if on display. One bore Beadle's sly visage.

The other twitched as the slivers of Jack's face that the mirrors had captured struggled to lock into a whole aspect.

"Honestly, you haven't done anything," Peter's voice drifted. "In fact, killing Rachael? That was a huge favor. I only wish I'd been there in person to see her sizzle. At least I like to imagine that she sizzled when you burned into her.... Did she?"

"What the hell?" Jack demanded. "Rachael was one of our own. One of us."

He heard Peter's footfall a little closer and tensed. Peter fired wide, shattering a vase on a bookcase to Jack's right. Jack bounded from his cover, and scraping the muzzle of the ivory gun against the wall, he traced an invisible line beneath three of the mirrors. Another bullet ripped past, this time blazing so hot that it cauterized the flesh of Jack's left arm as it dug out a furrow of skin and muscle.

Jack dropped behind a display of bronze figurines. Sweat soaked his body and his hands shook as adrenaline flooded his bloodstream.

"You brought the ivory gun."

"Yeah," Jack just managed to keep his voice calm and level. "Rachael insisted."

"The bitch!" For a moment even the storm and machine gun fire outside seemed to quiet. Peter's voice rose softly. "So, you know?"

"Yeah, Beadle. I know," Jack replied. He hadn't wanted it to be true but he couldn't deny it any longer. "I just don't understand. Why did you do it?"

Beadle forced a dry, dull laugh and Jack stole a glance at him from between the muscular thighs of the bronze nude.

"Because we were betrayed, Jack. At the end of the revolution, we were gods. People fell to their knees in fear of us. We could've done anything—everything we wanted. The world was ours!" Peter's youthful visage lit with excitement but then his countenance dimmed to a sneer that Jack had seen on Beadle's face countless times before. He contemplated the gun in his right hand.

"But Peter and Rachael conned me into supporting some stupid republic. Like I'd be satisfied filling out paperwork and making endless speeches. We could've gutted our enemies and made any laws we wanted. But no, they'd had enough fighting. They wanted to settle down and debate endlessly with bureaucrats."

Beadle looked straight at Jack and, flashing a wry smile, held his gaze for a heartbeat. Then Jack flattened as Beadle fired off another shot. The bronze jerked as a bullet embedded into its polished torso.

"You were the only one who knew better," Beadle went on speaking conversationally. "I should have paid attention to you, Jack. Gone back down and had myself a fine time kicking asses and slitting throats on the Bone Ledges, just like the good old days. But Peter conned me with all his sweet talk about greater power and shaping future governments." Beadle looked momentarily sick. "All he actually did was pander and wheedle for votes like every other boot-licker."

"You could have just left him." Jack suggested but he was only half listening to Beadle now. Beadle hadn't come this far to have one conversation reform him.

"I did one better," Beadle responded. "I buried him in my place and became a more potent Minister than he ever could have."

"You did always want to be a natural blond." Jack stretched his arm back though it hurt like hell and started his shoulder bleeding. He just managed to draw his line below another two of Beadle's mirrors.

"True." Beadle sounded closer, his voice tinged with nostalgia. "It really was touching to see you at the funeral. You always look so handsome when you're heartbroken."

Jack's gut clenched like he'd been kicked. He'd wept at that funeral.

He'd wanted to die and here was Beadle congratulating him like he'd won a six-buck circle-jerk.

A furious, cleansing fire rumbled through Jack's mind. He fought it down. He couldn't let Beadle prod him into exposing his Way yet.

"And doesn't that just return us to the question of why you're trying to kill me?" Jack ground out. "The only person who bothered to look sad when you died?"

"Harsh, Jack." Beadle didn't sound the least perturbed but his voice did seem to be nearer and more to Jack's left than it had been.

"Though to be fair, you are right," Beadle went on. "I never was one of the popular ones. Not like you. You don't do crap and people adore you. They snap up your posters and swoon over every broad-shouldered prick who plays you in the films."

"Are you listening to yourself?" Jack answered as he edged closer to the dark wood desk. "You're the Minister of Security, how much more popular do you need to be?"

"Minister!" Beadle shouted. "It's just a crapload of paperwork and campaigning for a pathetic crumb of power. And then Rachael wouldn't even let me enjoy what little there was of that."

Beadle fired his pistol and Jack leapt behind the desk, though an instant later he realized that Beadle hadn't shot at him but instead drilled a hole into the decorative ministry shield hanging on his wall.

Seven shots. That likely left five more bullets in Beadle's clip, and one in the chamber. Beadle liked to build his guns to hold a baker's dozen.

"She wouldn't stop nagging about civic responsibility and how I could channel my drive into lasting reforms." Beadle shook his head. "It was pathetic. She used to be tough—the goddamn Shadow of Death! But ten years on and she just turned into another soppy old auntie. Made me want to puke, hearing her nag my soldiers about limiting use of lethal force against civilians. The Shadow of Death squawking when a couple of my boys have a little fun gunning some pissants down."

Jack stared at Beadle, feeling a strange kind of dissonance. He'd been prepared to hear Beadle excuse his actions on the grounds of self-preservation or even ambition, but not because Rachael had lost the murderous edge she'd possessed as a furious teen.

"So, you spiked her?" Jack asked.

"As if she gave me a choice. She was going to expose me and press charges. Talk about disloyal. She deserved the spike." Beadle shrugged. "Not that I got a chance to drain her. I'd forgotten how fast you could fry a bitch, Jack."

A meaningless protest caught in Jack's throat. It hardly mattered to Beadle that he hadn't wanted to harm Rachael.

"What I wouldn't have given to smell her burn," Beadle's expression turned wistful. "The tapes just don't do you justice. Still, it was beautiful to see you cook that mouthy nag. Less than a minute of film, but it's so much more pure than any of those idiotic, sanitized films that the Ministry of Culture turns out about us every other year, don't you think?"

Jack took in Beadle's wide admiring smile from the shadows of the desk. He realized that he'd gotten it all wrong thinking that Beadle had betrayed the ideals of their shared youth. Beadle hadn't changed at all. The same gleefully murderous and fearless creature that Jack remembered from their first meeting stood before him now.

"You really murdered Peter and Rachael because they didn't want to keep pretending they were still seventeen?" Jack asked. He managed to drag the muzzle of the ivory gun across the bookshelf, but he had to use both hands to keep steady. The smell of his own blood wafted on the filthy odor of the gun.

"You weren't there," Beadle replied. "They betrayed everything we were and everything we did."

"People change. That's life." Jack choked back the bile rising in his throat. "We all have to grow up sometime."

"Not me." Beadle sounded serious. "And you aren't exactly one to talk either, Jack. I mean, how long are you planning to drag out the heart-broken loner routine?"

"Honestly, I'm done with it." Jack eyed the last line of mirrors. Two leather chairs and a drink table offered sparse cover.

"Good, because if you aren't over me by now I don't know what's wrong with you," Beadle said and in spite of himself a tired laugh escaped Jack.

For just an instant he remembered how they'd laughed and teased each other all those years ago.

"I hadn't originally planned on putting you in the ground in my place." A hint of melancholy drifted through Beadle's tone. "There was this younger guard, Finch or something like that. The dark, sincere type you go for, actually. Perfect and he didn't even know he was one of us. But Rachael had him transferred. She just made it fucking impossible for me."

The mention of Finch crushed the faint nostalgia threatening to temper Jack's outrage. And realizing that Rachael had protected the young man made Jack doubly furious at the way Beadle had betrayed her.

He edged forward as Beadle went on, "There was a time when you would have gladly laid down your life for mine."

Yeah, and there had been a time when I thought a blowjob in a public toilet was the height of romance.

"It's not as if you're doing anything much with your life—"

It hurt like hell but Jack lunged from the cover of the desk. He swung his arm out, slashing the muzzle of the ivory gun under the last four mirrors, and completing the circuit. He released the rings of smoke from around his fingers with an electric crackle. The blue smoke rolled up from the line Jack had traced, obscuring the faces of Beadle's mirrors like a shroud.

"No!"

Beadle fired a spray of bullets after Jack, tearing apart the gold moldings of the wall. Jack hurled himself behind a bookshelf. Wood splintered all around him. A hard kick landed against his left shoulder and knocked him to his knees.

"Those took me months to build, you ass!" Beadle shouted.

Blood poured down Jack's left arm and the edges of his vision narrowed, as if he were falling into a dark tunnel. Jack gripped the ivory gun, focusing on the solid feel of it in his hand. Its sour stench hit him like a whiff of smelling salts. He forced himself up to his feet and swung the ivory pistol up, to take aim.

Beadle drew a bead on Jack at once.

"I know you, Jack." Beadle's tone was soft, almost pleading, but his grip on his pistol didn't waver. "You aren't going to murder me."

He was right, of course. Even if it killed him, Jack was going to do Beadle worse than the fast death of a bullet through his skull. Jack fired into the bone mask on Beadle's shelf, shattering it in an explosion of gold light.

All the tremendous power of Beadle's Way kicked back against the assault. An arc of gold light slammed Jack to the floor and burst the ivory gun apart. Then it flooded back along the course Jack had traced, ripping through wood paneling and bursting Beadle's mirrors. Like a reflex it struck against the source of its devastation: the power that had crafted the ivory gun.

Realization and horror transformed Beadle's expression.

"No! Jack, you wouldn't—not to me." He swung the muzzle of his pistol down to Jack's face.

The golden light smashed into Beadle's chest, hurling him back onto his heavy wooden desk. The mahogany radio crashed to the floor. Beadle fired as he jerked and twitched in the blaze.

Then the gold light burned itself out and Beadle lay supine, trembling across the desk. Jack wasn't sure if a bottle of ink had overturned or if Beadle had pissed himself. Liquid gleamed in the security light as it dribbled off the edge of the desk.

Jack tried to push himself up to his feet but pain flared through his right hand as he pressed his palm to the floor. Glancing down Jack noted that shards of the ivory gun had raked open dozens of shallow gashes in his hand and forearm. A spent bullet jutted from the floor only inches from Jack's thigh.

His right side hurt with each breath he took and rivulets of blood soaked down his left arm. He should have been in agony but mostly he felt exhausted. Maybe he was dying. Or already too dead to feel anything more.

On the desk, Beadle whimpered and held his shaking hands to his head. Piece by piece, Peter's countenance cracked off and fell away. The skin peeled from his arms and clumps of blond hair fell across the floor, exposing the gaunt terrified face of the boy Beadle had been so long ago, when he'd first hidden himself away in a mirror.

He was broken down to his very Way. Most likely, they'd have to carry Beadle out on a stretcher when they came with the warrant for his arrest in a few hours. But he would live to stand trial. Beyond that, Jack didn't have it in him to give a shit.

He stared at the ceiling, thinking of nothing. Then he wondered if Finch was up yet. Probably getting dressed and preparing to come here and arrest Beadle.

Gritting his teeth against the pain now shooting through his side, Jack rolled onto his knees. He stood.

He didn't want Finch seeing him laid out and bloody as a dog somebody had put down. Finch didn't need to know what breaking Beadle had cost Jack. That hadn't been the point of doing it.

Slowly, Jack made his way out of the office, down the hall and out to the balcony. The storm he'd raised still hurled down rain and howling wind. Exhausted guards staggered across the muddy grounds, the fight drained from them by an enemy utterly unscathed by bullets or rage.

As Jack slipped over the balcony the clouds whirled around him. The wind wrapped him in sleet and flung him out into the sky. He felt the first rays of sunrise strike his face as he fell.

9

He woke on Hanford Terrace again, drifting in an inner tube through a familiar swimming pool full of water lilies. A glossy black mastiff watched him from the water's edge. She studied him as he blearily trailed his bloody hands through the water. Then the dog leapt in and paddled to him. She caught the cuff of his coat in her teeth and steadily pulled him into the shallows.

The cracked tiles of the cerulean ceiling rolled over Jack. He managed to turn his head and saw Finch standing at the edge of the pool, stripping off his heavy coat. His dress uniform suited him. Jack guessed he'd worn it especially to emphasize his rank when he and his friends from the Ministry of Justice went to arrest Minister Tyber.

Finch waded down the granite steps, and hauled Jack out of the water, while the dog padded alongside them. As Finch lowered him to the ornate tile floor, the dog melted into Finch's shadow.

"Got your man?" Jack asked, though his words came out in a rasp.

"In both senses. Yes, I think so," Finch replied. "We took Minister Tyber into custody two hours ago. Only he wasn't Tyber— I guess you already knew that."

"Yeah," Jack managed.

"You shouldn't have gone alone." Finch pinned him with a hard stare, but then his expression softened and he stroked the wet hair back from Jack's face.

There were so many things Jack shouldn't have done, but this once he didn't regret his decision. He'd saved Finch.

And maybe he'd even fostered the beginnings of a new, better government. Who knew? He might as well indulge himself in the grandiose notion as he lay bleeding out.

And if he had to die, this wasn't a bad view for his last.

"Uniform looks good on you." Jack lifted a cold hand to the white linen and gold trim of Finch's cuff. His fingers left a bloody trail.

"You're not still bleeding, are you?" All the joy went out of Finch's expression. He pulled Jack's coat open, took in the mess of his blood-soaked, tattered shirt, and then tore the rags aside to expose Jack's cold skin and the bullet wound in his side.

His hands felt blazing hot on Jack's body.

"It's all right," Jack murmured. He didn't want Finch feeling sad. "First time I think I ever did the right thing for the right reason...."

"You are not going to die," Finch told him firmly.

"Sorry." And Jack was, because he hadn't wanted to hurt Finch. "Not for you to decide though."

"The hell it isn't!" Finch ground out as he gripped Jack hard and pulled his limp body into his arms. "If I'm a wizard then I can save you. You said that I could make what I want of it and I want you to live."

The heat of Finch's touch grew, spreading through Jack's chest and pouring out to his arms and legs. From the pool of his shadow the black dog rose up, snarling with all of Finch's fury and desperation.

"You can't die, damn it. You can't." Finch clenched his eyes shut in concentration.

Jack stared at the black mastiff. She sprang at him and hit him like the breath of a furnace pouring over his icy skin. Heat roared into his lungs and flooded his body.

Jack's heart lurched from its sluggish rhythm to an alert pace, like a pilot startling awake. His ears hummed and his nerves rang like chimes. All his scrapes and gouges flared to life. Finch still gripped him so hard that his muscular arms trembled. Jack drew in a deep breath of Finch's chest then lifted his hands and pushed Finch back slightly.

"Down boy. That's enough." Jack didn't need Finch to pour all of his power and life into him. His ribs hurt and every inch of him felt battered, but not in the dull, dying way he had before. This was the familiar ache of living—healing.

Finch relented, though he kept one arm wrapped around Jack. He looked flushed, dazed at having unleashed the full extent of his own power. Jack remembered the feeling as somewhere between an orgasm and a concussion. He stroked Jack's cheek then slid his hand down his side. Jack winced and alarm dispelled Finch's languid expression.

"You're still bleeding."

"Scratches, nicks. Nothing I can't survive." Jack caught Finch's hand and held it, then drew the palm against his chest to let Finch feel his heart beating, strong and steady. "I'm all right. You saved me."

"I did?" Finch asked softly then he offered Jack a broad grin. "I did. I am a wizard, like you."

"Yeah." Jack returned Finch's smile. All around them, dandelions growing up from between the cracked blue tiles spread brilliant gold blossoms. Tiny iridescent hummingbirds flitted between the violet trumpets of the flowering morning glories that entwined abandoned chairs and tables. Life went on even after desolation, not always in the same way, but still it could be beautiful, couldn't it?

"Not a bad day to end a revolution," Jack murmured. Beside him Finch nodded and gently squeezed Jack's shoulder.

"Not a bad day at all."

A Queer Trade

KJ CHARLES

"O, it's a queer trade, but there's many worse."
– Of the Street-Buyers of Waste Paper,
London Labour and the London Poor.

MARLEIGH WAS DEAD: to begin with.

Hepzibah Marleigh, gentleman of the parish of St. Alban the Martyr. Bent-backed, blue eyes bright in a face like crumpled parchment, teeth as brown as the meerschaum pipe they always clamped. He had lived in the cluttered house in Baldwin's Gardens for so long that it seemed impossible he should not be there.

But he was dead. He had been hit by an omnibus in the street and died under its wheels while Crispin spent a month at home lying to his parents, and while he doubtless hadn't been happy about that, it was Crispin who had to deal with the calamity he'd left behind.

"You sold his papers?" Crispin said hoarsely, staring at the old man's inheritors. "You sold the *papers*?"

"Well, and if we did? Nothing but a lot of old rubbish."

"It was my rubbish!" Crispin yelped. "He left it to me!" *To the individual serving as my apprentice at the time of my death*, in a document dated thirty years previously. Mr. Marleigh had said he intended to make a new will when Crispin had been summoned urgently to his mother's sickbed. He'd said they'd discuss it on his return.

Mrs. Burford swelled. "*You* may think we've nothing better to do than sit on top of piles of waste awaiting your convenience, Mr. Tredarloe. We're clearing the house and if there were things you needed there, then you should have been here to say so. I'm sure it's a pity if you *wanted* the old man's leavings, but it was hardly valuable, now, was it?"

"He left you his books and documents," Mr. Burford said firmly. "That's what the will said, and that's what we kept. Every book on the shelves and every paper in his desk or cabinet. You can't argue with that."

"He kept the most important papers on the *floor*." Crispin tried to keep his voice from shaking. He could see the scorn in Mr. Burford's eyes as it was. A big, foursquare man who would probably take great pride in telling the world how practical he was, and have nothing but contempt for a willowy, airy-fairy type.

"Rubbish. Ha, that's a good one, eh? If it's left on the floor, it's rubbish. You wouldn't run a business with paper strewn over the floor, would you? I'm a practical man—"

Of course you are, you stupid, swaggering clod, Crispin thought savagely. *And you don't have the faintest idea what you've done, or what I'd like to do to you, or what I could.*

"Now, really," Mrs. Burford said. "Don't make such a parade of a little thing. What did these papers matter anyway?"

They might kill other people. They'll probably kill me.

Crispin bit that back and said, as politely as he could, "Can you tell me what you did with it all?"

He headed down Grape Street, looking for the waste-man's premises.

The Burfords had given him the date of the sale, three days ago—three days! What might have happened in three days? They claimed to have forgotten the waste-man's name. Crispin doubted that. Mrs. Burford was no lady of refinement who would leave such matters to a steward; he would wager she'd bargained with the man herself. They knew perfectly well they were in the wrong, and were taking out their guilt on their victim.

He'd tried four waste-men already, with no success, but the last had considered the matter as if chewing a plug of tobacco, and at last given his opinion: "Baldwin's Gardens? Try Neddy Hall. Grape Street, room behind the Rag and Bottle."

Grape Street was a dank and noisome alley, on the edge of St. Giles. The houses on both sides leaned towards each other, and the cobbles were blackened with filth that stayed slimy no matter the summer heat. Ragged men and half-clad children stared as he passed. Crispin, in his lichen-green coat and pale gold waistcoat, would have been flash in any company; on this street, he looked like a butterfly among moths, except that the moths here had teeth.

There was no public house called the Rag and Bottle, or anything else. At length he asked a woman seated on the street, chewing the stem of the pipe she smoked as she twisted old newspaper round sprigs of wilting lavender and dropped them in her basket.

"Rag an' bottle?" she repeated, holding out her hand for the ha'penny Crispin offered. She gave a dry cackle. "Why, sir, it's right behind you."

He turned, and saw the shop front. It had seen better days but they had never been good: a little low place, its bull's-eye windows thick with grime. The woman gave him a nod and he shrugged, and went in.

The interior of the shop was bewildering. Bottles and glass of all kinds lined the shelves, and surfaces, and floor. The atmosphere held the ghosts of long-gone contents, with hints of perfume and gin, turpentine and cordials and orange-flower-water and oil. Barrels and crates were piled high with metal boxes, jars and tins. It was a heaping mound of discards, a dust-heap of a shop, and Crispin looked around him with horrified distaste, pulling his coat-tails to him for fear of the grime and dusty grease on every surface.

A dull-eyed man stood by a gimcrack chest of drawers, which he was filling with the contents of a battered sack. "Sir?"

"I'm looking for Mr. Hall. The waste-man."

The rag-and-bottle man gave a disappointed grunt and jerked his head towards the back of the shop, where a small door stood slightly ajar. "Froo."

Go through, Crispin interpreted that to mean, and so he went.

Ned Hall, waste-man, was not enjoying his day.

He was generally happy in his work. It wasn't a job for the weak, heaving waste down narrow stairs and hauling the barrow over cobbled or rutted streets, and after a while you could never get the paper dust out of your skin, but he liked it. Liked dickering over a ha'penny per hundredweight, liked seeing the odds and sods that came up in the piles, and mostly liked being his own master, a very long way from the docks.

It was a good life. A queer trade, to be sure, selling on psalters to wrap pork in, or dead men's love letters to go round an ounce of baccy, but it suited him. So it was impossible to say just what was wrong now.

Ned pulled at his ear, scratched inside it with a finger. He'd done that so often it was beginning to feel sore, but he couldn't stop, because he couldn't shift the feeling that he could almost, not quite, but maybe, if he could just turn his head the right way, *hear* something.

Except there was nothing there to hear, and it was driving him to Bedlam.

He clapped both palms to his ears, gave them a rub so vigorous that he felt they might come clean off, and was engaged in that undignified act when a knock came from behind.

"Mr. Neddy Hall?"

Ned turned to look, and blinked. A gentleman, of sorts, stood in the doorway, in a tentative sort of way, like he was trying not to be there. A flash sort, dandyish clothes. Slim, no great height, or age either: about twenty, Ned reckoned. A narrow, nervy sort of face, and a head of hay-coloured hair, that yellow-brown shade.

"That's Ned, if you don't mind. Something I can do for you, sir?" The 'sir' was for the clothes, mostly: there was something about the way the visitor stood, hip tilted and weight on one foot, that didn't say authority.

"Um, I'm trying to find some waste paper. Can you help me?"

Ned spread his arms wide, an invitation to look around that the young man took up, reddening as he grasped the silent point. The small room was paper from floor to ceiling, great piles and drifts of it, mounds of the stuff, white and yellow and browning, plain and printed and scrawled upon, a few bundles bound with string, most loose.

"You want waste, I've got it. How many hundredweight?"

"I mean, some specific paper," the young man said, a little reproachfully, as if Ned should have known that. He had a trace of one of those country accents that sounded like a stage pirate talking, so you could hear the *r* in 'paper'. "My ma—My, uh, teacher died and the house was cleared while I was away. They sold a lot of papers they shouldn't have and they wouldn't tell me *where* they sold them, and I *have* to find them. It's terribly important."

His eyes were wide, pleading, Ned observed, but the greater part of his brain was taken up with the observation that the toff talked like a molly. Not like the Cleveland Street boys, or anything. Just, a light voice that danced a bit and put a lot of stress on a few words, the sort of voice that made you think, *I know your sort.*

And the molly knew he knew, because the colour swept across his pale skin. "Can you help?" he asked, and there was an obvious effort to go a bit more manly there.

"What name?" Ned asked.

"Uh, Tredarloe. Crispin Tredarloe." The young man did something Ned would never have predicted: he stepped forward and put out his hand. "Pleased to meet you, Mr. Hall."

Ned extended his own hand, and Tredarloe's fingers wrapped round his palm. Long, slim, clean, soft fingers. Lucky for some.

"Good to meet you too, Mr. Tredarloe, but I didn't mean your name. I meant, who sold the stuff you're after?"

"Oh! Oh, yes, of course you did. Burford was the name, and the house was in Baldwin's Gardens, three days ago."

He was still holding Ned's hand. Ned glanced down at the slender fingers pale against his own skin. Tredarloe was missing the top joint of his little finger, the skin grown back smooth over the nub of bone that ended the second joint. Otherwise, he had lovely hands. Ned looked back up, at the man standing an arm's length away.

He was a little older, when you saw him up close, not quite so far off Ned's own twenty-six as he'd thought. Neat brownish brows over eyes that were a strange sort of yellow-green, like marsh gas or some such, not that Ned had ever seen a marsh. Freckles dusting his cheekbones. Full lips. Well dressed.

White, of course.

Ned pulled his hand away. Tredarloe let go. They both cleared their throats.

"Well, good news is, you've found your man," Ned said. "Your wasteman. I bought that load—"

"Oh, thank *God*." Tredarloe put a hand to his heart, miming relief.

"But if you're looking for something particular, there's a lot of waste here. I've been picking up all week."

"A lot of...you don't know where it is? You don't remember where you *put* it?"

"It's all waste." Tredarloe's expression made Ned add, "Was there anything I might remember? Books? I put books aside. Bundles of letters, ribbons? Binding? Pictures? Give a cove a hand."

"It was just handwritten papers," Tredarloe said wretchedly. "With some, uh, diagrams, but if you didn't know what they were, they'd look like scribbling."

Ned forced down the impulse to pat his shoulder. "Not to be disobliging, sir, but I pick it up, I bring it here, I sell it on. It's not a circulating library."

"Do you—I know you probably can't answer this—do you think you might have sold it yet?" Ned shrugged. Tredarloe glanced around and went on, hopelessly, "Do you mind if I search?"

"Search...what, for your waste? *My* waste," he added, because if Freckles here wanted it back, he could pay what Ned had.

"Yes. Um, starting where you're going to sell the next batch from? I really do need to find it, you see. Please?"

Ned looked around at the tons of paper that surrounded them and back to the pretty young man gazing appealingly at him with those marshlight eyes, and said, "Well, it's your funeral."

Three hours later, Crispin's hands and shirtsleeves and knees were filthy, his back hurt, and he was beginning to despair.

There was so much paper. So much, so heavy, tied tightly into bundles with twine so he split his fingernails trying to prise the ends apart and see what was within, or loose, in piles that, he had rapidly realised, would be all too easy to send spilling across the dusty floor. He couldn't stop sneezing.

No wonder Ned Hall was that colour. Grey-white dust over brown skin.

It had been hard not to stare. For one thing, Crispin was from Cornwall, where he didn't think he'd seen a man of colour in his life. There were many in London, he knew that, but, like the Jews and the lascars, they mostly made their homes in the East End, that dark and alarming place of manual labour and poverty where Crispin had rarely set foot. He had a West End life in his odd, specialised little society. He'd only seen men of colour as itinerant street-sellers, never actually spoken to a black man before, certainly never touched one.

Hall's hand had felt...well, Crispin was sure he should assert that it felt the same as any other man's hand, but he'd never before touched a hand so ingrained with paper dust that it felt dry and slippery. He'd rarely felt a hand so strong, either. Hall was not more than three inches taller than Crispin, but he was all muscle. Sloped shoulders, powerful legs, and his *arms*! His shirtsleeves were rolled up against the heat, and the strength visible in those forearms made Crispin's mouth go dry. Unless that was the paper dust. The thought set him coughing again.

"Gets in your throat, don't it?" Hall's voice came from behind him. Crispin jumped like a cat, papers cascading from his hands. "Steady!"

"Oh, blast. I'm so sorry, you startled me."

"Leave it," Hall said, as he scrabbled to pick the papers up, and offered him a tin mug. "Here."

"What is it?"

"Tea. Gets the dust out of your throat."

He held the mug a little further forward. Crispin took it tentatively. Tea didn't sound a terribly good idea in this heat, and in truth he would prefer Darjeeling or Pekoe to whatever navvies' brew this was, but he didn't want to be rude. The first sip, stewed and tannic, made him wince, but the second seemed to sluice down his throat, washing away what felt like an inch thickness of dust. He gave a moan of bliss.

Hall grinned at his expression. "Good?"

"Wonderful."

Hall swigged from his own mug. He looked a little heated, as though he'd been working hard, and he was covered in fine dust. Crispin could wet a finger in his mug, or his mouth, and run it down one of those forearms, leave a shining line of skin...

"Any luck?" Hall asked.

Crispin gave a guilty start. "What? Uh. No. No. I haven't found it."

Hall made a face. "I've to load the handcart up. S'pose I could let you know if I see your bits and pieces. What's it look like again?"

That was an offer of help, Crispin realised. "Oh, thank you! It's handwritten papers. Cramped handwriting, with symbols and diagrams. Uh, can you read?"

"Be a dull job if I couldn't."

Blast. That made it a little more delicate. "Well, it probably won't make a great deal of sense to you anyway. It's a specialised form of mathematics. I dare say it will look like utter gobbledegook."

Hall was giving him what he could only describe as a Look. "Too clever for my sort, is it? Got you, sir, thank you very much."

"I shouldn't say *clever*," Crispin said hastily. "Just a very obscure branch of, of study. I shouldn't expect anyone to recognise it as anything meaningful. Well, the Burfords threw it all away."

Hall grunted, and went to a pile, riffling through a sheaf. Not precisely next to Crispin, but close enough that he could feel the man's presence. He'd been sweating—manual labour, a hot day. Male scent and paper dust, blending together in his nose.

Pay attention. He flicked through a clump of what turned out to be sheet music, then a railway prospectus, down to a closely written sheet that made his heart jump for a second until he saw it was merely a set of accounts.

"Where does it all come from?" he asked.

"Waste? Everywhere. Publishers, coffee-shops, printers, lawyers. Schools. House clearance when someone's dropped off his perch. If you've waste, I'll take it."

"Just waste paper, or do you deal in..." Crispin indicated the rag and bottle premises with a thumb.

"Just waste," Hall said, much as a King's Bench barrister might deny he carried out lowly conveyancing work. Clearly there was a hierarchy of the men who collected London's discards, and paper was at the top. Clearly, also, the word 'paper' was not used, for some arcane trade reason. Crispin knew all about specialist vocabulary. "I'm a waste-man only."

"I had no idea," Crispin said. "I never thought what happened to the, uh, the waste." He felt slightly self-conscious adopting the term, but it seemed only polite.

"Most people don't. Some just put it out with the dust. Crying shame. I'll take it off you for a penny a pound any day."

Crispin heaved a load of waste to another stack so he could inspect further down. The sheets here were smaller in size, closely written. He peered closer. "Oh! There's letters here. Personal letters."

"It's amazing what you get. Well, someone's passed on, what are the family to do? Mostly they don't even look twice. Old Great-Auntie's love letters from Great-Uncle—or someone who wasn't Great-Uncle, come to that—all tied in old ribbon with a lock of dried-up hair in the knot. She keeps 'em safe for years, then five minutes after she shuffles off, they're sat on my piles with the songsheets and schoolbooks."

"That's awful," Crispin said.

"It's the way of things. Burn your love letters, or have 'em put in the ground with you, or they'll be tomorrow's packing paper." Hall gave a slightly rueful smile. "I put 'em aside for packing, when I notice, rather than foul use."

"That's... I'm glad you do."

"Soft, that's my trouble." He shrugged. "It's all waste. Some of it used to be hopes and dreams, but I pay a penny a pound, same as for any other sort. It's a queer trade, but there's many worse."

"Who do you sell it to?"

"Going into business for yourself?" Hall sounded a little threatening, but when Crispin hastily looked around, a two-inch stack of paper in his hands, he saw a broad grin, and felt his own mouth curve responsively.

Hall really was rather handsome. It hadn't quite struck him at first, in the unfamiliarity of looking at a man of colour. He'd noticed brown skin, broad nose, not much more. After three hours of surreptitious glances and casually exchanged words, though, he was seeing deep-set dark brown eyes with creases that suggested Hall laughed a lot, and a bottom lip that dipped in the middle to devastating effect when he smiled. Crispin had always had a weakness for smiles.

And he'd said something. "Um, no," Crispin managed, after a hasty mental search for the question, then kicked himself for not returning the joke. "Well, not unless the study doesn't pay off. Do you need an apprentice?"

Hall laughed at that, a rich chuckle. God, that smile. "I'll let you know if there's an opening."

"So where *do* you sell it?" Crispin asked, to keep his mind off the response he might have made in different circumstances.

"Provisioners, mostly. Wholesale and retail."

"Provisioners?" Crispin repeated, flirtation vanishing like smoke. "What—why—?"

"To wrap food. Where'd you think the newsprint round your pound of sausages comes from?"

"The paper will be wrapped round *food*?"

"That's what I said." Hall was giving him an odd look.

Crispin didn't care. His mind felt like it was seizing up. "But... Not actual food. Not for *people*."

Hall's dark brows came together. "Yes, food, for people. Cheese, butter, fish, sweetmeats— Oi, mate!"

The papers slid from Crispin's numb hands to the floor in a whispering rush. He staggered back a step, bumping into another heap that swayed and, inevitably, fell. His foot slipped on a sheet underfoot, and he found himself on his arse, a small avalanche of paper under him, and Ned Hall squatting in front of him with a worried look. "You all right?"

"I have to find the papers," Crispin croaked. "You have to help me. It's so important. Please." He grabbed Hall's hand, unbalancing the man on the slippery paper-strewn floor. Hall came forward to one knee to steady himself.

Crispin was half sprawled on the floor, and a very handsome, sweaty, muscular man was kneeling between his legs, holding his hand.

Panic, utter panic and wild urgency thudded in Crispin's chest, but that didn't stop part of his mind noting the way Hall's eyes widened a fraction, and the clasp of his fingers, quivering but not letting go.

They stared at each other. Didn't move.

If I just pulled him forward again, Crispin thought. Under other circumstances this would have felt like a terrible missed opportunity, but he had no damn choice and no time to waste. He cleared his throat. "Please help."

2

Ned was not enjoying his day.

He had been, for a while. Tredarloe improved the view no end, and he'd liked the company and the chat. It made a change: you wouldn't get a posh fellow in here in a month of Sundays, and Ned was no more averse to admiring looks than the next man. Tredarloe's marshlight eyes were expressive enough to get him into a pack of trouble, and Ned had felt them on him all afternoon.

He might even have squatted a bit deeper and lifted a bit more in the way of weight, accordingly. A wispy fellow like that might well have a taste for a man with muscle to him, and Ned had had too many compliments on his legs and arse to bother with false modesty.

Mostly, compliments from men who didn't look much higher than his waist. Tredarloe *talked*. He had sounded interested in the trade, and friendly, and funny once he relaxed a little. There'd seemed to be quite the lively fellow behind the nerves, in fact, someone Ned could have chatted to for a while longer. Until he'd said that about the food.

And now Tredarloe was on the floor, just how Ned had been picturing him for a while now, pulling him close with a plea on his lips and need in his eyes…and all the sod wanted was a hand sorting the waste.

Ned gave a moment's consideration to pushing him flat on his back, since they were down here anyway, give Freckles something else to think about. He sat back on his heels with a sigh. "Help you what, find your waste?"

"It's not waste." Tredarloe scrabbled to sit up, drifts of paper shifting under him. "It's very, very important and if it gets wrapped around food…"

"What?" Ned demanded. "The inks are poisonous?"

"No. Well, not like that. No. Um. I can't really explain."

"Well, you can look for it yourself, then." Which wasn't kind, but there was only so much silly buggers he could take when it wasn't the kind of silly buggers he wanted to play at.

Tredarloe bit his lip. He had to know what that looked like, white teeth against dusky pink.

"Come on, get up." Ned extended his hand. Tredarloe took it and allowed himself to be heaved to his feet. "Look, I got work to do—"

"I'll pay you. For your time and labour and...and if you'll let me do something."

"If I'll let you do something," Ned repeated, making it slow and incredulous-sounding because he was, he had to admit, disappointed. He'd taken money, had once had some toff in a shiny silk hat pay a guinea for the privilege of having Ned's cock in his mouth, and that beat hauling paper by quite some way. Nothing wrong with it, and coin was always welcome, but he'd just had this idea that Tredarloe had been treating him like a person, not a transaction. He'd thought they'd been getting on.

That said, Tredarloe was looking horrified, the colour sweeping across his face like scarlet fever. "Not like that!" he blurted. "I mean—can you keep a secret?"

Ned could throw him out now, or he could find out what this was about, which, he had to admit, was starting to make him curious as a cat. "Yes, I can keep a secret. And you can hire my time, and labour. Five shillings for the afternoon." A high figure, but Tredarloe didn't flinch. "Anything else you want to pay for, that's extra." Which made Tredarloe go even redder, pleasingly.

"And I've your word?" Tredarloe said, sounding urgent. "Secrecy. I need your word as a—a—"

"Gentleman?" Ned suggested, with a little sarcasm.

"Man of honour." Tredarloe got that out with surprising dignity.

Ned considered, then extended his hand. "Man of honour, word of honour." Tredarloe grasped it—they were getting quite familiar with the feel of each other's palms—and gave him a little nod, man to man.

"Well," he said. "The thing is. The papers. They're, uh, magic."

"Magic," Ned repeated.

"I don't expect you to believe me, but please just listen," Tredarloe said sharply. "My master, who died, whose papers they were, he was a very powerful magician who did a lot of theoretical work, and he wrote it down, and he never filed his papers properly. And when he died I was away, and you cleared the house, and the papers you took are *covered* in, uh, in spells. Do you understand?"

"Covered in spells." Ned crossed his arms. "Right."

"For five shillings, you could at least pretend you're listening," Tredarloe snapped.

"Make it ten and I'll believe every word you say." Thank the stars he hadn't fucked the lunatic. Who knew where that might have led.

"That's a bargain," Tredarloe said. "Ten shillings and you believe that my master was a magician, *I* am a magician, a huge amount of inscripted—magic—paper has passed into your hands, and some of it might even now be wrapped round a pound of sausages that someone is going to *eat*, do you understand?"

"And what would that do?" Ned asked, drawn in to the fantasy despite himself.

"I don't know, but nothing good. Words have power. We use a written system for the magic, you see. Anything he wrote with a certain pen, well..." He did look worried. Ned could swear he believed every word of his own nonsense.

"All right, then. You want me to look for your magic paper now?"

He did his best to make that sound serious, but evidently failed, because Tredarloe glared at him. "No. I want to compel you."

"That'll cost you a lot more than ten shillings."

"Will you stop it!" Tredarloe's voice cracked. "I'm serious. I have to know what you did with the paper, so I need to make you remember. That means a compulsion, a kind of spell to bring your memory out."

"You want to do magic on me?" Ned felt a strong inclination to say, *Bugger that for a game of tin soldiers*, and had to remind himself that Tredarloe was a bedlamite. Let him play his game. "Go on, then."

"Have you any paper?" Ned just looked at him. Tredarloe glowered. "Clean paper. Not written on."

Ned plucked a sheet from the stack where he kept blank waste, for the writer types who occasionally dropped by. Tredarloe pulled a pen from his pocket. It looked like silver, covered in fine engraving that caught the light, with an odd yellow-white nib.

"That ivory?" Ned asked.

"Uh...bone." Tredarloe sounded just a little evasive. "What's your full name?"

"Edward Isaac Hall." Ned peered at the page as Tredarloe wrote his name, in flowing script. The ink was a bright deep red, and what was odder, he didn't need an inkwell, like the ink was kept inside the barrel of the pen. Must be some new-fangled invention. "How does that work?"

"Ssh." Tredarloe was writing, swift and confident, symbols that Ned didn't know. Odd shapes, too. Ned had once picked up a child's book of what they called optical illusions, pictures that were different depending on how you looked at them. A black candlestick became two white faces, that sort of thing, and it had given Ned a bit of a funny feeling to have his eyes not know what to do. That was what these characters were like. They gave the impression that if you looked hard enough they'd turn out to be another shape altogether.

The pen scratched, with a dry noise like the rattle of rats' feet on dusty boards. The ink rolled out from the pen, no shortage of it, glistening red. Tredarloe drew a line on the white paper and it looked like a razor cut on skin. *Not on my skin*, Ned thought, and then realised he was reassuring himself with the jest, because the hairs were standing up on the back of his neck.

He could smell something metallic. A bit like iron. A bit like blood.

Tredarloe looked pale, eyes intent on the page. He wrote a word in joined-up letters—*memoria*— doubled the line of the pen under it and slashed the word through with a flourish, and Ned

—carried in the armload of waste. The Burford lady had been a harridan to bargain with and it had only just been worth his while with all the clearing work, but it was good quality foolscap. The room was full, because he'd had a couple of windfalls and a few of the provender merchants he usually supplied had shut up shop for the seaside, lucky sods. He dumped it on a not-too-teetering pile by the wall, shook his head at a funny feeling in his ear, went back for another load—

lurched forward with shock so that Tredarloe had to grab his arm to stop him falling.

"Did that work?"

Ned moved his mouth, couldn't make any noise. It hadn't been just remembering. It had been like going back in time, it was so vivid. Like living the moments again. Like magic.

"I need to know," Tredarloe insisted. "It was just a memory compulsion, it won't have done you any harm—"

"Harm?" Ned said explosively, jerking his arm away. "*Harm?* You put a spell on me!"

"I did say I would. Look, I dare say you're very angry and surprised, but I'm paying you ten shillings to believe me and find the paper, so please can we do that first? Where is it?"

Ten shillings, Ned told himself, and *Not mad*, and *Magic*.

"I—Over there." He turned to indicate the wall and as he did, almost heard that not-there sound again. A set of impressions connected in his mind: dry paper, scratching pen, things that rustled in shadow. "Is that your stuff making that bloody noise?"

Tredarloe's mouth dropped open. "You can hear it?"

"I *can't* hear it. That's the problem."

"Yes!" Tredarloe said. "That's exactly what it's meant to sound like!"

"It sounds like something you can't hear?" Tredarloe just gave him a look, and Ned shrugged. "All right, yes. It sounds like something I can't hear, and I've been not hearing it for three days."

"I wish you'd *said*. I could have used that."

"Can't you hear it?"

"No," Tredarloe said, with a regret that Ned found entirely misplaced. "The paper, please? I mean, the waste?"

Ned went to the wall where he'd put Tredarloe's waste. He'd brought in a fair bit more in the intervening days since this accursed load, and not moved any of it on. That was, he realised, because the noise he couldn't hear was louder on this side of the room. He'd been avoiding it.

He had to put his back into it to clear a path. Tredarloe hovered, twitchy, and darted in as soon as there was a sufficient gap, hands reaching like a miser for gold.

"Yes," he hissed, after a moment. "Yes!"

Between them, they pulled out the piles. Ned could see it, as soon as Tredarloe brought out the first lot: this was his stuff all right. It just *looked* peculiar. The ink was a funny brown shade, rather than red, and it was a different hand, sort of, but there were symbols in those odd, wrong shapes, and words that weren't English, some crossed and some not.

Ned heaved out another double armful of the stuff, squinting at the odd ink, and wondering why you'd choose a brown that looked like—

He flung the lot away from himself, a violent gesture of revulsion that sent sheets cascading over Tredarloe as he squatted on the floor.

"What the—!"

"It's blood!" Ned said with explosive disgust, batting at his hands as if that could take the touch of the fouled paper away. "Isn't it? It's bloody written in bloody *blood,* you…you bleeder." He couldn't seem to think of any other oaths. "Oh, my days. I *touched* it." He sat on the floor, hard, and put his head between his knees.

Tredarloe came over and rested a tentative hand on his shoulder. "Um, Mr. Hall? Ned? It's not as bad as all that, really. It's only Mr. Marleigh's blood, I promise, and he chose to use it. That's how the magic works."

"Like yours," Ned rasped.

"Yes, but look, you use your body to work, don't you? Your muscles, your strength." His fingers closed a little on Ned's shoulder, in unconscious illustration. "Well, I use mine, my blood and bone. It's not that different."

He ought to push Tredarloe off, not let the man touch him. Writing spells in his own blood, right there in front of him. It was unlawful, was what it was: unlawful and unnatural and wrong.

Which, admittedly, was a pack of words he'd heard before. That was why he didn't live in Shad Thames where four generations of his family lived, where he'd grown up, where every street held people who looked like he did, or like other kinds of foreign, and he wouldn't be glanced at twice. They looked at him here. Not the other waste-men, or the Grape Street people, who had got over the novelty of a man of colour, but there was always some new passer-by, or the rookery brats, or the drunks.

But he'd needed to get as far from Shad Thames as he could, because looking was a lot better than prayers and curses and talk.

Ned had definite ideas of his own about what constituted *wrong*. Having a bit of fun with one of the lads off a trading ship was not wrong, in his view. Putting a boot into your sixteen-year-old brother's guts because you'd caught him kissing a sailor and then running off to tell the whole neighbourhood: *that* was wrong, and Jem could go to the other place along with the rest of his family, if they wanted to be like that. Writing magic spells in your own blood…

He looked at Tredarloe's face, so close to his own, at the concern in his marshlight eyes, and decided he'd wait to pass judgement. He'd always felt a cove had a right to use his body as he liked, as long as he did no harm.

Tredarloe's lips were slightly parted, his breathing quick, and he wasn't moving his hand off Ned's shoulder. There were probably lots of things worse than magic, or blood, if Ned thought about it, which he wasn't inclined to do because he had other things on his mind.

He swallowed. "What did you say your name was?"

"Crispin." Breath ghostly over Ned's skin.

"What's that accent?"

"Cornwall."

He was very close indeed, and not moving, and Ned thought *Oh well*, and gave him his best smile. "You do anything except magic, Crispin?"

"Sometimes I fuck," Crispin said, the word sounding odd in his soft, country voice. "How about you?"

"I do that," Ned agreed. "And, I wouldn't like to say *magic*, precisely, but…"

The smile that curved on Crispin's lips was a thing of wicked joy. "Well, I showed you *my* magic. So if I can just check that all this paper is here and stop worrying, I think it's your turn."

That was a promise he wanted kept, but—

Ned put a hand behind Crispin's head and pulled him over.

He couldn't bear men who didn't kiss. He'd been a working man for a toff too often, and a novelty for white men too, and he couldn't find the fun in it any more. If Crispin was one of those, ready to fuck but not kiss him, he'd rather know now.

Except he wasn't, because Crispin was kissing him back, warm and supple, tasting carefully rather than diving in but not for lack of enthusiasm, or confidence. He had his hands over Ned's shoulders, mouth open, tongue darting, and then he pulled harder, deepening the kiss, and Ned shuddered with response, taking a handful of that soft, straight hair. Crispin might be slender but he wasn't feeble, and he didn't need telling what to do. His long fingers were driving up over Ned's neck and through his tight-curled hair, making goosebumps of pleasure rise, the other hand pushing downwards over his shirt like a man who wanted to feel skin, and they could just go over sideways onto the paper-strewn floor right now—

Except, he wasn't fucking on *that*.

Ned pulled away, not without reluctance. Crispin blinked at him.

"Waste, Freckles."

"What? Oh. Yes. Right."

"And then—"

Crispin's mouth was wet, a little pink, extremely kissable. "Absolutely."

"I'd say do it now, but the floor's covered in spells," Ned added.

"Oh, you've no idea. It's a constant trial to me." His smile was as wide as Ned felt his own to be. "All right. Let's get it finished."

Crispin shuffled over, back to kneel amid the papers, unable to stop smiling. The whole miserable day had turned into sunshine. Mr. Marleigh's papers retrieved, no harm done, and Ned Hall kissing him like a man.

Crispin was all too used to the way people responded to his willowy frame and light voice. He'd had sneers and taunts all his life. Even this last visit in Liskeard, there had been the usual thing from his brothers and old schoolmates, and he'd had to grit his teeth to prevent himself saying, *Do you realise who I am now? Do you know what I could do?*

People had ideas of the type of man he was. Even other men of his sort made assumptions, and he'd been pushed away more than once for failing to be suitably passive and pliant. But not today, not in those marvellously muscular arms, and he couldn't help shooting a glance at Ned, who was grinning back at him.

"Work," he reminded them both. "That is, *I* must work. Don't touch the rest of it if you don't want to. It won't hurt you, but I understand if you'd rather not."

"I've touched nastier things in my time," Ned assured him. "And if it means you'll take that that blasted noise out of here, I'll be happy."

"I will. I promise. It's rather unusual to hear it, you know," he added, carefully.

"Is it?" Ned didn't seem to be listening. He was staring down at the sheaf of inscripted paper in his hands. "Uh, Crispin?"

"Mmm?"

"What if I'd sold some of it?"

Cold sank through Crispin's warm cloud of happiness. "Do you think you did?"

"Ugh. It's not like you remember selling waste unless there's something special about it. But..." He looked at the paper he held. "Nice feel to it, this has. Good texture, weave, whatever you call it. And the writing, the, uh, ink. It's fairly..." He made a face. "Special."

Crispin sat back, and reached into his breast pocket for his pen. "May I compel you again?"

Neither of them wanted to, that much was clear. Ned set his jaw. Crispin had to take a few deep breaths. Compulsion was one of his least favourite practices. As with all the scripti that affected minds, it seemed to suck the blood from the back of his neck, leaving a nauseous ache and dizziness.

Then again, he doubted Ned would have suggested this without reason.

He wrote the name, Edward Isaac Hall, feeling the snake-bite as he started, the cold suction at the top of his spine. His blood, red on the page, running through the bone nib, forming the litterae that gave the scriptus its power.

He whispered the name of *memoria* as he bisected the scriptus with a slash of his pen across the page, and felt the stroke like a knife across the back of his neck. There would be no wound there, he knew that, but the knowledge never stopped him flinching.

Ned jerked, instantly compelled. His eyelids flickered wildly as the memory hit him, then snapped open, and he said, "Drat."

"You sold some?" Crispin said, voice rising, and had to quickly add, "You weren't to know. It's not your fault." He swallowed, envisioning a ream of scripted paper used to wrap raw meat at the butcher's counter, blood soaking into the scripti. "How much of it did you sell?"

"Well, not much," Ned said. "I mean, for waste, not much. I took just the one bit from that pile, but there was that blasted noise that wasn't there, and I loaded up from a different stack."

"How much is not much?"

"About yea big," Ned said, and indicated a pile perhaps twelve inches thick.

"Jumping Judas." Crispin stared at him. "A foot of it? That must be…" He couldn't begin to calculate how many sheets. "To whom?"

Ned grimaced. "Billy Harkness. He's a gaffer at St. George's Market."

"A…"

"One of the fellows who runs the market, deals with the costers, sorts out pitches. The costers bring their own waste, but he keeps a stack on hand for selling on if anyone runs out. He'll hand 'em a pile and they'll use it."

"Market," Crispin said, voice hollow. He'd been to St. George's often enough. A mass of stalls and barrows and shop fronts. Gleaming tin or copper saucepans here, bright painted crockery there, people shouting their tea trays, old shoes, blacking, combs, corn-plasters. Peep shows of historical events, or targets for the boys to shoot at. Flower-stalls and half-starved lavender-sellers. And food. Onions, turnips, cabbages, bunches of herbs. Slabs of meat, beef and pork and strings of sausages. Serried ranks of glistening herring and tumbled heaps of oysters, whelks and eels…

"We have to go there," he managed. "This is a disaster. We have to go, we have to go now." And he knew it, but he couldn't move. "They're going to kill me. If anyone gets hurt… They're going to kill me. I'm going to die."

"Crispin!" Ned's hands, warm and dusty, closed over his face, a gentle touch. "Stop. Calm down."

"I can't!"

"You got to. Right, look, give me a handle on this. This paper, it's got spells on it, like you wrote, right? What spells? Would they do memory things, make people remember stuff?"

"Uh." Crispin pulled himself together under the questioning. "Only if the scriptus was *memoria*. Each of the scripti, the words of power, does a different thing, you see, and Mr. Marleigh was very versatile. He wrote different ones, a *lot* of them. He experimented." Crispin swallowed at the recollection of some of those experiments.

"Like what? Come on, give me an idea what we're talking about. Name three."

"Um… *Ignis. Glacio. Dolor.*"

"Which means, for them as don't have your education?"

"Fire. Freeze. And, uh…" He wished he'd said a different one. "Pain."

"Pain," Ned repeated. "Why— No, just tell me this. Say someone brought home a nice bit of mutton wrapped in one of these papers. In the one that says *pain*. What happens?"

"I don't *know*. This isn't how it's supposed to happen. Maybe nothing at all, Mr. Marleigh's dead for heaven's sake. But...raw meat, blood on the scriptus..."

"Right." Ned drew the word out. "I sold Billy the waste maybe two hours after it came in, Crispin. It's been in his lock-up for three days, and if he ain't moved it on yet, it'll be soon. Let's go."

3

It was late afternoon by the time they reached St. George's market, which was raucous and heaving with people on their way home, picking up a bit of something for dinner. The summer sun was still bright, still hot. It wouldn't be dark for hours yet. Ned wondered if his companion would prefer darkness.

They're going to kill me. I'm going to die. Crispin was a bit of a panicker, Ned could tell that, but he'd sounded like he meant it. He hadn't said who was going to kill him—they'd had no time to talk about it—but it was giving Ned a case of the chills.

He hadn't said why anyone would want to write the magic word for pain, either, and that was something Ned wanted a good explanation for, but it could wait till later.

Assuming there was a *later*, because Crispin had gone fishbelly white at the idea of a foot-thick pile of what he called inscripted paper loose on the world, and to be honest Ned wasn't feeling that chipper about it himself.

"All right, let's try Billy first," he suggested as they approached the stalls. "Look on the bright side, there's nothing to say he's started using that lot of waste yet."

"Um," Crispin said. "I think there might be."

He was staring over towards a coster's barrow, where an argument was in process. A stout woman was holding a basket at arm's length, and maybe she just wasn't that strong, but it juddered and leapt so it looked hard to keep a grip on.

"Well, what am I s'posed to do about it?" the coster demanded. "I sells the fish, that's all. Good fresh fish, I sells."

"Too bloody fresh! I wanted 'em gutted!"

"I gutted 'em, didn't I?"

"Well you didn't gut 'em enough!" shrieked the woman. "Because they're still bloody moving!"

"Oh God no," Crispin said. "Oh *no*."

"What is it?" Ned demanded. "Crispin?"

"Don't give me that," the coster was shouting. "Any lunatic can put live fish in a basket—"

"Without their guts!" The woman was bellowing full-throated now.

"Moving and flapping with a hole where their innards came out! I won't have it in my kitchen! You bloody have 'em!"

She raised the basket high and upturned it, opening the lid, as the coster roared protest. Fish fell in a silvery stream, hitting the barrow and the cobbles, making the small crowd that had gathered to laugh at the bedlamite leap back.

A man picked up one of the thrashing, jerking fish. "Gawd above," he said, staring. "She's right."

Ned darted forward and seized a fish. A herring. It was moving, oddly dry against his hands. Its eyes were bright; its mouth opened and closed.

It was scaled, its belly gaped open and empty, and it had come out of a basket, not a bucket. It wasn't even wet.

"It's not dead." Ned couldn't make sense of it. "Why's it not dead when it's got no guts and it can't breathe?"

"*Vita*," Crispin whispered.

Ned didn't know much Latin, if that was even what those words were. He wasn't of the Romish faith, hadn't had a deal of education beyond dame school. But it didn't take a scholar to work out what *vita* meant.

"Life," he said. "You can make life?"

"Not really. It never works for long. Mr. Marleigh spent years trying to improve the litterae, the things that make the words work. It was his hobby, his obsession. He tried so many...so many times..." Crispin tailed off.

Ned looked around. At the fish, the slabs of butchered meat, the chickens hung by their legs. There was a shriek from further up the street, followed by a chorus of additional screams, getting closer, and a parting of the crowd as people stumbled back. Something small, pink and bare shot through the legs, past Ned, and out of the market. A mongrel dog set off in pursuit, but almost immediately veered off.

"What was that?" Ned asked.

Crispin swallowed. "A, uh, skinned rabbit, I think."

Ned started to laugh. He couldn't help it.

"*Not funny*," Crispin hissed.

"No. No, it ain't. Come on, let's find Billy."

The gaffer Billy Harkness, red-faced, with a black crepe band round his arm and another round the crown of his hat, was at the centre of a frantic and growing crowd. A flower-seller was waving an extremely healthy-looking bunch of dahlias in his face. "I'll have whatever you've got!" he cried hoarsely. "Two shilling a bundle!"

"Three," a woman said. Her purple asters were sadly wilted by comparison. "It ain't right to favour one over another, Billy Harkness. I want the stuff he had. The preserving paper!"

"I don't know what he had!" Billy shouted. "I don't know what's going on!"

"It's the wrapping what does it, that's what," the flower-seller said, but her voice was drowned by the furious tones of half a dozen other costers.

That was going to be a problem. Word would be spreading like wildfire if there was a way to keep flowers and green stuff fresh, in this hot summer, and Ned would bet the shellfish hawkers would twig to it any minute, if they hadn't already. He nipped over to the edge of the street and clambered up on the windowsill of a shop.

Crispin had followed. "What are you doing?"

"Having a look-see." He squinted over the heads and tried to get a view on things. The market crowd was heaving like the Thames, with waves and eddies of people clustering to get a view, cut by the determined tugboats of people on a mission. Flower-sellers and costers, combing the market frantically for the 'preserving paper'. Ned could see at least three auctions going on, as fishmongers and the rabbit-man waved precious handfuls of waste.

He bent down towards Crispin. "Is it all going to be life stuff?"

"I don't know. Mr. Marleigh kept the piles together. But after you'd picked it up and moved it and piled it…there could be anything else in there."

Ned straightened again, so he could commit the locations of the auctions to memory for easy finding, and that was when he saw the trouble. Up ahead, to the east, the crowd was parting, drawn away on both sides like Moses and the Red Sea, and a figure was walking jerkily down the middle. There was a strange sort of silence there, too, spreading over the people like a charm.

"What's that?" Crispin had hopped up on the sill in front of him, crouching a little so they could both see. "Who's that? Why is everyone looking at him?"

Ned couldn't quite make it out. "Can't see. Why's he walking like that?"

"He doesn't look well." Crispin peered forward, wobbled slightly. Ned grabbed him, a hand on his shoulder, the other to his waist, steadying him. "I don't think he's well at all."

The figure was closer now, his gait slow and halting, and now people were starting to move. Not just parting to leave a path but turning and pushing and running, and as Ned stared, he heard the first scream.

"Oh, right." Ned's voice sounded oddly calm and distant in his own ears. "It's George Foster. Well, there's a turn-up."

"Is he poorly?" Crispin asked, with a thread of panic. "He looks very poorly."

"None too chipper. We were going to bury him tomorrow."

"Oh, fuck," Crispin said, and fell off the windowsill.

It was like his knees just buckled, and it caught Ned by surprise, what with his hand was very comfortably settled on Crispin's hip, and he was watching a man whose funeral he'd been planning to attend walking down the street. He lurched, and came off sideways, and found himself landing more or less on top of Crispin in a heap. It was a good thing there was an old man's corpse strolling through the market, or somebody might have laughed at them.

He grabbed Crispin by the lapels. "What the hell! What the sodding—He's bloody dead! Why did you do that?"

"I didn't!" Crispin yelped. "It's the paper!"

"Well, make it stop!" Ned hissed. "That's Billy Harkness' father-in-law, you country cracker. He didn't like him alive, he's not going to be pleased to have him turn up dead."

"I can't just make it stop," Crispin hissed right back, shoving himself to his knees. "I don't know *how*."

"How can you not know?"

"I didn't do this!" Crispin repeated. His marshlight eyes were wild. "I didn't write the scriptus, it wasn't my pen, I don't know how Mr. Marleigh got *vita* to work, I have no idea why it would have started working now, and I don't know what to write!"

"Death," Ned said. "Write him dead, like he ought to be."

"I don't know how! Why would I have learned to kill people?" Crispin demanded. "It was bad enough having to do pain!"

"Oh my days." Ned grabbed his hand, hauled them both to their feet, and headed over to where Billy Harkness stood and stared, face a horrible puce shade. He stood alone because everyone who knew Billy Harkness knew that the gaffer and his pa-in-law had had no love lost, and Billy was free with his fists. If old George had come back, you might think you knew the reason, and people were melting from around Billy like river foam.

"All right, Billy," Ned said, dragging Crispin up to him.

"All right." Reply by rote. Billy couldn't shift his eyes from the thing making its slow approach. Old George, in his best clothes for the laying-out. He was moving funny, one shoulder down, one leg not working right, head on one side. Face sagged, mouth slack, eyeballs rolled back and showing white against yellowed skin. "Oh, my Gawd. Do you see that, Ned? *Do you see it?*"

"Those preserving papers everyone was talking about—"

"Not now!"

"Did you bring anything back home in 'em, at all? Like, a couple of days ago?"

"What?" Billy sounded vague, then he turned, gaze sharpening. "What did you say? Was this *your* fault?"

"Mine," Crispin said, his voice shaky but clear. "Not Ned's."

"It wasn't his either, he's trying to sort it out," Ned said. "That waste you took off me, did you bring anything home in it? Baccy? Meat? Anything old George ate?"

"The bloody paper."

"Yes, but what was *in* it?"

"No, he ate the paper. He'd tear off these strips, roll it into little balls and mumble away at it, toothless old goat. Done it all his life. Fair turned my stomach, it did."

"He ate it," Crispin said. "Jumping *Judas*."

"That help at all?"

"Not really."

They were all staring at George Foster, dragging and lurching his way towards them. He was quite close now. His blank eyes seemed to be fixed on Billy and he began, slowly, to raise an arm. There were some high-pitched noises from the watching crowd.

"I'm going to get out of the way now, I reckon," Ned said. "Billy, mate, you might want to scarper."

Billy nodded slowly, not moving. George Foster made a sound in his throat.

"Um. Bill?" Ned took his arm, turned him around, and gave him a push. Billy took one stumbling step, then another, then fled. Behind him, George Foster's corpse let out a wet, slurring noise that sounded angry, and set off stumbling after him.

When Ned turned, Crispin had vanished. He looked around in disbelief, and saw him squatting over by the wall, pen in hand and paper on his knees from the sheaf he'd pocketed as they left the rag and bottle.

"What was his name again?" Crispin demanded as Ned approached. "George Foster? Any middle name?"

"How would I know? What are you doing?"

"Nothing useful." Crispin was scribbling frantically, those odd, boxy little shapes and symbols. "I'm trying to cancel the scriptus but he *ate* it, and I don't even know if the name is any use any more, considering he's dead, and it's not my scriptus! I didn't write it!"

"I'm not saying it's your fault," Ned said. "Nobody is."

"They will, believe me, but I meant that it matters who wrote it. Whose pen." He slashed the off-white nib of his own pen through a word on the page, and made a frustrated noise. "This won't work. I can't overwrite Mr. Marleigh. He'd been using his pen for sixty years, his blood and bone. That's where the power's from. I can't compete with that."

"His blood and bone," Ned repeated. "Crispin...what happened to your finger?"

Crispin flinched. An actual, visible flinch, like at a blow. "It doesn't matter."

"That's the nib, isn't it? Your finger bone?"

"Sssh!" A frantic hiss. "Don't talk so loud."

"Bloody hell." Ned stared down at him as he scribbled, face white and drawn. His actual finger. Why would anyone do that?

He hopped up on an upturned crate to get another look round, and avoid thinking about it. The market was half empty in front of George, with little eddies of people darting up to get a look and legging it away again. Behind him, the crowds were flowing back together, and the bargaining for the paper seemed to have restarted, with handfuls being brandished all over the market. Amazing, Ned thought. They'd seen George Foster walk by and they still wanted the damned stuff to keep their dahlias fresh.

He glanced back at George, and saw him stagger. Not in his shambling way, but as though struck. As he watched, the corpse lurched again, and a small man darted forward out of the crowd, arm up, finger pointed. He was shouting something Ned couldn't hear over the hubbub, and George made a howling noise, like a dog. A sturdy youth followed, dragging Billy Harkness in an arm lock. Further down the market, a dark-haired woman was striding towards the paper auctions in a meaningful way, a path clearing for her as though by magic.

"Oi, Crispin," Ned said. "There's some people, sort of...doing stuff."

Crispin was on his feet like a jack-in-the-box. He propelled himself upwards with a foot on Ned's crate, said, "Oh *hell*," and dropped down again. He shoved his pen into a pocket and scrabbled up the papers he'd written on. His hands were shaking. "Hell!"

They looked like coppers, Ned thought, though they weren't in uniform. "Police?"

"Justiciary. Police in charge of magic."

"Well, but don't we need them?" Ned said. "You didn't sell the paper, it wasn't your fault it got out. Or, I could just go tell them—"

"*No.*" Crispin grabbed his arm. "You can't. They'll know it wasn't you and they'll make you say what you know—"

"What d'you mean, make?"

"Trust me, they can. They will. And then they'll have me."

"But you didn't do anything wrong!"

"Yes, I did." It was almost a whisper. "I really did."

Ned opened his mouth without knowing what he was going to say. He never found out, because there was a massive *whoomph* behind him, and he turned just in time to see a tongue of flame erupt over the heads of the crowd.

"*Ignis,*" Crispin said, sagging. "Of course it would be *ignis.*"

Ned jumped up onto his crate again. People were panicking in earnest now, screams erupting from different parts of the market, and more gouts of flame too. The two men, justiciary or whatever, had disappeared into the mob, but the dark-haired woman copper was looking around, frowning, nose wrinkled like she was sniffing, and as Ned stared, her eyes met his.

He hopped down. "Can those police sorts of yours deal with the fire and stuff? As well as you could, I mean?"

"Yes, of course. Better, probably."

"Right, well, let's leave them to it. Come on, quick."

He pulled Crispin behind him, a tight grip on his sweaty hand, heading up Bury Place, and ducked into the little entrance to Pied Bull Yard as the closest opportunity for private talk he could think of. Nobody about, nobody paying attention. He pushed Crispin against the bricks, cold even in summer under the arch. "Right. What's going on? What did you do?" He grabbed his right hand, with its truncated little finger. "What's *this* about?"

"It's unlawful." Crispin spoke in a whisper. "Blood magic, any magic that uses human bodies. I'm sure the law's meant to stop people using, you know, *other people*'s blood and bone, but that's not what it says. Blood and bone makes you a warlock." He mouthed the word rather than said it. "And the justiciary hunt warlocks."

"And that's what you are."

"It was *my* bone," Crispin said tensely. "*My* blood. I never hurt anyone else."

"You said *pain—*"

"I didn't want to!" He looked sick. "We used a rat—Mr. Marleigh said I had to learn— I didn't want to do any of that!"

Ned tightened his grip on Crispin's hand, staring at the little finger, with the skin grown so smoothly back. "How old were you when he cut off your finger?"

"Fifteen."

Ned remembered being fifteen, the resentment, the helplessness. Would he have cut off a chunk of his little finger to command the powers Crispin had? Like that was even a question. He sighed. "What happens now?"

Crispin sagged back against the wall, eyes wide in the gloom. Ned didn't release his hand. It was warm under his own, and somehow their fingers had shifted so he wasn't as much gripping Crispin's hand as holding it. "They'll have found the papers by now. They'll know someone's been using scripti. And if they find me, if they see my finger, my pen—"

"Well, throw it away," Ned said. "Or break it or burn it or whatever. Lots of folk have bits missing, my old man lost three fingers to a dropped packing crate. How would they know why you lost yours?"

"I," Crispin began, and then stared at him, mouth open. "Oh Ned, the pen, Mr. Marleigh's pen. I could...*break* it." He whispered that as though it was blasphemy, as though he was speaking treason.

"Would that stop all this?"

"I think it could. I can't be sure, Mr. Marleigh didn't tell me how to stop him doing things, but I can't think of anything better, and it certainly can't do any harm."

"Right, well. Let's go and get it, then."

"Wait." Crispin tugged at his hand. "Ned, why are you helping me? I'm a warlock. The justiciary will be after me, and you really don't want to get on their wrong side, and none of this is anything to do with you. You shouldn't be doing this."

It hadn't even occurred to Ned that he might walk away from this muddle, or from Crispin. "What, and stick you with all this on your own?"

"Well..." Crispin looked bewildered. "Why not?"

Because you shook my hand. Because you need someone to help you, and I don't see anyone else lining up. Because those freckles are killing me. "You want me to go away?"

Crispin's fingers tightened. "No. But—"

"This isn't your fault," Ned said. "I can't say I like the sound of this blood and bone stuff, but I *saw* you, doing your best to get that waste back before it hurt anyone. You didn't mean any of this to happen, did you?"

"No. I swear it."

"Well, then." Crispin with his back against the wall, Ned against him, eye to eye. Their entwined hands. A dark and little used alley. What the hell. Ned leaned in and kissed him.

"Mph." Crispin's other hand landed on his arse, pulling him in, and Ned returned the favour, delving up under the tails of his fancy coat, feeling his warmth through the fine shirt. Crispin might be scared and guilty, and a warlock, whatever that was, but his tongue was in Ned's mouth like that was the only thing that mattered, his lips receptive and demanding all at once. And that wasn't the only demanding thing, either, because Crispin had his thigh between Ned's now, putting pressure on his very interested prick, and their joined hands were squashed between their two chests, a hard lump like a love-knot of ribbon that would send the whole stack of waste tumbling. Ned mumbled into his mouth, pressed his hand against the curve of his spine.

"Oi!" It was a furious yell from the yard. Crispin jerked in shock, his teeth banging painfully against Ned's lip. "Bloody mollies, fuck off out of it! Piss off to Cleveland Street!"

Ned shouted back a few choice words to the angry yardman even as he tugged at Crispin's hand. "Come on, Freckles. Let's get that sodding pen."

4

"Right," Ned said. "And how are we doing this?"

Crispin had no idea either. He looked round, feeling the doom settling on his shoulders.

The Burfords had taken all Mr. Marleigh's books and papers from every shelf, and crammed the lot into the little study of the house in Baldwin's Gardens for Crispin to take, as though he had anywhere to put it all. It looked like Ned's storeroom, filled floor to ceiling with books and papers. The desk, which Crispin knew to be six feet away, was completely obscured from view by the heaps.

They stood together in the doorway because they couldn't get any further in. They weren't even meant to be in the house; Crispin had used *recludam* to open the locked door. He hoped the Burfords weren't coming back.

"I suppose it'll be in the desk? If we move everything…"

"To where?" Ned waved an indicative hand. The narrow hallway was full of Mr. Marleigh's old, heavy furniture: evidently it was all to be sold. The Burfords were losing no time in emptying the place of every trace of the old man. Crispin felt his throat tighten unexpectedly, and bit his lip. Ned frowned. "You all right?"

"It's just… I only found out he was dead this morning. I came back from Cornwall, and he was gone and the house half emptied already. The Burfords can't rid themselves of him fast enough. They've stripped the place of everything portable, the silverware and plates and everything down to the paper on the floor, and now this. Vultures."

Ned shrugged. He saw it all the time, Crispin reminded himself, made a living of clearing dead words from dead people. "Condolences and all, but we got a problem here. This is a good few hours' work to shift if there was even space to do it and there's probably people on fire by now. Can't you do something?"

Crispin wanted to say, *Such as?* He wanted to point out that he hadn't eaten since breakfast and writing four scripti had left him sick, drained and shaky. He also wanted to see the expression on Ned's face again, the awestruck look when Crispin had written *recludam* and the door lock had clicked. He didn't think Ned often let himself look impressed, and come to that, Crispin wasn't used to being impressive.

Unfortunately he couldn't think of a thing to do. There was no word of power that would shift that weight, or if there were, it wouldn't leave a drop of blood in his body. Setting it on fire would very much not help. What else was there?

"We need the pen," he said aloud, making himself focus. "The point isn't moving the paper, it's finding the pen. Mr. Marleigh could call it. He'd sometimes put it down and forget, he was very old, and he'd whistle and hear something. Ned, would you mind?" Ned made a face of reluctance but not refusal, so Crispin, with equal reluctance, reached for his own pen.

"*Calamus*," he murmured to himself, scribbling the words. "*Canticum.*"

It was like a bucket of ice water over his head. He staggered, and felt Ned's arms around him. "Crispin? What's wrong?"

"Too much," he mumbled. He felt hatefully weak. "Haven't eaten. And the pen hurts."

"You look sick as a dog." Ned pushed him gently to a sturdy sideboard that had been dumped in the hallway. "Sit on that."

"Can you hear anything?"

Ned tilted his head, scrubbing at his ear with the heel of his hand. "I can hear... Well, it's singing all right, but I'll swear it's coming from yours."

"Is it?" Crispin stared vaguely at the silver pen, with its thick, engraved barrel. Ned gently took it from his fingers and replaced it in his inner pocket then turned his head, listening. "No," he said a moment later. "Just yours. Maybe there's too much paper in the way, or it's in a different room, but not a thing. I don't suppose you can try something else?"

No, he couldn't. He felt like bursting into tears at the thought, but he set his jaw, reached for his pen, pulled it out of his pocket—

Ned's hand closed on his. "Hang on. Is that silver?"

"Yes."

"It looks expensive."

"What? Does that matter?"

"Your man's pen, the old gentleman. Was that the same sort of thing?" Crispin blinked. Ned gave him a gentle shake. "Look around. Look at this place, stripped bare. Would they have left a flash pen like that behind?"

Crispin's mouth moved a couple of times. "The Burfords. If they took the pen..."

"What happens if someone else writes with it?" Ned asked.

"They can't. It was his blood and bone for sixty years, doing his will. Nobody else can write with it. They *mustn't*."

"You reckon the Burfords know that?"

"Oh sweet bloody jumping Judas," Crispin said. "We have to find them."

He pushed himself off the table, and almost fell. Ned caught him—he was making quite the habit of that. "Whoa there. You look dreadful. Is there something I can get you?"

"Food." Crispin leaned into his strong grip thankfully, feeling his legs wobble. "I just need something to eat. Plum dough, or fudge. Biscuits. Anything sweet." Even the words made him hungrier. His head swam.

"Right. You stay here, get your breath back. I'll be five minutes."

"Ned—"

"Food first."

He let himself out. Crispin slid to the dusty floor, careless of his clothes, and put his head between his knees.

He'd wanted to say something. Maybe *thank you*, maybe more. He wanted to hold Ned's strong forearms and tell him exactly how much it had meant not to be alone on the worst day of his life to date. He wanted to explain himself and the pens and why he wasn't, truly, a bad person no matter what the law said, and he wanted to kiss Ned somewhere they wouldn't be interrupted, and he wanted food with a clawing hunger that tempted him to gnaw at his own hand. If Ned brought him sugared biscuits, the kind with fine crystals on top that melted on your tongue, and you felt the butter and sugar running down your throat... He dizzily imagined cramming them into his mouth, kissing Ned while he did it, crumbs on their lips and groping hands, and was lost between two hungers when the door opened.

"Ah, Crispin," said Mr. Marleigh.

His head snapped back so hard, it banged on the table behind him.

It was Mr. Burford in the doorway, his big, bulky form silhouetted against the warm evening light. But it had been Mr. Marleigh's voice, and it was Mr. Marleigh he sensed, with the instant recognition between one practitioner and another. His mouth dropped open.

"I must say, I'm disappointed." Mr. Marleigh's voice was stronger, younger. He moved in, leaving the door open behind him. Crispin scrambled to his feet, bracing himself against the table, staring at Mr. Marleigh's bright blue eyes in Mr. Burford's face. "I did assume it would be you."

Crispin's mouth moved a little before he could control it to answer. "What would, sir?"

"This." Mr. Marleigh jerked a hand at his, Mr. Burford's, body in its serge suit. "The person to write with me, the person I should become. Surely you wanted to. All that power, all that potential, and you were going to let it go to waste? Throw the pen away? I thought you had ambition."

"I wasn't there," Crispin said numbly. "You died when I was still at home." And if he had been there, if Crispin had been the one to clear the study and pick up the pen, so vibrant with power, compared to his own feeble creation, might he have been tempted? Tried how it fitted to his hand, attempted to write, and felt the snake-bite of Mr. Marleigh's pen in his spine?

"And that was damned inconvenient," Mr. Marleigh said. "Look at this oaf I'm wearing. An earthbound clod without the slightest sniff of power. What am I to do with this?" He took a step forward. Crispin took a step back. "No, no, it won't do. We'll have to do better than this." Words he'd heard so often, always in that weary yet kindly tone. "I've tried the powerless, and they're no good to me. I need a practitioner. Someone young, with power, with *potential*. Someone very like you."

Crispin took another step back. His foot hit some damn great piece of furniture. "Who are you?"

"My dear boy, you know who I am."

"No, I don't think I did," Crispin said. "You're the pen. Aren't you? You're not Mr. Marleigh at all."

"I'm the Mr. Marleigh you knew," said the man, the being, who faced him. "And before that I was Miss Cotton, and before that...what was it now...Higson? I forget. It's been a long time. And now—"

"You're not going to be Mr. Tredarloe," Crispin said. "You're *not*."

"Oh, do think, boy," Mr. Marleigh said, a little testily. "I share, you know. You'll be present too. We'll work together, just as we did before. And I am so powerful. You've no idea how powerful I am, and you want power, Crispin, I know you do. You want strength and admiration, and never to be the weakling or the outcast or the joke again. Don't you?"

"You sat in a cramped old house your whole life, writing scripti," Crispin said. "I don't want to do that."

"But Marleigh did, that's the point. Research made him happy. We'd do what made you happy too. We got on, didn't we? You were so hungry to learn from me, and wasn't I the best and kindest of masters? Can't you see how well we'd work together?"

Crispin stared at Mr. Marleigh's bright eyes. Remembered his patience, and kindness, and the world of magnificent potential he'd unrolled like a bright Persian carpet before Crispin's uncertain feet. Remembered his smooth explanations of the nonsensical laws against blood magic, and the hidebound minds of the justiciary. Remembered the knife going through the joint of his finger, he holding the hilt, and Mr. Marleigh's hand over his, pressing down.

"You have to help me now. I'm so close." The words hissed. "I have spent four lifetimes on *vita* and I have nearly achieved it. I *will* achieve it, with you. I will have life itself under my command and then we shall rule, you and I."

Crispin wondered, in a distant sort of way, what would happen if he told Mr. Marleigh that *vita* had finally worked. Just a few weeks ago they'd have shared the success with such joy. "Rule? Rule who?"

"Whoever I want." Mr. Burford's coarse features curved into Mr. Marleigh's sharp smile. "What can we not have in exchange for life? Think of it, Crispin. Think of the power we will command. Think of the women who will fall at our feet."

"I don't want women to fall at my feet. I don't want *anyone* to."

"Ambition!" He shouted the word, making Crispin flinch. "Where is your ambition, boy? Do you want to be negligible all your life? Here." Thick fingers reaching inside his jacket, pulling out that familiar silver shape. "Take it. Write with me."

"I don't want to," Crispin whispered.

"You do." Mr. Marleigh's eyes were on his with serpent intensity, unblinking. "I know you. You want power. You want to show them all, and you will. I'll give you more strength than you can imagine. You only have to reach out and take it."

He could feel the pull, feel the shape of the pen in his hand, the engraving under his fingers, how easy it would be. He could feel the power too, realised just how much Mr. Marleigh had hidden from him all this time. It was out now, throbbing in the ether, distorting the air around him. He could have it for the taking, and he could use it. No more looks of contempt then. No more mockery. He swallowed, closing his eyes. "I..."

"Who the hell are you?"

Crispin's eyes snapped open. Ned had walked around Mr. Marleigh, or Burford, glowering. He had a paper bundle in his hand, filling the dusty hall with the sweet smell of plum dough.

"Ned," Crispin said urgently. "Go."

"What is this?" said Mr. Marleigh softly.

"That's *who*, not what," Ned said. "And what's that noise?"

"Ned, go," Crispin repeated. "Now!"

"Oh," Mr. Marleigh said, softly. "Yes, he can hear me, can't he? Not like you, Crispin. You have no senses at all, but this one has got a pair of ears.

Potential." He tipped his head to one side, a little too far for a normal neck. "Not much, little more than a flit. But there."

"I don't know what you just called me, sunshine, but mind your tongue or I'll help you do it. Crispin—"

Mr. Marleigh's hand shot out, landing on Ned's bicep. He wrenched savagely, muscles bulging, and Crispin saw the second it dawned on him that for all his strength, the other man was unmoved.

"I could use him," Mr. Marleigh said thoughtfully. "He'd last me longer than this carcass."

"No," Crispin said. "No, you can't!"

"I don't much want to. A negro is scarcely the most useful face to wear. But if it will not be you, it must be someone." He smiled at Ned. "Are you ambitious, boy? Can you dream? Can you imagine freedom?"

"I'm free right now, you balmy old sod." Ned jerked unavailingly at the hand that held him. "And I'd like to know why you're singing like that pen, and— Crispin, what's going on?"

"Now, *that's* will," Mr. Marleigh said. "Do you see, Crispin? Or perhaps you simply don't have it in you. Perhaps you aren't good enough, after all."

Crispin swallowed. "Give it to me."

"Are you sure?" Mr. Marleigh's smile curved. "Do you have the nerve?"

"I'm your apprentice. I learned from you. You can't give the power to anyone else. I *want* it."

"Crispin!" Ned snapped. "What are you doing?"

"Be quiet! I want it, I want the power! Give me the pen!"

"Write for me," Mr. Marleigh hissed. "Write with me. Be mine." He held out the pen, and Crispin seized it.

The power. He felt it instantly, rushing up his arm, the sheer strength of blood and bone, hundreds of years of slowly building force.

And lives too. Not just the pen-wielders'. Dozens and dozens of lives, sucked in and drained and discarded.

As if one should use one's own blood and bone when there were so many other people there for the taking. No wonder he'd been so weak, consuming his own flesh rather than devouring those around him. What a fool.

And with the pen in his hand he could see, and hear too, the senses his weakling talents had denied him. He could hear the song of the pen, a keening cry, and he could see the power that spilled out from it, like the rainbows in an oily puddle, limning Mr. Burford's body with Mr. Marleigh's glory. And he saw Ned, solid and dark in contrast, with the faintest flicker of talent around him, and a bag of sugary pudding in his hand.

"Crispin?" Ned said.

"Write," Mr. Marleigh said, and the words rang like an operatic chorus in his ears. "Write with me. Be me. And we will be magnificent together." He released Ned, sending him stumbling with a shove.

"I couldn't promise magnificent." There was a tremor in Ned's voice. Crispin could see his fear. "But I reckon you and me would be all right, Freckles. Put the pen down, eh?"

"*Write.*"

Crispin settled the pen carefully in his hand, where it nestled as though made for him, and pulled a sheet of paper from his pocket. He put it on the table.

"Ah, don't do this. It ain't you," Ned said. "I don't even know you, but I know you're better than this."

Crispin didn't look at him. He turned the pen in his hand, feeling, for once in his life, absolute certainty of his course. He nodded to himself. Then he smashed the nib into the table with all his strength.

It didn't break.

"Boy!" roared Mr. Marleigh, and lunged.

Crispin couldn't fight him. He wasn't a fighter, even when he had the strength to do more than stay upright, and the power rolling out from Mr. Marleigh's body was terrifying. There was only one thing he could do. He shouted, "Kill it!", swiped his hand over the tabletop, and sent the pen flying towards Ned a second before Mr. Marleigh's blow hit.

5

NED SAW THE silver cylinder skidding towards him and hurled himself forward. He snatched it up before it hit the floor

—*hot to his hand, a screaming like cats in his ears, and colours wild to his vision, like they said opium did you in the penny shockers*—

wrapped one hand round the other for grip, and whacked it against the wall as hard as he could.

Didn't break. Bloody thing didn't even give. The shock resonated through his hand so he almost dropped it.

The big man with weird eyes was up and turning, face distorted with rage, reaching for the pen. Behind him Crispin was a slumped form on the ground.

Ned bolted. Legged it out, and right, and straight down Baldwin's Gardens to Gray's Inn Road, knowing that *thing* was after him, whatever it was, because he was pretty sure it wasn't a person by any definition he'd recognise.

What the hell had Crispin done?

And what was he going to do? The pen was hot as coals in his hand and it felt like it was squirming, like he was holding a snake, and how did you kill a pen anyway?

Chuck it in the Thames? He'd never make it that far. Anyway, he'd learned his letters off a book of fairy tales, and if you could trust that, which you might as well after everything today, throwing magic stuff in rivers never worked for long. Could he get to someone with a forge who could melt it?

"Thief!" roared a voice behind him. "Stop thief!"

The sod. Heads turned, looking at the black man fleeing a well-dressed cove, and nobody was going to stop and ask if it was a fair charge, were they? He sidestepped a burly coster by a fraction of an inch, elbowed a shopboy viciously, and charged out onto Gray's Inn Road with hands grabbing at his sleeves and no ideas at all except to keep running.

A fully laden brewer's dray was rumbling along, pulled by two great plodding horses. The iron wheel-rims sent showers of sparks flying up from the cobbles.

Iron.

Ned threw himself forward, dragging a clutching boy behind him with the strength of desperation. He hit the cobbles within arm's length of the massive vehicle, knocking the breath out of himself, and shoved the pen under a wheel.

Back in the day, when he'd worked the docks with his dad and brother, he'd once seen a man fall in by the side of a mooring coal barge. It had swung sideways so gently, without a pause, to bump off the stone quay. That had been the worst thing, the implacable, unaffected movement of the boat. Somehow, he'd felt like it ought to have reacted to the crunch of bone.

This was like that. The dray rolled on, oblivious, as the pen splintered into shards, and the scream shot through his head like knives.

He rolled over, gasping, as the wide-eyed amateur thief-taker let go, and saw the big peculiar man stood in the road. His mouth was working, hands clawing, eyes fixed on the broken ruin of the pen, and then his face began to collapse inward as though it was being sucked down his own throat.

Ned got up, skirted well past him, and ran. In a real panic now because what the hell, what the hell had he done...

He charged into the house, and skidded to his knees at Crispin's crumpled form. "Crispin! Crispin, mate, are you all right? Freckles?"

"Urgh." Crispin's face moved, then he blinked. "Ned?"

"Oh, thank God." Ned grabbed him, holding tight. "Oh my days."

"Ned," Crispin slurred. "Run. Mr. Marleigh—"

"That bloke? I reckon he's got his own problems. I broke the pen."

"You— I love you," Crispin said. "How?"

"Brewer's dray. Iron wheels. Or half a ton of cart, I don't know which it was that worked, but it broke."

Crispin's eyes widened. "Oh, that's brilliant. You're brilliant."

"Hold on." Ned extricated himself from Crispin's grip. "I got you food."

"I *do* love you." Crispin grabbed the plum dough he held out, and shoved about a third of it into his mouth in one go.

"Nice to be appreciated. That bloke...what did you say his name was?"

"Marleigh," Crispin mumbled through a mouthful.

"Right. Wasn't he dead?"

"Mmm."

"Right." Ned sat on the floor, feeling just a bit wobbly. "Well. There's a lot of *that* about today." Crispin shot him a look, eyes lightening with amusement, and Ned found himself starting to smile back. "You think breaking the pen did it for the other stuff, the other magic?"

Crispin swallowed. "Yes. I'm quite sure the other scripti will stop working. I mean, if things are on fire, they'll keep burning, but at least Mr. Foster will be dead."

"Good to know. Now, do you want to tell me what just happened?"

"It was Mr. Marleigh. He was...possessed, I suppose, by the pen, and he wasn't the first, either. Someone made the pen three or four lifetimes ago, and fed it, and when they died someone else used it, and it fed, and it wanted to live. It, or what was left of its owners? I don't know. I suppose Mr. Burford used it, and it took him, but it *wanted* a practitioner to live in. It wanted me."

"Who's Mr. Burford?"

"The body he was using, the man in serge."

"He didn't look too chipper, when I broke the pen," Ned said carefully. "Did I hurt him?"

"The pen did, not you. It *killed* people. I thought Mr. Marleigh just used his own powers. I asked him, even, how was it that he could write so many scripti when every one I wrote drained me, and he said a lifetime's expertise. And all the time he was using other people, blood and bone, I felt it when I took the pen. He was a murderer, Ned, and I worked for him. I *believed* him. And he was keeping me around, training me up, so the pen could pass to me. Because he thought I'd take the power at any price. He was going to change his will in my favour—mine, whichever apprentice he happened to have when he got too old—and then take me over so he'd keep his money. If my mother hadn't fallen ill... I'm such a bloody fool."

Ned couldn't really argue. "What about your pen? If you keep using it, like he did..."

Crispin stared at him, marshlight eyes stricken. Then he fished it from his pocket with a trembling hand. "Will you kill it for me?"

"Is that going to hurt you?"

"I never took strength from mine. It fed off me. And I don't care anyway. Break it. Please."

Ned hesitated, but the fairy stories were in his mind and he couldn't shake the idea of how this ought to go. "Don't you reckon you should be the one to break it?"

"I don't know if I can," Crispin whispered. "It's my power, and years of my life, and my *finger*...please, Ned, do it for me? So it's gone, and I can't change my mind?"

Ned put a hand to his face, cupping it carefully. "Freckles, I saw you with that other pen. Even I could feel how much power that had, and you made a damn good stab at smashing the thing to bits. You aren't going to change your mind."

"No. No, I suppose I'm not." Crispin took another bite of plum dough. "Would you hold it for me, though, till I've eaten? I'll break it then."

"I'll do it with you. We'll get rid of it together."

"Actually, I'll take it," said a woman from the doorway.

Ned jumped like a scalded cat, and from Crispin's reaction he wasn't the only shocked one. She was leaning against the doorframe like she'd always been there, a strong-faced woman with dark hair and an irritable look. The woman copper from the market.

"Esther Gold," she said, swinging into the room. "Justiciary."

"Now, just a moment, miss," Ned began urgently, rising to his feet to stand between her and Crispin.

She ignored him, looking down at Crispin, who stared up, white-faced, mouth full of half-chewed plum dough. "So. An entire marketplace rendered chaos by blood magic on scripted paper, some sort of vivified pen, a remarkably dead man on Gray's Inn Road and an even more impressively animated one on Oxford Street. You may consider yourself officially in trouble. Pen."

She held out her hand for the pen, commandingly. Ned glanced to Crispin, then handed it over. She turned it in her fingers, nose twitching. "Tsk. Right, up you get. I'm going to take you in."

"Now wait, miss," Ned said. "None of this was his fault."

"Mrs, and I'll be the judge of that."

"No, ma'am, you need to listen—"

"I did," she said calmly. "I was listening to you both with interest for some time. It seems to me, young man, as though you have committed the very serious offence of being an utter fool. Although...you were his apprentice, yes? Who apprenticed you to him?"

"Uh...he came and found me."

"Full of plausibility and ambition, and lots of warnings about the evil justiciary with their baseless distrust of warlocks?" Crispin flushed. Mrs. Gold made a sour face. "If I had a shilling for every time, honestly. Now, get up. You are coming in to the Council and I am going to establish what exactly happened, armed with this pen which will tell me if you have indeed used only your own blood and bone. It's a good thing you didn't smash what may prove to be vital evidence for you. Imbecile," she added, just under her breath. "And if you're Ned Hall, I'll have you in as well. There's a gaffer at St. George's Market who's threatening to twist the head off your shoulders, so we may as well keep you out of his way while we untangle this mess."

"But I'm a warlock," Crispin blurted out. "I thought the justiciary killed warlocks."

"We don't like them," Mrs. Gold agreed. "And the reason we don't is, they tend to leave a trail of victims in all shapes and sizes. I am prepared to consider the possibility that you might be one of them. Come and help me find out."

For the second time in his life, Crispin headed down Grape Street to find Ned Hall.

The rag and bottle man seemed not to have moved since his first visit, several very long days ago. He nodded Crispin in, and he walked through the shop with hope and fear quivering in his belly, and into the room full of paper.

Ned was there, in his shirtsleeves, heaving in the last armful of paper from his cart. He looked up, and that smile lit his face for a second, then dropped away.

"Crispin. You all right?"

"Yes. Yes, I think so. Do you have a moment?"

"Had plenty of 'em," Ned said. "I wasn't sure I'd be seeing you again."

Crispin shut and bolted the door to the shop behind himself, and as if in response, Ned pulled the door to the street closed.

"I'm sorry," he said. "They only just let me out. I've been there for four days, being questioned and interrogated and talked at. It was appalling. All the things Mr. Marleigh did, all the people, and poor Mr. Burford... God, it was dreadful, and there were so many people who wanted to blame me—"

"The coppers?"

"No, they were wonderful, actually. There were people looking for a scapegoat, or saying that a warlock was a warlock and I should be punished, and Mrs. Gold simply wouldn't stand for it. I mean, they haven't let me off scot free, or anything like. I'll be on watch for the rest of my life, probably. But they decided this morning, they're going to give me a chance, remedial training, teach me how to use my powers the right way. It's going to be all right, Ned." He gave a tentative smile. "Um, how are you?"

Ned blew out a breath. "Well, your Mrs. Gold had a word with Billy Harkness, seems like, because he's not tried to take my head off after all, but I doubt I'll be selling paper to St. George's any time soon."

"Oh. Oh dear."

"Eh, there's plenty of others." Ned shrugged, carelessly, but his eyes were on Crispin. "So, you came round, why? I mean, nice to hear you're all right, anything else?"

"Well, I mean... the thing is..." Crispin took a step forward. "You said we'd be magnificent, you and me. I wondered if you'd like to see if you were right."

Ned didn't move, didn't smile, but the skin round his eyes creased, giving them all the welcome Crispin needed to see. "Pretty sure I didn't say that, Freckles."

"Yes, you did. In the house."

"I said we'd be all right. I said I *couldn't* promise magnificent."

Crispin found he was smiling now. "No, that's right. And you said you couldn't promise magic either, before. Now I think of it, I'm not sure why I bothered coming."

"Low expectations." Ned took a step forward, lips curving, and then Crispin was in his arms, kissing him, tasting dust on his mouth and feeling it under his fingers. Paper dust and sweat, the smells of Ned. He bit at Ned's lips, wrapped a leg around his hips, felt a strong hand under his arse, hoisting him up. They kissed, and grabbed, and crashed down together on top of a stack of paper that slithered underneath them. He got his leg between Ned's powerful thighs and hands to his shoulders, pushed him away a little so he could get his mouth to Ned's neck.

"Mph. Freckles. Do that again."

Crispin nipped his ear. "Do you have to call me that?"

"Your freckles are stunners. I want to lick them all up."

"You can lick them right off, if you like."

Ned grinned blindingly down at him. "I'll give it a go. You're out of trouble?"

"I really am."

"And there's no more of this warlock stuff? No more setting fire to markets?"

"None. I promise. I'm going to be a model of good magical practice, honestly." Crispin bucked his hips invitingly, and felt Ned's hand descend, taking assured hold of him through the straining cloth of his trousers. He ground up, into the hold, gasping.

"Glad to hear it," Ned muttered. "Just rabbits out of hats and whatnot?"

"Well, sort of." Crispin fumbled urgently with buttons. "Is that all right? Do you mind?"

Ned's hand delved below his waistband, skin to sensitive skin, making

Crispin jerk and moan. "I can live with magic. How are you with paper dust?"

"I dare say I can put up with it," he managed, strangled. "Oh God, Ned!"

"That's all right then." Ned was lying over him, holding him, smiling at him, and Crispin's heart was pounding as hard as his prick in Ned's hand. "Couple of queer trades we've got."

Crispin put an arm round his neck to pull him close for the kiss he needed, even as he pushed up into his hand, rocking with increasing urgency, feeling Ned's arousal hard and solid against him, waiting its turn. "Anything wrong with that?" he mumbled against Ned's lips. "Oh. Oh."

"Not to my mind, Freckles," Ned murmured, as Crispin cried out. "Just about nothing at all."

Magically Delicious

NICOLE KIMBERLING

Special Agent Keith Curry didn't like going nowhere. But where else could a guy go on a stationary bike? Not that he didn't like to work out. He liked free weights just fine. Cardio day? He wished he could pass on it. But even when he was in top shape, being one hundred percent human in NIAD, NATO's Irregular Affairs Division, had some disadvantages. When arresting an extra-human suspect, he could not turn invisible, shoot geysers of flame or fly. The only magic he had access to resided in his shoulder holster in the form of his mage pistol.

And besides, he had to try and compete with Gunther. Well, he couldn't compete with his boyfriend, but he could try not to look too bad by comparison.

Tall, dark, handsome and naturally fit, Gunther did not need to tag along with Keith to the company gym. His perfect physique had been bestowed on him by the mages who had transmogrified his goblin body in utero so that he could be consistent with the human world. But most mornings he came along to the gym anyway. Insofar as Keith knew, Gunther only ever worked out to be social.

Whereas Keith could have epitomized the word "average." Not good looking or bad looking. Brown hair and eyes. Nothing beyond that to report. He was the kind of man nobody noticed for very long. And that worked out well for him when he was on an investigation, but was a constant source of mild unease for him the rest of the time.

Gunther was hot enough to get any so-inclined man and maybe a few who were just curious. His blue eyes twinkled like chips of lapis lazuli as he sat his duffel bag down on the gray carpet and started scrolling through the messages on his phone.

"Looks like strike force is on call for the Saint Patrick's Day parade again," Gunther commented.

"Damn leprechauns," Keith muttered.

"Their labor dispute looks like it's getting intense." Gunther held up his phone to display a photo of six nasty-looking specimens forming a three-layer pyramid that stood about hip high to a normal man. The one on top held a sign reading, "Pixies Go Home," another held a card that said, "NIAD Busts Unions!"

"I do not envy you. They look like ball-biters," Keith observed. "What's their beef, anyway?"

"They worked for one of the NIAD contractors, who replaced them with pixies because they came cheaper."

"So angry ball-biters." Keith let out a low whistle. "Be careful."

"I'm always careful. And I'm a good planner. I brought you some breakfast." He reached into his gym bag and pulled out a can of Primal Thunder Power Shake and waggled it at him.

"That's not breakfast. It's a meal-replacement product." Keith pushed the pedals harder as his velocity-free vehicle simulated a steep incline. Sweat prickled beneath his Slayer t-shirt and trickled down his stomach. "It tastes like baby aspirin sprinkled on sawdust."

"But it has nine grams of protein and its new, improved flavor makes it taste like a ray of creamsicle-flavored sunshine." Gunther sat on the bike next to Keith's and idly pushed one of the pedals around.

"I've got my own breakfast."

"I hope you don't mean that baggie with a tofu dog in it I saw you put in your pocket this morning." Disapproval darkened Gunther's expression.

"No, that's my lunch." Keith kept a straight face, unable to stop himself from winding Gunther up. They'd been living together for a year now and although many of their domestic conflicts had been smoothed out, Gunther still found Keith's eating habits appalling. Which Keith thought was pretty rich coming from a guy whose goblin origins allowed him to eat cigarettes and swig lighter fluid.

"Are you sure you used to be a chef?" Gunther asked.

"Either that or I just loved wearing checkered pants and a ridiculous hat." Keith grinned up at his boyfriend. "Seriously though, I've got a hard-boiled egg as well. And a couple of dijon mustard packets I swiped from the fancy grocery store. I'm fine."

Keith reached a plateau in his imaginary bike ride and took the opportunity to get his wind back. He glanced out the fifth-story window. If he looked between two buildings he could just see the Washington Monument poking up at the midpoint of the National Mall. Beyond that lay the Lincoln Memorial, where, in the vaulted basement beneath, NIAD mages worked strange spells that controlled the flow of magic in this, the earthly realm.

But if Keith and the other agents did their jobs right, neither the chilly tourists nor the tired commuters filing into office buildings all around would ever know about the mages, the leprechaun labor dispute or any other magic.

To them it was business as usual in the nation's capital. Dismal winter fog still clung to the tops of the buildings. Dirty slush coated the sidewalk below.

As a native Californian, Gunther had been game about his first East Coast winter, getting very excited about owning his first pair of snow boots. But then Gunther's outgoing nature and high spirits were hard to deflate by any means—the exact opposite of Keith's own inborn pessimism and suspicion.

"Is there any more news on the security breeches?" Keith asked.

Gunther returned his attention to his phone. "No one has claimed responsibility and the spells leave no residue to analyze. Pixie-pure magic. That's what they say."

Keith rolled his shoulders to try and remove the tension building there. Over the past three weeks, seven NIAD agents had been attacked by a bizarre and completely incapacitating spell that caused severe hallucinations that lasted from hours to several days. During that time, the agents became convinced that they'd been abducted, recognized no one around them and often had to be physically restrained. Afterward, the agents remembered little about the experience, but seemed mostly to be unharmed.

While it was true that many extra-humans, especially in the fey community, might regard this sort of attack as more of a prank than a terrorist assault, NIAD took a dim view of any kind of breech of security.

"I suppose they haven't bothered to interview the local pixies yet, then," Keith asked.

"Anybody with a handful of jelly beans can score a thimble-full of pixie dust these days," Gunther replied, giving a shrug. "It's half of what the leprechauns are so pissed about. Apart from being made redundant at work, all that magic dust flying around is completely ruining the market for three wishes, or so they say."

"I would say the three wishes racket also suffers from some credibility issues that are unrelated to pixies." Keith didn't like to think of himself as prejudiced, but the antics of leprechauns often rubbed him the wrong way.

"Such as?" Gunther glanced up from his phone.

"Oh, like a bald guy wishes for hair and ends up getting a rabbit. You know, a hare? Douchebag leprechaun humor."

"Yeah, that's probably true. Still, if the pixies don't get on the self-regulation ball, our brass is going to step in and do it for them. Then nobody will be happy. Especially not that sugar junkie Buttercup," Gunther said, absently, his eyes still glued to the small screen.

Doubtless he was scanning some social media feed for news of his huge West Coast family. Gunther had more cousins than anyone Keith had ever met, as well as apparently endless interest in looking at photos of their babies, pets and favorite outfits. Suddenly his expression brightened and Gunther glanced up at him.

Keith steeled himself against the shock of whatever photograph he was about to be shown.

Snow goblins—that is goblins who had not undergone transmogrification—looked like creatures of nightmare. They seemed to be made entirely of spiky, white bone. Blood red pits smoldered where their eyes should have been and they had more teeth than a barracuda, even when just born. Keith had now gazed upon many small, toothy creatures being held by proud parents or grandparents.

He mentally crossed his fingers, hoping for a pink or blue hat that would help him figure out the gender, at least. Instead Gunther turned the phone around to reveal a photograph of Keith's old restaurant.

"It's a five star review!" Gunther offered his phone for Keith's perusal.

Keith broke into a smile. Before coming to NIAD, he'd owned his own place, called KC's. When he'd decided to use his knowledge of food to help NIAD root-out extra-planar contraband, he'd sold the tiny diner to his sous chef, Candy. At first she'd kept the place going strong using his menu and recipe book. But lately, she'd been switching it up—making the joint hers, which made Keith proud. He'd picked a winner when he hired her. That was for sure.

Though as the reviewer glowingly described the cozy surroundings and carefully crafted plates, it still gratified him to see that one of the five stand-out dishes mentioned was his own.

"This is great. We should definitely go see her next time we're in Providence," Keith said.

"Maybe we can make a weekend out of it in June. I hear their pride parade is the only nighttime parade in New England."

"That is correct," Keith said.

"And KC's is right on the parade route."

"Have you had this plan for a long time or did you come up with it now?" Keith felt he should ask.

"Just now." Gunther took his phone back, pocketed it and picked up the Primal Thunder again. "If you're not going to drink this I will."

"Knock yourself out." Keith bore down on the pedals again, pushing against the last incline in the computerized interval training. Sweat slicked his palms. Beside him Gunther cracked the top of the can and chugged the entire twelve ounces. Even then he looked good, like a guy in a commercial. He finished, crumpled the can in his hand and gazed out the window.

"I'm also really looking forward to seeing the cherry blossoms this spring," he said. "I just missed them last year."

"They're pretty good... if you like pink trees." Keith dismounted from the bike and scrubbed his face with a dry towel. When he glanced back up he found Gunther's expression had filled with sadness.

The sudden change of mood puzzled Keith, as it went against Gunther's usual equanimity. He stepped forward and put a hand on Gunther's shoulder.

"You okay?"

Gunther didn't reply. He moved closer to the window until his forehead pressed right against the glass and his breath fogged the pane. Though his lips moved, Keith couldn't hear what he said.

Keith glanced around the workout room. They were hardly the only agents present. Eight or nine other agents occupied the space. A couple of Gunther's strike force buddies gathered at the back, pumping iron. One of them noticed Gunther's dejected posture and gave Keith the stink eye.

His name was Haakon and he was half-dark elf, though Keith would never have used the word *fey* to describe him. He always stood too close to Gunther in the cafeteria lunch line and Keith suspected him of unnecessarily flexing his big black 3-D delts while using the free weights. To Keith, Haakon always seemed to be thinking something like, "How does a scrub like you keep a stone cold fox like Gunther? He could definitely do better." Or at least that's what Keith assumed Haakon thought, since they were the only two sentences Haakon had ever spoken to him.

Keith ignored Haakon's glower and turned back to Gunther. Quietly, he said, "Hey, what's up?"

Slowly Gunther turned to face him. His blue eyes shone with tears.

"I have to get out of here," Gunther whispered.

"Out of DC?" Sure, the city could be dreary at this time of year but he thought Gunther might be overreacting a little. Could it be homesickness?

"Out of *here*!" Gunther's voice rose with each word. "I have to get *out*!" He spun to face the window and smashed his fist directly into a window designed to withstand a mage blast. Blood exploded across the glass as his knuckles split and popped against the unyielding surface.

Gunther howled with rage and threw himself at the glass, thrashing against it like an eel caught in a net. Keith lunged forward and caught him around the waist, pulling him back from the impenetrable barrier.

"I need some help here!" Keith bellowed.

Gunther fought him, throwing an elbow that caught him like club in the gut. Keith curled over in pain, but managed to keep hold of his boyfriend long enough for Gunther's strike force buddies and a couple other agents to get across the room. While Keith tried to stand, Haakon tackled Gunther like the high-school linebacker he'd probably been. Someone hit the alarm. A red light coalesced in the center of the room, spinning and flashing like the light atop an old-time cop car.

Gunther struggled against his opponents, wailing and writhing on the gray carpet. His already injured hand smashed against the pedal of an elliptical trainer. Blood spattered across the device. Being goblin inside, Gunther easily overwhelmed the men restraining him. He kicked Haakon back against a weight rack, sending dumbbells crashing down.

On-duty security came through the door, stun guns drawn.

"Clear off!" one shouted.

"What the fuck are you doing?" Keith rushed forward, but not in time. The point man leveled the gun and fired. A silver bolt of magic flared from the muzzle, slamming into Gunther's chest. Gunther went still.

Completely still. Keith couldn't even see the rise and fall of his breath.

For Keith all time stopped. Though he knew that the security guy had fired a stun gun, he also knew that stun guns could kill, especially when fired at close range.

Keith dropped to his knees, leaning forward to listen for breath, and heard nothing. Suddenly he felt hands on his shoulders urging him away from Gunther's unmoving body. Blind with rage, Keith shook them off launched himself at the shooter, screaming. "I'll kill you, you stupid fuck!"

Two on-duty agents caught Keith by both arms and held him back. One of them was shouting something in Keith's ear.

"...he's been compromised. That's what happens when you stun a goblin. Calm down. He'll be fine."

Keith stopped struggling as he saw a medical team also coming through the door. They crowded around Gunther's fallen form so densely that all Keith could see were Gunther's feet. One of his running shoes was missing—lost in the struggle.

"Let me go," Keith growled. "I want to see him."

"No, you'll just get in their way." Haakon came forward, rubbing his shoulder as he did so. "You need to let them do their job."

"Where are they taking him?"

"To the medical unit." Haakon did not actually look at Keith as he spoke, which did nothing to soothe Keith's nerves. But he stopped fighting and the two security guards holding him loosed their grip.

"What the hell just happened?" Keith tried to mute the panic in his voice, but he couldn't.

Haakon finally met his eyes and said, "I think he just became the eighth agent to get pixie-dusted."

2

Keith went to the medical unit, but wasn't able to enter as Gunther had been quarantined until he regained cognizance. The witchdoctor in charge shook a couple of rattles around Keith's head to make sure he was clear of magical influence, then said, "We'll call you when you're allowed to visit. Would you like me to inform Agent Heartman's family?"

"I can call them," Keith said quickly. He knew Mr. and Mrs. Heartman would react badly to any official NIAD phone calls.

Phoning Gunther's family with bad news was harder than Keith had imagined possible. It had been a long time since he'd been a contributing member of a family and he'd forgotten how it felt to participate as an insider. Now he would have to tell them that their son had been attacked, while he stood by, powerless. But at least he knew that Gunther's parents were the only two people in the world who loved Gunther as much as he did.

Despite Keith's delicate wording, Gunther's mother, Agnes broke down right away, crying and handing the phone to Gunther's bewildered father, Gerald, who seemed certain that Gunther had been killed.

Once Keith managed to explain that Gunther was at the hospital under sedation and was expected to make a full recovery, he had to wait while Gerald explained this to Agnes. Finally, Gerald finished with the phrase, "We'll be there in five minutes. We'll just have to tell our supervisor what's happened."

Since Gerald and Agnes worked in the translation office of the San Francisco NAID branch, they had access to the travel portals that connected all the offices. This proved convenient during the holiday season, but could be overwhelming as well.

"You don't have to rush," Keith said. Even he hadn't made it into the medical unit yet. "They won't let you in to see him anyway. Not until he starts to come around. And I still have to go be debriefed about the incident."

"Agnes and I would rather be there just in case," Gerald said.

"At least go home to pack a bag," Keith said.

"No need. Gunther keeps a suitcase of ours in the closet of the spare room. We'll have everything we need for a few of days." Gerald had the tone of a man announcing an obvious fact that Keith should have already known.

"Right." Keith sagged against the wall. Of course Gunther would have an emergency suitcase for his parents. He'd only moved out of their place to move in with Keith. "Look I'm not at home right now. But I guess you probably have your own key."

"That's right. You just get on with what you're doing." This last came from Agnes, who had apparently just found the extension handset.

On the one hand Keith was relieved to know that someone understood how he might feel about Gunther, but he also felt a twinge of annoyance at how easily the not-even-inlaws-yet decided to invade his space. He pushed it aside. He needed to get on with things right now so he said, "Thanks, you two."

Clad all in black and seated around a circular table of the dim, circular room beneath the Lincoln Memorial, the twelve men and women in charge of maintaining the magical barriers surrounding NIAD DC headquarters looked like they'd come directly from some big funeral for a corporate incense manufacturer. Thin, perfumed trails of smoke coiled against the ceiling and swirled into the recessed lighting fixtures like gravity defying serpents.

For a group of people who had all decided to wear the same color to work, the mages varied wildly from one another in their personal style in that they appeared to have chosen to survey the entirety of fashion history. One man looked like he'd stopped moving forward with fashion in the mid-seventeenth century. The female closest to Keith wore latex pants that were arguably inspired by the dystopian necro-future. She held a lit cigarette that smelled like cloves.

Keith thought, *Things to bring up to my union rep: mages being unfairly exempt from dress code* and *flouting citywide indoor smoking ban.*

The joke helped calm his nerves.

Taking turns, the mages quizzed him on his and Gunther's actions leading up to the event. As he spoke, spells moved the smoke in the air to re-create his actions in a three-dimensional representation.

"And you did nothing unusual?" Another mage asked. She was a dead-ringer for Morticia Addams, and Keith wondered whether she imitated the costume ironically to creep people out, or if the character herself had been the inspiration. "No one contacted Gunther or handed him any packages, for example? Tapped him on the shoulder, maybe? Was there anyone smoking a cigarette on the street nearby that Agent Heartman could have inhaled the smoke from?"

"Not that I know of," Keith replied. The mention of this caused a twinge of anxiety about the amount and contents of the smoke he currently inhaled.

The Morticia-clone steepled her fingers and leaned back in her chair. Another mage, an elderly man whose neat Savile Row suit contrasted sharply with the jewel-encrusted crown he wore, leaned forward to take his turn as interrogator.

"You said Agent Heartman was looking through his phone messages just before the attack? Did he receive any calls?" As the King spoke, Keith thought he caught a whiff of formaldehyde.

"I don't think so. But I have his phone here. You can check." Keith slid the device across the table toward the King. The man removed a silver pen from his pocket and used that to manipulate the phone while murmuring a string of incantations. Finally he said, "There's nothing here," and pushed the device back to Keith who caught it just before it spun off the edge of the table.

Morticia straightened in her seat. "That will be all. You may return to your duties, Agent Curry."

As one, the mages turned from him. Without speaking, they stretched out their arms and linked hands. Then, following some unknown cue, they began a loud, slow chant in what sounded like Latin, but could have been anything.

Keith didn't know if he'd ever experienced such a summary dismissal in his life. He'd wanted to ask questions—find out if they had any real leads. But they just kept chanting as if he didn't exist.

Dejected, he mounted the stairs and climbed back up into the chill winter air, and headed back to his office. By the time he got there, his co-workers had both already gone on their assignments so he was left alone in his undecorated cubicle.

As an agent, Keith specialized in investigations involving contraband food items. Everything from illegal unearthly fruit importation to busting human protein rings fell within his purview. Among the new cases in Keith's inbox were fresh allegations of glycerin adulteration of vampiric meal-supplements. He also needed to finish up the paperwork on what had turned out to be spurious allegations of mermaid-flesh dealers working the Florida Keys. After a cursory investigation, Keith had determined that the mermaid flesh was really manatee—also illegal, but not his department—and passed the case along to the Department of Fish and Wildlife.

He needed to file paperwork for both but he couldn't just file reports knowing that the person who had caused Gunther to break his own hand was just waltzing around somewhere free and happy.

He considered asking his supervisor, Nancy Noble, to reassign him to Gunther's case, then realized it would be quicker and easier to just reassign himself as his supervisor had stepped out to lunch.

Gunther had said that the magic was pixie-pure and the biggest known dealer of pixie-dust just happened to be an associate of the Heartman clan. Her name was Buttercup and she, like a lot of fairies, spent a lot of time dressed up like an insect—a moth, to be precise. She lived in the Elysian Fields, a former paradise that now served as a kind of way station en route to the Grand Goblin Bazaar. Keith could have easily traveled there via the official system of NIAD portals, but he would have had to file a travel plan, so he elected to use the goblin market transportation system instead.

The Grand Goblin Bazaar exited over many different realms simultaneously, linked together by portals that allowed a shopper to move from one market to another via a system of entry points. On Earth these were usually disguised as disused bathroom stalls at farmer's markets.

Prior to being associated with the Heartmans, Keith had disliked this method of travel, fearing both uncertainty and ambush. But since becoming close with Gunther's family, Keith had lost nearly all fear of goblins. More than that he wore a tooth-shaped pendant affiliating him with the Heartman Clan, which had helped a lot on the one occasion he'd gotten lost.

The only market currently open in DC in March was the fish market at the wharf, so that's where Keith headed. He donned his spectral lenses, which allowed him to see objects concealed by magic. These might include living creatures who altered their appearance to blend better with human society, or signs and symbols written in spectral ink. In DC, as with the entire Eastern Seaboard, leprechaun graffiti covered the bottom foot of most walls.

He walked through the lunchtime crowd, heading toward the bathrooms. There he found an out-of-order stall marked with a sign whose plain block letters glowed vibrant green when viewed through the spell-revealing lenses and changed from reading "out-of-order" to "Grand Goblin Bazaar."

Unfortunately the glasses also revealed the presence of a line of six leprechauns forming a blockade in front of the stall. Standing shoulder-to-shoulder with their arms linked, they formed a barrier the approximate height of a rabbit fence. Easy to step over? Not if a guy wanted to come out of it with his nut sack intact. After glancing at the urinals to make certain no other guys were present, Keith pulled out his ID and said, "Official business. Step aside."

The leprechauns looked at each other with expressions of such exaggerated incredulity that Keith thought it might have been faster to file the paperwork to use the NIAD portals after all.

"He's from NIAD, don't you know?" The leprechaun whose crinkly, orange beard poked down toward his pointed shoes like a fuzzy carrot spoke not to Keith but to a compatriot, whose green felt hat sported not one, but three decorative buckles.

"NIAD, you say?" Three Buckles said. "Doesn't that stand for something?"

"Nasty, idjit, arsehole, dingleberries, I think it is," Carrot Beard replied.

"Oh no, them letters means nosey, insulting, arrogant, dickholes," a third leprechaun who was clean-shaven but sported a nose the relative size and shape of a toucan's beak chimed in.

Keith remained unmoved. Years of experience had proved to him that he couldn't out-insult a leprechaun. Instead he pocketed the ID and crouched down to as close to their eye level as possible.

"What are you doing here, guys? What's the point of hanging out in this shitter all day?" He tried to sound reasonable rather than frustrated, as the wee men tended to thrive on conflict and general strife.

"We're committing an action!" Carrot Beard cried, his ruddy face reddening even further.

"It's our right to demonstrate," Three Buckles said.

"So this is a protest?"

"That it is." Carrot Beard nodded. "Against them damn union-busting scabby pixies, may they rot in eternal hell forever."

"May their wee heads be squashed like grapes and may goblins suck the marrow from their tiny broken femurs," Toucan Beak added solemnly.

"I don't think it's wise for professional wish-granters such as yourselves to be cursing anyone aloud. It could constitute a criminal threat," Keith remarked. He kept his tone calm, and resisted the urge to crack his knuckles, an action that he tended to perform unconsciously when irritated.

"I was merely speaking figuratively." Toucan Beak pulled an obsequious pout.

"Look I'm not here to bust you. I just need to use this portal. Do you have any literature I could take? A pamphlet maybe?"

"Yes, sir, we do!" Three Buckles reached into his small waistcoat and pulled out an even tinier piece of paper. From what Keith could make out, the leprechauns had been on strike against their employer, Taranis Inc., for several weeks. The leprechauns claimed that the pixie scab labor had been brought in by NIAD itself, to ensure production would continue uninterrupted.

"It's an interesting theory," Keith said.

Carrot Beard grinned, "How about a monetary donation to help our cause then?"

"How many wishes do I get for it?" As Keith said it, he realized that this was how people fell for the wish racket. He knew if the little bastard said yes that he would pay up and wish for Gunther to be better.

"None. Ha! We wouldn't grant a dirty badge's wishes even if we weren't on strike which we are so fuck off, ball bag!" Carrot Beard said.

Keith didn't know if he was happy or sad about the wish being denied, because whatever emotion he felt was immediately subsumed by a wave of overwhelming anger. His hand was around the butt of his mage pistol before he even registered that he'd made a decision to draw it.

Five leprechauns scattered but Carrot Beard stood his ground spitting, "You don't have the guts!"

Keith's finger tensed around the trigger but some part of his mind that had remained free from homicidal rage stilled his hand.

"Don't count on that," Keith said. "I'm an East Coast chef. I've killed more living creatures on a busy Friday night than most agents grease in a lifetime. But I don't want to kill you. I just want you to know that I'm serious about going through this portal."

"And I'm telling you no! I know what you really want."

"And what's that?"

"To buy the dust from Big Wings. Her and her mob are the reason we're here protesting instead of working. Why can't you badges shut her down?"

"By Big Wings I assume you mean Buttercup?" Keith said. "What do you know about her customers?"

"Don't tell him anything," Three Buckles shouted from behind the toilet.

"I'm no squealer," Carrot Beard yelled, as much at Three Buckles as at Keith. "You'll get nothing out of me."

"But I think we can both agree that I caught you, so you do owe me three wishes," Keith said. "So for the first, I wish you would tell me everything you know about pixie dust being used for terrorist attacks on NIAD agents."

Keith watched Carrot Beard's face writhe and contort, but he had the little man dead to rights. "I only know that nobody's claimed responsibility. Nobody knows who's doing it. What's your second wish? For me to know the answer? The Magic doesn't work like that. Even if you wished it into me, chances are I'd be whisked away and changed into one of the villains doing this and then I wouldn't be interested in telling you, and owe you nothing. The Magic does what it wants and takes its own payment. It obeys your words the way it wants to."

Keith considered this. He'd often wondered why leprechauns were so consistently obstructive in their wish-granting. He hadn't considered that magic might be capable of creating perverse manifestations of its own accord.

"All right then, I wish you'd step aside and allow me go though the portal."

"Fine, you may." Carrot Beard did as Keith asked and beckoned him forward.

Keith holstered his pistol and took a step inside.

"Wait, what about the third wish?" Carrot Beard rushed up and caught the leg of Keith's pants.

"I'll keep it for when I need it," Keith replied, shaking the little creep off.

"Careful, badge-boy, one slip of the tongue and your Mother's on the surface of the moon."

"I'll take that under advisement."

Then he stepped inside the portal.

The experience of travel through portals was unnerving because of its lack of drama. There was no sense of vertigo or travel at all, just a slight tension in the air and a strange bending of the light, and his surroundings changed from the dingy bathroom stall to the interior of a blue plastic port-o-let. Opening the door, Keith squinted at the intense light flowing in from the vast green meadow outside.

The wind smelled sweetly of flowers and hay. A brilliant sun shone in a blue sky. Keith had been to this plane three times now and it always seemed to be the same time of day—around three o'clock when the shadows lengthen slightly.

Maybe it was the only time the portal opened there. Then again, maybe time held still in this realm. Who knew?

He scanned the verdant grass for his target.

Finally, about fifty feet away he saw a large yellow moth fluttering toward him. As it drew near it fluttered in a circle around him, then hovered in the air around his belt. A swirling ribbon of yellow light shimmered through the air as Buttercup expanded her body. When she was finished she stood about belt-height. She wore nothing, and her small breasts jiggled as she put her hands on her hips. He was crotch to face with Buttercup, the undisputed master of this realm.

"Well met, badge," she said. As she spoke Keith could see that her tongue, like her lips and hair, was a vibrant yellow.

"Well met, Miss Buttercup." Keith produced the badge of which she spoke, just as a formality. Obviously she'd already pegged him as a NIAD agent.

"Spooky to see a badge wearing a goblin pendant," Buttercup said. She flapped her wings to bring herself closer to his throat, twisting her head this way and that as if looking at hidden dimensions in the jewelry, which for all he knew, she could see. Finally she squeezed her eyes closed and crinkled up her nose to take a long sniff. "You smell like kerosene kisses and forbidden love! How romantic...." She rolled back in a little flip, as though bowled over by the wonderfulness of it. Tiny yellow hearts manifested in the air between them.

"There's nothing forbidden about my love," Keith said. It wasn't true. Not by a long shot. But he wasn't going to let some half-pint fairy yank his chain again. He'd already committed a major infraction drawing a mage pistol on civilians engaged in a legal protest. Even if they were leprechauns, they still had rights.

"Love between a goblin and a human? Only as much as the adoration of a cat for a mouse." Buttercup's face went serious. "You want to watch out if she brings home a pot big enough to hold you, badge-boy."

Keith considered correcting any of Buttercup's erroneous assumptions, but decided that, on the whole, it wouldn't be worth it. Instead he pulled out his notebook.

"I came to ask you a few questions," he said.

"It took you long enough."

"Oh? Why would you say that?"

"I've sent hundreds of letters," Buttercup said.

"Letters?" Keith couldn't help glancing around for any sign of even a building, let alone a post office box on the broad, green expanse of the fields. The lone structure was the blue port-o-let that he'd stepped out of minutes before. As he gazed at it, wondering where the letter slot could be, the port-o-let vanished as the layover ended. The sight of the gate fading caused a cold stab of anxiety to move through his gut.

It will reappear in three minutes, he told himself. *And then disappear again three minutes after that. It's the way the gates work.*

Still, he checked his watch.

"You said you've sent letters?" he prompted.

"Every day. Hundreds and hundreds of messages. I've written about it on every single leaf and flower petal I could find, but no one answered." Buttercup raised a sorrowful hand to her forehead then added, "Until you! Forget what I said about your forbidden love. I'm sure she's very nice. And you! You must be a great knight! Pray, illustrated stranger, find my little pixies, I beg you. They are so tiny. And cats are everywhere in the earthly realm."

The "illustrated" took him aback until he realized Buttercup was staring at the tattoos on his forearms. Keith resigned himself to missing several cycles of the gate. He sighed and said, "Okay, describe what happened."

"I was just fluttering over there by the riverbank when I saw three men come through the port-o-let. They wore white paper clothes and smelled like bleach." Buttercup wrinkled her nose. "One of the men began to sprinkle wondrous delights on the ground."

"Do you know what they were?"

Buttercup nodded vigorously. She leaned forward, venal desire showed in her yellow eyes. "Pop Rocks."

Of course, Keith thought. He wondered how Buttercup would respond to the string of Zotz he had in his pocket, but decided not to play that card yet.

"And these attracted the pixies?"

"I knew it was a trap right away," Buttercup said. "No one just throws magical marvels such as those on the ground! I yelled for my little girls to stop, but they were already there, swarming. Then out came the butterfly nets. I tried to stop them but they had a hateful orange cat, and then in an instant they snatched my girls away through the stinky toilet door."

Keith finished writing this down, as well as the names of each of the pixies, Butterbur, Artemesia, Lorraine—the list went on and on.

"I don't suppose you have any pictures of them?"

Buttercup cocked her head then swept her hand over her heart and pulled away a bit of gray dust. This she cast into the air where it became a glittering image of a small woman with wings like a dragonfly and shimmering azure hair and lips.

"That's Lorraine," Buttercup said.

Keith pulled out his phone and took a photo. Out of the corner of his eye he saw the port-o-let begin to coalesce into existence. Knowing he was about to leave he said, "So the leprechauns say that you deliberately sent your girls into the earthly realm to eliminate competition for sales of your pixie dust."

Buttercup looked aghast. She jumped back and flitted up into the air. "That's a dirty lie! What do they know? Little finks."

Keith pressed the issue. "But you do sell pixie dust, right?"

"To my friends," Buttercup conceded. "Or to people with candy."

"When was the last time you sold dust?"

"You're not a knight after all, are you fish-foot? You're another nasty badge trying to put your laws on my body." Buttercup zipped into the air. "What I do with my dust in my kingdom is my own business."

"Wait!" Keith whipped the Zotz out of his pocket and waved the string of candies in the air. "I didn't say I believed them. I was just telling you what they said."

Buttercup circled, just out of reach, eyes never leaving the Zotz. She dived in and snatched at them, but Keith pulled them away.

"Give it!"

"Tell me who you last sold dust to."

"Another badge called Half-dead. He used it to disguise a *boy* who smelled like Half-dead's *semen*." Buttercup's humor seemed to have returned.

"I remember the case. The guy was in protective custody," Keith said nodding. Half-dead was a veteran NIAD agent and also Gunther's godfather, so chances of him being the kidnapping culprit were slim. "But no one else since then?"

"No one."

"But there's been a lot of illegal dust around DC recently," he said. "Where do you think it could be coming from?"

"How do I know?" Buttercup came back to ground, crossing her arms in a sulk. Then her expression changed to one of total distress. "Those bleach men. What if they're taking it from my little girls?" She threw back her head and let out a wail that filled the air like a siren, and grated like the screech of an owl. It reverberated through the air, shaking the petals from the yellow flowers nearby.

"We don't know anything for certain," Keith said, shouting through the terrible noise. Buttercup did not relent. In desperation he pressed the strip of Zotz into her hand. It took her a moment to notice them, but when she did she tore open one of them and thrust it into her mouth, sucking it violently as saffron-colored tears streaked her cheeks. Keith glanced at his watch. He had one minute. He said, "I'm going to file a report. And I'll make sure that another agent contacts you with an update. Don't worry. We'll do everything we can to find your girls and bring them back safely."

3

As he walked back through the fish market to the Metro, Keith took stock of what he'd learned. A group of humans—or at least humanoids with human candy—had kidnapped more than twenty pixies. That meant that there was more than enough contraband power of illusion floating around the earthly realm to perpetrate the intrusions on NIAD. But who had those so-called bleach men been? Few humans knew how to use the port-o-lets to travel, and fewer still would be so familiar as to know that one of them had a layover in Buttercup's realm.

As he stood, swaying with the motion of the subway car, Keith pondered the circumstances of Gunther's attack as rationally as he could.

What if it had been an inside job? A mole in NIAD was hard for him to imagine. The pledges of loyalty, secrecy and disclosure an agent took when being instated were magically binding. But pixie dust was powerful stuff—strong enough to allow an infiltrator to cast a glamor on himself and appear to be any agent.

The key would be to review the security camera footage, he decided. He should look at every single agent entering the building that morning and establish that they were really there, as well as scanning for duplicates. He entered NIAD headquarters with the plan firmly in mind.

The moment he stepped past the security door, two agents escorted him straight back to the Lincoln Memorial where he once again descended into the vaulted chamber beneath the scrotum of Honest Abe to meet Morticia and the funereal fashion of the mage gang.

They did not seem happy. And neither did Keith's direct superior, Nancy Noble. She stood at just inside the doorway, arms crossed and eyes narrowed.

Usually Keith liked Nancy. Though she was in her early forties, she shared his taste for metal music. He found her boxy pantsuits and perennial frosted eighties mullet soothing. But Nancy's adherence to rules could sometimes cause a rift in their relationship.

"Agent Curry has arrived, Mage Melchior," Nancy intoned.

The mage who Keith had dubbed "the King" slowly turned to face him, looking for all the world like an animatronic figure in the world's creepiest theme park.

"What can I do for you?" Keith asked, trying for a pretense of nonchalance.

"We have received a complaint from a member of the extra-human community regarding your conduct." As Melchior spoke, a coil of smoke slithered down from the ceiling and wormed its way into Keith's nose.

Keith sneezed and tried to rub away the tingling sensation it left behind.

"Now please tell us how you've been spending your morning." Melchior smiled as he spoke. Keith took a breath to collect himself and to figure out how to put the most positive spin on his actions. While he was thinking, he heard a voice begin to relate his actions. With mounting horror, he realized that the voice was coming out of his own mouth. The mages had put a spell on him. Rather than being able to choose his own words, the spell drew an account that sounded like court testimony, as if his sub-conscious had been duped into giving evidence.

He could do nothing to stop speaking long enough to collect his thoughts and nothing to stop himself from cracking his knuckles, one by one, as he grew more and more furious.

"And then I returned to the office with the intention of reviewing the security footage to scan for the presence of doppelgangers," Keith heard himself finish.

Melchior gave him a long, appraising look and then, with the expression of a man who has been offered chicken gizzards when he expected foie gras he said, "Agent Curry, your job is to act as a food inspector. You are neither cleared nor qualified to investigate security breeches. If you persist in making incursions beyond your station I will ask for your dismissal. Is that clear?"

Still under the influence of the smoke he said, "Yes, I understand. And just for the record, you don't need to put the whammy on me to get me to tell the truth, you ridiculous old mummy. I'm an agent, not an offender."

The mage's eyes flashed wide. Keith thought he could see tiny lightning bolts flashing across them. Necro-future girl snickered, then took a hasty drag of her cigarette to cover it.

"We're within our rights to use enhanced interrogation," Morticia said. "So long as your superior officer is present."

"And I'm within my rights to file a complaint about it anyway," Keith said. "Which is what I'm going to do."

The King narrowed his eyes and said, "Agent Noble, please escort Agent Curry back to his desk."

Nancy nodded, caught Keith by the elbow and guided him out of the room. Once they'd reached the chilly winter air of the mall, he expected her to turn to him and crack a joke—possibly about which archeological dig the King might have been unearthed during. Instead she stalked silently alongside him. Keith spent the walk sneezing over and over, causing his already traumatized abs to ache like hell by the time they reached the NIAD building and climbed up to their floor.

Nancy remained wordless as they returned to their department, not even giving him a single gesundheit. She motioned him to follow her to her private office.

"Shut the door behind you," she said.

"So..." he said. "Am I in big trouble?"

Nancy turned to face him. At that point he noticed her right eye twitching slightly.

"If you embarrass me like that again I will rip off your dick and shove it right into your disrespectful, permission-avoiding rectum," she said. "Do you hear me?"

"Yes, ma'am."

"I don't like apologizing to those creepy old fossils," she said.

"Right. I get that. I'm sorry."

"And I hate being summoned to their underground lair. Now I'm going to smell like I threw a séance at an undertaker's all goddamn day." Nancy threw herself into her rolling chair and unbuttoned her suit coat.

Nancy had never been this angry with him before. He felt hurt and slightly scared, which was weird for him. Normally being admonished by his employers evoked sensations of rage and personal affront.

Maybe worrying over Gunther's condition was affecting him more than he knew.

"Do you want me to pay for your dry cleaning?" Keith didn't know if it was appropriate to offer but needed something to say.

"No," she said, sighing. "But you are going to have to hand over your mage pistol."

"What?" *Here comes the affronted rage*, he thought, with grim satisfaction.

"Your weapons privileges have been revoked pending the investigation into allegations that you brandished it at innocent civilians." Nancy held out her hand to receive the weapon.

Keith left it snuggled into his holster, protesting, "Those were not innocent. They were *leprechauns*."

"What the hell were they doing? Jacking your Lucky Charms?"

"You and I both know those little runts are dangerous."

"One of those little runts also claims that you extorted three wishes from him." Nancy leaned back in her chair. "Did you?"

"Not extortion, exactly. I caught him, fair and square."

"Agents soliciting or accepting magical items from extra-humans is expressly forbidden!" Nancy said, eyes wide. "You *know* that, Keith."

"It happened in the heat of the moment," Keith said. "I just wanted to find the people who attacked Gunther."

"Listen, I know you do, but unfortunately Mage Melchior is right. You don't have any authorization to investigate anything outside of this department. Now give me your pistol."

"You can't take my weapon. It's not fair. It's the only thing I have against all that magic. When I'm killed out there by some shitty vampire, my blood will be on your hands." Keith felt his face flushing. His hands shook with rage.

"Don't be so dramatic. It's only temporary."

With the reluctance of a drowning man letting go of a life preserver, Keith handed over his weapon. He knew he'd broken the rules, but why did that mean he had to part with the sole piece of equipment that gave him any chance of surviving a magical encounter?

"When do I get it back?" Keith asked, abandoning all pretense at civility.

"It could be as long as a week, presuming you get it back at all." Nancy stood and locked the pistol into the office armory cabinet. "Until then you can help catch up on permitting paperwork."

Keith had thought that NIAD could not insult him any further. "You aren't seriously confining me to the office, are you?"

"Not confining, but without your weapon all you can safely do is permits and recertifications." Nancy spoke as though everything she said was perfectly reasonable, rather that salt in his open wound.

"So what? For trying to find the bastards who attacked my boyfriend, I really have been busted down to being some kind of food safety inspector?"

"Now you know why the rest of us don't wave our pistols around in public bathrooms," Nancy said with a shrug. "Now get back to your desk. Or better yet, go visit your boyfriend at the hospital."

"He isn't allowed visitors yet."

"Apparently the situation has changed. He called while you were gallivanting with the fey folk. When you see him, give him a big hug from me."

After a brief detour at Gunther's locker, Keith made his way back to the elevator and up to the on-site medical unit, which took up an entire floor of NIAD's primary office. While standing in the hallway waiting to be admitted his phone rang.

"Curry speaking," he said.

"I prefer my curry silent and in a bowl, but we can't have everything we want." The voice on the other end had a lilting accent—distinctly reminiscent of an Irish Spring deodorant soap commercial.

"Okay, who is this?"

"Never you mind my name, let's just say we have some unfinished business—a matter of an unfulfilled wish."

Carrot Beard, then.

"So why are you calling me?" Keith leaned against the wall, scanning the hallway from behind his mage-enhanced spectacles, wondering if he would spot the leprechaun hiding out behind a chair-leg, whispering down his sleeve. The only knee-high creatures he saw were a couple of brownie orderlies dressed in white smocks.

"I was hoping you wouldn't mind going ahead and making your wish now to settle the business between us," Carrot Beard said.

"I was hoping you wouldn't run tattling to my boss like a little snitch, but we can't have everything we want." Keith wouldn't normally have antagonized one of the fey folk like this, but the loss of his mage pistol left a raw mark on his pride and temper. "But you did, so why would I do you any favors?"

"That wasn't me! I was against it! The others forced me against my will," Carrot Beard protested. "Listen Agent Officer Curry, sir, you've got to help me out. My nerves are shot. The Magic wakes up and listens every time you say a word. It's driving me fucking bonkers! Just close out your wishes, for the love of God."

"You can hear everything I say?"

"Not me, the Magic," Carrot Beard said. "It's giving me the mother of all headaches."

"Good. I think I'll let it go a little longer then." Keith hung up, despite the continuing protests coming from the phone's tiny speaker.

He got directions to Gunther's room. As he went, Keith passed other, stranger rooms. One had held what looked like an incubator full of sparkling red smoke, while another, completely blacked-out room had a sign that read, CAUTION! VAMPIRIC PATIENT! ADMIT NO NATURAL LIGHT!

Gunther lay on a regular-sized hospital bed, near a window in a regular room designed for the more human-looking of NIAD's extra-human agents.

He looked surprisingly well. He reclined casually, wearing a faded blue and white checked hospital gown. His hair was tousled but still silky and black as a raven's wing. His right hand had been extensively splinted and bandaged, so that only the tips of his fingers were visible. And those looked swollen.

Keith went to him immediately. Gunther's expression lit when he saw Keith approaching.

"Hey there, how was your day?" Gunther spoke with such casual ease that Keith simply told him, ending with Nancy's revoking his gun privileges.

"So, I guess Haakon's right," Keith finished. "I'm a fuck-up and you could definitely do better."

"That's just mean," Gunther reached out to pat his hand. "And it's not even true."

"I'm pretty sure it is." Keith stroked Gunther's long fingers. Then, remembering he'd brought a gift, he reached into his pocket and produced Gunther's half-finished pack of Lucky Strike filterless. "But I did remember to bring your smokes."

Gunther's eyes lit up. He snatched the pack with his good hand, shook a bent white tube out, folded it in half and popped it in his mouth. Gunther chewed and then swallowed the entire thing, paper and all. His eyes closed in bliss as he leaned back against the pillows.

"Thank you so much," he said. "All those little brownie orderlies only eat Drum shag."

"There's no accounting for taste," Keith remarked. As surreptitiously as he could, he took stock of as much of Gunther's body as he could see. He didn't appear to be hooked up to anything but a pulse monitor, which Keith found infinitely relieving. "So you ready to talk about what happened to you yet?"

"Well, one minute I was in the gym and the next I was tripping and then I woke up in here," Gunther said, shrugging. "The witchdoctor said I recovered from the hallucinations more quickly than the fully human agents on account of my goblin blood. But that didn't help my hand at all. I broke almost every bone in it. It's going to have to be magically reconfigured once the swelling goes down."

Keith winced, "I am so sorry. That's awful. You must feel like shit."

"I don't know about *shit*. More like really weird," Gunther shifted on the propped-up pillows.

"When they took you away, I didn't know what to think," Keith admitted. "I thought the security guys had killed you."

"I heard you unleashed your fury on them," Gunther teased.

"Don't laugh about it," Keith said, still feeling raw over the incident.

"I'm not. I'm touched. I'm pretty sure you could have taken at least one of them out before the rest of them started tasing you."

"So everybody's talking about how I lost it?"

"No, just Haakon. He told me when I came to." Gunther smoothed the pale yellow blanket that lay over his lap.

"He was waiting here?" Keith tried to keep the outrage from his voice but seriously: Did the guy have no shame? Trying to bird-dog Gunther in a hospital bed?

"No, they paged him because he's my team leader. They paged you first but you were still out pounding the pavement." Gunther gave him a warm smile, as if proud that Keith would be so dogged in his pursuit of justice.

"It was mostly standing around in a lush green, sweet-smelling field," Keith said.

"Yeah," Gunther said, closing his eyes. "It smelled pretty green where I was too."

"Where? In your hallucination?"

"That's right. I can't really remember too much about it but it smelled really green—like grass or something. And there was this big pile of gold coins. It was so weird." Gunther opened his eyes. "I was really scared but there wasn't anything to be afraid of. Like how in a nightmare sometimes blue is terrifying."

Keith gripped his good hand harder. "I haven't ever been scared of *blue*, but I get what you mean. Do you remember what you were saying when you were first attacked?"

"Not at all."

"You were saying that you had to get out."

Gunther shrugged. "I don't remember anything about that."

Keith thought a moment. "But you did see a pile of gold coins?"

"Right." Gunther peered into the middle distance as if trying to access the hallucination again.

"Like a pot of gold, maybe?"

"If it was a pot of gold, I definitely don't want to go to find the end of the rainbow again," Gunther said. He flashed a smile, then his expression dimmed. "You don't think leprechauns had anything to do with this, do you?"

"When I met them this morning they said they were committing an action. Maybe attacking you was part of that action."

Gunther lay quiet for a moment, staring silently out the window, which caused a thrill of alarm to go through Keith. His face had the same sad expression that had crossed it moments before he'd flung himself at the exercise room window.

Then he said, "I don't like that word."

"What word?" Keith spoke as gently as he knew how.

Gunther looked right at him, "Attack. What happened to me didn't feel like an attack. It didn't feel like I was being targeted to be hurt. It felt like…like I stopped being me."

Keith did his best to hide the intense relief he felt at Gunther's lucidity.

"Did you tell that to Haakon?"

"Sure. Him, the medic, the witchdoctor, that mage who looks like Elvira—"

"I thought she looked more like Morticia Addams."

"Oh, yeah, right, I see that. Anyway I told everybody who came to question me."

Keith sighed, and lifted Gunther's good hand to his lips. He pressed a kiss against Gunther's skin.

"Do you know how long they're going to keep you here?" he asked.

Gunther cocked his head as if he didn't understand Keith's question then said, "They're not keeping me. It's voluntary. I can check myself out whenever I like."

"Then why are you still here?"

Gunther's hunched slightly and whispered, "My parents came."

"I know they came. I called them."

"They're going to be at the house when we get home." Gunther's expression went furtive.

"Is there something wrong with that?"

"I just hoped I could avoid talking to them about what happened." Gunther looked miserable then sat up straight and rang the bell to summon the nurse. "I guess I just have to face them like a man."

"We could always run away to a motel. Dye our hair. Buy fake beards."

Gunther gave him a tired smile and slid his hand across Keith's now-stubbly jaw. "It wouldn't work. My mom would just hunt us down by scent. Her nickname used to be Bloodhound back when she was a mercenary in the old country. Best to just go home."

4

EVEN BEFORE KEITH reached his front door, he could tell Agnes was making dinner. And not just any dinner. She was making a good old-fashioned goblin dinner to help her little Gunther regain his strength. Keith's eyes began to water preemptively as he imagined the capsaicin-laden steam that would be filling his house.

It wasn't that Gunther's mother was a bad cook—indeed, in goblin circles she was considered a model homemaker—it's just that she wasn't human and therefore did not cook to human tastes. She didn't stew meat, so much as weaponize it by use of fistfuls of hot peppers.

On the day that Gunther had moved in with Keith, she had taken Keith aside and pressed a small spiral notebook into his hand. Written on the pages were her precious, famous and well-guarded recipes for goblin favorites such as Cracked Hot-Pepper Marrow Bones, Sheep Skull Surprise (the surprise turned out to be extra eyeballs sewn into the sheep's mouth), and Goblin-style Pig Trotters, which were traditionally served raw in a bowl of vinegar, and garnished with whole bulbs of garlic cut crosswise and seared on the edge of a heated scimitar. On the first page of the notebook she'd made a special note that Gunther, like all goblins, was sensitive to salt and could only abide the smallest amount on special occasions. Then she'd drawn a little, anatomically-correct heart.

When she'd handed over the book, Agnes had made him pinky swear to never reveal the secret blends of peppers, and Keith had done so without even crossing the fingers on his other hand. He'd had been touched by the gift and, after reading it through, dutifully hid it in a locked filing cabinet, where it remained unconsulted to this day.

As he turned the key in the lock of the front door he glanced over to Gunther, whose worn-out expression lifted as he obtrusively sniffed the air.

"Mom's making knuckle bones," he said, with a grin. Then, anticipating Keith's reaction added, in a whisper, "Maybe we should order you a pizza?"

Keith shook his head. "I'm sure she's made me something too."

As they crossed the threshold into the living room, Keith sneezed. Gunther's father looked up from his seat on the new sectional couch that Gunther had purchased specifically with his parents in mind.

Like Gunther, Gerald's body had been reconfigured to appear more human. Gunther had once told Keith that the magician who had chosen his parents' human appearances had been a big fan of romantic comedies and that was the reason that they closely resembled Gary Cooper and Barbara Stanwyk. Though Gerald was an older version of the great screen actor now, but not less formal, wearing shirtsleeves and a tie while watching television.

Gerald appeared to be using the television's screen within a screen function to watch two separate curling tournaments simultaneously. He stood when they entered and embraced his son with an affection that Keith found embarrassingly dorky, yet couldn't help but be jealous of Gunther for inspiring. Keith's own father had given up dispensing hugs the second Keith had acquired secondary sex traits, as was the way in his family. So when Gerald next turned to embrace him, Keith found himself paralyzed in confusion. Gerald didn't seem to notice. He turned his attention back to Gunther.

"Your mother went straight to the butcher shop from the hospital," he said. "There's no stopping her when she's in a cooking frenzy."

"I guess I'm the lucky one today," Gunther replied. Gunther's father's expression faltered as Gunther passed by him to the kitchen. There, Gunther's mother had every one of Keith's six burners cranked up to high. The blue flames heated stockpots full of bubbling liquid. Keith did a quick volume calculation and decided that it would be a tight squeeze, but yes, he could have fit into the biggest pot. Bones protruded from the top of one, while another held a tangled knot of simmering chicken feet so big it could have been mistaken for a tumbleweed.

Agnes smiled at them as she shoved a bobbing organ that Keith thought might be a lamb's heart back under the simmering broth with a long wooden spoon. The end of the utensil she used was stained vivid orange from peppers and grease. The kitchen table had been set with the plain white plates that Keith preferred. In the center of the table sat a heaping dish of peeled raw onions.

"Dinner's almost done, so you boys should go wash up," she said.

"Thank you, Mom." Gunther kissed her on the cheek.

"You're welcome, sweetheart," she said. "And don't think I've forgotten you, Keith. I bought those veggie burgers. It has... carrots. I hope you don't mind."

"I have no beef with carrots," Keith said.

"Oh thank goodness," she replied.

For reasons that Keith had never discovered, snow goblins like

Gunther's family despised carrots above all other vegetables. Rabbit food, they called it, with a look of extreme disgust.

Keith took the upstairs bathroom, while Gunther used the one on the ground floor. He considered losing his shoulder holster and mage pistol, then, with a dismal, sinking feeling remembered that he was no longer in possession of his mage pistol. He divested himself of the impotent holster immediately.

Back in the kitchen Agnes used tongs to heap hunks of meat and bone down onto three plates. The fourth contained eight veggie burgers and a party-sized bowl of potato chips. Keith noted that she'd drawn the curtains, and failed to put out any utensils.

This dinner would be fully goblin style. There was no getting around it. But Gunther needed it. Keith would just have to man up and endure the spectacle.

Though Gunther and his parents had been transmogrified to appear to be human, they were still magical creatures who retained certain qualities and abilities. They could and did consider substances like kerosene beverages, for example. And they could crush and eat bones with their deceptively human-looking teeth.

True goblin dinners were hands-on affairs full of chomping, gnashing and splintering of bone. Gunther tucked into his bowl of ribs with gusto, chomping the slender bones as one might eat a French fry, alternating with bites of raw onion, which he ate as though it were an apple. Agnes elected to start with a whole heart, which she bit and shook as though it were still alive. Her gold earrings glinted with the motion.

Gerald seemed unusually reserved as he slowly munched a chicken foot.

"You okay, Gerald?" Keith asked.

"Well, no Keith I guess I'm not," he replied. "Not after what happened today."

"I'm completely fine." Gunther rolled his eyes like an exasperated teenager.

"Your father's not talking about the pixie dust attack," Agnes said.

"He isn't?" Gunther glanced askance at Keith, who could only reply with a shrug. "What's up, Dad?"

"I guess I'm just hurt, Gunther," the older Heartman said.

Keith took a bite of his veggie burger in order to completely preclude his entry into the conversation. Gunther's parents, despite their frightening eating habits, were nice people.

"Why are you hurt?" Gunther's immediate guilt showed on his face.

"You fibbed," Agnes did not look up from her bowl.

Gunther froze, then hung his head in shame, which caused Keith to nearly choke. What could Gunther have possibly been lying about? He couldn't imagine. The veggie burger went thick as concrete in his mouth. Finally, he managed to swallow and ask, "What did Gunther fib about?"

"Why don't you tell him, son?" Gerald said.

"I said that I worked in the mage office as a researcher," Gunther said.

Keith felt his brow furrow in puzzlement. But before he could ask for clarification, Agnes said, "When really he's in the strike force!"

Again Keith paused not sure what, if anything to say. Then, inspired, he said, "How do you know Gunther's on the strike force?"

"Well," Gerald said, "his team leader was wearing a jacket that had those very words stenciled on the back in big white letters. That was my first indication. Then he introduced himself as the leader of Strike Force Team A and said that Gunther was a valuable member of the team. So after that I had a notion that it might be the case." The scorn in Gerald's voice could have been used to peel paint from the wall if the hot pepper steam hadn't already been hard at work there.

"I suppose you knew, Keith," Agnes said.

"Well, yeah," Keith replied.

"Do you know how dangerous that is? Gunther could be deployed to battle anything! Monsters, even!" She spoke with conviction that subsumed the fundamental irony of goblins being worried about attacking monsters. "We absolutely forbade him to interview for strike force. Gunther has gone directly against our wishes."

"He is a big boy now," Keith ventured into the conversation though he worried where it might lead. Family arguments in his own childhood home often led to fistfights and rivers of tears. He didn't think he could take Agnes, or shoulder the guilt of making her cry, for that matter.

"Son, we want you to resign," Gerald said. "Strike force is too dangerous."

"Dad!"

"Absolutely not." The words were out of Keith's mouth before he could weigh the consequences—not that consequences would have mattered. Once he decided to say his piece nothing could stop him. "Gunther is exactly the agent strike force needs. He's strong, he's smart and he's ethical. And he's not afraid to bring a gun to a swordfight."

All three Heartmans stared at him in shock. Then Agnes said, "You've been in a swordfight? Oh, Gunther! How could you be so reckless?"

"Hell, yeah Gunther's been in a swordfight," Keith cut in before

Gunther could reply. "More than one! And he's also rescued baby centaurs from an illegal breeding farm and gone on a shitload of other operations that are too classified for any of us to know about. I'm proud of him. You should be too."

"We are proud of him, but we don't want to see him in the hospital ever again," Gerald said.

"That had nothing to do with strike force," Keith said. "That was a random attack that could have hit any agent. The one thing we do know, though, is that Gunther recovered three times as fast as a born human would have. Besides, the other guys on strike force would never let anything happen to Gunther. They all love him. It actually creeps me out how protective they are."

"Of course they love him. How could they not?" Indignation colored Agnes's cheeks at the implication that anyone could fail to love her son. "And yes, they were very nice to us when they came to visit Gunther in the hospital."

Silence, punctuated by the muffled snapping of bones beneath goblin teeth, descended over the table. For reasons mystifying to Keith, Gerald, Agnes and Gunther seemed to have come to an accord. Did that mean Gunther could stay on Haakon's team? For the sake of Gunther's pride and dignity, he hoped so, though privately he would have been relieved if Gunther transferred to a less-violent unit.

"So I don't mean to tell you your business Keith, but I couldn't help but notice that we didn't see you there," Gerald said.

"Keith had to work," Gunther said. "His job is important."

"I'm sure his supervisor would have given him the day off if he'd asked," Gerald said.

It was the truth, and it stung. Sure, he could have been there holding Gunther's hand. He probably should have been. But he'd never been that guy.

"I thought my time could be better spent investigating the attack than hanging around the hospital hallway," Keith said. His reply sounded terse and defensive, even to him.

"And it was!" Gunther said. "Keith found out the probable source of the pixie dust used in the attack."

After a short silence, Gerald sighed and picked up a chicken foot.

"It's nice to see you boys are so quick to defend each other, I suppose." He bit off a long toe and chewed it.

"Oh, I know! Isn't it?" Agnes said, flashing a sudden smile. "Now you two finish your dinner."

Following the meal, Agnes started washing up, despite Keith's protests that he should do that since she'd cooked. Finally she relented when Gerald called her into the conversation to help him relate all the gossip Gunther had been missing since he moved away from the West Coast trans-goblin community. Keith scrubbed the greasy pots while listening to tales of abject normalcy. So-and-so went to college, someone else had a nice vacation in Hawai'i. Only once did the tone of the conversation falter—when Gerald revealed that one of Gunther's distant cousins had been cited for violating the Secrecy Act and revealing that he was a goblin to a human reporter.

The leak had been sealed and sufficient disinformation broadcast to discredit the cousin as well as the journalist, but he was now unable to return to the earthly realm, even though he'd been born here.

Creatures with fey blood lived a precarious existence here, whether they be sprites, dark elves or goblins—facing deportation or exile for ever revealing their true nature. Keith didn't know if it was right or not. But it was the way it was.

Still, hearing of the sadness of Gunther's aunt and uncle, he wondered if it always had to be.

The conversation lightened after that and Gunther brought out the brand-new Scrabble game that he'd bought in anticipation of his parent's first overnight visit. Being professional translators, Gerald and Agnes wiped the floor with Gunther and him, even when they gave them a handicap and allowed them extra tiles. But it was a pleasant way to pass the evening—certainly different from Keith's own childhood home where the television was a necessary guest at every meal.

Just after nine, yawning and stinging with defeat, he and Gunther adjourned to their bedroom. As the door shut, he pulled Gunther close.

"Do you think your parents are really mad at me for not being at the hospital?" he whispered.

Gunther shrugged, then shook his head. "When they're angry they don't say anything at all. I think.... They think they know how we should be acting but we're not them, you know? You're not my mother. You don't have to be standing around next to me ready to feed me your own leg to show me you love me. You can just text."

"What the hell are you talking about?"

"You know, the story where the mother secretly cuts off parts of her body to feed to her starving husband and children?"

"I've never heard of that—ever. I'm completely sure I would remember if I had ever heard that story," Keith said. "It must be a goblin thing. Is it set on a craggy, snowy mountaintop under a blood red sky?"

"It is, but.... Are you sure you don't know that story? There's a children's picture book and everything," Gunther said.

Keith just shook his head, partially to answer Gunther's question and partially at the idea that he would have ever come across such a book. Though now that he thought of it, it did sort of resemble the plot of *The Giving Tree*.

"Anyway, that's not the point," Gunther continued. "What I'm saying is that they don't understand you, but they're trying. And at the same time they're trying to accept the fact that I'm grown up now and can make my own decisions. That's probably harder for them."

He stripped down to his boxer-briefs and climbed onto the bed, careful to shield his injured hand from harm. Keith followed suit, though he removed all his clothes, as was his habit.

Nowhere did Gunther's physical superiority become more apparent than when they were alone and naked. Accessories like clothes and jewelry and epic attitude gave Keith moderate visual impact. Once they were removed, he had only his tattoos and his imperfect body to represent him. Whereas Gunther—Gunther achieved male perfection to Keith's eye. He could have been carved from marble and put on a pedestal in some Italian museum.

For the first year that Keith and Gunther dated, Gunther still lived with his parents. For that reason, Keith had a lot of experience not only having quiet sex, but also having sex while knowing that his boyfriend's parents lay sleeping only a floor away.

It had been a year since then and Keith had to remind himself to be quiet—very quiet—when he slid into bed beside Gunther. The first thing he noticed was the red mark where the bolt from the stun gun had slammed into Gunther's chest.

"Does it hurt?"

"A little. It's not too bad though. We all get mage-stunned during strike force training. It doesn't hurt as much as being tasered, but it makes you super-groggy."

"Too groggy for this?" Keith ran his hand down Gunther's perfect abs to find the warm flesh beneath Gunther's boxer-briefs. Keith couldn't actually believe that Gunther still wore anything to sleep with him, but he supposed that's the kind of habit a guy developed after living with his parents into his thirties.

And besides, if he was honest, Keith had to admit that he enjoyed the sense of transgression every time he slid his hand beneath the flat elastic band. It recalled the thrill of his first high-school gropes.

"I can fight through the fatigue." Gunther began to roll toward him, then winced, rubbing the red mark on his chest where the mage bolt had hit him. "Maybe not on my side though."

"Don't worry. I got this one." Keith leaned in for a kiss and found Gunther shying away. "You really want me to stop?"

"No, I'm just…" Gunther turned away. "I can't believe my mom served raw onions."

"You're worried about your breath?" Keith almost laughed but stopped himself. Gunther could be sensitive about his extra-human qualities. "You brushed your teeth for practically an hour. You're fine."

"If you say so." Gunther allowed himself to be coaxed into a kiss, which, when deepened, tasted mostly of cinnamon toothpaste.

Keith luxuriated in the moment, careful not to put his weight on Gunther's chest or jostle his bandaged right hand. He decided the best course of action would be to head south. Not only would that avoid the injury zones—it would keep Gunther from trying too hard to get Keith off. Because the fact was that Keith owed him one.

He hadn't come to the medical unit when Gunther needed him. Why? 'Cause he would have broken down. No matter what kind of man-of-action rationalization he gave himself or others, the fact was seeing Gunther hurt tore at him worse than he'd imagined it could. And he hadn't wanted to break down in front of those people. So he'd been absent instead.

He definitely owned Gunther a righteous pole-smoking.

Gunther's reaction when Keith closed his lips around the head of his cock was both charming and predictable. He nestled closer into the pillows, smiling down at Keith as though he'd never seen anything better in his life. He tucked his bandaged hand over his stomach and reached down to stroke Keith's shoulder.

Keith decided then to make a performance of it. Not just to give the best head he could but look good doing it. He tried to incorporate a sense of drama and flair to his long licks and tongue swirls. He tried to keep all the eye-contact he could while working Gunther to a feverish tremble, quivering right on the edge of orgasm, then withholding it at the last moment, causing Gunther to writhe against the pillows and clench his fingers in the screwed up sheets.

Keith reckoned this must be the best job, blow or otherwise, that he'd ever done getting Gunther off. And the pride he took in that went straight to his dick, making it stand up to accept the honor, as if and saying, "I'd like to thank Gunther's smoking hot cock and its two ball companions for giving me the inspiration to be fucking amazing."

He dropped one hand down to his own tool to give it a little pat on the head, to acknowledge its participation in this award-winning event. Then he dived back down for his closing move, bobbing, nuzzling, snuggling and sucking with the confidence of a man who knows his efforts are appreciated.

He managed to time it so they came almost at the same time, with Gunther lagging a couple of seconds to watch Keith work himself before surrendering to Keith's final deep kiss.

He lay on Gunther's thigh, panting to catch his breath while Gunther stroked the sticky hair back from his face. Finally, he urged Keith back up into place beside him. They kissed again, which made Keith's already reddened lips tingle.

Just as he started to slip from the edge of consciousness, Keith heard Gunther say, "Even if I could do better. I wouldn't want to. Cause you're the best to me."

5

THE NEXT MORNING brought news of another agent attacked—another member of the strike force. Keith found out about it from Nancy, who shook her head sadly as she related the information. "They now seem to be targeting the Strike Force A directly. A lot of people are worried that it's a specific retaliation."

The idea of a person or persons going after the strike force specifically twisted Keith's gut and sent him rummaging around his desk for the antacids before he even sat down.

He told himself Gunther would be fine. His parents were staying on a few days to help until his bandages came off so he wasn't alone and would be taken care of if he had a relapse or there was a new attack.

He forced himself to focus on his work.

Keith shared his office with two other employees, Inspector Daisy and Inspector Sandborne. Together with Nancy they constituted NIAD's Division of Magical and Extra-human Drugs and Food or "MED/Food" for short. Normally, Daisy and Sandborne carried out site inspections and recertifications while Keith investigated—*investigated*, despite what that tiara-wearing mage puke King Douchebag Melchior thought—cases of criminal wrongdoing.

Stripped of his weapon, Keith had very little to do. He finished his paperwork just before lunch. Then both his coworkers donned their MED/Food jackets and headed out.

Keith was left alone with the backlog.

A better punishment could not possibly have been devised for his insubordination. He spent three hours shifting paper, checking stamps and dispensing stamps on up-to-date companies before getting to the "request delay in filing paperwork" pile. Here he found a wide variety of semi-literate and partially illegible forms wherein the owners of various magical businesses alternately pleaded for more time in filing or attempted to explain their circumstances.

The forms ranged from weird, "primary stakeholders disappeared while dealing with trolls—request more time to acquire ransom" to the lame, "flood in records room makes it impossible to submit appropriate documentation." He gave the poor woman dealing with the troll kidnapping a ninety-day extension and flagged the flood for investigation.

It just sounded too much like a "dog ate my homework" to

him—especially in this digital age. Moreover it was Taranis, the company that manufactured Primal Thunder Power Shake. That wouldn't have, in itself, been a cause for punishment. But Keith happened to note that Mage Melchior served on the board of directors for that particular company. He figured as long as the mage was set on thinking of Keith as a mere functionary in the bureaucracy of the NIAD lunchroom, he should act the part. And in his experience, Hell hath no fury like a health inspector scorned.

He grabbed a MED/Food windbreaker prepared to be the most pedantic, unfeeling obstructionist dick imaginable.

He paused only to stick his head into Nancy's office to tell her where he would be.

"You're doing a site inspection?" She lifted a quizzical brow.

"Primal Thunder has an exclusive on the exercise room vending machine. I'd hate for all those strike force guys to go thirsty because Taranis allowed their permit to lapse," Keith replied.

"I thought you didn't want to investigate without your gun."

"I'm not investigating. I'm just helping out Daisy and Sandborne." He brandished his new weapon for her to see. "Have Clipboard—Will Travel."

"I find this suspicious, but I'm going to let you do it anyway, since this is the second time the company has missed their deadline for filing and it's all the way out in North Dakota." Nancy took a moment to write him the portal permit to the NIAD office in Bismark, then said, "No expenses. I want you back here by five."

"Yes, ma'am."

The portal to Bismark deposited Keith in the closet-like toilet of a run-down filling station. There, a single, grizzled attendant sat behind a counter, reading the paper. He glanced up in mild surprise as Keith emerged from the out-of-order toilet. Keith thought he was human, but couldn't be sure.

"Didn't know I would be expecting a traveler today," the attendant remarked. "Especially not from MED/Food."

"That's why it's called a surprise inspection." Keith flashed his badge. "But not for you," he added when the old man began, very slowly, to become alarmed. "I'm on my way to the Taranis corporate office. My boss told me I'd have a car to use here?"

"Let's see." The attendant grunted slightly as he bent to perform some unseen preparation that Keith sincerely hoped did not include retrieving a shotgun or hiding some half-eaten human body. He didn't want to be suspicious of the guy, but since he'd entered law enforcement, he'd become cautious as a hypochondriac.

To keep from staring at the man like a creep, he took stock of the refreshments on-hand. The tidy rows of cigarette packs, candy bars and breath mints looked strange and antiquated next to the Primal Thunder Energy Drink machine's splashy blue facade.

The attendant straightened up and handed Keith what turned out to be a battered old key on a Bismark State Capitol building souvenir key ring.

"It's the silver Escort around back," he said. He rang some numbers into the register then printed out a thin paper receipt. "No need to fill it up before you bring it back. Just sign here to take it out."

Outside, the weather in North Dakota was not as cold as Keith had expected. Crisp, but the air was pleasantly sweet and distinctly free of the smog and sorcerous residue that clogged the air filters of his home base. He found the car and slumped down into the seat, taking time to adjust the mirrors before donning his spectral lenses. Through these he could see two small, hidden readouts. These were located near the speedometer and alerted him to the presence of portals nearby.

The spectacles also allowed him to see the leprechaun sitting on the seat next to him.

Carrot Beard stared straight ahead with his arms folded in front of him, though because of his height the only thing to glare at was the bottom of the glove compartment.

Only NIAD's extensive agent training kept Keith from jumping. Instead, after a steadying breath he said, "Trespassing on NIAD property can result in exile from the human realm for no less than one hundred days up to one hundred years."

"You think I care, badge? I have to protect myself from your loose lips," Carrot Beard said. "No jury would convict me."

"I think you'll find that even if you were entitled to a jury, which you are not, that would not be the case. Now scram."

"Wait now, Agent Curry, let's not be hasty," Carrot Beard backpedaled in the way that Keith had come to expect, alternating between bluster and obsequiousness. "You don't want to go into that beverage facility alone, I guarantee."

"Why is that?"

"I used to work there, you know, before the pixies did me out of my job, curse their—"

"Watch it now."

Carrot Beard scowled, "Bless their little scabby hearts, I meant to say."

"So why would I need you with me to do a routine inspection?"

"Come on now, Agent Curry, you and I know you're not an inspector. You're the filth, if you'll pardon my vernacular."

"I don't think I will," Keith leaned back. "But okay, go on. What do you think I would be investigating there?"

"Any of their so-called natural flavorings, for one thing," Carrot Beard replied.

"Are you saying that they're made with contraband food items?"

"I'm saying that many of them are what you'd call magically delicious." The leprechaun pulled a smug smile, which almost caused the tip of his chin and nose to touch.

Keith took a moment to consider Carrot Beard's offer. He did have a floor plan of the factory—all food producers were required by law to submit one—but his specialty did not lie in factory-scale productions.

But it would never work. If leprechauns had been employed at Primal Thunder, then Carrot Beard would be spotted immediately.

Besides, he really wasn't investigating anything.

And yet, if Carrot Beard's accusations were true, there could be unauthorized adulterants in the company's line of energy drinks. The fact that Gunther liked them so much was reason alone to make sure that the ingredients were authorized.

As he thought this, Keith felt a wave of intuition sweep over him. Now that he was thinking along these lines, Gunther had been drinking a Primal Thunder beverage seconds before he'd been attacked or possessed or whatever had happened to him. The mages had asked if Gunther had inhaled any second-hand smoke before his attack. What if the magical agent that had allowed interlopers to take control of Gunther's body had been contained in the drink instead?

Of course Keith knew his immediate urge to condemn Taranis Inc. was based partially on his dislike of Mage Melchior, but still, once the idea entered his head he couldn't let it go.

He could think of one man who might know.

He got his phone and dialed a number he never thought he'd call on purpose.

The dark elf used a single word to answer and that single word was his name. "Haakon."

"It's Keith Curry."

"Yeah?" Haakon clearly didn't find Keith hard-core enough to handle entire sentences.

"When Santiago went down this morning, what was he doing?" Keith asked.

"Nothing," Haakon said.

"Was he drinking a Primal Thunder drink, by any chance?"

"What?"

"The energy drink," Keith said. "Did he drink one before his attack?"

"Well," Haakon paused and Keith worried that that was the end of the sentence, but Haakon continued, "now that you mention it, he was drinking one just before he was compromised."

"Do you remember what flavor?" He glanced askance at Carrot Beard, who nodded at him in an I-told-you-so fashion.

Another long silence, then, "Orange. I remember it spilled on the sidewalk."

"That's what I needed to know. Thank you."

"What does this have to do with Santiago?" Haakon's tone grew demanding, but also tinged with worry. He truly did care about his team, Keith supposed.

"I'm not sure yet. Just don't let anybody drink any of that shit until I get back." Keith rang off and turned to Carrot Beard. "How good are you at casting a glamor on yourself? Not turning invisible. A real glamor."

"It's interesting that you should ask, because I do have one fine disguise I use quite often." Carrot Beard's chest swelled with pride.

"Show me."

The leprechaun took a deep breath then pinched his fingers over his nose as though he was about to jump into a dunk tank. Then he made a motion as if to blow out, but instead of opening his mouth, he kept it clamped shut.

He began to grow. His neck stretched upward and his legs stretched down. Another deep breath brought his head up to the level of Keith's shoulder and a third lengthened his legs to the floor. Then as Keith watched, the leprechaun's beard retracted into his face, only to emerge from the top of his head in a shock of bushy red hair.

Carrot Beard's face had changed as well, growing younger, his cheeks covered with a smattering of freckles. When he spoke it was with the voice of what he appeared to be—a ten or eleven year old boy. Keith glanced over his spectacles to make sure Carrot Beard appeared the same to the human eye. He did.

"It's good, isn't it?" the boy, whom Keith now mentally referred to as Carrot Top, asked.

"That's not going to work," Keith said.

"Don't you worry. All I need is a clipboard and I'll make a fine assistant. I won't swear at all. I promise."

Keith rubbed his eyes in annoyance and said, "Little kids don't have jobs as food inspection assistants."

"Just tell them it's Take Your Son To Work day," Carrot Top blinked. His green eyes twinkled. The freckles spattered across his milky cheeks seemed even more adorable than before. He leaned close to Keith. "I'd be ever so happy if you'd show me how you make money to buy me toys, Daddy."

Keith didn't know what was worse—the sudden horror and revulsion at some apparent kid calling him Daddy or his guilt at feeling revolted by it. Still, Carrot Top had come up with a pretty workable strategy. It would be foolish not to take advantage of it.

"Okay, we'll go with you being my son, but don't call me Daddy," Keith said.

"Whatever you say, Pops." Carrot Top immediately started playing with the electric window, rolling it up and down. Keith briefly wondered at the location of the child-safety control panel then decided it didn't matter. If the leprechaun-now-posing-as-a-child fell out the window, it would be one less thing he had to worry about.

6

Driving through Bismark's wide streets, under the big clear sky would normally have been a pleasure. Keith only spared a glance for the historical town center and well-kept lawns before heading to the outskirts of town.

There, nestled between two rolling hillocks covered in winter-yellowed buffalograss, stood the head office of Taranis, and the adjacent Primal Thunder Bottling Company. It looked much the same as any other facility of its kind. A gray and cream corporate façade that somewhat resembled an airline hanger on one side with loading docks along the other. Shining blue trucks backed up to the docks to receive pallet-loads of fruity drink.

No fence encircled the facility, but two security guards flanked the front entrance, which Keith supposed was not that unusual in corporate buildings these days—even in North Dakota. Keith's spectral lenses revealed that though one was human, the other appeared to have some ogre blood. Again, Keith found nothing suspicious about discovering extra-humans working in a facility with a NIAD contract.

The entry foyer held a big, round desk staffed by a bland receptionist. When Keith flashed his NIAD badge, the young man directed him to Mr. Taylor's office on the third floor.

While Keith negotiated the large, echoing room and over-sized elevator buttons, Carrot Top tagged along behind him, staring up at the ceiling and occasionally picking his nose.

"Stop that," Keith said.

"It's part of my character," Carrot Top replied. "It's what boys do."

Keith watched Carrot Top twist his hand around to get what appeared to be a deeply satisfying dig on. Then, as if possessed by some innate reflex, he dope-slapped the leprechaun in the back of the head.

Carrot Top whipped around, furious, but before he could speak, Keith said, "It's what fathers do."

Carrot Top just scowled. The mirrored interior of the elevator reflected back the image of them together, plausibly father and son, he supposed. The sight unsettled him more than he would have thought. Probably because it reminded him so much of his childhood interactions with his own father.

Gunther had most likely not been the recipient of even well-deserved dope slaps. Gerald and Agnes had probably been the type of parents who used their words and expected Gunther to, as well. The many photographs of Gunther and his assorted family members that hung in the home he shared with Gunther spoke of a close-knit, understanding, non-dope-slapping crew.

A thought occurred to him that had never before crossed his mind: did Gunther want to be a father? The notion of Keith himself acquiring a taste for parenting seemed ludicrous, but Gunther had a nice family and traditional tastes. Would he truly be telling some kid to get his finger out of his nose someday? Time would tell, he supposed.

The elevator reached the third floor, happily releasing Keith from any further contemplation of his future as a parent or how apt Carrot Top's imitation might be of any future progeny.

The letters stenciled on the door said, Rick Taylor, CEO. The rest of the office said, "I love hunting." From the framed page from *Bowhunting Magazine* featuring Taylor in camo gear standing over a fallen moose to the head of what Keith suspected to be the very same moose mounted on the wall, Taylor's office transmitted a pervasive interest in trophy-centered aggression. Several gold plaques identified Taylor as a winner, just in case Keith had failed to notice. Taylor had trounced the competition at numerous shooting and archery competitions, and had even achieved excellence in bowfishing, which Keith hadn't even known existed before this moment.

Taylor stood just slightly taller than Keith—somewhere around five ten, but outweighed him by at least twenty pounds. He had a thick shock of hay-colored hair and a mustache that looked strong enough to jump off his face and go on safari by itself.

He'd been named CEO of the year by *Food and Beverage Weekly* for his management of the Primal Thunder Power Shake brand for six consecutive years, if the series of plaques on the wall were to be believed.

Taylor shook Keith's hand and smiled at Carrot Top when introduced. Then he turned and gestured to the two chairs. "Please have a seat."

Keith did so, noting that Taylor failed to sit himself. Rather, he perched on the corner of his desk in a relaxed, informal, congressman-meets-his-constituents way that Keith, as a resident of Washington DC, immediately mistrusted. But Taylor wasn't looking at Keith, instead he kept his eye on Carrot Top.

Keith glanced back at Carrot Top, whose illusory boy-like form turned out to be the perfect disguise for standing and gawking at the assorted deer and antelope heads keeping the prize moose company.

"What do you think?" Taylor asked.

"You must be descended from Herne the Huntsman!" Carrot Top said.

"No," Taylor laughed, then continued. "We're not related, but we do take down an elk together now and again."

Keith hoped that this was not literally true, but feared it might be. Taylor winked at him, which didn't clarify.

"Now what can I do for you?"

"I'm just here to finish your inspection." Keith held up his clipboard as though its presence proved his veracity. "You haven't had a walk-through in at least three years."

"Has it been that long?" Taylor asked, smiling.

Keith resisted the urge to put a check mark in an imaginary box on the form marked: *This asshole is jerking me around*. Instead he said, "That's right. And this year I gather your paperwork hasn't been submitted either."

"That would be because of the flood," Taylor said. "Five hundred gallons of orange beverage all over the floor. Mage Melchior himself came to help us with the cleanup. He's on the board of directors, you know."

"That's right, isn't it?" Keith said. He wondered if he should play it hard and question Taylor's obtrusive namedrop or just play dumb. Dumb seemed like a better option—easier to sustain. "Will Mage Melchior be joining us for the inspection then?"

"Oh, no, he's much too busy to hang around here." Taylor gave a laugh. "So what can I do for you?"

"I just need to establish that this floor plan is still accurate. It will only take twenty minutes or so. I've even brought my own hardhat." Keith rapped his knuckle on the thing to emphasize its sturdiness.

"I brought one too!" Carrot Top chimed in. He plopped the over-sized headgear onto his ginger noggin. "Do we get free samples, Daddy?"

Keith fought not to roll his eyes. "You'll have to ask Mr. Taylor that."

"Can we, mister?" Carrot Top exuded the breathless excitement of a high school thespian chewing the scenery.

Taylor didn't seem to notice the over-acting. He just said, "Sure, big guy, let's get started. I just have to make one phone call to let them know we're coming down. It might seem like fun, but this is a real factory and parts of it are dangerous. Do you promise to behave?"

Carrot Top nodded solemnly, though from his vantage point, Keith could see that he had his fingers crossed.

Taylor picked up the phone, dialed and, in a casual and cheerful voice, explained to some unknown person that he would be bringing visitors down to the floor. He didn't seem to be speaking in code, but then Keith didn't think he needed to. Any visitors would be suspicious to an organization that had gone to such great lengths to avoid inspection.

Down in the bottling facility, the equipment seemed fairly standard and in line with the floor plan on file. Along with the wildly popular Primal Thunder brand, the facility manufactured nutritional supplements for extra-humans living in the earthly realm. Most of the production line consisted of vats of colored sugar water into which various additives were inserted via nozzle. Some of the additives, Keith recognized as arcane nutrients found only on other planes, as well as the ubiquitous platinum, a nutrient needed by most creatures of fey descent. Gunther himself took it in tablet form. The other supplements appeared to be a murky sludge of whey protein and fiber.

Keith made sure to glance at Carrot Top every now and then. The leprechaun was doing a good job of using his boyish guise to peer and stare at everything. Halfway through the tour he pointed at a series of copper tubes that ran along the ceiling. Each tube ended in a nozzle that hung above a mixing cauldron.

"What are those?" Carrot Top asked.

"Those lines contain our secret flavoring agents," Taylor said. "They're what makes Primal Thunder taste so good."

"And what exactly are they?" Keith asked.

"The ingredients and exact formula are proprietary, though we did submit a formula to the MED/Food office before production began," Taylor said.

"I don't seem to have that list." Keith leafed through the papers.

"If you need a new list I can have one sent to your office," Taylor said.

"That would be best, I think." As Keith spoke he watched a thin, red stream of fluid spray down into a vat. Even with his spectral lenses on, he could see nothing remarkable about the substance. He wished he could get a sample of pure flavoring, but the nozzles were at least twenty feet in the air.

He continued the inspection, going down the checklist, reviewing the equipment and checking for the appropriate number of hand-washing stations and recessed floor drains.

He was on his knees checking one of these when he spotted something odd slinking along the floor.

At first he thought it was a trick of the light, then he realized that it was a fluffy yellow cat.

Even regular human food facilities didn't allow cats.

This one crouched across the room beneath the noisy bottling line, ears flat, clearly disturbed.

Just as Keith was about to mention it to Taylor, a worker in a white clean suit swooped down and scooped the creature up.

He disappeared through a side door.

Keith checked the floor plan. The side door that the worker had gone through went to an area labeled "employee break room." Could one of the workers have snuck his or her cat into work for some reason? And the worker had been wearing a clean suit. That, in itself was not unusual, but Buttercup had mentioned that the culprits who had kidnapped her fellow pixies had also worn a paper outfit and threatened her with an orange feline.

And although neither the cat nor the clean suit was suspicious on its own, together, and combined with lost paperwork, they aroused Keith's interest. As he neared the end of the route he diverged to glance through the single, high window in the break room door.

Inside, the room appeared to be exactly what it said it was. A few tables and chairs. A microwave. A faded OSHA poster on the wall. The only unusual thing was that there didn't seem to be anyone in it, which Keith found strange, given that he'd just seen one man and one cat step into the room that appeared to have no other exit.

"How are we doing, Inspector?" Taylor's too-loud voice broke through Keith's concentration. "No violations, I hope?"

"Everything seems to be in order here." Keith deliberately avoided lingering at the break room door. He'd have to find a way to get in without Taylor dogging him.

Because there was definitely something going on here and he aimed to find out exactly what. What had started as a fairly childish attempt to harass Mage Melchior's company might turn out to yield a real result. Excitement bubbled up inside as he felt himself gravitating toward discovering what Taylor wanted to keep hidden.

Unfortunately, Taylor seemed dedicated to personally escorting him off the property. He walked them straight to the front door and offered Keith a firm handshake.

"It was a pleasure to meet you," he said, his tone laden with finality.

Keith stopped to leaf through the papers on his clipboard to buy himself some time. If only he could get Taylor to leave him alone for five minutes he was sure he could get back to the production floor.

"It's too bad you don't have a list of your flavoring additive ingredients,"

Keith said, glancing up from the meaningless remarks he was writing on the inspection form. "I could certify you right now."

Taylor seemed to weigh this before giving a shrug. "I'm sorry, but the I.T. guy says it will be at least another week before he can get the backup restored."

"I'll keep an eye out for it then." Keith smiled and started ambling slowly toward the two security guards flanking the front entrance. Both eyeballed them with bland interest. Behind him he heard Taylor answer a phone call. Then the man's voice faded as the elevator doors closed behind him. Keith knew he had to think fast. His shoes squeaked loudly against the tiled floor of the big foyer.

"We need to get back to that production line," he said under his breath.

"I know that," Carrot Top growled.

"If you have any ideas, now's the time." Keith glanced around again, trying to decide if he could just make a break for it.

Suddenly, Carrot Top loudly announced, "Daddy, I have to pee."

Keith stopped in his tracks. He didn't know the leprechaun's game, but at least this gave him an excuse to stop walking toward the exit.

"I thought you said you didn't have to," Keith replied. Was this some kind of code? Was he talking about using a portal?

"I have to go!" Carrot Top squirmed and pressed his hands to his crotch in a very authentic display.

Still adrift, Keith said, "Can't you hold it?"

"There's a bathroom right there!" Carrot Top pointed back down the long hall that they had traversed. Indeed, there was a bathroom.

"Oh for God's sake," Keith seized Carrot Top's hand and headed back down the hallway. Once they were out of sight of the security guards, Carrot Top yanked his sweaty palm free of Keith's grip.

"Quit holding hands, you queer."

Keith snorted, "You wish your tiny fey ass was good enough for me to want."

"Are you actually a queer then?" Carrot Top asked. "I'd have never thought it. You look so manly with your dainty little clipboard and lack of weapon and all."

After considering a couple of ways he could turn his clipboard into a weapon and use it against the leprechaun, Keith decided to ignore the comment. He did not want to risk any onlookers intervening, as he would appear to be beating a child. Plus, he just didn't have the time.

He said, "Shut up and follow me and look bored."

He headed back to the production floor and reentered the big, cavernous room without fuss. He didn't walk too fast or too slow. He kept a determined look of vague annoyance on his face, which ensured that he would be noted then disregarded by most employees. After all, they had just seen him there performing normal duties. Carrot Top tagged along behind him. His expression of petulant child ennui verged on perfection.

They made it into the break room without incident. The space was still void of people as well as felines. Two vending machines stood against one wall. One sold Primal Thunder drinks and the other contained a variety of energy bars as well as a single apple.

"Ah, the old break room." Carrot Top turned in a slow circle. "It seems smaller than it used to be. Or maybe I'm bigger."

"No, it's definitely smaller," Keith said, checking the floor plan. "They've moved this back wall up twenty feet or more. That would mean there's a twenty by twenty foot space behind it?" Keith ran his hand over the wall, feeling for seams, or some kind of hidden door. The wall was smooth as could be. He kept going around the room then he noticed something odd. The Primal Thunder machine wasn't plugged in.

Not only were vending machines approximately the height and size of a door, they were engineered for the entire front to open so that the machine could be filled and serviced. He suspected he had found his door. Now all he needed to do was get through it.

Carrot Top drifted over, watching as Keith felt up and down the side of the machine for any kind of latch.

"You trying to break in? You should use the code."

"What code?"

"The access code." Carrot Top reached up and pressed 54321 then hit the button. The door popped open. "Those cheap bastards couldn't make us pay for drinks that we made."

"Quiet!" Keith whispered. With great care he pulled the door open and found exactly what he expected—not cans of beverages, but a narrow corridor leading toward the back of the room.

"That's new," Carrot Top remarked.

The air flowing out of the corridor was thickly scented with leaves and earth as though it were a greenhouse filled with exquisite blooming flowers. Automatically, Keith reached for his mage pistol, then cursed himself for doing it.

As quietly as he knew how, Keith called for backup. Or attempted to anyway. As the dispatcher attempted to patch him through to Bismark, Carrot Top seized his arm.

"Pixie dust! I smell it in the air."

Then from down the corridor he heard the yowl of a cat, followed by a tiny, high-pitched shriek.

Keith instantly started forward. Carrot Top caught him by the arm, but Keith shook him off easily. The leprechaun's hands grew smaller and smaller in his hand as the creature reverted to his normal small, bearded form. Oddly, as he did this, his strength seemed to increase exponentially weighing Keith down like a sinker.

"Let go of me," Keith hissed.

"Hello? Who's there?"

The voice Keith heard did not belong to Taylor, but that gave Keith scant comfort. He now had two choices—go forward and reveal himself or retreat and wait for backup.

Keith spent exactly half a second considering his options. He felt the chances of making it out of the facility without being caught were slim. So he reached into his inside coat pocket and got out his badge.

He strode decisively into the room. There, on rows of steel tables, with rubber hoses feeding into them stood ten of the largest aquariums he had ever seen. Each was easily as big as a coffin. But they didn't hold water. Lush, low-growing plants carpeted the bottoms while chicken wire covered the tops. Nestled among the foliage, Keith made out a small plastic fixture that had once hidden the bubbler. It had been fashioned into a treasure chest spilling out plastic pieces of eight.

Exactly like Gunther had described.

The man in the white clean suit that he'd spotted before stood next to one of the aquariums. Now in addition to the clean suit he wore a respirator and held the yellow cat. Inside, Keith could see dozens of colorful moths fluttering right at the bottom of the terrarium. Though as Keith drew nearer their movements seemed strange. They almost flickered. One moment he'd see a moth and the next a cowering little female figure with candy-colored hair.

He'd found the missing pixies.

"Blood of Menses! They've enslaved the wee women!" Carrot Beard exclaimed. "This is worse than hiring them as scabs. This here is an insult to all fey creatures!"

"Quiet." Keith started towards one of the aquariums trying to assess the health of the Pixies trapped inside. They looked terrified.

"Look out!" Carrot Beard yelled. "The bastard's brandishing a cat!"

Keith turned his attention back to the room's lone attendant.

"I'm Agent Keith Curry from NIAD." He held up the badge as if it were itself a magical amulet instead of a piece of silver-plated brittanium. "Put the cat down and put your hands up."

Though the man's eyes were shielded by thick goggles, Keith could see the panic in them. Suddenly he hurled the cat at Keith. While Keith sidestepped the incoming missile of claws and fur, the man lunged to the side and hit a large, red button on the wall.

An alarm began to sound. As the cat came to a skidding landing on the tile near them, Carrot Beard leapt from the floor to the top of the nearest terrarium. He curled his now-tiny fist around the twisted wire, yanked it free and wriggled into the terrarium through the opening to the plants below.

"I'll just be bunking up with you all in here so long as there's a ferocious moggy cat on the loose," Carrot Beard told one of the moths.

Keith kept his eyes on the man in the clean suit. He didn't seem to be armed, but it was hard to be sure given the amount of pixie dust in the air. He positioned himself between the man and the hallway.

"I repeat! Put your hands in the air!" he bellowed over the siren. The man complied then, as suddenly as it had begun, the alarm stopped. The man in the clean suit dropped his arms to his sides and stared at something just beyond Keith's shoulder.

That did not give Keith a good feeling about who, or what, might be standing behind him.

"You know, Agent Curry, for a minute there I actually thought you were really an inspector," Taylor's voice sounded from behind him.

Keith slowly raised his hands and turned to face him and his bwana mustache.

Of course he was holding a pistol, what had Keith expected? A crossbow? Taylor looked disappointed, but not angry.

"I am really an inspector today," Keith said.

"What happened to your so-called son?" Taylor craned his neck, scanning the room.

"I told him to wait in the bathroom." He hoped Carrot Beard had the good sense to keep hidden.

"He had a leprechaun with him," the clean suit guy chimed in. "I didn't see where he went."

Taylor leveled his gun at Keith's head and said, "Show yourself, or he's dead."

"Piss off, dick hole!" Carrot Beard's voice seemed to be coming from everywhere in the room.

Taylor turned to Keith and shrugged. "Can I assume that was your so-called son? Looks like you've failed as a father. Turn around and get down on your knees."

Keith knew that if he turned around it would be the end. Taylor would shoot him. They'd hide the body and wash the blood out with an industrial hose. Maybe Carrot Beard would report the crime, or maybe he'd just be glad to be free of that unspoken wish.

The wish—he still had it!

He wanted to be careful, but he didn't have time.

"I wish—" Keith said, then stopped. What could he say? He felt the pressure growing, almost as if the magic itself was urging him on. Despite his dire situation he felt the strange need to giggle. The whole world took on a surreal and comical tone, as if the air had been replaced with laughing gas.

"You wish?" Taylor repeated. "Is this your last request?"

"I wish you were the worst shot in the world," Keith blurted out.

"I guess you're out of luck," Taylor said. "Now turn around."

"No," Keith stood firm. "If you're going to kill me you'll have to look me in the face."

"No problem. I was just trying to keep the janitorial hours low." Taylor pulled the trigger.

Keith stayed still as a statue as the deafening crack of the pistol firing less than a foot from his face split his right eardrum. A high-pitched whine replaced all other sound. In his left ear only, he could hear the rapid-fire rat-a-tat of the bullet ricocheting all around the room. Strange laughter filled the air as the bullet went on and on for what seemed like a full minute, shattering the aquariums, hitting the ceiling and the floor. Then the clean suit guy grabbed his leg and fell, cursing.

Freed from their cages, the pixies zipped and zinged into the air by the dozens, flying like rainbow-colored confetti, all the while being cheered on by Carrot Beard.

Taylor's mouth hung open in astonishment. He raised his arm to fire again and the fluorescent light fixture on the ceiling creaked, then one end swung down, smacking him directly in the face. He fell straight back to the floor. Keith rushed forward, kicked the gun away, then knelt to check his pulse. He was unconscious but still breathing.

As Keith reached for his handcuffs he saw Carrot Beard trot up alongside Taylor's head.

"What a wish, my boy! The magic loved that one! True spirit of comedy."

EPILOGUE

"So the special flavoring in Primal Thunder was pixie dust after all?" Gunther asked. He sat at their kitchen table patiently waiting for Keith to put the finishing touches on his vegetarian shepherd's pie. After spending so much time with the little people, he'd found himself wanting to take a crack at the wholesome, sturdy fare of the Emerald Isle. He had spent the last five days in Bismark, overseeing the seizure of Taranis and the Primal Thunder Bottling Company, and taking statements from everyone involved. When he came home he found that he'd just missed saying goodbye to Gunther's parents, which saddened him more than he'd thought it would.

"Even worse," Keith said. "It was grade B sorghum syrup given a glamor via the use of pixie dust. The system was ingenious, really. They got a cat, slapped an enchanted collar on it and made it into a good little menace for the pixies. Then they'd have a pixie cast a glamor on the sorghum giving it whatever flavor they wanted. Apparently, this service used to be provided by the leprechauns at extortionate prices."

"Then Taylor figured out a way he could cut costs," Gunther finished. "But wait—doesn't that mean that the leprechauns knew all along the pixies were being held captive there?"

"They knew the pixies had stolen their jobs, not that they were being kept against their will. They thought Buttercup had rented them out as scab workers during the labor dispute."

"Why didn't any of them report Taranis? You'd think they'd have done it out of spite alone."

"Well, because that kind magical food adulteration is supremely illegal, mostly." Keith slid his hands into his oven mitts and transferred the bubbling casserole to the table. Then he returned to the stove to give the six lamb sausages he had in his skillet a good shake. Just because he was a vegetarian didn't mean Gunther had to be. "I think they're going to cut a deal for immunity in exchange for testimony."

"That would be smart." Gunther folded his hands and mumbled the few quick words that comprised the goblin version of saying grace. His right hand was still supported by a cast, but the bulky bandages had gone. "But I still don't understand how the attacks on NIAD agents figure in."

"They weren't attacks at all." Keith slid the sausages onto a plate, retrieved his half-empty beer from the countertop and seated himself at the table. "One of the pixies, Lorraine was her name, was sometimes able to work little spells into the pixie dust she dispensed that allowed her to send messages. The problem was that they were incomprehensible. She was only able to press her immediate feelings into the dust."

"So I really was possessed—sort of. Possessed by a memory."

"Exactly." Keith helped himself to a serving of salad, then to the buttermilk dressing.

Gunther served himself a paperback-sized portion of the shepherd's pie. He topped this with two sausages, then asked, "So why is there a cat in my parents' bedroom?"

Keith couldn't help but smile. It was so like Gunther to wait until halfway through dinner to ask about the cat.

"Well, it took a while to catch it, but we did. After we removed the enchanted collar that allowed them to control it, it turned out to be pretty friendly. The pixies wanted it tried as an accessory but dropped the charges once we explained that it was acting against its will. I couldn't find a no-kill shelter in Bismark so I was going to take it to the rescue shelter in Arlington, but it was already closed." Keith took a more modest portion of the casserole and gave it a taste. The French lentils had melded well with the mushrooms, he decided.

"So you brought it home?" Gunther forked shepherd's pie into his mouth, heedless of the scalding temperature.

"Until tomorrow," Keith replied.

"Then why did you buy it all those toys?" Gunther asked.

"It seemed like a pretty nice cat, deep down. I thought it would be bored in there by itself." Keith kept his eyes down. In truth the cat had charmed him right from the second the enchanted collar came off. It had a pretty face and a sweet, chirpy meow. It had kept him company in his motel room in Bismark. On the second day Keith had named him Cheeto.

Gunther regarded Keith for a long moment then rose and went upstairs. He heard the door to the spare room open. Seconds later the cat came slinking down, followed by Gunther.

"It's no use keeping him up there all alone." Gunther reseated himself. Immediately, Cheeto jumped up onto his lap.

Keith shook his head, "You better watch out. You don't want to get too attached. You have a weakness for scruffy things."

"Yeah," Gunther said, smiling. "I do."

Everyone's Afraid of Clowns

Jordan Castillo Price

Halloween is magical for some folks. Me, I mostly see it as a chance to sneak a big bag of candy into the shopping cart. Ghosts and monsters and things that go bump in the night don't need a special holiday to put me through the wringer. I deal with weird entities all year long. But there's weird, and then there's weird. I had it on good authority there'd be actual children at the party where we'd agreed to put in an appearance.

"We don't have to stay long," Jacob assured me. "An hour, tops."

I hadn't breathed a word about my lack of enthusiasm for this particular social obligation. Hadn't even rolled my eyes. Jacob, though…he knew. Maybe not in a telepathic way, but what difference did it make when he could read my thoughts in the set of my shoulders and the gaps between my sentences? I've got an obscure paper license behind my badge, one that declares *Victor Bayne - Level 5 Medium* is clearly too important to be expected to show up at social events. At least that's what my last few boyfriends made of it. But since I've paired up with another PsyCop, and a clever one at that, I'd need a more plausible excuse to play hooky when I wasn't in the mood for people. Either that or tag along for the ride and do my best to fly under the radar.

Sure, I'd daydreamed about weaseling out of this particular shindig, but I'd never thought it could actually happen. Being half of a couple isn't all easy kisses and inside jokes. It's occasionally doing things you'd rather not, especially when you'd prefer to stay home and half-watch scary movies you've seen umpteen times. Luckily, it was easy to take cues from Jacob. While I don't expect him to act as my crutch, when I need to navigate a social setting, being with him really is a valuable perk. For instance, I'd voted on bringing the extra wine in the back of the cupboard to the party, but according to him, wine wouldn't quite cut it. Halloween was one of those occasions where you were expected to be seasonally appropriate…even if you threw everything together last-minute, which due to our crushing work schedules, we typically did.

Only the truly prepared have time to drive all the way out to a suburban cornfield just to find a stupid gourd. It was a lot easier to hit the old lot on Montrose, the one that had been a car wash in its previous life.

Maybe one of these days we'd plan far enough ahead to escape Chicago for a few hours and take a trip to the country. But not this year, not today.

The only thing worth looking at in this particular pumpkin patch was Jacob. Sure, he can rock a suit, but tonight he was a study of dark-on-dark, black hair, black goatee, black jeans and black leather jacket. Even though I'm pushing forty, I'm still as much of a sucker for a leather jacket as I've ever been. Sadly, even a vision of Jacob in leather looking dashingly intent couldn't elevate the lame-o surroundings. There was a fly-by-night quality to the lot's setup, and its flimsiness contrasted with my mental image of how "things" were supposed to be. Neat, square hay bales outlined a perimeter, and a puny scarecrow stood watch over bushels of apples and winter squash. Tarps covered the old blacktop, where pumpkins were arranged in clusters according to size and price. Streetlights shone down, obliterating any potential view of the stars. Shoppers were sparse. People bundled in winter coats milled around despondently. The single animated person there was a guy trying to pump up his kids' enthusiasm and get them to pick something out. They were too busy texting to notice.

Thankfully, Jacob wasn't invested in creating any memories. His family life has been as close to picture-perfect as a family can be, so he doesn't get all sentimental over things that might have been. Tonight we were on the same page—we usually were—and all he wanted to do was score a random pumpkin and get going. "Vic? What about those painted ones?"

"Sure." That way it would look like we'd put in some extra effort without actually having to carve something.

The painted pumpkins were stacked beside the register on a hay bale, perfect for grab-and-go shopping. But although I marched up with every intention of choosing one at random, I've always had a soft spot for Halloween, so I couldn't help but try to pick out something good.

I couldn't find anything.

All of them were smiling. Cats, ghosts, monsters too. All of them wore the same, identical gap-toothed leer. Seeing them all together like that, the attempt at differentiating one design from another seemed all the more half-hearted. Even the clown-painted pumpkins weren't scary. And everyone's afraid of clowns.

I doubt any of the foster families I'd lived with had enough means to hire a clown to traumatize us on our birthdays. My suspicion of clowns came from the movies, though not in the way it usually happens.

I'd started sneaking into R-rated films when I was way too young to understand them, but tall enough to pass for a burgeoning adult, which I'd been doing since I was thirteen. (Sometimes I think I'm still doing it.) Once in a while, the employee in the ticket booth would call my bluff and demand to see a drivers license. But most of the time, they couldn't be bothered.

The moldering second-run cinema a short bus ride from my high school had never once carded me. I think they just needed the business. They were always running gimmicks and promos, like guess the number of beans in a jar to win a free ticket, or free small popcorn to the first twenty customers, or half price Halloween double feature to anyone who came in costume.

I'm not big on advance planning, but that year, I was prepared—getting into the double feature meant getting out of the boring duty of accompanying the younger kids trick-or-treating. Most days I wore all black anyway, but that day I upped the ante with a black blazer, sleeves pushed up, naturally. After gym period, I gelled my hair into a cheesy widow's peak. Add a set of plastic dime-store fangs, and I was ready for my close-up. Okay, so I wouldn't be winning any vampiric costume contests, but it did save me $2.50 on my ticket.

Thanks to Patrick Swayze, ghost movies had started losing their edge by the early 90's, but gory, predictable slasher flicks were still a dime a dozen. This was good. Not because I couldn't appreciate subtlety, but because armpit hair and random boners weren't the only thing puberty had brought me. Ghosts. Sometimes movies get 'em right nowadays— especially the creepy Japanese flicks with English subtitles. But back before I figured out I possessed anything more than an overactive imagination, movies weren't actually that scary. Cinematic boogeymen were nice and blatant, hockey masks and chainsaws. And the characters who ended up minced and mangled had done something so stupid—opening that door, venturing into the basement, going off to have sex in the woods—that whatever those lamebrains got, they deserved.

I'm not sure why the dilapidated theater bothered opening its doors for a weekday matinee. Even with the half-priced Halloween double deal, attendance was sparse. By the light of the decaying snack bar promotion, the cavernous space with its rows and rows of stained seats felt hollow and forbidding. All the other moviegoers had spaced themselves out, ten or twelve seats away from their nearest neighbor. Was it some natural law, maybe a magnetic field that caused strangers to distribute themselves so carefully? Hard to say. That'd be an awful lot like physics, and I had trouble maintaining a steady C- in loser math.

It wasn't the fear of blocking others' view of the screen that sent me creeping toward the back of the theater. The place was so empty I didn't need to worry about getting in anybody's way. It was more that I'd developed an overall preference for slinking in at the last minute and sitting the back of the room. Not the very last row, though. Those seats were up against the wall at a rigid angle. The second-last row, right in the middle. My seat. Really, it was. I'd carved my initials in the armrest and everything.

Just to be clear, my main reason for sitting all the way in the back was not the anticipation of an anonymous hand-job. It only happened that one time. I could hardly call the handiwork anonymous, either, because I was fairly sure my five-minute friend was the kid with the braces who worked at the sub shop across the street. At least I hoped that was why he smelled like cold cuts.

Sitting all the way in back did make it harder for me to lose myself in the movie, since I could see the edges of the screen, the point where the projected reality met real reality and the glamour fell away. Not only was I there to indulge in some distraction, but I'd positioned myself to be distracted from the distraction itself, so I couldn't get sucked in too deep. Even that young, I'd had some high level avoidance techniques all figured out.

Film rolled. Same plot, same setting, and only nominally different actors. A group of kids in the middle of nowhere, and wouldn't you know it, the car breaks down and it's nearly dark. The very blonde girl is wearing heels, so we all know how she's gonna end up. And the guy who's too much of a smartass for his own good? He'll buy it ironically. They always do.

I was postulating this detail almost a quarter of a century later, of course. Other than tiny flashes of clarity that I tend to question, my actual recall is not nearly that good. Mainly I do remember sitting in my initialed seat, sipping from a can of warm Pepsi I'd smuggled in, and watching a movie that was supposed be scary, but was actually comfortingly predictable.

It was entertaining enough until someone crept into the row behind me. That's when my memories start feeling different, less like something I've conjectured in my 20/20 hindsight and more like the physical, visceral experience of something that came surging right back, juicy with adrenaline and fear.

I remember straightening. I remember flexing my toes in my sneakers, like I could grip the tacky floor with them right through the worn rubber soles if I needed to make tracks fast. I remember the smell of fake butter-scented oil covering traces of scorched popcorn hull. I remember the horsehair-and-innerspring cushion creaking beneath my bony ass as I shifted my weight, trying to look casual. And I remember the thread of apprehension coiling like worms through my innards as I warred with the thought of leaving. Because I'd put actual planning and effort into my costume, dammit, and I wanted my half-priced movie.

I remember all that, the pissed off clench of high alert. And I remember rolling my eyes when the creep in the back row sidled his way across several seats and planted himself just behind my right shoulder.

In my dozen years as a PsyCop, I've seen enough gruesome shit to instill a better sense of self-preservation. But at that age I was such an ignorant twerp, I was all sneer and swagger. I turned around to confront the guy—probably with a brilliant remark like, "Excuse me?"

There was nobody there.

I remember it with utter clarity. I heard the guy. Knew it was a *guy*, even. Knew exactly where he was positioned in relationship to me. Except he wasn't.

Even though the rest of the sparse crowd was too busy watching the movie to be paying any attention to me, I hunched in on myself, feeling stupid. Apparently someone had used the narrow back row to cut across. No big deal. I settled back in my stiff, creaking seat, took a cautious sip of my warm pop, and stared straight ahead. In the movie, flashlights were dying, a storm was rolling in, and the soundtrack was starting to get spooky. Though I'd been jostled out of the moment, it wasn't exactly an intricate plot. I slipped right back into the experience of the film—at least as deeply as I ever allowed myself to—and I watched the smart-aleck guy fight with the snotty kid brother while the high-heeled blonde tried to make peace...and I saw movement out of the corner of my eye. Not up on the screen, but just over my right shoulder.

Okay, asshole. I vividly remember thinking that. *Now I got you.*

I held my head very, very still, and I looked only with my eyes. The guy behind me was leaning forward, sprawling across the seat-back, cradling his chin in his hands. Dozens upon dozens of empty seats, and he was right there in my personal space. If not for that hand-job, I would've whipped around and told him to get lost. Instead, I continued to scope him out in case I might get lucky. Pale. That was all I could see without turning my head. Angling for a better look, I scratched the nape of my neck so I could tilt my head, and finally, then, I caught a decent glimpse.

Not only was the guy behind me in costume, and not only was he at least a venerable forty years old, but he was dressed as a clown.

Even the potential of getting fondled didn't cancel out my revulsion. I stood up to move, and turned at the last moment to shoot the clown a dirty look for creeping me out of my own damn seat.

He was gone.

Clown or no clown, I wasn't about to put up with somebody fucking with me. I threw myself against the seatback, fully prepared to find him huddled down in the back row, dick in hand, snickering to himself. But other than a scattering of trash on the floor, the row was empty.

2

Heebie Jeebies—the gift that keeps on giving. A quarter-century later and I was still chafing gooseflesh off my forearms.

"Do you see something?" Jacob murmured. He gets off on watching me do my thing.

"No. Not really." I scanned the parking lot. It was clean. "Just thinking."

"Tell me."

Although Jacob was crowding me worse than a dead clown in a run-down movie theater, my barriers didn't shoot up. He was allowed in. Take that any way you care to. It was a comfort, actually, to have hooked up with the one guy who thinks *Hooray!* when the dead start bleeding through. "Not much to tell. It was a long time ago."

Jacob picked up a massive, ugly smiling pumpkin and headed for checkout. Twenty bucks—highway robbery—plus tax. The teenaged boy behind the hay bales needed to count my change three times. I'm guessing he would've preferred I put it on my card, but knowing what I know about electronic surveillance, I just can't bring myself to swipe it through a tablet. Everyone knows those things are only good for YouTube videos and solitaire.

Jacob handed me the smiling whatever while he beeped the lock and opened the back door, then took it back so he could settle it in carefully for the ride. I would've just thrown the damn thing into the backseat and let it fend for itself. Then again, I would've ended up scraping pumpkin guts off the upholstery after we took a sharp turn and ended up playing roller derby.

Pumpkin situated, we buckled ourselves in. He pulled into traffic, went a few blocks, and stopped.

Red light.

Not anywhere near us, more like two blocks up the street, but traffic was frozen for the whole stretch of road. Was it a clean intersection? I wasn't sure—I didn't drive this route often enough to have every haunted crash site memorized. I craned my neck to see if I noticed anyone wandering in and out of traffic...literally. But it was cold and dark and miserable out, and the only pedestrians were huddling in their coats, not rambling around hoping to get in the final word with the driver responsible for their current state of deadness.

"So," Jacob ventured, since it seemed we were settling in for a nice long wait. "This thing on your mind—the long time ago...how long?"

I considered how much emotional scar tissue surrounded the clown memory. Not much. I'd only had a glimpse, after all. He hadn't followed me home to lurk in my closet. He hadn't touched me. He hadn't even said anything. Any anxiety I currently felt was due to the anticipation of a house full of shrieking tweens, not the clown ghost.

My decision to go ahead and talk was based mainly on the knowledge that Jacob would really get off on hearing about it. And when he's looking all slick in a leather jacket, I can't resist. I eased my hand onto his thigh, dropped my voice down low, and said, "I was sixteen. It was a darkened movie theater. Typical nineties slasher flick. I was sitting there alone in the second-last row—"

"The one on Sheffield?"

"I dunno. Could be." I gathered my thoughts and put on that ghost story voice he digs so much. "So I was sitting there. Alone. In the second-last row...."

"It was that general area, though, right? Near the El? Or was it the one on Broadway?"

"Maybe." I struggled to keep the annoyance out of my voice. "It was a run-down, turn of the century, single screen theater with floors like flypaper, and horsehair hanging out of the seats. Does that set the stage for you?"

"The Mercury? Biograph? The Music Box?"

"I don't know. I was just a kid."

"But was it in Lakeview or New Town?"

"Lakeview. I guess. Probably." I paused to see if he had any more urgent questions. Apparently he had his bearings. I regrouped, imagined the feel of the darkened theater, gave his thigh a subtle grope, and said, "It was Halloween, and anyone in costume got in for—"

Jacob braked, a little too hard for the flow of the creeping traffic. "Halloween, to the day?"

"Whose story is this—do you mind?" Apparently, he did. In one of those decisive police driving moves that no one ever seems to question, he nosed out of line and swung a U-turn. "What are you doing?"

"If we drove past, maybe it would spur your memory."

"I remember the important parts." Damn it, who the hell cared which specific theater it was? Couldn't he tell I was trying to put on a sexy-voice? "What's the deal? Usually when I talk ghost, you stop and listen."

"I was listening. You were sixteen, it was Halloween, and you saw something." He swung around a poky driver trying to parallel park and high-tailed it toward Lakeview. "Whatever it was...what if it's still there?"

I spared a glance in the direction of the backseat. The ugly pumpkin grinned back at me. "I thought we were late."

"It's not that far out of the way."

No, not as the crow flies. But Halloween was as big a hindrance to traffic as a freak October snowstorm or a Bulls NBA championship win. Despite Jacob's assertive driving, it took us nearly forty-five minutes to traverse three neighborhoods. And once we were in a spot where I could've used some extra time to get my bearings, traffic picked up while I tried to fit together my jigsaw puzzle of a memory. We were zipping down Broadway when I finally spotted it—a tall, narrow building with a green awning where the marquee used to be. I checked the opposite side of the street. An old McDonalds. The kid who gave me a cheap thrill hadn't smelled like salami after all. It was fries. I felt the pieces fit into place with a satisfying snap, and said, "There."

"The coffee shop?"

"It wasn't a coffee shop then."

In fact, it could hardly be called a coffee shop now. It looked more like a catch-all meeting place for every obscure group from Boystown to Wrigleyville. We crept by it four more times in search of parking, and each time I scanned the gaps between the handbills plastering the windows to determine if the overhead lights were even on. On our final lap, I saw someone at the door usher in a few guys with a flashlight, money changing hands, so I kept my mouth shut while Jacob pulled another U-ey to grab a spot opening up just across the street.

"How's that for parking?" Jacob said. I was gracious enough not to mention I could hear him muttering a little bit louder each trip around the block. "And they're open, too. Perfect timing."

With whatever renovations had occurred over the past few decades, the façade didn't feel quite like the old theater to me. And yet there was a sense of deja vu as I approached, where if I really concentrated, I could feel myself swallowing spit around those cheap plastic fangs. Before I could get too self-congratulatory about finding the place, it occurred to me that I was barging into a big old building that was probably haunted, with no anti-psyactive drugs, not even a packet of salt in my pocket, and I grabbed Jacob by the elbow before he could barrel on through the door and charge right into who-knows-what. "Hold your horses, mister. Let me get my bearings."

Jacob stopped and looked at me, dark eyes sparkling with eagerness.

I'm still putty in his hands when he gives me that calculating leer. Unfortunately, before I could bask in his approval, he turned his attention toward the door. Sure, he got off on the idea of me being a medium. But when it was all said and done, he was way more interested in the ghosts.

I considered saying it was a long shot we'd find anything at all based on a single glimpse I got back when I only needed to shave once a week, but why rain on his parade? We hardly ever had the chance to go out together, and wasn't ghost hunting preferable to a Halloween party full of strangers and their kids? That was probably overly optimistic on my part. I do still have a healthy fear of ghosts. Seeing what I've seen and knowing what I know, of course I do. In all likelihood, though, if we found anything at all, it would probably just be a repeater. Those things were tame, more like a smattering of leftover death energy than a ghost. I could disrupt the signal, Jacob would get all hot n' bothered watching me do my thing, then he could take me home and do *his* thing. Win-win all around.

Or it could be seriously haunted.

I ignored Jacob's eager body language and shifted my awareness.

White light. It's not really light, and it's probably not white—but since the shorthand works, that's good enough for me. I visualized it streaming down from the heavens, surging in through my third eye. And I felt it filling me with the mojo that allows me to break the death barrier. This power source isn't tangible and it's definitely not measurable, but that's just because no one's come up with the right equipment to see it just yet. I've tapped it enough times to trust it's there, and to know with certainty that in some clumsy or rudimentary way, I'm able to use it.

If it's awkward for me, it's twice as bad for Jacob. He can't see this stuff like I can—but I've learned the hard way he can suck up my white light without batting an eyelash. He moved to take my hand, and regretfully, I had to step away. "You had your shot back in the car. Look with your eyes, not with your hands. I'm charging my batteries now."

"Sorry." He cocked his head toward a rainbow flag. It felt natural to be grabby in Boystown. "Habit."

I was wearing my black wool peacoat, and those pockets went deep. I stuffed my hands in to keep from discharging my light into Jacob, and also hoping I might find some prop I could call upon in case we were blundering in on something scary. The more I searched—and the more I came up with nothing but spare change and gum wrappers—the more spooked I felt. Jacob was raring to go, holding open the door, and it occurred to me that I'd grown phenomenally blasé if I was willing to face off with a freaking *ghost clown* just to give him a few jollies. Blasé, or stupid.

I headed in.

3

It was dark inside, except for emergency exits and flashlight beams. I dug deeper into my pockets looking for a pen light, but it wasn't my work overcoat, and I didn't even have that. A guy in an old-timey carnival barker costume with a wooly fake mustache told us, "Ten dollars." Jacob paid the guy, who handed him a pair of plastic wristbands, and said, "Down the hall and to the right."

We headed down the darkened hallway, me trying to place it in my memory, Jacob with a flashlight out. Of course he had his flashlight, even in his leather jacket. He's nothing if not prepared. He flicked it over the wristbands and read, "Men 4 Men Haunted House."

"Huh. Guess I can't say you never take me anywhere."

"Tonight's the last night."

"Yeah, they'll need to start putting out the Christmas decorations soon as they lock up behind us."

Jacob passed me a wristband and I took it, careful not to brush fingertips but now regretting that we'd ended up at some big gay Halloween thing and couldn't even touch each other. I fastened the band and scanned for something familiar in what little I could see. "I'm not sure this is even the place."

"Slow and steady. I've got your back."

I was on the verge of surrendering to the obvious smartass reply when Jacob pushed through the swinging double doors and a jolt of memory hit. Me, shouldering through the lobby doors and smelling that intense fake butter popcorn smell, then wishing I had a few more bucks to buy a popcorn, even a small one, and hoping no one searched my backpack for the contraband carry-in Pepsi.

Yeah. This was definitely the place. Luckily the doors hadn't changed, because once we were through them, the darkened lobby looked nothing at all like it had in my high school days. The concession stand was covered with espresso machines and pastry displays. The arcade games were ancient history. And the old smoking lounge off to the side? Now it was a makeshift stage with a big chalkboard on the wall inviting everyone to next Thursday's open mike. The secondhand tables and chairs were deliberately mismatched, and stilted art that screamed "local" crowded the walls. It felt crappy and cluttered, but only five years' worth of clutter and crap. Not twenty-five.

"This way," a chunky guy in a skeleton T-shirt called out, gesturing with his flashlight for us to stop drifting toward the empty cafe and go through the balcony doors. I'd never been up in the balcony—I'd always presumed it was in total disrepair. Not sure what had me more spooked, the thought of digging up a ghost or my fear of falling through a rotten floorboard. But Jacob plowed on ahead, and I tried to tell myself that if the floor could support his bulky gym-rat physique, my skinny butt would make it through unscathed. Despite my attempt at a positive, can-do attitude, the farther in we got, the more my blasé confidence leached away. My heart fluttered as the passage narrowed, turned, and narrowed again, and I felt like a steer being prodded through the processing plant. It was dark and close and warm and musty. I opened up my internal valve and let white light surge in, then pushed out a protective membrane to cover both Jacob and me, straining so hard to do it that I broke a sweat. We approached a final door, lit by a single red bulb. Jacob gathered his courage and reached for the doorknob.

The door flew open and a figure burst through. "Bewaaare!"

I jumped back, grabbed for my sidearm and came up with a handful of nothing. Lucky for the guy in the zombie mask I was off duty—although it was quite possible Jacob might deck him right through the fake rubber skin.

"You are about to behold sights and sounds that would drive a lesser man insane. You will be called upon to reach down deep and connect with your primal masculine nature to navigate the horrors within. Are you ready?"

When it became apparent that Jacob was too busy keeping himself from smacking the guy to answer, I muttered, "Sure."

The guy handed me a restaurant pager. "Only when you receive the mystical signal may you progress to the next ghoulishly diabolical level."

I stared stupidly at the piece of plastic. It flashed red and buzzed.

"Step up to the gaping maws of terror—and proceed."

Jacob shot the guy a nasty look and strode through the door. As I followed, the guy quietly added, "In the event that the overhead lights come on, follow the instructions to the emergency exit."

Lame. My adrenaline ebbed, and I shifted my attention to pulling down more white light. Maybe the douchebag in the mask was just a guy, but with live people wandering around in costume, I reminded myself, the dead ones would be a lot harder to spot. Our flashing plastic disc urged us forward, and we trooped down a short hallway and passed through the door at the end marked SECOND CLASS CITIZENS. I was steeled against the probability of some poor schlub of a volunteer leaping out in front of me, yet poised to scan the room for something scary, when a light flashed so brightly it blinded me. Not metaphysical white light, either. A strobe, aimed right in my face.

"Fuck." I turned aside and knuckled my eyes. Technically I should be able to see spirits whether or not my retinas froze. It's not like I see them with my physical eyeballs. But I've got to navigate all the planes of existence at once, and I needed my physical sight to at least get through the damn room.

"You okay?"

I gave Jacob a disgusted "pff" and blinked for all I was worth. "If you can still see anything, make sure no one gets the bright idea to jump out and grab me."

"It's okay. We're alone."

I blinked harder and forced a few deep breaths, but the relentless strobe kept the spots from clearing. I closed my eyes and just listened, then, and the room's soundtrack swelled around me. What had first sounded like crackly, worn speakers was actually the recorded sound of a fire. And the sirens in the distance weren't real, either. Shielding my peripheral vision with cupped hands, I slowly opened my eyes. Still strobing. But I could see, sort of. The balcony had received a major remodel sometime in the last few decades. The seating was gone, the floors were leveled, and it had been closed off from the auditorium below to create a long, narrow room. Sheer nylon "flames" hung from the ceiling, rippling in the breeze of a few small fans. They probably didn't look like much with the lights on, but in the suffocating red light punctuated by the white-hot flares of the strobe, they were practically alive. Not exactly like flame—but creepier, like the way things from the other side are no longer exactly alive. The soundtrack welled around us, crowd sounds threading through the fire sounds, and behind it all, someone called out, "Women and children first! Women and children first!" Over, and over, and over...and the lights strobed, and the nylon flames danced, and all the while I struggled to determine if that voice was actually on the recording at all, or if we were walking directly through a ghostly repeater.

A dry ice machine gasped out a cloud that looked eerily substantial in the strobe light. It was the perfect place for some kind of fucked-up entity to hide. "I need to get out of here," I said.

Jacob tends to play by the rules—except when he doesn't—and he wanted out as much as I did, whether or not he had permission from the flashing piece of plastic. "The door should be on that wall." He strobed between the fake flames, I followed, and between the two of us, we located the door just as the stupid vibrating puck lit up.

We crowded into an antechamber. When the door closed behind us, the crackling flames and sirens fell silent. The building may have been old, but it was a theater, and the acoustics were deliberately engineered.

"This was a bad idea," Jacob said. "Let's turn around and go back."

I almost slid an arm around him, but in the interest of keeping my white light to myself, I couldn't. Which meant I'd need to articulate something that would've been so much easier to convey without words. "Just a few colored lights. Big deal. It's fine. We're fine."

He took a breath and nodded, and I crossed the empty, darkened space to the far door, which had CASTRATION STATION painted on it in drippy glow-in-the-dark paint. The room beyond was dark—at least until Jacob broke out the flashlight. Good thing. I narrowly avoided caving in to my gut reflex of grabbing his arm and discharging the light I was hoarding. Even with the flashlight beam, the room was plenty creepy. The scent of institutional antiseptic was strong, and my gut said "hospital" before my mind even registered the beep of a heart monitor playing in the background. Given my less-than-savory history with the medical profession, and the room had "panic attack" written all over it.

"That's enough," Jacob said. "Turn around."

"No, I'm good." That wouldn't be the case if the soundtrack played the metallic clatter of a gurney, but for now I just gorged on white light and repeated *not real, not real, not real.* "There's the door, straight across. Let's keep going."

4

A FEW STEPS in, Jacob snarled and batted at something. The flashlight beam bounced around the room, disorienting me. And then I felt it, the whisper touch against my cheek. Annoyance spiked, not fear. If a ghost was pawing me, I'd damn well know it. Something was hanging from the ceiling, that's all. That cottony fake cobweb stuff? Or maybe sewing thread.

I stretched my awareness for anything that might truly raise my hackles, anything lingering on the wrong side of death, and came up with nothing. I stepped around Jacob to lead the way. "Keep going, just ignore it."

And again I was looking in exactly the wrong place when the room flooded with light. An activation strip of some kind was stretched across the middle of the room, and I'd marched right up and stomped on it. "Sonofabitch." I tried to blink away the spots, but all I could see was the afterimage of a bank of lightbulbs. I did my best to fix the room's layout in my mind—the split second I'd glimpsed between all the strobes—and groped my way toward the far wall. I reached out with more than just my hands. My psychic feelers were out, too. But other than the fact that a bunch of really stupid special effects had thrown me for a loop, nothing had the kind of supernatural wrongness I associate with spirits lingering where they shouldn't, tricking death.

The stuff dangling from the ceiling thickened, brushing my hair and my shoulder. I ducked my head and opened my eyes just a crack, but it wasn't enough to really see what was going on, just erratic strobing that revealed a field of dangling stuff. Pendular. Like dozens of hairy potatoes hanging from the ceiling in stretched-out pantyhose legs. If the group running the house was something a little more innocuous, like March of Dimes, I'd figure my own sick imagination was the reason I felt like I was wading through a field of testicles. But Man-On-Man, or whatever these jokers called themselves? It had to be intentional. Maybe most people would only get their hair ruffled, but lucky me, tall as I was, the fake balls kept bopping me in the face. I'd never been teabagged by a haunted house before. Can't say it was anywhere near as fun as it might've sounded.

Jacob gave an exasperated huff and began batting the danglers out of his way. "Could you stop aiming them at the back of my head?" I asked.

"Damn it." He swatted a scrotum. I ducked and hopped forward to make sure it missed me on its return trip...only to trigger another pressure-activated mat. The strobing stopped, the room plunged into darkness, and the screaming began.

White light. I sucked it down like an ice cold fountain drink, and I reassured myself that if there was anything impinging on us from the other side, I'd see it whether or not the lights were on. But even knowing what I know, the canned screaming—combined with the meaty sawing noises and the bleeps of an EKG—had the back of my shirt soaked through with sweat and my heart rate climbing like I was attempting to tackle a Stairmaster. A single small, high-intensity light reappeared, Jacob's flashlight. It lit on the door at the far wall. "There," he said. "Go."

Before he could forget the touching moratorium and short-circuit my white light, I went...right across yet another floor trigger.

The room lit up red, and a pair of animatronic figures burst into motion right beside us. *Fake*, I told myself, *all fake*. Of course it was fake. I could hear the motor whirring beneath the soundtrack of the screams.

But fake or not, the scene made my brain start pumping out panic-juice.

It was a patient and nurse scenario, played out by a couple of second-hand department store mannequins. The nurse had a rusty, blood-covered saw fixed to her hand with clear tape, wound around her wrist at least two dozen times. She was on some kind of mechanized belt that made her whole body tilt forward and back between the legs of another mannequin. The male patient was splayed on his back, hospital gown rucked up around his hips, arms and legs out stiffly...in restraints. The restraints had been made for sex-play, and not very vigorous bedroom hijinks at that. Even so, freakout mode hurtled toward me, threatening to not only take my carefully gathered white light, but my dignity. The last thing I needed was a debilitating panic attack with a football team's worth of testicles swinging around my head.

I made myself look with my third eye. Nothing there, nothing dead. I put one foot in front of the other, and I forced my way to the door. The plastic disc hadn't given me permission to go, but just let it try and stop me. I spilled out into a hallway, a small square passage where we could gather our wits. In front of me, the next door was closing. I heard a group of guys laughing together. They were having *fun*.

Jacob joined me, the door on the nightmare castration hospital closed, and everything went quiet except for my pulse pounding in my eardrums. His flashlight beam traced the emptiness of the hall. I scanned too. My sixth sense saw nothing. "We should go back," Jacob said. "It's not worth it."

I visualized what I remembered of the theater, its layout, the angle of the balconies. Right, center, left, each connected by an angled hallway. "No, this has got to be the last balcony coming up. It'll be faster to go through."

"I guess." Jacob shone his light back toward the door we just exited, then sighed. "Castration? Seriously? If this is the new kink, then I'm getting old."

"Good thing. I didn't find it even remotely hot." Call me a stick-in-the-mud, but I like balls just as nature intended, firmly planted between a pair of hairy thighs. I focused on my white light, on reinforcing the protective membrane around us both, and I caught my breath in that calm pocket of silence.

The puck lit up. Oh joy.

The word PRISON was stenciled on the door to the third (and hopefully final) room. A fake cell shouldn't trigger a panic reaction from me, not like a fake hospital ward. Though you never know. I hadn't ever landed myself behind bars, but as a PsyCop, I had introduced my share of residents to the system.

My inner eye told me we were all clear, so I went on ahead. The first thing I noticed was that the lighting was a lot calmer. It wasn't exactly steady—it rose and fell to illuminate one part of the room, then another—but it didn't flash in my face and blind me. Behind some bars made of wooden dowels, one wall was muraled with hangdog men in orange jumpsuits. Since this *was* Boystown, I expected at least one of the inmates to be getting his jollies in the shower with a hunky, tattooed convict. But no. All the poorly-drawn prisoners just gazed out through the bars looking pitiful and morose.

A two-dimensional cutout of a prison guard whirred toward me, set to roam back and forth along the bars on a simple parallel track. Not the musclebound type of guard you'd find in a tasteless gay prison porno, either. A woman...a woman who looked like she'd dressed as a slutty prison guard for Halloween. She stood in profile with her back arched and her pouty lips slightly parted. Her skirt was so short you could see her butt cheeks peeking out beneath the hem, and the shadows her perky nipples cast against her tight, skimpy uniform top had been painted with excruciating and deliberate attention.

Jacob passed me cautiously so as not to brush together and discharge the juju, scanning the room with his flashlight. Me, I was fixated on those lush nipples, baffled, watching the 2-dimensional guard glide back and forth, back and forth, while the prisoners gazed straight ahead. Once I could tear my eyes away from the figure, I gave the room a scan. No ghosts. Just some cutouts and murals, with a soundtrack of clinking and clanking chains. And on the wall behind us, a bunch of photocopied handbills. That must've been why the lights weren't strobing, instead fading tastefully in and out—to give people time to get a look at the writing. Jacob was right up against that wall, reading intently by the beam of his flashlight. As I approached him, I passed a speaker with more high-end than the others. The whisper, "falsely accused...falsely accused..." came clear, looping through the clank of chains. Maybe if I wasn't so juiced up I would have taken it for a repeater. But my white light was shining bright, and it was obvious there was nothing in that old balcony but a bunch of weird paintings, flimsy bars, a soundtrack, and some amateur animatronics.

What a relief. I'm not the most social guy, but I was more than ready to write off our Boystown date as a bust and get to our obligatory party when Jacob grabbed a handbill off the wall and whirled to face me. "Whoever's in charge of this *event*—he's answering to me. Now."

Okay. Or not.

I backed up a couple paces to give him room to charge through the exit, then surreptitiously pulled down another handbill before I followed. It was a wanted poster—not the Photoshopped old west party-gag type, either, but the sort we'd see posted at the precinct. Nope, no gag. This one was authentic. The guy was wanted for aggravated sexual assault. And the word INNOCENT had been stamped beneath his photo in inch-high red letters.

I'd been so focused on keeping an eye out for the clown ghost, I'd totally missed what was really going on. Second-Class Citizens... Castration Station...Falsely Accused.... These Men 4 Men bozos had nothing to do with leather chaps and rainbow flags—their sole mission was to hate on women. No wonder the haunted house was a total turn-off.

Jacob banged through the door, leaving me to fumble along behind. Old ghosts could wait. He had fresh horrors staring him in the face.

Sometimes I feel like I'm nothing more than a bundle of baggage, and anything can set me off. The sound of a gurney, the sight of a restraint, a whiff of antiseptic. But I don't suppose anyone lives this long without knowing things they'd rather not know, without developing a sore spot. Jacob's put in a lot of years working sex crimes, so he's seen a lot. Maybe too much. And he's just as haunted by his ghosts as I am mine.

By the time I made it off the balcony and down the far stairwell, Jacob had his rage under control. He asked the worker in a perfectly nice, perfectly reasonable tone to speak to the manager. And either he was so charming—or the guys running the event were so oblivious—that maybe they even thought he wanted to pay his respects and congratulate the guy on a job well done. The worker led us to a long, narrow room that buffered the old theater from the concession stand, a disused staff break room crammed with plastic furniture stacked halfway to the ceiling, plain chairs too unhip to populate the new bohemian coffee shop, clunky tables beginning to warp and yellow, all of it peppered with old graffiti and cigarette burns. One corner of the room had been cleared and set up with a single set of table and chairs. The open laptop looked weird on the furniture of my misspent youth. And the guy tapping at the keys didn't quite fit, either. He was Caucasian and mid-thirties, maybe a handful of years younger than me, average height and weight. Not bad-looking. His hair was neat and his clothes matched.

He didn't seem like the type of guy who'd be involved an anti-woman cult. He looked so...normal.

When Jacob interviews someone, his attention doesn't waver. He tractor-beamed this guy in and began asking him questions in a tone that was very, very interested. And when Jacob's interested, who can help but be flattered? Good-looking guy like that, nailing you with those shrewd, dark eyes. Maybe a straight guy wouldn't find himself squirming in place as desperately as I had. But no one's immune to the charm. And once Jacob had the guy right where he wanted him—bragging about their membership numbers, reveling in the haunted house's attendance, taking credit for the theme of the displays—once the guy was firmly planted in the casually laid snare, then Jacob picked up the strings, and pulled.

"And this statistic...." he produced a handbill from his pocket and smoothed it onto the yellowed plastic tabletop. His voice stayed smooth, but its friendly tone took on a cautionary chill. "*Three in five reported rapes are false accusations.* From which credible source did you draw that?"

The guy froze up as he realized the adulation he'd been basking in was nothing more than bait, and he'd fallen for it, hard. "Well. We have a reference sheet." He started shuffling papers that looked mainly like menus and random receipts to me. "A handout. A pamphlet. Somewhere." His hands started to tremble as Jacob's cool, collected gaze bored into him, unflinching. The moment stretched, awkward and increasingly painful. Or satisfying, depending on who you were. I personally enjoyed watching the creep squirm. "Well, I can send you the resources if you give me your address."

"You do that," Jacob said, voice like silk. With deliberate, slow, precision, he pulled out his badge, dropped it open it in front of the rapidly paling woman-hater, and extracted a business card from a pocket in his ID. There's nothing on his badge the guy would recognize, and nothing on his card to indicate which agency he actually works for. But it all looks very important and vaguely threatening, just like Jacob, when something rubs him wrong. When he handed his card over, the guy flinched as if he was worried Jacob might take him out in a stunning papercut ninja-move. "And if I don't hear from you by the end of the business day tomorrow, I'll be in touch."

The guy shuffled it into his stack of scrap paper. "Sorry, I'm all out of cards."

"That's fine." Jacob poured on the sinister charm. "I have a database."

I presumed he'd made up that database thing to spook the guy. But then I realized something like that probably did exist—and even if Jacob didn't have the clearance to scan it himself, he could at least put in a request.

Jacob delivered a long, uncomfortable look, a look that was in itself a threat. He was utterly still, while the haunted house guy fidgeted and squirmed, and a sheen of sweet broke out across his upper lip. Better to let the creep imagine what he'd been caught doing—and to worry about what the consequences would be—than to spell it all out. Jacob allowed the lingering badass look to stretch a moment more, then finally turned away before the guy's head exploded.

I tried to catch his eye for a subtle show of support. We locked gazes. Only briefly, but that was plenty. The control I presumed came so naturally? It was hanging by a thread. If the sweating guy was stupid enough to rally with a parting shot, he might end up with a black eye for his troubles. Then Jacob would be the one suffering consequences.

I shifted into their line of sight to put myself between them, and gestured toward the exit with my chin. "Let's go. We're already late."

Jacob snapped around and strode out the door. To most people, he might have seemed agitated. Ticked off. Miffed. But to my surprise, I was actually pretty fluent in his body language. His posture was too rigid, his footsteps too forceful. He wasn't merely annoyed—he was furious.

I've got a pretty good long-legged stride, so I was right behind him in the hallway when the punch he'd been holding back finally landed. I didn't feel the physical impact, but it jarred me nonetheless. It was only my mundane sympathy at work, though, nothing physical, and nothing psychic either. No one actually felt the blow but Jacob...not unless the shabby wall had developed some kind of consciousness.

I grabbed for Jacob's hand, but he angled away from me and shook it out. "I'm fine."

Uh-huh. "We should put some ice on it."

"It's fine."

I thanked our lucky stars he'd whomped paneling and not cinderblock. Otherwise our night could've ended in the emergency room. "At least run it under cold water." As I suggested it, my shoddy memory offered up a glimpse of a bathroom that should be close by. We'd delved pretty deep into the bowels of the building tracking down management. But if I recalled my exits correctly, there was a side door not far from us, and beside that, restrooms.

Jacob's knuckles must've been smarting pretty good, because he let me herd him down another hallway instead of charging out toward the car. I was rifling through my mental rolodex, trying to figure out who I could call about these Men 4 Men assholes, when we strode under a bank of black lights and I lit up like someone had just trod on my motion sensor.

"What the hell?"

My entire front was glowing. And glittering. Glowing *and* glittering.

Fucking pumpkin.

5

Jacob turned and got a load of me, then glanced down at himself. There was a single smear of glowing glitter on his leather jacket, which he buffed off neatly with the heel of his palm.

I swallowed back a groan.

"I have some napkins," he offered.

"Don't bother. You'll just grind in the glitter."

"Not if we're careful."

"But, your hand...."

"It'll just take a second. C'mere."

I rolled my eyes and eased into the alcove beneath the UV bulb, where a poster proclaimed in luminescent letters, *Men's Rights Are Human Rights!* Maybe it was best for him to take a stab at cleaning me up in case there'd be black lights at the party. After all, he couldn't make it much worse—plus, if he was focused on my peacoat, he wouldn't need to dwell on his throbbing knuckles—or the poster's stupidity.

Jacob pulled out a napkin, hunkered down in front of me, and dabbed.

My heart skipped a beat, and my field of vision went white.

There was no big boom, no smell of ozone and crisped hair, no dancing afterimages, but it seemed like there sure as hell should have been. At least Jacob felt it too, the energetic smack when the white light I forgot I'd been hoarding arced from me to him, and he lit up brighter than a well-positioned strobe light. He gasped and staggered back, and then he gave a long and heartfelt shiver.

Well...that was one way of distracting him from his shitty evening.

He resettled his jacket with a shrug and rubbed the back of his neck. "I can't believe I...I'm so sorry." He shifted around as if he was suddenly uncomfortable in his own clothes—or, heck, maybe even his own skin.

There weren't really words for this energy swap phenomenon—not yet, anyhow, since the field of Psych is so new. The give-and-take routine is uncharted territory. Whatever Jacob does, he's strong. But even so, I worry that someday I'll channel more juice than he can absorb. Maybe the overflow would just go back wherever it came from—maybe not. I haven't overloaded Jacob's mojo-receptors yet, but I wasn't keen on testing our limits when we had no idea what the consequences might be.

"Are you okay?" I asked.

Jacob took a deep breath and let it out slowly. "It tingles."

I'm visual, he's somatic. The energy I label as white light feels effervescent to him. "C'mere." I opened my arms. "Pass some of it back."

It was as good a time as any to experiment. I'd generated a bunch of protective energy, and the only scary thing in that old theater was the fact that the people in it actually believed their own idiotic hatespeech. He reached toward me, just one hand, and we pressed our fingertips together. And waited. The sixth sense can be elusive. Unless I've got a visitor from the spirit world chatting with me, everything feels subjective, and frankly, somewhat made-up. It seemed as if I could feel the energy teeming beneath Jacob's skin, but it also felt like a figment of my own imagination. He scowled at our point of contact, and he tensed. But all the physical straining in the world wouldn't channel energy. I watched, less invested in the outcome. I'd been dealing with my "gift" for a good hunk of my life and was nowhere near as motivated to prove anything.

It was when I acknowledged my relaxation that everything shifted. It's like looking through a window on a sunny day, that moment where you stop seeing your own reflection and get an elusive glimpse at whatever lies beyond the glass. My barrier shifted, and some of that energy Jacob had grabbed flowed back in. Not through my crown chakra, but through my fingers. I saw it glow—and I felt it. Kind of.

Or maybe I just imagined that I did.

Jacob gazed deep into my eyes with a look so tender, I suspected he felt it too. Especially when he redoubled his efforts at transferring the charge back to me. "Hey, c'mon." I enfolded his punching-hand in both of mine, drew it up to my chest and blew on his knuckles. We both shuddered. "Keep some for yourself. I'll find more."

Here's the thing with energy—it can make you a little loopy. When I pulled Jacob up against me, our bodies sparked together. Maybe I was just imagining the fireworks...but I don't think so. Suddenly we were grappling together, and he crushed his mouth to mine so decisively it was as if he was trying to replenish not only my energy, but my oxygen. As if all the air had gone out of the world, and the only thing left to do was pass the last breath back and forth between us. No, we didn't need to worry about wasting the energy. Most folks go their whole lives without even feeling this psychic current. Jacob and I, we had plenty.

"Do you feel it too?" he murmured against my lips. I nodded. "Is it always like this?"

"Only with you."

Jacob wedged a hand between my legs and stroked me. Aggressively.

Like everything he'd held back when he was talking to the manager was now straining at the seams. Me, I was a goner even before we'd started snowballing the white light. His intensity does that to me, creates a feedback loop of need. Now I ached to be touched, humping myself into his hand like a horny teenager getting his rocks off in the second-last row of a crappy afternoon matinee.

Theaters are full of oddball passageways, places for actors to make their surprise entrances, or ushers to skulk through in search of rule-breakers to terrorize. I tore my mouth from Jacob's and picked out a door painted to match the wall with a yellowed STAFF ONLY sign hanging crookedly at eye level. Lucky for us, whatever staff currently used it was too lazy to lock up behind themselves. We spilled through it into a darkness that felt so still, so vast, it could only be the auditorium itself, with three-story ceilings and an utter absence of light. The rest of the building felt as if it was cycling through a revolving state of decay and repair, but in the auditorium, time stood still.

Maybe I was still sixteen after all, and maybe the guy cramming his hand down my pants was some stranger from a fast food joint across the street. Maybe the last twenty-five years were a wacked-out scenario I'd invented to kill some time during a tedious study hall.

And maybe somewhere over my right shoulder, there was a ghost clown taking the whole thing in.

"Wait," I whispered.

Jacob paused, and whispered back, "What?"

I listened. Or looked. Or whatever it was I did with that elusive piece of my brain that connected with the dead.

Nothing.

My caution threatened to kill the mood—and me with a raging hard-on that really needed some attention. Telling ghost stories from the safety of the car was one thing. But barging into a haunted theater on Halloween? "Just making sure we're...alone."

Lucky for me Jacob's got some majorly screwed up turn-ons. My back slammed up against God knows what, and his tongue subdued my mouth. He worked at my fly, groping hard, while I fumbled with his belt buckle. The huff of our breaths attempted to punctuate the dark, but they were no match for the smothering acoustics. We grappled together in the suspension of time and place, sight and sound, and my awareness filled with the wet slide of Jacob's mouth against mine, his lips and his tongue, and the insistence of his urgent stroking. That would've been enough to bring me off—not only the feel of his mouth and his hand, but the force of his arousal. But Jacob doesn't do anything halfway. Before I could think too hard about the mundane horrors lurking on the theater floor, he knelt.

If the kisses and strokes were intense in the muffled darkness, his mouth was capable of short-circuiting my brain. The sensory deprivation knocked my perceptions out of balance. I'd been reduced to a single neural pathway—and Jacob was working it for all he was worth. I tend to waffle about whether to murmur words of encouragement or simply keep my trap shut, but in that rare and strangely condensed moment, I felt free to simply lean back and enjoy the sensation while he gave me head. Vaguely, I noticed the soft friction of his hand pumping his own dick, and the occasional grunt where he throated me especially deep. And maybe I uttered some sounds, but mostly I was caught up in the climb. The teetering brink. The delirious release.

I grasped ineffectively at his short hair when I came, and he squeezed my ass hard enough to leave a pattern of fingermarks behind. Jacob doesn't just get off on ghost stories, he gets off on getting me off. I'd even go so far as to call him an overachiever, not that I'm complaining. I cradled his face against my groin and shuddered while the last few twitches played out, and I counted my blessings. I'm lucky to have him. I'm fully aware of it, too.

I sighed, and said, "I'll finish you."

"I'm good," he assured me—and not like he needed to wait 'til later, either. Oh well. The auditorium floor was no stranger to a little DNA. I knew that for a fact.

Only once we'd gotten ourselves tucked away and straightened out did I start feeling all turned around, wondering where we actually were in relationship to the rest of the room, and what I'd been propped up against while he gave me my jollies. "Lemme see your flashlight," I said, and Jacob pressed it into my palm.

When I hit the light, I saw shapes. Not ghostly forms—but not anything I'd been expecting, either. Like the rest of the building, the auditorium had been repurposed. Currently, from one end to the other, it warehoused towering stacks of carpeting rolls. No wonder sound wasn't carrying right. The entire room had been drinking up the acoustics. And now that I had a visual on our surroundings, I registered the peculiar odor of man-made fibers and glue. I wouldn't say I was saddened—after all, when I knew the place it was already well into its decline—but I did feel kinda melancholy. At least back then it was still entertaining people other than a group of sorry men with self-esteem issues.

I sought out the second-last row, but with the seating gone, I couldn't quite place my reserved spot. I scanned the far wall, the ceiling. Murals, too dark to make out, and some fancy plasterwork more or less intact. "Carpet storage?" I said. "That sucks."

"You'd think someone could do more with it in a location like this."

Who's to say why some things thrive while others decay? At least the theater was still standing, I supposed. Maybe someday, a new owner would revive it and do it justice.

On Jacob's request, I aimed the beam toward the floor. No spilled drinks or popcorn were there to camouflage our evidence, so he swabbed up after himself with the napkin he'd used to clean up my peacoat. He wasn't being all that thorough. But if anyone did a walkthrough with a UV light, maybe they'd see some transferred glitter and presume the fluorescing smears on the floor were just craft paint. He tucked the napkin into his pocket and said, "Let's get out of here."

With pleasure. I slipped back into the hallway, already calculating the quickest route to the party, when Jacob snagged me by the sleeve and stopped me from storming out through the lobby. "Line of fire." He pointed toward my feet. By the black light, my jeans showed a telling splatter mark glowing purple across the hem. "Sorry."

It really looked nothing like craft paint.

6

"There." Jacob pointed out the old restroom I'd half-remembered. It looked as disused as the rest of this far corner of the theater, but as long as the plumbing still worked, it would do. We ducked in. It was dark, and the overhead lights took another second to flicker to life. The room must've last seen regular use in the discount cinema heyday. It had a vaguely 80's feel, but with everything more scuffed, chipped and discolored than I remembered. I paused at the sink, briefly considered taking off my jeans entirely, then decided that plan held way too much potential to take a mortifying turn. I hauled my foot up to sink level instead, belatedly hoping I wouldn't pull a groin muscle.

At least the tap worked. And if I didn't manage to get my pant leg entirely clean, I could at least disguise the evidence well enough to blame the painted pumpkin if anyone noticed me fluorescing inappropriately. Beside me, Jacob ran his knuckles under a stream of cool water. They didn't look too bad. Guess he'd experienced a last-moment whiff of common sense and pulled his punch.

"You'll live?" I asked. He shook his head ruefully. "Don't worry. Maybe we don't personally have the resources to target their knucklehead group. But one of us is bound to know someone who does. First thing in the morning, we'll make some calls."

Jacob's shoulders slumped. "I guess that's the downside of digging around, looking for trouble. You might not like what you find."

"It's a shame, though. This place. It wasn't all that stellar back in high school, but at least it wasn't full of carpet rolls and misogynists."

"Especially with the location," he agreed. "I could see a place like this going to pot in an iffier neighborhood. But here?"

I was still scrubbing off his spooge when Jacob shook the water off his hand and went looking for somewhere to dispose of the sticky napkin in his pocket. He tried one door, then another, then another. Of the dozen stalls, only one wasn't locked from the inside. Easier for the cleaning crew, I supposed. While he rattled a toilet handle, he started making those grumbling noises he makes when he's trying to park the car. I reached for a paper towel to blot my shin dry. The dispenser was empty. Of course. And I was too soaked to just shake it off.

I joined Jacob by the stalls and said, "Pass me some toilet paper."

"Hand some over here too, while you're at it."

I jumped at the sound of the stranger's voice. Jacob didn't. Good thing. Otherwise I would've probably stuck my hand over the top of the stall without verifying whether I was dealing with a corporeal being... which, judging by the fact that it was locked, not to mention the pair of big transparent shoes visible beneath the toilet door, I was not.

I took the wad Jacob handed me, set it on the floor, and edged it under the door with the toe of my shoe. A transparent hand reached down and grasped for it, then passed right through. And then, a heavy sigh.

As calmly as possible, I murmured, "We're not alone."

Jacob stopped rattling the toilet and turned around with exaggerated care. I opened my internal spigot wide and called down as much white light as I could picture. I also edged away from Jacob so he didn't brush up against me and siphon it all off.

"If you want to talk," I told the bathroom ghost, "we can talk." With a curt hand gesture, I motioned for Jacob to fall back to the row of basins so we'd have more room to maneuver. I followed, crouched, walking backward with my eyes fixed on those ghostly shoes. "But don't try anything funny."

"What the heck is that supposed to mean?"

"It means that talking is talking, and that's all. Not touching." And definitely not an invitation to slip inside and take my body for a joyride.

"Oh." The ghost stepped through the stall door and into the aisle—in costume. And makeup. "Here I figured you were being a weisenheimer."

I backtracked as fast as I could.

As he squared up with me, I noted his shoes were at least a couple sizes too large. He wore gigantic trousers with bright patches sewn on the knees, wide suspenders, and a pencilled in five o'clock shadow that followed the curve of a painted frown. He was bald on top, but what hair he had left stuck out sideways, and a tiny bowler was perched at a jaunty angle on the curve of his smooth pate. Now that I got a good look at him, I could see his makeup looked more like the pre-painted pumpkins than a circus clown's. He wasn't a clown per se, more like a vaudevillian hobo. I wouldn't have known the difference when I was sixteen, but even if I had, I would've figured that no matter how you slice it, a clown's a clown.

"What's it doing?" Jacob asked.

"He, it's a he. Just talking."

"So if the both of you are lit up like a night game at Comiskey Park," the hobo said, "why is it that you can see me, but the other one can't?"

"Different skill sets."

"Huh. Whaddaya know? Mesmerists, table rappers, mind readers—I've seen every kind of mentalist you can imagine. Figured it was all some kind of schtick."

"Probably not all of it."

"I guess not. So, you got some history with this dump?"

"Not as much as you, I'll bet."

Jacob said, "Does he know he's…?"

"Dead?" The hobo pulled an exaggerated, wide-eyed look of shock. He patted down the front of his costume and said, "So that's why I've been walking through walls."

"He knows—and he can hear you just fine."

Jacob put on his best reasonable authority-voice and said, "Everything's okay, we'll work it out, just stay calm."

"He's plenty calm," I said.

"And if there's something you need to say, now's the time. We're listening—and we'll do what we can to help."

Jacob was making an awful lot of promises he had no way of knowing we could keep. Or was he? He's notoriously slick about doling out no more of the truth than is absolutely necessary, and I supposed "do what we can" is all anyone ever really does.

"I knew you fellas were good eggs when you told off that creep in the office." The ghost took a couple steps forward in his oversized shoes and I motioned for Jacob to back up toward the door. Sure, the ghost wasn't wailing or rattling chains or blasting us with cold spots. He wasn't chanting a phrase over and over or regaling me the details of his death. But he was still a ghost. And mediums can get bumped right out of their own drivers seat if they get careless around the dead. "But there ain't nothing you can do for this old place, not unless you know the Mayor. You don't, do you?"

I didn't. Jacob might have shaken his hand a time or two, but that probably didn't matter. The Mayor would be less likely to invest his influence in protecting a single building nowadays than he would have in vaudeville times—back when a cup of coffee cost a nickel and nobody had yet uttered the words Wikipedia or Facebook. Things were complicated in this brave new millennium. Sure, PsyCops were elite. Yet we were so specialized, I doubted we even had enough influence to shut down a bunch of blowhards like Men 4 Men.

"Sorry, no. Real estate's completely out of my league. Maybe you should just go toward the light."

The spirit glanced up at the cruddy light fixture.

"Not that. The *white* light." While I had no personal experience with whatever lay beyond the veil, I've seen my share of ghosts cross over. Stuck spirits tended to cheer up once they took the leap. "I'm sure you've got a lot of good memories invested here, but it's not the end of the road."

"The good old days? Maybe. Once. Hard to say. All's I can think about is what a knucklehead I was. My pal Bernie owned the joint, and these wiseguys would come by three, four times a week and shake him down for protection money. And finally I says to him, Bernie, you gotta go to the cops with this. If you don't, I will."

"And whoever was shaking him down, they found out you reported them?"

"And how." The ghost crammed his hands in his pockets and schlepped toward the basins. I put an arm across Jacob's midriff—just short of touching—and backed us both out of its way. "After that, the payments doubled. One for the wiseguys, another one for the cops in their pockets."

Ouch.

"So Bernie started putting in more hours, booking racier burlesque acts. I doubled up on my shows for the same pay. It didn't help. We were working ourselves into the ground and the only ones to benefit were the dirty cops and the mob. I was on my way to try and convince Bernie to sell, get out while he still could, when all them bouts of angina finally caught up with me." His eyebrows twisted together and his hand fluttered across his chest. "The long hours. The drinking. The wondering about who would come sniffing around next, looking for another handout."

"Do you know what happened to Bernie?"

"He sold. Without me helping him book the acts and keep all them crazy actors in line, he barely rode out the final month. Last I heard, he'd made tracks for Florida, scoping out some properties in the Everglades."

Damn. I was hoping maybe this Bernie guy was still lurking around so I could dig him up, negotiate some kind of reconciliation between the two of them and herd them along to their afterlives. But Bernie was long gone, and the thing that tied the hobo to this godforsaken theater was his own regret.

"Hanging around here, thinking about what you could've done different...it's not gonna change the past. It's time to move on."

"I'll go find some salt," Jacob said. But I caught him by the sleeve and gave my head a subtle shake. Laying a mindless repeater to rest was one thing. But a ghost with free will—one who wasn't doing anything worse than moping around and second-guessing a decision he couldn't unmake? I'd feel like a grade-A jerk if I tried to force it to cross over before it was ready.

"Cops aren't as crooked nowadays," I offered. Maybe that would make him feel better.

"Yeah? Then how is it the numbskulls in the back office get away with charging ten smackeroos for a traipse through the balcony?"

"Well...I didn't say the police were perfect. Just that they're not *all* on the take." I thought about how different the theater was from the movie house of my teens. Then I imagined how much it must have changed since the time of snappy hats and unfiltered cigarettes. "Things change. No amount of regret's gonna make bit of difference. What good does it do for you to watch the place backslide?"

Before the hobo could answer, I realized maybe it wasn't random bad luck that this prime piece of real estate was being used for open mics and carpeting storage. I said, "Ever stop to think that maybe the savvy type of developer—a prospective buyer who'd really spruce up the place—decides to take a pass 'cos the theater gives him the willies?"

"What're you getting at? Other people besides you can see me?"

See would be an awfully strong word. But *sense*? On some level, some deep and subtle level, absolutely. "It's notoriously difficult to sell a haunted property," I told him. "Even if most folks'll tell you they don't really believe in ghosts."

"I never thought of this place as...haunted."

The last thing I wanted to do was give the poor guy more regret to wallow in. "Look, I'm not big on making promises, but one thing I'm sure of is that the next step, whatever it is—it's good. Maybe you can resolve things there, or heck, maybe it'll be enough to get the long view and see how it all works out. But first you've got to let go."

Did he shimmer? Or was that just my own wishful thinking? I cranked up my internal faucet and flooded myself with white light. If he'd been a mindless repeater, I would've strengthened my light armor and given him a good hard shove. But since his personality was intact, it just didn't feel right. He'd need to cross over himself.

Though that didn't mean I couldn't help.

I glanced at the door and lit up the whole thing in my mind's eye. The room around me, the row of basins, the spotty mirrors, all of it went a bit dimmer. And although that doorway led to nothing more than a dingy little hall that smelled like a thrift store, it glowed. "It's easy," I said quietly. "Just as easy as walking out that door."

He gazed at the exit. It was difficult, but I did my best not to oversell it. And just as I wondered if maybe I really should send Jacob to find some salt—after all, there'd be plenty in the cafe—I saw the ghost was most definitely shimmering. He took one step, then another. Reached for the knob...then glanced back over his shoulder, at me. "If you think of anyone looking for an investment—artist, architect, I'm sure a guy like you knows plenty of them *types*. Put in a good word for this place, okay?"

A guy like me. Huh. "Okay."

With a shrug and wistful smile, the hobo ghost turned, and in his oversized shoes, walked through the glowing door, and was gone.

My shoulders relaxed. Jacob, as tuned in to me as ever, widened his eyes. He was dying to start asking questions, but he contained himself and waited for me to speak.

"We did it," I said. I didn't need to open the door and make sure the ghost wasn't lurking out there in the hall. I'd felt the shift when he crossed, like a change in the barometer. Given the way Jacob started fidgeting around, like he was trying to resettle himself in his own skin, he'd felt it too—or maybe he was just trying to will away some goosebumps.

We headed out to the car in silence, part companionable, part stunned. Connecting with a supernatural entity is a game changer in itself. Add to that the glimpse of another era that feels nearly as visceral as time-travel, and you've got yourself one hell of an experience. I slumped in the passenger seat, slightly buzzed, but mostly worn out, and wished we could skip the party. What I really wanted was to go back home, kick off my shoes, order a pizza, and process everything that had happened. Just Jacob and me.

He may be no telepath. But he can read me like an open book.

At first I worried it was wishful thinking when the route Jacob chose didn't lead toward the party, but pretty soon it became clear it wasn't just some shortcut, and I'd successfully dodged an awkward night of social niceties and small talk. All it took was a trip through a truly horrifying haunted house and an exorcism. He pulled up in front of our place. My hand dropped to his knee, and a shiver coursed through me and into him as my surplus white light redistributed itself between us. Carrying around too much mojo is a strain. It felt great to finally allow myself to relax.

He covered my hand with his. I tactfully ignored the bright scuffmarks on his knuckles. "What did he look like?"

"The ghost? Caucasian. Fiftyish, maybe. Hard to tell—he was in a clown costume."

"We were talking to *a clown ghost*?"

"Or a hobo. More like a hobo."

Jacob shuddered. "You're fearless. You acted like it was nothing."

"It wasn't nothing. I was watching to make sure he didn't try anything… funny."

"See? You can even joke about it. If I didn't know you better, I'd worry."

But he did know me. And he knew that I was plenty cautious. I wasn't exactly fearless, either. A good part of my current state of relief came not from laying a ghost to rest, but knowing I wouldn't be expected to fumble through a bunch of awkward chitchat.

He gave my hand a squeeze. "So…was the clown ghost confined to the bathroom, or could it see what else was going on in the theater?"

What was he talking about—the balcony atrocities, or the hummer? I gave him a sidelong glance. "We're totally busted."

Jacob quelled a smirk.

"Don't even think about developing any new kinks, mister," I warned him. "Ghost exhibitionism is not a thing."

He quelled harder. And didn't quite succeed. "You're sure? That he saw us, I mean."

"He mentioned something about me probably knowing artist-types, so yeah. I'm sure."

Jacob sighed. "I wish I could've heard both sides of the conversation."

Maybe someday he could. Back when I'd first glimpsed that ghost in the last row of the theater, most people thought psychics were doing some kind of act—Mesmerists and table rappers. And only a few years later, science gave its blessing and put us psychs under the microscope. They've already developed drugs that can quell or boost psychic talent. Unpleasant, sure. But they exist. Maybe someday those pills will be as safe and common as penicillin and aspirin. I wouldn't be surprised if it happened in our lifetimes.

We unbuckled our seat belts and leaned in for a kiss. Who's to say which of us initiated it? As different as the two of us are, more often than not, we're in synch.

We even flinched in unison when we glimpsed something leering at us from the backseat. I cut my eyes to the floor.

Fucking pumpkin.

I fixed my attention on Jacob, brushed my lips across his, and murmured, "I'll get it." I'd only held the damn thing for a few seconds, but I knew it was heavy. It would feel phenomenally satisfying to haul it to the alley and pitch it in the trash—plus it would be a great way for me to show my appreciation for skipping the party without coming right out and saying it.

Besides, it wasn't as if it could do me much more damage.

I was already covered in glitter.

The Thirteenth Hex

Jordan L. Hawk

"Terrible deaths!" a newsboy yelled from the corner as Dominic Kopecky hurried past. "Twelve killed by patent hex! Pharmacy hexman arrested!"

Dominic hesitated, casting a glance at the crowd eager to read about the latest tragedy to strike New York. He tried to follow as many cases involving the Metropolitan Witch Police as possible. This would make a nice addition to his scrapbook at home, and perhaps the article would contain information on what had gone wrong. Had the hex's angles been incorrectly calculated, or an improper symbol used? The wrong jewels ground into paste and mixed with ink could cause awful consequences. If the newspaper article mentioned the symptoms, he might be able to determine....

A quick glance at his pocket watch showed he'd be late to his desk if he stood in line for the paper. Blast—given the interest in such a case, they'd surely be sold out by the evening. Perhaps a second edition would have even more information, though.

He hastened the last few blocks to the MWP main offices. Reporters thronged the marble steps leading up to the brass doors, shouting questions about the patent hex case at every witch who passed by. Most of the familiars had taken animal form to avoid having to answer, so the morning bustle was unusually full of an assorted variety of animals including but not limited to birds, toads, and cats.

There had been a time when Dominic had dreamed of striding through those brass doors. He'd dared give it voice once, when he was fourteen and considering what he wanted to do with his life. He could still remember his parents' horrified looks when he spoke up at the dinner table, asking if he might go to city hall and be tested for magical aptitude.

"*There's no magic in our family!*" his mother had exclaimed. She'd lived in America long enough not to make a sign against evil, although her fingers twitched.

His father had been more diplomatic. "*We only want what's best for* you, son. Put aside these foolish notions. You're good at math, you have a steady hand—perhaps you could study architecture."

Not that it had mattered, in the end. He'd taken the tests anyway and failed them, to the relief of his parents. Still, Dominic hadn't been able to bring himself to forget about magic altogether. It haunted him, just as his longing for men did, a need he couldn't seem to stamp out no matter how hard he tried. So he'd managed the next best thing.

Perhaps it was just as well. Most witches couldn't even calculate a cosine, let alone apply the correct theorem to determine the proper circumference a magical circle required. Hexmen filled a real need. There was no reason to be dissatisfied with his life. And if his relatives didn't think it entirely respectable, well, it was his life and not theirs in the end.

Tamping down a sigh, he bypassed the grand entryway in favor of a discreet side door meant for the non-magical employees. After hanging up his coat and hat, he entered the great drafting room of the Metropolitan Witch Police.

Desk after desk filled the enormous chamber, each one equipped with paper, pens, and a dozen different inks. Reference books of every kind lined the walls, to make calculations easier or to help an uncertain hexman choose the proper ingredients for the requested hex. Enormous windows let in plenty of natural light. Gaslights and candles abounded.

A few other hexmen—and women—were already at work. Dominic went to his desk near the center of the room. Two small wooden boxes stood atop it, the one on the left already full of requests, the one on the right empty and waiting for his completed hexes.

Taking his seat, Dominic removed the top request. A poison detector—a routine appeal, given how many suspicious deaths occurred in the city. MWP and the regular police preferred to keep a stack of them on hand, ready to be infused with magic, then activated by the correct phrase when the need arose.

The first few hours passed quietly. Dominic worked his way steadily through the pile, calculating circumferences and angles, choosing inks and symbols, and employing a steady hand aided by protractor and ruler to create perfect hex signs. Right now, they were only ink and paper, but in the hands of a witch and their familiar they would become so much more.

Which was why it was so important to get everything just right. Because with magic behind it, a badly drawn hex could turn deadly. Just as the patent ones in the news had.

"Mr. Kopecky?"

"Yes, that's...." Dominic began as he lifted his gaze from the paper. Then his tongue tangled, and he forgot how to speak.

The man standing in front of his desk was...well, he'd never thought of a man as *beautiful* before, but it was the only word that came to mind now. The white of his shirt collar contrasted with rich, brown skin. Silky black locks brushed his shoulders, and wide lips shaped into a rather cheeky grin.

"...You?" the man prompted, when Dominic only stared.

God! He dropped his eyes quickly, willing his reaction under control. He couldn't forget himself at work, in full view of everyone. As he glanced down, his eye snagged on the badge pinned to the man's vest.

A familiar? Here?

"Y-Yes," Dominic said. Forcing his gaze up, he met a pair of eyes so dark he couldn't tell where pupil began and iris ended. "I'm Dominic Kopecky."

"Rook." The man didn't offer a last name. Or perhaps that *was* his last name?

Dominic swallowed hard. "A pleasure to meet you, Mr. Rook."

Rook extended his hand. Dominic shook it in a daze. Rook's skin was warm against his, the palm soft. How would it feel against...?

He definitely had to divert his thoughts to business. "Is there anything I can help you with?"

"Actually, yes. I have need of an expert hexman, and your supervisor tells me you're the best."

"Mr. Buchanan?" As if he didn't know the name of his own supervisor. Rook must think him an idiot. "That is, of course. I'll help in whatever way I can."

"Excellent." Rook turned away, then glanced over his shoulder. His thick lashes dipped low over his dark eyes. "Coming?"

Upstairs? To the MWP offices? What in the world could the familiar want that would require Dominic to accompany him there?

Dominic scooped up the soft leather wallet that held his tools. "I...yes. Lead the way."

2

"So, you're a familiar?" Dominic asked as they traversed the corridors leading to the upper levels of the Coven. As soon as the words were out of his mouth, he cursed himself. The man would hardly be wearing a familiar's badge otherwise.

Rook didn't seem to think him stupid—or didn't let on if he did. "Yes," he replied easily. "A crow, if you didn't guess."

"You can fly? I mean, of course—I'm sorry." Every sentence out of his mouth was more idiotic than the one before. "It must be wonderful."

Rook glanced over his shoulder. "Do you dream of flying, Mr. Kopecky?"

"Not anymore." He had once—often, in fact. But it had gone the way of so many of his childhood dreams. "May I ask what you need help with, exactly?"

Rook's lips thinned as he pressed them together. "It's not precisely a case," he said. "Or, it is, but everyone else considers it solved. I wanted another opinion, however."

"I'm not certain I understand," Dominic confessed. "You want an opinion on a case that's already solved?"

They came to a small office deep within the warren of the MWP building. Two desks had been shoved inside, both of them rather battered and scarred. One desk was unoccupied, but a lithe man with kohl-rimmed eyes lounged at the other. The fellow reminded Dominic of some of the dancers at Columbia Hall, and a blush scalded his cheeks at the memory. If anyone knew he visited such a den of vice....

"Cicero," Rook said, "can you find somewhere else to be for an hour?"

Cicero leaned back slightly, regarding Dominic through yellow-green eyes. A cat? He certainly had the haughty look and boneless mannerisms of one.

"Is this him?" Cicero asked.

"Yes." Rook frowned slightly. "So clear out, unless you're looking for trouble."

"Trouble?" Dominic asked. What exactly did Rook want from him?

Cicero stretched languidly, rising to his feet. "Don't get your feathers ruffled, darling," he said to Rook. "I'm going to find a nice, warm place to curl up for a while." He winked at Dominic as he left. "And I'll see *you* later."

"Out!" Rook squawked.

Cicero sauntered out. Rook closed the door forcefully behind him. "Ignore him." He gestured to Cicero's vacated chair. "Please, sit down. Sorry about the mess."

"It's quite all right," Dominic said. "But you mentioned trouble?"

Rook sighed. "It won't be trouble for you. And hopefully not me, either. As I said, everyone else thinks the case is solved. If you say they're right, then that's the end of it. If you say they aren't...well." He grinned slyly. "That's where things get interesting."

Dominic had the feeling Rook's definition of "interesting" differed quite a bit from his own. "What case? Who are 'they?'"

"*They* are Hilda Trojak and Bruno. Witch and a bulldog. Not bad detectives, but they tend to see what's in front of them and nothing more. And when you suggest there might *be* something more..."

"They don't want to hear it?" Dominic suggested.

"Especially not from an unbonded familiar," Rook agreed ruefully.

"You don't have a witch yet? That is, I'm sorry."

Rook arched a black brow. "Are you?"

Dominic fidgeted in his seat. "Well...they keep you busy doing paperwork, don't they? Until you choose your witch?"

"A bit more than that." Rook shrugged. "But it's true—a familiar isn't much good without a witch to channel his magic."

"That's not so, I'm sure." Dominic objected. "Here, tell me, what is it you wish help with?"

Rook leaned back in his chair. "If you follow the papers, you've probably read about the deaths caused by the patent hexes?"

Dominic straightened. "Yes. That is, I haven't read the latest paper, but I heard an arrest was made."

"What you haven't heard—what no one outside of these walls has heard—is there were thirteen victims. One survived, due to prompt magical attention to remove the hex."

Dominic frowned. "Why keep it a secret?"

"Because the thirteenth victim was Commissioner Roosevelt."

Dominic felt as though all the air had left the room. "Surely you can't mean the police commissioner?"

"Yes." Rook watched him through thick lashes. "By sheer luck, Captain O'Malley came into his office to deliver a report. O'Malley and his familiar were able to remove the hex before it proved fatal."

"Why hasn't this been made public knowledge?"

"And make the commissioner look weak in front of his political opponents?" Rook snorted "Perish the thought. The assumption is he was merely one of a number of victims of a shoddy hex, and that there's no reason to look any deeper."

"But you don't think so," Dominic guessed. "You believe he was the intended target."

"I see we think alike." Rook's grin faded. "Heaven knows, Mr. Roosevelt has made plenty of enemies, from the common citizens no longer allowed to spend their Sundays relaxing at the beer garden, all the way up to the mayor himself."

Rook opened the drawer of his desk and took out four pieces of paper. "These were taken as evidence. I'd like you to just look at them and give me your professional opinion of each."

Dominic had the distinct feeling that Rook hadn't asked for permission before making off with the evidence. If the detectives in charge didn't like Rook sticking his beak into their investigation, they might make an example out of Dominic. He could lose his job.

Rook watched him with black eyes, a faint, teasing smile on his mouth. As though daring Dominic to do something naughty.

Why did he have to be so handsome? As if aware of Dominic's regard, Rook licked his lips, just a tiny flicker of red tongue against their plumpness.

Dominic's cock swelled against his trousers. Swallowing hard, he looked hastily down at the papers, praying Rook didn't notice the blush heating his cheeks. The paper squares were decorated with brightly colored hex signs. The phrase to activate the magic caught within the lines and sigils was printed across the top, and identical on each: *Nothing Soothes the Stomach Like a Wendelson Hex!*

He picked up first one, then the other three. Taking out his jeweler's loupe, he examined the inks closely. "The paper isn't of the best quality, but it's better than what the street hexmen use. The design is twice as elaborate as it needs to be, of course."

"Is it?" Rook asked, cocking his head to one side.

"Oh yes. It's something one sees often in commercial hexes. People assume the more elaborate the better, so you get all sorts of frivolous loops and swirls that don't actually do anything." Dominic sniffed. "All brightly colored to further distract the eye."

Rook grinned slyly. "Prefer to keep things simple, do you?"

"Simple isn't bad," Dominic objected. "A clean hex, well-drawn, has a-a power to it, if you will. It focuses the magic poured into it, like a sunbeam through the lens of a magnifying glass." He gestured to the hexes in front of him. "This is more like a kaleidoscope. Pretty, but weak."

"Fascinating." Rook folded his hands beneath his chin. "So the hexes in front of you were all drawn by the same person?"

"They certainly appear to have been, at first glance." For better or worse, the printing press had proved unable to create hexes capable of containing magic. Something about the act of drawing them by hand gave them magical potential, or at least that's what Dominic's teachers had speculated. As a result, even the most meticulous hexes tended to have a certain signature betraying the hand that had drawn them. "Allow me to examine them more closely, if you will."

Rook propped his shoes on the desk and folded his hands over his vest. "Take all the time you need."

3

"These have been altered," Dominic said an hour later.

Rook leaned across the desks, his look intent. "What do you mean, altered?"

"It's difficult to see—those unnecessary flourishes I mentioned earlier confuse the eye. But the measurements don't lie." Dominic pointed at the leftmost hex. "See this line? Its angle has been changed just slightly. And here, the symbol has been painted with a different ink. Red spinel instead of ruby, if I know my gemstones."

"I'm sure you do. But why do you say altered? Couldn't the hexman have simply made a mistake? Perhaps he wasn't entirely sober when he drew that one?"

"For one thing, both of the incorrect hexes are wrong in precisely the same way. Of course, the man could still be a maniac and have done this deliberately," Dominic went on. "But look here. It's very faint, and again, the blasted—pardon me—ornamentation helps to hide it. There is a slight divot in the paper from the pressure of the pen, where the original line and symbol were scraped away."

Rook snatched up first one, then the other, peering at them closely. "You're right. Kopecky, you're a genius."

Dominic looked down hurriedly. "Anyone would have noticed it," he mumbled.

"And yet, no one did." Rook hopped to his feet. "All right. Let's go."

Dominic found himself trailing behind the crow through the labyrinth of corridors, until they came to a more open area. Here were the desks of the MWP detectives, arranged in a large room similar to the one for the hexmen below. Witches and familiars sat at the desks, the shuffle of paper, buzz of speech, hoot of owls, and purring of cats forming a low rumble.

"Hilda!" Rook called.

A blond woman glanced up from one of the desks. A bulldog lying beside it lifted his head. At the sight of Rook, the woman scowled.

"What now?" she asked. "I've work to do, in case you haven't noticed."

Dominic hung back uncertainly while Rook approached the witch and familiar. "I want to talk to you about the Wendelson case."

"Not again." Hilda's scowl deepened, and Bruno growled. "We have the murderer, Rook! Let go of this insane theory of yours before you muddy the waters too much. Keep things simple for the jury."

"But this *isn't* simple." Rook beckoned Dominic closer. "I had one of our own hexmen examine the hexes. The ones that caused the deaths have been altered."

The bulldog surged to his feet, transforming into a short, squat man in a puff of smoke. He wore a bowler hat low over his brows, and a tweed suit that bore evidence of recent meals on the lapels. "That don't mean nothing!" he barked.

Hilda touched his arm, quelling him. "What it means is that Wendelson poisoned his customers deliberately, then," she said. "I'm sure the prosecutor will be glad to hear these new findings. They should make it easier to secure a conviction."

Rook looked taken aback. "Why would Wendelson do such a thing?"

She shrugged. "Do I look like an alienist? He must be crazy. That's good enough for me."

"But why draw them one way, then alter them after?" Dominic asked, even though he'd meant to stay out of it. "Wouldn't he just draw them incorrectly in the first place?"

"You heard Hilda—he's crazy." Bruno's frown showed teeth. Dominic had to force himself not to step back. "As for you, crow, this ain't your case. You ain't even got a witch, so keep your beak out of what don't concern you."

Rook nodded tightly, then turned away. Dominic hastened after him. Once they'd crossed most of the room, Rook said, "Fetch your hat and coat, Kopecky."

"Whatever for?"

Rook cast him a crafty look. "We're going to view the scene of the crime."

Dominic's eyes widened in surprise. "But Bruno told us—you—to let it go."

"I'm bad at letting things go." Rook winked at him. "We're going to find evidence that even someone as thick-headed as Bruno can't dismiss."

Examining hexes was one thing, but now Rook meant to drag Dominic into other parts of his unauthorized investigation? Mr. Buchanan might forgive the first, but certainly not the latter.

"I can't," he said, backing away. "I'm—I'm sure you'll find someone better qualified to assist you."

Rook's expressive face shifted. He looked...not disappointed, exactly. More as though Dominic had struck him in the face. No doubt his good looks meant he usually got his own way. "But...."

"I'm sorry," Dominic mumbled, turning his back on Rook and hastening toward the stairway.

One of the doors leading deeper into the building swung open, and a deep voice said, "There's nothing I can do for you, Mrs. Wendelson."

Dominic wasn't certain if the man's voice was truly loud, or if it only seemed so because everyone else had fallen silent at his appearance. Startled, he turned, and saw a large man with an extravagant mustache, speaking to a woman who was clearly distraught. Tears streaked her face, and she clutched at his sleeve.

"Please, Mr. Cavanaugh," she begged. "My husband would never do such a thing. He only wanted to help people!"

Cavanaugh? Chief of the Metropolitan Witch Police Cavanaugh?

Cavanaugh gave her a look of distaste, carefully extracting the woman's hand from the sleeve of his expensively cut suit. "As I said, Mrs. Wendelson, it's for a jury to determine his guilt or innocence."

"But that could take months! The children and I have no other means of support." Mrs. Wendelson swayed, seeming on the verge of collapse.

"Well, then, your husband should have considered that before he murdered a dozen people," Cavanaugh said, without so much as a trace of pity. "McDougal, see her out."

Dominic stood back as a young witch escorted a sobbing Mrs. Wendelson past. Cavanaugh certainly seemed to have made up his mind as to Wendelson's guilt. Just like Hilda and Bruno, and most likely the prosecutor.

Dominic wavered. It wasn't his job, he reminded himself. He wasn't a witch. He had no business working with any familiar, let alone one he found as personally appealing as Rook.

He could go back downstairs. Hope justice was served despite everything. Hope the sobbing woman and her children got their husband and father back, before they found themselves destitute.

He found Rook leaning against a wall near the napping cats, arms folded over his chest.

Dominic cleared his throat awkwardly. "Er, Rook?"

Rook's head snapped up. "Dominic?"

God, Rook would think him the most inconsistent man in New York. "I...I've changed my mind. I realized I couldn't stand by and just hope an innocent man isn't condemned. Not and look myself in the mirror, anyway." He straightened his shoulders. "Let me know what you need, and I'll do it. I am at your disposal."

4

Dominic followed Rook out of the MWP building and onto the street. Pushcart vendors made their way through the crowds, urging hungry pedestrians to try noodles or hot pot. Carts and wagons of every description jammed the thoroughfare. The scents of dung, perfume, and garlic mingled in the air.

As they walked, Dominic's eye was drawn to the bright hexes painted on the buildings, most of them intended to guard against fire. Rook must have noticed Dominic's interest, because he said, "Why did you decide to draw hexes for the MWP? You know, instead of finding employment somewhere like there?" He gestured to the nearest shop. Ladies hats crowded the display window, and the signage proclaimed: "Each of Madame Lily's Hats Comes with a Hex Guaranteed to Give a Pleasing Cast to Any Countenance."

"Fashion isn't really my thing," Dominic said, glancing down at his rather out-of-date tie.

Rook let out a cawing laugh. "I'd never have guessed it! But I don't mean fashion, necessarily. You could have worked for a pharmacy like Wendelson, or gone west and painted hex signs on barns to keep the cows giving milk, or worked in a factory making certain the equipment doesn't jam. There are a hundred different jobs for a skilled hexman such as yourself. Why choose police work?"

"Why does anyone choose police work?" Dominic countered.

"Prior to the mayor appointing Roosevelt as commissioner, for the rather large amounts of money to be made by looking the other way when it comes to certain crimes," Rook replied wryly. "Although I doubt hexmen saw much of the spoils."

Dominic bristled. "Certainly not! Are you implying you did?" Curse it—he'd been starting to like the familiar.

Rook only laughed again. "Don't be daft. I sit around doing paperwork, remember?"

"So why did *you* join the MWP?"

"Because for all its faults, the MWP makes certain familiars are treated properly." A dark cloud passed over Rook's face, his mouth dipping into a frown and his eyes becoming unfocused.

"I don't understand. I thought familiars chose their witches?"

"In ideal circumstances." Rook stuck his hands in his pockets, hunching his shoulders. "But how often are circumstances ideal in this world? I'm an unbonded familiar. If a witch trapped me in a cage they would have me at their mercy. They could starve me, refuse to give me water, pluck out my feathers. Eventually, I'd give them what they wanted just to survive."

Dominic's belly turned over, and he was glad he'd only had a light breakfast. "And you'd be bonded to them after? Forever?"

"Yes." Rook removed his hands from his pockets and shook himself, as if flinging off the idea. "And on that note, we seem to have arrived."

Judging by the size of the pharmacy, its business must have been good at one time. But as Dominic stepped inside after Rook, he found that the wide aisles and open displays gave the place an empty air. Would the place survive the scandal?

At the sound of the bell, a man dressed in an apron and sporting a prodigious beard hurried out to meet them. "Welcome, gentlemen," he began. Then his eyes dropped to Rook's badge, and all enthusiasm vanished. "This way," he said brusquely. "Sarah, mind the till!"

A salamander scurried to the edge of the counter as they passed, and the man held out his hand so it could climb to his shoulder. He must be the witch who charged the hexes for customers.

As soon as they were safely in a back room, the witch turned on them. "Haven't you lot done enough to destroy my business already?"

Rook held up his hands. "We just have a few questions, Mr...?"

"Greene. As if you didn't already know that."

"I prefer not to assume," Rook replied. "I'm Rook, and this is my associate, Mr. Kopecky."

The salamander nudged Greene's ear, as if whispering to him. Greene's brows drew together. "Your associate? Not a detective?"

Dominic shook his head. "No. I'm a hexman."

"What's this all about, then?"

Rook folded his hands in front of him. "We're looking into the possibility Mr. Wendelson isn't guilty. I can't promise you we'll be able to clear his name, but we need to ask some questions if we're to at least have a chance."

The pharmacist looked stunned. "You want to clear him? I thought the MWP wished nothing more than to lock him away and lose the key!"

"Not if it means an innocent man goes to jail, and a murderer walks free," Dominic objected.

"Hmph." Greene looked skeptical. "And why are you telling me this? I'm not a suspect?"

Rook shrugged. "Your shop is teetering on the brink of ruin. If you did decide to commit murder and blame it on your partner, you guaranteed the destruction of your livelihood at the same time. Are you really that bad of a businessman?"

Greene snorted. "You have a point." The tension eased out of his shoulders. "What do you need to know?"

"According to what you told the investigating witch, surplus hexes were kept in a locked cabinet, until needed to replenish the stock out front," Rook said. "Who else had access to the cabinet besides you and Mr. Wendelson?"

"Just Sarah—the girl out front, manning the till—and Bobby Marlin. He sweeps the floors, maintains the stocks, and makes certain the displays are always full."

Rook nodded. "We'd like to speak to them both."

"Of course." Greene gestured to the door leading out of the storeroom opposite the one they'd entered through. "Bobby's break began just before you arrived. He's probably back in the alley smoking."

"Or listening in," Rook said sharply. He lunged for the door, yanking it open just in time for Dominic to catch a glimpse of an aproned figure fleeing down the alleyway.

5

"After him!" Rook ordered. There came a burst of gray smoke, and an instant later a glossy black crow took to the air.

Dominic raced after the fleeing figure, determined to keep the man in sight. Unfortunately, actually doing so proved difficult. The alley was crowded with crates, barrels, refuse, and loitering men. Marlin dodged every obstacle with seeming ease, while Dominic had to work to keep from slipping on rotten vegetables or tripping over broken crates. Within minutes, his lungs burned and his legs ached. What would he do if he managed to catch the man? He had no weapon past his fists, and no idea of how to properly use even those.

"Stop!" he shouted. "MWP!"

Marlin ignored the shout, instead ducking into a side street. Swearing, Dominic skidded around the corner and almost collided with the fugitive.

Marlin seized him by the lapels and shoved him into the rough brick wall. Up close, he was young, barely even old enough to be called a man. He had a man's physique, though, going by the muscles bulging under his shirt.

"I won't let you do this to me!" he cried.

Black wings swooped down, right into Marlin's face, so close their tips brushed Dominic's cheek. Marlin jerked back instinctively, and Dominic twisted hard, breaking the loosened grip. Rook continued to bombard Marlin, cawing loudly as he dove at the man's face, weaving between the flailing arms trying to knock him away.

Dominic snatched up a short length of broken lumber. Unsure what else to do, he swung it hard, striking Marlin in the back.

Marlin staggered forward, then went to his knees. Emboldened by his unexpected success, Dominic said, "Surrender! Or I'll be forced to give you some more!"

"I s-surrender! Please, don't!"

Rook landed on his feet in a puff of smoke. "Bobby Marlin, you're under arrest for assault."

"No, don't!" The youth was sobbing now, his face pale with fear. "What do you want me to say? I'll say it! Testify to it in court if I have to!"

Dominic glanced uneasily at Rook. Marlin hardly struck him as a hardened murderer, let alone someone who would do in thirteen people.

Rook watched Marlin through narrowed eyes. "How enterprising of you," he said. "On your feet. We're taking you in."

6

"Do you really think he's our murderer?" Dominic asked as the police wagon disappeared down the street with Marlin securely inside. They stood on the corner beside one of the new police call boxes installed under Roosevelt's orders. After securing Marlin, they'd tracked down the policeman walking the beat, and had him summon a wagon. Rook had suggested the policeman take credit for the arrest and charge Marlin with assault. Naturally the fellow had been more than happy to do so.

Now Rook turned away, hands once again thrust deep into his pockets. "Directly? No. But if someone else asked him to remove thirteen hexes from the stockroom, then put them back in, I doubt he'd ask many questions if the money was good enough. And once he realized what he'd been involved with, he became too frightened to admit his guilt. No doubt he'd rather see Wendelson in the electric chair than himself."

"No doubt," Dominic agreed. "What a sorry state of affairs."

"Quite. Still, hopefully a night in jail will loosen his tongue. Especially if I imply he might yet escape by cooperating." Rook removed his hands from his pockets and stretched first one arm, then the other. "But enough of this depressing business. Are you free for dinner?"

Dominic knew he should protest. It was still early, not yet five o'clock, and he might get a few hexes drawn if he returned to his desk immediately. But Rook's mischievous smile stole all of his resolve. "Yes. I am."

They dined at a small tavern around the corner from Dominic's apartment. Rook kept the conversation light, relating various pranks the unbonded familiars pulled on one another in their barracks.

"Doesn't it ever get awkward, though?" Dominic asked. "Cats and dogs living together, that sort of thing?"

Rook laughed, an infectious sound that did funny things to Dominic's chest. "A bit, a bit. But Cicero is good friends with a mastiff, if you'd believe it."

"I wouldn't."

"It's true, I swear!" Rook pushed his empty plate away. Leaning forward, he laced his fingers together beneath his chin. His dark eyes took on a warm glow. "So. Why don't you show me your apartment?"

Dominic nearly dropped the tankard in his hand. Had Rook noticed his attraction? And if the familiar had, could he possibly return it? Or was he simply looking to continue their friendly conversation?

Rook's shoe nudged lightly against Dominic's ankle. Even though there was no skin involved, the simple signal sent a bolt of heat straight to his groin.

"Y-Yes." He coughed and cleared his throat. "I mean…yes. I think I'd like that."

"Oh, don't worry," Rook murmured as he rose to his feet. "You will."

7

AN HOUR LATER, they stood on the roof of Dominic's apartment building.

When he'd unlocked the door to his rooms with a trembling hand, he'd expected...well, he'd expected the encounter to go as such things normally did. Instead, Rook had asked if there was an access to the roof.

"I've never been up here before," Dominic confessed as he looked around warily. Clearly someone had, because there was a blanket and a few chairs, although the place was deserted for the moment.

"Don't like heights?" Rook teased.

"It isn't that." Dominic followed Rook to stand near the edge. "It just never occurred to me."

"I see." Rook tipped his head back. The wind stirred his black hair like a lover's hands. "You never answered my question."

"Your question?"

"As to why you chose to work for the MWP, instead of some other, more lucrative, employer."

"Oh." Trying to formulate an answer, Dominic stared out over the expanse of the city. The sunset painted the brick walls a warm shade of orange and lent color to the slate roof tiles. The tangle of wires, from telegraph to electrical, hung black against the reddening sky. The character of the sounds drifting up from the street had shifted, from the frenetic pace of the day to the more leisurely stroll of early evening.

"I suppose I didn't know what else to do," he said at last. "I might have turned my hand to medicinal hexes, or fashion, or something else, you're right. But none of those felt...important. When I was young, I dreamed of joining the MWP as a witch." Heat scalded his face at admitting such a folly in front of a familiar. "Stupid, I know, but I guess some part of me never quite let go of that dream."

"Why was it stupid?" Rook asked.

"My parents tried to talk me out of taking the tests." He stared down at his shoes. "They were from the old country and didn't approve. But I did it anyway. I...I failed."

Rook frowned. "Failed?"

"Of course I did." Who was he, to have imagined even for a moment that he was magic? "I left town for a month to help my uncle in Boston. When I returned, my mother confronted me. My results had come back while I was gone. She'd opened the letter and was absolutely furious."

"And the results?"

"A high aptitude for hexing. There was that, at least. But as for being a witch, nothing outside of the general populace."

He'd cried himself to sleep that night, the hot ball of misery in his chest compounded by his mother's anger and father's disappointment.

"At any rate, it was for the best," Dominic forced himself to say. "Got my head out of the clouds and on the ground where it belonged."

"No wonder you stopped dreaming of flying." Rook took Dominic's hand, twining their fingers together. The touch made Dominic's mouth go dry and his cock stir. "Would you like to fly again?"

It took him a moment to parse the words. "I don't know what you mean."

"I can give you this. Let you see out of my eyes." Rook gently brushed his thumb across Dominic's cheek, before sliding his long fingers through Dominic's hair. "Not actually feel the wind beneath us, that would only come with practice. But you could at least see."

Dominic's limbs trembled, although he wasn't certain how much came from desire for Rook's touch and how much for what the familiar offered. "How?" he asked, and his voice broke on the word.

Rook grinned. "Take a deep breath and close your eyes."

Dominic obeyed. He felt Rook shift even nearer. Lips feathered across his closed eyelids, the touch shockingly intimate. Rook's hand slipped around to cup the back of his neck, fingers pressing gently against tense muscles, encouraging them to loosen.

"Relax, Dominic," Rook whispered. "Let me in."

Dominic felt a little tingle across his skin, as though lightning had struck nearby. For a moment he tasted blood, and lights flashed behind his eyes, a small explosion of fireworks.

Then Rook withdrew. Startled, Dominic opened his eyes again, saw the familiar perched on the low wall surrounding the flat roof. An almost triumphant grin creased Rook's face, and he threw back his head and laughed in such delight that Dominic couldn't help but join in.

"Now the fun begins," Rook said, and toppled backward off the building.

8

DOMINIC LEAPT FORWARD with a strangled cry. An instant later, a black shape soared back up out of the abyss between buildings, feathers gleaming the light of sunset.

"Close your eyes and concentrate on me."

Dominic gasped. It was as though Rook had spoken directly in his ear, even though he currently swooped idle loops above the roof. How could such a thing be?

Magic. For the first time in his life, he was truly touching magic.

He did as ordered. Instantly, he found himself flying.

No, he wasn't flying—he still felt the building firmly beneath his feet. But seeing the world through Rook's eyes was the next best thing.

New York spread out beneath them, the setting sun casting a golden glow across the jumble of buildings. A flock of pigeons startled into the air as Rook passed over their roosting place.

Then they were spiraling down, down, between the cliffs of the buildings and toward the street. Dominic's heart beat faster, and a cry rose to his lips.

But he didn't open his eyes.

At the last moment, Rook pulled out of the dive, gliding low over the heads of the crowd. His claws scraped the hat of a cab driver, and Dominic imagined he heard the outraged shout as they swooped away.

Rook's wings beat hard, taking them higher. The tangle of wires laced across the sky provided both obstacle and challenge. Rook danced among them, each easy flick of feather twisting him like an acrobat. This was freedom—freedom and wonder and the sheer joy of being alive.

Rook circled back and Dominic had the disorienting experience of seeing himself through the familiar's eyes. Dominic blinked hastily, just in time to see Rook flutter in and land on human feet.

"Did you enjoy?" Rook asked hopefully.

A laugh of wild delight bubbled up in Dominic. Without thought, as naturally as breathing, he stepped forward and slid his arms around Rook.

Rook's eyes widened slightly, and for a fraction of an instant Dominic thought he'd misunderstood everything. Then Rook kissed him.

Rook tasted of the beer they'd drunk at the tavern, and of something else, warm and a bit wild. He caressed Dominic's lips with his, then nipped lightly at the lower one, before diving back in. Dominic opened to him, tongues touching, exploring each other's mouths in turn. And maybe it was the drink, but this felt different than any other time. There was no awkward fumbling, no bumping of noses or excess saliva. His skin hummed, still attuned to Rook, and Rook to him, and their hearts beat like caged birds against their ribs.

Dominic drew back reluctantly. "Someone might come," he said, glancing at the blanket and chairs.

"I certainly hope so," Rook said with a wink. "But it might be better if we do that in your apartment."

9

As soon as Dominic had the apartment door shut and locked behind them, Rook pounced. Dominic found himself shoved against the door, Rook's mouth on his once again, a lean thigh slipping between his own.

"I've been wanting to do this since the moment I laid eyes on you," Rook murmured when they came back up for air.

It hardly seemed likely. "Even when I was staring at you like a fool from behind my desk?"

"Of course." Rook ran his thumb across Dominic's lower lip. Dominic caught the digit between his lips and sucked hard. Rook swore and pressed more tightly against Dominic. "I want you."

"Then let's get away from the door."

They stumbled through the apartment, shedding clothes as they went. Rook was gorgeous, all rich brown skin and lean muscles, lithe as a dancer. Such a contrast to Dominic, who had spent too much time sitting at a desk. Rook was so beautiful...what if he was disappointed by Dominic's softer form?

"Mmm, just look at you," Rook said with a grin, stalking toward Dominic across the small bedroom. "Good enough to eat."

Before Dominic could reply, Rook went to his knees. His long fingers wrapped around Dominic's erection, tugging a few times, before he leaned forward.

Dominic gasped and reached blindly for the bedpost to support himself. Rook's mouth was heaven, warm and wet. His clever tongue teased Dominic's slit, inspected the underside of his cock, and gave a long, slow lick before his mouth finally engulfed Dominic to the root.

Dominic's free hand trailed through Rook's silky black hair, gripping lightly. Just the sight of Rook on his knees, Dominic's cock slipping in and out of his lips, sent a tingling through his sack. With a gasp he pulled back. "Too good," he mumbled. "Not yet."

Rook rose to his feet and pulled Dominic to him. The feel of skin against skin, from thigh to chest, was a paradise of a different kind. Dominic ran his hands across Rook's back as they kissed, sliding down to shape his taut buttocks.

"It is good," Rook agreed, when their lips parted. "Now get on the bed and let me make it even better."

Dominic obeyed, and a moment later Rook slid between the sheets on top of him. The friction of skin against his cock drew a sigh from Dominic. Rook grinned. "Tell me what you want." He kissed Dominic again. "Anything."

"I'd like to touch you."

"But of course." Rook rolled off and onto his back. "And once you've touched me all you like, I want you to fuck me."

Dominic's cock jerked in anticipation. His blood pounded in his veins, and Rook's taste filled his mouth. He wanted all of it, everything, anything. Not trusting himself to speak coherently, he ran his hands across Rook's nearly hairless chest, pausing to tweak the dark nipples. Rook groaned and arched as Dominic tugged. "Harder, if you want."

Dominic lowered his head and caught one nub between his teeth, worrying at it lightly. Rook swore and arched even further, his hands clenching Dominic's shoulder. Pleased with the response, Dominic turned his efforts to the other nipple, then trailed his mouth down to Rook's belly.

Rook's cock brushed his cheek, as if asking for attention. Dominic rubbed his lips across the darkened skin, nibbling carefully. "Yes," Rook encouraged. "You can use your teeth. Anything."

Dominic slid his mouth further down, breathing deeply of Rook's musk. He licked the wrinkled skin of Rook's sack, then caught one ball in his mouth and sucked. Rook groaned in response. As he trailed his tongue back up the shaft, Rook said, "Damn it, Dominic. Need you. I don't want to wait any longer."

Dominic teased him, tonguing his slit and drawing yet another frustrated curse. Taking pity on them both, he leaned over and opened the nightstand, fishing out a small jar of petroleum jelly. "How do you want me?"

Rook's teeth gleamed in the dim light. "Lay back."

He took the jar from Dominic's hands and gently pushed him back on the bed. Dominic went willingly, watching as Rook dipped his fingers into the slick lubricant. When he smeared it down the length of Dominic's shaft, Dominic had to grit his teeth to keep from thrusting into the slick tunnel of Rook's fingers.

"Watch," Rook invited, and leaned back on one elbow. He lifted one leg, exposing himself without the slightest apparent embarrassment. His unselfconsciousness made Dominic's cock ache even more. How had he been so lucky as to end up in bed with this man?

Rook slicked his fingers again, then touched them to the puckered ring of his ass. "Mmm, yes," he moaned, head falling back as he pushed them in.

"Does it feel good?" Dominic asked hoarsely, even though it clearly did.

"Fantastic." Rook writhed around the intrusion of his own fingers. "Not as good as you're going to feel, though."

Rook set the jar back on the nightstand and moved to straddle Dominic. Grasping Dominic's cock, Rook shifted into position, his own erection all but pointing at the ceiling in apparent excitement.

Dominic bit his lip, quelling the urge to thrust upward as Rook slowly worked his way down. He was hot and wonderfully tight, body gripping Dominic's cock as if he wanted to pull him in and hold him there. Finally, with a deep groan, Rook seated himself fully.

"Damn," he whispered, head back and eyes closed. "Hold on for the ride, sweetheart, because there's no way I'm going to last long."

Before Dominic could even think how to respond, Rook began to move—and then thinking at all was out of the question. Rook rolled himself forward and up, the muscles in his long thighs bunching beneath Dominic's hands. Just the sight of him, handsome face distorted by pleasure, muscles moving beneath warm brown skin, was almost enough to push Dominic over the edge. Coupled with the hot slide of his body around Dominic's cock, the feel of Rook's heavy member slapping rhythmically against Dominic's stomach....

Dominic's hips twitched despite all his efforts to remain still. He let go of Rook's thighs and wrapped his hands around the other man's cock, making a sheath for Rook to thrust into as he rode Dominic. Rook's eyes flew open. "Fuck...yes...Dominic!"

Rook clenched around him, and he could take no more. His hips jerked up, and he buried himself deep while he spilled inside Rook. Hot semen struck his chest as Rook lost himself to ecstasy.

For a long moment, Rook held still, his breath coming in shallow pants. Then, with a contented sigh, he pulled free of Dominic's softening cock. "Now look at the mess I've made of you," he said with a smile.

"I like it." Feeling uncharacteristically bold, Dominic dipped his finger in the warm puddle of spunk and brought it to his lips to lick.

Rook's gaze followed the gesture. "If you're trying to get me aroused again, it's working. Although as hard as I came, I think I need a bit more time."

Dominic felt boneless and limp. "I enjoyed this. With you," he said, feeling suddenly shy. "When you find your witch, you won't have to...to give this sort of thing up, will you?"

Give me up, he meant. But one evening of passion hardly gave him a claim to Rook's affections, no matter how deeply they seemed to have connected.

A pensive look passed over Rook's face. "Some witches and familiars sleep together," he said slowly. "But plenty don't. The bond doesn't imply anything romantic or sexual. It would be...be up to him."

"Or her," Dominic suggested.

Rook's dark eyes avoided his. "Go to sleep," he said, pulling Dominic tighter against his side.

"Have I said something wrong?"

"No." Rook shook his head, but his gaze remained elsewhere. "You haven't. We'll talk about it in the morning. Put out the light."

Dominic did so. But the last thing he saw before the lamp flickered out and plunged them into darkness, was Rook's look of regret.

10

Dominic woke alone the next morning. The window stood open, letting in the cool morning air—no doubt that was how Rook had left, to keep from disturbing Dominic's sleep. The sounds of the street drifted up, including the call of the newsboy, which was what had wakened Dominic.

He reached out and touched the empty sheets beside him. They still smelled of Rook's skin, and a stupid ache started behind Dominic's sternum. Had Rook left silently out of a polite desire to let Dominic sleep? Or had the look of regret Dominic thought he saw been real?

Rook had said they'd talk about it in the morning. Except he'd left without saying goodbye or leaving a note.

It didn't make sense. Rook had been so open, so enthusiastic. Why would he be sorry about any of it? Had Dominic's question about his future witch hit a nerve?

Maybe the question had sounded too needy. Perhaps Rook feared Dominic meant to tie him down somehow. Clip his wings.

Or maybe once lust was satisfied, he'd realized someone like Dominic wasn't the sort he wanted to wake up in bed with. Too common, too ordinary. Unmagical.

Dominic dressed slowly, all his limbs weighed down by the lead in his chest. He should have known it was too good to be true. Yesterday had been magic of a sort he'd never been meant to touch.

He settled in at this desk determined not to think about Rook or what they'd so briefly shared. He would put it behind him, just as he had put his youthful failure of the witch tests behind him.

Which he hadn't done a very good job of, considering where he worked. He'd claimed to let go of that childhood dream, and yet he'd spent his adult life in its shadow. What had he been thinking? Rook was right—he ought to leave police work. Charm hats, or keep the cows giving milk, or whatever he could find as far away from the MWP—from Rook—as he could.

At any rate, he needed to work now. Shaking his head, he focused his attention on the hex he'd drawn. He'd just scrawled the activation phrase: "Reveal Poison."

Only that wasn't what he'd written. Instead he'd somehow managed to inscribe: "Help me."

What the devil? Dominic hastily tore up the hex into tiny pieces. How could he have made such a mistake? Why would he write such a thing?

"Dominic!"

"Rook?" he exclaimed, looking up in surprise at the frantic cry.

But Rook wasn't there. Only the other hexmen and women, all of whom now stared at him in curiosity or disapproval.

"S-sorry," he mumbled, ducking his head. Was he losing his mind? Writing strange things, hearing Rook's voice...perhaps he ought to leave for the rest of the day, before he made some irrevocable mistake.

"Dominic, please, I don't know if you can hear me. God, I hope you can."

Dominic blinked. The words sounded as if Rook had spoken them in his ear. Just as they had yesterday, when he'd seen the world through Rook's eyes for those few, precious minutes.

Except now, instead of pleased, Rook sounded terrified.

"Marlin is dead. They say he hung himself in his cell, but it seemed suspicious. I started asking questions—too many. They grabbed me—I'm in the dark, and I can't see. I'm scared. Please, if you can hear me, you have to help!"

Dominic surged to his feet, heart beating a frantic tattoo against his ribs. His co-workers were all staring by now, but he didn't care.

Rook was in danger. Pausing only long enough to scoop up his tools, Dominic ran for the stairs.

11

"Rook's in danger—you have to help!" Dominic shouted.

Cicero stared at him. "What?"

Dominic knew he looked like a madman, out of breath from running all the way from the drafting hall, clutching his tools in his hand, without hat or coat.

And no doubt Cicero would think he *was* insane, if he claimed to hear Rook's voice in his head. "Please, can you put in a call to the jail? Find out what happened to the suspect from last night? Robert Marlin?"

Cicero frowned, but didn't hesitate, instead leading the way to the bank of telephones in one of the outer rooms. When he ended the call, his face had gone pale beneath his shock of black hair.

"Marlin is dead," he said, turning to Dominic. "What happened to Rook? Where is he?"

"I don't know!" Dominic took a deep breath. "It's going to sound absolutely mad, but I—I heard his voice in my head. He said he thought Marlin's death suspicious, he'd asked some questions, and someone grabbed him. He was in the dark and afraid!"

To Dominic's shock, Cicero didn't even question his wild tale. "Blast. Have you heard from him again? Can you reply? Try."

"I...I wouldn't know how," Dominic said.

"Of course you wouldn't. Damn it, Rook." Cicero shook his head and pushed past Dominic. "Follow me."

The familiar led the way back through the building, until they reached the large room where the detectives had their desks. Hilda looked up as they approached and scowled. "You again," she said to Dominic. "What do you want?"

"It's Rook," Dominic began.

"Of course it is," she cut him off. "Whatever he's gotten you involved with, forget about it. I don't want to make a complaint to your supervisor, but I will if I have to."

"I don't care," Dominic said. "Rook is in danger!"

Bruno shifted into human form. "What are you talking about?"

"Stop growling and I'll tell you," Cicero said sharply. Rook had obviously conferred with the cat that morning, because Cicero gave a succinct description of everything Dominic and Rook had learned. "And now the prisoner is dead and Rook is missing."

"I see." Hilda let out a heavy sigh. "All right. You two come with us."

Had Cicero finally gotten through to them? Were they actually going to help, or was Hilda going to drag him in front of Mr. Buchanan and demand he be fired on the spot? "Where are we going?"

"The jail. That's where Rook was last seen, wasn't it?"

Relieved, Dominic nodded. Hilda led the way down the stairs and out to the MWP's stables. Horses milled about, and a number of police wagons meant to transport prisoners waited for use. "We'll take one of these," Hilda said, gesturing to the nearest wagon. "It'll get us there faster than going on foot or hiring a cab."

Bruno scrambled into the driver's seat at the front, and Hilda opened the back. She climbed in first, followed by Cicero and Dominic. The wagon wasn't meant for comfort, with only two unpadded benches along either side. Once they had settled, Hilda tapped the front wall to signal Bruno.

The wagon lurched into motion. Hilda stared out the window, watching as they left the MWP behind. Then she turned back to them. "I'm sorry you had to get caught up in this," she said.

Reaching into her pocket, she drew out her police issued Colt and leveled it at them.

12

Dominic froze, his heart pounding in his chest. The black bore of the gun seemed to swallow the world, metal gleaming in the gray light filtering through the wagon's small windows. Beside him, Cicero let out a gasp of horror.

"Hilda?" the cat asked, green eyes going wide in disbelief. "No. Not you. You'd never become involved in something like this. You're too good of a policewoman."

Misery showed on Hilda's face. "I didn't want to," she said heavily. "I was glad when Roosevelt was appointed commissioner. Clean up the streets and clean out the ranks. But when we started to investigate the patent hex case…they made threats, Cicero. My daughter is only six. The chief said she'd never live to see seven if we looked for any other suspects."

Dominic felt all the blood drain from his limbs. If Chief Cavanaugh was involved…

Bobby Marlin's strange offer, that he would say whatever they wished, made sense if it had been the MWP who had come to him in the first place. He must have thought Rook and Dominic were there to tie up a loose end.

No wonder he hadn't survived the night in jail. And Rook…oh God. Rook had strolled in, thinking the case merely a matter of a stubborn witch and bulldog convinced they'd done the right thing. Not a betrayal of justice by the very people sworn to uphold it.

"I know you're afraid for your daughter, but if you went to Commissioner Roosevelt directly, surely he could protect her," Dominic said. "Let us go. Tell Bruno to take us to the commissioner straight away."

Hilda shook her head. "It's too late for that. I'm too involved."

That didn't sound good. "Did you grab Rook?"

"He wanted Bruno and me to come to the jail with him. Hear what Marlin had to say." She shook her head. "Couldn't he have just minded his own business? I'd barely gotten back from dealing with him when you two showed up." A frown creased her face. "How did you know he was missing?"

"He missed an appointment with Kopecky this morning," Cicero lied, although why he bothered Dominic couldn't guess.

"You said you dealt with Rook." Dominic clasped his hands to keep them from shaking. "What did you mean? Are you taking us to him?" Surely Rook wasn't dead. Hilda and Bruno had already returned, or at least were on their way back to their desk, when Dominic had heard Rook's plea for help. He must still be alive.

But for how long?

"You'll see," Hilda said gruffly.

"Hilda," Cicero said, "we've known each other for years. You can't just—"

"Don't tell me what I can't do, cat." She pointed the gun at him menacingly. "Not when it comes to protecting my daughter. Now be quiet. I'm done talking."

The wagon ride seemed to go on forever. Dominic was aware of every jolt through a pothole, every creak as they made a turn. Gradually the sounds of the streets faded—they were heading out of the city and into the surrounding countryside. The breeze through the little windows became fresher, bringing with it the murmur of waves.

The wagon creaked to a halt. A few moments later, Bruno swung open the doors. Once he had done so, he resumed bulldog form with a growl.

"Don't think about running," Hilda warned. "It'll either be my bullet or Bruno's teeth for you if you do."

Under the watchful eyes of witch and dog, Dominic climbed out, followed by Cicero. They stood on a low rise, a ramshackle cabin before them. Time and weather hadn't been kind to it, and the hungry sea had eaten away the beach until the waves lapped almost at the foot of the rise.

"An old smuggler's den?" Cicero guessed.

"Too smart for your own good," Hilda said unhappily. "Just like that damned crow. Get inside."

The lone room was devoid of furnishings and looked to have been abandoned for some time. Bruno resumed human form to open a trap door in the floor. It led to a small basement, which in turn had a second trap door. Marks on the floor showed where some furnishing had once concealed it, but like the cabin above, the tiny basement was completely empty. A large, shiny new padlock held the trapdoor closed.

Hilda handed Bruno her gun, took out her hex wallet, and flipped through it. Pulling out a piece of paper, she placed it on the padlock. A shimmer of light spread from her fingers, charging the hex with magic. "Open."

The padlock clicked obediently. Hilda swung open the trapdoor. The smell of the ocean rose from below, and the sound of waves grew suddenly loud. "Get in."

Cicero shrank back. "The tide's coming in. You mean to drown us!"

Hilda's face had gone white. "Don't make this any harder, Cicero."

"Harder for whom?" Dominic drew himself up. "Why should we let you keep the blood off your hands? If you mean to kill us, at least have the decency to do the deed yourself, instead of leaving it to the sea."

A loud squawk sounded from below. Cicero clutched Dominic's arm. "That's Rook!"

Despite everything, relief flooded through Dominic. Rook was still alive—that had to count for something. "All right." He held up his hands. "We'll go."

"I'm sorry about this," Hilda said as Dominic stepped onto the creaking ladder leading down. "I didn't have a choice. If Rook had just minded his own business..."

Dominic didn't dignify her with an answer. The trapdoor swung shut, cutting off the light, and a moment later the sound of the padlock snapping back into place sealed their fate.

13

"Rook?" Dominic cried. He heard the frantic beating of wings, accompanied by desperate caws, but could see nothing. The stench of the ocean was strong, and cold water lapped at his shoes.

"I've a match," Cicero said.

"And I have a candle—well, a bit of one." Dominic fumbled through his hex wallet until he located it. "It's meant to make sealing hexes, so it will melt quickly, but it's better than nothing."

The light from the candle was feeble, but enough to give them some idea of their grim situation. Smugglers had dug out this passage beneath the cabin, shoring up the walls with stout beams and fitted mortar. At one time it must have let out onto the beach, but storm and tide had done their work, and now the lower end of the gently sloping tunnel vanished beneath the water. Every surface was slick with damp, and from the marks on the walls, the tide regularly reached the ceiling.

The candlelight gleamed from iron bars. A birdcage sat on the floor, its lower half already in the water. Rook clung to the bars, wings striking frantically in a futile attempt to free himself.

Dominic ran to the cage. He flung open the latch, and Rook squeezed out, landing briefly on Dominic's arm before hopping off. A moment later, he crouched there in human form. The bridge of his nose was raw and bloody, as were his wrists, where he'd battered himself against the cage.

Overcome with relief, Dominic put his arms around the familiar. By the time he could spare a thought for Cicero's presence, Rook clung to him in turn. Water already lapped around their knees, cold and remorseless.

"Are you all right?" Dominic drew back, although he didn't let go of the other man. "I was so afraid for you."

"We both were," Cicero said. He hugged to the ladder, clearly averse to touching the water even in human form. "Damn Hilda!"

"Hilda?" Rook asked.

"She said she brought you here."

"I'm not sure. I was hit from behind." Rook touched the back of his head and winced. "The next thing I knew, someone had used a hex to force me into crow form and I was in a cage. There was a blanket draped over it, and by the time I managed to knock it off to see my surroundings, they were already gone. I never thought Hilda would stoop to something like this. At least I wasn't dumb enough to take the altered hexes with me. They're still in Dominic's apartment."

"Not that it will do much good when we've drowned here. Unless either of you can swim?" he added hopefully.

"Swim?" Cicero exclaimed in horror.

Rook shook his head. "After I dislodged the covering, I got a look at the tunnel. It's long, and goes deep. And we'd be swimming against the force of the incoming tide."

That was it, then. They were going to die as soon as the tide came fully in. An innocent man would go to the electric chair, his family left to starve in the gutter. And Chief Cavanaugh would be free to try a second assassination attempt, or whatever mischief his twisted mind invented to get rid of Roosevelt and reinstate the corruption from which so many police had benefitted.

Rook's hands closed around Dominic's. "The candle—you've brought your hexing tools with you?"

"Yes, of course." Dominic shook his head. "But it won't do us any good. We don't have a witch to activate it."

"Cicero, move out of the way," Rook said. "Dominic, I want you to draw an unlocking hex on the trapdoor, as strong as you can make it."

"But I hate getting wet," Cicero complained.

"You'll like drowning a lot less! Move!"

"You don't understand." Dominic let Rook lead him back through the water to the ladder. It lapped almost at their waists now, and Cicero let out a distressed hiss as he gingerly lowered himself into it. "The hex won't *do* anything, Rook! It isn't magic on its own."

"I know." Rook clasped Dominic's shoulders and stared into his eyes. "I need you to trust me, Dominic. Just this once more. Please."

Dominic swallowed. "You left," he said, stupidly perhaps, but they didn't have much time remaining to say anything. "You said we'd talk this morning, but you left."

"Idiot," Cicero said.

Rook shot him a glare. "Yes, you told me that earlier." Turning back to Dominic, he said, "I'm sorry. I'd hoped to put this business to rest first, but that was just an excuse. I know you must feel you have no reason to trust me, but I'm begging you. Please, just this one last time. Draw the hex for me."

The grief in Rook's dark eyes caught him off guard. Fear he would have expected, given their circumstances, but sorrow?

"Very well," he said.

14

"Hold this open," Dominic ordered as he scaled the ladder. Rook obediently took the leather wallet and held it unrolled over his head in both hands. Dominic selected a stick of charcoal—it would cling to the wood better than ink—and set himself to work.

He'd drawn thousands of hexes in his time, but none like this. This was the application of raw materials to rough, water-slimed wood. Even worse, the work was above his head, forcing him to crane his back into a painful angle. The terrible light didn't help.

A part of him knew it was folly. Whatever Rook had in mind, it wouldn't work. They needed a witch to activate the hex, and a familiar of some power to provide the magic for the hex to reach through the barrier of the trapdoor and act on the lock. While they might have the latter, they lacked the former.

But Rook had asked him. And if this was to be the last hex he ever drew, Dominic would make damned sure it was up to his standards.

"Could you hurry it up a bit?" Cicero called.

Water lapped around Dominic's thighs, even though he stood on the ladder. A quick glance showed him the two familiars floating in the waves, Rook still holding up Dominic's tools, Cicero holding Rook with one hand and anchoring himself to the ladder with the other. The cat's eyes were wide with terror, but Rook didn't look afraid at all.

"A proper hex takes time," Dominic replied, his voice shaking. The cold seawater sapped warmth from his limbs and made it more difficult to keep his hand steady.

"Shit," Cicero whimpered. "Oh shit, we're going to die here. You stupid crow!"

The water crept to Dominic's waist. Panic scratched madly at the back of his thoughts, distracting him, and for a moment he couldn't remember the next sign. Not that it mattered—they were going to die, here in this awful place. They'd gasp out their last, mouths pressed against the final pocket of air against the trapdoor, until there was no more—

"You can do this, Dominic," Rook said above the lap of waves. "I know you can."

He drew the final symbol. "There. It's done." He let the charcoal fall into the water that now flowed about his chest.

Rook dropped the wallet; it vanished beneath the waves as well. "Now we just need to activate it."

"We need a witch," Dominic said bitterly.

"We've got one." Rook grabbed the ladder with one hand, and wrapped the other around Dominic's. "You."

The bitterness surged like the tide, and Dominic snatched his hand away. "I failed the tests, remember?"

"*No!*" Rook grabbed his hand again. "It's what I meant to talk to you about this morning. What I should have told you before we slept together. Instead I let myself get carried away by the moment, and I'm sorry, Dominic. Sorrier than I can tell you."

"Get on with it!" Cicero shouted.

Rook kept his eyes fixed on Dominic's. "You are a witch." His grip tightened on Dominic's hand. "My witch."

It wasn't possible. Couldn't be possible. "I failed the tests."

"I don't know what happened back then. If your mother altered the letter, or if your talent for hexing skewed the results, or if there was just some stupid mistake. But I do know what's happening now." Rook let go of Dominic's hand and cupped his chin, forcing him to look at Rook. "We've already started to bond—do you think just anyone could have seen the world through my eyes last night? Or heard me call out this morning? There's just one last step—you take magic from me and use it to infuse the hex."

He blinked rapidly, and to his horror Dominic saw tears clinging to the thick lashes. "I didn't want it to happen this way. I wanted to give you time to think about it, so you could decide if...if I'm what you really want. I should have told you before we ever slept together, so it wouldn't cloud things, but I didn't. I made a mistake, and I didn't know how to tell you." The water lapped around his jaw now. "We're out of time, and I'm so sorry, but I know you can do this. I know it."

For a moment, every fiber of Dominic's being rebelled against Rook's words. It couldn't be true. The one thing he'd always wanted, but it wasn't for him. It couldn't be.

"Do this," Rook whispered. "Fly with me again, and trust I won't let us fall."

Dominic closed his eyes. Instantly, Rook was with him as he'd been the evening before, when they'd flown over New York. When their bodies had joined in bed later on, moving as one thing, better than anything Dominic had ever known.

He released the ladder and thrust his hand blindly up, making contact with the hex.

And the magic *flowed.*

"Open," he gasped, as the water filled his mouth.

Rook darted up the ladder, slamming into the trap door. It flew open, and a moment later, he reached down and hauled up Dominic, then Cicero. The three of them scrambled away from the trapdoor by common consent, hastening into the cabin above. Thankfully, it was deserted, and only a lonely stretch of beach met their eyes when they stepped outside.

"This is *awful.*" Cicero complained, wringing his sodden clothing. "I'm not your friend anymore, Rook."

"I've some fresh cream back in the barracks."

"Fine." Cicero tossed his head. "I *might* reconsider. After the cream. Now use your wings and go to Commissioner Roosevelt before anyone else gets hurt."

Rook took a step away, then turned back to Dominic. Desperation showed in his dark eyes, but all he said was, "We'll talk later."

Then he was off, a black shape cutting across the sky.

15

Dominic sat in his apartment later that evening. He and Cicero had managed to flag down a passing wagon to return to the city. By the time they arrived, Rook had already gone to Police Commissioner Roosevelt with the evidence and their story. Cicero and Dominic had been met by non-witch police officers, who questioned them closely. By the third iteration of the events of the last two days, Dominic felt utterly wrung out.

But it had been worth it. Even now, a newsboy below flogged the evening edition to passers-by. "MWP Chief Cavanaugh arrested! Patent hex deaths used as a cover up for assassination plot!"

Things would be interesting—to put it mildly—at the MWP for a while. It almost made Dominic wish to return to his desk in the hex department, just to avoid the fuss.

But he wouldn't. He'd never sit at that desk again.

He'd ventured to ask Cicero if it could possibly be true, if he really was—had always been—a witch. The cat had rolled his eyes, asked how Dominic thought they'd unlocked the trapdoor otherwise, and insisted even a feather-brained familiar like Rook would know his witch.

Had Dominic's mother altered the letter? Painful as the thought was, she might have done so, believing she protected him from his own worst impulses. He hoped not, though, preferring to believe there had been some mistake, clerical or otherwise. He didn't want such suspicions, however justified, to taint his memory of her.

There came a rap on the window behind him. Startled, he turned and saw a hunched crow peering in at him.

He hurried to open it. Rook hopped in, taking human form as soon as his feet touched the floor.

"Thank you for letting me in," he said, looking abashed.

"As if I'd leave you there on the ledge," Dominic replied with a smile. "I hope I'd treat my familiar better than that."

Just saying the words sent a thrill through him. Rook looked up, eyes widening slightly in surprise. "You aren't angry?"

Somehow, all the doubts Dominic had felt over the course of the afternoon melted away now that Rook was with him again. He'd felt the connection between them even before he'd understood what it meant. Having Rook here with him felt *right* in a way nothing else in his life ever had. "Well, I do wish you hadn't waited until we almost drowned to tell me. But no, I'm not angry."

Rook folded his arms over his chest and hunched his shoulders. "I should have been honest with you," he said unhappily. "After I decided to look into the patent hex case, I came to talk to your superior about his best hexmakers. I saw you that day, although I don't think you saw me. And I knew."

"How?" Dominic asked. "That is, I've never been clear on how a familiar chooses."

Rook smiled ruefully. "We try to keep it private. The other familiars told me I'd just *know*, but I never believed them. Until it happened to me." The smile faded. "I thought I'd try to get to know you better first, before committing to the bond. Cicero thought I should be at least honest, but I didn't listen. I wish I had."

"Well, it certainly would have been helpful to know we weren't going to drown," Dominic said. "Let alone that I wasn't going mad when I heard your voice speaking in my head. But...Rook...I'm a *witch!*"

A gleeful laugh escaped him, and it drew another smile from Rook, although even more quick to fade than the last. "You always were. You didn't need me for that."

Dominic stepped closer, slipping his hands around Rook's waist. "I needed you to show me."

"Anyone could have, who appreciated you as they should." Rook sighed and looked away. "The truth is, I didn't expect to find myself smitten with you. But I was, from the first moment. And I kept telling myself I'd explain everything. I meant to tell you on the rooftop. But you were so sad, and I wanted to *show* you I could be the familiar you deserved, so badly." Rook shook his head angrily. "Then I slept with you, and...and how were you supposed to decide with a clear head after that? I was so ashamed of myself. So I flew away from my problems, just like I always have." His shoulders sagged. "I'm sorry, Dominic. Just...just tell me what you want. If it's to work for the MWP, or do something else. Or... or never see me again."

Dominic shook his head. "Silly crow," he said. "How could I not want you? And you already know I wanted to work for the MWP. This business has strengthened my resolve, to see that justice is done no matter who it inconveniences."

Rook glanced up uncertainly. "Do you mean it?" he asked tentatively. "You want to-to stay with the MWP? With me? They might not make us start with a beat, after uncovering the plot to assassinate Roosevelt."

Dominic pulled Rook closer. "Even if it was the most wretched beat in the city, I'd walk it with you, and count myself lucky. You're everything I ever dreamed of, Rook." He tenderly cupped Rook's smooth jaw in one hand. "You're beautiful and clever, and I would have wanted you even if you weren't a familiar. But you are, and you've given me magic."

Rook's eyes darkened, and a cunning smile spread over his mouth. "Then shall we celebrate by making a different sort of magic?"

"I thought you'd never ask," Dominic said, and bent to kiss him.

The Soldati Prince

Charlie Cochet

Who would be slaughtered next?

Riley studied his prey, his eyes narrowed and focused on his first potential victim before he moved his gaze onto the next one. He had to choose. Or did he? His lips curled into a wicked grin. Who said he couldn't have both?

"Sorry, fellas. Looks like you're out of luck."

Riley stuffed the remaining slice of lemon cake into his mouth, moaning in delight as the frosting melted on his tongue. God, these were so freaking good. He washed it down with the frothy cappuccino he'd made himself while cashing out the register. Once the lemon cake was no more, he moved on to the old fashioned glazed donut. He could never choose between the two.

The café's front doors opened and Riley swallowed the remainder of his donut. He took a quick sip of coffee before addressing the two men in dark jackets and jeans.

"Hey, guys. I'm real sorry but we're closed." Hadn't he locked the door? He was pretty sure he'd locked the door. Maybe he should've been paying more attention to his closing duties and less to stuffing his face. It wasn't like Clara minded if he took the leftovers home. Getting rid of the remaining stock at the end of the day was one of his many responsibilities at Tiger Tails Café. If he had to eat a few tasty cakes in order to perform his duty, well, that was a sacrifice he was willing to make.

The men came toward the counter and Riley straightened. Maybe they were tourists and didn't understand English very well. Riley motioned politely to the door.

"I'm sorry, we're closed. Tomorrow. We open tomorrow."

"Are you Riley Murrough?"

So much for not understanding him. Riley eyed them warily. "Um, yeah. Can I help you guys with something?" His gut twisted and he casually removed his orange and black apron. The taller of the two smiled, his lips spreading and curling freakishly up the sides of his face before they opened wide, releasing a horrific, gurgling shriek.

"Holy fuck!" Riley reeled back. What the hell? The glass display case shattered, followed by the shop's windows and doors. The shriek intensified, forcing Riley to cover his ears, the noise piercing his skull. A black tar-like substance leaked from the men's eyes and ears, their faces elongating and contorting, their skin growing veiny and ashen. Riley had no idea what he was seeing, but he wasn't sticking around to find out. He tossed the apron at their faces and bolted into the backend of the café, forgetting about the trash bags he was supposed to have taken out half an hour ago. He tripped over a bag and hit the linoleum tiles hard. Behind him, the men—or whatever the hell they were—emerged, their eyes nothing but hollow sockets.

The putrid smell of decay and rotted filth made Riley gag, and he scrambled to his feet, covering his mouth to keep himself from throwing up. The smell made his eyes water, and he tried his best to breathe through his mouth as he threw open the side door. The alley was plunged into near darkness. The lights had been working just fine last night when he'd closed. What the hell was going on?

Riley's attempt to make it to the street was quickly thwarted by the appearance of another shadowy figure. Maybe it was just a regular guy and not some decomposing monster. Riley considered asking the man for help when it began oozing the same black tarlike substance as the others. *Nope*. Riley spun on his heels and bolted down the alley, hoping to make it to the other side of the street. He was halfway there when he made the mistake of looking up.

"Oh, Jesus." He came skidding to a halt, his heart leaping into his throat as terrifying creatures in various stages of putrefaction scurried down the side of the brick buildings like roaches. They came out from the shadows, from trashcans, and from the very ground itself shrieking and hissing, fangs dripping with tar, eye sockets empty voids, and long mouths emitting a rancid stench. Riley turned but they were closing in on him from every direction.

This couldn't be happening.

Snatching up a discarded trashcan lid, Riley held it out in front of him. It seemed like an absurd move, but there was nothing normal about this whole situation. He backed up away from the closest mass of screeching creatures and swung the lid in front of him in hopes of staying out of their reach a little longer. Something told him being touched by one of these things would lead to unpleasant results. He screamed for help but his voice was drowned out by a ferocious roar that echoed through the alley, sending an icy chill up Riley's spine.

Was that...? *Did I just hear a tiger roar?*

From out of the depths of who the hell knew where, four huge tigers bared their fangs and roared. Now there were tigers? Had they escaped from a zoo somewhere? He slowly backed away from the huge cats lined up across the alley, their eyes on him. Gingerly, he crouched down and attempted to hide as best he could behind the trashcan lid. Wait, tigers had a really good sense of smell, didn't they? Crap. He was a dead man. Not like they didn't know he was there. Another roar froze him to the spot. He stared wide-eyed and helpless as the largest of the four tigers broke into a run, heading right for him. Riley screamed, the trashcan lid brandished as a shield as the tiger leaped. To Riley's disbelief, the tiger soared over him.

Dumbly, Riley turned. The tiger jumped into a mass of shrieking creatures, its fangs bared as it slashed with razor sharp claws. Holy shit, they were fighting! Before another genius revelation crossed Riley's mind, the other three tigers joined the battle. They fought viciously, tearing and clawing at the dripping, rotting corpses of indefinable creatures. Their claws left behind strange colored lights as they tore gashes into their enemies. Riley had never seen anything like it, not during any number of late night National Geographic marathons nor any of his favorite geeky TV shows. Man, he really needed to get out more.

Riley inched away from the battle hoping to slip away unnoticed. Maybe he could make a break for it now that everyone was busy. There was a good chance the lemon cake he'd eaten had somehow been laced with LSD and he was high as a fucking kite grinning like an idiot and sitting on the café counter stuffing baked goods into his mouth. One could only hope.

The alley darkened and Riley gasped. More creatures emerged from the shadows, scurrying toward the tigers. How the hell were four supposed to fend off hundreds, maybe more? The tigers roared and leaped. They twisted their muscular bodies to lash out at their attackers with massive paws, their ears flattened back against their big furry heads. It was both mesmerizing and terrifying. Riley breathed through his mouth as he slowly retreated when one foul creature turned its empty eye holes in his direction. How the hell did they know he was there?

"Shit." Riley took off, glancing behind him as the bastard shrieked, calling to the others. A mass of the things abandoned the fight to chase after him, several blocking the end of the alley and bringing him to a halt. Something solid slammed into him from behind and he hit the ground hard, but it didn't hurt as much as the burn that seared his flesh when one of the bastards grabbed his arm. Riley cried out at the pain, a tiger roar soon joining his shout. He rolled onto his back just as a shadow moved over him. This was it. It was all over. Riley shut his eyes tight. He regretted not having been able to clear his browser history. *Sorry, Mom. I wasn't disturbed, I swear. Okay, maybe a little.*

The burn disappeared from his arm and he felt the heat of a heavy mass over him. His eyes flew open and he was met with orange, white, and black fur. The larger of the tigers stood over him fighting off the approaching creatures. His green eyes vanished, replaced by a glowing white light. He snarled and opened his jaws, a blinding light burst out, forcing Riley to squint his eyes. The light flared, exploding through the alley before fading. Then silence.

Riley sat stunned. The alley was empty. Every last foul smelling creature was gone. The tiger turned its large head in his direction and Riley gave a start. Its eyes were once again green. It stared intensely at him, as if it could see into his very soul. It was weird and a little bit creepy. With a series of roars and mewls, the tiger began to contort itself, its fur drawing inward and its body changing. *Now what?* Before him the tiger changed into a man with intense green eyes.

The man's muscles twitched and flexed as he slowly stood. His jaw was chiseled, his brows thick and as pitch black as his hair. There were several nicks on his tanned skin. Riley had no idea where the black boots, leather pants, and tight T-shirt had come from, but they made him look even bigger, more menacing. Both arms were covered in tribal tattoos, from the patterned bands around his wrists and forearms, to the more intricate designs disappearing under his shirt sleeves.

"Please don't kill me."

The man's eyes widened. "You see me?"

Shit. "Um, no. Didn't see a thing." Riley got up and held a hand up in front of him. Two equally muscular men and Wonder Woman joined their friend. The others had changed too. This was crazy. Riley backed away slowly. "I'm uh, I'm gonna go check myself into a hospital about my uh, not seeing you guys. Excuse me."

"Khalon, look!" The fair haired man pointed to Riley's arm. He followed the guy's gaze and cursed under his breath. There were four bands of tribal markings around his left forearm where the creature had grabbed him. Had it somehow marked him? If it had, why did the marks look like a tattoo? Wait, the patterns looked just like the ones on this Khalon dude's arms.

"What is this?" Riley looked up and nearly jumped out of his skin. The one they'd called Khalon stood in front of Riley. He took hold of Riley's wrist and held his arm up to inspect it.

"It can't be."

Just when Riley thought this night couldn't get any weirder. Khalon shook his head before releasing Riley. His jaw muscles clenched as he grew pensive, his eyes narrowing.

"We're taking him with us."

"What?" *Hell no.* Riley tried to make a break for it, but Khalon threw his arm around Riley's waist and pulled him up against him. "What the fuck? Who the hell do you think—"

"Sleep, human."

Khalon waved his hand over Riley's face and everything went black.

2

"It cannot be."

Khalon paced his study. He refused to believe it. There had to be a mistake.

"He has the mark. *Your* mark," Rayner said. Beside him, Adira nodded her agreement. Ezra was silent as usual.

"I'm aware," Khalon snarled. He stepped up to the Eye and placed his hand on its smooth golden surface. Was that why the orb led them to Riley Murrough? It would explain why the human could see Khalon and his warriors. It didn't explain this... *insult*. A human? For centuries he'd waited patiently for his mate to be revealed to him, only to be ridiculed with this farce. How could the priestess mock him so?

A knock at the door brought him out of his vexing thoughts. Toka entered the room and bowed. "Your prince awakens, your majesty."

"He is *not* my prince," Khalon growled, causing the young servant to start.

"Khalon," Rayner warned. "There is no need to take out your displeasure on Toka. He's merely doing his duty." Rayner shook his head in disapproval before meeting young Toka at the doorway. He spoke softly. "Forgive his majesty. It has been a trying day." He placed his hand to Toka's cheek and smiled warmly. "Return to the prince. Our king will be in shortly."

Toka smiled and nodded before hurrying off. Rayner rejoined his brethren, receiving a scowl from Adira.

"You shouldn't encourage his sentiments. He is a servant, Rayner. Bed him if you wish, but do not fill his heart with false hopes."

Rayner rolled his eyes. "Yes, mother."

"Could we perhaps focus on the problem at hand and not the delusional desires of a foxling servant?" Khalon grumbled. He was in a foul mood and had no time for Rayner's dalliances.

"Very well." Rayner smiled sweetly. "Your warrior prince awaits."

Khalon stormed toward the door, stopping to thrust a menacing finger in Rayner's face. "You are an insufferable bastard."

Rayner bowed graciously. "Surpassed only by my glorious king."

"Bite me." Khalon stormed off to the laughter of his second in command. Why did he put up with such insolence? *Because he's your fiercest warrior, trusted confidant, and your best friend.* Khalon let out a scoff. Friendship was terribly overrated.

Khalon entered the royal bedchamber and scowled at the sight before him. The shackled human was up and brandishing an iron poker in his hands, swinging it at the servants.

"So help me if you touch me again I'll skewer you like marshmallows!"

With a growl, Khalon marched over to the puny human and snatched hold of the poker. He jerked it away and grabbed him by the collar.

"Get your hands off me, asshole!"

The human twisted and attempted to land a punch, but Khalon made certain to keep him out of arm's reach. He shoved the human down into the wingback chair and tossed the poker at one of the servants who caught it and returned it to its rightful place beside the stone hearth.

"Leave us," Khalon barked, waiting for the last servants to dart out of the expansive room. He turned his glare on Riley Murrough. The man dared to scowl at him? Khalon tried his best to summon patience. They had, after all, taken the man from his home. "You have questions."

Riley fumed, his indignant hazel eyes watching Khalon's every move. "Damned right I have questions. How about we start with what those things were, and why they were trying to kill me?"

"Those *demons* were trying to kill you to get to me." Khalon clasped his hands behind his back and paced slowly before the human. Just the sight of him was enough to boil Khalon's blood.

"Why? We've never met before today. I don't even know who the hell you are."

"I am Khalon King of the Soldati, and I am your mate." Saying the words alone pained him greatly.

"Hey, if you want to be friends, that's cool, but friends don't kidnap each other or chain each other up. Okay, maybe some do, but why don't we start small? Maybe grab a cup of coffee instead?"

Khalon stopped pacing. "What?"

"You said you were my mate. Are you British, a little Australian maybe? I can't make out the accent."

"I am neither. Why would you assume as such?" Khalon waved a hand in dismissal. "Never mind." It was quite possible the man was an idiot. "I meant mate as in lover. Partner. You are fated to rule and hunt at my side as my prince."

"Whoa," Riley let out a laugh and held his shackled wrists up before him. "Let's not get ahead of ourselves. You chain up all your dates? On second thought, don't answer that."

"The Great Priestess has made a mistake. A terrible, horrible mistake." Khalon was certain of it. He was king of the Soldati. His destiny was to be united with a great prince, a warrior like him. Not some frail human with wispy hair. Khalon's frown deepened. He stopped before the human and crouched down, his head cocked to one side as he studied him.

"Finally we agree on something. So, why don't you let me go and you can square things off with the… Great Priestess, is it? Square things off with her, and we'll just pretend this never happened. I won't press charges. I'll go back to my ordinary life serving up scones and lattes, and you go back to… whatever it is you do, and we're good. I'm good. You're good."

"Be quiet." Khalon reached out to take a lock of the human's hair between his fingers. It was golden like the sun. Not entirely unpleasant. For a human. It was also soft and reached his brow. His lashes were somewhat long, and there were faint freckles strewn across his nose and cheeks. There were flecks of amber and green in his eyes. His lips were pink and full. Not an entirely displeasing exterior. Pretty, for a human male. He was rather small, but then most humans were, compared to Soldati.

"What are you doing?" Riley sank back into the chair, squirming in the seat. Khalon ignored him. He took hold of Riley's arm and pushed up his sleeve. Not as scrawny as he expected. Taking a handful of Riley's shirt, he attempted to push it up only to get his hand smacked away. Khalon narrowed his eyes.

"I don't give a shit who you are," Riley ground out through his teeth. "Don't touch me."

Khalon threw a hand out, wrapping it around Riley's slender neck. "You are mine until otherwise released." He brushed his thumb across soft skin, the stir it caused in Khalon's stomach unsettling.

"Screw you! I'm not scared of you."

Khalon leaned in, his fangs growing as he grinned at the all but trembling *prince*. "Then why do you reek of fear?"

Riley lifted his chin in defiance. "I reek of a guy who got chased by a bunch of demons down a piss-stained alley."

The impudence! Khalon let out a snort of disgust and released the incorrigible human. Unbelievable. How could he be expected to mate with this…this impertinent pixie? The man was about as fierce as a newborn fawn, all wide eyed and fluffy-tailed. It was humiliating to say the least.

Riley rubbed at his neck, his glower on Khalon. "You have some serious anger issues, my friend."

With a frustrated grunt, Khalon tugged on the golden rope near his wardrobe, ringing the bell to summon the servants. Toka was promptly at his door.

"Get him out of my sight before I finish what those bastard demons started. Clean him up and feed him. I need time to think of my next course of action without him and his incessant babbling."

Riley gasped. "And you're still single? How is this injustice possible?"

What sounded like a giggle escaped Toka before he clamped a hand over his mouth. Was Khalon losing his touch? Now the servants were laughing at him!

"Forgive me, your majesty. I meant no offense." Toka's big amber eyes grew glassy and Khalon sighed. The last thing he needed was to make the foxling weep. Rayner would become irate with him and Khalon had enough to deal with at the moment without one of his friend's insufferable lectures.

"Just go."

Riley pulled his arm from Toka's reach. "Now hold on a second. I demand—"

"Go!" Khalon roared, balling his hands at his sides before the urge to strangle the man overpowered him.

"Going." Riley turned and fled from the room with several servants in tow. Toka excused himself when Khalon called out to him.

"Keep an eye on him."

"Yes, your majesty." With a bow, Toka turned and left him alone to his thoughts, the room blissfully silent. How could one human cause so much discourse? So much noise? With a sigh, he dropped down into the chair Riley had vacated, his lip curling with a snarl. Now his chair smelled of the man. Something flowery. Lavender? Sandalwood? What the hell did it matter? He'd just closed his eyes when he heard Rayner's footsteps.

"Can I not have a moment's peace in my own chamber?" Khalon grumbled. "What do you want?" He opened his eyes and peered at his friend who boldly took a seat on the footstool before Khalon without invitation.

Rayner's amber eyes filled with concern. "Do you truly believe the priestess has made a mistake?"

Khalon leaned forward, his hands clasped between his knees. "You saw him. I was to be mated to a fierce warrior. Not *that*." He sat back and ran a hand through his hair. "He's frail. I have swords taller than he."

"Strength does not lie with size alone."

Khalon narrowed his eyes, aware of his friend's amused expression. "Remind me why I have yet to imprison you for your insolence?"

"Because the last time you imprisoned someone, humans were still defecating in holes inside those ridiculous little wooden sheds. Also because you love me."

Khalon scoffed. "You overestimate my attachment to your miserable carcass."

"I love you too," Rayner replied with a chuckle.

"Are you saying I'm growing soft?" Was it possible?

"I'm saying perhaps you're growing into your own skin." Rayner patted Khalon's knee, his eyes still alight with amusement.

Khalon would not dignify that with a response. He was not going soft. "The answer to your previous question is yes, I believe the priestess has made a mistake."

"Then there is only one thing to do. We take Riley Murrough to the Great Priestess. Request she remove the mark along with his memories of us."

Khalon considered this. "It means a new mate will be revealed to me."

"Isn't that your wish?" Rayner asked as he stood. His expression turned guarded and for once Khalon could not decipher his friend's thoughts. Did Rayner not wish him to get rid of the human? As soon as the thought crossed his mind he quickly dismissed it. Ridiculous. Rayner was a Soldati, the most powerful next to Khalon himself. He understood the desire to have a warrior as great as he at his side, to share his life, his heart, and his bed. Rayner might be taken with the foxling servant, but it was merely another passing fancy of his. The idea that a Soldati would take a servant as his mate was laughable.

Khalon stood. "Inform Adira and Ezra. We leave for the temple of the Great Priestess in the morning."

Rayner bowed. "Yes, your majesty." With that, he turned and left the room. No jovial ribbing, no innuendos, or playful insults. Did his friend not agree with his decision? Riley Murrough was a human. He was neither strong enough nor honorable enough to be a Soldati, much less a Soldati prince. As soon as they reached the temple of the Great Priestess, everything would be set to rights.

3

"So uh, you guys just sit around waiting to bathe people?"

Riley felt a little self-conscious undressing in front of a bunch of strangers, but then again it wasn't anything he hadn't done countless times in the locker room at the gym. Of course the locker room hadn't resembled a palatial Turkish bath. He had to admit, it was pretty impressive. The brown and gold tiles shaped into intricate designs along with the mosaic tigers along the walls of the circular room were gorgeous. The glowing wall sconces gave the place a warm, cozy feel.

"It's our honor to serve the Soldati," one of the servants stated gently as he led a stark naked Riley to the expansive bath. He entered the steaming water and sighed. It felt damned good, and he did kind of stink. He would have preferred to be alone in the bath, but that was looking less likely with every servant that joined him. One poured a nice smelling substance on his hands before moving onto wash Riley's hair. A second servant lathered up Riley's right arm, another his left, while a third massaged Riley's shoulders.

"Do you... turn into things?" Riley asked a red-haired servant. He seemed to be the only one who talked, and when he spoke, the others jumped to it.

"I am a foxling. My animal form is a fox."

Cute. He kind of looked like a fox with his heart-shaped face and bright amber eyes. His eyes were outlined in dark kohl, his hands, wrists, and forearms were a dark smoky color that faded into his bronzed skin. "Is that makeup on your hands?" Riley asked.

"No. That is my skin," he replied with a smile. "As I said. I am a foxling."

"Right. Sorry, not used to all this. What's your name?"

"Toka."

"Toka, where am I?"

"You are in the home of Khalon King in the realm of the Soldati."

"And where exactly is that?"

Toka smiled impishly. "Upstate New York."

One of the servant's hands travelled lower and Riley gave a start. "Hey, whoa, I appreciate the assistance but I can scrub my own nads, thanks."

The servants giggled and Toka scolded them, though Riley noticed he wasn't harsh or unkind. "You have a way with words, Riley Murrough."

"You can call me Riley." He finished washing himself up and allowed the servants to escort him out of the bath where he promptly took the towels from them. "Thanks, guys, but really. I can dry myself." As soon as he was done, he slipped his arms into the lush, intricately decorated robe held out for him. He tied the sash and followed Toka to a different set of doors than he'd come in from. There was a large bedroom decorated in rich hues of red and gold, from the elaborate rug to the canopy of the giant four-poster bed. A delicious scent made his mouth water, and for a moment he thought he'd died and gone to heaven. There was a carved wood table set with more food than Riley could eat in a week.

"Come. You must be hungry."

Riley didn't need to be asked twice. Had he wanted to refuse just on principle, his stomach would betray him. The need to inhale some of this delicious food overtook any concerns regarding his current outlandish predicament. He tried not to talk with his mouth full, but he wanted to eat and get some answers. *Ooh, chicken*!

"So, if we're in New York, how come I've never heard of this place? You'd think someone would have spotted it." And probably try to book a wedding. Khalon would make a mint. Not many castles in New York these days. The décor was pretty extravagant too. He knew a few people who would have happily given their firstborn to get married in a place like this.

"In your world you must have come across magic."

Riley cocked his head to one side. "Like, Vegas magic? Because I hate to break it to you...."

Toka chuckled and poured Riley some tasty fruit wine concoction. "No. Like monsters, mermaids, witches, things that go bump in the night."

"On TV. Lot of weird stuff on TV." Actually, lot of weird stuff in real life lately too.

"Well, that *weird stuff* is real."

Riley swallowed a mouthful of tasty chicken. "You're telling me ghosts, vampires, werewolves, it's all real? You expect me to believe that?"

"You were just saved from demons by a group of magic wielding warriors who can change into tigers. Yet you can't believe the rest exist?"

"Touché."

"Our world has always existed, protected by a veil. Over the years, the growing discord in the world has begun to weaken the veil, allowing those bound to our world to slip through into the human world. Demons are notorious for slipping through, but the Soldati have hunted them since before humans walked this earth."

"Speaking of Soldati. What's the deal with King Crabby-Pants?"

Toka took a nibble of what looked like a sugar cookie only fancier. "He's not as bad as he seems."

"You mean he's only a self-absorbed prick some of the time?" Riley moved onto some of the other meats. There were all kinds and cooked to perfection. There were bowls of fruits, platters of cheeses, vegetables, and plenty of mouthwatering desserts. He plucked what looked like a lemon bar. One thing was for certain, the Soldati knew how to feast.

"I'm sure your boss is a great guy, and this is all just a big misunderstanding. So why don't we expedite this process a little and you tell me how I can get back home." He gave his most charming smile. "How about it?"

Toka's troubled expression gave Riley pause. "You're safer here. The demons are searching for you. They won't rest until you're either dead or have been claimed."

"Claimed? Are we talking joint taxes, or...." He had a feeling Toka wasn't talking about taxes.

"Physical union."

"Sex. I have to have sex with Mr. Personality so the demons don't tear me apart? Wow, okay. I can do that. A few drinks and it'll be like any other night at the club." He reached for the wine bottle only to have Toka gently lay a hand over his.

"It's more than sex."

"First it was just sex, now it's more than sex? What's he want, a commitment? It's going to take more than one night chained up in his basement with him growling at me to win me over. Okay, and an amazing dinner, but I'm not that easy." He popped a couple of grapes into his mouth. Khalon and his warriors had saved Riley's life, and he was grateful for that, but it didn't give the guy the right to have him locked away in his castle like some medieval princess, or prince apparently.

"Khalon is a Soldati king and a great warrior descended from the fiercest Soldati warriors. Every Soldati king is destined to be mated with an equally powerful creature, one of the Great Priestess's choosing. This mate will rule at his side as his lover and prince. The union makes the Soldati more powerful. It's a position of honor and privilege. Khalon's mate is meant to bring greatness to him and his kind."

"And instead he gets stuck with me. Yeah, I can see why the guy would be pissed." No one had ever mistaken him for a warrior much less a prince. Four years of art school and what did it get him? A string of crummy jobs and a long list of clients who wanted him to either work for a pittance, or give his art up for free. His mother was right. He should have been a pharmacist.

Toka leaned over and took hold of Riley's wrist. He pushed up the sleeve, revealing the tribal bands around Riley's forearm. "This is Khalon's mark. It was imprinted on your soul from birth by the Great Priestess, waiting to be revealed the day your king arrived to claim you. Today was the day you were to be claimed, which is why the demons found you, and why you were able to see them. The all-seeing Eye led Khalon and his warriors to you." He released Riley's arm and Riley couldn't help but run his fingers over the black tribal patterns.

"Has the Great Priestess ever been wrong?"

Toka shook his head, his delicate red hair swishing with his movement. The guy was adorable. "You've been chosen for a reason."

"I hate to break it to you, but I'm just a regular guy. Unless cooking the perfect poached egg becomes a superpower, I've got nothing."

Toka smiled sweetly. "We'll see."

The room grew quiet and Riley wasn't feeling so hungry anymore. "There's no way out of here, is there?" Even if there was, Riley believed Toka. If he went out there on his own, there was a chance he'd run into more of those demons. It would be kind of tough serving up Frappuccinos with demons tearing at his mortal flesh, and he wasn't talking about the morning coffee rush.

"I know you have no reason to trust us, Riley, but you saw the demons for yourself. They will kill you."

Riley couldn't help his curiosity. "And if they do?"

"If claimed and a Soldati King's mate is killed, the king is destined to live without a mate for the rest of his immortal life. There will be a void he will never be able to fill. If unclaimed, a new mate will be revealed."

Riley swallowed hard. Well that sucked either way.

The doors opened and Riley recognized the tall dark-haired guy who walked in. It was one of Khalon's warriors. Toka swiftly jumped to his feet, his hands clasped in front of him and his head slightly lowered. Riley noticed the way his cheeks flushed.

"Rayner."

"Toka." Rayner smiled warmly. He took hold of Toka's hand and put it to his lips for a kiss. "Thank you for taking such good care of our prince."

"I'm only doing my duty, sir."

"Of course." Rayner released Toka's hand and turned to Riley. "I hope you have enjoyed the king's hospitality. In the morning we set out to the temple of the Great Priestess. Khalon will present his case in the hopes of getting the mark removed. You will be returned home."

Riley stood. "The priestess can remove the mark?"

"The Great Priestess can do anything. She is the one who marked you, and therefore the one who can remove it. Khalon will be given a new mate, and you may return to your life unaware of what has transpired." Rayner bowed and turned to go.

"Wait, what do you mean I'll return unaware? I won't remember?" Riley wasn't sure he liked the sound of that.

Rayner bowed his head. "That is correct."

Before Riley could say another word, Rayner bid him good night and excused himself. Riley sat back down, moving his gaze to Toka and watching him smooth down his embroidered tunic. Seeming to realize he wasn't alone in the room, Toka cleared his throat and motioned to a long gold rope hanging from the ceiling beside the bed.

"Should you need anything at all, simply pull on that rope and someone will arrive immediately. The servants shall be in to clean up. Sleep well, Riley. May you find what you seek on your journey to the temple. Is there anything else I can do for you before I go?"

"So, you and Rayner...."

Toka smiled bashfully. "Goodnight, Riley Murrough."

"Goodnight." Riley returned Toka's smile and watched him go. He liked Toka. The foxling was really sweet. He clearly had a thing for Rayner, though Riley had a feeling servants and Soldati warriors rarely mingled, much less dated. Did Soldati warriors date or did they just carry off their lovers and *claim* them? An image of Khalon claiming him entered his head and Riley jumped to his feet, his face burning up. *Nope. Not going to happen.* His arm itched and Riley scratched at the bands. He had to get this off. If the priestess could do that, then he'd go along on this crazy adventure.

After the servants came and took what was left of the food away, Riley walked around the room in hopes of easing the fullness of his belly, at least that was his story and he was sticking to it. He was not nosing around. The wardrobe was huge, and it was filled with all kinds of snazzy clothes. There were candles everywhere and a huge stone fireplace with a comfy looking chaise lounge in front of it. The walls were decorated with intricately woven tapestries of tigers frolicking. Once he was done walking off his fullness, he cleaned up in a bathroom that was bigger than his tiny apartment.

As he lay in bed, he thought about what their journey might entail.

He sat up and ran his fingers over the tattoos on his arm. Soon, they'd be gone. He'd be back in the café none the wiser of any demons or sexy tiger men. But the demons would still be out there. Would they come for him once the mark was removed? Would Khalon bother protecting him if they weren't connected?

What he needed to do was get some sleep. With every question he asked himself, half a dozen more popped up. He had no idea what lay ahead tomorrow. He had a feeling getting a decent night's sleep would be about as easy as facing Khalon King again in the morning. Maybe he was being hard on the guy.

"You know what? I should cut the guy a break. Start fresh." Yep. That's what he'd do. Maybe Khalon just had a rough day. Who didn't have them? Tomorrow things would be better.

4

Khalon King was an asshole.

He was a sexy asshole, but he was still an asshole. The guy spent most of his time growling at Riley, muttering the occasional order, and then cursing Riley some more. Did the king of the Soldati ever smile? How was the guy not emotionally and physically exhausted from all that brooding? Rayner was more fun. Mostly because his life's mission—aside from killing things—was to annoy the ever living fuck out of his king. Riley kind of liked him. Adira was more serious, though she did tease the guys. She was also very motherly. Even if at times she dispensed some tough love. Tough as in kicking their asses. Ezra barely spoke. When he did, everyone listened, even Khalon. Of course Khalon did his own thing anyway, but he genuinely took Ezra's advice into consideration.

And then there was Riley. At least Khalon hadn't shackled him for their trip. They'd left to the well wishes of the castle's residents, from Soldati to servant. It was the first opportunity Riley had gotten to see the castle from the outside. It was extraordinary and huge. Kind of like those Scottish castles in the movies, but with plumbing. It was a strange mix of ancient and modern. The gray stone façade was covered in ivy, while expansive and lush gardens surrounded the castle on all sides. Beyond the gardens were thick forests and above them, the bluest sky he'd ever seen. Riley had been horrified to discover they'd not only be going into the forests, but they'd be making the journey on foot. Well, after the first skirmish with a couple of rogue demons, Khalon decided it would be best for Ezra and Adira to change into their tiger forms.

Riley stopped to rest on a fallen log. They'd been at this for hours. "Really? You guys don't have cars, or horses? Carriages? Something that moves you can sit down on?"

"We have no need for vehicles or horses."

"How do you get around?" Riley's question was met with a chuff from Adira who sat close by, her tail thumping against the ground. "Right, the whole tiger thing. Question, where do your clothes go when you change?"

Khalon folded his arms over his broad chest. "Our clothes are like a second skin. When we shift, it simply becomes one with our fur. Clothes are an invention of man. Unfortunately, even our world has conformed to your nonsense and we've been forced to adapt. Entering your world unclothed yields... undesired results." Khalon motioned it was time to get going. Hey, a whole five minutes. Fantastic.

Reluctantly, Riley got to his feet and started walking again. "If it's a second skin, do you feel pain when you get your sleeve caught on something or your boot steps on a rock?"

"No."

Cool. So because Riley couldn't shift into anything more than a couch potato, they were all forced to walk. Way to make friends. At least the forest was scenic and not some creepy dark fairytale woods. It was sunny but not hot. There was a nice breeze and Riley felt good in his new clothes. He wasn't used to wearing such heavy boots, or with so many laces and buckles, but he liked them. They went up his calf over his black pants. They'd given him a brown leather tunic thing with green stitching and a black shirt with long flouncy sleeves he could smuggle a whole chicken in. He noticed the Soldati were partial to leather. They had a sort of modern-day-Robin-Hood-in-bondage look going on.

Something had been bugging Riley since last night. "Is it really necessary to wipe my memories? I mean don't you think humans have a right to know about what's out there?"

Khalon came to an abrupt halt and spun on his heels. Uh-oh. He'd angered Tigger. Again.

"A *right*?" Khalon loomed over him, which wasn't difficult considering he was about a foot taller than Riley. "You humans are so arrogant. You believe your mere existence entitles you to whatever you fancy. That you are the center of the universe. For centuries, my warriors and I have risked our lives to keep you safe, and yet year after year you find new ways to destroy yourselves. There is no greater threat to the human race than itself."

Wow. Okay. Not a fan of humans, clearly. "If you dislike me so much, why are you going through so much trouble to keep me safe? You haven't claimed me, so you'll just get a new mate right?"

"Despite my *issues*, I won't allow any demon to get its hands on you. Also, your death would weaken me."

This was news to him. "How?" Riley almost had to run to keep up with Khalon's strides. Unsurprisingly, the guy was certainly in a hurry to get rid of him.

"The mark on your arm connects you to me. If a Soldati's mate is killed, the Soldati warrior will grow weak and vulnerable. This will weaken the rest of the Soldati, leaving them susceptible to attack. Full recovery for a Soldati warrior can take years, if he survives that long. As I have not laid claim to you and you have not accepted your position as my prince, the demons will do their best to kill you in the hopes of killing me shortly after."

Riley didn't like the sound of that, not just the whole him being dead part, but Khalon left vulnerable along with the rest of his warriors. He didn't want to be the cause of anyone's grief, even if he hadn't asked for any of this. For all of Khalon's gruffness, Riley had seen the way his warriors looked at him, the affection and pride in their eyes as they wished him safe travels.

"And hypothetically speaking, if I was claimed, would they still come after me?"

"Hypothetically speaking if you were a Soldati prince, you would be a warrior and could easily dispatch any demon intent on harming you, if they were stupid enough to attempt it."

Right. Ask a silly question, get a snarky answer. Up ahead a colossal fallen tree blocked their path. Khalon climbed the huge branches with incredible grace, leaping up to the top before disappearing over the other side. Adira and Ezra did the same, leaping from branch to branch until they were up and over.

"Um...." How was he supposed to get up there? He could climb the branches, but they only went halfway up the tree. There was no way he could jump the rest of the distance.

Rayner landed at the top and for a moment Riley thought he'd be left behind. Instead, Rayner turned and got onto his stomach. He reached down, a wide smile on his handsome face.

"Use the branches to climb up then take my hand. I'll pull you the rest of the way up."

Riley did as he was told and carefully climbed, like he used to do when he was a kid. He'd been pretty good at it then, surprisingly still was. When he ran out of branches, he stood on his toes and stretched himself as far as he could to take hold of Rayner's hand. The guy pulled him up like he didn't weigh a thing. If Rayner was this strong, how powerful was Khalon? Rayner motioned for him to stay then leaped down, landing perfectly on his feet. He turned and held his arms up.

"I'll catch you."

Riley felt a little silly, but there was no way he could jump from this height without hurting something and he hardly needed another reason to piss Khalon off.

"What's going on here?" Khalon asked, appearing beside Rayner. He frowned up at Riley. "What are you doing? We've no time for games."

Patience, Riley. Patience. "I'm being assisted by your second since the all mighty king has forgotten I can't leap skyscrapers."

Khalon rolled his eyes. "That's a fallen tree, not a skyscraper."

"It's like a freakin' Redwood. I'm sorry if I've disappointed you yet again with my human frailty and inability to leap tall buildings in a single bound."

"Oh for heaven's sake." Khalon turned to Rayner. "Adira is mewling about being hungry or something to that nature. Go see what she wants."

Rayner bowed his head and was off, leaving Riley with Khalon and the royal stick permanently wedged up his ass. Khalon raised his arms.

"Jump."

Riley sat down on the edge of the tree, eyeing Khalon warily. "How do I know you won't drop me?"

"If you don't hurry up I just might."

Riley swung his legs back and forth, a sweet smile on his face. "Tell me something. When you court your next prince, do you plan on being this charming, or am I just special?"

Khalon growled a deep rumble that came up from his chest. Okay, maybe he shouldn't poke the grumpy tiger with his witty repartee.

"Fine. I'm going to jump." Riley took a deep breath and pushed himself off. He managed to maintain his dignity by not flailing—too much. Khalon caught him, his arms wrapped tight around Riley as they stared at each other. They were nose to nose, their lips inches away from each other. Well that escalated quickly. Khalon's scent invaded Riley, an earthy mix with the faintest hint of some fragrant blossom. His green eyes were hooded and he poked his tongue out to brush his bottom lip, brushing against Riley's lips in the process. He could feel Khalon's hot breath against his skin, and he was suddenly consumed by a sudden need to kiss Khalon. All he had to do was lean in just a little. What would Khalon taste like? Would his lips be soft?

As if reading his thoughts, Khalon parted his lips. His pupils dilated and he angled his head slightly. He dropped his gaze to Riley's lips, his grip on Riley tightening.

"Forgive me," Khalon said gruffly.

"For what?" Riley's voice came out almost whispered. His body felt hot, especially his face, and his fingers had somehow found their way to Khalon's shoulders. Khalon's body was hard against Riley's, his warmth radiating off him. Riley's heart pounded, his pulse raced, and a desire he'd never experienced before coursed through his body. What was happening to him? It wasn't that he felt attracted to Khalon, it was more. His body needed Khalon's touch the way his lungs needed air.

"I'm...not certain," Khalon replied quietly. Confusion crossed his ruggedly handsome face and he gently put Riley down on his feet, though his hands remained on Riley's waist. "Stay close, human."

"Riley."

Khalon cocked his head to one side. "Excuse me?"

"My name is Riley, not human." Was he blushing? *Oh God, please don't let me be blushing.*

"Very well. Riley." Khalon cupped his cheek and Riley leaned into the touch before he could stop himself. "Stay close to me. We near the temple."

Riley nodded. He wasn't quite sure what was going on. He felt...weird. Did Khalon feel strange? He looked a little unsettled. Riley dropped his gaze when he noticed Khalon's tattoo was moving. The bands were turning on his arm, some in opposite directions.

"Your arm."

Khalon followed his gaze down to his arm. He pulled away from Riley as if he'd been burned.

"What's wrong?"

Khalon placed his hand over his arm as if he were trying to stop the movement or cover up his tattoo, neither of which was working. He shook his head. "It's nothing. We should keep going." He turned and strode off, leaving Riley feeling...disappointed for some reason.

Riley felt a tickling on his arm and he moved his sleeve to scratch the itch when he saw the bands on his arms moving. They spun around his arm, some in different directions just as Khalon's had. He needed to get some answers, but he had a feeling he wouldn't be getting any from their fearless king.

As they continued ahead, Riley waited for the right opportunity. Khalon seemed lost in his own thoughts and he was walking at a brisker pace than the rest of them. Riley took the opportunity to sidle up to Rayner.

"Hey, can I ask you a question?"

"Of course."

"What does it mean when his tattoo starts moving?"

Rayner looked surprised by his question. "Why do you ask?"

"Well, when he caught me, we kind of ended up a little closer to each other than expected. When he put me down, I noticed his tattoo was moving, but when I asked, he said it was nothing."

Whatever he'd said seemed to amuse Rayner greatly. He let out a laugh, his eyes twinkling with mischief. "Is that so?"

"Yeah, what's it mean?"

"It means he's made an emotional connection with you, one from the depths of his very soul."

"Oh. Is that a good thing or a bad thing? Because you know, most of his emotional connections leave me thinking he's close to following through with a physical connection of his fist to my face."

Rayner threw his head back and laughed. He wrapped an arm around Riley's shoulders. "You are something else, Riley Murrough."

Ahead of them, Khalon paused long enough to glare at them over his shoulder before grumbling something under his breath and marching off again.

"Tell me, Riley. Did your mark do the same?"

"Yeah, it did." Riley stared at him. "Wait, are you saying I had an emotional connection with him?"

Rayner nodded. He lowered his head and spoke quietly to him as they walked. "I think you are each as stubborn as the other. I also think the priestess was not mistaken. You were marked as his mate for a reason. Before this adventure is through, we shall discover the purpose. I'm certain of it." Rayner stopped in his tracks, his expression turning hard.

"What is it?"

Rayner's eyes went wide and he pulled Riley behind him. "Khalon!"

Khalon growled and hissed as he shifted into his tiger form. He took off toward them and as soon as he reached them, Rayner swiftly changed. Before Riley could ask what was going on, the four Soldati formed a tight circle around him, hissing and baring their sharp fangs. Their collective roars were terrifying. Whatever it was it couldn't be good.

Riley crouched down, his hand instinctively going to Khalon's fur. It wasn't difficult to differentiate Khalon from the others. He was much larger than the other three Soldati. Yet even if he hadn't been, Riley would've been able to pick Khalon out from among a hundred tigers. How he knew that was beyond him.

Khalon's whiskers twitched and his ears flattened against his head but he didn't object to Riley's hand on his fur. Around them, the forest plunged into silence. No birds, no rabbits, squirrels, or leaves rustling. Riley squinted as he tried to see past the trees and bushes into the dense forest. It was dark. Why was it so dark? It was still mid-afternoon. The shadows moved as one and Riley gasped, dread sweeping over him. It wasn't shadows, it was demons. And there were thousands of them.

5

KHALON ROARED, HIS call echoing through the trees, a warning to the demons that he would tear each and every one of them apart if they dared to lay a hand on Riley. He summoned the power within him, channeling it through his body, the heat spreading until a white glowing light emitted from his eyes and body. He had only to brush near a demon with his light and it would crumble to dust. With another fierce roar, he sounded the attack. His warriors drew from their own power, each one with a unique light force.

The four of them charged, slashing and leaping into the ocean of demons, all while maintaining a perimeter around Riley. Khalon would not allow them to hurt him. Perhaps the priestess had been mistaken, perhaps not. Whatever the reasons for her bringing Riley Murrough into his life, Khalon would not lose him at the hands of demons.

A wave of foul creatures gurgled up putrid poison, their stench irritating Khalon's nostrils and their shrilling cries resounding through the forests around them. Their razor sharp claws scraped at the earth as they crawled, scurried, and hobbled toward Riley.

"You have to give me something to fight with!" Riley shouted at Khalon.

Khalon hissed. No simple weapon could kill these demons. *Leave this to us,* Khalon said in his mind.

"Did you just telepathically talk to me?" Riley looked startled and Khalon would have rolled his eyes if he could. He swiped his claws at another demon, slaughtering it.

How else do you think we communicate while in this form?

Riley kept himself away from clawing demons, skirting their rotting limbs as they attempted to get nearer. A tide of demons rose, its shadow washing over Riley.

Rayner! Khalon sped toward Riley and skidded to a halt. He braced himself as his friend leaped and bound off Khalon's back to give himself the height needed to eradicate the wave of demons from its center. He landed on his paws and they continued to extinguish the foul beasts. Khalon was taken aback by Riley's resourcefulness. Despite his lack of weapons or power, he found ways to outmaneuver any approaching demons, at one point leading a hoard straight to Khalon for him to pounce on and destroy. Riley caught on fast, using himself as bait to lead the demons straight to their destruction. Demons weren't very bright, and Riley discovered this quickly. There were but a few dozen left when a demon slipped passed Ezra and hurtled toward Riley.

Behind you!

Riley didn't hesitate. He leaped out of the way, but not before the demon clawed at his arm.

Riley! Khalon swiftly dispatched of the foul creature and rushed over to Riley who sat up in the grass. He sucked in a sharp breath as he held onto his arm. *Are you all right?*

"I'm fine. Just a scratch. It burns though."

Let me see.

Riley held his arm out, his sleeve torn where the demon had caught him. The small gash was quickly turning black around the edges. Khalon licked at it, the foul stench and burn enough to make his eyes water.

"What are you doing?" Riley watched curiously.

Removing the poison. Hold still. Almost done. There.

"Thanks." Riley smiled and gave Khalon a scratch behind his ear, causing him to purr. Why the blasted hell was he purring? Riley's eyes went wide, a shadow casting over them.

"Khalon!" Riley shoved Khalon off of him with a strength Khalon hadn't known Riley possessed. Khalon went rolling. He jumped to his paws in time to see a demon slash at Riley, its claws catching him across his stomach.

Riley! No!

Riley fell onto his back spurting and coughing up blood, his hand covering his stomach as blood seeped through the shredded jerkin.

Oh Gods, no. Khalon's fury rose from within his very depths as he stood over Riley's broken and bleeding body. It was a primal rage he had never felt before, one that threatened to tear him apart from the inside out unless released. Khalon's roar shook the trees. His fur bristled and he called upon his Soldati power to free the rage demanding vengeance. A bright white ring of lightning burst from him with a deafening boom. It swept through the forest all around them, consuming and obliterating any darkness in sight and beyond, its force knocking over trees and shooting leaves in all directions. The demons screeched pitifully before bursting into ashes. Khalon destroyed them all.

"Khalon."

Riley's soft whisper caught his ear and Khalon quickly returned to human form. He pulled Riley into his arms and ran a hand over his head.

"Why would you do such a thing? After everything.... Why would you sacrifice yourself for me?"

"I know we haven't known each other long, and we kind of got off on the wrong foot, but you're a good guy, and from what I hear, a good king. You deserve your warrior prince."

Riley's words splintered Khalon's heart. "You would think me so cruel as to wish you dead, so I might claim another mate?"

Riley smiled up at him, a tear running down his cheek. "No, I don't think you're cruel. An asshole sometimes, but not cruel. Neither of us asked for this, but you needed me. I did what I had to...." Riley gasped for breath and Khalon gently shushed him. There was so much blood, and the demon poison would have spread too deep and too quickly for Khalon to stop. What good was all his kingly power if he couldn't save one human? No, not merely a human.

His prince.

Why had he fought so hard against what had been right in front of him?

"You must rest," Khalon said, placing a kiss to Riley's cheek. He held him close and let his head rest against Riley's. Soon, he would be at peace. "Forgive me, for my behavior and arrogance. You are far from frail. You are strong, brave, and worthy of the Soldati. If there is any unworthiness here, it is mine."

Riley nuzzled his face against Khalon's, his hand on Khalon's chest. "I would've liked getting to know the real Khalon." Riley's face grew ashen, his lips darkening. Khalon had been drawn to those lips only moments ago when he'd held Riley in his arms. His heart had chastised him, telling him there was more between them than he pretended. It had been evident in the connection they'd made. They could fool themselves all they liked, but they couldn't fool their hearts. Their fate had been forged since the beginning. Khalon had waited centuries, and now his arrogance had robbed him of the chance at a life with Riley.

Khalon wished he'd given in to his desire to kiss Riley earlier. Not wasting what little time remained, he placed his lips to Riley's, though their previous warmth faded quickly and Riley went limp in his arms.

As Riley departed from their world, so did Khalon's strength. The warm white light in his soul dimmed at the loss of his mate, as did his power. He had brought this upon them. "Forgive me."

Rayner crouched down beside Khalon and wrapped his arm around him, his voice laced with sorrow. "We failed you."

"No." Khalon shook his head, his body racking with shivers as the last of his Soldati strength left him. "*I* failed *him*."

"Khalon King of the Soldati, why does your heart weep for this mortal man?"

Khalon's head shot up. "Priestess."

The priestess neared, her bare feet leaving trails of tiny flowers in the grass as she walked. Her dark skin was smooth as silk, her long dark tresses untamed. Her golden eyes sparkled like the stars and her beauty was unrivaled by any other. She stopped beside him, her thumb wiping his tearstained cheek.

"I allowed my self-importance to blind me, and my mate has paid the price with his life."

"You believe the mark was placed in error. I shall therefore return to you your strength and power. You shall be gifted another mate, one who is not unsuitable to a Soldati king."

"He's *not* unsuitable," Khalon growled then recalled to whom he was speaking. "Forgive me." He drew a deep breath and released it slowly. Why was he finding it so difficult to keep his emotions under his control? Calming himself, he continued. "It's true, he is a human, and perhaps not as strong as I, but that does not mean he is unsuitable as a Soldati prince. He is strong of heart, courageous, and heaven help me, as willful as any other I have known. He did not deserve this death. This is all my doing. Had I not placed unwarranted judgement upon him, he would still live." He lowered his head in prayer that the goddess would take good care of his prince in the veil beyond.

The priestess cupped his cheek and raised his head. He was taken aback by her warm smile. "Khalon King, there is purpose in all I do. What would you sacrifice to have your prince returned to you?"

Khalon did not hesitate. "Anything."

"Your majesty," Adira interrupted cautiously. "Forgive me, but you must think about what you are saying. The loss of the human is regrettable. He was most certainly a noble man. But you are our king. What if the price is too great?"

Khalon swallowed hard. Adira was right. He had a responsibility bigger than himself, and he had known Riley for such a short time. Yet as he brushed Riley's hair from his brow, his long lashes resting against his pale cheek, Khalon's heart spoke a truth even he had been unaware of.

"He *is* my prince." Khalon gave the priestess a decisive nod. "Do what you must, but please, return him to me."

The priestess stood and stepped back. She raised her arms to her sides, her eyes glowing white. "You shall have your Soldati prince, Khalon King, as was intended." A fierce wind swept through the trees, rushing out to surround Khalon and Riley, the noise drowning out the concerned cries from his brethren. Khalon held Riley tight against him, watching as Riley's body illuminated from within. The Soldati markings around Khalon's arms moved and shifted, while Riley's marks grew. What had begun as a few bands now travelled up his arm in a pattern matching Khalon's own markings. The color returned to Riley's skin and Khalon felt his strength returning to him, along with his power.

Riley arched his back violently, his mouth opening as the white light burst free, disappearing into the sky high above them. With a groan, his prince blinked his eyes open, and Khalon noted the gold spreading from the center of Riley's irises until his eyes turned bright amber. A lock of hair on his brow darkened to pitch black.

"Riley?"

"What...what happened?" Riley frowned before turning his face to the priestess and giving a start. He clung onto Khalon, making him chuckle.

"It's all right, Riley. May I present the Great Priestess."

The priestess smiled kindly. "Welcome, Soldati prince."

Riley looked puzzled. "I don't understand. I...died. Didn't I?"

"Your king has made a great sacrifice to have you returned to him. I have granted you life, and in your true form. That of immortal Soldati."

"You mean, I can change into a tiger?" His jaw went slack. "Wait, did you say *immortal*?"

The priestess laughed softly. "You were always a Soldati. Your true form would have been revealed once your king claimed you. I simply sped up the process. All that you have been, what you will become shall be revealed to you in time. This is your destiny, Riley Murrough."

Riley's troubled gaze landed on Khalon. "What did you sacrifice to bring me back?"

They all turned their attention to the priestess who addressed Khalon, her tone gentle and void of ill will.

"A Soldati King must never deem himself worthier than those whom he protects. Your arrogance and pride have led you to this. Yet you are of kind heart, and have ruled your warriors with fairness and goodness. Your sacrifice is thus, Khalon King. Every full moon, you shall live your life as a mortal man, susceptible to mortal wounds, pain, and the frailty you so feared."

"What?" Rayner shook his head in disbelief. "But—"

"I accept," Khalon stated firmly.

"Your majesty," Adira began, her protest cut short when Khalon held up a hand for silence. He bowed his head to the priestess.

"Thank you, for your kindness and mercy. I shall do everything within my power to be worthy of you and those I have been blessed to share my life with."

The priestess put a hand to his head. "I know you will." With that, she disappeared, leaving behind the scent of blossoms and a night sky filled with dazzling stars. Each full moon would leave him vulnerable as never before, but that hardly meant he would be weak. He had his warrior heart and his prince to guide him as he discovered his human strength.

Khalon stood, bringing Riley up with him. Taking hold of his hand, he pressed it to his lips for a kiss. Near him, his warriors lowered themselves on bended knee and placed their fists over their hearts. The four of them spoke in unison.

"We honor you, Prince Riley Murrough of the Soldati, and eternally pledge our blades, our hearts, and our fidelity to you."

Riley swallowed hard. He nodded to their warriors before turning his bright amber eyes to Khalon. "I'm sorry. I don't know what to do."

Khalon kissed his cheek, the scent of his prince filling his senses. His desire and call to claim his mate threatening to overwhelm him, but he maintained a firm grip. Now was not the time. "Let us return home. There is much to discuss." Riley appeared uncertain. "What troubles you? If you fear leaving your former life behind, know you are free to visit the human world whenever you wish. You are my mate, Riley, not my prisoner." Was it possible…? Khalon swallowed hard and forced himself to speak the words. "If your happiness lies elsewhere and not at my side, I will honor your wish. You have only to speak it."

Riley stood on his toes and kissed Khalon, the taste of him awakening something deep inside him. He threw his arms around Riley and pulled him against him, deepening their kiss as the fire spread through them. Khalon could feel the heat coursing through his mate. Riley's desire for him, his need was as fierce as Khalon's, answering any misgivings Khalon possessed on whether Riley wished to remain at his side as his mate. Riley's soft moan sent a shiver through Khalon and he slipped his knee between Riley's legs, pressing up against his mate's hardening length.

A distinct clearing of the throat brought their passion to a screeching halt. Khalon pulled abruptly away, his face heated and undoubtedly as red as it felt. "I, um, forgive me," he said, sounding breathless. Goddess above, what was the matter with him? Behaving like some fledgling Soldati.

Rayner gave him a wicked look. "Perhaps we should return to the castle. We'll sneak you in the servants' entrance so that you might make it to your bedchamber without incident."

"Rayner!" Khalon scolded, his face going up in flames. Beside him Riley groaned and buried his face in Khalon's jerkin as the others giggled like children.

"Do you wish to get on with your *discussion* in private without the realm seeking to celebrate the union of you and your prince?" Rayner asked innocently, his intent anything but. "Or shall we announce your arrival and begin the festivities. It will be at least a week before you get to any...*discussing*. And then there's the coronation, the reception, the—"

"I get it," Khalon huffed. "Stop discussing our—" He made finger quotes. "Discussion."

Rayner threw his head back and laughed. He turned and walked off to the sounds of Khalon cursing him. Adira and Ezra followed, chortling along. Khalon turned to Riley who looked up at him with a bright smile.

"I think I'm going to like it here."

6

Yep, he definitely liked it here.

Riley arched his back and let out a low moan. It was taking everything he had to keep himself in control. With his newfound strength and power, he had no idea what could happen if he wasn't careful. Unfortunately control was difficult with Khalon's hard naked body pressing him into the mattress. Not that Riley was complaining.

"I find those little sounds you make very pleasing," Khalon purred before trailing kisses up Riley's torso. His strong hands roamed over Riley's body, over his stomach, down his thighs, and in between his legs. Khalon took his sweet time as he explored every curve, ever patch of skin, as if he were mapping Riley, committing every inch of him to memory. With every touch, he followed up with a taste then a kiss. It was driving Riley absolutely fucking crazy.

Riley had no idea what came next. They'd somehow managed to sneak into the castle, but not without some sleight of hand from Rayner and the others. Apparently the whole realm wanted to meet its new Soldati prince. As much as Riley wanted to oblige, neither he nor Khalon could stand to wait any longer. Every second that Khalon didn't lay claim to Riley became torturous. Their bodies were drawn to each other, a magnetic pull that caused Riley's body to physically ache with his need to have Khalon inside him. It was kind of scary.

"Are you sure this is what you want? That *I'm* what you want?" Riley asked, his toes curling and his breath hitching when Khalon's lubed finger found Riley's entrance. "I know the priestess said this is who I really am, that I've always been a Soldati prince, but I don't feel all that different. I mean, I feel stronger, and there's this weird, pulsing, warm glow inside me that I can't explain, but I'm still *me*."

"And I would not wish you to be any different." Khalon nipped at Riley's neck. "We shall face this new adventure together, guiding each other. I know you might be," he pushed a finger inside Riley, causing him to cry out in surprise, "overwhelmed."

"Bastard," Riley huffed.

Khalon chuckled and continued to stretch Riley. "But all will be well. I will be here with you, at your side. Once I have claimed you, our bond with grow stronger. More of your true self will be revealed. Whatever happens," Khalon's tone softened and he placed a kiss to Riley's lips, "we are one."

Riley slipped his arms around Khalon's neck, unable to believe this was all happening. Yet somehow it felt right. He had no idea what being a Soldati prince entailed, but he trusted Khalon. With a shuddered sigh, Riley closed his eyes and gave himself over, spreading his knees farther apart. Khalon settled in between them and lined himself up. Riley braced himself. He slipped his fingers down to Khalon's shoulders and held on tight as Khalon stretched him. His fingers dug into his lover's skin. For all of Khalon's strength and ferocity, he was also very gentle. Soon the pain and burn gave way to sweet pleasure and Riley groaned, a soft gasp escaping him as Khalon began to move.

"Khalon...."

"I love the sound of my name falling from your lips," Khalon murmured, taking hold of Riley's wrist. He brought it to his lips for a kiss before moving to the bed and lacing their fingers together. He lowered himself carefully and Riley moved his other hand to the bed so Khalon could take hold of that one as well. "You're so beautiful."

Riley looked away, embarrassed. "I'm not."

"You are, and I will spend my immortal life showing you how beautiful and good you are. The Soldati realm is fortunate to have you, Riley, as am I."

Had this happened back home, Riley would have thought he'd gone crazy. It was too soon to feel so strongly about someone who he knew so little about, yet it felt as if Khalon had always been with him. If the mark had been with Riley since birth, simply hidden, then what about his connection to Khalon?

"My prince?"

"Yeah?" Riley looked up at Khalon and the amusement evident in his sparkling green eyes.

"You are thinking far too much. Close your eyes and give yourself to me." The low husky order sent a shiver up Riley's spine and he nodded, allowing himself to think of nothing but Khalon and the slow deep thrusts that had Riley gasping for breath.

Riley's brow beaded with sweat, his skin was hot and flushed as Khalon's movements became a little quicker, his breath more ragged. It was clear he was trying his best to go slow. Riley wrapped his legs around Khalon's waist, his voice hushed in Khalon's ear.

"Give yourself to me."

Khalon smiled, a sexy crooked grin that went straight to Riley's painfully hard dick. He pulled out of Riley, and got on his knees. He twirled his finger and Riley did as he was asked. He turned onto his stomach and got on his knees, his head on the pillow. Riley expected Khalon to plunge inside him, instead Riley let out a surprised gasp when Khalon began making a meal out of him. He cursed under his breath and grabbed fistfuls of the bedsheet. Moving one hand to his dick, he stroked himself, his moans and cursing seeming to urge Khalon on. Khalon's mouth was soon replaced by his thick, hard length and Riley groaned as Khalon pushed himself in deep.

"Please." Riley wasn't above begging. He needed to feel Khalon's release.

Khalon gave him what he wanted, driving himself into Riley with deep, powerful thrusts that made the bed tremble beneath them. His fingers dug into Riley's flesh and the sound of skin slapping against skin was glorious. Riley kept up with Khalon's pace, his hand moving faster as Khalon's thrusts began to lose their rhythm. The bands on Riley's arms spun furiously as the patterns of his markings danced and shifted.

Khalon changed his angle and Riley cried out, his orgasm exploding through him, and the white light inside him flaring out through his body ignited the room like a lightning strike. He came hard, his limbs shaking from the force of his release. Khalon soon followed, his heat filling Riley and his cry drowned out by the roar of his inner light being released into the room, the thunderous sound fading only when Khalon collapsed onto the bed beside Riley. The white light in the room faded until only the warm glow of the wall sconces remained.

With a satiated smile, Riley turned and snuggled up close to Khalon who wrapped his strong arms around him. He kissed Riley's lips before they were both forced to come up for air. Riley smiled up at Khalon.

"Wow. That was... impressive."

Khalon chuckled. "It was rather exhilarating wasn't it?" He planted a kiss on the tip of Riley's nose. "My prince has quite a wicked streak."

"Admit it, you like that about me." Riley nipped at Khalon's jaw, loving the low growl his lover released.

With a playful roar, Khalon grabbed hold of Riley and rolled him onto his back. He nipped at Riley's neck before moving his lips onto Riley's for a long, deep kiss. When he pulled back, he smiled warmly down at him.

"There is much to like, my prince. You've been in my life for such a short time, yet you've changed it so much."

"So what happens now?"

"Now, you search your heart. I have claimed my prince, and in return you have laid claim to my heart. Close your eyes and listen."

Riley did as he was asked. He wasn't sure what he was listening out for, but he listened. He could hear the water flowing in a nearby fountain somewhere outside the bedroom window in the garden below. Birds chirped and crickets came out to play now that nightfall had come. All of Riley's senses were heightened, and he felt *everything*. From the gentle breeze against his skin as it drifted in past the curtains, to Khalon's heart beating in his chest. He could feel the white light inside Khalon, as if it were his soul. They were connected. Whatever Khalon felt, Riley felt. A scary thought occurred to him and his eyes flew open.

"Can you feel me? I mean, if something happens to me, can you feel it?"

Khalon took Riley's hand and kissed it. "We are one." Khalon took Riley's finger and he watched mesmerized as Khalon put the tip to one of his now elongated sharp fangs. Gently he pushed Riley's finger until he drew blood, causing Riley to suck in a sharp breath at the same moment Khalon winced. "We are connected. Your pain becomes my pain. My pain becomes yours."

Riley worried his bottom lip. "What if I'm not strong enough? I don't want you to feel pain just because I can't handle it."

"Fear not, my prince. I shall train you, show you the ways of the Soldati." His hand went to Riley's heart. "Great strength lies in you, we've only to bring it to the surface."

God, Riley hoped Khalon was right. Before he could say anything else on the matter, a huge glowing orb caught his attention. "Um, Khalon? There's a weird gold orb thing floating in your bedroom."

Khalon cursed under his breath and turned. That couldn't be good.

"What is it?"

"It's the Eye." Khalon sat up with a heavy sigh. "It sees all. It also informs us of demons slipping into the human world."

Riley sat up, his gaze on the strange orb. "So, it's kind of like an alarm system?"

"A little more complex than that, but yes. It informs us when humans are in danger and lets us know where the attack will take place. It's how we found you."

"So what now?"

"Now," Khalon stood and stretched his long muscular body much like the tiger dormant inside him would stretch. "I'm afraid I must leave you." He kissed Riley's lips and headed for the wardrobe.

"Leave? Wait, you're going after those things?" Riley climbed out of bed and grabbed the discarded robe on the wingback chair.

"That is what we do, Riley. We protect against the demons." Khalon opened his wardrobe and began removing clothes from it.

"Then I'm coming with you."

"No." Khalon tossed his clothes onto the chair and crossed the room to draw Riley into his arms. "You have yet to grow accustomed to your Soldati body. You haven't even shifted yet. When you do, your limbs will seem to be uncooperative and it will be almost like learning to walk anew. Please, I cannot allow you to face this danger until you are ready. It could be perilous for the both of us. You know I speak the truth."

Riley wrinkled his nose. Khalon was right. Didn't mean he had to like it though. Was he supposed to just sit here while Khalon faced those bastards without him? He wanted desperately to help but he didn't want to put anyone in danger, which is what would happen if Khalon had to be worrying about his safety while trying to take down a bunch of demons.

"Stay here," Khalon said softly, delivering a feathery kiss to Riley's temple. "Explore the castle, get to know the realm. I will assign guards to accompany you."

"Can Toka come with me?"

Khalon looked surprised by the request. "If it would please you."

"I like talking to him." He also had a feeling Toka knew what it felt like to watch someone he cared about walk off to battle.

Khalon's smile reached his eyes. "Then all the more. Now dress. I would like for you to see me off."

Riley nodded. He quickly got dressed in his princely garb, which was another thing that would take getting used to. It was a lot more leather than he usually—ever—wore. He finished lacing up his boots then took Khalon's hand, pausing at the door long enough to take a deep steady breath.

"They will love you. Simply be yourself." Khalon kissed his cheek and they left the room. As they walked hand in hand down the castle corridor, everyone they walked by bowed. It was the strangest sensation. Usually when Riley had walked down the street it was like he'd been invisible. There were times when he'd had so many people bump into him he'd felt like one of the bumper cars at the fair. Now, everyone bowed and addressed him as His Highness. They looked at him like he was some kind of movie star.

Outside the main doors, Rayner, Adira, and Ezra waited, along with what seemed like everyone in the realm. Khalon's warriors all knelt the moment they saw Riley. With a proud smile, Khalon turned to Riley and pulled him close. He leaned in to whisper in his ear.

"Your people care greatly for you, Riley Murrough, as do I." He wrapped an arm around Riley and pulled him close, a wicked smile on his face before he kissed Riley to the sounds of cheers and catcalls. When Riley was all but out of breath, Khalon pulled away. "A little something to keep me in your thoughts until I return."

"Bastard," Riley said through a shaky laugh, the rest of the crowd joining him. He put his hand to Khalon's cheek, telling himself he'd be joining Khalon soon enough. "Be safe."

Khalon turned his face to kiss Riley's palm. "I shall." With a wink, he turned and motioned for his warriors to follow. With the wave of his hand, Khalon stepped forward and disappeared, the others swiftly following. Riley inhaled sharply at the sudden sense of loss. He put his hand to his heart and rubbed at his chest. He didn't like that feeling one bit. Toka stepped up beside him, and Riley spoke so only Toka would hear him.

"Does it ever stop feeling so horrible?"

Toka shook his head sadly, his eyes on the spot where Rayner had disappeared. "He takes my heart with him every time he goes off to battle, leaving me hollow until his return."

As Riley stood there, the breeze sweeping through his hair and before him a magical realm he wouldn't have been able to conjure up even in the greatest depths of his imagination, he felt a warm loving glow spread through him. His arm itched and he looked down at it, smiling when the bands and the patterns of his mark began to move.

"He's thinking of you," Toka said with a warm smile.

Riley's heart swelled and he hoped Khalon could feel Riley thinking about him as well. He turned to face his people, all of whom had waited centuries for his arrival. Riley had no intention of letting them or Khalon down. There was so much to do and get used to. There was his warrior training, his tiger training, and a coronation to prepare for, not to mention finding a way to tell his mom about his new boyfriend/mate without the whole moving to another realm to live as a tiger shifter prince part. That should prove interesting.

His life as barista Riley Murrough might be over, but his life as Prince of the Soldati was just beginning. With a confident grin, Riley headed toward the castle's main doors. He was going to rock at being a prince.

One Hex Too Many

LOU HARPER

I KNEW IT was going to be a taxing day the moment I pried my eyelids open. Perhaps it was precognition, perhaps the sight of dark clouds through the many windows of my loft. After a long Indian summer, October barged in baring its teeth. Those clouds were ominous enough to have floated off a pulp horror cover.

The alarm clock I hadn't set showed 9 a.m.—time to drag my sorry ass out of bed. Tossing covers aside, I rose and shambled off to the bathroom. I drained the snake and turned on the tap to splash cold water on my face.

A blond man with blue eyes and cheekbones sharp enough to etch crystal looked at me from the mirror. Even my regrettably caffeine-starved brain registered the wrongness of this image. I knew for a fact that my own coloration was dull brown and the less was said of my cheekbones, the better.

Mirror-man waited patiently while I stared. His good looks were as overdramatic as the sky outside. His left brow twitched in a familiar way. "Good morning, Detective Mulligan."

"Good morning, Leslie," I said. "To what do I owe the pleasure?" I was aiming for sarcasm but I'd had too few hours of sleep to hit the bullseye.

He gave me a toothy smile. "I'm happy to see you too, Buttercup. Or should I say Teddybear?"

I scratched my—admittedly hairy—chest. "Whatever you want, Les, just get on with it." Leslie Morland, assistant to Captain Karl Parker, my boss, had many excellent qualities. Short-windedness wasn't one of them.

"The Captain wants to see you as soon as you get in."

"You could've called on the phone, like normal people. Or, even better, leave a note on my desk."

"Biannual test of alternate communications—Captain's mandate." His lips formed a lewd curve. "And I wouldn't want to pass up my chance to see you in your morning glory. Besides, I wanted to be sure you actually made it in before noon."

"I had a late night," I grumbled, and it was true—I hadn't gotten home from the stakeout till the wee hours.

"So I heard. Nonetheless, Captain Parker would love to see you in person, the sooner the better. I've been waiting for you to rise for the last twenty minutes. You should really put a mirror into your bedroom." His leer deepened. "Over the bed would be ideal."

"Not in your dreams," I retorted. Departmental use of mirrors for communications was strictly regulated and safeguarded with multiple layers of security hexes, but nothing was ever a hundred percent safe. There was always a small chance one of those rogue hacker wizards—wackers for short—could get through. In over a decade on the Force I developed a healthy dose of paranoia.

Leslie pursed his lips—they got a lot of exercise. "I beg to differ, Mike. Everything's possible in my dreams." His voice switched to business—more or less. "Pleasantries aside, when can we expect you to grace us with your manly presence?"

"Forty minutes. Now go away; I need to shave."

The Extramundane Crimes Division took up the entire fifth floor of the new Downtown Police headquarters. Not because there were so many of us, but because a history of unfortunate incidents had proved the necessity of keeping most things extramundane at one self-containable area. The last thing you wanted was for a runaway warlock to stumble into Vice summoning flame imps. True story.

The old station had had buckets of nineteenth century architectural charm and zero twenty-first century functionality. Fortunately, when the city of New Skye finally coughed up the money for the construction of a new one, the architects kept our particular needs in mind. How we hadn't ended up in the basement was a miracle.

The squad room was a large space populated by office desks in a random arrangement, as a result of new theories of workplace design. They stood in pairs as if ready to breed. Chief Parker's office stood at the far end of this sprawl.

Leslie's desk—with Leslie behind it—held guard up front, though he was in charge of all our administrative needs. And the office supplies, naturally.

As I approached he looked up from his computer and jerked his head toward the office. "Go right in, Mike."

Through the open blinds I could seen Parker's massive figure behind the desk. He wasn't alone—another man sat across from him, shoulders slightly hunched in the pose of a subordinate. I tapped the glass door once and stepped in. "Captain?"

"Detective Mulligan. Come in." He swept a large hand in the direction of his other guest. "This is Detective Hugh Fox. Detective Fox is joining our department."

The man in question stood, smiled too amiably, and offered his hand. "Honored to meet you."

I took a quick assessment of him: height average, age no more than thirty, body lean, hair short and dirty blond, face eager. His whole body radiated eagerness, but I caught a brief but sharp glint in his eyes—he was reading me as I read him.

I nodded, murmured something polite, and we sat.

"Good job last night on the Stilton case," Parker said, training his eyes on me.

"Yes, sir. And thank you." I waited for Parker to tell me why I was there.

"Detective Fox served five years in uniform in the Twelfth Precinct and recently passed his detective exam with flying colors. He's a high four on the M-scale and is a Perceptive."

"Naturally," I said. A Perceptive was someone with acute ability to sense magic, aka theurgic energies. All Extras were Perceptives; it was a job requirement. So why was the Captain telling me this? For him it practically counted as gushing, and he wasn't the gushing kind. Parker went on. "But we all know there's more to this job than book-knowledge and theurgical talents. Detective Fox will need to learn the ropes from a seasoned investigator."

The penny dropped, and kept flitting and pinging. "Me?" I asked in disbelief.

"Of course. Who better? You have plenty of experience and happen to be solo at the moment."

A very long moment. "But—"

Parker cut me off, directing his benevolent smile at Fox. "Detective Fox, would you mind stepping outside? I'm certain Leslie has a stack of paperwork for you to sign."

Fox sprang to his feet. "Of course. Thank you for your time, Captain Parker." His gaze brushed past me as he marched out.

"I work alone," I said once the door shut.

"Because you're a maverick cop who plays by his own rules?" Parker had a good poker face, only the slightest twitch in the corner of his mouth betrayed he was mocking me.

I ignored it. "You know why."

"Do you really believe you're cursed?" he asked.

I didn't know what I believed. I tipped my head, indicating the squad room. "They do."

He snorted. "Cops are more superstitious than a clutch of old crones. Extras especially. You've been tested. By the foremost experts of the field. They all declared you curse-free."

"I lost six partners in five years. That's a hell of a run of bad luck," I retorted.

Parker didn't budge. "Only one of them died, and not even on duty."

"What about Carillo?"

"Carillo was careless. He should've known better."

Parker was right, of course. I spread my hands. "So you give me a rookie. Isn't it like playing a game of Russian roulette with the Fates?"

Parker bestowed a benevolent smile on me. "I'm sure it'll be fine. Besides, nobody else wants to partner with you. It's a simple administrative decision."

He didn't fool me. He was a black man in a white man's world. Built like a brick outhouse, he could intimidate a suspect simply by looming over the poor fucker. He'd made captain young, but he didn't get where he was just by his looks; Parker was smart. People who underestimated him based on his looks lived to regret it. If they were lucky. I was no such fool. "What's the catch?" I asked.

"No catch. He's what I told you. You take him around the block and show him what's what. If he has what it takes to be an Extra, we keep him. If not, we throw him back into the pool. Now, don't you have some work to do?" I was dismissed.

I found my new partner at his new desk—the one butting against mine. Leslie was leaning against it, explaining office policies in a sensual drawl that made duty rotation sound X-rated. Since I'd last seen him, Fox had gone through a remarkable transformation: his face had acquired a rosy hue and droplets of perspiration condensed on his temple. In many ways he resembled a boiled crab. *Time for a rescue.*

I stepped up and said, "Dial it back, Les. The kid's brand new, can't you see? You'll break him."

Leslie gave me a look of smoldering defiance. "Mike, your concern is duly noted. I'm about to show Detective Fox around."

"I'll do it. We wouldn't want to keep you from your many duties," I said.

"Spoilsport." He sashayed away.

I motioned at Fox. "C'mon."

Out in the hallway he sighed with obvious relief. "Thanks, man. Leslie has a very strong charm. And I'm not even gay. Not that there's anything wrong with it," he added in a rush. He turned even redder. So he knew about me. Good, it saved time. "What I meant—"

"I know what you meant. The magic is strong with Leslie Morland."

"Clearly. I've heard the Extramundane Division did things differently, but isn't it against regulations to use charm spells at work? Not to mention sexual harassment issues."

I had the urge to come to Leslie's defense. "It's not what you think. Leslie's antics are part of our training. Using charm spells, especially on detectives, is a common practice among theurgically abled criminals. Fortunately, regular exposure builds up tolerance. In a few weeks you won't even notice Leslie."

He considered this. "Is this a standard practice? I've never heard of it before."

"Nah. Parker's experimental initiative."

"I see. What about the glamour?"

"Ah. You noticed. Good job," I added because not everyone cottoned on so quick. "Leslie changes body and face about once a week. Sometimes male, sometimes female."

"Is it also part of the training?"

"Beats me. But don't even try to see through it. You'll only give yourself a headache—it's impenetrable, I tried. We all did."

"Oh." Fox wore the expression of a man who had too many questions and didn't know where to start.

I decided to dump all the answers on him at once. "No, we don't know what he really looks like, if Leslie is male or female." *Or if he's even fully human*, I added only to myself.

Official policy prohibited hiring of non-humans in any capacity to the Police Department, although the Fae Rights League was lobbying hard to change the status quo. Surely, Parker wouldn't thumb his nose at departmental policy, would he?

I shook the suspicion out of my head. "You can call Leslie he or she—he has no preference. I go with he because it feels right. Les changing bodies will be confusing as hell for you at first, but you'll soon get used to it."

"How do you know it's really him?" he asked.

"You just do. Probably the body language," I replied, though I knew there was more to it. We arrived to a heavy door at the end of the hall. "Here we are: Extramundane Forensics."

As I'd promised, I introduced Fox around. After the forensics I showed him where everything was, including the interrogation rooms—magic-shielded, of course—and left him at the armory to collect his vest, weapon, etc.

I was busy boxing up the Stilton files for the archives as he returned. He proceeded to check his desk drawers, procuring necessary office supplies, and generally settling in.

Our domesticity didn't last long; Leslie marched up with purpose, his aura of charm dialed to a low hum. "Got a new one for you, Mike." He dropped a piece of notepaper on my desk.

"What's the case?" I asked, looking at the address.

"Suspicious death."

Our destination proved to be in Colby—an all right neighborhood, with small houses of the working middle class, sliding toward shabby to the South. 7523 Brighton Street was a three-story apartment building with four apartments on each floor, two on either side of a central staircase.

Detective Jablonsky from Violent Crimes greeted us on the third floor, at the door of apartment eleven. We'd worked together on a case once, years ago. I liked him; he was thorough and a good cop. "Mulligan," he said in greeting, but his eyes, full of questions, were on Fox. I introduced them to each other.

"Whatcha got?" I asked.

He jabbed his thumb in the air, pointing behind him. "Stiff's in the bathroom." He glanced at his notes. "Dan Roberts, thirty, single. Downstairs neighbor noticed the water coming from his ceiling. When Roberts didn't open the door, the manager used his key to enter the premises and found the deceased in the tub, the water still running." All the while he talked his gaze kept returning to Fox as if calculating his bet for the office pool. The tale of my curse had spread far and wide.

"Gonna let us in?" I asked pointedly.

He stepped back and waved us in. "The photographer's with the stiff at the moment. You can take your turn soon enough."

It became clear right away why we'd been called in. The living room could've been a magic shop display case—dreamcatchers, witch balls, candles, bundles of herbs, figurines, and tokens were everywhere. Completely useless, the whole bunch of them—the occult equivalent of snake oil. Their combined power couldn't have averted a bloodthirsty mosquito.

"Protective charms, but inert," commented Fox. He noticed it too. Good.

Slater, the assistant coroner, appeared. He was one of the rare people whose physical appearance perfectly matched their professions. With his gaunt figure, sallow face, and nicotine-stained teeth he couldn't have been more cadaverous, short of being one of his own clients. Strangely, he'd looked exactly the same when I'd first met him a decade ago.

He mumbled a greeting while peeling wet latex gloves off his hands. He stared at Fox too.

"Mulligan's new partner," Jablonsky explained.

"So young," he said in the somber tones of a funeral director.

They were getting on my nerves. "Cause of death?" I snapped.

Slater turned his mournful eyes to me. "Drowning. Reason unknown. I'm ordering an autopsy."

"Sign of struggle?"

"None. No visible injuries or marks."

The police photographer stepped out of the bathroom and I motioned to Fox to follow me. We donned our gloves as we went. I stopped at the doorway to take in the scene. It was a narrow room, toilet and sink to the left, towel rack to the right, tub straight ahead. Not particularly clean or orderly, but not in great disarray either. The dead man lay under the water, mouth open, eyes staring. He appeared surprised.

Not unlike a chemical reaction, magic spells left their mark on their subject. Perceptives like us picked up this residuum like dogs a scent. The name for this talent was Extramundane Perception—EMP for short.

Every type of magic, every spell, left subtly different residuum. I could sense this one from the door, but up close to the dead man it was strong enough to make my skin crawl and ghosts stir in the back of my mind.

But this wasn't my first trip around the block; I kept my face blank and my voice level as I motioned to Fox to switch positions. "Tell me what you feel," I said as he crouched by the tub.

Fox closed his eyes. Shutting off your other senses, at least the ones you could, opened up your magic perception, but it was a rookie move. I'd have to lecture him about it later but not right now, not in front of others.

He wrinkled his nose. "Decay, slimy and putrid. Something else..." he hesitated. EMP was not as tangible as the other senses, closer to emotions and memory than anything else. Everyone experienced it differently. "Acrid," he said at last. "Is it…?" He turned to me, looking a little green.

I nodded. "Theurgy of Virulence, aka dark magic." The chances of Dan Roberts having had a stroke or epileptic seizure was down to zero. Dark magic was heavy shit, right up there with kidnapping and murder, barely a notch below terrorism. It was on the top of the List of Prohibited Practices.

Regular cops left the collection of trace evidence to the forensics people, but magical evidence had an impermanent nature. We all kept an evidence kit in our cars, just in case. I'd grabbed mine before we came up. Now I retrieved an enchanted glass vial, took a sample of the bath water, and labeled it.

A natural body of water, especially running water, was a piss-poor medium for retaining residua, but a tubful of tap water was a different matter. I put the sample away and proceeded to inspect the contents of the medicine cabinet and the cupboard under the sink. I came up empty.

"Foul play then?" Jablonsky asked, watching us from the door.

"Deadly use of prohibited magic if I ever saw it. Have him wrapped up and rushed to the morgue."

On account of the ephemeral nature of theurgical evidence, magic-related homicides always jumped to the top of the autopsy queue.

Fox and I walked through the rest of the apartment, but aside from another clutter of faux-occult junk we found nothing magic related. Since Jablonsky's people were already on the scene, we left it for them to collect the rest of the forensic evidence, while we went off to talk to the building manager.

"Mr. Kovaltchek complained about Roberts a lot, loud music, whatnot, but Kovaltchek complains about everyone," explained Shamon, a worn-faced, middle aged man. "But the water was really dripping from his ceiling, so I went up there and banged on Dan's door, and when there was no answer, I unlocked it and went inside." He yawned and scratched his chest through his T-shirt.

"And found the deceased," I said to move things along.

"Yeah. He was floating in the tub like a drowned rat. The water was still running. I called the cops."

Instead of serving up the next logical question, I kept scribbling on my notepad. I wanted to know if Fox would jump in without prompting.

He did. "Did you touch anything, Mr. Shamon?" Fox asked.

The manager shrugged. "The tap, of course. I had to shut the water off, didn't I? And the doorknobs."

Fox continued the questioning. "Did you notice anything unusual?"

"Aside from him being dead? No."

"How about the occult items in the living room?"

He shrugged. "That junk? Seen worse. We once had a hoarder. And a guy with a half a dozen pixies. You wouldn't believe the mess they made. He was evicted." No surprise, pixies were nasty little buggers, and didn't belong indoors.

Fox hesitated and I took back the reins. We were starting to develop a rhythm. "How long has Roberts been living here?"

Shamon screwed up his face. "Let's see... He moved in last the spring, so it's been a year and a half."

"Did he get along with the other neighbors?"

"You'd have to ask them. I work nights, so I don't see much of them."

"Do you know if Mr. Roberts had any enemies? Did he mention anyone giving him trouble recently?"

"If he did, he didn't tell me. My wife will be home around five—she'd know more."

I asked him for a list of all the tenants, names, apartment and phone numbers. "You'll only find Mr. Kovaltchek in. Everyone else is at work."

"We'll be back in the evening," I assured him.

He gave an approving nod. "They should all be home by six or seven. Except Miss Yeates."

"How so?"

"She's a traveling nurse. Off for weeks at a time. Been gone for days."

The manager was right. The sole tenant home in the whole building was Mr. Kowaltchek, and he had a grievance about all the others. "They must think they're the only people on earth from the way they behave," he griped with an asthmatic wheeze. "And if you remind them to turn their music down after ten or wipe their feet before coming in so they don't drag the mud all over the stairs others have to use too, then they tell you to mind your own business. Well, it is my business! I'm a tenant here too, just like them, and it's my right not to live like a swine!"

The old guy was ready to gallop off on his hobbyhorse, and I needed to rein him in. "How well did you know Mr. Roberts?" I asked.

He scowled. "Well enough. Heavy footed, inconsiderate clod. Just last week he was hammering at eleven at night. Eleven! When I knocked on his door and asked him politely to comply with the lease terms that state clearly no loud noises after ten o'clock, he called me a nosy old fool. Can you believe it?"

I declined to comment. "Has Roberts ever mentioned anyone who wanted to do him harm?"

"He didn't tell me anything. But I'm not surprised," he said with glee.

I did another go at prying something useful out of the old guy. "Is there anything else you could tell us about Mr. Roberts? Not noise related?" I added quickly.

"He used to drive a flashy car until he smashed it up. Served him right." Kowaltchek's already sour expression turned acidic. "And he brought women home all the time. Different ones, and not very respectable ones, if you ask me."

"Did you talk to any of these women?" I asked, hiding my excitement. Finally we were getting somewhere.

He glared at me from a depth of indignation. "Absolutely not! I do not consort with women of that kind."

Doth protests too hard, I thought, but said only, "You must've seen them coming in." I pointed at the living room window looking onto the street. A worn old chair faced it—perfect perch for people watching.

"I'm a member of the neighborhood watch," he huffed and it turned into a cough.

"Most valuable undertaking," I said mildly when he stopped hacking. "The neighborhood watch program is a vital tool of crime prevention."

"Exactly," he said, placated. "All sorts of hoodlums hang around here."

"I'm sure. So about Mr. Roberts' lady friends...."

"Lady...." He made a phlegmy sound, but didn't fall into another coughing fit. "I couldn't have seen them because they came through the back door from the parking lot. One time—" he said with emphasis— "I happened to be going out that way when they were coming in. I was taking the trash out, you see, the dumpster's out back. But that jackass was so rude to me, afterwards I made sure I stayed out of his way."

"So how do you know they were different women?"

"I heard them. I have good hearing, and they'd never even tried to keep it down. Lots of talking and laughing, and other noises, if you know what I mean. Though lately, for several months I think it was the same woman. I don't know who."

I kept the interview up for a while longer, but didn't get anything relevant out of him.

We knocked on the doors of the remaining apartments, but as predicted, nobody was in.

2

The silence in the car teemed with unspoken words. I glanced sideways—Fox's eyes were on me, narrowed, assessing. This time he kept them on me instead of retreating behind the polite façade. I hadn't been the subject such intense scrutiny by another man for long time. An uninvited but not unwelcome thrill skipped down my spine like a playful pixie.

I turned my attention back to the road and concentrated on getting us back to the office.

"Something you're not telling me," Fox said.

I had an inkling what he meant but played ignorant. "I haven't told you a lot of things. You'll need to narrow down the field."

"Something to do with you and me partnering up," he replied, brushing aside my lame evasion. "It started this morning; whenever I told someone I'd be your partner they were giving me an odd look. Like they knew something I didn't. And now Jablonsky and Slater were doing the same."

"Perceptive. You might make a detective yet," I joked.

He must have had the patience of a golem, because he went on without a hint of irritation. "Thanks. So, what is it?"

There was no point in trying to keep it a secret—sooner or later someone would spill the beans and it might as well be me. "I'm supposed to be cursed."

"Supposed to be?" He asked more amused than concerned.

"I've gone to three different specialists, who put me through every test that exists, and every single one came up negative." I lifted a finger before he could speak. "On the other hand, none of my partners have lasted a year."

He blanched a little. "They died?"

"No! Well one, but it was a car crash, nothing to do with the job."

"What happened to your other partners?"

"Oh, this and that. Transfer, early retirement, one of them moved to Australia to become a shark conservationist—it had been his childhood dream and just couldn't resist the call any longer. And then there was Carillo. He was the last one." The memory of Carillo's mishap still sat heavily on my chest. He'd been my favorite partner.

"Go on," Fox prodded.

I sighed and dove into the story. "We were on a low-key case, battery and assault—a mugging gone wrong. Carillo was following up some flimsy lead, just to be able to cross it out. I was at court that day. To cut a long story short, Carillo knocked on the door of a potential witness and got the full blast of a polymorph spell straight in the chest. He turned into a gray tabby."

Fox gasped. "A cat?"

"Yup."

"Cripes!"

"I'd never seen anything like it." Shape-changing humans—with a few notable exceptions—was prohibited, and not to mention damn difficult.

"But how and why? And who?"

"A level seven animist from Alabama on the run from his guild and the police. Somehow he'd managed to scramble his own brain communing with the flora and fauna too hard."

Something didn't come from nothing; active use of magic drew power from the Practitioner. Overexertion, whether through prolonged strain or one big burst of magic, had harmful physiological effects. To put it bluntly: you could turn your own brain to jelly.

"He thought Carillo was there to arrest him. The guy was deep in paranoid delusions by then. And Carillo, the stupid bastard, didn't wear his vest. He'd said it made him itchy."

Anyone could go through the motions of magic, just as anyone could bang on piano keys. But it took talent, work, and discipline to make music. And a shit-ton of all three to become a virtuoso. Most people worshipped and envied virtuosos. I didn't. The higher the M-level, the bigger the danger of the Practitioner becoming unstable. Especially if they lacked self-control.

Theoretically, the scale went to twelve, but there had been only a handful of confirmed tens in the past two centuries, and even eights were uncommon.

"Did you catch the perp?"

"Sure, but it was no great feat. That last spell did him in. He was a gibbering mess curled in a fetal position when we found him. As far as I know, he's still at the Beanham Sanatorium talking to his mashed potatoes."

"And Carillo?"

"Doctor Watanabe over at the Panacea Theurgical Hospital eventually succeeded in reversing the spell and put Carillo into human form again, but not quite as good as new. He developed narcolepsy. A detective who nods off at random moments isn't much good. They offered him a desk job, but he took medical retirement instead."

"That's one fucked up story. Now I see why people think you're jinxed."

"Carillo's doing fine," I said, mostly to my own comfort. "He took up vegetable gardening, and spends most of his time in the backyard, puttering about between naps. I suspect his wife prefers him this way. Last time I paid a visit I came away with a bag of heirloom tomatoes."

Fox took a moment to consider the information before passing judgment. "I don't see how what happened to Carillo has to do with you. You weren't even there."

I could've tried to argue, but didn't. Fox was growing on me by the minute, and hoped he stuck around for a while.

Upon returning to headquarters I suggested lunch at the cafeteria, but Fox had some paperwork to take care of at HR. So I took the elevator straight to the fifth floor and dropped off the water sample at forensics. Before I could go back down Leslie caught me—Captain Parker wanted a word.

"How's the case?" he asked without preamble.

"Definitely dark magic," I told him. "No solid leads yet." I filled him in on the few things we knew so far.

"Any chance of PB involvement?" he asked when I finished. Preternatural Being was the official term for the fae—the non-human sentient beings and their minions who lived with us.

I shrugged. "So far nothing has suggested more than human magic." Fae magic tended to be either inconspicuous or brutally obvious. This in-between stuff wasn't their MO.

Parker expressed his satisfaction with the curtest of nods. "What's your take on Fox?"

The change of direction startled me only for a second. "Too early to tell, but he seems fine so far. Good senses, observant. Eager to learn."

Parker expression was suspiciously neutral hearing my answer. "Good. Keep me updated." He didn't specify whether on the case or on Fox.

I inhaled lunch and legged it back to my desk. Fox joined me shortly after.

"What do we do next?" he asked. Following my example, he'd loosened his tie and was rolling up his shirt sleeves. His jacket hung from the back of his chair.

I took the list Shamon had given us, tore it in half and handed half to Fox. "We find out everything we can about the other tenants. See if any of them is a Practitioner. This type of targeted magic is easiest to do from close by."

Fox had misgivings. "You think the perp is registered?"

"We'll see." In the US, federal law required everyone at M-level one or above to be registered, even if they didn't practice. It was printed on driver's licenses as well. Of course, when there was a law, there were lawbreakers, but you couldn't join an accredited guild and receive proper training without registering.

Fox took his half of the list but didn't spring straight into the search. "That acrid sensation at the scene, does dark magic always feel that way?" He winced at the recall.

"To you, yes." I replied with a twinge of empathy. The first time was always the most unpleasant. The residuum of dark magic touched your worst memories. To me it brought back the heart-pounding horror of watching the boy I loved destroy himself. But this wasn't about me, so I put a positive spin on the situation. "You're lucky to run into it so soon. They teach you about it at the Academy, of course, but don't show you—it's too dangerous." Dark magic was addictive, and didn't I know it.

"Have you ever come across it before?"

"Once or twice." The first time it nearly killed me. "It's the vilest and most dangerous thing out there. And not just to its victim. Dark magic takes a piece of your soul every time you use it." It sucked your life force too. Dash was turning gray at sixteen. If he wasn't so blond others would've noticed it too, not just me.

He must've heard this before. "Makes you wonder why anyone gets into it at all."

"For the same reason people try crystal meth. Stupidity. Arrogance. They think they can dabble with it, just for kicks, but it's like the worst drug squared—once you start you can't stop." Dark magic turned my beautiful vibrant Dash into a wreck, but he still couldn't quit it. If only I'd done something sooner... The inescapable wave of guilt stole my breath for a moment.

"You okay?" Fox asked with a deep frown of concern.

I had to pull my shit together, so I did. I shoved the past back into the dark corner where it belonged. "Yeah, I'm fine. What I was going to say is that there are easier and safer ways to kill a man. This murder was personal." I waved my half of the list. "My gut tells me the answer is here."

So we set to work. I called the offices of the management company that owned the Roberts' building, and told them to fax over the lease applications of all the current tenants. The next step was to search them through various databases, starting with DMV records.

Most of a cop's job consisted of mundane stuff like this. TV shows like *ECD, New Skye* and its many spin-offs made people think the workday of an extramundane investigator was full of car chases and deadly exchanges of magic. Oh, and spiffy gadgets that could tell you the perp's magical specialization from a whiff of residuum. As if.

In reality, you rarely cast a serious spell on the job. The paperwork that followed was punitive. But I figured the realistic portrayal of a cop's job would've made for boring television.

A tickle to my sixth sense made me look up from the computer and I saw Fox watching Leslie by the file cabinets. With a tiny jolt I recognized something very familiar in Fox's gaze—lust. Definitely. Our boy wasn't half as straight as he claimed to be. *Well, well.*

I followed his gaze. Bending and stretching, Leslie showed a fine figure, but it did nothing for me, because it wasn't real. I knew, I was strange that way, but I'd always preferred the gritty and flawed reality to the glossy magazine version of it.

Speaking of gritty reality, I turned my attention back to Fox, and gave him the once-over he deserved. He had an unremarkable face at first glance, but at closer scrutiny I noted the sensuous curve of his lips. The willful line of his jaw balanced out his otherwise boyish features. His eyes were his best feature though—they betrayed a quick and inquisitive mind.

His body—what I could see—was made out of streamlined muscles. Yeah, I wouldn't have kicked him out of the bed for eating crackers. For an idle moment I imagined the two of us in bed—sans crackers. It was a compelling picture, one I'd have to explore later, under different circumstances.

I felt no shame over my fantasies. I was a healthy hot blooded male; I sized up other men, gay, straight, or undecided. It didn't mean I was going to do anything about it. My hetero counterparts did the same regarding women. And I bet the women's thoughts weren't any more pure either. Good thing too, purity was a dull business.

Apropos of dull business, I turned my attention back to the DMV database. Fox too stopped ogling Les, and we sunk into the routine of police work.

"What level are you?" Fox asked out of the blue. "If you don't mind me asking."

I shrugged while trying to look innocent. "At last evaluation I registered at low five." Yearly checks were mandatory for cops, along with weapons qualification and a full physical. For some, their M-level was a matter of pride or shame. Not for me. It's not the size of your magic talent that counts but what you do with it.

Fox nodded and went back to his search. I tried to do the same, but my attention wandered. This case stirred up memories I preferred unstirred.

The talent generally emerged in puberty, and every child between the ages of twelve and sixteen went through yearly mandatory testing. There were the rare child prodigies who manifested early. They usually ended up in specialized boarding schools—either private or government run—where they were monitored 24/7 to keep them from frying their little brains.

I was a late starter—my abilities didn't manifest till I was sixteen. Good thing too, at least by then I was past the whole sexual awakening thing, though still raging with hormones. And in love with Dashiell Fairthorne, a talented and reckless young practitioner-to-be who thought he could handle a little dark magic. He'd been wrong, and I, like an idiot, had stood by, watching him go off the rails and turn into a warlock. The memory chilled me to the marrow.

Leslie's hand on my shoulder roused me from my ruminations. He squeezed and dropped a handful of faxes on the desk before drifting away. You had to give it to Les—he knew when not to say a word.

I studied the tenant applications. There were eleven of them—the one for Erin Yeates was missing. I called the management company and got an unenthusiastic secretary on the line. I gave her my name and purpose, and stressed how much she didn't want to see me in person. She gave in and went off to search for the missing record.

As I waited, my gaze wandered around the squad room. Most detectives were out, except for Nash, who was furiously tapping away on her laptop, and her partner Martindale, who was on the phone like me. Leslie sat behind his desk pensively rubbing his cheek. When he noticed me looking he gave a smile, but a small one, without the usual innuendo. For the millionth time I wondered what the real Leslie Morland looked like.

"Hello? Detective Mulligan?" came the secretary's voice from the phone.

My attention snapped back to work. "Yes, I'm here."

"Ms. Yeates never filled out an application," she said.

"How's that possible?"

"Simple—she was added to somebody else's lease. A relative's."

I got the original tenant's name out of her—Mrs. Camille Holland—and hung up.

Soon I learned that our Erin Yeates had no driver's license or ID card issued in this state. There were only four people with that name in the records, but their addresses didn't match. All four were M-negative, but I printed out their driver's license photos anyway.

"Found something?" Fox asked.

I told him.

"Yeates is the traveling nurse in apartment twelve, right?"

"Right next door to the victim. Have you found anything yet?" I asked.

"Not much. Dan Roberts was arrested for drunk driving in January. He'd already had too many points because of a slew of speeding tickets, so his license was suspended. A little over a month ago his car was found wrapped around a lamp post. There was blood on the steering wheel but there was no driver to be found."

"Interesting."

"He reported the car stolen minutes before the police knocked on his door. According to Officer Russwell, Robert had a black eye that he claimed he'd got in a fight."

"Did they get him for driving without a license?"

"Not quite. Roberts hired himself one of those traffic lawyers who advertise on the sides of buses. The lawyer got him off the hook."

It must've cost Roberts a pretty penny. "The man sounds like trouble waiting to happen."

"You think there's a connection with the murder?" Fox asked.

"I don't know. Let's keep digging."

My prime suspect was Ms. Yeates, but it was no reason to disregard the others just yet. The obvious solution was the correct one far more often than crime novels would lead you to believe, but not always. Everyone had their secrets, something in their past they didn't want you to know about. For example, Mr. Randolph Kowaltchek was not only three times divorced, but one of his wives had taken out a restraining order against him. On account of harassment.

I checked for Erin Yeates in the central guild registry, but came up empty.

The clerk from the Medical Examiner's office called at quarter to four, letting me know that Mr. Robert's autopsy was done.

I thanked him and told him we'd stop by to pick up the report in person.

"C'mon, we're gonna go see about a corpse," I told Fox, rolling down my shirt sleeves. "Grab your jacket, it's cold down there."

When we arrived at the autopsy room, Jablonsky and Dr. Anika Nayar were discussing the weather. I couldn't help but notice how the normally slouchy Jablonsky stood ramrod straight. Dr. Nayar had this effect on most men. She had the kind of exotic beauty that turned heads. It also made people forget how good she was at her job.

The mortal remains of Mr. Roberts were there too, under a white plastic sheet, thank goodness. I'd seen plenty of stiffs in fifteen years on the Force, but bodies laid out on stainless steel gurneys like slabs of meat still gave me the chills.

"The Extra special Duo is here," Jablonsky said theatrically. "Give it to us straight, doc." The poor man turned into a clown around pretty women.

"Extramundane, as in exceptionally dull," I corrected him.

After the obligatory introductions and Dr. Nayar giving Fox a pitying look, she launched into a speech about corpus-this and cingulate-that.

"Could you dumb it down for us dum-dums?" asked Jablonsky, voicing a collective sentiment.

I smothered a snigger. Dr. Nayar, like most men and women of science I'd met, loved using big, scientific words that flew over the heads of most cops.

She glared at us, disgruntled, but proceeded with the smallest words in her medical vocabulary. "I took tissue samples and forwarded them for further testing, but my initial assessment is that the deceased has been the passive subject of deleterious theurgical energies over a prolonged period."

"How prolonged? Give us a guesstimate," I added, knowing how much her ilk hated inexact answers.

"Roughly a year," she admitted reluctantly. "It's only a ballpark, but definitely more than six months."

"So the perp was slowly poisoning the guy with bad juju till he finally croaked in the bath?" Jablonsky asked. It was not a bad analogy—dark magic could work like that, slowly building up in the body like arsenic.

But Anika shook her head. "The vic received one massive dose, less than twelve hours ago. He was blasted with enough dark magic to kill an elephant."

This unpleasant news put a smile on Jablonsky's face, though he tried to hide it. He turned to me and Fox with all the solemnity he could summon. "Obviously, this is a case for the Extras; us normal cops would just get in your way. I'm sure your captain and mine will agree." Jablonsky loathed cases involving hocus-pocus, as he called it.

But he was right too—you didn't want someone without EMP chasing after a warlock or whoever did this. "Agreed," I said. "Send over your case files and whatever else you have."

"Will do," he said and left with a spring in his step.

Dr. Nayar looked after him with an amused little smile. Tough guy, it seemed to say in tones of irony, but when she opened her lips, the words were all business. "There's something you'll find interesting: the magic wasn't what killed the victim. Not directly."

"No?" Fox and I asked in a dumbfounded unison. "What did, then?" I added.

"He drowned," she said with the expression of a poker player laying a Royal flush on the table.

"You're saying the perp used a shit-ton of magic to drown the vic before his brain fried?" I meant the victim's brain, though it couldn't have done much good to the perp's either.

"That's exactly what I'm saying."

"Fuck me sideways with a broomstick." The words tumbled out of my mouth.

Instead of taking offense she snickered and slapped the folder containing the written report to my chest. "Take your sexual deviancies somewhere else, Mulligan. I have cadavers to disembowel, and you've taken up too much of my precious time already."

We thanked her nicely and left her to her gruesome job. Out in the hallway I flipped through the pages of her report. The electronic version was probably already in the archives, but bureaucracy loved redundancy, just as much cops loved tangible things.

"What now?" Fox asked. His eyes gleamed and his whole body tensed with a ready excitement—like a hound dog on the scent.

"Fox, do you realize the depth of irony in your name?"

I failed to confound him. "Because cops are hunters, and fox is the hunted?" he asked.

"Something like that."

"Ah! But fox hunting had been outlawed even in the old country, and foxes are hunters too. Cunning ones, I'm told."

"You win," I said, bowing down to logic. "C'mon, let's pay the DA's office a visit and have them obtain a search warrant for Ms. Yeates' apartment.

"You think we have enough for a search warrant?"

"If this was a garden variety triple axe murder, I'd say no, but the justice system takes a grim view of dark magic."

3

We returned to Brighton Street at half past five, in the company of a couple of forensics guys. Mrs. Shamon had been expecting us. She lifted her brows at the sight of our small army and the warrant, but she grabbed the keys and let us into the apartment with the stoicism of long-suffering building managers everywhere.

"Stay outside," I told her, even though she didn't show the slightest desire to put a single foot into the apartment.

I didn't have to say anything to the forensics people—they knew to wait till we declared the place safe to enter. Fox and I edged in warily—people who dabbled in this type of magic had been known to set booby traps.

I wanted to remind Fox to be cautious, but he didn't seem to need it. One had to go through two months of intensive training to become an Extra.

All our vigilance turned out to be for naught. The apartment was neat, clean and devoid of personality or magic, except for a small amount of residuum in the bathroom. It filtered through the wall from Mr. Roberts' apartment.

Not only did the rooms have the minimum necessary furniture, but there were no books, no pictures. Every closet and every drawer gaped empty.

"I don't think Ms. Yeates plans to return," Fox said, staring into an empty medicine cabinet.

I shared his suspicion. I sent in the forensics guys to dust for fingerprints and any trace evidence they could turn up, but my expectations were sub-basement low. Fox and I headed for the manager's apartment.

She offered us coffee and we gratefully accepted. It was a good brew, full bodied and smooth. *Just the way I like my men,* I would've joked in different company, though it wasn't the whole truth. I liked them every which way.

"How long had Ms. Yeates been living here?" I asked Mrs. Shamon.

"About a year." She ran her fingers through her hair. Like her husband, she was work-worn and middle-aged. "She seemed like a nice girl. Do you think she had anything to do with Dan's death?"

I sidestepped her question. "She was added to the previous tenant's lease, correct? Mrs. Camille Holland's."

She nodded. "Camille had lived here forever, longer than anyone. Her apartment is rent-controlled, so my husband and I were a little suspicious at first, but Camille did need the help. She was close to eighty and had a hard time just climbing up and down three flights of stairs. And her niece, Erin, was a very nice girl, and a nurse. It made sense for her to move in and take car of the old lady."

"But she's a traveling nurse," I pointed out.

"Back then, she wasn't. Erin was here every day."

"Anything happen to Mrs. Holland?" I asked, because of the many things we hadn't found in the apartment, an old lady was at the top of the list.

"Oh, she had a stroke not two months later, poor soul. They rushed her to the hospital but she died a few weeks later. At least she had a family member with her at the end."

How convenient for Ms. Yeates, I thought. "And Ms. Yeates started traveling after that?"

"She told me once there was more money in it," Mrs. Shamon explained. "After Camille passed away, she had no reason to stay put."

"Did you know her well?" I asked.

"No, not really. She was gone for weeks, and when she was at home she kept to herself."

"Was she on friendly terms with the other tenants?"

"I don't know."

"How about Mr. Roberts? Did they spend time together?"

Mrs. Shamon gave a reluctant shrug. "I wouldn't know. They were up there on the third floor and I'm down here, and I have better things to do than keep tabs on the tenants. That's Mr. Kowaltchek's hobby." The scorn in her tone had barbed edges.

As I expected, she had no photographs of Erin Yeates, but described the young woman as pretty, average height, slender with long blond hair. I showed her the driver's license pictures of the four Erin Yeates I'd dug up, but she shook her head at all of them.

We thanked her for the coffee and her time, and shuffled on.

Our next move was to interview the other residents of the building. Their response to us ranged from friendly to suspicious, but they all buzzed with curiosity about the murder and their own potential for being a key witnesses. Some tried to hide it but it was in their eyes.

Sadly though, not one of them could tell us much we hadn't already known. Still, it was a good exercise for Fox and me to find our rhythm. I had him take lead on half the interviews, and soon we worked like a well-oiled machine. The truth was, I liked having a partner, and I'd missed this.

Most of the tenants didn't mind letting us walk through their apartment, but a few had to be pressured first. We found no magic residuum of any sort in any of the apartments.

It was well past seven in the evening by the time the last door closed behind us. The forensics guys were long gone by then, having had little to do to begin with.

Fox and I drove back to the station and dropped the car at the motor pool.

"Can I buy you dinner?" he asked, unexpectedly. "You know, since we're partners and as my thanks. Unless you have plans." His smile flickered.

My only plan was a TV dinner and going to bed early, and had nothing against an upgrade. "Me? Not a thing. I'm all yours." I meant no innuendo. Truly. I was between partners in my *pursuit of serial monogamy*, as my mother liked to call it, usually followed by a sigh.

At my suggestion, we settled on Roland's—it served American cuisine with a spicy southwestern twist. It was a short drive away, but far enough that it hadn't become a cop hangout. Not that I minded those, but sometimes I preferred privacy. We got into our separate cars and met up at the restaurant twenty minutes later.

Roland's had been in business for seventy years or so. The current owner was the granddaughter of the first one, old Roland himself. Underneath the food smells lurked a scent of leather and old wood. Fox and I sat at one of the small booths.

"It's been an illuminating first day," he said, putting his menu aside.

"If by illuminating you mean learning how unglamorous a detective's job is, then I'll bet." I didn't even bother looking at the menu; I always ordered the same thing.

Fox disagreed. "Not at all. It's an unusual case. The Yeates woman was blighting Roberts slowly, for a year or so. What was her motive?"

Being able to talk out details of an investigation was a major benefit of having a partner. To get the best out of the process, I took the adversary position. "Who knows? They lived next to each other. Maybe he played his music too loud. Obnoxious neighbors can drive the most patient person to homicide."

"But then why blast him and drown him in the tub? She had to know it would get too much attention. If she just kept up what she'd been doing before, he could've died from an aneurysm or something similar, and nobody would've suspected foul play."

He was right—it wouldn't have been much different from a poisoner escaping justice because the death seemed to be from a natural cause. "Maybe she was fed up. Maybe she thought she'd get away with it," I said.

"Then why did she clear out? And the other thing: she used a fake name from day one. It suggests premeditation."

"It could be unrelated. She might be running from the law," I replied, although I agreed with him on every point. "You seem awful sure Erin Yeates is our perp."

"Aren't you?" As questions went, this one was mostly rhetorical.

"I am," I admitted. "But it's good to keep an open mind."

Our waiter arrived and I ordered the Roland burger with house fries, and Fox opted for a turkey burger with spicy mango salad.

"What sticks out to me is that she performed the last spell from a distance," I said as we were left alone again.

"Maybe she did them all from elsewhere," he suggested.

I shook my head. "Not feasible. Targeted magic depends on proximity. Line of sight and physical contact are a bonus. Obviously, it can be performed from a distance once or twice, but not regularly for a year."

"Why not?"

They didn't teach much about the mechanics of dark magic at the Academy, on the premise that it was best not to give the students ideas. What I knew I'd learned the hard way. "It requires blood sacrifice, and she would've needed a whole flock of black pullets to keep it up for a year. But a drop of her own blood from a pricked finger sufficed if she performed the ritual right next door."

"Blood sacrifice?" Fox stared at me, as he processed the information. I could tell when he'd finished connecting the dots from the way his brows jumped. "The last spell was a big one, and animal sacrifices go only so far, am I right?"

"You are. Chances are we have two murders on our hands, we just haven't found the other body yet. I suspect that last spell was the one she couldn't execute without the sacrifice to begin with, and it's the reason she didn't use the apartment. Couldn't be too far away though, somewhere in this city."

"She won't be easy to find."

"I arranged for a sketch artist to pay Mr. Kowaltchek and Mr. Shamon a visit tomorrow morning. Once we have a face we can put out a BOLO."

"She could be anywhere by now," Fox expressed his doubts.

"I doubt it. Casting any kind of magic saps your energy, proportionally with the magnitude and difficulty of the spell. Square it and you got dark magic. After this morning's performance, Ms. Yeates must be drained. I'll bet she can barely move."

Fox reluctantly gave in. "And what do we do while we wait for someone to recognize her?"

"We put the victim under a microscope."

Our food arrived and we shelved the shop talk. Roland's was easily the best burger in town—two beef patties grilled to juicy perfection, topped with melted cheese, onions, and house pickles. Even the roll had been made in-house. The Roland burger deserved and received my undivided attention.

I caught Fox watching me intently. Our eyes locked and he blinked away. There was something about him...I couldn't put my finger on it just yet, but it both drew me to him and made me wary.

"So what made you want to be an Extra?" I asked to break the awkwardness of the moment.

"I have the qualifications and graduated from the academy at the top of my class."

I didn't understand his defensiveness. "I have no doubt. But not everyone with necessary talents and skills becomes an Extra. You could've gone to any other department. Not to mention far better paying civilian jobs."

"Why did you became one?"

For the time being I overlooked him sidestepping my query and shrugged. "It runs in my family. I'm a fourth generation cop with extramundane talent on both sides of the family. Possibly the fifth. There are some speculations about my great-great-grandfather on my mother's side. Though he was only a police constable in a small town." I fixed him firmly in my sight. "I gave you my story. It's your turn."

He relented. "To be entirely honest, I wanted to show up my father. His old man was an Extra, but Dad's an M-negative. A dud."

"It sometimes skips a generation. I take you and your father don't get along well."

The resistance was there again. "We...have a complicated relationship."

"Say no more," I said to shut the door on the subject. In truth I would've liked to learn more. Fox was a bit of a conundrum. His open-faced eagerness mixed oddly with evasiveness. Fox had secrets, probably having to do with his family. Well, who didn't? But I was intrigued.

"I do care about what we do," he added hurriedly.

I shrugged. "You have a knack for detecting, but it takes time to see if you got a knack for the magic stuff too." Parker's words came to my mind: *If he has what it takes to be an Extra, we keep him. If not, we throw him back into the pool.*

"What's Chief Parker like?" he asked, momentarily blindsiding me. He wasn't a mind-reader. I would've known.

"Why do you ask?"

Fox hesitated before replying. "He's... intimidating."

"That he is," I agreed. "I'd love to tell you how looks are deceiving but I'd be lying. Captain Parker's a tough sonofabitch. He might turn a blind eye to a touch of creative policing, but bend the law too far and he'll not only throw the book at you but will beat you into the ground with it first. Other than that, he's a fair man."

"Thanks for the warning," he said, smiling.

We let the waiter on patrol know we were ready for the check. When it arrived Fox slapped down his credit card and I let him.

"You don't always investigate homicides, do you?" he asked.

"Of course not. We're only called in when there's a possible occult element, and citizens of our fair city still murder each other using ordinary methods far more often than not. Mostly because M-positives are in a distinct minority. Though, after a few years on the job you'll start doubting the statistics."

"Isn't it hard to be a jack of all trades?"

I'd heard this question many times and had a ready answer. "It keeps you on your toes, but all of us in the squad have our specializations. I'm, along with Nash and Martindale, specialized in violent crimes—assault, battery, robbery. Hyde and Basalla do fraud and embezzlement, and so on."

"So, what kind of cases have you worked on lately? I don't mean only you. I'm trying to get a feel for the whole squad. At the Academy they teach you the principles but there's nothing like practical knowledge, is there?" There it was again: that intense gaze trying to burn a hole into my skull. He wasn't after me, only my professional knowledge, I reminded myself, but the thrill was back.

"Don't you have a girlfriend waiting for you?" I asked.

"Nah, nothing of the sort."

I had no reason to be pleased by the answer, but I was. "Okay, but not here," I said. The restaurant was filling up and the hostess had been shooting longing looks towards our table. "I know a place, a real dive bar. You'll love it." I gave him directions.

Cabal was the kind of bar where you had to get your own drinks because nobody was going around with a tray and a friendly smile.

"I don't know if I love it, but it's certainly different," Fox said as we claimed our table deep in the dark bowels of Cabal. He was eyeing the mummy hanging from the ceiling.

"It's not real," I told him.

"I figured." He took a sip of his drink and kept studying the decor.

There was plenty to see—mounted animal heads and various other objects of taxidermy adorned the walls. They were all unusual, either by nature, like the two-headed calf, or by the hand of the taxidermist. "The other room has a wolpertinger," I said.

Only the Gods knew what purpose the building served before Charlie Cabal took it over, but it hadn't been a bar. The place had strange side rooms connected by a narrow hallway. We sat in the bigger one—the one with the billiard table. Two men with pool cues stared at the colored balls in solemn interest. They paid no attention to us sitting in a far corner.

Fox turned his attention from a fake demon skull to me. "How did you find this place?"

"Walking around. I live just a block away." I considered adding that Cabal's proximity to my own lair had had nothing to do with me inviting him here, but it would've sounded suspicious, even to me.

"Oh." He took another sip. "So, how long have you been flying solo?"

And we were back onto the safe ground of shop talk. "Over a year, almost two. Ever since Carillo got zapped. Do me a favor: always wear your protective gear."

He dug three fingers under his shirt collar and tugged out a corner of the familiar beige fabric. In the darkness of the room the cotton-wool-magic blend shimmered faintly. "I used to be on foot patrol in the Ninth, before transferring to the Twelfth."

"Hoofing it in the Ninth? I'm impressed." The ninth was down by the docks, a rough neighborhood.

"The upshot was that now I don't leave home without the vest."

Technically it was a shirt, but the name stuck from the times when it had been a bulky, sleeveless garment. "At family dinners my dad still tells the story of how in his day the vest was half an inch thick and you'd still break a few ribs if you caught a bullet or a spell from up close," I commented.

"Do you have a big family?"

"Oh yeah. Scattered all over the country, but we all come together for Beltane and Samhain. In between, those of us who live in town have dinner on the last Sunday of every month at my parents' house. How about you?"

He shook his head. "Not much of a family." Then in a change of tone he said, "You promised to tell me about your last case."

"Ah, Stilton. Wrapped it up last night." Late, late last night. I'd drunk only half a bottle of beer so far but the fatigue I'd suppressed all day popped its head up.

"Who's Stilton?" Fox's eyes lit up with keen curiosity, and I rallied for his sake.

"It's a kind of cheese. We busted a counterfeit cheese ring. The FDA guys chipped in," I explained.

He laughed. He had a good laugh, unbridled and warm. "How would you forge cheese and why?"

"You take some cheap cheese add magic and presto, you have expensive gourmet *fromage*. The actual process is more complicated, of course, you need a fairly high level practitioner—or several, in this instance—with specialized skills. And there's also the printing of the packaging and so on."

"And there's money in it?" His face radiated bemusement.

"Oh yes. Some cheeses can command high prices because of their rarity, like the Mongolian Yak cheese. But a smart forger goes for the mid-range stuff—it's easier to move in bulk without attracting attention. They were very good imitations too. Even the cheese experts could hardly tell the difference."

"Does it really matter then?"

"Sure it does! It's fraud. The average person on the street couldn't tell cubic zirconium from diamond, but they wouldn't want to pay the same price. Plus there are the FDA regulations. Some of those cheeses weren't even made of dairy of any sort."

"I see your point. But didn't you say you took cases involving violence?"

"One of the members of the cheese consortium managed to displease the others and got himself whacked. But the person doing the whacking bungled the job and the whackee landed in the emergency room with a cracked skull and third degree magical burns. He died, but not before uttering the word Stilton to the attending nurse."

Fox straightened up in alarm as the sound of a high-pitched wailing filtered to us from the main bar area. "What's that?" he asked, ready to spring to action.

I slapped my forehead. "Oh, shit, I forgot—it's karaoke night."

"I thought we were under attack by a banshee."

"Almost as bad. Well, we might as well join in."

Fox had a nice singing voice—possibly baritone, but I was no expert. Unfortunately, he couldn't carry a tune in a bucket with an extra large handle. I had the exact opposite condition—good with the melody, but my voice put crows to shame. Our duet of *All Along the Watchtower* made ears bleed and earned us standing jeers. All in good humor and in the spirit of Karaoke, of course.

It was several drinks later by then. I yawned loudly, climbing off the low stage. "I should call it a night," I said to Fox.

"Yeah, me too," he agreed. "I should call a cab," he added.

"Or you can crash on my couch if you want," I said without thinking. I would've suggested the same to Carillo in a similar situation. Probably.

"You sure?"

I shrugged with all the nonchalance in the world. "Yeah. Why not?"

"Okay then," he said and we took off on foot toward my building. There was no point in driving a block, and I could pick up my car from Cabal's lot in the morning. The car had enough wards on it to keep it safe from thieves and vandals. I assumed the same of Fox's.

There was a cold bite to the night. Fox looked up at the moonless sky. "There will be a storm."

I sniffed the air and smelled no promise of rain. "Nah, not yet."

He chortled. "Are you sure you're not a weather witch?"

"Bite your tongue!" I elbowed him in the ribs for good measure. Weather witches were the butt of jokes. As the saying went, even a blind weather witch gets it right sometimes.

We arrived to my building in good spirits, chatting about infamous instances of weather witches getting their forecasts disastrously wrong. "The place used to be a warehouse," I explained as we stepped out of the freight elevator on the third floor.

"I can tell," he said, looking at the steel sliding barn door of my place.

I let us in and switched the lights on. It was a typical converted loft—exposed brick, a wall of windows, high ceilings with exposed beams. The style was minimalistic, more out of my laziness than conscious effort. "Home, sweet home," I announced, making a sweeping gesture. I tried to disregard the presence of my unmade bed but it wasn't easy. The bed was a massive piece of furniture, prominently placed, and this week's bed linen happened to be red—a gift from my sister.

Naturally, Fox's gaze tracked straight to it. A blush like a distant reflection of those linens appeared high on his cheeks. "Nice," was all he said, and our eyes met.

I didn't know what made me lean in and kiss him. I wasn't that drunk; I had no excuse.

For a flicker he returned the kiss, but immediately after he shoved me back with true force. His face was angry red now. "What the fuck are you doing?" he yelled.

I opened my mouth to apologize but he was already out the door, leaving me gaping like the idiot I was. "Fuck," I said to the empty room at last. I'd really done it this time. This was going to be a record even for me—losing a partner in under a week. I was suddenly exhausted beyond exhaustion or the ability to think. I stripped off my clothes and face-planted on my big red bed.

4

My mood hadn't improved by the next morning but at least I had a full night's sleep, and arrived to the station fresh and early. Fox was already there, eyes darting back and forth between the sheets of paper in his hand and the computer screen.

I dropped into my chair and scanned the room—there was no one in earshot. "Look, about last night—"

"Oh gawd, I had way too much to drink," he said in a bright voice. "I took a cab home, and then this morning couldn't remember where I'd left my car. I swear, I'll never drink again." He gave a sheepish grin.

It took me two blinks to process his demeanor and know where we stood—we were going to act as if the kiss had never happened. Probably the best choice, I had to admit. I cleared my throat. "My sentiments exactly. So whatcha got there?" I asked motioning at the papers.

"Jablonsky dropped off his files," he said solemnly. "He'd already gotten the credit card statements. Roberts had lunch in various restaurants in Oakfield almost every day. He must've worked around there somewhere."

"Good thinking. Van Cleef Boulevard has a bunch of car dealerships. We can start there. Let me just do one thing and then we can hit the pavement." I pulled up the electronic version of the autopsy record, extracted Mr. Roberts' fingerprints from it and fed it into IAFIS. The Integrated Automated Fingerprint Identification System was tech-only for security reasons, and thus the search would take a while. I didn't have high expectations, since we already had our vic's records, but I'd been raised to be thorough in everything in life.

We struck gold at the third dealership, called *Dream Car Deals*. They specialized in imported luxury vehicles.

Mr. Devereux, the manager, was a neat man in a neat suit. When we asked him about Roberts his expression soured, spoiling the overall effect. He had the secretary fetch Roberts' file for us. It was a thin one, containing little beyond the address and phone number we already knew.

"He just came in one day, asking for a job and you hired him without references or job history?" I asked.

Devereux didn't actually shrug—it would've been incompatible with his tidy image, but he implied a shrug. "Those things are worthless in this trade.

You can either move inventory or not. He presented himself well, so I took him on a trial base. He sold a Jaguar on his first day, so I hired him."

"And fired him a week ago," I added, reciting what I'd learned from the file.

The sour expression was back in force. Devereux pressed his fingers together. "Roberts has been acting erratically of late and it culminated in an unfortunate incident."

"Incident?" I glared at him.

"Roberts got into a fistfight with a customer," Devereux admitted with palpable discomfort. "He had to be forcibly removed from the premises, and I had no choice but terminate his employment."

"Was he drunk?" I asked.

"Apparently so," he said with great distaste.

Devereux had no further information of use but he let us talk to the other employees, as long as we did it discreetly. We did, and learned nary a thing. Dream Car Deals was clearly not the place where employees hang around the water cooler, discussing their weekends. Or if it was, Mr. Roberts didn't partake. Everyone from the sales people to the janitor agreed that Mr. Roberts was a friendly man, yet he hadn't opened up about his personal life, past or present.

"That was a waste of time," Fox summed up the experience as we hopped into the car.

"I wouldn't say so." I put the key into the ignition but didn't turn it.

"We haven't learned anything new."

"Don't you find it intriguing how tight-lipped Roberts was about his personal life? His neighbors didn't know anything about him, and that's normal. But even the most reserved man lets a few things drop to coworkers. Yet in a whole year of working at Dream Cars, nobody heard as much as an ex-girlfriend's name from him. And he didn't sound like an extrovert to me."

"What are you saying?"

"Mr. Roberts was hiding something. Possibly something big, big enough to get him killed." I scratched my chin—it helped me think. "Do you have the bank records on you?"

"Yep." He pulled the printout from his inside pocket and unfolded it.

I went over every expense one by one. People hardly ever used cash anymore, and this was a godsend to us cops. Roberts charged everything, meals, hair cuts, clothes, gas, liquor, you name it. Mundane stuff, but one thing jumped out at me. "He went to the same magic shop at least once a month, sometimes twice. We should pay them a visit."

Fox looked at me puzzled. "I saw it, but I figured he had to buy all that pseudo-magic junk somewhere. I didn't think it would be of much use."

I saw it differently. "Customers of this kind of store often reveal personal information to the shopkeeper. It's like going to the drug store—people ask pharmacists for advice."

Comprehension lit his expression. "He might have told the salesperson why he needed the protection."

I put the car in gear and peeled away from the curb.

Mr. Murble's Magic Emporium was nestled between a used bookstore and an Ethiopian restaurant on Hyssop Street in Gipsyville. The neighborhood's name originated almost two centuries ago when a throng of east European immigrants settled in the area. Only some of them were Romani, but in a predictable spirit of prejudice, the older settlers called this new influx Gypsies. The name stuck, but the derogatory edge gradually wore off.

Nowadays Gipsyville was a bohemian, multi-ethnic neighborhood, in fast danger of becoming trendy. Starbuns coffee shops and other chain-stores were popping up already on every other corner.

Anyone who could do magic knew the only place to find genuine occult supplies was in Faetown. But that part of the city was notoriously intimidating to outsiders. Say or do the wrong thing there and you'll end up being chased out by goblins. Shops around the city like Murble's served the magically-challenged.

A doorbell jingled daintily as we entered. The front section contained an extensive selection of what the experts called "useless junk." Pretty, colorful things with feathers and seashells, scented candles that were supposed to bring luck, prosperity and the like. Judging from the fine layer of dust over them, business had been slow.

But—to my surprise—there was real magic here too, and plenty of it. Its aura filled the air, becoming thicker as we proceeded toward the back. I scanned the high shelves for the source and saw murky shapes floating in jars, boxes without labels, and even a Hand of Glory—a gray market item at best.

I glanced at Fox and saw him grimace. I knew how he felt—for a Perceptive, a place like this could be overwhelming. This was how a dog in a spice store must've felt.

The elderly woman sitting behind the counter was the spitting image of the main character from one of my childhood books: Madame Petuska, the hedge witch. Mme Petuska lived in a forest populated with talking animals. Both had the same wizened face, wind-tousled hair, and generally rumpled appearance. Though, the shopkeeper's hair was brown and silver, not black like Mme Petuska's.

Her name was Miranda Murble, as we soon learned.

"So there's a Mr. Murble?" Fox asked.

She bobbed her head bird-like. "Yes, yes. But he's taking his nap right now, like he does every day at this time. I myself can't sleep during the day, and somebody has to mind the shop. We had a girl but she went back to school. I suppose I should put a sign into the window. What can I help you with?"

I showed her Dan Roberts' photo. She held it at arm's length and squinted. "Oh, yes. Handsome young man, comes in every few weeks, buys silly things. His name is...now, let's see...oh, I remember, Dan. Something happened to him?"

"Why would you think so?"

"Oh you know, he insisted that someone put a hex on him. I asked him once if he'd seen an expert about it, but he got angry and said they were all quacks. He had peculiar views, I can tell you."

"Peculiar how?"

"Well, when I suggested he should see a witchdoctor or a shaman—everyone knows they're the best for hex removal—he wouldn't hear of it. He didn't trust practitioners, he said. He'd rather buy his own magic protection, but it didn't make much sense. The things he picked couldn't be much help for any serious kind of malediction."

"Did you tell him that?"

"I tried but he wouldn't listen. Young people often don't—they think they know everything better. He always had a list and bought nothing but what was on it. What could I do?" she shrugged.

"Did he say who cursed him?"

She frowned, pursed her lips, and frowned some more. At last, she said, "You know, I can't recall. I always assumed it had been a jilted lover, since he was so handsome, but I don't think he ever said it outright. But my memory's not what it used to be. When I was a young girl I could recall the name of all my classmates from kindergarten through high school. And whom they dated when. It drove my sister nuts."

"Did Dan mention a girlfriend or family?" I asked to steer her back on topic.

She thought about it. "No, I don't think so."

"What did you talk about?"

"Oh you know, this and that, the weather, that TV show about the girl with the hobgoblin."

After another fruitless fifteen minutes we extricated ourselves from Mrs. Murble's hospitality. Not a single person entered the shop the entire time. I wondered how they managed to stay in business at all.

On our way to the squad we stopped to grab tacos from a food truck. I paid.

"What I can't figure out," said Fox between bites, "is this: Roberts must've made pretty good money on commissions, but where he lived is anything but luxurious. What did he spend his money on?"

"I wondered about it myself."

"Gambling?"

"Possible. We'll have to pull his bank statements and search his apartment again."

As soon as we sat down at our desks, Fox got on the horn with the bank and I checked to see if the fingerprint search had turned up something. It had. "Ho-ho. Lookie here," I crowed.

Fox thanked the person on the other end of the line and hung up. "What is it?" he asked, ears practically perking.

"Our friend, Mr. Roberts, was arrested for DUI three years ago, but—here comes the kicker—he was using a different name then: Robert Daniel Lamprey."

"An alias?"

"I'm inclined to believe Dan Roberts is the alias." It was a popular practice among those who wanted to disappear to switch around elements of their real name. And Dan Roberts was far more ordinary than Lamprey.

Fox's grin mirrored my glee. "The plot thickens!"

It felt as if we were back to our pre-kiss new-partners-getting-to-know-and-like-each-other state. But could we ever really get back there? Maybe, if I managed to stay totally professional.

I tore my gaze from Fox's lips and turned back to the arrest report. "He was a resident of a place called Thistlewood at the time."

"Never heard of it."

I thought I might have. "It's a few hours due south, if I'm not mistaken."

"This is for you, Sweet Cheeks," Les purred and dropped a few fax sheets in front of Fox. Les was still blond, but this time, the buxom female variety. I still couldn't think of him as a she, though.

"Thank you, Leslie," Fox said, giving Les a cursory smile and not blushing in the least. He must've already gotten used to the charm and the glamour spells.

Les gave me a sultry smile before wafting away.

"Is that from the bank?" I asked.

"Yes. Check it out." Fox handed the papers to me. "Roberts made large cash withdrawals at least once a week. What do you think, gambling, drugs, hookers?"

With renewed zest we threw ourselves into finding out everything possible about Robert Daniel Lamprey. I soon knew everything subject to official records, from his parents' names and marital status to every last traffic ticket he'd had. There were quite a few of those, going back a decade. Fox searched the Thistlewood Herald's web site for the Lamprey name. For a small town newspaper it had a surprisingly professional site.

An hour later we compared notes. I started. "Robert Daniel Lamprey, thirty. Born in Thistlewood and apparently raised too, because he married a local girl, Sophie Walsh. Two kids. Divorced two years ago. Parents deceased. What do you have?"

Fox scratched his chin. It was smooth, unlike mine that had already started to bristle. "The usual, marriage and birth announcements, appearance at local events. There's one interesting tidbit: seven years ago Lamprey's name was mentioned in connection with a girl's death."

"Oh really?" My curiosity piqued and peeked all at once. "What was her name?"

"Rose Breen. She apparently drowned in Lake Thistle at the outskirts of town. Her mother, Petronella Breen publicly accused Robert Lamprey of murdering her. However, the ME ruled the death accidental."

"The mother couldn't have been happy about it." The tingly anticipation cursing my nerve endings had nothing to do with magic, and everything with a detective's figurative sixth sense.

Fox felt it too—I could see it in his eyes. "I wouldn't think so," he said.

"Other family?"

"Rose's younger sister, Violet."

I fed both names into the M-registry. Violet's returned nothing, but Petronella's scored. She'd been ranked at level three and had once been member of a reputable druid guild, though not any longer. Further search revealed that she'd passed away a few years ago. I told Fox.

He'd been looking up Thistlewood on the map. "The town is only about ninety minutes' drive from here," he said, and I knew we were on the same page.

5

We made it to Thistlewood in an hour-fifteen. While I drove, Fox was furiously tapping away on his laptop, digging for information about the Breens and the town, and filling me in as he went. By the time we arrived, we'd learned plenty enough to know what questions to ask and to whom.

Thistlewood was nothing like burbs that popped up around the city with soulless precision. No, it was an honest to goodness small town full of quirky old houses and huge trees that stretched their bare branches toward the gloomy sky.

Fox glared out the windows with deep suspicion. "This place is too quaint—like the beginning of a horror movie."

I laughed. "You haven't been out of the city much, have you?"

"How did you guess?"

"Sixth sense," I quipped. "I like small towns. They have a slower pace and everyone knows their neighbors' business." A big boon to a detective.

Fox screwed up his eyes. "I thought you were a city boy like me." His tone was light, barely stilted.

"I am, but I spent many happy summers of my childhood in a place like this." I rolled down Main Street slowly. The two-story red brick buildings lining it housed the usual shops and cafés. "Not a Starbuns in sight. I wonder how they managed that. Where's the newspaper office?"

Fox glanced at the map open on the laptop's screen. "Should be coming up on the right. There it is."

Thistlewood Herald, declared a modest hand-painted sign over a storefront. We parked in front, next to a real classic—cherry red station wagon with wood paneling. Fox gave it an admiring once over. "I haven't seen one of these outside of my grandmother's old magazines."

But we were here on business. "Talking to a journalist is a kind of dance," I warned him. "So this time you sit back and watch. Let me do the dancing."

The Herald's front office contained a cozy clutter of old-fashioned office furniture, stacks of papers and three people. One of them, a young woman, led us to the second floor once I introduced us as police detectives. I left the Extramundane part out.

The office of Herbert Pomfret, the Herald's owner, editor, and chief contributor was even more chaotic than downstairs. A huge mahogany desk dwarfed his already slight figure. He was a middle-aged, balding man with bright, inquisitive eyes. They darted between Fox and me as I explained our purpose.

He offered us seats. "Rose Breen. Beautiful girl. But it all happened ages ago. Now here you are, detectives from the city, asking about her. How extraordinary." He rubbed his hands together. "I'd love to help you gentlemen with anything I can. Just don't ask me to reveal my confidential sources." He winked.

I gave him my most irreproachable look. "We're simply collecting background information for a case that may or may not be related. As the head of the only newspaper in town, you probably know Thistlewood and its citizens better than anyone else."

"A case, you say?" The journalist's trademark hunger for information burned in his eyes.

And here we were, stepping and swaying around each other. "You wrote several articles about the death of Rose Breen and related events seven years ago."

"Yes, indeed. The investigation ruled it as an accidental drowning. Are you telling me it wasn't?"

"Did or does anyone around here think it wasn't?"

He smiled, no doubt taking my non-answer as a confirmation. "Her mother, Petronella—she made quite a fuss too."

"What kind of fuss?"

"She was convinced young Robert Lamprey had murdered Rose, and was rather vocal about it. Sheriff Drummond took the boy in for questioning but then let him go. Petronella became unhinged right after. She went around town complaining to everyone who'd listen about the miscarriage of justice. It didn't do her much good."

"How so?"

"Well, you see, she wasn't from around here and never quite managed to fit in, perhaps because she was the only theurgist in town. People made an effort to be welcoming for her husband's sake—Doug's family had lived here for generations, but she didn't go out of her way to make friends. After Doug died she didn't really have anyone but her daughters."

"How about Robert Lamprey?"

"Quite the opposite—his ancestors were among the town's founders. The family had lost most of their fortune, but the name alone carried plenty of weight around here. He was also a handsome, well liked boy. Although, there were rumors," he added, leaning forward.

"What kind of rumors?"

"Robby was especially popular with the female sex. The most desired bachelor in Thistlewood. All the single girls were jealous of Sophie Walsh for having caught him. And some of the not-so-single ladies too." He winked. "They were a handsome couple though, most people agreed. But some less charitable souls suggested that the match had plenty to do with her family's wealth, and that he had a roving eye and other roving body parts, even after the nuptials. But I don't know how useful these rumors could be to you."

I glided past the implied question. "Rose Breen had a sister, Violet. How did she react?"

Pomfret showed no disappointment, no doubt preparing for his next move. "Poor child, barely eighteen. She was devastated, but we didn't see or hear of her much. She sort of just faded into the shadows. Mrs. Breen's antics took the spotlight. The sheriff tried to talk sense into her, but with no effect. But when Petronella attacked Robert with a pair of kitchen shears the Sheriff couldn't let things slide any longer. The Lampreys agreed not to press charges if she got professional help. So she spent six months in a psychiatric hospital. It must've worked because she stopped agitating after her return. Funny thing though..." he trailed off.

It was a fine move of tease and I followed. "What is?"

He smiled. "Well, old Babcock, the barber happened to see the whole thing going down, and he had the theory that Petronella didn't try to kill Robby with those shears but to cut off a lock of his hair. Babcock supposed she meant to use it in a voodoo doll, or something like it. I told him druids didn't do voodoo. Do you think he was onto something after all?"

"We have no such evidence," I said evasively. And it was true—so far all we had were our suspicions and hunches.

"Could I see your badge?" Pomfret suddenly asked. *The wily old fox.*

It wasn't a request I could refuse. He took one good look at the shield and glee spread across his face. "You didn't tell Lori you were Extras," he said. "I don't blame you though. I need to have a talk with that girl about being more attentive."

I put my badge away. "Does Violet Breen still live here?"

"No. She left over a year ago." His brows twitched. "Come to think of it, just after Robby Lamprey skipped out." His choice of words caught my attention.

"What do you mean *skipped*?"

"He cut and ran after the divorce and the rumor is he's not paying child support. You wouldn't happen to know where he is?" It was a bold move and he couldn't have hoped it to work.

"How did the divorce go down?" I asked.

"Bad, very bad. As I said, Robby was a libertine. It was a constant source of speculation around town. Bad enough, but in the last few years he threw caution and discretion to the wind. Rather foolhardy considering how financially dependent he was on his wife. Sophie's father owns several business in town, including our only car dealership."

"Lamprey worked there, didn't he?"

Pomfret pursed his lips. "Not after the divorce. He had no job or prospects. When his own father died, he hadn't left much more than the family name to Robby."

I thanked Pomfret for his cooperation, and he magnanimously instructed Lori to dig up a few old photos from their archives. There was one of Robert Lamprey, looking young and far too handsome for his own good, and another of all three Breen women, taken at a Mayday celebration a year before Rose's death. Rose and Petronella were both pretty and blond, but Violet slouched between them like an awkward ugly duckling. Her brown hair fell into her face, shielding her eyes from the photographer.

"Pomfret was surprisingly forthcoming," commented Fox in the car.

"Yeah well, he saved us time for sure, but didn't tell us anything that wasn't public knowledge. I suspect he received more than he gave. Let's pay a visit to the sheriff."

Sheriff Drummond was not happy to see us, and made no bones about letting us know. But the law was the law, and after a few minutes of macho posturing he acquiesced to talking to us. He even had a secretary dig up the Breen file. It was a thin folder, took me two minutes to scan the pages before handing them over to Fox.

One detail in the medical examiner's report had caught my attention. "Rose Breen was pregnant? This wasn't in the newspaper."

He snorted derisively. "We didn't make it public, didn't want to cause embarrassment to the family. Not that Mrs. Breen showed any gratitude."

"Did you do a DNA test?"

"Of course we did. Do you think we're some kind of backwoods hicks here?"

"And?"

"The DNA indicated Robert Lamprey as the father, but it meant nothing. The boy didn't deny having had a sexual relationship with the girl," he grudgingly admitted.

"While engaged to another girl? I call that a motive for murder."

His expression started to take on a purplish hue. "There was no murder. She went for a swim and drowned. A tragic accident. And Robert Lamprey's movements were well accounted for."

"By his own father and fiancé," I said, not bothering to keep the scorn out of my voice. There was no point.

Sheriff Drummond's color darkened to an apoplectic eggplant. It clashed badly with his uniform. "Get the hell out of my office!" He went on shouting some other stuff, but it didn't much matter.

We left him to it. Getting into the car I noticed a cherry red classic station wagon with wood paneling parked across the street. Pomfret sat behind the wheel. I waved to him.

"You'd think he could use a less distinctive car for snooping," Fox remarked.

"Why bother? Around here everybody would recognize him anyway."

Fox shrugged. "Before we were thrown out, I read in the report that several witnesses saw the girl cycling toward the lake at around 2 p.m. Her body was discovered at half past five, washed up on the shore. Now, if she drowned in the middle of the lake as it supposedly happened, the body would've sunk and wouldn't have resurfaced for days. Right? And lakes have no strong currents to wash a body ashore."

I started up the car. "That's usually the case with floaters."

"And of course, the exact time of death would've been difficult to pinpoint. But it wasn't an issue with Rose Breen's death."

"Making life easier for someone who might come under suspicion. Or in need of fabricating an alibi," I said, finishing his train of thought. Damn, I'd missed having a partner.

Fox even anticipated my next step. "Are we headed to see Mrs. Lamprey?"

"Yup."

"Nice digs," Fox said appreciatively as I pulled up at Mrs. Lamprey's house.

I had to agree. The two story home had an old-world charm with its gabled roof, exposed rafters, and wrap-around porch. It sprawled in the middle of a well-kept flower garden, though only the dahlias were in bloom this late in the year.

She must've been expecting us because my finger barely touched the bell before the door flung open and a tall blonde woman appeared in its frame. "What do you want?" Anger made her beauty hard, but under pleasanter circumstances she must've been quite fetching.

"Mrs. Lamprey?" I asked.

She nodded angrily.

"May we come in? We have information regarding your husband."

She shook her head emphatically. "Ex-husband. Say what you have and make it quick."

"I'm sorry, Mrs. Lamprey, your husband has been killed."

She didn't even blink. "Was he driving drunk again? I hope he didn't take anyone else with him. Unless it was one of his whores."

"No, he was murdered. Drowned in his own bathtub."

Her face turned ashen as the hardness fell from it. She looked much younger now, like a scared little girl. "It was magic, wasn't it?" she muttered.

I nodded. "Mrs. Lamprey, you—" The door slamming in our faces cut me short.

"Go away! I don't want to talk to you," she practically screamed from the other side. Hurried thumps of footsteps faded into the distance.

Fox huffed. "Well, fuck."

"I could've handled it better," I admitted. I took a business card out and scrawled a few words on it before dropping it into the mailbox.

"Wouldn't have mattered." Fox pointed at an expensive black car coming to a sudden stop at the curb. A red-faced older man hopped out and charged straight at us.

He was Don Walsh, Sophie's father. No, he didn't want to talk to us, neither did his daughter, and we would do wise clearing off; he knew his rights.

We cleared off.

The red station wagon was idling on the other side of the street, a little way down but still in a spot with a good view. I strolled over and knocked on the window. Pomfret rolled it down a circumspect two inches.

"We're headed to the Breen house," I told him. "Do you know the best way?"

A happy grin spread over his face, replacing his initial wariness. "Sure thing. Just follow me."

"Will do."

Fox gave me a quizzical look as I started up the car.

"Pomfret's not doing anything illegal tailing us, and it's not like we could easily lose him. We might as well make use of him," I explained. "Small town folks don't readily open up to outsiders like us."

We followed the red car as it led us in what seemed to me a circuitous way across town. The Breens' home sat literally on the wrong side of the tracks. The houses here were small and even the well-kept ones had an air of shabbiness. The one Pomfret stopped in front of didn't even make an effort. The building skulked behind overgrown weeds like a stray dog trying to stay out of sight.

The journalist hopped out of the car and waited with keen curiosity while we clambered out from ours.

"Did you canvass the neighbors back at the time of Rose's death?" I asked him.

"There was no need," he replied, a touch defensively.

"Right. Well, I want you to talk to them now. I want to know what they thought of the Breens, any stray gossip, if anyone was close to them."

Journalistic voracity lit up his face but he didn't move. "What's in it for me?"

It was time for me to dangle the carrot. "If you deliver, I'll give you a very interesting piece of information. You'll like it, I promise."

He gave in. "All right. Anything else you want to know?"

"Find out if there was any unusual activity after Rose's death, but especially in the last few years."

"Magic unusual?"

"Any kind at all."

As Pomfret scuttled off, Fox turned to me. "You're going to tell him about Lamprey?" He asked, keeping his voice low.

"Why not? It's not state secret. Mrs. Lamprey and her father probably won't splash it around town, but the cat's already out of the bag." I popped the trunk open, took out a pair of flashlights and handed one to Fox. Technically, we could light up the whole street with a couple of spells, but regulations required us to follow standard police procedures whenever possible.

"We're going in?" he asked.

I schooled my face into an expression of solemnity. "Nah, that would be illegal. Unless we had probable cause. But we can look around the yard and peek through the windows."

We waded into the weeds. Curtains blocked the view through the front windows so we tramped around the house. Unknown critters scurried in the knee-high vegetation.

Fox tensed. "Are there snakes here?"

"I don't know. Possibly. Why?"

"I hate snakes." It was the first truly spontaneous thing he'd said all day.

"It's a rat," I replied, spotting a gray fur and skinny tail.

"Oh good," he said with a sigh of relief. Our eyes met and we both loosened up a good deal.

I pointed to the curtainless window of the back door. "Look inside and tell me if you see anything suspicious."

He leaned close to the glass, holding the lit flashlight with one hand and shading his eyes with the other. "It's hard to tell, but I see something that could be a dead body," he said a few seconds later. He stepped back. "There, through the door. Take a look."

I did. The beam of my flashlight couldn't penetrate the darkness past a few feet. All I saw were shadowy shapes that could've been anything. "Yes, I think you're right," I replied.

"Well, that's a probable cause. We must go in now." Fox's tone was dead flat. Neither of us conveyed anything that could've been called the least bit conspiratorial. We were professionals, after all.

I lay my hand on the lock. It was a cheap thing, simple mechanics combined with the most basic ward. Any M-positive burglar could've picked it. I did it under two seconds. We stepped inside.

Fox dragged his finger through the layer of dust covering the kitchen counter. "Doesn't look like anyone has been home in a good while."

"No," I agreed, peering into an empty and dark fridge. I tried the light switch but the room remained dark. "Electricity is off."

He turned the tap. Nothing, not even a gurgle came out. "Water too."

The cabinet contained only a can of sardines and cleaning supplies under the sink. We moved on. The house had only two bedrooms—the girls probably shared—and one bathroom. The latter was more empty and disused than the kitchen. Neither of the bedrooms yielded anything of interest, not even a wire hanger.

"Someone cleaned the place out pretty well," Fox noted.

The living room looked equally unpromising—it had furniture and a carpet on the floor, but no pictures on the walls, no books on the shelves. I pulled the drapes open and daylight filtered into the room. We switched our flashlights off.

Fox stomped around, then stopped and stared at the floor. "There's something here." He crouched and lifted the edge of the carpet.

I stepped closer to take a look. It was a simple dark stain but I thought I recognized it. "Burn mark."

He pulled the carpet back more but the stain kept going. We moved the furniture to the side and rolled up the carpet.

"A pentagram," Fox said, staring at the exposed floor.

"Not just any pentagram." I got on my knees for a closer look. The floor seemed scorched but there was no real damage to the cheap laminate other than the discoloration. I only knew of one thing that left such mark. I patted the floor. "Come." Fox kneeled next to me and watched intently. "Look at it from a low angle, like this." I showed him. He copied my pose. "What do you see?" I asked, straightening up myself.

"There's a purplish sheen." He sat bolt upright. "Someone summoned a demon here. But not recently—there's no residuum whatsoever."

I nodded. Demon was the name we used for the creatures of the other side. They were powerful and dangerous. Fortunately, only those already steeped in dark magic could summon one. And it was frequently fatal to the summoner. "Mrs. Breen most likely."

He frowned. "This makes no sense. Petronella Breen died years ago."

"From a stroke," I reminded him. "Probably caused by the summoning."

"Still doesn't make sense. If she summoned the demon why didn't she have it kill Lamprey?"

"It doesn't work that way. You can bribe a demon to grant you powers or tell you secrets, but only as long as it's confined by the summoning circle. If the circle is broken and the demon is set free, all bets are off. The summoner has lost control."

Fox's face lit up. "Demons don't like being bossed around, do they?"

"Nope."

"Okay, let me see if I can sort this out. Mrs. Breen summons a demon, dies in the process, leaving it to Violet to deal with. But wait, Violet Breen is M-negative; I checked the records. She couldn't make use of the demon."

"Or banish it," I added.

So she can't be our mysterious Erin Yeates. There had to be a third person present to deal with the demon. Violet can't be the murderer."

"She still could've been involved in many ways. We don't know to what exact purpose they summoned the demon."

Concentration etched deep lines into his forehead. "Some demons can raise the dead. Do you think—?"

I shook my head. "They can animate the bodies of the dead, but can't give them life. Revenants are creepy but not all that useful."

"You think they involved a third person?"

I was starting to have a hunch of what had happened and how, but I decided not to share it with Fox yet. It was a wild idea with too many possible ramifications. I needed time to think it through. So I skirted around the subject. "We know far too little about demons and the range of their abilities. They are difficult to study."

"I take Violet Breen is still our lead suspect?"
"She's our best bet," I said truthfully.

We took a few pictures, then we put the carpet and furniture back in place and closed the drapes before exiting, and locked the door behind us. I was just putting the flashlights away when Pomfret appeared at the far end of the street. He waved and hastened to catch up with us.

"What did you find inside?" he asked, the moment he was in talking distance. I gave him my blankest expression. Fox stared off in the direction where the sunset would've been if you could see the sun.

Pomfret stopped at two paces and shrugged. "Can't blame me for asking."

I gave him my full attention. "What do you have for us?"

"Let's see..." He scratched his head. He was holding a notebook but didn't need to look at it. "General background first. Mrs. Breen wasn't popular. She didn't make friends and the neighbors thought she was hoity-toity. And there was the witch thing."

"She was a druid," I corrected. There was a difference, mainly in the philosophical approach to theurgy.

"It's all the same to people around here. I personally think Petronella might have merely been reserved."

"What about the girls?"

"Violet took after her mother—shy and quiet, but Rose was outgoing and generally well-liked, despite her family. When she died sympathy swung in Petronella's favor. The Lampreys and other rich folks are not as popular on this side of town. But then she started acting out."

"Don't spare us the details," I said.

"Aside from what I'd told you earlier, several neighbors attest to having seen Petronella and Violet dancing around a fire in the backyard while chanting. Otherwise, Violet stayed inside the house, but Mrs. Breen was seen about, always muttering to herself. According to Mr. Litwick, she was crazier than a bag of frogs." He checked his notes. "Ah yes, on one occasion the Medrano's boy threw a stone through the Breens' window. Two days later he fell off a roof, broke both his ankles and was in a cast for months. The Medranos cried bloody witchcraft."

"What was the kid doing on the roof?" I wondered out loud.

"Good question. It wasn't even their own roof, but one of the neighbor's. Ralph Medrano is the local troublemaker. He's not doing much climbing these days though. Mr. Litwick says the little bastard got what he deserved."

"Mr. Litwick has lots of opinions."

Pomfret chuckled. "That he does. Wanna know the rest?"

"Shoot."

"So, after Mrs. Breen came back from the crazy house everything became very quiet. The women barely came out of the house, they even had their groceries delivered. Unprecedented luxury in these parts. Things changed after Mrs. Breen's death—various people started coming and going at odd hours."

"Men or women?"

"Both. All sorts of rumors started from prostitution to drug dealing, but aside from the comings and goings, the house remained as quiet as before. Then, a little over a year ago Violet did a spring cleaning. As Mr. Litwick says, she put half the house at the curb. Nobody from here would touch any of it, of course, but others drove by and took things. The leftovers she had hauled to the city dump." He flipped his notebook shut, signaling this was the extent of his discoveries.

"And the next day she drove away and nobody has seen her since. Am I right?" I asked.

"You sure are. I did what you asked. Now it's your turn." Good thing Pomfret had no magic talent because he was glaring at me as if trying to drag information out of my brain by sheer willpower.

Fair was fair. I told him about the lamentable death of Robert Lamprey.

Pomfret whistled. "So handsome Robby's luck ran out at last." He didn't appear struck with grief. "And you believe it might have something to do with Rose Breen's death?"

"We couldn't possibly comment," I said.

"Of course, you couldn't." He made a gesture of tipping his nonexistent hat. "Well, gentlemen, it's been a pleasure. Now you'll have to excuse me, I have a feature to write."

I stopped him. "I have one more question."

He halted. "Yes?" The question mark hung suspended between us.

"What's the best place around here for a bite to eat?" I asked.

His whole body sagged as the anticipation for further tidbits drained away. "That would be the Thistlestop Café, hands down. But stay away from any dish of prairie duck."

"Why?"

"Well, you know how prairie oyster is really bull testicles?"

"So what is prairie duck?"

"Nobody knows, but it's not duck."

◇◇◇◇◇◇

The Thistlestop Café bustled with famished locals but the friendly waitress found us a table. Prairie duck risotto was the dinner special, she informed us. The gazes of other patrons had followed our every step already, and now hung on us expectantly. Fox and I both opted for the ranch burger with coleslaw, and our audience turned back to their own meals. I sensed a collective disappointment.

In a room full of eavesdroppers, Fox and I couldn't discuss anything more significant than the weather.

"I hate this gloom," he said. "I'd rather have a big storm than the constant gray skies."

Without thinking I said what I knew in my bones. "Not yet, but soon. Probably tomorrow."

He opened his mouth, possibly to riposte, but closed it again, and awkwardness took a seat between us. And we'd been doing so well.

It was still there in the car on our way back to the city. The night had fallen and the tunnel of light the headlights bore into the darkness offered little distraction. Fox had sunk into his seat and thoughts, picking at his cuticles. Tics and quirks reveal a lot about a person, the parts beneath the surface. Fox was anxious about something.

"See, we made it out alive," I said.

After a disoriented moment he grimaced. "Don't jinx it. It could be one of those all-roads-lead-back-from-where-you-started things. I won't relax till I see the city lights." The humorous tone rang false but he stopped bothering his cuticles.

I wanted to keep the conversation alive. "Small towns aren't so bad."

"Says you. What was so great about the one you spent your summers at?" His curiosity was genuine, and the unease between us started to thin.

"What wasn't? Frostcombe was even smaller. I don't suppose it has gotten any more populous in the last couple of decades."

"Did you have relatives there?"

"Uncle Frank was the local sheriff. Great-uncle, to be technical, but it's awkward to say. We kids called him Uncle Frank. The townsfolk called him Sheriff Mulligan. He did his twenty years on the force in the city before retiring to Frostcombe. He became sheriff by popular demand."

He frowned. "Didn't the locals consider him an outsider?"

"His wife, Aunt Myriam, was a local girl."

"Mrs. Breen married a local too."

"Uncle Frank was an outgoing man; he knew how to talk to people. It makes all the difference."

"Ah. Was he M-positive?"

"Yes, but only as a low-one. He wasn't an Extra at any point."

Fox tilted his seat back a couple of clicks. "So tell me about those summers," he said sleepily.

A blast of old memories hit me—the smell of grass, the heat of the sun on my skin, and the rough dirt under my bare feet. "As I said, Frostcombe was a small place. Everyone knew everyone else; nobody locked their doors. We kids, me, cousins, local youngsters, we ran around practically unsupervised like a pack of wild dogs. But of course the whole town was keeping an eye on us, and if we got into the wrong kind of mischief, Uncle Frank would hear about it by dinnertime."

"Was there a lake?"

"Only a creek. Plenty big enough to arrive home at the end of the day covered in mud."

"Yeah, but what did you actually do all day?"

"What didn't we? We rode our bicycles everywhere, went frog hunting—we let them go, by the way—played out our favorite movies in the abandoned barn, explored the woods...you name it."

"Stop, you're making me gag. Are you sure these are your own memories, and not some old TV show you've seen?"

"Real as the day, as Aunt Myriam used to say. I didn't realize how good I had it till it was over."

"What happened?"

"Oh, nothing extraordinary. They grew old, Aunt Myriam became sickly; they couldn't take us on any longer. We kids got older too, more interested in our cool city friends." It occurred to me I'd been jabbering about myself too much. The conversation had a strangely intimate quality. I didn't recall having discussed my childhood in more than passing with any of my previous partners. Fox had a way of making me open up. Not a bad skill for a cop. "How did you spend your summers?"

He pulled a face. "Not doing anything as rustic as you. Mostly reading books about history, going to museums and science exhibits with my mother. She also signed me up for summer camps every year—always something educational. She was of the opinion that young minds had to be nurtured every way possible."

"You poor thing."

"It wasn't bad. I liked them. Most of them, anyway. But my childhood was fairly regimented. Mother would've fainted if I arrived home covered in mud."

"I can imagine."

"We had a swimming pool though, and neighborhood kids were welcome—as long as they abided by Mom's schedule."

"Sounds like a strong woman."

"She is. Has to be to live with my father."

"I take you don't get along with your old man too well."

He hesitated. "We're very similar in some ways, and very different in others, and both too stubborn to give an inch."

He didn't elaborate further, and we sank into a different kind of silence, one without eggshells. Fox leaned his head back and closed his eyes. His hands rested in his lap, motionless.

It hadn't escaped my notice that during our tête-à-tête I'd divulged far more than he had. Detective Hugh Fox was a crafty and elusive man. A mystery I would've liked to unwrap.

My thoughts wandered back to the Lamprey case. By the time the city came into view a plan had emerged. I kept it to myself.

6

Fox wasn't in the squad room when I arrived the next morning. He'd been summoned to complete his mandatory sensitivity training—Les informed me. It could take a while. I set to work by myself.

By the time Fox showed up, I'd confirmed my suspicions by way of online databases, some public, some restricted to Law Enforcement. I'd also had a short but tense conference with Captain Parker, and consequently took a trip to the equipment room.

"What are you up to?" Fox asked, motioning at the litter of papers surrounding my laptop.

"I'm writing up the report on yesterday's findings. We need to start the crime book. Should've done it on day one." I said it all on one breath. "Grab a binder, will you?"

He strode off to the supply closet and I kept tapping away at the keyboard. The crime book was something we did with every major case, definitely when dealing murder. It contained not only all the reports, but everything we picked up along the way, as long as you could punch holes in it or slide it into a sheet protector. Some of these—like newspaper clippings—didn't always make it into the electronic archives.

Fox came back with a 5-inch thick binder and started putting the papers in chronological order.

"The forensic reports came in," he noted, picking up a stack and starting to read.

I already knew what was in them. No surprises or big revelations. Dr. Nayar's tissue samples confirmed her initial assessment, narrowing the time range of dark theurgical exposure to 350-400 days. So about 12-13 months.

Ms. Yeates' apartment yielded nothing. Not a smudged fingerprint or stray hair anywhere. In itself it was a telling statement—you couldn't obliterate evidence so completely without the use of industrial strength chemicals or magic, and there was no trace of the former.

I typed my report slowly, including every painstaking detail. I needed to kill time—most shops didn't open till ten. Fortunately, the sketch artist came by, dropping off his portrait of Ms. Yeates.

Arthur, the artist, had a touch of magic in him, and his portraits always were as vivid as if he drew them from a live model and not from other people's memories. This one showed a lively young woman with a willful line to her jaw.

Fox lay the sketch on his desk, next to the photos we'd acquired from Pomfret. He frowned and tapped the drawing. "Look at this."

I leaned forward to peer at the pictures he was pushing from his desk to mine. I knew right off what must've grabbed his attention.

"It's as if Ms. Yeates was put together from the best parts of Rose Breen and Sophie Walsh," he said.

"The girlfriend and the wife. Robert Lamprey had a type," I said lightly, and flopped back into my chair. I didn't want Fox to charge down this path just yet. "I wonder what's on the front page of the *Thistlewood Herald* this morning?"

"I'll check." And clickety-clack his fingers danced on the keyboard.

I watched the reactions flitter across his face as he scanned the screen. They went from curiosity to dismay to amusement. "Want to read it?" he asked.

"Nah, just give me the condensed version."

"Well, the title is *Local Bad Boy Meets Grisly End*."

"Suitably lurid."

"The article starts with the drowning of Robert Lamprey and makes an immediate leap to the drowning of Rose Breen. Pomfret used our visit to Thistlewood to substantiate the connection."

"A reasonable assumption," I conceded.

"True, but the way he words it...the article reads like pulp fiction. It's a few facts and a whole lot of insinuations. And the colorful descriptions..." He shook his head. "I could never write like this," he added with a hint of admiration.

"Fortunately, you don't have to. The preferred prose of police reports is dry and dull. You do your job well if you put your readers to sleep while recounting a murder spree."

"Hah. There's even a picture of us talking to Mrs. Lamprey." He swiveled the screen around.

The photo was never going to win any awards, but it was us, all right. Taken with a telephoto lens, no doubt. "Pomfret, the sneaky bastard. I didn't even notice he had a camera. I'll bet the breakfast crowd at the Thistlestop Café had a lot to talk about over their prairie duck omelets. Print a copy and add it to the crime book for laughs."

Fox punched a button. "What are we doing next?"

Ah. It was exam time. "What would you do?"

He pulled himself straight and gleamed. "I thought about it half the night. We need to find the connection between Violet Breen and Erin Yeates. Won't be easy since we haven't recovered any personal items of either of them, and the Thistlewood Police is not likely to be cooperative. We should start with finding the car the Breen woman was driving when she left town. It must be registered either to her or to her mother."

I liked his plan. "What else?"

"Put out a BOLO for both. Possibly even put their pictures on the news and ask for help. Set up a hotline. Also, talk to Ms. Yeates' neighbors again, see if any of them recognizes Ms. Breen."

"Good. So you know what to do."

He was taken aback. "What about you?"

I stood. "I have a court date, to which I'll be late if I don't leave right now. You can handle this, and ask Leslie for help with getting in touch with the news outlets. I'll catch up with you as soon as I can."

I left but didn't go to the courthouse. Mr. Murble's Magic Emporium was still closed at five minutes to ten when I parked across the street. I didn't quite expect it to open up, but at ten sharp the old woman appeared behind the glass door and flipped the sign from *closed* to *open*.

I pulled out my phone and dialed Fox. "Change of plans," I told him. "Mrs. Lamprey just called me. She wants to make a statement, but only to one of us, and in person. Since I'm detained you'll have to do it."

"But—"

"I have trust in you." I hung up to cut off further inquiries.

The sky hung above the city as dark and foreboding as a sky ever could. I squared my shoulders and stepped into the shop. The door jingle echoed through the deserted room. I re-locked the door behind me and flipped the sign back around. No need for innocent bystanders to be stumbling in. From my right pocket I took out a box and slid it onto a shelf between candles promising prosperity, and at the same time patted the small lump in my left pocket for luck. I feared I'd need it.

The old woman emerged from a backroom through a beaded curtain just as I reached the counter. She gave me a tired smile. "Detective. Nice to see you again. Do you have more questions or are you here to shop?"

I didn't smile back but studied her wrinkled face and tried to see the young woman she'd once been beneath. Only the eyes showed a trace of her. "The former, I'm afraid. Why did you wait seven years to kill Robert Lamprey...Miss Breen?"

She blinked at me bewildered. "I'm sorry, I don't know what you're talking about."

She was very convincing, but not to me. "Really, Violet... May I call you Violet?" She only stared open-mouthed, so I went on. "What's the point of keeping up the charade? You achieved what you wanted, and let's be honest, you have nothing left to live for. You might as well clear your conscience."

She shook her head and graying locks of her once brown hair fell into her face. "You're mad. None of what you're saying makes any sense."

If I'd had any doubts, the dark coils of magic reaching for me would've removed them. They were like a burning itch under my skin. I shrugged. "No? Then let me tell you how I think it all went down. Stop me if I'm getting anything wrong."

"You're mad."

She was probably right, because I kept talking. "You and your sister were close. Very close. Rose was everything you weren't—pretty, popular. You could've been jealous but you weren't. You worshipped her. I'll bet she told you all her secrets, the ones she kept from your mother. So you knew about Robert Lamprey. He was a cad, a skirt-chaser, and a liar. But Rose didn't know this; she assumed the best of everyone. And she was in love with him. Am I right?"

The pretense of confusion fell from the wizened face and the eyes stared at me with cold hatred.

I went on. "Lamprey probably promised to marry Rose, even though he was already engaged to another girl. Who knows what lies he made up to get into her panties, but he succeeded."

"You're disgusting. All men are disgusting," Violet hissed.

"No doubt. In truth, Robert never had the slightest intention of marrying a penniless girl from the wrong side of the tracks. Sophie Walsh was pretty and blonde too, and she had her father's fortune behind her."

"Rose was just a plaything for him." Loathing of the deepest kind etched Violet's words.

"But he got her pregnant. Most inconvenient. He asked Rose to meet him in secret, but she told you about it. When she was found dead, you just knew he killed her. You told your mother everything. You thought her magic could bring him to justice, but she wasn't that kind of practitioner."

"Mother tried, but she was useless. Couldn't even make a working Voodoo doll." Her magic wrapped tighter around me.

"Sympathetic magic is not a druid specialty," I agreed before resuming my tale. "It would've been the end of it, but then something unexpected happened—your own talent began to manifest. The emotional shock must've had something to do with it. Late bloomers are rare, but not unheard of. There was a man in France who was twenty-eight when he first manifested."

She sneered. "Thank you for the theurgy lesson."

"You knew what kind of powers you wanted, and your mother was mad enough with grief and rage to help. Even so, it couldn't have been easy, but when there's a will, there's a way. And slowly you became a warlock."

"A priestess of Lord Alastor," she corrected me haughtily.

This was new information. "Ah, so that's the name of the demon you and your mother summoned. What a foolhardy thing to do—you must've known the act would kill your mother."

Violet showed no hint of remorse. "There had to be a sacrifice. Lord Alastor demands it."

"Her soul for your powers. Just so you could take your revenge on Robert Lamprey."

"Mother did it willingly."

For Violet it was just the price of doing business. I had no hope of making her understand the monstrousness of it, but kept talking anyway. "You didn't want to simply kill Lamprey. You wanted to torture him for a long time and enjoy every second of it. So you were careful not to use any of your magic on him or any of the people close to him. But anyone else in town was fair game. You got into their heads, you played them like chess pieces. All the while using glamour to appear as someone other than yourself. How did you pull it off? In a town as small as Thistlewood, people notice strangers. And if you impersonated a local it would've inevitably caused a ruckus."

She smiled smugly. "It was one of Lord Alastor's gifts—the ability to blend in and be forgotten."

I nodded; it made sense. "Of course. You weren't good at it at first though—the neighbors noticed strangers coming and going at your house."

She shrugged it off. "Nosy fools. I couldn't care less what they thought."

"You kept tormenting Lamprey for years. Pushing temptation in his way, mostly women and booze. He was no saint to begin with but you made sure he sank as low as possible. At last, Mrs. Lamprey had enough and kicked the cheating bastard to the curb. Robert Lamprey fled Thistlewood with his tail between his legs, but you were just getting started. Should I continue or would you like to take over?"

"Nah, go on. You've been doing well so far, and I like the sound of your voice."

Doubtlessly, she preferred to know how much I'd figured out on my own. I obliged. "It's much easier to get lost in the anonymous crowd of the city. Taking up a new identity, you followed Lamprey and moved in for the final act. But you couldn't resist showing off, just a little. The first six letters of you new name—Erin Yeates—spells Erinye. Erinyes are the Furies, the goddesses of revenge and punishment from Greek mythology."

"You're a smart one," she said, mocking. "Robert never got it. I knew he wouldn't."

"You got Miss Hollands under your influence and compelled her to put you on her lease, then you got rid of her."

"She was old. Would've died soon anyway," she said blithely. A minor murder was nothing in her scheme of things.

"Right. You got into Lamprey's head at the same time you wormed your way into his trust. He must've been exceptionally wary by then, even if you looked like his wet dream, but he had no defense against you. At the same time you set yourself up here as Mrs. Murble. How did you manage to find a genuine magic shop outside of Faetown?"

"This place was full of useless garbage when I moved in," she sneered. "I had to buy all this stuff with my own money." She motioned with her head to the vials, jars, and boxes filling the shelves behind her.

"You mean with Robert Lamprey's money?" I asked.

"Same thing."

Naturally. "It was a clever move, surrounding yourself with magic—it would mask you in case someone like us, Perceptives, showed up. Making our skill useless. Kinda like hunters use the scent of skunk to disguise themselves. What I don't get though, why such an elaborate setup?"

She rolled her eyes for real. "For fun. I convinced Robby that I knew how to alleviate the curse and sent him here for supplies. I could never get this close to him in Thistlewood. When he put up his useless trinkets, I made him feel good for a few days, then turned the screws again. It was delicious to watch him swing between hope and despair. I wish I had the time to do the same with you. Alas." She seemed genuinely saddened.

Oh yes, time. I was coming to it, but not quite yet. "You drowned Robert Lamprey in his own bath tub exactly seven years after he drowned your sister in Lake Thistle. Did you reveal yourself to him in his final moments?"

"Of course, stupid. He had to know. I had to hear his mind begging to me, to God, even to Rose, the fucker. I had to taste his fear, to drain every last drop. An eye for an eye, a soul for a soul."

"That had to be one bad-ass spell. You cast it from here, right? In a back room somewhere?"

"This place has everything I'll ever need."

I didn't like her use of the future tense. She had to be even more delusional than I'd thought. "I take it you got hold of the embryo and used it—the unborn child of your sister and Robert Lamprey—for the ritual. Aside from his inherent occult power, it also provided a special connection to Lamprey. You kept it all these years, preserved. But was it enough?" Her expression dared me to guess. I did. "No, it wasn't. You needed more. A blood sacrifice. Where's Mr. Murble?"

She threw her head back and laughed like a young woman. An utterly mad young woman. "He was a virgin! Fifty years old and he'd never been with a woman. Or a man," she added in a mocking tone. "Too perfect. Saved me so much time."

I felt the coils of her magic in my bones now. "Yes, time. I know what you're doing. Dark magic is impossible to give up. When you made your pact with Alastor you signed away your own soul too. The demon has been draining it away, slowly savoring it, like you savored Lamprey's suffering. A soul for a soul. Your life is slipping away with every second of dark magic. When I came in you had maybe a year. Now it's down to months, soon to weeks, days."

"But I can take you with me."

"It won't work."

"You think that silly shirt will stop me."

"Not by itself, but you see, I'm a bit like you. My talents emerged late—not as late as yours—I was sixteen. Just as they did, I was hit by a hefty dose of dark magic. By some miracle it didn't kill me but I was in a coma for a long time. Eventually I woke up and made a full recovery, except there was one little aftereffect—the incident left me immune to dark magic." In truth, it was a very high resistance, not complete immunity, but she didn't need to know it.

Her eyes grew big, full of uncertainty, doubt, and curiosity. She hit me with what was probably all she had. A saw in her face the toll it took, the furrows in her skin visibly deepened and her skin turned ashen. I myself felt as if an icy hand grabbed my guts and twisted them, but I kept my face straight and didn't so much as rock back. "I told you. You can't kill me like you killed Lamprey. Was it worth it? You threw away everything worth living for and for what? Would Rose have wanted you to turn into this lonely wretch for her?"

"Don't utter her name with your filthy mouth," she growled, but it was all show. Her strength was gone. She swayed and had to grab onto the counter to steady herself. Her head dropped and she was taking slow, deep breaths. When she looked up there was only a tired old woman left. "It doesn't matter what happens to me," she said. "The bastard is dead and he died slowly and in agony. It was worth it. I'll make a full confession; it'll give those fuckers in Thistlewood something to talk about." She chuckled. "Come, let me show where I cast the spell. It's right here in the back room. Murble is still there—I didn't have the strength to move him and he's starting to smell." She turned and disappeared through the beaded curtain.

I was ready to hand the scene over to forensics and followed Violet Breen only to take her into custody. I got only as far as the curtain. The strings of beads whipped around me faster than I could react. I jerked back with all my strength but the strings just cut deeper into my flesh. They were no ordinary beads—they held me in their grip like the tendrils of a jellyfish held their prey.

Violet had to lean on the wall for support but she laughed. "A Babylonian mantrap," she explained wheezily.

"Killing me won't do you any good," I said loudly.

The coquettish smile was disturbingly out of place amid her decrepit features. "Oh, but it will," she cooed. "Lord Alastor promised. He'll give me back my youth and a new, beautiful body, and wants only your soul in exchange. Lord Alastor has always kept his word."

Through the open doorway to my right I glimpsed sight of a pentagram, much like the one in the Breen house. Wisps of smoke emanated from it. One thin strand trailed through the door to Violet, like a ghostly umbilical cord, and through her to the spot where the mantrap joined the ceiling. The pentagram was giving them power. Not good, not good at all.

I could just twist my left hand enough to squeeze it into my pocket. My fingers curled around an object the size of a car beeper. I squeezed the button and a deafening boom filled the air. The device I'd left on the shelves would do minimal physical damage, but it sure made a lot of noise.

Multiple things happened at once. Violet jerked back while her hands shot forward and magic flew past me. It came not from but through her—she was merely a conduit. The fleeting taste of the magic set my mind roiling with my deepest and darkest memories. I felt and heard the fireball exploding in the shop behind me.

As the demon, using Violet as his puppet, set the shop ablaze, he momentarily lost connection with the mantrap. I tore myself free. In the other room, burning shelves tumbled on top of each other blocking the way out. The flames licked up the walls and spread with unnatural speed.

Claw-like fingers gripped my arm. "You're mine at last. I've been waiting." The words came from Violet's mouth but the voice wasn't hers. It poured from her lips in a fetor of sulfur and nightmares, and squeezed my chest in a searing pain. The demon clutched me tight with Violet's fingers, but her body was spent.

Gasping in pain, I thrust my own magic against them, as my mind screamed DESIST! They let go and recoiled in a hiss of disgust. I spun on my heel and sprinted down the hallway. There had to be a rear exit, I told myself. The flames chased after me, their hot breath singeing the hairs on my arms. A high-pitched sound came from far behind me—it could've been a scream of laughter. I didn't know or care.

A door, a door, a door, I kept chanting as I ran down a twisty and narrow passage. It was supposed to help me find the exit, but it's fucking hard to do magic when you're scared out of your mind. How fucking big was this building? I made a turn, opened the door, and found myself in a room full of broken furniture and piles of cardboard boxes. The smoke rushed in behind me and filled the space in seconds.

I could've blown a hole into the nearest wall in the hope it would open to the outside, and give myself a raging migraine. Better option than being suffocated or burned alive, but there was also the danger of bringing the whole building down.

I was about do it anyway when a *BANG* shook the walls and a metal door shot past me like some oversized shrapnel. Without wasting time on thinking, I darted in the direction of the blast. I flew through the remains of the rear door and into the alley like a bat out of burning hell. Straight into the furious figure of Detective Hugh Fox.

I gulped breathable air. "What the fuck—"

"I'm gonna strangle you," he rasped while dragging me away at high speed. "You fucking lied to me!"

Well he was right about that, and I didn't argue. A florist's van screeched to the curb just as we reached the mouth of the alley. Doors swung open and the driver—Captain Parker himself—shouted at us. "Get in!"

Under Parker's insistent glare Fox hurled me into the back and hopped in up front next to Parker. We were already moving as I slammed the sliding door shut.

The back of the van didn't contain a single flower, unless I counted the redhead by the surveillance equipment, with a headphone around her neck. I didn't. It was Nash and she would've punched me in the face if I called her a flower.

"The fire—" I gasped

"The fire department is on its way," she said, and I could hear the distant wail of sirens.

"Did you get all of it?" I asked, unbuttoning my shirt.

She pulled a face. "The magic-only mike crapped out almost immediately, the hybrid died when you were jabbering about the unborn child, but the tech-only lasted till the end."

"Good." I peeled the tape securing the mikes to my chest carefully, trying not to turn the procedure into a spontaneous manscaping event.

"You really know how to piss off a woman. No wonder you had to turn to other men for company," she snickered.

I gave her my winningest smile. "Aww, c'mon, Nicky, you know there's only one woman for me and it's you."

She sighed, exasperated. "You're a dumbass." And gentler she added, "And you burned your hand."

She was right—a red welt decorated the back of my left hand. I hadn't noticed it thanks to the adrenaline rush, but I knew I would feel it later.

Nash was already digging for the first aid kit.

7

WE DIDN'T LEAVE the scene immediately. Captain Parker advised the Fire Chief of the situation and I gave my account of the interior layout. Sending men into a burning magic shop was just about as bad as sending them into a burning fireworks warehouse. They hosed the building with fire- and magic-retardant foam from a safe-ish distance.

The situation could've turned ugly, but the fire died down as fast as it had started. I suspected that it had run out of life force to feed on, and the foam prevented it from acquiring more. We left close to noon, just as the HAZMAG team arrived in their orange head-to-toe magic protection gear.

I was sitting in Captain Parker's office smelling like a barbecue pit, and I kept my mouth shut while he was giving me a proper chewing-out. At least he'd closed the blinds and thus hidden my ignominy from the prying eyes of the squad room. Well, Leslie did.

The Captain was generally a man of few words, but once he started it was like a tidal wave. I let the tirade of departmental regulations, insubordination, and bone-headed idiocy wash over me.

"...I should suspend your sorry ass," he said and let his ham-size fist fall on the desk. He didn't exactly pound on the furniture but the pens and pencils jittered nervously in their holders.

Fortunately, I was made of tougher stuff and managed not to jitter. "Yes, Captain," I replied solemnly.

He stared at me with deep distaste. "When I let you talk me into your hare-brained scheme we agreed on a strategy. Your task was to pussyfoot in there, confirm your suspicion, then waltz your lily-white ass out. Riling up the Breen woman was not part of the plan."

"I couldn't stop myself," I said.

"Yeah, that's your problem right there—piss poor impulse control. Dealing with warlocks is a job for the SMAT team."

I had great respect for the men and women of Special Magic and Tactics. They were the best of the best. But. "Captain, we both know Violet Breen was not going to surrender without a fight. She was too far gone, and had nothing left to lose."

"I fail to see your point." Parker glared at me with the expression of a peckish werewolf.

A smart man would've kept his mouth shut and his tail tucked between his legs. Naturally, I kept talking. "Even the triple layer of magic Kevlar of the SMAT team can't provide sufficient protection from a demon-powered and trained, half-mad warlock high on dark magic. They're the most powerful before termination. There would've been casualties."

"So what, you decided to help her burn herself out? Literally?" he growled, far from appeased.

"No, of course not. That would've been disobeying a direct order." I knew my face was a mask of sincerity. "I didn't anticipate her torching the place." That part was at least true.

His chair groaned as he leaned back in it. He gave me a long, silent look, and I could make out the marks of stress and weariness in his posture. "You could've died. You realize how much paperwork a dead detective generates? I'm knee deep in bureaucratic bullshit already because of the fire."

I grinned at him. "I'm touched you care, Captain. Anyway, I'm here and barely scathed." Nash had made a neat bandage, though the pain had started despite the ointment she'd put on the burn.

Parker let out a snort that would've made a horse proud. "My fault for letting you talk me into this." He leaned forward with renewed purpose. The chair groaned again. "Consider yourself reprimanded. Now get out of my sight; I'm sick of your ugly mug."

"I love you too, Captain," I said and cleared out before he could hurl an insult or possibly office furniture at me.

Leslie looked up from his work as I exited Parker's office. "How did it go, Mike?" His voice was heavy with concern. The Captain's office had the department standard magi-tech soundproofing, so even Les, sitting right outside, couldn't have heard a world.

"My head's still attached to my body, so pretty well," I said while trying to keep my gaze off his breasts. I couldn't get past their wrongness.

"His bite's as bad as his bark, but luckily he likes you." He reached out and gently squeezed the fingers of my left hand. His touch was cool and brief, over before I could register surprise.

"I'd hate to be someone he dislikes," I muttered and slogged to my desk.

I badly wanted to go home, take a nice cold shower and find a diversion that would keep me from thinking of dark magic and what it did to people. But I had a report to write, so I popped the laptop open. I was at the part of the magic shop combusting when my sixth sense made me look up and see Fox barging through the doors with grievous bodily harm in his eyes.

I squared my shoulders and readied for the onslaught but it wasn't to come. Fox was still several steps away when he met with Leslie on an intercept course. How Leslie did it, I don't know, but he had a special talent for conflict-prevention. He herded the reluctant Fox into Captain Parker's office. As they turned, Leslie gave me a pointed glare.

Message received. I shut the laptop, and took my leave. The report could wait.

But I didn't go home—the big, empty loft and only my thoughts for company didn't appeal. I debated visiting by one of the bathhouses of Glynwood, but it would've just been exchanging one kind of loneliness for another. Drinking never cheered me up either, unless I was already in a good mood.

Fortunately, the perfect escape was only a short drive away. An hour and a half later I was sitting in a small airplane with a parachute strapped to my back, because there was nothing like soaring high in the air to clear the fog out of your head.

My newly improved mood lasted all afternoon and well into the evening. All the way till I stepped out of the elevator at my floor. Fox stood in front of the loft door. I could tell from the rigid lines of his shoulders and the way his jaws clenched together that he wasn't any less disgruntled than before. If anything, he'd had time to simmer.

Neither of us said a word at first. We eyeballed each other like a couple of street thugs ready to get down and dirty.

"How long have you been waiting?" I asked, just to gage the extent of his ire.

"About an hour," he replied, scowling.

"You should've called."

He exploded. "You're a rank bastard!"

"You have a right to think so—" I started but didn't get far.

"You bet your ass I do! Did you enjoy making a fool of me? What was it? Couldn't stand to share the glory?" He wanted very much to hit me, I could tell.

"There was no glory. Believe me. How did you find me out?" I asked, because I had to know.

"Funny thing," he started without a mark of humor. "I was on my way to Thistlewood but little details were bugging me, like the police sketch and your sudden court date, and you sending me alone to an important interview. So I called Mrs. Lamprey, and she knew nothing about it. Imagine my surprise." His voice had the strained rumble of someone trying not to shout or throw a few punches.

"Uhm."

"So I went back to the squad to find out from Martindale that his partner and my partner went off on some magic shop bust with Captain Parker, leaving us behind. We commiserated for a while before I decided to find you and have a word." He'd curled his hands into fists.

My skin prickled realizing violence was a distinct possibility. I threw my hands up in a gesture of peace and submission. "I'm truly sorry I misled you, but it's not what you think. I kept you out of the mess for your own safety." I talked in a slow calm voice.

"I'm not some girl you need to protect," he sputtered.

"I know many girls who'd take offense to that. The point is, I couldn't trust you not to do the wrong thing at the wrong time."

My words only fed his ire. "Trust? After you just said—"

"I'd said I had trust in you. To do your job well. And I meant it. But handling a warlock is something else completely. I couldn't be sure you wouldn't try to do something heroic and get yourself killed. With my track record, I couldn't risk it." And I'd been right because he did rush in, but fortunately for both of us, exactly at the right time. So I'd been wrong too.

My calm words had succeeded in cooling the mood to some degree, but Fox was far from placated. "Oh, so it was okay for you to face her down alone."

"I was never in real danger. You see, I have a freakishly high resistance to dark magic."

This, at last, took him aback. I could practically see curiosity wrestling control from anger. "How?"

"It's a long and pathetic story. I promise I'll tell you one day, but not tonight. I'm exhausted. I'm truly sorry about misleading you."

He stood silent for a while, wavering. "You're obviously not fire resistant." There was still a bite to his tone, but only a nip, not the rip-your-head-off kind.

"Touché." I lifted my bandaged hand—I'd completely forgotten. It had stopped throbbing. When did that happen?

Fox still stood there, blocking the door, but his scowl had turned into thoughtful scrutiny. "You should've told me."

"I don't know you well enough, we're not truly partners yet," I replied, because it was the brutal truth.

Fox digested this for a moment. His eyes took on a clarity of purpose, as if he'd come to a decision. He stepped up. "Well let's fix that. We should get to know each other better."

He stood close enough for me to feel the heat of his body—there was no uncertainty what he'd meant.

My nostrils flared to take in his scent—warm masculinity breaking through a fading layer of a woody aftershave. A vein pulsed rhythmically in his neck. He was so alive, so tantalizingly real. I took a step back. "I don't think it's a good idea," I said, using up my last shred of common sense.

Fox took a step forward, grabbed my shirt, and pushed me against the wall. "I think you think too much," he whispered before our lips met.

I knew this was a bad idea, but I didn't listen to myself. Traces of his anger still danced in the air, and it was there in the roughness of his touch, the way he ground his groin against mine. I was only made of flesh, flawed, weak, but very hard flesh. A question crossed my mind, regarding how this fit in with my supposed curse, but at the moment I couldn't care less.

I fell upon him with all the bottled up craving I had, and I had quite a lot. Parker had been right about my poor impulse control.

Somehow we managed get through the door and all the way to the bed, tearing at each other's clothing along the way. The linen wasn't red anymore; I'd changed it since last time to virginal white.

For a supposedly straight boy, Fox displayed firm zeal for our sweaty wrestling. A remnant of his fury still pulsed between us, raising temperatures and passions. He wasn't gentle, and neither was I. We were locked in a mock-struggle for power, giving and taking. Here it was at last, the real Hugh Fox under the prim and proper surface: fierce and wanton.

We froze in a pornographic pose as a blaze of bright white light filled the loft. It went as quick as it came, and the boom of thunder followed half a second later. It'd been a close one. The sky opened and fat rain drops began to tap on the windows like tiny fists.

"I told you," I said, breathing heavy.

"Fucking weather witch," Fox growled and claimed my mouth in a vicious kiss.

The rain kept coming down hard for hours, while we explored and exhausted each other's bodies.

It was a dark and stormy night, at last.

Josh of the Damned vs. The Bathroom of Doom

ANDREA SPEED

(N.B.: For those who are continuity sticklers, this story takes place between Plaything of the Gods! and Josh vs. Destiny)

Josh was having a weird but surprisingly erotic dream about Colin, his boyfriend, somehow getting the lead in the reboot of Plan 9 From Outer Space when something cold and wet shocked him awake.

He jolted up to find Doug standing over him, pressing a can of Mountain Dew to his forehead. Before he could ask his stoner roommate what the hell he thought he was doing, Doug asked, "Aren't you working tonight?"

Josh stared up at him, uncomprehending, until he glanced at the overturned milk crate he used as a table, and saw the clock read 10:33. "Holy shit, my alarm didn't go off?" For some reason, Josh instantly reached for the clock, even though that did no good at all. Why the hell did he do that?

"Um, no," Doug said, answering his question as he jumped out of bed and scrambled for the bathroom. Since Doug almost always responded like he was on a satellite delay, this was no surprise at all.

Josh quickly took a leak, and then struggled into his work clothes. He could skip the shower, because he had one before going to bed anyway. "Can you give me a lift?" he shouted, deciding to skip brushing his teeth too. He was going to get coffee breath no matter what happened. "I missed the bus." He worked the overnight shift, eleven to seven, at the Quik-Mart. The worst, most dreaded shift of all overnight workers, except for him. Josh had actually grown to love it—mostly—in spite of all its challenges. And there were many weird ones.

There was a longer than average pause before Doug replied, "Sure." How much pot had he smoked? Maybe he was on edibles. One of Doug's dubious friends brought some pot brownies over the other day, and they smelled a little too much like poop for Josh to find them at all enticing (and he liked brownies), but Doug had a higher tolerance for that kind of nonsense.

Josh had pulled on his hated Quik-Mart smock and was struggling into his boots when he finally remembered, "Hey, aren't you working tonight?" Doug was a pizza delivery guy for Tony's, or at least he usually was. Tonight was apparently different.

"I have the flu," Doug said.

Josh stumbled out into his bedroom, zipping up his jeans, and gave Doug a scrutinizing once over. He was barely done before Doug shrugged. "I'm playin' hooky. I mean, fuck it. Didn't feel like workin' tonight."

Unbelievable. Josh had no idea what Doug had on Tony, but he seemed to get a lot of days off with no consequences. Then again, Doug was his number one delivery guy, probably because he drove like a fucking maniac. "Good for me, I guess," Josh said, deciding to not let it bother him. That was how Doug approached life, and he seemed to have no stress at all.

Josh grabbed a soda and an apple he could eat in Doug's shitty car, and they went out to the apartment parking lot, which was full of cars but empty of people, and never stopped being eerie. As soon as he got in Doug's beater car and slammed the door, his hybrid hula Jesus doll on his dashboard—the top half of a plastic Jesus glued to the bottom half of a female hula doll—started swiveling his hips ferociously. Hula Jesus was a shameless flirt.

He probably shouldn't have let stoned Doug drive, but he was actually a better driver on pot. He lost his maniac tendencies, or at least the edges were smoothed down. It shouldn't have worked that way, but somehow it figured with Doug. He was kind of unusual that way.

Josh felt a tickle on his arm hair, and looked down to see a mosquito there. Not for long, as the Medusa bracelet on his wrist had its eyes briefly light up, and the bug turned to stone. He flicked it off, and it went up in a tiny cloud of dust.

Medusa ran the dimension on the other side of the dimensional portal behind the Quik-Mart, and she wanted to keep it open and safe from interference on either her side or the human side. She made Josh her human eyes on this side of the portal, and the bracelet wasn't a gift, but protection for the poor, weak human. If anyone grabbed him or touched him with the intent to harm him, they turned to stone. So fast it was both impressive and frightening at the same time. It was death, sure, but it was so bizarre it was hard to fathom it on that level. People didn't turn to stone, and they certainly didn't turn into it just because the Medusa head on the bracelet started glowing, except yes, they did. Josh still hadn't quite wrapped his head around it. He also had no idea how she did it, or how the bracelet worked, or how it managed to sense the intentions of people who interacted with him. After all, Colin could give him a nice love bite, and the bracelet didn't turn him to stone. But he didn't understand any of this, and he was pretty sure he wasn't meant to. While Medusa seemed to treat him as an equal, he couldn't help but feel he was the lowest man on this totem pole. Probably because he was. He wasn't supernatural, he wasn't even a shitty necromancer like Mr. Kwan, he was just a regular guy, and on top of that, a gay boy who really didn't like to fight. He was the last person that should have been involved in any of this.

Despite the pot slowing Doug down, they made it to the Quik-Mart before Josh's shift began. The lot was quiet, and Josh was always struck by how peaceful the lot seemed. At first. If you didn't notice the clots of thick shadows by the ice machines were actually werewolves waiting for an opportunistic snack, or even just a bumper of a car (they liked chrome). As soon as they got out, Josh made a hissing noise, which Colin told him was a noise vampires used back in Dev to make werewolves back off. It sometimes worked.

And yeah, werewolves and vampires didn't get along, but mostly because werewolves were just big, dumb dogs, and vampires were apparently notorious dicks (according to Colin—Josh hadn't enough experience to say if that was true or not). It was weird how quickly soap opera monsters got once you were dealing with them all the time.

Josh went in, followed closely by Doug, who made a beeline for the ice cream freezer. The clerk on the late shift was glad to see him, as it had been a boring night. She left without noticing the werewolves lurking in the parking lot. It was funny how normal people never seemed to notice them, or just dismissed them as regular dogs.

She didn't know about the dimensional portal behind the store that opened up at night and closed at sunrise, that let all the monsters from the hell dimension of Dev come over and buy snacks. There were types, and certain types of monsters liked certain kinds of snacks. The lizards like salty crunchy things, the zombies loved frozen burritos, and vampires occasionally had a sweet or boozy tooth. What shifters bought depended on what kind of shifter they were, although he wasn't sure if an unshifted werewolf had ever been in the store.

Doug came up to the counter, already eating his Drumstick, and dropped a dollar in quarters in front of him. "Would you mind if I hung around for a bit?" Doug asked, before biting off most of the chocolate crust on the cone.

Josh shrugged, scooping the coins into his hand before dumping them in the cash register. "I don't care. Although if Mr. Kwan comes by, you'll have to split."

Doug rolled his eyes. "Don't I know it. What's that guy got against me, anyway?"

"Well, according to him, you remind him of his nephew Cullen, who is, and I quote, an 'obnoxious little shitweasel'."

Doug snickered, taking a seat on the edge of a small display case. "Shitweasel."

Josh had just officially started his shift and not even decided on the snack he wanted to steal when a lizard guy came in for his nightly chips. The lizard guys (no gender was apparent, although Colin said they did have them) were exactly that: bipedal lizards. They varied in colors from moss green to a sort of ashy gray, and while they spoke no language Josh understood, they always seemed nice, and never wanted change. They just bought their chips, paid, and left. He never had any trouble with the lizard guys. Except sometimes he spent half the night refilling the chip displays.

"Whoa," Doug said, sitting forward and watching the lizard guy waddle stomp down the aisle. "They really are big lizards."

"What, did you think I was lying?"

"No. I just figured it was a nickname."

The lizard guy came up to the counter with an armful of chip bags, and noticing Doug staring at them, the lizard stared back. Since they had big yellow eyes the size of tangerines, this was very noticeable. "Ignore him, he's new to this," Josh said, hoping that would be enough.

"Sorry," Doug said.

Maybe the lizard guy forgave Doug, because he stopped staring at him. He dropped his money on the counter and left with his many bags. It was especially nice because it left Josh two dollars and sixty three cents in change, which he could totally pocket, because Mr. Kwan didn't care. It might not sound like much, but it added up. One night, he cleared seventy five bucks in "tips".

As soon as it was out the door, Doug sat forward, sending ice cream cone crumbs falling to the floor. "Dude, your job is awesome."

Josh shrugged. "A lot of the time, yeah. Sometimes it sucks. Like, when the loony monsters come in, or the werewolves piss all over the parking lot."

"It's still better than customers who don't tip or bad traffic."

A zombie shambled in, making its slow, methodical way toward the freezer case, where the burritos were kept. Doug sat forward and stared at it, but zombies never seemed to notice and/or care about the looks they received. This one was a pretty decent one, a string bean of a guy with rotting but mostly intact clothes and body. That was a nice change from some of them, as he'd had zombies come in almost naked and lose bits. Usually it was just skin or clothing, but sometimes it was more. He'd had to sweep up more fallen off feet and ears than he'd ever thought possible. "They look more gnarly on The Walking Dead," Doug noted.

Josh shrugged. "Hollywood. They exaggerate for effect. Although sometimes ones come in here that are pretty ugly. I told you about the zombie who lost his foot, right?"

"You were serious?"

"Hell yeah."

"How do you dispose of that kinda shit?"

"You throw it out in the lot. Werewolves eat everything."

"Ew."

It took ages for the zombie to get his burrito and shamble up to the counter, so Josh decided to help himself to a candy bar while waiting. Doug, for his part, opened a can of soda, and watched the zombie as it made its plodding way through the store.

Once he bought his burrito, took it, and made it slowly out the door, Doug said, "I'm not sure I'll ever buy zombies as a threat again."

"Don't let their sluggishness fool you. They can move faster when they want, and in a group they can overwhelm you with numbers. Zombies are relentless."

"Oh, right, you were attacked by zombies once."

"Yeah. Before I realized the Medusa bracelet would turn them to stone if they tried to bite me, they ate a customer. They're still a threat, just in a group."

Doug nodded and burped. "Got it. Don't mess with the zombies."

"I wouldn't mess with any of the customers."

"What if they start somethin'?"

"Case by case basis. Most of 'em you can ignore, but never engage with a yeti. Under any circumstances. Even if they seem friendly."

"Right, they eat everything."

Josh nodded, hoping he was doing it emphatically enough. "They are the scariest goats you will ever meet. Also, indestructible."

Doug pointed toward his braceletted arm. "Could you turn one to stone?"

Josh paused and looked down at it, as if the Medusa head would spring alive and tell him. "Uh ... good question. Well, I guess, if it was gonna hurt me, yeah."

"So they're only mostly indestructible?"

How fair was this? Doug was a stoner who spent most of his day high as hell. How did he always come up with these great questions? Josh rarely did any controlled substances, and these things almost never occurred to him. Was he just stupid? Was Doug really a genius derailed by pot? He never seemed overwhelmingly bright when sober. Of course, he didn't see him sober for very long. "Dude, how do you do this to me? You've been in my world like, five seconds."

"Not true. You've told me about some of this stuff for a while, dude."

"You know what I mean, it's the principal of the thing."

Doug shrugged, sliding off the case. "Is there a place where I can piss around here? Or do I hafta do it in the alley with the werewolves?"

"If you did, there's a good chance they'd bite your dick off." Josh pointed toward the back room. "Employee toilet. But don't smoke up in there, 'cause Kwan'll blame me."

Doug nodded, slipping into the back, and Josh wondered if he should trust him. Could you trust a straight guy? It probably wasn't politically correct, but everything he'd ever seen on the internet told him no. But this was Doug, and while he was a relentless druggie who accidentally showed him up at times, he was a pretty decent guy, straight or not. Besides, he couldn't help being straight, could he? He was born that way.

Josh had eaten his candy bar and started flipping through a trashy magazine when a guy came in. Only the guy pulled Josh's attention hard, hard enough that he knew he must have been a vampire.

Unless they went all fangs and copper eyes on you, vampires looked just like regular people, except a little bit hotter. More than a bit, as a matter of fact. It wasn't an accident either. According to Colin, vampires generally tried to turn people attractive to them, so as a mass, vampires were prettier than any other group you could think of, including actors and supermodels. There was the occasional unattractive or odd vampire, but they were few and far between. It only added to the fact that most other monsters thought of vampires as huge pricks.

Vampires also had a kind of pull, an ineffable magnetism that always made them the center of attention. It was super easy to catch prey when they were drawn to you. This guy was tall, with silky looking brown hair and a manly jaw line that just begged to be in an ad for a super expensive razor. His lips were well shaped but pale, and his eyes were the cold blue of a raspberry popsicle. So, if Josh was single, he'd totally do him, but Colin was actually a bit cuter, so tonight's vamp could go suck someone else.

He wandered back toward the cooler section, as if looking for beer. Which was possible. Most vampires lost their taste for anything except blood once they turned, but some still had a few lingering traits. Colin had a sweet tooth for example, and sometimes he drank alcohol, even though he said it did nothing for him. But he did like to be social.

Josh felt a breeze, and looked to see the vampire had left the door propped open. How was that even possible? Josh tried to do it once during the summer, when the air conditioner stopped working, but the thing refused to stay ajar. But it was possible the werewolves messed with it. Werewolves messed with everything, on the off chance it was edible.

Doug came out of the back, and he didn't smell any more like weed than he usually did. But Josh gave him a scrutinizing look. "What?" Doug exclaimed. "I didn't have time to even light up, I swear. I just—"

There was a strange noise, kind of like the squeak of a squeeze toy, and Doug stopped and looked down. "Dude, what the hell?"

Josh looked over the counter, and saw that Doug had stepped on something. It wasn't immediately clear what, but there were several others crawling over the floor. His first thought was rats, except rats had long tails and these didn't have those. Also they seemed fluffier, and smaller, but only fluffy in a relative way. Because a lot of them didn't have much fur, or only had it in patches. One looked like it had a bite taken out of it. Josh picked one up by its stubby tail to get a better look at it. It writhed feebly, its tiny paws gray and its eyes filmy and seemingly blind. He could see a gash in its side, where bones were visible, but there was no blood, and it didn't appear to be breathing. Its tail even felt cold. "I think they're hamsters," Doug said.

"Dead hamsters," Josh said, putting the creature back on the floor. "Zombie hamsters."

"What? Hamsters can be zombies?"

"Apparently." Josh noticed the majority of the hamsters—there had to be at least a dozen, maybe two dozen or more—were making their way to the chip aisle. "Oh no you don't, you lousy rats. Not unless you're paying for it." Josh retrieved the silver broomstick from under the counter. Yeah, he usually used it to shoo away werewolves, but it would sweep up hamsters. And once outside in the parking lot, there was a good chance the werewolves would eat the undead rodents.

He'd just started sweeping up the zombie hamsters when the vampire appeared at the end of the chip aisle, watching the undead rodents make a concentrated beeline of destruction for the Cheetos. "Oh, goddamn it," the vampire said, lip curling in disgust. "You just can't even pay for good help these days, can you?"

"You know about these?"

"Yes. I hired a necromancer to throw in some distractions and cannon fodder. I can't believe he went with hamsters. How much of an idiot do you have to be to think hamsters would eat human flesh? He's been in Dev too goddamn long." The vampire's eyes went copper, and suddenly he didn't seem remotely hot.

"So he's a vampire, right?" Doug asked.

Josh ignored him. "What did you expect to accomplish with this?"

"Oh, is this the exposition part, where I tell you everything, giving you enough time to stall and hope help arrives?" In the blink of an eye, the vampire was gone from the aisle, and suddenly behind Doug, one arm around his throat. "Do what I say, Medusa's bitch, or I rip his head off."

"Dude," Doug said, giving him wicked side eye. "Not cool."

Josh needed a few seconds to absorb this, and attempt to figure out what was going on. That was the hardest part. "Hold on a second. What exactly do you expect from me? Free burritos?"

"Call your boss, tell him to get down here now."

"Umm ... you don't know my boss at all, do you? I can call him, but I can't guarantee he'll show up any time soon, or even tonight."

"If he doesn't want his store burned down, he'll show. Tell him that."

Josh propped the broomstick up on the counter, and reached for the phone. There was no point in trying to goad the vampire. They were supernaturally fast, and this one clearly knew he couldn't engage Josh without turning to stone, so he was keeping his distance and threatening Doug instead. It was nice his necromancer gambit failed so spectacularly. How in the hell were zombie hamsters supposed to help anyone at all?

Josh picked up the receiver and dialed up Mr. Kwan's number, but his call went straight to voicemail. It said, in all its thrilling entirety, "This is Kwan. You know what to do." "Umm, Mr. Kwan, it's Josh. There's a vampire here threatening to burn down the store if you don't show up.

And also, the store is full of zombie hamsters. These things seem to be related. Well, bye."

As soon as he hung up, the vampire said. "That's all?"

"What did you expect? There isn't exactly a button back here for vampire emergencies."

In the silence that followed, there was audible crunching, as the hamsters chewed through the bags and got into the Cheetos. They were spilling all over the aisle like a neon orange waterfall, quickly subsumed by fuzzy gray bodies. It was a zombie feeding frenzy, but because they were hamsters it was adorable.

Josh picked up the broom, and the vampire snapped, "What do you think you're doing?"

"I'm gonna try and clean up the chip aisle," he replied. "I know you're a vampire, and I can't get the drop on you unless you allow it, so I'm not gonna try. I'm just gonna do my job. 'Kay?"

"You could try somethin'," Doug said.

He shook his head. "Really can't. These guys are the Flash of monsters."

The vampire narrowed his copper eyes, but said, "Fine. No sudden moves, or I rip his head off."

"Dude," Doug said. "We get it. Seriously. Stop bein' a drag."

"A drag?" The vampire had a questioning tone to his voice, suggesting he had no idea what that term was supposed to mean. Josh didn't feel like enlightening him, so he didn't.

Just as an experiment, Josh picked up one of the zombie hamsters, to see if it would turn to stone. It didn't. He held it in his hand, but it didn't even try and bite him. Why would it? He wasn't made of corn, and it wasn't like hamsters had much intention in the first place. They had the same drives most creature had: to eat, fuck, sleep, shit, be safe. That was about it.

Oh, weird. That sounded kind of like him. Now he was really depressed.

He used the broomstick to shove the hamsters off the shelf, and with the rain of undead rodents went a split open bag, which spewed fluorescent orange cheese puffs all over the aisle. The obvious, easy food was an instant draw, and even hamsters who managed to climb the shelves were jumping down to join in on the feeding frenzy. He really needed to film this for YouTube. He could say it was a special effects test or something, and hopefully no one would ever call him on it. The noise of hamsters noshing on Cheetos was strangely loud.

"Don't ignore me,'" the vampire said.

Josh sighed and rolled his eyes. "I'm not, but there's nothing I can do, is there? I can't make Mr. Kwan show up, and I can't attack you. So where does that leave us?"

There was a long silence, filled only with crunching. Once Josh got back to the counter and stowed the broomstick away, Doug finally broke the silence. "I gotta a vaporizer, if anyone wants to toke up."

"Satan on a unicorn, is getting stoned all you think about?" The vampire exclaimed.

"I'm a pizza delivery driver with a useless degree, and debts I'm never gonna pay off. So what else am I supposed to do?"

That was actually a very fair point. Chalk another one up for Doug.

"How about a name?" Josh wondered. "I mean, he's Doug, I'm Josh, and you are…?"

"What is this, a fucking tea party?" The vampire's eyes were glowing like embers now. "Am I your fucking friend?"

"No, you're a fucking hostage taker, but I'll call you dickhead if you don't want to give us a name."

The vampire snarled, showing one of his fangs. Which looked kind of stubby next to Colin's, but Josh knew better than to say it. At least right now. "Fine. My name is Carey."

Doug burst out laughing. "Your name is Carey?" He dissolved into a fit of giggles, and Josh found it hard not to join him. He suddenly pictured the vamp in a prom dress and a tiara, covered in pig's blood. Actually, that image was surprisingly hot.

Now Carey looked even more pissed. "What's wrong with my name?"

"It's not exactly macho, is it?" Josh said. "And, when you think of a badass vampire, the name Carey doesn't really fit very well."

Doug stopped giggling, but he was still grinning broadly. "It's somewhere between Floyd and Rutabaga."

"Like Josh and Doug are such macho names," Carey said. He couldn't have sounded more bitchy if he were on a reality show. "You sound like you should have your own brand of ice cream." While both he and Doug tried to figure that one out—okay, sure, like Ben and Jerry's, but Josh wasn't certain what the insult was exactly—Carey started showing his impatience. "Where the fuck is Kwan?"

"I told you, I can't just snap my fingers and have him show up. Besides, what's your endgame here? He shows up, curses you out, possibly beats you with your own shoe, then what exactly?"

"Like I'm telling you shit," Carey spat. "And Kwan's just a human. He can't do shit to me."

"He's a necromancer. Aren't you technically dead? Can't he control you?"

"No, that's not how it works."

"Why not? Why can necromancers control dead things, but not vampires? You're dead too."

Carey rolled his eyes. "Idiot human. We're undead, not dead."

Josh scratched his head. Mr. Kwan had tried to explain it to him before, but Josh kind of spaced out, 'cause he just didn't get it. He didn't get half this supernatural shit. It was really confusing. "Yeah, but what does that mean exactly? Why are vampires vampires and not zombies?"

Carey glared at him. "You can't be this dumb and work for Medusa. What do they teach you in this dimension?"

"That the Earth is six thousand years old, at least in some schools," Doug said.

Oh, more confusing shit. "So what the hell are dinosaur bones?" Josh asked.

Doug shifted his weight from foot to foot, clearly tired of standing, but since he had a mad vampire standing behind him with a hand to his throat, he probably wasn't sitting down anytime soon. "Hoaxes and lies of a secular media. Or something like that. I used to date this girl who was home schooled by her ridiculously religious parents. They made the Flanderses look like Iggy Pop, y'know?"

"Do you ever shut up?" Carey roared.

In the silence that followed, the bell over the door dinged, and they all looked to see a hot guy standing there, a tall brunette with hazel eyes and lips just made for kissing. In other words, Colin, Josh's sexy vampire boyfriend, had arrived. It seemed like time stopped for a single second, as everyone realized what was going on. Colin saw there was another vampire here, and he wasn't doing anything good. And Carey saw there was another vampire on the premises—maybe one he recognized, if he had done his homework at all. Josh knew shit was about to go down, but wasn't sure what.

Josh opened his mouth to speak, but never had a chance. The next thing he knew, Doug was catapulted into him, and they both went down in a tangle behind the counter, as the noise of things breaking and being thrown suddenly littered the store like so many zombie hamsters.

"Ow!" Josh complained, pushing Doug off him. He did indeed smell like weed.

"What are you complaining about?" Doug said, pushing off him and sitting up. "A vampire was threatening to tear out my throat."

There were some brief but dreadful squeaks between slamming noises, suggesting the hamsters were becoming accidental casualties of the vamp battle. They both peered over the counter, but it was very hard to see what exactly was going on. Carey and Colin were moving so fast they were essentially blurs, although collapsing shelves and flying cans were damn well visible. Also, a hamster on the floor would occasionally and suddenly become a red smear, as if smashed flat by the invisible hand of a god. "What the hell is going on?" Doug asked.

"Vampire fight. I told you they were the Flash of monsters."

"How come I still got a throat, though?"

"Colin was faster than Carey. Meaning, Colin is probably older than Carey."

"Being old makes 'em fast?"

Josh shrugged. "Kinda. Older equals stronger in the vampire world. New ones are at the bottom of the bar graph, and really old bastards are at the top."

Doug looked away from the smears of light and motion. "How old is Colin anyway?"

"He doesn't like to talk about it. But he's somewhere in the late two hundred/early three hundred range." Josh hated gay stereotypes, and the fact that Colin was reluctant to talk about his age, in spite of the fact that he no longer aged, was a real bummer. If he had to have one stereotypical trait, did it have to be age insecurity? He would have preferred Colin being into show tunes rather than that.

"So it's not so much May/December between you two as it is May 1999 and December 1842?"

Josh glared at Doug, but before he could think of a good response, Colin suddenly came to a stop in front of the counter. He had a small bloodstain on his cheek, and his hair was slightly mussed, but otherwise he looked normal. Except his copper eyes were out, but you had to expect that. "Are you all right?"

"Yeah. He couldn't hurt me, so he was using Doug as a substitute."

"I'm fine, by the way," Doug said.

Colin lobbed something one handed into the far corner. Only after it hit the wall, leaving a dent, and fell to the floor, did Josh realize it was Carey. He was trussed up like a rodeo calf, ankles and wrists together, in fine silver chain. "Talk, you stupid piece of shit," Colin snapped. "Who sent you?"

"Fuck you, old man." Carey's defiance was slightly undercut by the fact that he was saying this directly into the floor.

"Where'd you get the chain?" Josh asked, returning to a full standing position. "Also, how is that holding him?"

"He was trying to use it on me, but he's an idiot." Colin said. "It's an Atropos thread."

"That's a thread?" Doug exclaimed. "Wow, this really doesn't make sense."

"It's a special artifact. It can't be broken by anyone but a god." Colin said. He glanced back at Josh. "Kind of answers the question of who he works for, doesn't it? Not just anyone could've gotten a hold of one of those."

Josh stared back at him, confused, and started shaking his head, but then pieces began falling into place. What gods did he know? Medusa, who scared the shit out of him, but wouldn't do something like this. Then there were her sisters ... and that's when the penny dropped. "Oh shit, Sterno and Urinal. How can they be up to stuff again? Didn't Medusa exile them to another dimension?"

"Sthenno and Euryale," Colin corrected. Not that it mattered to Josh, because he was never going to get their names right. What kind of fucked up family did you belong to when Medusa was the *normal* name? "And she's exiled them before. They always seem to find their way back."

"Then why not kill them and be done with it?" Doug wondered.

Colin gave him a withering glance. "You'd kill your own family members just 'cause they're crazy?"

"Well ... no. It's just they're trying to overthrow her or something, right? So wouldn't it be better if she never had to deal with them?"

"They're not trying to kill her," Josh said. "I'm not sure they can. So they're just targeting other things, which usually means me. And I'd take it as a personal favor if she locked them up somewhere they couldn't escape and threw away the key."

Colin's look was sympathetic, but Josh knew what he was going to say before he even said it. "She's tried, believe me. It's hard to lock up gods, crazy or not."

"Medusa's crazy," Carey said, his voice muffled by the floor.

"If you'd met Sterno and what's her pants, you'd never say that," Josh said. He had, and not only were they even more visually fucked up than their snake haired sister, but they acted like their brains were hives of angry bees. You couldn't get crazier, even if you fed meth and bath salts to an entire mental ward and set them loose at Burning Man.

Colin stalked over to Carey, and lifted him one handed off the floor, by the thread binding him. He then dropped Carey like he was a fifty pound sack of wet cement. Vampire or not, that had to hurt. "What was the plan, asshole? Don't tell me this pathetic show was it."

"You didn't tell me your boyfriend was a badass," Doug whispered.

Josh looked at him with his eyebrows raised in disbelief. Should he be offended by that or not? "He's one of Medusa's handpicked soldiers. Of course he's a badass."

"I was just the first part," Carey said, still speaking into the floor.

"The first part of what?" Colin asked.

Then there was this weird noise. Josh wasn't sure what it was at first, and then his mind sort of grasped it. It was like something heavy being dragged over pavement, something made of...metal? No, not metal, but something kind of like that. It was weird, whatever it was. And it sounded like it was getting closer.

He went over to the windows, and was about to look out when the door burst open, and...Josh was pretty sure it was a prank. Either that, or he'd just had a psychotic break. Because he would swear he was looking at a bathtub.

One of those old fashioned claw footed bathtubs, white porcelain like a toilet, only this one seemed to be dragging itself forward on its clawed feet.

"Oh for fuck's sake," Colin exclaimed.

"You're seeing this too?" Josh took a couple of steps back as the tub struggled to drag itself through the doorway. Part of him wanted to help it, before he remembered it was an inanimate object that never should have been moving in the first place. "Well, I guess it proves Sterno and Uranus are behind this, 'cause they always monsterize the wrong things."

"Oh, they were the ones that did that giant slug?" Doug asked.

"Yeah. They did a giant mustache as well, and a mop thing." Josh reached the counter, and thought about grabbing the broomstick again... but for what exactly? Did silver work against bathtubs? Wait, what the hell was he thinking?

"I didn't hear about the mop thing," Doug said.

Josh looked at Colin, and gestured at the bathtub. "What do we do here?"

Colin stared back at him, with his eyebrows raised and his mouth set in an uncertain line. Since indecision was uncommon with Colin, Josh knew this was bad. "I'm not sure." He kicked Carey. "What does this thing do? Does it have a mouth?"

Carey looked up, and spied the bathtub still working to squeeze its awkwardly sized bulk through the door. He let his face collapse to the floor again before he responded. "I have no idea what that is."

Colin kicked him again. "Yes you do. This is the second part. Are you telling me that you didn't know what part two was?"

"No."

The bathtub was through the door. While the front part seemed to have moving feet, it appeared the back part didn't, which was why it was finding moving so awkward. But this brought up so many questions Josh wondered where you started. Did it have a circulatory system? A brain? How could it be moving around if it didn't have these things? What exactly was it supposed to do? Loofa them to death?

Josh retrieved the silver broomstick anyway, and decided to poke the bathtub with it, to see what it would do. "If I'd dropped acid before I came here, I'd be screaming my head off," Doug noted. He was staying well behind the counter.

"I haven't ever done acid, but I'm considering screaming my head off anyway," Josh said, edging closer to the tub. This was a billion kinds of wrong, and the hell of it was, he kind of felt sorry for it. What kind of bastard god would give some semblance of half-life to a bathtub? Cutting the batshit crazy out of it, it was weird and seemed cruel somehow. Especially since only its front two feet worked. What was the point of this?

Josh reached out and touched it with the broom handle, and the next thing he knew, he was looking up at Colin, who was hovering over him, looking as concerned as possible with his copper vampire eyes and fangs still visible. "You okay?"

Josh's right arm was alternately numb and tingling, and his head felt like it was spinning like a broken turntable. "What happened?"

"We think the tub's electrified."

"You flew across the room like a dummy made of boomerangs," Doug added, even though Josh currently couldn't see him.

Josh had no memory of this. Of course, if he was electrocuted, he wouldn't. "Who the fuck has ever heard of an electric bathtub?" He sat up, and saw the tub was standing in front of the door, as if waiting. Could a bathtub ever be said to be waiting for anything? "This is fucking mental." Looking down at his arm and the Medusa bracelet, a thought suddenly occurred to him. "Wait. How come it hasn't turned to stone?"

"I think this is why it's not so much crazy as brilliant," Colin pointed at the tub. "It has no intent whatsoever. It's just an accident waiting to happen."

Josh attempted to wrap his mind around that, but he was sure the electrocution was keeping his brain fuzzy, as this still didn't make a damn lick of sense. "Wait ... what?"

"I'm saying while this is fucking crazy, it's also brilliant. It has no intent, and even though it's been animated, it's hardly alive, is it? And by giving it a natural electrical field, it isn't attacking anyone. But if you touch it, it's gonna hurt you. Clearly they know about the bracelet, and know they can't attack you successfully."

"Call me crazy, but I fail to see how this is good news."

Colin scowled. "Well, it's not. But it's kind of fascinating."

Josh glared at him so hard he was kind of hoping he could sting him with his gaze alone. Maybe the bracelet would accommodate him in this respect. (Alas, no such luck.) "I was just electrocuted, but it's fascinating? I so wanna kick you in the shins ..."

"Maybe we should just focus on the bathtub?" Doug suggested.

Josh threw up his hands, which he could now feel completely. "Great. What the fuck are we supposed to do about it?"

There was a very long silence, with only the faint crunching from the zombie hamsters audible. "Call a plumber?" Doug finally offered.

Josh rubbed his forehead, wondering if his hair got singed. "Does anyone have a sledgehammer? Col, couldn't you just bust it into pieces?"

Colin looked back at the tub, the uncertain twist of his lips pretty much saying it all. "The electrical field might be an issue with me too."

"Fantastic."

"What's that?" Doug asked.

Both Josh and Colin looked around, but saw nothing new. "What's what?" Josh asked. "You're gonna hafta be a lot more specific."

"I thought I heard something, kinda like a bang."

It was then there was another noise, kind of like scraping porcelain, but the tub wasn't moving. Also, it sounded really muffled, like it was coming from a different room. Which was truly weird, because there wasn't another room. Just the bathroom, and the ... storage room ...

"Oh shit," Josh said, climbing to his feet. The outer back door to the storage room was impossible to open, since the werewolves bit the doorknob and warped it, but if something could kick in or force the door, it could surely get in. "We gotta bar the—"

But the words were barely out of his mouth before the storage room door was pushed open, and they saw, in the doorway, a toilet.

Doug started giggling. Josh shook his head in disbelief. "You have gotta fucking be kidding me."

"This is a new one," Colin said. "Besieged by bathroom fixtures."

"So what do we do?"

"Umm." Colin didn't even attempt to make a sentence of it. He just gave up there.

"I could probably piss in it," Doug said. "Would that help?"

"You could try," Colin said. He didn't sound hopeful.

Josh's head was starting to hurt, and he assumed it was psychosomatic, unless electrocutions gave you headaches. Or it was impact.

The toilet was somehow dragging itself into the store. It wasn't clear how. Its lid moved a little but otherwise it wasn't doing anything but propelling itself forward. Colin went over to Carey and lifted him up by the thread. "What's the point of this?"

Carey sighed. "To take over the store. The store is the access point, and whoever controls it controls the way to and from Dev."

"How are a toilet and a bathtub going to help you take over the store?"

Carey needed a good, long minute to consider this. "I don't know."

"There's a Home Depot down the road, right?" Doug asked. "Why don't I hop in my car and go buy a sledgehammer? That should take care of it, huh?"

"That's a good idea," Josh admitted. Also, possibly the only idea. "Why don't you go do that, and hurry. A sink might be showing up next."

"Or a hamper," Colin said, dropping Carey on his face again.

"Not cool, man," Carey said.

Doug pushed himself over the counter, avoiding the toilet, and managed to sidle his way out the door, avoiding the tub. This was like the worst haunted house novel possible. The bathroom was attacking, even though it had no reason to, wasn't exactly haunted, and was mostly just doing this because it was made to do this.

Josh pushed himself up onto the counter, to stay out of the way of the attacking appliances, assuming they could attack at all. Josh wondered why he was trying to understand this. None of the Sisters' monsters ever made sense, but he really didn't have much time to think about it when it was going on, as they were busy attempting to kill him. Of course, they both failed, but they put up a better effort than you would have thought considering what they were. It begged the question how Sterno and Urinal animated these things, and why they bothered, but, again, crazy. It was probably surprising they didn't wear wigs made of oatmeal and claim the CIA was bugging their fillings.

"Do you think the toilet's electrified?" Josh wondered.

Colin looked at it and shrugged. "No idea."

The silver broomstick was on the counter, so Josh nodded at it. "Wanna check? It's your turn."

"I'd rather not. Why don't we check in a new way?" Colin went over to Carey, picked him up by the thread, and tossed him at the toilet.

"Hey!" Carey shouted, as he impacted the toilet and ended up draped over the lid. "That really wasn't cool, man."

"Guess it's not electrified." Colin said.

"Then what good is it?"

"It has teeth," Carey said.

They both stared at him, not sure if they dared believe him or not. "How do you know?" Colin asked.

"I can feel it chewing," Carey said. "I think it's trying to throw me off but doesn't know how."

"I should feed you to it, you piece of shit," Colin said. But he grabbed Carey by the legs and dragged him off the toilet, which did indeed raise its lid up and slam it down, showing jagged teeth, each the size of a fifty cent piece.

"Now that's disturbing," Josh said. Because it was. It was like the nightmare of a child undergoing traumatic toilet training.

"I wonder if it has a tongue," Colin said.

Josh winced at the mental image of this. "Oh my God. Like I wasn't gonna have enough nightmares due to this."

"I was just curious."

"Well, stop it. You can examine it when Doug gets back with the sledgehammer."

The bell sounded, and Mr. Kwan came stomping through the door, his shoulders in the hunched, tightened position that signaled he was ready to bite someone's head off. (Not literally.) "Where's the motherfucking bitch ass vamp—" he stopped, coming up just short of the bathtub. (Lucky him.) "What the hell is this? Why is there a tub and a toilet in my store?"

"They're bitch ass's back up," Colin said, lifting Carey up so Kwan could have a look at him.

"And you might want to stay away from the tub, it's electrified," Josh said.

Mr. Kwan scowled at the bathtub like it was an annoying customer. "What, is it from an old CIA testing facility? How are these things even moving?" Before Josh could respond, he heard the crunching. "What the fuck...?" Mr. Kwan walked around the back of the aisle, and saw the undead hamsters having their Cheeto frenzy. "Oh for fuck's sake! Did Count Chocula bring these things too?"

"He did. He's working with a crappy necromancer."

"Really crappy," Kwan grumbled. Josh couldn't see him from where he was, but he heard the weird squeak of one of the hamsters. "Goddamn rats. Stop eating my stock. You're dead. You can't even digest it." Mr. Kwan stomped back towards the front, though he stayed farther away from the tub. "How do we get rid of these goddamn things?"

"Well, Doug's buying a sledgehammer," Josh said. "We figure that oughta do it."

"You aren't squishing these hamsters. The dead smell will linger for weeks."

Josh was revolted by the very idea. "Eww. No, we're taking out the toilet and the tub. We have no idea what to do with the hamsters. Maybe lead them to the portal behind the store with Cheetos."

Colin dropped Carey with a thud, and he muttered some curse, but Josh didn't catch it. "You're a necro too, aren't you? Can't you take them over?"

"I'm a shitty necromancer," Kwan said, craning his neck to look at the hamsters. "But so is the guy responsible for this." Kwan said something weird, something Josh had no hope of understanding, and held up a raised fist. The hamsters stopped crunching, and slowly but surely, the surviving zombie rodents started grouping behind him. It was undeniably creepy, and also, kind of weirdly cute, as long as you didn't notice most of their bodies were rotting. "Now, I wish I could make them eat vampires."

"Oh, I'll take care of this guy," Colin said, nodding down at Carey. "I'll take him back to Medusa. She can decide what she wants to do with him."

Carey looked up at him. "Please don't."

"You knew, when you aligned against her, it would come to that if you lost. Don't chicken out now."

The toilet clacked its lid noisily, making Mr. Kwan jump. "Holy fuck. Does that shitter have teeth?"

"It does," Josh said. "It's pure nightmare fuel."

"How do ya kill a toilet?" Kwan asked. "I mean, beyond Taco Bell."

They considered that for a long moment. Josh looked at all the zombies behind Kwan, and wondered aloud, "Can we choke it with hamsters?"

"Oh, hey," Colin said, slapping him on the back. "That's a great idea."

Kwan frowned. "Would that work? It's not like it's breathing."

"Why not?" Colin countered. "It's moving and has teeth. It's worth a shot, at any rate."

Kwan shrugged, and made a motion with his hand. The zombies started moving forward, but slowly, because they were corpses with degraded muscle tissues, and hamsters to boot.

Josh grabbed the silver broomstick, and tried to pry open the toilet lid, but the thing was actively fighting him, and it wouldn't budge. Colin noticed he was having a hard time and grabbed the broomstick to help. Adding Colin's strength made all difference, as suddenly the lid jumped open and was pinned back to the tank. The teeth were even more disturbing the longer you looked at them. There was no water—and no tongue—in the bottom of the bowl, which appeared to be empty, but it begged so many questions. Oh hell. Crazy crazy crazy. Josh mentally chanted that to himself as the hamsters started climbing the base and pouring into the empty bowl.

This was his work day. Watching dead hamsters crawl into animated toilet mouths. If he ever filed for unemployment, should he just slam that on there? His last job covered zombies, animated toilets, man eating mustaches, a horny Yeti stalker, and Cthulhu's loser half-brother. Looking for a job that included none of those things.

Finally, there were enough undead hamsters in the bowl to keep the lid open on its own, and he and Colin pulled the broomstick away. It tried to bite them, the lid attempting to chew up the hamsters, but it was like trying to eat a candy apple with a mouth full of gum. Two or three packs of gum, at least. And zombie hamsters didn't feel pain, so even when the lid bit them, unless it got them directly in the head, they didn't notice, and kept filling in all the spaces of the bowl.

Once all the hamsters got in there, the lid was all the way up. It couldn't close, and after a while, it stopped trying. If that wasn't dead, it was probably close enough for an animate toilet. (Crazy crazy crazy.)

"Should we consider that a win?" Kwan asked.

Josh shrugged, and Colin said, "Why not?"

Kwan grunted, apparently accepting that.

"I was misled," Carey said. "I was taken in by Gorgons."

"Tell it to Medusa, 'cause I don't give a damn," Colin said.

Doug came back in, dragging a pair of sledgehammers behind him. "These were far more expensive than I thought they would be. You got forty bucks?"

"I'll pay you back," Josh said, although he wasn't sure how. He'd worry about it later.

He took one of the sledgehammers, and was astonished at how heavy it was. Josh needed both hands to grasp the handle, and lifting it up was almost impossible. But he managed, and Doug lifted up his sledgehammer, and they both hit the tub. The tub cracked and chipped, and Josh felt a little buzz of electricity, but that may have been psychosomatic, as the handle felt like some kind of polymer plastic that wouldn't conduct it.

Doug dropped his sledgehammer. "Okay, if I do any more, I'm gonna pop my shoulders out of my sockets."

"Wimp," Kwan chided.

Colin picked up the spare sledgehammer, and swung it as though it weighed no more than a broom. Whereas Josh's hits made cracks, Colin's hits instantly pulverized the porcelain, rendering it dust. Show off.

Between the two of them, they had the tub busted down to nothing but porcelain powder in a couple of minutes. Without being asked, Colin then turned his sledgehammer on the toilet, and reduced it and the hamsters within to a red paste. It did smell pretty bad. "What did I tell you about not smashing them?" Kwan said.

"I'll get Gary to bring in some stuff," Colin replied. "He can get the smell cleared off in no time."

Kwan's sharp gaze turned to Josh. "Gary?"

Josh sighed. "He's a reverse tooth fairy, and he's a real prick. But he works for Medusa, so he could probably get the job done. Still, he's a spiteful little bastard."

Kwan shrugged. "As long as he gets the job done, I don't care."

He wouldn't. But he hadn't had to deal with that foul mouthed, deranged fairy before. Maybe Josh could take that night off, call in sick or something.

Kwan then started walking around the store, making noises of disgust. "Holy shit, we got a lot of work to do. Pretty boy, why don't you put your vamp speed to good use and straighten this all up."

Colin rolled his eyes. "Would you please not call me pretty boy? For one thing, I'm older than you." Still, he stalked off toward the back of the store, at normal, human speeds for the moment. He probably wouldn't protest too much because Kwan was his boyfriend's boss, but Josh knew Colin well enough to know he wouldn't capitulate instantly either. He only did that with Josh. Sometimes.

Doug sighed, propping himself up against the counter. "If I ever ask to come to the store with you again, remind me of this."

Josh almost laughed. Yeah, this job wasn't for everyone. He decided to try and sweep up the remains of the toilet while Colin and Mr. Kwan had a spirited debate. He then saw a blur of motion out of the corner of his eye, and a few racks righted themselves before Colin came to a stop, and said, "You don't pay me to clean up, so that's on you."

Colin came up to him, and said, "I gotta drop jerkass off at Medusa's. Then I'll be back." He game him a quick kiss before grabbing Carey by the thread and slinging him over his back like a pack. He was still protesting as Colin left with him.

"Medusa's gonna turn him to stone, isn't she?" Doug asked.

Josh shrugged. "Probably."

Kwan appeared at the head of the chip aisle, fixing Doug with a nasty look. "If you're gonna stay here and eat my stock, you can at least do some cleaning."

Doug pointed to himself, like there might be someone else around. Josh wasn't sure Doug was getting out of this one unless he left now.

Sometimes he was sure he'd be better off somewhere else. But how empty would his life be without zombie hamsters, and his sexy vampire boyfriend? Josh didn't want to know.

The Trouble With Hexes

ASTRID AMARA

Tim Keller coughed up a nasty splatter of phlegm and blood, wiped his mouth, and stepped from the alleyway beside Renegade Tattoo. "Hey, beautiful."

Vincent stopped in the middle of locking up the shop. He narrowed his eyes. "You've got to be fucking *kidding* me."

"I've missed you too, sweetheart."

Vincent's expression was both stony and hurt. He locked the door and slammed down the security gate with unnecessary force. "What do you want?"

"You."

Vincent snorted. "Too late for that, Tim. You lost booty call rights when you threw me out of the house."

Tim wavered for a moment, unsteady. His balance was the latest thing to be affected, and he clumsily lurched into the messy graffiti and rain stained bricks of the alley.

Vincent looked pissed. "Are you drunk?"

"Me?" Tim laughed-coughed. "You know I don't drink anymore."

"You also don't stop by anymore. Maybe today's the day for breaking all the rules." Tim stepped closer, and Vincent's eyes widened. "Jesus, Tim. You look horrible."

Tim couldn't argue with that. He'd lost forty pounds since he last saw his ex-boyfriend. He'd once been an obsessive weight lifter with a killer body and thick brown hair. Now he looked scrawny and had thinning hair. He was also pale as a ghost, asthmatic, and his balance and sense of body coordination were shot.

At least Vincent's looks hadn't gone to pot in the six months since they'd broken up. He was as exotic looking as ever, with those sharp cheekbones, refined nose, and thick, unruly dark hair. His neck tattoos seemed to bring out the piercing blue of his eyes. His hair was wilder than Tim had remembered it, and he still looked too skinny for his own good. But he looked like...

Home.

Tim shook his head.

"What the hell happened to you?" Vincent asked, moving closer.

Tim could see rage tempered by concern across Vincent's face. Vincent had always been so easy to read. He'd never hidden anything in the two years they'd dated. It had probably been their downfall.

"I need your help," Tim said.

"Why?"

"Because I think I've been hexed."

Vincent actually stepped back in surprise. "Bullshit."

"After everything, you think I would joke about this?" Tim pleaded. He coughed, wincing as he drew breath. The wax and wane of his breathing abilities was the most worrisome symptom of them all.

"I don't know what to think," Vincent said. He walked alongside Tim. "You don't even believe in hexes, remember?"

Tim smiled coldly. "That was before blood started coming out of my lungs."

Vincent put his hand against Tim's chest, holding him still. He narrowed his eyes now, but not in anger—in consideration. "You still got that tattoo I gave you?"

"Which one?" Tim shook his head. "Wait—yeah. Of *course*. They're tattoos. They're permanent."

Vincent arched his eyebrow, and a feeling of nostalgia, affection, and sadness washed over Tim in a powerful wave. He'd missed Vincent more than he'd allowed himself to admit.

"I figured you'd get them covered up or lasered off, considering your opinion of me the last time we spoke."

"I'd never get rid of your art," Tim said, shocked that Vincent would even consider him doing something so petty. "Besides, I paid good money for them."

"Not all of them. Show me the freebie I gave you."

"What, now? Here? It's the middle of the night."

"Yeah, and I'm not going anywhere with you until you show me."

Tim didn't understand why, but did as he was told. He lifted the hem of his T-shirt, embarrassed to show a stomach that was once washboard sexy and now resembled the belly of a thirteen-year-old boy coming out of a cold swimming pool.

Just above Tim's navel, Vincent had tattooed a complex colored foo dog, one of Vincent's pieces of flash art that Tim had found particularly compelling. He loved the play of color over the image, and the symbolism of a guardian lion that was also canine in design. But at the moment the dog looked more sinister than normal. In fact...

"Wait, did you color its eyes red? I don't remember that." Tim frowned. Was he losing his mind?

Vincent only glanced at the tattoo briefly, then went very still. "Jesus. Tim, we got to get you home."

"I just came from home," Tim complained. "I'm out of food and too sick to get more. And the whole house smells like me. Which isn't nice. I smell like salami, for fuck's sake."

Vincent smirked at that. "Always have a romantic turn of phrase at the ready, don't you?" He started walking again, gripping Tim's shoulder to steady him. "I mean *my* home. I've got some things that can alleviate your symptoms for the time being."

"Really?" Tim hoped his desperation wasn't too obvious. "So you think I'm—"

"Hexed? Yeah. No doubt about it, dear ruiner of my life."

Tim smiled at that. "Aw. Did I really?"

"Fuck you. Where's your car?"

Tim motioned with his head in the direction of Pike Street. "It's about a mile away. Parking's a bitch in this neighborhood even at midnight. Can you drive? I'm trying to minimize my time behind the wheel when I'm like this."

Vincent hesitated. "Yeah...uh, I lost my license again."

Now it was Tim's turn to scowl. "What? How many?"

"Only one. But since it occurred within a year of the last one, they took it away."

Tim sighed. "And I suppose you refused anti-seizure medication again."

"I don't need medicine," Vincent snapped, and it was déjà vu. How had they skipped past all the months of sex and love and laughter and ended up right back in the same fight they last had? "I've told you, the seizures aren't related to epilepsy. They're related to hexbreaking."

The insult lingered at the tip of Tim's tongue. All those fights over what Tim belittled as Vincent's "voodoo religion" and his "new age bullshit," and now here he was, desperate and on his last chance for help. He couldn't argue against Vincent's claim that hexbreaking gave him seizures when he himself was asking for help in breaking a hex.

Six months ago, he'd have scoffed at the idea. He was a private investigator, a believer in science and rationality and clear cause and effect. And what had started as Vincent's weird extra-curricular activity with his crazy Aunt Charlotte soon became an all-encompassing side job that Tim not only had zero faith in, but clearly took a toll on Vincent's health.

But now? He wasn't scoffing at the idea anymore.

Tim's sickness had started as a regular cold, but progressively worsened as it spread across systems. It now affected his nerves, his bones, his joints. Every part of him was falling apart, and doctors had no explanation. He had been diagnosed with lupus, pneumonia, severe asthma, pleurisy, chronic fatigue syndrome, and some unidentified form of cancer. He'd spent four months getting injections, x-rays, blood transfusions, and alternative therapies, all to no avail.

"How long have you been sick?" Vincent asked, breaking Tim's self-pitying train of thought.

"About four months."

"And you didn't come to me until now?" He shook his head. "Do you know how stupid that is?"

"No, I don't," Tim agreed. "I don't know anything about this. All I know is that nobody else can tell what's wrong with me, and something about it feels..." he paused.

Vincent glanced at him. "Feels what?"

"Intentional," Tim mumbled. It embarrassed him to even say it out loud. But he couldn't shake the sense that every ache and pain felt as deliberate as if someone were standing over him, breaking his ribs one by one.

Vincent nodded. "Well the good news is, you're doing something about it now."

"And the bad news?" Tim asked.

Vincent kept his eyes on the sidewalk. "I won't know for sure until I examine you, but I think you've got a withering hex. Witherings take about two to three weeks to activate, but when they do, they are very hardcore. And mortality follows within four to six months, tops."

Tim's skin went cold. "*Mortality*?"

"We'll figure something out," Vincent said, giving Tim a weak smile that wasn't fooling anyone. "Don't panic."

"I'm too tired to panic," Tim admitted. They finally reached his car, a nondescript silver Nissan Altima that he'd purchased specifically for its unremarkable appearance. He clicked open the doors with the remote and leaned against the driver's side door, closing his eyes. He felt drained these days, whether he did anything or not. It had gotten to the point that he had to postpone almost his entire case load. He'd already handed over as much of his work as he could to his friend and business partner

Jonah Cohen. But Jonah could only take up some of the slack—he had his own cases too.

That very morning Tim had had to look the latest prospective client in the eye and refer her over to Intelligus Inc., a corporate soul-sucking private investigative and security firm, and it left him feeling sicker than any hex he could suffer. Intelligus had been stealing clients from Keller Cohen LLC for the last year, practically running them out of their own home town, and now he was what—handing over the keys? Rolling over and letting them take it all?

Sickening. The thought alone made him feel nauseated. He grabbed his stomach.

Vincent looked panicked. "Oh God, please throw up before you get in the car. I can't drive all the way to Wallingford with puke on the floor."

"I've been worried about you too, sweetheart," Tim mumbled. He climbed into the driver's seat. Once Vincent got in the car and buckled up, Tim turned over the engine. "Where am I headed?"

Vincent looked away. "Fifty-Second."

Tim frowned. "You live on the same street as me? What happened to being in gay central?"

Vincent shrugged. "The landlord was raising the rent, and Wallingford seemed like a better fit for me. There are a few tattoo shops along the university strip I might hit up for a vacant space, get off the hill if I can. It would be nice to walk to work."

Tim concentrated on the road. His years of being a patrol officer made him a focused, deliberate driver. He was grateful for this, since so much of his mental capacity remained focused on minimizing attention to his pain.

"So how have you been?" Tim asked after a few minutes of awkward silence.

Vincent huffed. "Fine."

"How's Crazy Charlotte?"

"Fine," Vincent said. He clearly wasn't going to make this easy.

"Okay then." Tim got the hint.

By the time Vincent directed him to an older Victorian house that had been divided into separate apartments, Tim's exhaustion nearly overwhelmed him. It was a short drive, only fifteen minutes, yet it felt as though hours had passed since he'd gotten in the car. He parallel parked outside Vincent's home, turned off the engine, then rested his head against the steering wheel. He closed his eyes.

A moment later, Vincent's long, bony fingers rubbed the back of his neck. "Come on."

"Mmm. I missed you," Tim muttered into the wheel.

"All the charming words in the world aren't going to get me to carry you up the stairs," Vincent replied. "Come on. Stand up, big guy."

Tim blinked awake, then hunched over, the wave of nausea blowing through him like a stale gust of death. He scrambled out of the car and leaned against the side of it, puking up a steady stream of blood, and what could be internal organs, he had no idea anymore.

Organ-less at forty. There was a future he hadn't planned for himself.

Vincent said nothing, but rushed to Tim's side. He guided Tim up a steep, narrow set of stairs to the second story.

"Couldn't…get a place…with an elevator, could you?" Tim gasped.

Vincent fumbled with his keys to open the front door. It was pitch dark that night, the clouds low enough to almost touch, and no star visible in the sky. It was the witching hour, Vincent used to say. The hour of magic and mystery. The hour for tattoo artists, private eyes, and criminal liaisons.

And hexes.

Tim followed Vincent inside, half leaning on, half-groping Vincent as he did so. Vincent steered him through the dark to a brown L-shaped couch, where Tim collapsed.

Vincent closed the front door and switched on the lights. As he fiddled with something in the kitchen, Tim leaned back against the thick cushions of the couch and peered around the room. It had many of its traditional features, including wainscoting and filigree trim, and some large, single-paned windows overlooking the Seattle skyline and letting in an un-environmentally friendly volume of wind through the cracked seals.

Tim had half expected that Vincent on his own would make his place of voodoo business look like a fortune teller's, with mirrored tapestries and incense and florid, extravagant oriental carpets piled atop one another on the floor.

Instead, it looked like the apartment of any busy man who spent little time at home. A wall contained a large bookshelf full of art books he referenced for his work. Speakers and an ancient stereo system took up half the shelves.

In front of a large window that peered out over the city was a tilted drawing table covered in numerous sheets of tracing paper, with a few illustrations and photographs clipped out for reference. The pile at the top showcased Vincent's custom designs for clients—intricately detailed ravens, a guitar on fire, a massive mermaid, a spaceship. Each design differed yet they all held the characteristics of Vincent's unique drawing style—detailed with entangled decoration, shadows and light playing over the image.

It was the one all-encompassing image Tim had of his former lover: Vincent, hunched over his desk, sketching all night long, from the moment he got home from the studio until the sun started to peek from under the horizon, a soft smile on his face, the look he got when he did something he loved.

"Here's some water to rinse your mouth out." Vincent placed a glass on the large coffee table in front of Tim.

"Can I borrow your toothbrush?" Tim asked.

"No."

"Why not?" Tim pouted. "You've had your mouth on my asshole."

"Because I only share body fluids with people I'm sleeping with, and you are no longer one of them."

Tim sulked, drinking the water in one long gulp. He didn't realize how dehydrating dying could be.

"I'm brewing tea; it'll be ready in a few minutes," Vincent said, coming around the couch to sit on the opposite end so he could stare at Tim.

It was nice. It was kind of like old times, except in old times they'd be sitting next to each other and groping. They'd had amazing sex for the two years they'd dated, and even now, the memory of all those fucks was fresh and colorful in Tim's mind. He almost snaked a hand toward Vincent, except he wasn't sure he had enough blood left in his body to get a boner, let alone enough energy to actually get off.

So instead of acting on his frisky instincts, he simply looked his ex over.

There were subtle differences, he realized, as they studied each other under light. Vincent had coloring done on the Celtic cross of his neck tattoo. He had new tattoos on his hands, but that wasn't surprising. He always had one or two tattoos in the midst of healing.

He wore the same faded black jeans he always sported, and a tight-fitting thermal under a grey T-shirt from some band Tim didn't know. The beginnings of stubble were making their appearance on his chin and cheeks, meaning he hadn't shaved in several days. His facial hair grew slowly.

Tim, on the other hand, would have a full-out beard by the end of the night. As if mocking the fact that his hair was thinning, his beard seemed to grow extra fast these days.

Vincent studied him as well. When the kettle whistled, he made his way to the kitchen, returning with a steaming pot of something that smelled strongly herbal and unpleasant, like licorice and fish.

Tim grimaced. "No."

"Yes," replied Vincent, pouring him a cup. The tea was a light green color. "It'll make your feel better, I promise."

Tim took a deep breath, then nodded. "Okay."

"It's not a cure," Vincent cautioned. "It can dull the effects, but the hex will continue to take effect until I break it."

Tim sipped the hot beverage. It tasted sour, but the flavor of anise overpowered everything else. "So what's a withering hex?"

Vincent stretched his legs out between them and leaned back, blue eyes staring straight at Tim. "There are several kinds of hexes, and hexmakers specialize in one or two. Only a few can create any type."

"Hexmakers," Tim repeated. "The opposite of you, I take it."

"Yes."

"Couldn't someone who breaks hexes make one?"

Vincent raised an eyebrow. "Yeah but why would they? Hexbreakers like me spend all our free time working to break them apart. We wouldn't manufacture more." He sighed. "It's so strange, telling you all this. You threw me out on my ass when we started this conversation six months ago."

"I know. I'm sorry." Tim swallowed. "Let's just say I've grown, shall we?"

Vincent snorted at that, a hint of a smile curling the corner of his pouty lips. "So hexmakers usually specialize. Spot hexes are the easiest to weave, and take effect immediately. However, they only last for a week or so, a month at most. They target direct pain to a specific location on the body.

"Memory hexes are more debilitating," he continued. "They also go into effect quickly, and can lead to severe mental illness, and occasionally death, although that's typically self-inflicted. They mess with your sense of self, your sense of time and place, and memories. They warp who you are and what you remember."

"Fuck." Tim shivered. "Glad I don't have that."

Vincent's eyebrow quirked up. "No you aren't. Because you have a withering hex. They are hard to make and even harder to dismantle. And they always end in death."

Tim sipped more of the tea in response. "So how do we go about breaking it?" The more tea he drank, the more he felt disembodied, as if the pains radiating from his joints and bones belonged to someone else.

"There's no *we* here," Vincent said. "Charlotte is too busy with her own work and you're too sick to do anything but rest. I'll hit the streets tomorrow and see what I can find out."

"Oh come on," Tim scoffed. "Do you think I'm the kind of person who would sit on my ass and wait for someone else to solve something?"

Vincent did smile at that, his gaze turning affectionate for a moment. "No. But this isn't a case of a missing person or insurance fraud, Tim. There are a lot of steps involved, and even if we work together night and day, the chances of us solving this are slim."

That sobered Tim right up.

Vincent shook his head. "A hex is made with smoke and intention, and is woven into a pattern with intent to kill. I can untangle the smoke threads knotting this together in your body, but there's a hexroot, an object binding the hex on the other end that will continue to grow the structure until the root is destroyed. We need to find the object that's binding the hex to you. That usually stays with the hexmaker's client, which means we have to find out who hexed you. If we can retrace the who, and what, and why, then there's a chance I can unravel the pieces."

"And if not?" Tim asked. "Can we call it back or something? Cancel it out with another hex?"

"It doesn't work like that. You can't eradicate one illness with another. Once a hex is created, it's a thing, living and breathing, and it can't be nullified. It can only be broken or, in some cases, transferred."

"Transferred?" Tim perked up at that.

But Vincent scowled. "I won't do that. I swore an oath that I would never in my life hex another human being, and transferring one is as bad as creating one from scratch."

"Can't you transfer it back to the person who bought it?" Tim asked.

"Theoretically, yes, if we knew who that person was." Vincent shook his head. "But I won't. I'll never do that, not even for you, and not even if the person is the vilest piece of scum on earth."

"Why not?" Tim asked. "It's self-defense."

"It's morally abhorrent. Besides, there are better ways to get hexmakers to stop that don't involve murder."

"Like what?" Tim asked.

"It's complicated."

"You think I got something better to do tonight?"

Vincent sighed. "Everyone has a unique personal symbol, we call it a marker. It's a source of power for an individual, and it's what hexmakers use to tie their hexes to their victims.

"I can deface a hexmaker's personal symbol in such a way that I remove the source of their power."

"Deface how?" Tim asked. "Like beheading?"

Vincent snorted. "Not that dramatic, Tim, we're not *murderers*." He shifted though, looking a little uncomfortable. "It's a brand, made specifically to eradicate the hexmakers own symbol."

Tim made a face. "You're *branding* people?"

"It's more humane than transferring a hex," Vincent replied, looking defensive.

Tim shook his head. "I don't get how science hasn't figured any of this out."

Vincent laughed at that. "Because science and magic aren't compatible."

Tim finished the tea. It left him feeling woozy, almost drunk. "So what do you need from me?"

Vincent stood up. "Strip."

Tim clumsily obliged. His hoodie came off easily, and he kicked off his shoes. He slowed at removing his t-shirt and jeans, embarrassed to display his weak body. But when Vincent motioned for him to continue, Tim hurriedly pulled off his shirt and jeans, and gripped the elastic band of his underwear.

Vincent held out his hand. "Whoa, that's enough. Skivvies on please."

"It isn't like you haven't seen my balls before."

"This isn't foreplay." He moved closer to Tim, eyes narrowing. "Damn. Whoever it is, they're good. I can't see shit. Hold on." Vincent walked back to the kitchen, and returned with a very large gel pill filled with yellow liquid. He swallowed it, and washed it down with a swig of water.

Almost instantly Vincent's pupils dilated. His skin went a shade paler.

"What did you just do?" Tim asked.

"It's crowpepper." Vincent moved to stand beside Tim again.

"What's that?" Tim asked.

Vincent narrowed his eyes at Tim's chest. "A type of poison. Hold still."

Tim stepped back. "Wait, *what*? Is this going to hurt you, helping me?"

"Stop moving." Vincent stared at Tim, looking him over slowly from head to toe, his glance lingering on Tim's chest and throat.

"Answer me," Tim demanded. "Is helping me going to give you another seizure?"

"Maybe. Unlikely. Shut up for once, please. I'm trying to concentrate."

Vincent studied Tim in such a detailed, methodical way, any burgeoning libido Tim may have drummed up the energy for withered and died. The examination was thoroughly unflattering. "You strip all the people you examine, or only the ones you used to fuck?"

"*Tim.*" It was a scold, not an invitation. At last Vincent stepped back, wobbling a little as he did. Tim shot out his arm and grabbed him in case he fell over. "I'm fine," Vincent said. He collapsed back onto the couch. "It's hard transitioning from micro to macro, that's all."

Tim had no idea what that meant. But while Vincent's attention was elsewhere, he took a chance and sat right next to Vincent.

"Someone really hates you, Tim," Vincent said, rubbing his eyes. "Anyone come to mind?"

Tim snorted. "Are you kidding? I'm a private dick. I can list ten people off the top of my head who hate my guts and wouldn't mind me being dead. I wouldn't know where to begin."

"Begin four months ago, when you first got sick. It would have been someone who hired a withering hexmaker early that month, in the first two weeks of June. The kind of person to know about occult practices and the existence of curses, and who had access to some possession of yours that could serve as a hexroot. They'd also have to be someone with the money to buy a hex."

"Are they expensive?" Tim asked.

"Let's just say there's more money in hexmaking than hexbreaking."

"Are we talking a thousand here?"

Vincent scoffed. "For a spot hex, sure. For a withering? Especially the fucked-up, tangled mess around you?" Vincent shrugged. "That could be anywhere in the thirty to fifty grand range, depending on the abilities of the hexmaker."

Tim felt as though he'd been punched. Someone spent fifty grand to make him sick? He knew he had enemies, but the idea that someone had so much hatred of him they'd expend that sort of cash frightened him.

"It's the same as hiring a hit man," Vincent said. "Someone wants you dead, and they want you to die a slow, painful, agonizing death. It's the worst possible thing to wish upon another human being, and the malice of the wish gets woven into the hex, giving it barbs."

Tim shivered. He'd always prided himself on being stoic in the face of anger or pain or the end of his own life, but fear had slowly taken over his calm demeanor the last few months, and now it threatened to engulf him.

Something in his expression must have alarmed Vincent. He put his arm around Tim and rubbed his back. "I'll do everything I can, all right?"

Tim wanted to have a sexy comeback, or at least a derisive one. Instead he rested his head against Vincent's bony shoulder. The bone dug deep into Tim's temple, but he didn't care. For the first time in months, he felt safe.

"I missed you," he whispered again.

Vincent didn't reply. But he didn't stop rubbing Tim's back either.

Tim breathed in Vincent's unique scent, a mix of tattoo sterilization fluids, pine soap, and an exotic musk. "Vincent?"

"Hm?"

Tim whispered, "You seeing anyone?"

Vincent let out a breath of air. "Fuck, Tim. Now's not the time."

"Are you?"

"No. But that doesn't mean you get to pick up where we left off." He pulled back slightly, staring into Tim's eyes. "You broke my heart, you bastard. I loved you."

"I know." Tim swallowed. "I loved you too. Still do."

Vincent pulled back completely. "Your loss."

"Yeah." Tim rubbed a hand over his stubble. "The worst one of all."

Vincent stared at him for another long moment, then shook his head again. "You should take a shower. You smell like salami."

"Told you so." Tim followed Vincent down a narrow hall to a small but clean bathroom with an old claw-footed bathtub and hand-held shower head. Vincent provided him with some clean clothes, a towel, and a fresh razor.

"Do I need to pick up Bogart?" Vincent asked.

Tim shook his head. "Nah, my sister's been looking after him since I got really sick. You know how he is if he doesn't get a long walk every day. He drove me crazy."

Vincent smiled at that, and left, shutting the bathroom door softly.

Tim moved slowly, his body responding sluggishly, his mind a little like molasses. Whatever had been in that tea packed a punch. At least he didn't feel the pain in his lungs.

He washed himself, scrubbed his hair, and shaved. He would never have been able to wear even Vincent's baggiest sweatshirt four months ago. Now Vincent's T-shirt slipped over his frame easily.

The efforts of driving to Capitol Hill, finding Vincent, conversing, and showering had taken all of the reserves Tim had, and by the time he re-emerged from Vincent's bathroom, he was so tired he worried he'd fall over and pass out right there in the hallway.

Vincent seemed to understand this. He grabbed Tim's arm and led him down the hall to a sparsely furnished bedroom. Tim collapsed onto the futon bed. He passed out even before he had a chance to make one failed pick-up attempt.

Hexed indeed.

2

THE MEMORIES WERE bittersweet.

Vincent recalled those Saturdays of the two of them lying in bed, lazy blowjobs, playing on their laptops and eating breakfast under the sheets, Tim's Boston Terrier Bogart curled between them, the room scented with roasted coffee, cinnamon rolls, semen, and whatever Bogart had rolled in that morning.

For an entire year Vincent had harbored a crush on Tim from afar. They'd run into each other at parties of their mutual friend, and Vincent fell for Tim's rugged, powerful looks, his biting sense of humor, his unabashed self-confidence.

They'd hooked up, and the next two years did nothing but strengthen Vincent's affections. Tim Keller was reckless, brash, charming, and an asshole. He loved Vincent's artwork, he loved the same martial arts films, and he knew just how to bring Vincent off in such an explosive, all-encompassing way, sex with anyone else paled in comparison.

But everything changed after Charlotte recruited Vincent to help her break hexes.

In retrospect, Vincent had probably gone about it all wrong. Rather than bring Tim in, have him spend time with Charlotte and her clients, see with his own eyes the devastating affects hexes could cause, Vincent had chosen to cut Tim off from that world. He knew in his heart Tim would disapprove. It was unproven, unbelievable, and worse, dangerous.

Every time Vincent came home with blown pupils, a wobble to his step, or a killer migraine, Tim flipped out. He thought Vincent was on drugs. Or involved in some voodoo religion. Anything but the truth.

When the seizures started, Tim gave him an ultimatum: stop his dangerous bullshit with Aunt Charlotte or he'd kick Vincent out. He wasn't going to sit and watch Vincent kill himself for something that was a lie.

And now they were here.

Vincent tried to get comfortable on the couch. He closed his eyes and replayed those last fights over in his head. So much heartache, both of them brought to tears. Vincent never had a doubt that Tim loved him, more than Vincent loved himself, it seemed. But once Vincent had seen the devastating impacts a hex could wreak on an innocent individual, he *couldn't* stop. If given a real chance to eradicate evil in the world, what kind of honest man would step aside?

Not Vincent. He sat up, angry and regretful and bitter all at once. No way would he sleep now. He made his way to the kitchen and opened a bottle of beer. He'd stopped drinking in front of Tim when Tim decided to quit because it interfered with his work. That had been ages go and here Vincent was, sneaking the drink out of sight as if no time had passed.

Vincent gathered Tim's clothes off the bathroom floor and threw them in the washing machine hidden in the hallway closet, knowing Tim's clean-freak state of mind would recoil at the idea of wearing an outfit from the day before. He'd never understood how Vincent could comfortably wear the same jeans for a week straight. It was one of the ways they were different.

What did they say about opposites attracting?

Yeah. *Magnets*. Not really a good metaphor for people.

Vincent sat at his drawing table. He had two custom pieces to complete this week, and a client consultation that afternoon had been for a complex half-sleeve design that would take quite a bit of work.

But he couldn't relax with a beer and drawing while Tim lay dying in the other room.

Vincent hadn't forgiven him. Nothing that grandiose. But he did feel a surge of sympathy for the man. In his short time learning about hexes with Charlotte, he had never seen the type of crude, jangled knots that tightened around Tim's chest and throat. Hexes were like pernicious, thorny ivy crafted from smoke and ill will.

This hex had *layers* of hate. It was crude and rudimentary, and yet somehow also purer in its specific, malicious intent. It was designed to choke Tim off, one breath at a time. The bulk of the weaves strangled his chest and throat, crushing Tim from the inside out.

And Vincent had no idea who'd made it.

He decided that, if he couldn't draw, and he couldn't sleep, he might as well do a bit of research into what his known hexmakers had been up to four months prior.

The ones he and Charlotte had hunted down had been decommissioned with defacing brands, although the effects of the brand would fade over time. Sometimes the hexmakers would end up gaining back their powers. Charlotte even suspected there was a circle of hexmakers who worked together to heal brands.

Vincent was working on incorporating the defacing properties of the brand into a tattoo, something that wouldn't fade like the effects of the brand and would bind the restriction to the culprit forever. As far as he could tell, no prior hexbreakers had ever worked with inking their magic directly into their subjects, and the possibilities seemed endless.

However, with Charlotte being called to all corners of the country for her hexbreaking expertise, Vincent hadn't had much time to experiment. He was alone in the Pacific Northwest, and while it wasn't as bad as some places like New York or Detroit, there still was a lot of hate to spread around.

He booted up his laptop and looked at the database he'd created with another hexbreaker in New Orleans, an online resource for the small cadre of individuals who spent their free time eradicating hexes. The known hexmakers in the region of Seattle who were capable of weaving a withering were either still under the restrictions of brands, or AWOL.

His back ached from sitting on his stool. He glanced at the couch. It was comfy enough for sitting upright, but its pillowy softness brutalized an aching back. He brushed his teeth, changed into boxers and a T-shirt, and quietly made his way to his bedroom.

Tim sprawled unconscious across the bed, stretched diagonally, claiming seventy-five percent of the mattress. Vincent smiled. *Just like old times.*

This was a bad idea, he knew it. Sleeping in the same bed was an invitation. They'd both sport morning wood, and then what? They were supposed to ignore the fact that they knew each other's bodies so well? Ignore all those memories of mouths and hands and laughs, quiet sleepy morning delight?

Vincent scoffed. Tim would be lucky to have the strength to stand this morning, let alone jack off.

The idea that someone could hate Tim so much as to hex him with that deadly weave brought up a seething anger and protectiveness within Vincent. Regardless of how their relationship ended, he wanted Tim to thrive.

"Scoot over, Romeo," Vincent whispered, nudging Tim's shoulder. Even sound asleep, Tim obeyed his command. He mumbled something and rolled over, creating enough space for Vincent to slip in beside him. He used to turn into that big body and groan with contentment when Tim enfolded him in a fuzzy embrace. Now Vincent turned away so they slept back to back. Less chance of betraying his anger this way.

He woke up to the sound of puking.

Vincent startled upright, confused for a moment. Daylight streamed in from around the thick curtains, and the light illuminated the hallway and the open bathroom door. The sounds of Tim's distress knifed through Vincent. He hesitated—would it be worse to not be offered help or to be caught puking? He nearly crawled out of bed, when the toilet flushed, and the sound of running water and splashing emerged. A minute later, Tim returned to bed, looking like a ghost, awash of all color, dark brown eyes sunken in his face.

"Did I wake you?" he croaked. His hands were shaking. "Sorry. I tried to be quiet." He crawled under the sheets and didn't make a move toward Vincent, the ultimate proof he felt wretched. Tim curled into a ball and shuddered as if fevered.

Vincent reached over and felt his forehead. He burned hot.

"Do you get fevers often?" he asked.

"Yeah." Tim closed his eyes. "And I can't keep anything down. It scares me."

Worry wracked Vincent. He stroked the back of Tim's neck until the shaking subsided a little. Then he did get out of bed. He made another brew of block tea. While it steeped, he shaved and dressed. He was tired, but had too much to do to keep sleeping.

"Hey." He nudged Tim's unconscious form. He sat on the edge of the bed, beside Tim's head. He ran his fingers through Tim's hair. Several strands came out with his fingers, and he swallowed back his sadness. "Wake up, big guy. More tea for you."

Tim's eyes opened slowly. He looked exhausted. He blinked. "*Vincent?*"

"Yeah." Vincent smiled. "It's me."

"Thank *God*." Tim's arms wrapped around Vincent's frame, and his head rested in Vincent's lap. His hot breath warmed his crotch.

Vincent cleared his throat. "Hey. Sit up. You need more tea to block the effects of the hex." Tim didn't move. He seemed to have fallen back asleep.

The hot, rhythmic breathing of Tim's mouth on Vincent's crotch raised his neglected pecker to attention.

Vincent shook Tim's shoulder. "Wake up. *Now.*"

Tim shot up. "What?" He blinked, wiping his eyes. He glanced around the room, his eyes settling on Vincent. "Hey." He coughed, and something deep and terrible rattled in his lungs. "Sorry, I'm a bit groggy these days."

"Drink this." Vincent handed over the cup of tea, rising quickly to hide his unfortunate erection.

Tim drank the tea quickly, making a face at the sharp taste. "Ugh. Couldn't add some sugar or something could you?"

"No." Vincent opened the closet in the hallway to retrieve Tim's clothes.

"If you're looking for condoms in there, I have a few in my wallet," Tim called out, his voice hoarse. "I think one is even cherry flavored."

Vincent poked his head out of the closet. "Yeah? Didn't I give you that like two years ago?"

"Probably. I haven't scored much since you know...*lung blood*."

Vincent laughed at that. He grabbed Tim's dress shirt and threw it at Tim. Normal, healthy Tim would have caught it out of the air like a ninja.

Hexed Tim let the shirt hit him square in the face. "Hey!"

"Sorry." Vincent dropped the rest of Tim's clothes on the bed. "I washed these for you."

"You just want to get me naked, admit it," Tim said.

"Actually, I want you to focus. We need to head over to Charlotte's before she takes off again."

Tim scowled. "Why?"

"She can make a decoy. It's kind of like a voodoo doll—it will siphon the growth of the hex onto another object temporarily."

"Why can't you make me one?" Tim asked.

Vincent was at once embarrassed to admit how much he still had to learn, even after years of this work, and also flattered that Tim assumed he was an expert. Tim projected his own self-confidence on all of his friends.

"I've never needed to build one on my own until now," Vincent admitted. "But if she shows me how, I can be the one to hold the decoy, and its effects will be strengthened when I'm nearby."

Tim gave Vincent his cocky half-crooked smile. "So it looks like you're stuck with me."

"More's the pity. Drink that whole pot of tea," Vincent ordered. He then stepped out of the bedroom and made his way to the kitchen.

He set out two bowls of cereal, milk, and coffee on the coffee table. Tim emerged a few minutes later, dressed with his hair combed, but his face was very pale.

"Breakfast is served." Vincent sat on the couch and poured coffee for himself. He fished out his plastic pillbox and quickly swallowed the big yellow crowpepper pill with a slosh of coffee. He'd likely need a double dose of the poison to see the intricacies of Charlotte's work, but he'd learned months ago that taking too much at once set off his seizures.

Tim grimaced. "Oh for fuck's sake—"

"I'm going to live," Vincent interrupted, cutting him off before he started. "It's a *very low dose*. You're the one who needs to worry, so stop babying me." Vincent poured milk into his bowl, then fetched a pad of paper and pen.

"We need to narrow down suspects," Vincent said, returning to the table. Tim ate slowly, making a face. Vincent took a bite of his own cereal. Tasted fine.

Then he remembered one man he'd helped last year, who said everything he ate tasted like ashes in his mouth. Watching Tim try and choke down Special K made Vincent feel Special Angry.

"Let's start four months ago," Vincent said. "Who would have been mad enough to curse you?"

"Dozens of people." Tim shrugged. "I don't know. Who had fifty grand to spare? No idea." He pushed the cereal away.

Vincent sighed. He bumped his pen against his lips. "Okay, first thought? Jamie Santucci."

Tim scoffed. "No way."

"It's like murder, Tim," Vincent insisted. "The first obvious suspect is always the ex-lover."

"That would be *you* then," Tim argued. "You were my last steady date. I haven't seen Jamie in ages."

"But isn't he suing you?"

Tim grunted. "It won't amount to anything. Again. A judge already threw out his claim that I owe more for the sale of our condo because he covered the down payment. He got sixty percent of the sale already, so he's wasting his time."

"The fact that he's wasting his time doesn't negate him as a suspect, it strengthens suspicions. He isn't going to win a lawsuit against you so he's seeking revenge in another way."

Tim shook his head. "You don't get him. He's a greedy prick, not a vengeful one. Jamie doesn't care about anyone but himself. It's precisely why I broke up with him in the first place—he doesn't give a shit about *me*. The only way I'd peg him for it is if he'd sent a ransom note stating he'd kill me slowly and painfully if I didn't pay him a couple grand. But I haven't gotten any threats at all."

Vincent jotted down Jamie's name anyway. "Fine. Who else hates you?"

"Besides you?"

Vincent rubbed his eyes. "I don't hate you. That's the problem. You broke up with *me*, remember?"

"I didn't know any of this was real, did I?" He sighed. "I thought you were crazy. Only now that I'm experiencing this with my own body do I believe. You can't hold that against me."

"I can hold you accountable for the *way* you broke up with me," Vincent said. "You were such a dick about it."

A flicker of rage crossed Tim's tired features. "You were killing yourself!" His anger seemed as fresh as it had been the day they'd last seen each other. "You expected me to just let you go on getting migraines and seizures and God knows what else while you ran around doing something mysterious with your aunt?"

Tim motioned to Vincent's pill box. "Even now, you're poisoning yourself without a moment's hesitation!"

"If you were so worried about me, you had a funny way of showing it," Vincent said, unable to hide the bitterness in his voice.

"I *was* worried about you!" Tim cried. He ran his hand over his face. "God, you can be so careless. I worried, and I told you over and over, but all you did was dismiss my fears and tell me to leave it alone. So yeah, I left. I wasn't going to watch you die on me."

Vincent scowled down at the blank sheet of paper. "It's not your call. I can do what I want to."

"You can't kill yourself, not when I'm in love with you."

"I'm fine. I *will* be fine. And the work I do is important. God, you should see that by now. Look at you!" Vincent nodded at the half-full bowl of cereal. "You're the one who's dying. And I can do something about it. So what if I get a headache? I'm going to *live*, which is more than I can say for you!"

They stared at each other. Fighting, *again*. Always. How had they become so predictable?

Tim seemed as though he would argue more, but suddenly, as if the anger drained from him, he slouched and leaned back against the couch. "Let me check my calendar."

Tim reached into his pocket and pulled out a cellphone. He swiped through screens. "Four months ago...that was June. I'd finished up the... *oh*." Tim winced. "Oh yeah. *Mrs. Prelle.*"

"Who's she?" Vincent asked.

"A client. Well, she was a client. She then became the subject. She wasn't too happy about that."

"You got her address on file somewhere?"

"Back at the office, but—"

"Good. Choke down the rest of the cereal, we're going to stop by your place on the way to Charlotte's."

Tim seemed a little startled by the sudden action, but he did as he was told.

The tea was noticeably helping Tim. His uncoordinated lurching from one room to the other was gone, and his breathing sounded less labored.

"You still working out of your house?" Vincent asked as he sat in the passenger seat.

"Yeah. Jonah might be there. Be nice."

"I always am," Vincent said, although truthfully, there was a lot he didn't like about Tim's friend and business partner. While Tim seemed like the PI that starred as the good guy in detective stories, Jonah was the bad guy—weasely, suspicious, guilty-looking.

But Tim and Jonah had been friends a lot longer than Vincent and Tim had. They'd both worked for another security firm for a few years before opening up their own shop in Tim's back studio.

Tim's house was only a few blocks from Vincent's. It would have taken Vincent only five minutes by bike. But the lights and traffic made the journey twice as long.

"So what's the story with Mrs. Prelle?" Vincent asked.

"She hired us to collect evidence on her cheating husband. I got the evidence easily enough, but she never paid up. I called several times, but she kept saying she'd pay me after I coughed up the pictures. I explained that wasn't how it worked, and she got real pissy. So I went to her house and took pictures of her with *her* lover."

Vincent shook his head. "Yuck. Nice couple."

"I contacted her husband, and told him his wife was cheating on him, and he could have the evidence for a fee."

Vincent scowled. "That was a shitty thing to do."

Tim shrugged. "I'd already put several hours in and had nothing to show for it. I'd even waived my retainer fee for her since she'd made such a sob story about the whole thing. Seeing her cheating on her husband made me a little more callous I suppose."

"So what happened?" Vincent asked.

"What you'd expect," Tim replied. "Her husband confronted her, she confessed, then she spent the next three weeks calling me a dozen times a day to tell me what a shit I was."

As Tim pulled his Nissan up the small hill of the driveway in front of the single floor craftsman bungalow, a feeling of warmth filled Vincent. He'd loved living in this house with Tim.

Vincent half expected the sound of Bogart's barking and his goofy face smearing the window with slobber at their arrival. So when Tim opened the front door and no dog greeted them, Vincent felt a little empty.

"I miss Bogart," he admitted.

Tim smiled. "Me too. I can't wait to get him back. Every time I drop food on the floor I expect him to clean it up. It just sits there now, rotting."

"Torture for a clean freak like you," Vincent said.

"You have no idea." As Tim made his way through the living room, Vincent recalled all the routines that hadn't changed since they'd lived together. Lock the front door. Dump the keys on the table by the door. Peel off the coat. Turn up the heat. Vincent took in quick glimpses of the house as they made their way to the kitchen. Nothing at all had changed, other than the places where Vincent's art had hung remained bare. The space above the sofa even had a darkened rectangle on the wall where sunlight had faded the blue wall except where Vincent's painting had been.

Vincent stared at that rectangle. It made him inordinately sad.

"Come on." The back door clanged open and the blinds banged against the old window. They crossed the small yard to the tiny studio the former owners had rented out to college kids.

The studio backed onto the alley and consisted of a single room and a small bathroom. It appeared like a portrait in opposites—Jonah's desk looking like a cyclone had hit, Tim's orderly and clear of any paperwork. They had different working styles, different personalities, it was remarkable they even remained partners for seven years.

Jonah wasn't in, and Vincent let go of a breath he didn't realize he was holding. He'd expected Jonah to blame him for something. Jonah always took Tim's side.

Tim booted up his computer and plugged in his phone. He moved stacks of manila file folders off a wooden chair beside Jonah's desk and propped it beside his own, motioning to Vincent to sit.

"I hope you never bring potential clients here," Vincent commented. He shook his head. "How does Jonah work in that mess?"

"He's got a system, so he tells me," Tim said, yawning. He typed in his password and started sorting through his contact database. "And no, we never bring anyone here. We always meet in public spaces. Safer for everyone."

"Your latte bill must be enormous," Vincent said.

"That's why God invented business expense write-offs." Tim nodded to the screen. "Here we go. Prelle lives in Madrona, or did four months ago."

Vincent whistled. "Nice neighborhood."

"You can see why she wanted the edge over her husband. And why I didn't buy the whole 'I'm poor give me time' argument."

"Still, that was shitty of you."

"Well, business has been hard," Tim said. "Remember when I used to bitch about Intelligus Inc.? It's only gotten worse since they opened their Seattle office. We're barely staying afloat. Jonah wants to fold shop. He and Annie have had to put a second mortgage on their house to pay their bills, and our caseload drops every time Intelligus advertises. Annie's been nagging him for years to quit the PI business and go into private security, where there's more money." He ran his hand over his face. "So yeah, I felt a little guilty, but I figured the money would help us assist some more needy clients in the future. You have to make choices."

Tim pointed to the screen, and Vincent copied the address down in his notebook. Tim's phone vibrated on the desk, nearly falling off. Tim checked the screen.

"Keller Cohen," he said brusquely. Vincent used to tease him that he needed an actual secretary or referral service, but Tim considered it an extra expense they needn't bother with. That's what cellphones were for.

Shouting emerged from the other line. Tim winced and held the phone away, quickly disconnecting.

"Lover?" Vincent couldn't help himself.

"Ha ha. That was someone who should probably be on your list of suspects."

"Who was it?"

"Steve Lassiter," Tim said. Vincent wrote the name down as Tim continued. "I helped his wife about six months ago when he split town, taking their son after she'd been granted sole custody. I set him up and got their kid safely back to his mother, but the guy went off the deep end. He's been in and out of the drunk tank since then. I think he has a few battery charges to boot."

"Should we look him up?" Vincent asked.

Tim's eyebrows came together in a scowl. "Not unless you want to get shot. He mostly resorts to yelling at me a few times a week, from different phone numbers so I can't block the calls."

"We need to ask around, find out if he knows any hexmakers," Vincent said.

"Sure, I'll call him up and ask. As you can see, he's nothing but a gentleman on the phone."

Vincent looked at him blankly. To his surprise, Tim smiled, and reached his hand out to stroke Vincent's head. "I missed that look."

"What look?"

"That 'you're an idiot' look."

Vincent said, "I must give it a lot."

"All the time, sweetheart," Tim replied.

Vincent changed topics to keep his mind on the task at hand. He made Tim go through the lists of clients he'd had over the past half a year. They made note of everyone who was either possibly mad at Tim, had something to gain from Tim's death, including the head of Intelligus, which seemed like a stretch, and who would likely have the kind of money available to purchase a hex.

"I gotta make a few calls to follow up on Mrs. Oswald, okay?" Tim said. "She's a client with a missing daughter."

Vincent nodded. "Sure."

Tim flushed a little. "Sorry—can I..."

"Oh right. Privacy." Vincent stood. "I'll make you a sandwich in the kitchen."

Tim rolled his eyes. "I'm not hungry."

"Yes you are." Vincent left before he could hear any more.

Vincent easily navigated a kitchen he'd used for almost two years, though Tim hadn't been exaggerating when he said he had no food around. The fridge was bare of anything but condiments. Vincent briefly considered cooking rice and doing something with the dried lentils in the back of the cupboard, but decided that would be too much effort.

Maybe Tim would eat a mayonnaise and ketchup sandwich?

Yeah. That's likely to get someone turned off food to eat again.

He was still puttering around when Tim returned.

"You know, that tea makes me feel a little drunk." Tim smiled. "You sure as a recovering addict I should be drinking this stuff?"

"It's herbal," Vincent assured him.

"Yeah, so's pot."

"Let's get to Charlotte's," Vincent said.

Tim mumbled something Vincent couldn't hear. Nevertheless he dutifully led the way out of the house, reversing his arrival routine. Turn down the heat, put on his coat, pick up his keys, lock the front door. Vincent followed him out of the house.

It was a lovely autumn day in Seattle, the air crisp and sweet with the scent of moss and rotting berries. Everyone was outside, enjoying the rare sunshine. As they drove, Tim plugged his phone into his car and made several calls on speakerphone, following up on leads to find Mrs. Oswald's runaway teenager Zoe.

He then rang Jonah, holding up a finger to silence Vincent.

"Hey Jonah," Tim said.

"Where are you?" Jonah sounded exhausted. "I've been running around all morning trying to establish a pattern on this delivery detail—"

"Don't worry about that. Listen, I've got a lead on the Zoe Oswald case, I'm going over there this afternoon."

Jonah paused. "Really? Are you sure you feel up for that?"

"Sure."

"You going alone?" Jonah asked.

Tim hesitated. He glanced sheepishly at Vincent, then back at the road. "Vincent's with me."

Vincent heard Jonah's muffled expletive. "I thought you were through with that weirdo."

"Hey!" Vincent chimed in.

"You have me on speakerphone?" Jonah cried, "And we're talking clients? Tim—"

"Yeah, yeah. I know. No details. Listen I just wanted to keep you posted. You can drop the missing delivery for now, I know you have bigger things and I can postpone them another week."

"Call me if you need backup with Zoe," Jonah said.

"Thanks, champ." Tim disconnected, then shook his head. "I should be dealing with Zoe now, not in an hour from now. What good is it going to do to see Charlotte anyway?"

"Trust me, the decoy is going to make you feel like new." Vincent hoped he wasn't exaggerating the results. "We need you fit enough to fight off the effects until I can pinpoint who is holding the hexroot tying this to you. And I'd like to find out who out there is making these kind of messy hexes in the first place." Vincent grinned. "You know, usually with hex cases, it's pretty obvious who cursed who. Most people don't have such an extensive list of suspects."

Tim pulled into Charlotte's driveway. "Well, I'm special like that." He turned off the engine. He stared at his steering wheel as if gathering strength.

"She won't bite," Vincent assured him.

"I'll hold you to that." Tim followed him out. "I'm having second thoughts about this."

Before he'd even made it up the walkway to the front of the sprawling seventies rambler, Aunt Charlotte herself appeared, wooden spoon in hand.

"Well *fuck my eyes*. What's that son of a bitch doing here?"

Yeah—Vincent had second thoughts too.

3

Tim had the joy of watching Vincent squirm under the swearing, waving spoon violence, and vitriolic lecturing that made up Vincent's mother's sister.

They'd obviously caught her in the midst of preparing for a long trip. Half-packed suitcases littered the hallway, stacks of pre-prepared food in plastic containers covered the kitchen counter, and she was stirring some sort of meaty soup made on a massive scale. Maybe it was human baby soup. She punctuated every sentence by flinging the stirring spoon toward Vincent, splattering him with baby soup juice.

Tim never understood what had paired Vincent with Charlotte anyway. She was temperamental and brash. She'd been married three times and number four walked out before she could get another ring on her finger. She didn't look to be in her sixties—she looked like a pissed off forty on most days. She dressed like a teenager—miniskirts and halter tops that should have been banned once a person received their AARP card.

Tim left Vincent and Charlotte to argue over his mere presence and made his way to her living room. Her sprawling brick rambler had probably been quite the modern design that decade. Now the dark wood paneled walls, decrepit carpet and angled rooms made Tim feel trapped and depressed.

Cats slunk around the space in disconcerting numbers. Tim sat on an uncomfortable black leather sofa and immediately two cats sprung out from unseen places and occupied his lap. One started purring and sinking his claws into Tim's lap almost aggressively.

Tim's body had a spaced-out, drunken feel about it. His cough remained, his chest felt tight, and his bones ached. But nothing pulsed like it had been battered with a crowbar.

"If you puke on my couch I'm going to beat you, boy," Charlotte told him. She wore a summer dress, despite the plunging October temperatures. She sported several tattoos along her arms, all of them Vincent's work from the style of them.

"Nice to see you too, Charlotte," Tim mumbled.

"I'm inclined to do nothing for you, dickhead." She sat in the lounger across from Tim. "I've got enough to do today without helping the likes of you."

"Going to a cat lady convention?" Tim asked.

She whipped her wooden spoon down hard on Tim's thigh.

"Ouch!" Tim cried, flinching back. The cats didn't move.

"As it happens, I'm going to a hexbreaking summit in New Orleans. And in the midst of all my preparations here you come, another ugly problem. But I owe Vincent a favor."

"You owe him more than that," Tim replied.

"*Tim.*" Vincent shook his head.

Tim gave his innocent expression. "What? Don't scold *me*, scold your batshit aunt."

She slapped Tim with the spoon again, and this time the cats flew off his lap, claws sinking deep.

Vincent emitted a long-suffering sigh. "Charlotte, let's do this before the crowpepper effects wear off."

Tim watched him swallow another one of those horse-sized pills and narrowed his eyes. He wasn't going to yell at Vincent in front of his aunt, but he would definitely take him to task for it later.

It didn't help when Tim glanced back at Charlotte and she was shoveling pills down her throat. Within seconds her pupils spread wide, and her whole body seemed to vibrate.

"Take off your shirt," Charlotte ordered.

"What, no foreplay?"

"Don't antagonize her," Vincent said, sitting beside him. Charlotte knelt on the floor at Tim's feet watching him intensely.

Tim reluctantly took off his shirt. He felt humiliated by the way the two of them stared. Charlotte's lip pulled back in a silent hiss, but Tim couldn't see anything other than a shameful lack of rock-hard abs.

"We're going to need a ton," Charlotte said, though what she needed, she didn't specify. Instead, she clambered off the floor with a surprising amount of elegance for a woman her age, and started banging a frying pan around in the kitchen.

Tim noticed Vincent studied the eyes of the foo dog tattoo. "What's up with his eyes?" Tim asked him.

"I put ink in the eye sockets as a marker in case you ever got hexed. It serves as a litmus test of sorts. The brighter the color, the more power the hex has."

"What do you do for clients who aren't tattooed?"

"I tattoo them, idiot. It can be a small dot, nothing big. Even only a few millimeters of color will turn red when hexes are in the body."

"That was clever of you," Tim said. "But also sort of immoral. You didn't tell me about it ahead of time."

"And if I had?" Vincent raised an eyebrow.

Tim shrugged. "Yeah. I wouldn't have believed you. You got one?"

Vincent grinned and pushed back the left sleeve of his T-shirt. He had a serpent encircling the entire length of his left arm. The eyes of the beast were on his shoulder, and looked black.

"I like doing eyes," he said.

"I can tell." Tim glanced behind, into the kitchen, but couldn't see Charlotte. "So...we just sit here."

Vincent nodded. "She's going to burn the *Yisirik*. It takes about ten minutes."

"Ten minutes?" Tim smiled. "That's enough time for a quickie."

"No."

"I bet I could suck you off in ten minutes," he whispered.

"With blood coming out of your lungs? No thanks."

"Ugh, didn't think of that." Tim sighed.

"How are you feeling?"

Tim stretched back, kicking his feet up on the coffee table and lacing his fingers behind his head. "Actually, not bad. Whatever's in that tea packs a punch. I'm horny for the first time in weeks."

"There was a moment in your life when you *weren't* horny?"

Tim laughed. "The last few months my libido's been in hiding. You seem to bring it to the surface."

"Smooth talker." Vincent didn't seem upset though. "Well, the return of a sex drive is a good sign, but it's only a temporary fix."

"I know."

"We haven't gotten rid of the hex, we're only delaying its inevitable outcome."

Tim scowled. "Shit, have you always been such a party pooper? I don't remember that about you."

Vincent looked sad as he stared at Tim. He surprised Tim by reaching out and brushing Tim's bangs back from his forehead. "I don't feel much like partying when I see you like this."

There was a loud crash from the kitchen, followed by some vicious swearing.

"You okay, Charlotte?" Vincent asked.

Tim added, "If you need to burn off your hand in the process, go for it."

"Fuck you!" She sounded far away.

Vincent grinned. "You two are so *cute*."

Tim coughed. "She's probably making something to increase the agony. Not that I think that's possible."

"She may hate your guts for breaking my heart, but she has unshakeable moral standards. She swore to help anyone with a hex and she means it." He leaned over and whispered. "Besides, she only fights with people she actually likes."

"Really? Jesus, I feel bad for her enemies." Tim coughed again. His throat felt tight. He cleared it, and coughed once more.

A sense of panic began to fill him as his airways tightened.

He'd been through this before, and tried not to panic, but there was something so disconcerting about an asthma attack that rational thought lost to anxiety.

"Tim?" Vincent asked, looking worried.

Tim tried to smile, but he had to gasp for air. He fumbled in his back pocket for the inhaler he'd become inordinately attached to over the past month and a half, and took a deep pull of the medicine into his lungs. It had little effect.

Charlotte came in then, and without so much as a smile or a warning, she sliced Tim's forearm with a short knife.

"What the hell?" Tim gasped between chokes.

Neither Charlotte nor Vincent answered him. Charlotte squeezed the flesh around the cut on Tim's arm and collected the blood into a small thimble-sized receptacle.

Tim was too busy concentrating on breathing to focus on what they were doing. At some point Charlotte's and Vincent's heads were bowed together as they bundled a smudge stick of dried, smoking herbs together with twine.

Tim's vision got spotty. Vincent glanced up at him with huge black eyes and a worried expression. "Hold on, big guy," he said.

Tim concentrated on each rattling, closing breath. In, out. In, out.

Vincent and Charlotte stuffed the aromatic herbs into a small cotton satchel. Then Charlotte stared at Tim's bared chest, pulled out a fountain pen, dipped it in Tim's blood, and drew.

As soon as the pen touched the fabric of the satchel, Tim's throat loosened, and his airways expanded. He coughed and swallowed, and could draw a full breath for the first time in minutes.

She continued to draw.

When she finished, Tim was exhausted, but able to breathe normally again. Charlotte looked burned out as well, and wavered as she stood up. Vincent had to grip her and help her over to the couch.

"Tim?" Vincent moved to Tim's side. "You feeling better?"

"Yeah, thanks." Tim coughed one last time. He motioned to the satchel Vincent held. "Is that my voodoo doll?"

Vincent nodded. "It's called a decoy." He held it out for Tim, who took it with a sense of revulsion. The bizarre circular drawing on the satchel was in his blood. And the smell, while not off-putting, was very strong.

Tim pointed to the design. "Does this say, all hexes follow me?"

"No. It says Tim Keller." Vincent smiled. "You're lucky. Most people never get to see their own spiritual symbol. This is as unique to you as a fingerprint. The hex will continue to work its effects on the decoy, not you."

Tim reached for it, but Vincent pulled it back. "I'll keep it," he said. "It will be stronger with my will imbued in it. Besides, I can monitor it to see how much time you've got."

That wasn't very reassuring. Tim closed his eyes, a bone-weary exhaustion filling every pore of his body.

He nearly fell asleep there on Charlotte's couch. He felt something smack against the cut on his arm, and opened his eyes. Charlotte had slapped a band-aid over his small wound.

"You've pissed off an amateur," Charlotte stated. She sat on the other side of Tim. Her weariness gave Tim a momentary pang of guilt.

"No way that's an amateur," Vincent answered her. "It's too strong."

"It's strong, but it's ugly," Charlotte replied. "There's no craft to it. And I have no idea who taught this person to weave hexes."

"What do you mean?" Vincent asked.

She said, "Those who learn from others pick up their styles. Remember Marshall's weave? Looked just like Francesco's, and that's how I knew who taught him. But this mess... I've never seen anything like it, as if someone was reinventing the art."

"Your sense of artwork is pretty skewed," Tim commented, motioning to the weird, somewhat disturbing look of his personal symbol. It looked like a three year old hepped up on sugar was set loose with a sharpie and instructions to draw a maze. "Still, thank you," he forced himself to say.

She sighed. "You've got to rest now. Let the decoy do its job. You should feel better in an hour or so."

"I can't go home, I've got to find Zoe," Tim said.

Vincent said, "We'll go out after you've recovered. I'll come with you, all right?"

Tim blinked at Vincent. How easy it was to believe that this was how they would be now. Friends, sitting beside each other on the couch, trading good-natured barbs, angry only at each other's self-inflicted torments. It felt so good to look past the last six months of regret, and longing, and lonely nights. It was always easy, when it was something yearned for so desperately.

Vincent and Charlotte exchanged a few whispered words, and some anxious looking glances, but Tim was now too tired to try and eavesdrop. Every time he had a breathing attack, exhaustion washed through him.

Charlotte held her spoon up at Tim, and he appropriately flinched back.

"You take care of Vincent," she ordered him.

"Yes, Ma'am."

"If I hear you've broken his heart again, I'll beat you."

"Let's go back to my house," Vincent interrupted her tearful farewell. Tim couldn't hide his smile of relief at both leaving Charlotte's house and at returning to Vincent's. If Vincent was having him over, maybe his hatred had lessened. And maybe, where there was no hate, there could be forgiveness.

Tim wanted to talk but he was so tired, it took everything just to park the car and walk up that steep flight of stairs to Vincent's house. Vincent forced a whole pot of that horrible tea down his throat before letting Tim pass out on the couch.

Within seconds he fell asleep.

And woke up with a hard-on.

Tim blinked and stretched on the couch, yawning. He couldn't remember the last time he had enough energy for a boner.

It was mid-afternoon. He'd slept for three hours. He took stock of his body and realized he felt...*fine*.

No pains, no aches, other than a distant sense of something in his chest being a little off.

He stood, expecting pain in his joints, but they held his weight without protest. Amazing. He smiled to himself. That crazy Charlotte deserved a box of chocolates and a larger wooden spoon. The decoy made a huge difference.

Tim made his way down the hall to Vincent, who'd fallen asleep on top of his bed, curled into a fetal ball despite having the whole damn king bed to himself. It was another way that the two of them were so compatible.

Tim stood above Vincent and stared at him fondly. Vincent liked to look tough, with dark hair and tattoos and ripped punk clothing. But when he slept, you could see the little boy he once was. His long black lashes fluttered on those porcelain cheeks, and his cherubic lips formed a delicious pout that Tim desperately wanted to kiss.

Even the smell of him aroused Tim. He'd forgotten Vincent's woody, musky odor. He even *smelled* magical. Two years together and Tim had never appreciated the fact that his boyfriend, the love of his life, was literally magical.

Hexbreaker.

Was he a warlock? Wasn't that what a male witch was called? Weren't witches the ones who dealt with spells and magical brews? How could all of this be here, in the world, under a thin veneer of logic and normalcy? How could there be hexmakers haunting the streets of Seattle killing people from afar, and others entering trances to dismantle the magic havoc they created?

It was a whole new world and changed everything. If there were hexes, then there could be ghosts. Vampires. Hell, a weight loss pill that worked. *Anything* was possible.

And to think of Vincent, risking his life in that world to save people like Tim, people without hope, suffering despite all of the collective medical knowledge of mankind, choked Tim up. How lonely, he thought, seeing Vincent face these struggles without being able to tell anyone.

And of course, when he *did* tell someone, it ended up getting him kicked out of the house.

Tim sat beside Vincent's head carefully, not wanting the dip of the mattress to wake him. He took in the sight of Vincent like this a moment more, unable to disturb such a look of peace.

"You're at the wrong angle to strangle me, if that's your plan," Vincent mumbled, never opening his eyes.

"But I'm at the right angle to kiss you."

Vincent popped open one eye.

Tim felt tears wetting his own eyes. "Look. Vincent. I want to say how sorry I am. About how things ended with us. About not trusting you. I should have been more compassionate. Hell, I should have *listened*. And you'll never know how sorry I am."

Vincent blinked up at him for a moment. His eyebrows crumpled together, as if about to correct Tim. Instead he said, "I thought you said you were going to kiss me."

Tim smiled, something light and hopeful quivering precariously to life in his chest. He leaned down and gave in to his desire to kiss those pouty lips. He pulled back slowly, then kissed Vincent again.

The third time they kissed, Vincent wrapped his arm around Tim's neck and held his head in place. Vincent's tongue slipped between Tim's lips and a full-bodied groan came from somewhere in his chest. He needed this so *badly*.

Their kiss deepened. Tim leaned into Vincent, claiming him, tongue plunging deep into Vincent's mouth, sending a bolt of hot need through him.

Vincent broke the kiss, smiled, then flipped them over in one swift move. Tim laughed. He was used to being the aggressor, the one who called the shots. This was something new. The feeling of Vincent's weight along the length of his body was everything he needed at that moment, the hint of friction, the kisses that devastated all thought.

Vincent pressed down with his groin, and Tim let out a shaky breath as his cock rubbed against Vincent's. His fingers tightened around Vincent's arms.

"Just...just touch...oh God..." Vincent gasped, eyes dark, mouth red and slightly swollen from Tim's stubbly kisses.

Tim felt as though his erection claimed all the blood in his body, and a sense of lightheadedness crashed through him.

Vincent moved down the length of Tim. He laughed, eyes bright and shiny. He yanked on Tim's legs, pulling him to the edge of the bed.

"Stay right there," Vincent encouraged. He leaned over and unbuckled Tim's jeans, taking his time with the buttons on Tim's fly. Tim sat up on his elbows and watched with shivery anticipation. Oh this was so good, it was going to be *so good*...

Vincent reached for the waistband of Tim's jeans and underwear. Tim lifted his hips and Vincent slipped them both from him, pulling them off Tim's legs and tossing them in the corner of the room. He knelt at the foot of the bed and used his hands to spread Tim's legs wider.

The sight of Vincent kneeling there, in between Tim's legs and licking his lips in anticipation, made Tim almost come on the spot. His engorged dick leaked pre-cum as it awaited Vincent's sweet mouth.

Vincent reached for Tim's cock with one hand, and slowly, carefully, swallowed it down.

Tim's body electrified, every nerve flooded with pleasure. Vincent worked the underside of Tim's cock, swirling over the head with the hot, wet tip of his tongue. Tim blinked, torn between wanting to close his eyes in pleasure and not giving up a single second of the sight before him.

Vincent's eyes stayed on Tim's face as he sucked Tim down, watching every reaction. Tim groaned. He reached out with his shaking right hand and carded his fingers through Vincent's dark tangles. As Vincent sped the pace, Tim watched, mesmerized. The feeling was so good he tightened his fingers in Vincent's hair, letting go only when he realized he might hurt him.

Tim stroked the side of Vincent's bony face, stopping at his cheek, where he could feel his own dick in there, bulging under the skin. The feeling of his cock's contours under Vincent's skin sent a thrill of delight through him. The sight of Vincent's red lips stretched so tightly around the base of his big dick made Tim want to grab his camera and photograph it. It was obscene, the push of his own flesh inside that hot mouth. Tim ran his index finger over Vincent's lips, feeling the taut, wet flesh, and then he stuck his finger inside, working it alongside his cock, and Vincent let out a helpless groan. His hand plunged into his own jeans.

The sight of Vincent's cock poking out from the waistband of his jeans, combined with the deep thrust of his own cock down Vincent's throat, was all it took. Tim came with a breathy gasp, feeling like his whole life had led up to this one, great conclusion. It had been so long.

In the aftershocks of his orgasm, he felt Vincent stroking himself, and set about returning the favor. Tim joined Vincent on the floor, pinning him down on the carpet.

Vincent laughed. "Well, well. Look who's regained his strength."

Tim grinned, kissing his way down Vincent's clothed body. He unfastened the fly and got his mouth around Vincent's long cock in no time, swallowing at once to taste the salty bitter pre-cum. He yanked on Vincent's pants to get at his balls, and cradled the heavy softness of them in his palm as he took Vincent as deep as he could down his throat.

It didn't take long, which was a relief actually, because Tim's energy pretty much ran out by the time Vincent gripped his arms and came, filling his mouth with that unique taste that was so distinctly *Vincent*.

He crawled back up Vincent and lay splat over him. Tim's head rose and fell rapidly on Vincent's chest as they caught their breaths.

They lay like that for a few minutes, tangled in each other's arms on the floor. Tim couldn't remember ever feeling so relieved.

"We shouldn't have done that," Vincent said, breaking the spell.

"Why not?" Hurt filled Tim, and for a second, he worried, in his emotionally unstable state, he might start weeping. He sat up. "Jesus, what's it going to take to get your forgiveness? I love you, Vincent. I fucked up, and I'm sorry, and if you want me to grovel to be taken back I will."

Vincent shook his head. He scooted back and did up his trousers. "You wouldn't be here unless you needed me to save you."

"Only because I was an ass before. Trust me, I've learned my lesson." Tim smirked. "You sure *you* weren't the one to hex me?"

Vincent reached out and stroked Tim's face, shaking his head. "Don't joke about it." He stood, and offered a hand to Tim, who, embarrassingly, needed all the help he could get.

They dressed. While at Vincent's, Tim took advantage of Vincent's copy machine that he used to shrink and expand tattoo designs, and made a few extra copies of the picture of fifteen-year-old Zoe Oswald to hand out that afternoon. Vincent made them both sandwiches, and for the first time in ages, Tim felt hungry.

But the sandwich tasted like dirt. Even the texture felt wrong across his tongue. He choked down as much as he could because his body needed the calories, but he didn't enjoy a single bite. It had *looked* good. And he tried to do so as well, smiling and pretending to enjoy it, because Vincent's worried expression made Tim feel guilty for getting him involved in this whole mess.

Tim washed their dishes, knowing Vincent would leave them for the rest of the week if he didn't. Over his shoulder Tim yelled, "I have to go find Zoe now. If I put it off any longer she could get into real trouble."

"You can barely stand," Vincent replied. He came up behind Tim.

"I feel better than I have in weeks. Besides, I have bills to pay."

"Make Jonah do it," Vincent suggested.

"He's already taken on seventy percent of our case load. I can't make him take on more." Tim shrugged. "Besides, I want to do this one. I love missing persons cases."

Vincent stared at him. Then he nodded. "Fine. I'm coming with you."

"I thought you'd been kidding." Tim didn't bother to hide his enthusiasm. "You used to dread stakeouts."

"Well, I'm not volunteering to spend the next twelve hours in your sedan, and I have a tattoo appointment at six. But I can sketch here or in your car, it doesn't matter. Besides, the decoy is strengthened when I'm nearby."

Tim curled his arm around Vincent's neck, gently urging him closer for a kiss. "I should have gotten hexed a lot earlier."

Vincent allowed the kiss, but pulled back. "You're getting dish soap down my shirt."

"Sexy."

"I'll brew more tea for the road."

Tim groaned. He didn't know how much more of the stuff he could choke down.

They finally made it to the car, got gas, then made several stops throughout the downtown core and Pioneer Square district. Tim dropped off pictures of Zoe everywhere he usually looked for teenage runaways. His last stop was at Becky's coffee shop by the piers. A lot of kids came in and out of her place, because she offered free hot cocoa to the homeless kids. Becky commented on how awful Tim looked.

"Tim, you gotta' stop drinking or settle down or something. You look like a corpse."

"Thanks." Yet another great day in the life of Tim Keller.

With a little time to kill before six, Tim agreed to Vincent's request that they swing by Francesca Prelle's florist shop in Queen Anne.

It was easy to find, the only florist on a quiet street. It sat in the midst of a row of salons, high-end restaurants, and home furnishing stores. Across the street was a tattoo shop—"utter shit," Vincent declared—and a palm reader's. That piqued Vincent's interest.

They walked into Francesca's Flower Boutique, but the owner wasn't in.

"I don't suppose you know anything about the business across the street?" Tim asked, knowing Vincent was curious.

The young woman behind the counter shook her head. "No, I've never been in there. But you can ask Mrs. Prelle when she comes in tomorrow. She goes in there all the time."

Tim and Vincent shared a look. "You don't happen to know if Mrs. Prelle is planning on selling the business or anything, do you?"

The woman seemed surprised. "What? No! I hope not. I only got hired here a few months ago. Why?"

"I wondered if she planned any major changes in the next few months."

The woman shrugged. "Not that I know of."

"Thanks for your time," Tim said.

"Should I tell her you stopped by?" the woman asked.

Tim smirked. "Probably not. I'll surprise her tomorrow. She'll *love* that."

The woman smiled and waved them out. Without stopping, Vincent dodged an oncoming car and made his way across the street to the palm reader's.

Tim rushed to catch up to him, entering the shop behind Vincent.

It looked like every stereotypical palm reading joint he'd ever entered. It was what he'd imagined Vincent's apartment looking like. Even the proprietress sitting behind the counter was dressed like someone from the "Guide To Looking Like a Stereotypical Gypsy." Her long braided black hair hung down over layers of flowy maroon garments. Her eyes were deeply colored with blue mascara.

Vincent sauntered up to the counter. "Hi. You are...?"

"Zoya," The woman said. "Who are you?"

Vincent grinned. "*Zoya*. So nice to meet you in person." He offered his hand and she shook it tentatively. "I've heard all about you from my aunt."

"Your aunt?" For someone so exotic looking, Zoya didn't have an accent. Or if she did, it was distinctly Queens.

"Yeah. Charlotte Safi."

Zoya recoiled as if slapped. "Get out."

Vincent leaned over the counter, pointing his finger at her. "If I ever see your handiwork again, I'm going to come here and fuck you up. Personally. You understand?"

Zoya shot out of her seat. Tim's heart raced, looking in all directions, prepping for some sort of confrontation. Of course Vincent wouldn't plan this out with him beforehand. He would have to go by the seat of his pants.

Tim glanced between the back door and the front, but no one seemed prepped to rush to Zoya's rescue. And she wasn't making a move for any shotguns. Still, Tim rushed quickly to Vincent's side.

"Get out!" Zoya cried, hands waving in the air. "Get out, before I call the cops!"

Vincent shook his head. "He is a cop." He pointed to Tim.

Which wasn't actually true anymore, but Tim could act when the need suited. He slightly shifted his stance.

"I've heard several complaints about some sort of service you've been providing, ma'am," he said.

Zoya looked frightened. "It's nothing!" She shook her head. "Little spot hexes! They're over in hours. They have no lasting power. I swear it!"

"But I know what they look like," Vincent told her, "and if I ever see another one again—"

"Yes! I will stop! I swear. I swear to God!"

Vincent flinched as if to lunge at her. She screamed and jerked back. He then turned and left the shop. "You coming, detective?"

Tim lingered for a moment to glare at her. A *hexmaker*. In the flesh. For one fleeting moment, terror and rage threatened to overpower his ingrained sense of right and wrong. She made money inflicting pain on unsuspecting people. People like him.

But his sense of right and wrong had never abandoned him before, and didn't now. He turned to leave.

"You're very sick," she whispered, trembling. "I see, you know. I see what's happened to you."

Tim turned back and drawled, "Stay out of hexes, Zoya." He knocked his fist against the glass counter. "Or I'll be back."

"You'll be dead," she called out after him.

Tim dropped Vincent off at work right before six, then pulled in for fast food before heading home. He knew the food would taste like ashes. But he also needed to eat. So why not go for a huge grease bomb? It wasn't like he had to watch his figure, except to watch it waste away.

At home he changed, showered and shaved, and decided to get some work done before the inevitable nighttime exhaustion hit him hard and fast. He found Jonah at their office, looking small behind his mountains of paperwork.

Jonah had been a good-looking man in his twenties, but time and stress hadn't been kind. He'd lost his hair, but refused to accept it and shave it down. Instead, he tried hair treatments, which Tim didn't like, personally. He'd rather run his hands over a shaved head than plugs any day. He'd even told this to Jonah, but Jonah refused to take any advice from a man who sucked other men's cocks. Fair enough.

But Jonah had also gained weight in the last few years, and lost muscle mass. He looked primed for a heart attack. His eyes had gotten sallow, and his wife Annie threatened to put him on a heart health diet, or a Mediterranean diet, or worse, force him to go vegan. Which only served to make him eat worse while on the clock.

"Hey Tim," Jonah said. He sounded tired. "You get any leads on Zoe?"

"No, but her picture's out there. I checked in with Todd and the folks down at the docks. No one underage recruited as of yet. She might be okay."

Jonah sighed. "Sounds more positive than my day, at least." He tossed down a few photos. "I can't get a good shot of our fraud guy to save my life. He's a sneaky bastard, that one. Knows exactly what we're up to."

Tim slid into his seat and booted up his computer. "Keep trying. They always give up after a few weeks when they think they've nailed it."

"I know."

"You think you can set up the surveillance equipment at the apartment tomorrow in case Larry's got her?"

Jonah looked up quickly. "What? No! I told you, I'm not working tomorrow. It's Saturday. Aiden has a soccer match and I promised Annie I wouldn't miss it again."

"It'll only take a minute..." Tim's voice faded as the back door of the studio snapped open and Annie herself made an appearance, as if summoned by his wish not to hear her or think of her.

"Hi Annie," he said cordially. He started coughing and couldn't stop for several minutes, which caused Annie to merely lift her eyebrow at him.

"Sounds like quite a cold you got there Tim," she said.

"Thanks for your concern." He gasped. All that coughing had made him nearly throw up, but he was determined not to do so in front of others.

Annie glared at Jonah. "I thought you said you'd be a minute. I've been waiting now for ten."

"I know, I know, I'm coming." Jonah fussed over his papers, loading some in his backpack. He glanced at Tim. "My car's in the shop. Annie has to chauffer me today and tomorrow."

"Annie, can you be a sweetheart and swing your gorgeous husband past the apartment in the morning, before Aiden's game?"

Tim said it half-jokingly, knowing Annie would say no. He didn't expect her instant fury, however.

"How dare you!"

Jonah sighed, "Annie...."

"No, Jonah! He's taking advantage of you!" She crossed her arms. She was a pretty woman, dressed tastefully in a high-end business suit, no doubt fresh from showing a property. Although judging by the smears of black ink on her fingers, she might have been cleaning said property in the process. "You've had my husband running himself ragged for weeks now and it's got to stop."

"Annie," Jonah soothed.

"It's got to stop!"

Tim held out his hands. "I'm sorry, Annie. I was kidding. I'll do it myself. I know you guys are swamped."

Annie shook her head. "I'm so sick of this."

"I'm on the mend," Tim assured her, although he felt another coughing fit creeping up his throat. "I'll be back to full workload soon and I'll take on Jonah's cases. You can have a break, I promise. Just the two of you and Aiden. You could go on that vacation you want."

Jonah rolled his eyes. "All right, all right. Let's not book the tickets just yet." He ushered Annie to the door. On his way out, he turned. "Equipment's in the bag from this afternoon."

"Thanks," Tim said.

Jonah paused. "Oh! And I take it you won't be at practice Sunday."

Tim sighed. "Not a chance. Tell the fellas I love them."

"They'll appreciate that." Jonah winked and left.

Tim sat and stared at his computer screen. Jonah and he were on an amateur soccer league that played Sundays, and their team photo was his desktop wallpaper. It had been a lark, and a hopeful chance to meet some guy after he'd broken up with Vincent.

The team was pretty pathetic, and no one else was gay, but it had turned out to be a fun thing to kill time on Sundays, and a way for him and Jonah to enjoy themselves without work being the only thing they talked about anymore.

It had been two months since he last showed up to practice or a match, and he missed it now. He missed everything about being healthy. The wise bastards who said you never knew the value of health until it was gone were really spot on. He'd have paid any amount of money to have a functioning body again.

But wishing for something and getting it were different things. So instead he set about fixing a problem he could solve—namely the mountain of invoicing neither he nor Jonah had gotten around to in weeks.

He fell asleep in his office chair and woke after an hour or so, unable to keep his burger and fries down any longer. Thank God the studio had a small bathroom.

He took his miserable self back to the house, weaving and nearly toppling over on the slick cobblestones. His balance was shot to hell. The world spun as he fell across his bed. He closed his eyes, too weak to undress.

His dreams were sinister. Blackened barbed vines wrapped around his throat, choking his windpipe and sending whip-like sucker branches up his trachea and down into his lungs. They spread outward, puncturing the flesh and causing fountains of blood to burst from each wound, filling the inside of his body. The blood pooled under his skin, swelling him like a balloon. The pressure was so great he started to scratch at his wrist, trying to cut himself open to release the unbearable weight on his lungs. He scratched and poked at his wrist so violently, he thought he felt it snap.

And shot upright.

"Jesus!"

Vincent stepped back quickly, hands up. "It's me, sorry."

Tim blinked, gathering his senses. He reached for his wrist. No blood. No pressure.

"Sorry," Vincent whispered again. He stepped closer. In the darkness his body was only shadow. "I didn't mean to wake you. I wanted to check your pulse. You were pale as death and not moving at all."

"God." Tim blinked at the clock. "What time is it?" His voice was hoarse.

"One o'clock in the morning. I decided to swing by on my way home and make sure you were okay."

"How'd you get in?" It was unlike Tim to forget locking the front door. He was a man of habits, even now.

Vincent gave a little chuckle in the darkness. "Believe it or not, you never asked for your key back. I still have it."

"Yeah?" Tim snorted. "I'm surprised you didn't come in one day and trash the place."

"Oh, I thought about it," Vincent admitted. He came close enough now for Tim to see his face in the greenish glow of the digital clock. "But mostly I thought about stealing Bogart for a walk some afternoon."

"You wouldn't have had to steal him," Tim said. He scooted upright to make room for Vincent to sit. "I told you when we broke up that we could share custody. You said you didn't want to."

"It would have been too hard," Vincent replied. "Coming here, seeing him, seeing...everything. It was better to just move on."

Tim opened his mouth. Then shut it. Then opened it again. "Did you?" he asked quietly. He stared at Vincent in the dark. "Move on?"

Vincent didn't answer for a long time. He hovered there, not sitting, leaning down, as if weighing a decision. At last he let out a shaky breath and sat beside Tim. "I'm here, aren't I?"

Tim reached for him. They came together easily, heads turned just so, muscle memory stronger than the mind's. They knew what fit where, what each other liked, what stroke brought out the right kind of keening.

Tim set a slow pace, because he didn't have energy for more. He wasn't even sure he was capable of accomplishing anything at all, but Vincent conjured up a lazy erection with his ministrations. Vincent undressed them both, unhurried, taking in Tim's changed body as he ran his hands along Tim's pale flesh.

"You're so thin, Tim," he whispered. He kissed along Tim's breastbone. "It breaks my heart."

"Sorry I'm not as good looking as I used to be." Tim swallowed, feeling depressed with it all. "I'm a disaster. I'm sorry." He stroked Vincent's shoulders. "I'm sorry." It had become his mantra of late, the mantra of a dying man.

Vincent kissed his way down Tim's torso, and brought his lips to Tim's erection. Their moves were quiet and deliberate. Tim felt out of breath, his congested lungs working overtime, but it also felt nice, exerting some sort of control over his wounded body, demanding pleasure from this sad bag of bones.

"Move closer," Tim said hoarsely, tugging on Vincent's knee. He pillowed his head on Vincent's inner thigh, where a tattoo of a rearing horse covered the soft, pale flesh. He reached with his hands and pulled Vincent's long cock into his mouth, creating a rhythm in synch with Vincent's own sucking that filled the silence between heartbeats. They used to make a game of it, to see if they could time it perfectly, two releases at the same time, but Tim had no energy for games. He knew Vincent's need was more pressing, so he reached up and placed a finger inside him, slow and insistent, finding that space that was reserved only for lovers.

Vincent came with a moan around Tim's big cock, and the press of his muscle against the base of Tim's finger brought a flood of pleasure through Tim. As weak as he was, as sick as he was, Vincent could still wring an orgasm out of him, a bright burst of light behind his eyes in what was otherwise a sea of darkness.

Tim fumbled for Vincent when he turned around. They held each other for a moment, enjoying the natural fit of their bodies, chest to chest.

"Need water?" Vincent asked.

"Nah, I gotta get up and piss anyway."

"Good, then you can drink more tea."

"God, you're like my grandmother. She used to make us drink chicken soup until we had feathers in our eyes."

Vincent smiled against Tim's neck. "It works though, doesn't it?"

Tim nodded. "What's in it?"

"Lots of things."

"You're like a witch," Tim said. "Know any other kind of magic? Can you hypnotize me? Make me believe the last six months were an ugly nightmare?"

Vincent sighed. "I wish. I'd do the same to myself."

"I don't think you can hypnotize yourself," Tim said.

"I know I can't hypnotize anyone." Vincent's fingers twirled in Tim's scrawny chest hair. "I'm a beginner at all this. People like my aunt? They've been practicing for decades. I met an old hexbreaker a few months ago who's ninety years old and still practicing. She knows more than any hexbreaker on the west coast. There's hundreds of us. And for the record, no one I've met so far has died from seizures."

Tim woke up at that. "Do they all have them?"

Vincent shook his head. "My aunt doesn't, and this old lady didn't. But they both know hexbreakers who do. Trust me, I don't like it any more than you. One of these days I'm bound to shit myself, and that will not be good for client morale." He smiled. "But I'm fine, Tim. Really. I don't want to die any more than you want me to."

Tim sat up. He placed his palms around Vincent's face, framing it. How could he love someone so much that it hurt? Looking at Vincent's face made his heart feel heavy and full.

"I'd die if anything happened to you," he said, his voice breaking. "I mean it. I can't bear the thought. It's why I had to leave. It'll kill me."

Vincent stroked the hand caressing his face. "I'll live, Tim. But we got to get you better."

Tim's eyes were glassy. He cleared his throat and made his way to the bathroom before he completely embarrassed himself.

They stayed up for another hour while Tim drank the noxious tea. Vincent caught Tim up on all the current scandals and dramas at Renegade Tattoo. Tim could tell Vincent itched to open his own shop, one where he didn't have to listen to co-workers' crappy music and spend hours on end shooting the shit with people he didn't like. Tim gave him a quick rundown of the state of Keller Cohen, and their nemesis, Intelligus.

They slumped down in bed and kept talking after the lights were once again turned off.

"You don't think the head of Intelligus would have anything to do with your curse, do you?" Vincent asked.

"Who? Roger Titan?"

"Yeah." Vincent yawned.

Tim laughed at that. "Oh I wish. I wish I was such a threat to his national operations he'd need to hire hexmakers to get me out of the picture." He sighed. "Alas, I doubt Roger Titan even knows my name, let alone that I operate an investigative agency in the same town as one of his *sixteen* offices."

"He'd have the money, at least, which is more than that guy who is always calling and threatening you. What was his name again?"

"Steve Lassiter," Tim said. "And I agree, he's broke. No way he could pay for this. I'm still thinking Francesca Prelle is a good bet. She's got money and she spends money. And she hates me. And she knows a hexmaker. I'm going to send one of my temps over tomorrow to talk to Prelle."

Vincent didn't seem convinced. "Zoya's small time. She makes a few grand here and there offering to hex folks with throat polyps or vagina dentata."

Tim shuddered. "Christ, is that a thing?"

"It's an actual thing."

"Fuck."

"But no way could she come up with something as complicated as the mess wrapped around you, big guy. Her weaves have no artistry. It's like comparing a simple fat braid to a crazy crochet afghan that someone invented as they went along."

Tim said, "Well aren't I lucky that the thing that's killing me is very special."

Vincent smiled into Tim's shoulder. Neither had bothered to dress again. Tim loved the feel of Vincent's leg thrown over him, the gentle softness of Vincent's sac against his thigh. If *home* could be described in a singular feeling, it would have been this—Vincent's balls nestling against his hipbone. Nothing more.

Tim had more questions to ask, but that sense of serenity lured him deep, pulled him into the first real good night's sleep he'd had since this misery began four months ago.

Home.

4

Vincent awoke with the expectation of remorse.

After all, he'd succumbed to his wish to reunite with Tim despite the fact that he'd only end up hurt again. And it had taken—what? Twenty-four hours?

But he had no remorse. Waking up entangled with Tim's long body was everything he'd wanted, even during those months when he'd hated Tim's guts. Because that was the problem, wasn't it? Hate and love were not mutually exclusive.

Tim appeared drawn in the morning light, the shadows under his eyes dark enough to look like punches. Vincent despised the anonymous hexmaker at that moment more than he'd ever hated anyone or anything in his life. He couldn't even sit there and slowly work at the knots tied around Tim, because whoever had done this had created such a mess that Vincent couldn't see the damn weave unless he was chock-full of crowpepper.

He leaned over the bed and grabbed his jeans. He fished out Tim's decoy. The symbol was almost entirely gone now, faded into the fabric. Inside, the herbs had turned to ash.

Vincent got out of bed as quietly as he could and made his way into the living room where he'd deposited his backpack the night before. He swallowed his pill quickly, his body used to the funky, fuzzy feeling of the poison. It numbed his mouth almost instantly. He also grabbed his six inch curse scythe and the spare smudge stick.

Vincent returned to bed and carefully pulled the sheet back from Tim's lean body. With the crowpepper flush through him, he could see the intricate weave of barbed words.

While Tim slept fitfully, Vincent worked at untangling the knots. The intricate ones he could take apart by hand. The thicker knots had to be cut open with the curse scythe, waving the blade just above Tim's tattooed skin.

His efforts broke loose a patch of thick overgrown knots around Tim's throat. But the problem with dismantling a hex as complex as this without finding the hexroot was that as soon as he untangled a layer of the hex, it started repairing itself.

It was futile until they found whoever hexed him.

Yet Vincent couldn't stop picking at it. It was a scab covering the man he loved. As he concentrated, he felt his own temperature fluctuate.

Vincent managed to get an entire layer of the blackened barbs untangled around Tim's throat before he smelled something burning.

That should have been his clue. It always preceded a seizure. But by the time he realized, "Oh shit, it's going to—" it was happening.

"Vincent, sweetheart? Can you hear me now?"

Vincent's head ached horribly and his mouth tasted like hot metal. He swallowed blood.

"You're okay," Tim's voice soothed.

Vincent blinked, confused as to where he lay. There was Tim though, looming over his face, looking pale and shaken.

As he blinked up at Tim, Tim smiled. "And I thought *I* felt like crap."

"I tried to unravel your hex," Vincent said. At least he tried to say it, but the words came out slurred. He was so tired he couldn't form them.

Tim's mouth pinched tight.

"I want to sit up," Vincent said, slurring a little less. Tim reached around and helped him sit upright. Vincent's body ached and all he wanted to do was sleep.

"I woke up to you convulsing next to me," Tim said quietly. "Scared the shit out of me." He shook his head. "You want some water?" Tim stroked Vincent's hair. Vincent felt grateful, and leaned into him.

"Sleep," Vincent said.

"I like that plan," Tim said, "but we have to wait a bit."

"Why?"

"I called your aunt when I found you convulsing," Tim winced. "Sorry."

Vincent sighed. "Well, at least she can rebuild the decoy when she's here."

"It needs rebuilding? I thought they were supposed to last for days."

"Normally, yes. In this case?" Vincent's eyes felt like lead, and he closed them. "In this case, nothing is going the way it should."

Vincent almost fell back asleep, until Tim asked, "Is there a good reason I'm sitting on top of a really big knife? Trying to cut my heart out?"

Vincent managed a small smile. "You'd have to have one for me to cut one out."

"Ouch."

"I was cutting the hex," Vincent said, "but it's too powerful, it keeps repairing itself. We have to find the hexroot."

"It's a thing?"

"Yes, something of yours, probably small enough to fit in a pocket. They have to carry it with them always. Until we get our hands on that, we won't beat this thing."

"The decoy and whatever you did have made me feel much better." Vincent felt Tim's lips as they kissed his temple. "Sleep, sweetheart," Tim told him. "I'll talk to Charlotte when she arrives."

Vincent gripped his arm. "Don't go out without me."

"Never."

When Vincent awoke the second time, it was mid-afternoon. He would have to get to the shop in a few hours to finish a client's back piece.

Tim slept beside him. He did look better, color marking his cheeks.

And on Vincent's bedside table he found a repaired and refreshed decoy, along with a note from Charlotte.

He's got hours. You need to find the hexroot fast or you're going to lose him. I've cancelled my appearance at the conference so I can be near if you need me.
XOXO Ch.

With that sobering information Vincent woke up entirely. But he hated waking Tim when he looked so peaceful.

For better or worse, Tim's phone vibrating on the bedside table did it for him.

Tim startled awake, glanced around, and grinned like a kid at Christmas when his eyes caught Vincent's.

"Hey, beautiful." He kissed Vincent. Vincent kissed back, hiding a grimace. Tim's mouth tasted like death.

Tim grabbed his phone. "Keller Cohen. Yeah? Hey Becky, how are you, sweetheart?"

Tim listened, and Vincent got up to give him privacy. He made more of the tea Tim hated.

They showered together and shaved, and although Tim made plenty of innuendos while they slid naked and soapy together in the shower, he clearly had no strength to follow through with his groping. As it was, Vincent practically held him up under the water.

Tim dressed nicely for the day, as if meeting a client. He'd always looked handsome in a suit, having one of those swimmer's bodies that had the right proportion of shoulders to tapered waist to do the look justice. But the tailored snappy edge vanished when Tim's dress shirts billowed around his wasted frame.

Still, sick as he was, Tim had always been a handsome man. Clean shaven and in pressed slacks, he looked charming, if not a little rumpled.

Vincent gave him a kiss on his smooth cheek and handed him a thermos of tea.

Tim grimaced. "God in heaven."

"I also brought over fried chicken last night. You can eat it cold in the car."

"You coming with me?" Tim asked, his expression lightening. Vincent wondered if this was new, or if Tim would always have been so easily thrilled by Vincent's mere presence on a case.

Vincent held out his sketchbook. "I don't have to be in early today, so why not?"

"My hero." Tim kissed him back, then grabbed a duffel bag full of video equipment.

"Where are we headed?" Vincent asked.

"Becky called from The Cup. She thinks she saw a girl that looked like Zoe come in this morning, and she tried to get her to come back this afternoon by promising her a hot meal."

"That's good news right?" Vincent commented.

Tim looked grim. "Maybe. It also could mean she's run into Larry and his crowd, since they are the ones telling the kids about the free drinks at The Cup."

"Larry?"

"Low life pimp who prays on runaway teens," Tim clarified. He shook his head. "I need to set up the surveillance equipment at the apartment."

"Where's the apartment?"

"It's across from Larry's base of operations. We get enough clients to justify the minimal cost of renting the shitty space for surveillance."

Vincent asked, "The Cup is down at the pier, right? So we'll be passing through Belltown."

Tim glanced at Vincent suspiciously. "Why?"

Vincent pulled out his notebook. "Steve Lassiter's address is in Belltown."

Tim snorted. "I thought we agreed he was too broke to be the one." They both got into Tim's car.

"We have to check all leads, no matter how unlikely. You taught me that," Vincent said.

"Yeah, but I also don't believe in wasting my time on ridiculous theories. Steve's a fucked-up drunk who lost his son and is outrageously bitter about it. The fact that he takes his rage out on me is fine—it means he's not taking it out on his ex-wife. And he's had plenty of chances to hurt me over the last six months and he hasn't."

"Or he has, and that's why you can't eat a damn bite."

Tim pouted. "I ate a piece of chicken."

"Eat another." Vincent proffered the bucket of drumsticks.

Tim made a face. "I'd rather not."

"I know it tastes bad. You have to choke it down, big guy."

Tim sighed. He grabbed a drumstick, eating with one hand, steering with the other. "I feel like a caveman. I'm getting grease all over the steering wheel."

"Your clean freak status can be put on hiatus for one car ride." Vincent offered him a napkin.

Tim caught his eye and smiled. "What are you grinning about?"

"Nothing. You. How little you've changed."

Tim shrugged. "Same guy." He looked at Vincent. "Sorry though. I'm a sorry guy."

"Yeah, yeah. You've been over that. I believe you."

"Yeah?" At the stop sign Tim leaned over and kissed Vincent, his lips greasy, tasting like breadcrumbs. "Am I forgiven?"

"No. You owe me a fuckload of blowjobs."

"Deal!"

"When you're better."

"Obviously." Tim turned carefully, signaling first. Vincent nearly laughed out loud. Tim drove like a sixteen-year-old girl who just got her license. He was both one of the safest men he knew, and one of the most reckless.

Belltown had been a rundown, fading neighborhood in a bad part of town before it gentrified. All the old commercial properties got converted into expensive apartments with exposed brick walls and killer views of Puget Sound.

This morning, however, it looked pretty bleak, what with the cloud cover low enough to touch and the streets gray, ready for rain. There were a few dives in the neighborhood that hadn't gotten the memo about Belltown being upscale.

Steve Lassiter lived in one of these places, a soot-stained brick multi-story only accessible by alley with a view of other high-rises that cornered it in.

Tim parked illegally in the alleyway. He turned his blinkers on, then reached across Vincent to the glove compartment.

He pulled out his Glock 22 and fit it into the holster under his jacket that Vincent hadn't noticed. Vincent hated firearms; it was one of those things he'd conveniently blocked out about his ex.

Vincent gave Tim a look. Tim raised his eyebrows. "Hey, if it was only me, I'd leave it. But the guy is nuts, sweetheart. He's not laying a finger on you."

Vincent held up his hands in surrender, and got out of the car. A few droplets of rain fell.

A rain-damaged hand-written note over the security call system informed them that the front door was busted, and the second floor was now only accessible by the metal fire escape at the side of the building. They trudged around the building, past an overflowing garbage can. It was a gritty environment for a man in a suit, but Tim had this knack of blending in wherever he was. He took the stairs with focused determination, gripping the loose handrail. He smiled, but Vincent could tell Tim panted for air at the top of the staircase.

"You need a minute?" Vincent asked.

Tim shook his head. "Won't matter. I never have enough breath these days." He tried the old wooden fire door and it opened with a loud creak. They made their way down the hallway to unit #220.

Tim rapped on the door and barked, "Mr. Lassiter?" sounding like law enforcement. They waited a good minute or two before the door slid open, chain still on.

Steve Lassiter looked like hell. His eyes were bloodshot and he smelled unwashed. "What do you want?"

Tim grinned. "Remember me, buddy?"

Lassiter's eyes widened and his mouth distorted into a furious grimace. "You! Son of a bitch!" He slammed the door shut.

Vincent thought that was the end of it, but Tim apparently knew better, because he moved to the side. A second later the door flew open and Lassiter lurched out and lunged at Tim.

"I'm going to fucking kill you!" Lassiter cried.

Tim spun out of the way and turned back to Lassiter. Vincent's heart raced. But before he understood what happened, Tim had twisted the man up against the wall and pinned both his wrists behind his back. Tim shoved Lassiter's face against the chipped plaster.

"Calm down, Mr. Lassiter. I only have a few questions for you, then you can go about your business."

"Fuck you!" The man spat, struggling. "Let me go!"

"Ever hire a hexmaker?" Tim asked calmly, despite the fact that Lassiter writhed under Tim's arms.

"What? What's this about?"

Vincent stepped closer. "Where were you the first week of June this year?"

Lassiter looked like he didn't comprehend, his anger fading in confusion. "*What?*"

"First week of June," Tim repeated, shoving Lassiter harder against the wall for emphasis. "Where were you?" he barked.

"In Corrections, asshole!" Lassiter cried. "Check my fucking file! I was in Monroe until last month!"

Tim glanced at Vincent.

Vincent shook his head. "It had to have been that first week of June. And he would have needed something of yours to bind the hex."

"Not you, then." Tim shoved Lassiter back into his apartment. "Thanks for your time, Mr. Lassiter," Tim said. "And stop calling me, or next time I'll bring a few additional buddies."

Lassiter slammed the door shut. Vincent heard the chain lock slide into place.

They walked back to the car.

"Technically, just because he's incarcerated doesn't mean he couldn't have hired a hexmaker," Vincent said. "Prisons are a great source of income for budding practitioners."

"But you said he'd need an object of mine, something that would root the hex, and that he'd have to keep it. I haven't had anything stolen or go missing since this whole thing started, and it seems a bit of a stretch that they'd be able to get such an object back into prison."

"True," Vincent replied. Tim returned the gun to the glove compartment, and Vincent let out the breath he didn't realize he was holding.

Tim leaned his head against the steering wheel, looking woozy.

"You okay?" Vincent rubbed the back of Tim's neck.

"Tired, mostly. Hard to act tough when what you really want is a doughnut and a snuggle."

Vincent laughed at that. "I know a great doughnut shop on the way to the pier. My treat."

"You're my hero."

They did stop at the doughnut shop, and Tim made a good show of pretending to enjoy the cruller Vincent had bought him, although Vincent saw how hard Tim chewed to force the small bites down.

"Okay. Quick stop at the apartment, then The Cup."

They left the wealthier parts of downtown and went along Dearborn, past the international district and into a neighborhood of densely packed apartment complexes along the freeway.

"Nice neighborhood," Vincent mused.

Tim pulled into the driveway of the run-down apartment complex and turned off the engine. "Hey, it's Seattle. One day this is all going to be beautiful and expensive, you wait and see."

Tim removed the keys from the ignition, looked at them, and swore. "You're fucking joking!"

"What?" Vincent asked.

Tim rested his head on the steering wheel. "Fucking Jonah has the key. He didn't give it back to me yesterday." He called Jonah and stuttered something about needing the key.

Vincent didn't hear the entire conversation, but it sounded angry from Jonah's end. Tim could only get out bits of sentences. "Yeah but...I know and I'm sorry...but Becky called, so Larry...yeah. I could come by and pick it up if you...yeah. Okay."

He disconnected the call and ran a hand over his face. "Jonah's on his way over. And he's going to be pissed."

"Why?" Vincent asked.

Tim sighed. "Because his wife has declared today a no-work day and now he's breaking his promise."

"Should we talk to her, apologize?" Vincent asked.

Tim grimaced. "God no. She'll cut off my balls."

"She seemed nice when I met her last year."

"Yeah, well looks are deceiving. She's a homophobe with a stick up her ass."

This surprised Vincent. "She's homophobic and her husband is business partners with a homosexual?"

Tim shrugged. "I came before her, remember? She's had to deal. But last year she called me a fag. I almost clocked Jonah for it."

"Why clock him?"

"I can't hit his wife!" Tim scoffed. "A man's gotta have standards."

Vincent shook his head, then burst out laughing. "You really are a piece of work."

While they waited for Jonah, Tim made a few other calls, including one to a female law student who did side jobs for him on occasion, and would happily pay a visit to Francesca Prelle's flower shop for a small fee.

Tim ended his call when Jonah's large white SUV screeched to a halt beside Tim's Nissan. Before the engine had fully been killed Jonah sprang from the driver's seat, looking harried and upset.

"God damn you, Tim!" Jonah shouted. He hurled the key at the Nissan.

Tim got out of the car, wincing. "Hey man, it's your fault you forgot—"

"It's *one day*! I asked for *one* fucking day off! But no. You couldn't wait until tomorrow for this, could you?"

Tim straightened at that. "Should I tell that to Zoe's mom? Sorry ma'am, yes, your daughter may be selling her body for a place to stay right now, but it's my fucking *day off*."

Jonah shook his head, as if refusing to listen. "You're impossible, you know that? *Impossible*." He threw his hands up in the air. "I give up. I'm done." He spun on his heel.

"Don't be like that," Tim said, but Jonah didn't hear him. He stormed to his car and drove off, tires screeching in his haste to get back to wherever he'd been when Tim had so rudely extracted him.

Tim bent down, wincing, and picked up the tossed key. He walked back to the car slowly, feeding the key onto his key chain.

"Sorry for that scene," he told Vincent.

Vincent looked off to where Jonah's car finally disappeared, at the end of the road. "Who gets everything when you die?" he asked suddenly.

"Huh?" Tim reached into the car and pulled out his duffel bag of equipment. "You coming along? I have to set up the surveillance equipment."

"Who's in your will, Tim?" Vincent asked.

Tim scowled. "No."

"I didn't—"

"I know what you're thinking, and the answer is no," Tim said sternly. "Yes, Jonah is in my will and gets the whole business if I die, and no, he didn't hire a hexmaker to have me killed. There's no way he'd do it."

Vincent raised an eyebrow. "Yeah? From the sound of it the business isn't something he enjoys anymore. You said he's been begging to get out. His wife wants him out too. He'd like to sell it, but you won't let him."

Tim shook his head. "No way. Yeah, he has access to my stuff, but he doesn't have fifty grand to spare. We've sunk every penny into the business, and he's had to get a second mortgage on his house." He shouldered his surveillance gear and headed up the walkway to the apartment. Vincent hurried after him.

"Think about it logically, like the detective you are," Vincent encouraged, coming up alongside Tim. "The fact that they are broke is more of a motive. After all, your house alone is probably worth half a million by now."

Tim turned to him, looking surprised. "Jonah doesn't get the house if I die," he said. He swallowed and looked away. "That's still going to you."

Vincent felt floored. "*What?*"

Tim shrugged. "Jonah gets the business and all the assets associated with it. You get the house, Bogart, the car, and whatever pennies are left in my crap bank account. I didn't change it after we broke up."

Vincent felt at once honored that Tim had thought of him, even after their breakup, then guilty for assuming Jonah had planned a hit on Tim for cash.

But as Tim set up the equipment in the cold, unfurnished, little one-bedroom apartment, Vincent considered that perhaps the business alone was worth murder, for the right incentive. To get out of a job Jonah hated? To have the freedom to decide his own fate and not have to expend enormous amounts of cash to extricate himself from the business deal he'd roped himself into years ago?

And it wasn't like Jonah and Tim were friends. Well, not anymore. They used to be. But the years had eroded rifts between them. They both had relationships and drifted apart. Time and the stress of owning their own business in the face of stiff competition might have been the combination needed to break Jonah from feeling anything kind toward Tim.

The sound of Tim coughing a rattled, chunky cough drew Vincent out of his drifting thoughts.

"Okay, let's go downtown," Tim stated. Vincent realized he'd missed Tim setting up all his equipment.

"You don't need to be here to start the recording?" Vincent asked.

Tim shook his head, coughing again. "It's motion triggered and will start filming once the porch light next door switches on. If Zoe comes here, we'll be able to catch her."

"Clever." Vincent glanced out the window. The view was of another unit in the complex. It looked run down like the rest of the building. "It's hard to imagine what's going on in there."

Tim grimaced. "Evil. Evil goes on in there."

"Why don't the police shut them down?"

"Because it isn't that simple." Tim cleared his throat, and added, "They've gotten search warrants and gotten a few low grade perps arrested on human trafficking, but Larry and his gang are too clever to go down that way. It's going to take resources and time, two things Seattle PD doesn't have a lot of these days." He coughed again, and again, and suddenly he couldn't breathe. He gasped for air.

Panic rushed through Vincent. Tim fumbled for his inhaler, and Vincent fumbled for the decoy in his panic. Tim's symbol was completely gone from the bag—the hex had burned it off in hours.

The inhaler wasn't helping either—Tim's face turned white and he scratched at his throat, wheezing, before falling to the floor.

Vincent shook himself out of his shock and fumbled in his bag for more crowpepper and his curse-scythe blade. The short amount of time it took to activate the crowpepper felt like hours while Tim lay suffocating.

Vincent sat beside Tim's writhing body and motioned the blade through the air, slitting the invisible weaves that drew taut around Tim's throat. The way they had doubled and tripled in thickness and number alarmed Vincent. It was growing too fast.

The moment Vincent slit free a weave, it immediately started to rebuild, but at least he was able to cut enough from around Tim's throat that he could breathe shallow gasps of air. Vincent put down the blade and worked with his hands to untie the tangled knots of hate that closed around Tim's throat.

At last Tim took a deep breath of air. His face was ashen, his lips bluish. He had tears running down his face from the strength of his coughing.

"Sorry," Tim croaked, breathing deeply. He leaned against Vincent, his whole body shaking.

"When I find whoever made this, and I *will* find him, I will beat the shit out of him," Vincent whispered. He'd always harbored deep hatred for hexmakers, for using their powers to create such destruction. But seeing this person's malicious influence choke out Tim's life before his very eyes brought murderous intent to Vincent's mind. He was a hexbreaker, but Vincent found himself considering the possibility of reverting from his lifelong promise to not transfer hexes. It would almost be worth the risk, to give the sick bastard who made this a taste of their own medicine.

But Vincent didn't know who the hexmaker was, so he didn't have to weigh the pros and cons of injuring his conscience other than hypothetically at this point.

Instead, Vincent repaired the decoy now that he knew how. There were still enough herbs inside to lure the hex, and the cut on Tim's arm was still fresh enough to provide a little more blood to redraw Tim's symbol.

"If you're going to be slicing me open several times a day, I should probably just get an IV shunt for you," Tim wheezed, offering a smile that wasn't fooling Vincent.

Vincent shook his head. "Decoys are supposed to last days, not hours. This hex is too strong for it."

"Can we pump it up somehow?" Tim asked. "Make it bigger?"

Vincent shook his head. "Traditionally animal sacrifices were used for decoys since living flesh holds the symbol much longer. But my aunt and I made a rule that we would never use an animal or other living being for a decoy, it's morally unjustifiable."

"I know a really shitty terrier two houses down," Tim offered. "It wouldn't besmirch your virtue if you killed that dog-shaped evil thing."

Vincent laughed, then leaned back against Tim. All the crowpepper he'd swallowed was taking its toll. His exhaustion left him unable to keep his eyes open. The two of them held each other. He stroked Tim's back, feeling helpless.

They made their way to the pier and to The Cup. After a quick peek inside, Tim settled in the car to watch the entrance and Vincent pulled out his sketchbook.

Vincent remained silent for a few minutes. But the curiosity got to him. "Did she run away alone? I know you're not supposed to give me details, but maybe a few general points?"

Tim never took his eyes from the window. "I thought you were sketching."

"I am. But I'm also curious."

"She was alone," Tim said. "She ran off after a fight with her mom. Her mom thought she went to stay with her dad, who lives in Bellevue. But he hasn't seen her either."

"Family problems?" Vincent asked.

Tim shrugged, either because he didn't know or he wasn't going to disclose that.

Vincent watched out the window for a few minutes, but got bored and turned back to his sketchbook. How Tim could stare at nothing for hours on end, without music, without anything but a cup of coffee, boggled Vincent. What amazed him was Tim's incredible *focus* when he applied it. He watched the movements of every pedestrian in the vicinity, and every customer coming in and out of the restaurant, with eerie non-movement.

Vincent sank into his own focus, working on sketching out a design. He found himself checking the decoy every twenty minutes, terrified by the speed at which the hex moved.

About an hour after arriving, Tim suddenly cried, "Shit! Get my—"

The driver's side window shattered inward. Vincent flinched from the spray of broken glass. Someone huge reached through the window and yanked Tim out with a yell.

"Larry!" Tim gasped. "I'm not here for—"

"Shut your fucking mouth!" The giant man yelled at Tim. He was rough looking—at least six foot four, all muscle, ugly goatee, bald head. He shoved Tim's head against the pavement. "I told you to never come here again!"

"It's not for you!" Tim gasped. He started coughing. Vincent didn't know what to do. He had no fighting prowess. He could ram the guy with the car, but he was as likely to run Tim over.

Tim had wanted Vincent to grab something. Tim's gun. Vincent opened the glove compartment and withdrew Tim's Glock. Tim had wanted to teach him how to load and fire, if only for safety—as long as they lived together, Vincent would be living with a firearm.

But Vincent had chosen willful ignorance on the matter.

Good plan that turned out to be.

He gripped the pistol with a shaking hand, pointing the barrel down and away in case it had some sort of "auto-murder" button. He couldn't find any safety on the gun. But he knew the gun wouldn't fire as long as he didn't touch the trigger.

He pointed the gun at Larry.

Larry kicked Tim in the ribs.

"Back off," Vincent said, hoping his voice wasn't as terrified-sounding as he felt.

Larry stared angrily at Vincent, as if daring him to shoot. But Vincent must have looked pissed off enough to spook the bastard a little, because he backed away from Tim, never turning his gaze from Vincent.

Which is why he didn't notice when a white SUV came screeching to a halt behind him and Jonah hurled himself out of the car and into Larry's massive build, knocking him face first into the pavement.

By now a large group of folks along the pier gathered around. Someone must have called the cops—sirens could be heard in the distance.

Jonah scrambled off Larry and stood between the thug and Tim, looking furious. For an out of shape middle-aged man, Jonah could *move*.

"Go home, Larry," Jonah said.

Larry wiped at his mouth. His tumble to the pavement had cut his lip and he was bleeding. He sauntered off, but not before spitting at Tim on the ground.

"Tim!" Vincent ran to him, kneeling beside Tim's head. Tim was coughing again, unable to stop. "We need an ambulance," Vincent said to Jonah.

"Oh God. Hang in there, Tim!" Jonah fumbled for his phone.

Tim sat up slowly. "I'm...okay..." he gasped. His forehead was bloody, there were small shards of safety glass in his hair, and he was very pale. "Give me a minute."

Vincent and Jonah crouched around him. People continued to stare.

Tim's inhalations were labored and heavy, but he was able to catch his breath. But the toll of the day's activity was obvious. He looked weak and shaken to the core.

"What are you doing here?" Tim gasped at Jonah.

Jonah shrugged. "I felt bad leaving the way I did. I knew you were coming here next. I thought I'd offer to watch for Zoe since you looked so rotten."

Tim smiled weakly and placed his hand on Jonah's shoulder. "Thanks, buddy."

"Yeah, thanks," Vincent repeated. He knew tattoos and art and hexes but he did not do fights and violence and weapons. If Tim's rescue had been up to him, they might have lost.

And he realized now, there was no way the hex originated from Jonah, no matter what a logical fit it was. No man spent fifty grand to kill somebody and then risked their life to save him.

Jonah offered Vincent a tired smile. "You can get him home?"

"Yeah. Don't worry," Vincent assured him.

"Thanks." Jonah hesitated. "And it's good you're back. He's a dick without you."

"Hey!" Tim protested.

Jonah stood and headed back to his car.

"Hey! Hey!" Tim continued. He scrambled against Vincent, using Vincent's shoulder for support to pull himself upright. He staggered off toward the café. "Hey! *Zoe!*"

Vincent spun. A slight girl with shockingly black hair, heavy makeup, and grubby looking track pants turned at her name.

Vincent stared at her. He'd seen the picture of Zoe, and she looked so different. He'd never have recognized her. But somehow, Tim had.

I'm not the only one with magical powers, Vincent thought.

Tim talked quietly with the girl. Jonah sat in his SUV but with the door open, watching the interaction as well. Vincent moved to him.

"Guess we didn't need to set up surveillance after all," Vincent said. "Sorry to drag you away from your family for nothing."

But Jonah didn't look angry. He smiled. He shook his head. "That damned Tim. It's so hard to stay mad at him, because he's *good*. He's good at what he does, he has a good heart, he always means so well."

Vincent nodded. "I know how you feel."

Jonah frowned. "Do you think you can help him?"

"Help him?"

"With the...whatever he has. Black magic? He said he was going to you for help."

Vincent watched Tim put his arm around Zoe. "I'll do whatever I can."

"Well if there's anything I can help with, let me know." Jonah squeezed Vincent's shoulder. Vincent didn't think they'd ever shared so much as a handshake, let alone a shoulder squeeze, in the years they'd both been in Tim's circle of companions.

"Thanks," Vincent said. "If you find anyone with an 'I Hate Tim' bumper sticker give me a call."

Jonah laughed. "Anything in particular I should be on the lookout for? Oddly-placed ropes of garlic? Upside down crosses?"

Vincent smirked. "Nah. Well, if you find anyone burning bundles of *Yisirik*, give me a call."

"*Yisirik*?" Jonah asked.

"It's also called Syrian rue. It's a twiggy bundle that produces a magical smoke."

Jonah gave him an odd look and nodded. "Riight..."

He left soon after, and within a few minutes, Zoe was walking with Tim back to the car.

Tim grinned happily, despite his bleeding forehead and ghostly complexion. "Vincent, I'd like you to meet Zoe. Zoe, this is my boyfriend Vincent."

"Ex-boyfriend," Vincent said on principle, though he smiled and shook Zoe's hand anyway.

Zoe looked nervous. "You aren't going to tell my mom about where I've been staying, are you?"

Tim said, "Sweetheart, we're going to tell your mom whatever you want to say, but we're going to tell her in person, yes?"

She nodded. Tears filled her eyes. "Is she really mad?"

"She's scared. She loves you very much."

"I didn't mean to scare her."

"I know," Tim said. He opened his back door and let Zoe in. He gave Vincent a look.

"You sure you can drive?" Vincent whispered as Tim got behind the wheel and buckled his seatbelt. He nearly voiced the fear that had sunk within him since Tim's breathing problem back at the apartment—that this hex grew fast. Faster than any he'd seen.

But a glance at Zoe's frightened face made Vincent hold back his unwelcome revelation. There was enough regret and heartbreak in this car already. No need to exacerbate the issue over something he couldn't change.

"I can make it to Bellevue, where we can drop her off at her dad's house," Tim told Vincent. He managed a weak smile. "But after that, I'd be grateful if you'd take me home."

5

BLACK, EVIL DREAMS filled Tim's head, making it a relief to awaken, despite the pain in his chest.

It was late—the sky was pitch black, Vincent was at work, and Tim was alone.

He drank down a pot of Vincent's block tea, knowing Vincent would have forced him into it if he'd been there. He considered going to his office to do some work, but the idea of walking across the back yard sounded exhausting.

Luckily his temp help, Sarah, called just in time to excuse him from having to do anything else, so he lay in bed and listened while she detailed her conversation with Francesca Prelle.

Prelle wasn't friends with Zoya, it turned out. In fact, from what Sarah could determine, she didn't even like the lady. She simply provided fresh bouquets for her store every Monday morning, and the two would chat politely while Zoya made out the check. That was the end of the relationship.

And Francesca Prelle had moved on from her ugly breakup with her ex-husband. She had remarried only two weeks ago, this time to a wealthy semi-professional golfer who apparently made the world spin on its axis. Prelle was happy, she was wealthy, she was not friends with hexmakers.

She was off the list.

Tim stared at his phone long after Sarah disconnected. Prelle had been his last suspect. Now he was out of leads. Well, except for one.

He dialed a number he hadn't called in years.

"Tim fucking Keller," Jamie Santucci's voice said as soon as he picked up.

"Hey Jamie. Glad to see you still have my number programmed in your phone."

"What do you want?" Jamie snapped. Tim thought Jamie's voice sounded nasal and ugly. So much about Jamie's personality was ugly, Tim couldn't believe now that the two of them had actually once thought themselves serious enough to purchase real estate together.

But Tim had only recently come out before he met Jamie, and he desperately wanted to recreate his own sense of family after his own had reacted so coldly to his orientation. He had needed to belong to *someone*.

It wasn't a bad idea, just the wrong person to belong to.

"I've got one quick question for you. Afterward you can go on suing me from afar," Tim said.

Jamie scoffed. "I dropped that suit, you know. I don't need your money anymore. I've got someone else in my life who has shown me what love *really* is."

"Did you drop the suit because you have a different plan for ruining my life?"

"What?" Jamie asked, sounding genuinely confused. "Honey, I don't think about you *at all*. I've moved on."

"Really?"

Jamie scoffed. "Get over yourself, Tim. For your information, I've been in Aspen since January with Stephan. I only got back to Seattle in August. Seattle is so slovenly."

"I figured as much." Tim smiled, relieved. It had been a while since they'd been together, but Jamie had always been an obvious liar, and nothing he said now sounded artificial.

And Tim realized he was grateful it wasn't Jamie, despite everything. He didn't like the guy, but he didn't wish his relationship to have turned so caustic as to wish each other dead. "Thanks for the update. See ya."

"Wait, that was it?" Jamie asked.

"Yes."

There was silence. Then Jamie said, quietly, "Take care, Tim."

Tim swallowed. He was likely going to be dead soon, so it wouldn't hurt to let bygones be bygones. "You too, Jamie. Good luck with your new guy."

"Thanks."

Tim hung up and stared at the ceiling. The tea made him woozy, but the effect wasn't as strong as it had been the day before. The feeling of illness had changed. It was stronger. Everything in his body felt brittle.

He wanted Vincent. He felt lonely and pitiful and desperate. He was almost desperate enough to call his mother, then thought better of it. She'd likely tell him the only solution was God, and he couldn't stomach that argument.

As he lay there, a sense of intention filled his awareness. It was as though someone leaned over him and stared maliciously down. Fear filled him. A constricting sensation started at his ankles, and slithered up his legs. It was as though he were being wrapped by a massive invisible boa constrictor, tightening with all his might to crush Tim's body to a pulp.

Tim gasped in pain as the sensation reached his belly. He leaned over and retched as invisible hands gripped his stomach and crushed his ribs together.

Several of his ribs snapped. An unholy sob escaped him as pain unlike anything he'd ever experienced overtook him.

Something crunched at his sternum as the constricting sensation climbed higher. He couldn't draw a full breath. With desperate, uncontrollable fingers, he dialed Vincent's number and sobbed incoherently into the message.

Time stilled. Every breath was harder, like trying to breathe through heavy wet fabric. The crushing embrace strengthened. Another rib snapped. Tears ran down his cheeks. He shuddered on the bedspread and wished for the first time it would be over. He needed it to end. Death would be better than this agonizing strangulation.

It seemed like ages had passed since he'd called Vincent, but when Tim heard the front door unlocking he glanced at his phone and saw it had only been thirty minutes since he'd left his message.

Vincent called Tim's name. When he came into the bedroom, he stopped in surprise before rushing to Tim's side.

"Tim!" he cried.

Tim gasped for breath and pointed at his ribs. "Breaking..." he managed to cry.

"Oh God." Vincent pulled the decoy out of his pocket. It smelled completely burnt. Tim noticed that his personal symbol was gone from the bag, and when Vincent opened it, dozens of spiders scurried out of the satchel. Vincent dropped the satchel and the spiders skittered in every direction over his bedroom floor.

Vincent darted from the room. When he returned, Tim could tell he must have taken one of his poison pills, because his pupils were huge.

Vincent placed a pillow under Tim's head. He then reached into his backpack and pulled out a small metal tattoo machine. He fussed with plugs, needle packs, foot pedals, plastic wraps, o rings, and ink.

Tim was already in so much pain, he thought he'd probably look forward to the sting of the tattoo needle piercing his skin. But the tattoo machine wasn't for him. Vincent spread open his left palm and rested it against his bent left leg.

"What are you doing?" Tim choked.

"Everything I can," Vincent replied solemnly. And he lowered the needle to his palm.

If the inking hurt, Vincent didn't show it. His grim expression focused as he worked the needle in an intricate pattern over his left palm.

For one wild, irrational moment, Tim thought of cautioning Vincent. Palm tattoos were the kind of thing you needed to really think carefully about.

But he was in too much pain to voice his concerns. Besides, Vincent was a professional. He knew what he was doing. And the fact that he was permanently disfiguring his palm for Tim's benefit brought tears to Tim's eyes.

"Vincent," he cried.

"Almost done," Vincent said. He finished whatever he inked on his hand, then wiped at the mixture of black ink and blood with a clean paper towel.

He reached into his bag one-handed and pulled out a tube of tattoo ointment and rubbed this over the new ink, creating a thin, greasy layer.

He moved over Tim, but Tim grabbed Vincent's palm to see what he'd done.

It looked like a strange jumble of barbs, squiggles, and lines. Tim recognized it from the decoy. It was his own symbol.

But he was in too much pain to think about what it meant. He closed his eyes, gasping for air, as Vincent slowly waved his tattooed hand over Tim's body, eyes scrunched in concentration. Vincent methodically ran his hand above each and every part of Tim's body, and heat seared through him, followed by an achy numbness.

It might have taken minutes or hours. Tim lost all sense of time. He might even have dozed off. But at some point he blinked and found Vincent curled beside him on the bedspread, looking drained of all life. Tim fumbled with his hand and patted Vincent's head. His fingers no longer had that brittle about-to-break sensation he'd had earlier that night.

"You okay, beautiful?" Tim whispered.

"Tired," Vincent whispered back, not opening his eyes.

They slept.

Tim awoke and felt...

Totally better.

As in, nothing hurt.

Well, that wasn't entirely true—each breath was painful from his still-broken ribs. But every other part of him—his aches and pains, his rattling cough, the sensation of blood in his lungs—they were all gone.

It was as if someone had come in the middle of the night and lifted the hex from him.

Someone? Yeah, right. *Vincent.*

Tim looked down at himself and saw that Vincent had wrapped Tim's ribs at some point that night. Tim gingerly sat up from where he'd fallen asleep atop the comforter. Each movement hurt his ribs, but the wrapping held them tightly. He was going to have to get to the doctor at some point today.

Tim made his way slowly to the bathroom, still not trusting his newly recovered equilibrium. But at no point did the world waver or go sideways.

He had a morning erection which made peeing hard, but made the prospect of returning to bed with Vincent all the more appetizing.

And speaking of appetizing...

"I'm fucking starving," he said to his stream of urine. It didn't respond.

He washed his hands and face, marveling that something as small as the brush of his fingers over his scalp used to hurt. And now it didn't. He made his way to his empty kitchen and found the two-day-old cold chicken Vincent had brought over. He chowed down on one drumstick, then a thigh. They tasted like the best thing he had ever eaten in his entire life.

He brimmed with joy, so when crawled back into bed and startled Vincent awake, he expected a similar enthusiasm to greet him.

Instead, Vincent looked like death warmed over.

His face was ghastly pale, his eyes sunken in.

"You look awful," Tim said softly, leaning in for a kiss. Vincent kissed him back...

And that's when Tim *knew*.

Because Vincent's mouth tasted all wrong. It tasted like mold, something rotting.

Tim stared at Vincent, frozen.

"You feeling better?" Vincent croaked, blinking and trying to smile.

"Oh no, Vincent. Please tell me you didn't do what I think you did," Tim whispered.

Vincent frowned. "I don't—"

"Shut up." Frantically, Tim fumbled with Vincent's T-shirt, pulling up the sleeve on the left arm to reveal the head of Vincent's serpent tattoo. The eyes were not glowing red like his own foo dog had, but they were definitely no longer black. A strange pink tint seemed to vibrate from the eyes.

"You made yourself the decoy. You transferred the hex to yourself."

Tim knew he was right by the look of guilt crossing Vincent's face, before Vincent scowled and lowered his sleeve. "I didn't—"

"*You fucking transferred it to yourself!*" Tim shouted, suddenly furious and terrified, and so, so scared. Because he wasn't going to be the one to die now.

"I didn't have a choice!" Vincent finished, shouting back. He sat up. "You were out of time. I could see it in the weave. It's been sped up. You were going to *die*, Tim."

"And now *you* are!" Tears prickled at the corners of Tim's eyes. He wiped at them angrily, too pissed off to show sadness.

Vincent started, "It's not that bad—"

"Like *hell* it isn't! I've lived with this fucking thing for four months. I know how bad it is," Tim snapped.

"And I'm just starting," Vincent said. "I bought us more time. It'll take a few weeks to get to the level of deterioration you were at. By then we can track down whoever did this and-"

"What? Rush your dying ass over to Charlotte, so she can save you too? Of all the reckless, insane things you've ever done—"

"*Tim.*" Vincent's voice was quiet, and pleading. "Please don't shout. I've got a killer headache."

Tim bit back all the responses he had, and stared at Vincent. He shook his head. "I bet you do."

Vincent reached for him and Tim fell into him, curling himself around Vincent as if he could protect him from the curse.

But nothing could be done now. He wasn't a hexbreaker. He was an idiot who asked the love of his life for help and ended up getting him killed instead.

"Don't cry," Vincent whispered, hands stroking along Tim's back. "It was my choice. I couldn't bear it. I couldn't bear seeing you in that much pain. I'd gladly have given anything to help, and I did."

"So you know how I feel now," Tim said, voice choked. "You think it's any easier for me?"

"Yes," Vincent said. Tim pulled back to look at Vincent. Vincent smiled. "You're stronger than me and more determined. You gave up hope yesterday. Now you can't give up on me, or I'm dead."

Tim shook his head again. "You're a fucking martyr. I hate martyrs, you know."

"Yeah, but I'm a martyr who sucks cock like a champ."

"Very, very true." They held each other tightly. "So your hand is tattooed now."

Vincent shrugged. "I've been experimenting with using tattoo ink to permanently imbue intention. It seems like the surest way to keep the decoy active. And don't worry, palm tattoos fade quickly."

"So then it will be a big black faded ugly thing."

"Hey, it's your personal symbol. It will never be ugly to me."

Tim yawned. "You can still use it to jack me off, regardless." Tim said. He shook his head. "You said you'd never transfer a curse."

Vincent swallowed. "I shouldn't have done it. But I couldn't just watch you get crushed to death." He closed his eyes and fell silent.

At some point Tim thought Vincent had fallen back asleep, but when he stirred, Vincent pulled him back.

"No, stay," Vincent mumbled into his chest. "A bit longer, please. You feel good."

So they stayed, curled around each other in a desperate embrace, while Tim planned his next move.

It had been months since Tim last visited Jonah at the Cohen house in Lake Forest Park. Jonah and Annie owned a northwest style wood house tucked in a neighborhood of similar looking homes, all of them well manicured and sporting an assortment of children's toys in the front yards.

It was Sunday, and Tim knew Jonah and Annie had a long-standing tradition of a large brunch Sunday afternoons. He hoped he'd timed his arrival correctly—he was rabidly hungry, and the two burgers he'd eaten on the way over hadn't made a dent.

Annie answered the doorbell. If she was disappointed to see Tim, she didn't say so. Instead, she simply sighed and opened the door wider. "Hi."

"Hello Annie. Any chance you got some leftover pancakes?" Tim flashed her his most charming smile.

Even Annie seemed to fall for it. She nodded. "There's a few left over. Jonah's in his study."

"Thanks, darling." Tim winced as he entered the house.

"What happened to you?" Annie asked.

Tim shrugged. "Busted a rib or two. It'll be fine."

"Actually, you look a little better than the last time I saw you," Annie commented, tilting her head. "Maybe breaking some ribs cured your cough?"

Tim shrugged, making his way to Jonah's study off the entrance.

Jonah watched a golf tournament on his computer with his stocking feet propped up on his desk, his chair leaned all the way back.

"Hey, Tim." Jonah sat upright and pulled his feet from the desk. "What's up?"

"Trying to score me some pancakes," Tim said. He closed the office door.

"You look better," Jonah commented. He narrowed his eyes at Tim. "Actually, a lot better."

"Thanks. That's the issue I want to discuss," he said. He leaned closer. "I need to find someone, fast. We have to drop everything else we're working on."

"But—"

"I know it's a lot to ask. But if we don't find the person who is making hexes here in Seattle, Vincent is going to die."

Jonah looked as though he were about to interrupt, but shut his mouth instead. He sighed. He then grabbed a notepad off his desk and a pen.

"I'm not saying I believe this. But who do you suspect?"

Tim realized, for all the shit the two of them had been through, the pissy, petty disagreements, he loved Jonah. When he needed Jonah, he always came through. He felt so overwhelmed he leaned over and kissed Jonah on the top of the head.

Jonah hit at him. "Back off, dickhead!" He laughed.

The office door swung open and six-year-old Aiden appeared. "I just heard you say *dickhead*, Dad."

"Get out of here, Trouble!" Tim cried, roaring, flinging his arms out, looking huge. It was a game he'd played with Aiden since the boy was a toddler. Tim pretended to be terrifying, and Aiden pretended to be terrified and ran screaming. And then would run back to Tim and say "again," over and over.

Right on cue, Aiden shrieked and darted down the hallway.

"Be right back," Tim said, and slowly followed after Jonah's son.

He cornered Aiden in the laundry room, and while Aiden shrieked, Tim tickled Aiden until Aiden half laughed, half screamed "Mercy!"

Tim stopped, then tousled the kid's hair. "Go on, get out of here and let me talk to your dad."

Aiden grinned. "Bye Tim!" he took off down the hallway like his ass was on fire.

Tim turned, and that's when something caught his eye. He stared at the blue soccer jersey in the basket near the window.

His soccer jersey. The letters spelling KELLER were visible.

Tim nearly jumped in surprise as Annie stepped around him. She reached into the laundry basket and handed him his jersey.

"You left your shirt last time you and Jonah came back from a league game," she said. "I decided to wash it for you, but it was ripped. I meant to tell Jonah but I forgot."

"Thanks." Tim took the folded shirt and unfolded it. A hole punctured the shirt at the bottom, rough but circular, like it had been deliberately cut out.

The hairs at the back of his neck stood up.

Annie smiled, but it was a cold smile that never reached her eyes.

Tim backed away. "Fuck me," he said, realization dawning. It was her. *Of course* it was her. "I remembered I have an appointment," he lied.

"I've heated up those pancakes," she offered, but he already headed toward the door. He walked past Jonah's office quickly, but Jonah stopped him.

"Where are you going? You just got here," Jonah said.

"I forgot something important. I'll call you later, yeah?" He rushed to his car, cursing his stupid ribs. As he drove away, his mind raced through implications, reasons, actions to take. And permeating it all, a terrible sense of grief. He knew Annie didn't like him. But to hate someone with that kind of passion? It made Tim very sad, because his relationship with Jonah, his oldest and closest friend, would never be the same.

Vincent still lay in bed when Tim returned home, armed with grocery bags of food and painkillers. He unloaded the groceries and made two sandwiches, bringing Vincent's on a tray, with a birthday candle stuck in the soft bread.

"Wake up, sunshine," Tim called happily.

Vincent didn't look happy to be woken up. "Ugh."

"I brought you lunch." Tim placed the tray on the bed, grabbed his sandwich in one hand and lit the candle with the other.

Vincent sat up, blinking. He was pale and his eyes looked puffy. "I'm not hungry. I called today's clients and rescheduled. I don't want to be awake."

"But we need to celebrate," Tim urged, handing him the lit sandwich. Vincent smiled at it, shook his head, then blew out the candle.

"What are we celebrating?" Vincent asked.

"I know who hexed me," Tim said, clinking their sandwiches together in a toast. With his other hand he held up his damaged soccer jersey.

Vincent's eyes widened. "Who?"

"Jonah's wife."

"Annie? *Why*?" Vincent took a bite of the sandwich and grimaced.

Tim shrugged. "I know she blames me for interfering in their relationship by making Jonah work, although a person can't really force Jonah to do anything he isn't willing to do anyway, I'd like to point out." Tim sighed. "She hates that Jonah and I are business partners. She hates how little money he makes. She hates that I'm gay. The list probably goes on and on."

Vincent put the sandwich back on the tray, one solitary bite taken out of it. "I thought you said Jonah and Annie didn't have that kind of cash."

"They don't," Tim conceded. "I don't know how she paid for it. Maybe she offered hideous sexual favors. Maybe she sold the person's house? I can't think of other skills she has that would be any use to a hexmaker."

Vincent frowned. "If she didn't pay, then it would have to be someone she knows, some kind of favor. This is someone who is using a deep source of hate for their weaves and binds. It would change a person. If it really is Annie, then pay attention to her associates. Weaving that kind of blackness would probably permanently stain their fingertips black."

Tim froze, eyes wide.

"What?" Vincent asked.

"Stained black fingers," Tim repeated.

"Yes."

"Her fingers are black. Vincent, *her* fingers are black!"

Vincent and Tim stared at each other.

"She's self-taught," Vincent said. "Fuck me, she taught herself how to make her own withering hex."

Tim considered the hypothesis. It was definitely possible. Annie had hated him a lot longer than four months, which means she'd have had the time to learn how to make the hex. And she was clever, and picked up new things quickly.

"So how do we catch a hexmaker and the hexroot she is using?" Vincent asked.

Tim smiled. "I think it's time to whip up a little magic of my own."

6

THE PITIFUL CALLS Tim made to Jonah, and subsequently Annie, demonstrated to Vincent how good of an actor Tim was. Vincent himself felt near tears from Tim's convincing performance.

Tim had first sent Jonah on a pointless errand, begging off for the sake of his terrible sickness. He then called Annie ten minutes later, chokingly stuttering into the phone. "I've taken a turn for the worse, Annie, and Vincent's gone. I need someone to pick up my medication at the pharmacy. And I need to see you. To apologize for my behavior. To make amends before it's...over."

Vincent couldn't hear what kind of response Tim's performance received on the other end of the line, but it sounded like Annie begrudgingly agreed to come.

After the call, Tim enthusiastically retrieved a makeup bag that raised Vincent's eyebrows.

"Drag night?" Vincent inquired.

Tim smirked. "If you're lucky. Nah, it's for creating false injuries. You can get a lot of information out of people through sympathy." Tim whistled as he applied rouge to his cheeks, darkened his eyes, paled his lips.

Vincent found the transformation fascinating, but he couldn't stand and watch for long. He had his own preparations to make, getting his tattoo machine ready, props in place, curse scythe and crowpepper hidden but at arm's reach.

It didn't take long, but the effort exhausted him. In all his time helping Charlotte, he'd never actually been the victim of a curse, and he now felt sicker than he'd ever felt in his life. He threw up for the entire day, unable to keep down even the smallest amount of water. He tried to eat but food tasted repulsive—ashes wasn't the right metaphor at all. It tasted like he imagined cold vomit tasting, clumpy and horrible and with a vile, acidic aftertaste.

He brewed himself block tea until he ran out of supplies, but even that seemed to have little effect. By the time Tim's transformation was complete, Vincent felt near collapse from the pain in his chest. How the hell had Tim lived with this for four entire months?

Vincent returned to Tim's bedroom and almost stepped back in surprise at Tim's face.

Tim looked awful. He'd created dark, weary bags under his eyes and his stubble did little to hide his manufactured pale complexion. He'd even created a bruising effect around his throat as if he'd been throttled.

But Tim's expression was mischievous as he ushered Vincent into his closet. He gave Vincent a brief kiss, then shut the door almost entirely. Vincent left the door ajar just enough to see Tim lying in bed through the crack.

Nausea filled Vincent's stomach, and his throat felt tight, so he was glad he didn't have to wait long. Within minutes someone knocked at the front door. Tim croaked "Come in!" from his bed.

The sound of the front door opening could be heard. Annie came in slowly, pinching a paper bag of medicine in her hands. She eyed Tim cautiously.

Tim spoke so quietly Annie had to move closer to the bed to hear.

"I know you've wanted Jonah and me to fold Keller Cohen," Tim croaked, his face flush, eyes watering. "And I've kept him from doing so all these years. I want to apologize for that."

"It's too late for apologies," Annie said. She placed the medicine on Tim's bedside table. "Here's your medicine."

"There's no point to the medicine," Tim said. "It's not doing me any good. I've been hexed."

Annie's expression didn't change. She looked at Tim coldly.

"I know Jonah doesn't believe in hexes," Tim said. He cleared his throat. "But you do, right Annie?"

Annie's eyes narrowed. "Why would I?"

"That's what I keep asking myself," Tim said. "Why would you? I mean, I know you disliked how the business interfered with your home life, and you never particularly liked me. But why this? Why learn some black art to kill me slowly? Why do you truly hate me so much?"

Annie's smile never wavered. "Maybe because you're a selfish faggot who's ruined my husband's life?"

Vincent stepped from the closet. Tim leapt from the bed, starling Annie backward. She slammed into Vincent.

Annie tried to bolt. Tim grabbed her by the arm and yanked her back, pinning her arms behind her. Vincent quickly searched her, trying pockets first. He anxiously visualized finding nothing, the awkwardness of the whole situation.

But Annie clearly believed she was never a suspect, since she left Tim's hexroot in the back pocket of her jeans.

"Give that to me!" Annie screamed, struggling in Tim's grasp. "You don't know what you're doing!"

Vincent's breathing felt ragged. His body shook with fever. He placed the fabric in the metal bowl he'd prepared by Tim's bedside table.

"Preventing a murder," Vincent said. He pulled out his lighter.

Annie screamed as he lit the fabric. The material melted into a lump, offgassing toxic fumes.

Annie stopped screaming and went limp in Tim's arms.

"What the hell?" Tim cried. She had fainted in his arms. He lowered her carefully onto his bedspread.

"To make that kind of hateful hex, she had to be very connected with the hexroot," Vincent explained. "Destroying it hurt her."

"Good." Tim rushed to Vincent's side and gripped him by the arm. "How are you feeling?"

Vincent took stock of himself. He felt better. The overpowering sense of malice lifted and he breathed deeply for the first time since he became Tim's decoy.

With Annie unconscious, this was going to go easier, but they didn't have much time. "Grab her hand and turn it palm upward." Vincent reached under the bed and grabbed his tattoo machine and pedal.

He quickly pulled on gloves and laid out plastic over the surface of the bed. Years of blood-borne pathogen training as a tattoo artist had embedded itself into his procedures, even if he was also a hexbreaker who used blood in rituals.

"Will this work? Instead of a branding?" Tim asked anxiously, bracing Annie down on the bed.

"Only one way to find out," Vincent replied. He hesitated over her palm, and glanced back at Tim. "You sure you don't want me to do this the traditional way? I know it works."

Tim glanced down at Annie. "I hate her for what she's done to me, but I can't let you brand her. I'm sorry. She's still Jonah's wife, despite everything. Besides, by your logic the tattoo will last forever, as compared to the branding."

Vincent nodded. He swallowed the crowpepper, then grabbed the collar of her blouse and pulled it down to show her collar bones. Nestled between the bones, her invisible personal symbol became visible as the crowpepper flooded through his system.

As soon as the needle touched her palm, Annie flinched and regained consciousness. She struggled, cursing at Tim and Vincent, but Vincent was fast with the needles. He created the same image of her own symbol, and then blackened it out. He used white ink for the tattoo so as not to permanently disfigure her hand, although if it had been up to him, he'd probably have tattooed it big and bright red, just to make her suffer.

When it was done, he wiped clean the wound and applied ointment. The tattoo looked like a half-dollar sized circle of pale-colored scribbles on her left palm.

She's stopped struggling halfway through, and now just stared up at the ceiling, her face a study in fury.

When he finished he collapsed back, exhaustion overcoming him. Annie whipped her right hand back and slapped Vincent, hard, across the face.

"Get out of here," Tim growled. He stood in front of Vincent.

"I hate you!" Annie cried.

"You're going to leave now, and you are never going to do so much as give me or Vincent a nasty look from this point out, or I'm going to make your life a living hell," Tim said to her, his voice low with anger. "You think I've made your life hard? You have no idea. You will lose Jonah, custody of Aiden, your house, your job, your liberty. I will press charges and not rest until you are behind bars for the rest of your life."

Annie shuddered.

"But if you leave now, I will simply never see you again. Get out."

Tim didn't need to repeat himself. She stormed out of the house, slamming the door behind her.

Tim followed after her as if making sure she really left. Vincent lay back on the bed, feeling like he needed a week of solid sleep. But he had to finish dismantling the hex now. When Tim returned, he helped Vincent sit up. "Door's locked. She's gone."

"Good riddance."

Tim brushed the back of his hand gently over Vincent's cheek. "You feel okay?"

Vincent nodded. "I'll feel even better when this is over."

Tim leaned down and kissed Vincent on the forehead. "What do you need from me?" he asked.

"More crowpepper, my blade, and you laying flat on the bed."

"I like that part." Tim fetched Vincent's tools, hesitating with the crowpepper. "You want to call Charlotte and see if she can do this instead?"

Vincent smiled weakly. "No, but thanks. It should be easy now. I just want it done."

With a sigh, Tim handed over the pill. Vincent swallowed it, grimacing at the sickening lurch of too much crowpepper in his body.

But with it flowing through him, the weave of the hex shone like starlight over Tim's body. He grabbed his scythe, and went to work.

◇◇◇◇◇◇◇

Vincent managed to hold off his exhaustion long enough to cut the remaining hex weaves from Tim's body. Tim fell asleep halfway through the process, and Vincent followed suit as soon as the last barb was pulled free.

Vincent woke at one o'clock the following afternoon. Daylight streamed in from around the curtains. He'd slept for twelve straight hours.

And he felt ten pounds lighter, and famished.

He was alone in Tim's bedroom, the lights off, blankets pulled over his clothed body. In the other room he heard the television emitting sounds of explosions and gunfire. He smelled hot pizza and his mouth watered.

Vincent shuffled into the living room in his socks. He spotted Tim on the couch, watching television in shorts and an old t-shirt. An empty pizza box lay splayed open on the coffee table alongside a half-gallon of soda.

"You didn't save me any?" Vincent asked, stomach rumbling.

At once the blanket beside Tim exploded to life and a little face emerged from underneath. Bogart whined in joy and rushed out, jumping over Vincent with the most enthusiastic greeting Vincent had ever received in his life.

He forgot the pizza. Vincent knelt by the coffee table and allowed himself be lovingly mauled by the determined dog, who seemed to think the greatest sign of affection involved sticking his tongue into his loved ones' nostrils.

"I have another pizza just for you," Tim said, standing. "Covered in Canadian bacon and pineapple and all that garbage you love."

"Thanks."

Tim reached his hand down and pulled Vincent to his feet. He embraced Vincent tightly.

"How are you feeling?" he asked.

"Back to normal." Vincent smiled at him.

Tim nodded. He picked up Bogart and kissed the dog until he squirmed out of his grip. Bogart bee-lined for the bed.

Vincent sighed. "And here I thought we'd finally have a nice quiet night all to ourselves to fuck like bunnies."

Tim's eyebrow rose. "We can definitely do that. Bogart won't mind."

Vincent rolled his eyes. "He hogs the bed, you know that. He plants himself directly in the middle of the mattress and doesn't move."

"I guess we'll have to do it right here then," Tim said. He clearly intended to sweep Vincent off his feet and throw him down on the couch, but he must have forgotten his broken ribs. He got halfway through the move before swearing and falling back on the couch himself, dropping Vincent in the process. Vincent collapsed on the couch beside him.

Tim looked chagrined. "That was *so* much more romantic in my head."

"I think we should keep things lazy until you've healed." Vincent climbed over Tim, on his hands and knees.

"Lazy but still kinky?" Tim asked expectantly.

"Yes. Still kinky." Vincent's face hovered over Tim's, close enough for a kiss.

"Will you move back in with me?" Tim asked, a little breathless.

"Yes," Vincent said. He lowered his head to complete the kiss. But Tim pushed on his chest, keeping him out of reach.

"And do you forgive me?" Tim asked.

Vincent rolled his eyes. "Obviously."

"And do you love me?"

"Yes, but that might change if you don't stop being such a cocktease."

Tim's crooked smile transformed his beautiful face.

"Then kiss me before you change your mind."

About the Authors

Astrid Amara
Astrid Amara lives in Bellingham, Washington. She's a former Peace Corps Volunteer, an advocate for animal rights, and a bureaucrat by day. After work she can usually be found writing, riding horses, hiking, or else sleeping. Her novel The Archer's Heart was a finalist for the 2008 Lambda Literary Award.
www.astridamara.com

KJ Charles
KJ Charles is a writer and freelance editor. She lives in London with her husband, two kids, an out-of-control garden and an increasingly murderous cat.

KJ writes mostly romance, gay and straight, frequently historical, and usually with some fantasy or horror in there. She specialises in editing romance, especially historical and fantasy, and also edits children's fiction.
www.kjcharleswriter.com

Charlie Cochet
Charlie Cochet is an author by day and artist by night. Always quick to succumb to the whispers of her wayward muse, no star is out of reach when following her passion. From adventurous agents and sexy shifters, to society gentlemen and hardboiled detectives, there's bound to be plenty of mischief for her heroes to find themselves in, and plenty of romance, too!

Currently residing in Central Florida, Charlie is at the beck and call of a rascally Doxiepoo bent on world domination. When she isn't writing, she can usually be found reading, drawing, or watching movies. She runs on coffee, thrives on music, and loves to hear from readers.
www.charliecochet.com

Rhys Ford

Rhys Ford was born and raised in Hawai'i then wandered off to see the world. After chewing through a pile of books, a lot of odd food, and a stray boyfriend or two, Rhys eventually landed in San Diego, which is a very nice place but seriously needs more rain.

Rhys admits to sharing the house with three cats, a bonsai wolfhound, and a ginger cairn terrorist.

Rhys is also enslaved to the upkeep a 1979 Pontiac Firebird, a Toshiba laptop, and a red Hamilton Beach coffee maker.

But mostly to the coffee maker.

www.rhysford.com

Ginn Hale

Ginn Hale resides in the Pacific Northwest with her wife and three cats. She spends many of the rainy days tinkering with devices and words and can often be sighted herding other people's dogs, bees and goats. Her novel Wicked Gentlemen won the Spectrum Award for Best Novel and was a finalist for the Lambda Literary Award.

www.ginnhale.com

Lou Harper

Under a prickly, cynical surface Lou Harper is an incorrigible romantic. Her love affair with the written word started at a tender age. There was never a time when stories weren't romping around in her head. She is currently embroiled in a ruinous romance with adjectives. In her free time Lou stalks deviant words and feral narratives.

Lou's favorite animal is the hedgehog. She likes nature, books, movies, photography, and good food. She has a temper and mood swings.

Lou has misspent most of her life in parts of Europe and the US, but is now firmly settled in Los Angeles and worships the sun. However, she thinks the ocean smells funny. Lou is a loner, a misfit, and a happy drunk.

www.louharper.com

Jordan L Hawk

Jordan L. Hawk grew up in North Carolina and forgot to ever leave. Childhood tales of mountain ghosts and mysterious creatures gave her a life-long love of things that go bump in the night. When she isn't writing, she brews her own beer and tries to keep her cats from destroying the house. Her best-selling Whyborne & Griffin series (beginning with Widdershins) can be found in print, ebook, and audiobook at Amazon and other online retailers.

www.jordanlhawk.com

Nicole Kimberling

Nicole Kimberling lives in Bellingham, Washington with her wife, Dawn Kimberling, two bad cats as well as a wide and diverse variety of invasive and noxious weeds. Her first novel, Turnskin, won the Lambda Literary Award for Science Fiction, Fantasy and Horror. She is also the author of the Bellingham Mystery Series.

www.nicolekimberling.com

Jordan Castillo Price

Author and artist Jordan Castillo Price writes paranormal sci-fi thrillers colored by her time in the Midwest, from inner-city Chicago, to rural small town Wisconsin, to liberal Madison. Her influences include Ouija boards, Return of the Living Dead, "light as a feather, stiff as a board," girls with tattoos and boys in eyeliner.

www.jordancastilloprice.com

Andrea Speed

Andrea Speed was born looking for trouble in some hot month without an R in it. While succeeding in finding Trouble, she has also been found by its twin brother, Clean Up, and is now on the run, wanted for the murder of a mop and a really cute, innocent bucket that was only one day away from retirement. (I was framed, I tell you – framed!)

In her spare time, she arms lemurs in preparation for the upcoming war against the Mole Men. Viva la revolution!

www.andreaspeed.com

Lightning Source UK Ltd.
Milton Keynes UK
UKHW011032010620
364248UK00002B/489